Reign of Blood

Omnibus

ALEXIA PURDY

This is a work of fiction. All characters and events portrayed in this novel are fictitious and are products of the author's imagination and any resemblance to actual events, or locales or persons, living or dead are entirely coincidental.

TABLE OF CONTENTS

REIGN OF BLOOD

DISARMING

AMPLIFIED

RESONANT

ELIJAH
(THE MIEL CHRONICLES)

REIGN OF BLOOD

Chapter One

NEVER TEASE ANYTHING that wants to eat you. The ravenous eyes that bled death all around and peered from their window, drooling at the sight of us. The buildings loomed above as we rushed across the concrete and asphalt, hurrying to beat the sun as it set. They lurked in every window, shrouded by the shadow from the searing sun. The east sides of the buildings were crawling with vampires. They smirked and sneered their inhuman growls, hissing right at us as we jumped from sunbeam to sunbeam, racing to the awaiting van. Only the light kept them at bay. Only the light kept us from their sharp, gripping fangs.

Each block felt like it stretched longer and farther, growing with each of our steps. My mother ran hurriedly, as fast as she could with my little brother wrapped around her, molded to her chest, afraid to look up. I was dashing right next to her, afraid to get left behind and afraid to be first in any place. My backpack bounced on my back with each jump and step. I tried hard to not look up. To look upon them was to feel your soul drain of life, to wither away. Mom always said not to let them look into your eyes; they can steal your humanity and freeze you in your steps. But I did look, and I did study their red searing eyes. Even while running, I had glanced up into their pale, grey ashen faces. I waited for them to take my soul; I waited and discovered that I was immune. Immune to their mind control and their deepest desire. I wanted to smile and flip them off but I didn't think that my mother would appreciate that. I wasn't sure if she or my brother were immune. I wasn't about to piss her off by admitting that I had given in to such a temptation and had stared eye to eye with monsters.

So for now, we ran. We ran to our awaiting van where mom tied my little brother into his seat and slid quickly into the driver's seat, turning the ignition and slamming the gas as though our lives depended on it. Actually, they very much did. Soon the sun would fade, inhaled into shadows and we would be surrounded by monsters capable of draining our bodies of every little drop of crimson blood. They did not discriminate. They would rip even me and my younger brother to shreds. For now, they waited in their makeshift graveyard; the city's dilapidated buildings and streets.

I stared out the windows of the van and hugged my knees to my chest. Mom had her serious and stern face on. Sometimes I wish I could see her smile again, like the old days, before any of this happened. Before foraging for food had become an absolute for survival. Before running was a daily occurrence. Seeing her hair streaked with grey was not something I thought I would see so soon. She wasn't that old.

Times like these, even I felt old.

We left the city limits well before sunset. We were safer in the rural areas, where vampires feared to tread, too far from the shelters of the concrete jungles. I learned early on that some part of their humanity must still be intact because unlike the stories and movies I had heard and seen about vampires, these ones hated to sleep in the dirt. Oh, and all that crap about mirrors and garlic? Definitely not true. Stake to the heart? I had found that it did work but decapitation was a much more successful option. Missing the heart was too easy a mistake. Crosses and holy water? Well, that does work but you must be a believer for it to work as intended. If you did not believe, well, let's just say you might as well be throwing plain water at them.

An arsenal of swords, crosses and faith was pretty much all I needed. It had been just a year since the virus had turned more than three quarters of the population of the Americas into blood-seeking walking dead. Most died within days of contracting the strange ailment. I'd had all the practice I needed for a lifetime in learning how to kill vampires. It definitely made for an interesting life but I would give anything for my old one. Nothing beat a cold soda and movie on a Saturday night. High school issues seemed petty compared to the ones I had now. Stability, security, all gone. Staring out the dusty windows of the van as the trees grew thicker and the dusk seeped into the sky, I felt nothing but numb. Everything was all but gone.

Chapter Two

MY NAME IS April. I live in a bunker, somewhat hidden in the sparse forests surrounding what is left of Las Vegas, Nevada. I wish I could say that the nights would bring bright lights, slot machines ringing and an endless party, but that would not be so. The valley is a graveyard, black as pitch at night and a ghost city in the day. All that is left of a city that never sleeps.

My mother Helen and my younger brother Jeremy live with me in this makeshift home buried in the side of the mountains. It's pretty cool considering we could be out in the open where the vampires roamed at night. It was simple; we had found a door in a mountain cabin to what would've been part of a basement that led down a long hallway and into a cemented-in bunker. Located deep inside the bowels of the forest near Mt Charleston, this had become our home. It was ventilated somehow, had stores and stores of non-perishable food lining shelves and storage areas in a separate room.

Gallons of water sat in drums as big as me and a filtration system was set up for recycling the water that we did use. The place was wired with solar energy and generators if needed. The sleeping quarters were in a corner of the first room and consisted of three beds lined up next to one another. My mother and I took turns keeping watch during the night while Jeremy got to sleep the whole night. It wasn't much, but it was home.

The luck we had felt when we found this place was overwhelming. It was more than we could have hoped for. By chance we had searched the plain log cabin that sat atop the bunker and discovered this entombed sanctuary. Whoever had built it had had some money to burn and probably had been some sort of apocalypse-paranoid survivalist. It didn't matter in the end; it had not helped them any more than any money could've have helped in the end of times. The owners hadn't made it back here and it had remained untouched until we'd found it. I often wondered who they had been. It wasn't like they had lived here much, there had been no family photographs displayed across the walls or sitting on the coffee table. Nothing to mark it as lived in at all, like an abandoned and forgotten place, a just-in-case sort of place.

We still had to run down to the city for supplies. My mother did not like using up the stores in the bunker; she said she'd rather use what was widely available now in the abandoned stores and shops in the city than use what we had. It made sense; the city's abundance was for now, the bunker supplies for later. That didn't mean I didn't hate going down there. The city was crawling with vampires. They lurked in shadows of the evenings and stared hungrily at you as you walked about. A thousand eyes watching and sizing you up, it was the most uncomfortable feeling ever. As long as you didn't stay out too late, you wouldn't see them as much in the morning and afternoon hours. Dark buildings were an absolute no go. They holed themselves in the guts of structures until nightfall, when the burn of the sun no longer seared their ashen skin.

I hadn't always been so physical, but since I'd had it out with a vampire or two already, I had insisted on watching tape after tape of martial arts and weapons training after those near-fatal attacks on me and my family. My mother participated in these training sessions with me, too. Our slender muscles proved our dedication. We were femme fatales. I liked it that way. Delicate flowers were for the dogs.

The days went by slowly. Some weeks we didn't venture out at all, some weeks we explored the city every day. My mother really didn't want to go all vigilante and kill the hives of vampires we tended to find. I had killed some smaller ones, but my thirst to extinguish them grew with every kill. I spent my days sharpening my knives and arrows. I'd spend hours in the hunting stores, running my hands over the variety of weapons, guns, crossbows, all sorts of contraptions. I would settle on some shorter swords, machetes, daggers and crossbows. I had guns of course, but they were loud and tended to awaken the hives around us, getting them stirring earlier than we like.

This was the reason we were running that day. I had gotten in a bind and had to shoot a large hive of about 6 vampires that I'd come upon in small grocery store. I had cursed myself for letting them surprise me. I should have noticed their putrid smell before coming near them. But for some reason I had been distracted and hadn't been at my most-alert that day. Mom had been pissed. She'd had to join me to extinguish them, leaving my brother outside in the open daylight. This was a definite taboo.

4

He was defenseless, and at six years old, his haunted eyes made him older than he should've been. He couldn't handle a gun, let alone a sword or crossbow. He always had a knife which we had taught him how to use, but with his scrawny body, he was sure to not last long in a world of death all by himself.

After getting an earful that day, Mom had banned us from going to the city for at least a week. I hated being cooped up in the cabin and bunker. I had spent my time hunting animals for fresh meat, but it being the end of summer and the beginnings of fall, the animals were not so frequently available. Occasionally I would track a deer, but jackrabbits were more common. Coming across any kind of beef would be nice, but the vampires had ravaged the few farms around the north end of town ages ago. This had left us with little options in the meat department. Ever since the electricity had shut down in the city, the freezers stank of the rot of death in every market. Beef jerky was all we could really find to enjoy any kind of red meat.

So here I was, stuck on the mountain, staring down at the city that used to be our home. Watching the evening sun sink over the crests of barren rock near Mt. Charleston, at least the vampires didn't venture up here. Their inherent fear of being out in the open when the sun rose kept them near the buildings of downtown and the strip. They were such territorial creatures; they liked to group together in small hives. We thought it curious that we didn't find them in the outskirts of town, proving our theory that they preferred the clusters of buildings in the center of town. Still, the Strip was rich with food stocks that were nearly impossible for us to reach. It would mean treading into those bowels of darkness and silence, the remnants of the previously bright, noisy casinos. It was a darkness infested with death.

I tore myself away from my thoughts. Night was approaching. As the shadows fell across the cabin, we locked the huge, heavy metal door that was the entrance to the bunker and flipped the lights on inside to illuminate the concrete sanctuary of our isolated home.

Chapter Three

"APRIL, GRAB YOUR gear," my mother said. "We need to find more powdered milk and possibly any kind of meat products we come across. Also bottled water, detergent, and soap. Got it?"

Groaning, I snatched the page of lined paper with her neat writing pressed into it. Mom had been a teacher before the end of the world and teaching English year after year had been her passion. Now, only my brother and I were her pupils, more so Jeremy than me. I was seventeen and my eighteenth birthday would be coming in just a few months. I was no longer a child, being thrown into adulthood and survival mode faster than I ever would have thought.

"How far in are you planning to go today, Mom?" I tied my dark black hair into a tight ponytail and pulled on a thin jacket. The fall weather could get a bit chilly in the shade, but in the sun's warmth, it felt perfect. The dry air was still today as the usual wind made itself scarce. I slid daggers into the sheaths on my belt and one on the side of my boot then slung a quiver of arrows onto my back and a crossbow over my head to strap across my chest. I had come to love weapons. The crossbow was a bit bulky but I had chosen the lightest one I could find in the sporting goods store. It took some practice to get used to it but I could hit things dead on now. It was nice and quiet, which was a major plus. I favored it along with my machetes. Blade fighting was more intense and messy, but also quiet.

Mom pulled on her own gear as Jeremy fidgeted on the ottoman. He always got nervous seeing us prep for an outing. We always took him with us; leaving him was not an option. If we died, he would be all by himself in the bunker, a thought that sent a shudder down my spine. I ruffled his wispy medium-brown hair. It badly needed a cut. Mom hated trimming it because it was so thick it clogged the clippers with every pass. She tended to put it off as long as she could. He glanced up, giving me a nervous smile as he visibly relaxed under my touch. He always felt safer as long as he was near one of us.

"April, is it a short or long trip?" His small voice came out shaky as he gulped down his apprehension. I motioned him to move over on the ottoman and plopped down next to him, giving him a squeeze.

"Hey, trooper. Nothing to worry about, okay? What did I tell you before? Stick by mom or me and we got your back. Don't wander away and be extra quiet." Leaning down I whispered into his ear, "Short trip, I hope." I straightened up when mom turned towards us to grab a couple of duffle bags for the supplies. She tossed one to me and motioned for me to get moving. I stood up and winked back at Jeremy. "Come on, squirt, you want to have fun don't cha? How many do you want me to shoot today?"

"April, stop that!" Mom's tight voice pierced through the air. I rolled my eyes, making Jeremy giggle as he jumped off the ottoman and ran towards the door.

"Sorry, mom," I said sarcastically. Pressing my lips together, I gave her a feigned smile and batted my eyelashes at her as I walked by. Her eyebrows rose into arches as she shook her head and sighed. I was seventeen but she treated me like a child, even after everything that had happened. I was more adult now than a child, and I never would be one again.

Checking the monitor that connected to the camera that scanned the outside perimeter, I verified that is was all clear before turning the huge deadbolts, releasing the thick steel door. The cool autumn air rushed in along with some dust and dried leaves. There was a breeze dancing about and it kicked up the dirt and pollen like crazy. I sneezed, rubbing the itchiness that immediately stung my eyes, making them water. I hated fall and spring just the same; they sucked pretty bad for the allergy- plagued like me. I tacked a note to myself in my brain to snatch up more allergy meds when I hit the stores in the city today. A stock of them would be good; lord knows they would not be manufactured anymore.

"Hit the lock code, April. Jeremy, switch off the electricity to the house." Jeremy complied by flipping a dozen switches on the wall, deadening any electricity that would leak from the house above our bunker and clicking the lights off inside to conserve solar power inside our hideaway. We always tried to involve him with the technicalities of our survival; it made him feel like less of a helpless little man.

I waited as my mother locked the steel door behind her, tapping the numbers into the keyboard and closing the hidden door for the finger pad. We were lucky that the instructions to get into the bunker had been left in plain sight in a kitchen drawer up in the cabin or we'd never had been able to get in or out of the place. It was truly our home now.

I stretched and flexed my muscles, preparing for the scavenging ahead. My skin was a cool light brown which would deepen in the rays of the intense sun. In Vegas, it seemed to burn brighter than anywhere else I had ever been. I had already slathered sunscreen on me and Jeremy before we left, otherwise the nasty burns from the sun would not have been pleasant.

Jumping into our van, I strapped myself into the middle seat. Jeremy hated to sit alone so I either sat in the seat with him or he rode up front with my mother. Today he jumped in next to me and we spread out on the bench seat, laughing and giggling as I playfully poked him on his sides.

"Ok, guys, no playing around now, its work time."

"Aw," Jeremy moaned, crossing his arms across his chest and jutting his lower lip out at Mom. I shrugged and sat up straighter as she cranked the engine and started down the road. We would have to siphon gas while we were in town too. The van was efficient but the trek up and down the mountain still burned a lot of fuel. The engine hummed as the trees and asphalt raced by. I hated the forest around us; it was so sparse and ill-looking that I wondered why trees bothered to live here at all. Most were dead and strewed across the landscape in piles along with heaps of pine needles and mulch. The scattered cabins we passed were off the main road and looked dark and neglected.

I sighed, wondering how many humans were left after the virus had hit. I hadn't found one soul that I had known in my previous life. My mother had insisted on fleeing for the mountains when it became apparent that the vampires were not going to be leaving any humans alive. The massacre of the city, the chaos, had been a scene from a horror show. Blood and guts had been strewed across the streets; people's screams echoed in the night as we had desperately loaded up our belongings, what little we could salvage, and rode out onto the dark highways outside the city. That was the same night I had looked back, watching the lights of the Strip flicker on and off until the death shroud of darkness had swallowed it up. I could still hear the people screaming in my ears.

"Well?" My mother's voice broke through my thoughts. I peered up at her eyes glaring at me through the rear view mirror.

"What did you say?" I shook off my terrifying memories like a heavy fog that clung to my brain.

"What's wrong with you? I said 'do you want me to drop you off at the pharmacy first or do you want to scavenge the huge sporting goods store again?' I need you to stick to the list of food we need. Take the rolling cart with you." Mom looked away and returned her attention to the road as she sped along, avoiding debris and stalled cars.

"Um, yeah, that would be good. There's a pharmacy right next to the sporting goods store. Drop me there and I'll meet you at the supermarket that's down two streets from there. It should have some stuff left that's edible."

I took a deep breath in and shuddered, shaking off the past with one draw of air. I stretched my arms, rolling my shoulders and tilting my neck side to side, hoping to loosen the knots that formed while I anxiously waited to reach the city. It never failed to make me nervous. The buildings were not safe. Feral vampires could be lurking anywhere where sunlight did not touch. Even the stores I frequented had to be searched first before letting my guard down. The night sometimes brought new visitors to these places, in search of fresh blood.

I stretched to keep limber, too. If I had to fight one, it would be to my advantage to be ready. Jeremy watched me with studious eyes, filled with a knowledge he was too young to own. I smiled brightly to deflect the anxious energy floating in his eyes. He smiled and turned back toward the window. He knew that every trip into the city could be racked with danger. He didn't deserve this kind of life. He should have been allowed to be a kid, playing on swings and jungle gyms, eating cookies and ice cream under the intense sun of Las Vegas summers. Swimming in crystal blue pools and playing ball. I missed these activities myself but to deny him his childhood cut me to the bone. I wish he had had that before all this happened.

The van reached the first buildings after turning down I-95 southbound into the city. I watched the concrete speed by as the van swayed, dodging the debris and cars strewn across the way. Jeremy's eyes were staring at the back of the seat in front of him. He had averted them to avoid taking in the gruesome details outside. I wasn't so squeamish. I glanced over him through the window. Crashed and stalled cars alike were not out of the ordinary now. What bothered him was the endless array of corpses laid out in their last positions of death. Sitting in cars, hanging halfway out windows, lying in pieces across the highway after being hit when the panic of the masses had set in. Though they were mostly mangled and mummified now, I didn't blame him one bit. I looked at the bodies and emblazoned their empty eyes and terror-set faces into my head. I would not forget and I would not let it disillusion me. I couldn't.

Mom's voice softly interrupted the silence. "Coming up on the store, April."

I unbuckled my seat belt and, grabbing my weapons and equipment, nodded my acknowledgement to her. She slowed the van down to a crawl then lightly tapped the brakes to bring it to a full stop. I glanced out towards the huge Pro Shop sign that sat dusty in the bright morning sun. Butterflies fluttered their wings in my belly as I took a deep breath in. I loved these stores. So many fine weaponry and goodies, it got my heart racing. I needed to restock some of my supplies and today seemed like a mighty good day to do so.

I hugged Jeremy and kissed the top of his sandy brown hair. Smiling, I gave his fear-filled eyes a wink. "I'll see you in a bit, squirt." He nodded slightly but my reassurance was not convincing. I turned away, stepped out of the van and clicked the door shut behind me. I didn't look back as I heard the tires crunch away, rolling on the pavement toward the supermarket two streets down. I stood staring at the windows of the sporting goods store. Scanning the area around me, I expected nothing but I wasn't going to start getting careless.

The breeze was cool this morning, sweeping up small billows of dust and dead leaves. The street was desolate; cracked pavement, smashed windows and garbage were littered about. I closed my eyes. Standing by myself and listening to the eerie quiet made me feel naked, like I was exposed. I no longer heard the van and no steps betrayed anyone's presence. Opening my eyes, I sighed and said a silent prayer for courage as the flood of fear threatened to break. I'd done this dozens of times, but each time never got any easier.

I unsheathed my machete from my right side; it was perfect for close range combat and did the job. I didn't want to have to use it but that wasn't up to me. I had to secure the place before browsing the goods. Pushing the heavy glass doors to enter, I glanced around the store, looking for signs of movement, especially in the shadows. The air was stuffy but not sour, like the places that had rotting corpses and dead vampires lying around. This store wasn't frequented by the feral and wild vampires. The skylights high in the ceiling and the walls of glass windows kept it well lit and therefore, mostly vampire-free. I hadn't run into one in this particular store yet, but I wasn't taking my chances.

Systematically, I walked the perimeter of the isles then down the middle and zigzagged, stopping frequently to listen for footsteps or other noises. None came. Only the slight whistle of the wind outside broke the solace of the place. Having finished with the storefront, I made my way to the storerooms in the back. It was riskier there, darker. I lit a flashlight and scanned the area, shoving the double doors open to let the sunlight in. Luckily it wasn't a large area and the many boxes were stacked flush against the walls, since space was limited.

Satisfied, I closed the doors and turned back to the racks of camping stuff, weapons, bikes and more. A flutter of excitement now ran through my chest as I turned down my favorite isle of knives and arrows to restock my supplies. I grabbed a few boxes of ammunition and retrieved the wheeled metal cart to start piling it up with things. I opened some of the large duffle bags. These were for the smaller items, to keep them together and arranged as space efficiently as I could.

I slipped a few packages of arrows into the cart along with several daggers and throwing stars. I grabbed some extra boots—mine were wearing out–and a dart throwing set for Jeremy. Satisfied with my haul, I pulled the cart outside, letting the doors swing shut behind me.

I looked around and felt a slight chill down my arms. Even though I was wearing my thin jacket, it felt cold and I rubbed my arms. The sun was rising and would warm the air soon enough, but the feeling of dread seemed to stick to me as I scanned the area again. Nothing but silence greeted me. I shook off the feeling and turned towards the intersection. Turning east, I slipped my sunglasses down over my eyes and followed the road.

I scurried down the sidewalk, glancing around me and studying each building as best I could as I hurried down the road. When I turned down the second street, I felt silly for feeling skittish. I let out a laugh. Sometimes I felt like a fool, but living in this ruin of a world had made me so paranoid, I could swear that I was always being watched. The sun was brilliant and its intensity would burn the vampires to a crisp if they attempted to leave their shadowed sanctuaries. I talked myself down as I continued, calming my inner voice to silence as I approached the supermarket I was to meet my mother and brother at.

The van was nowhere to be seen but that wasn't unusual. They could have thought of another place they had wanted to visit before heading to our meeting spot. I looked around, repeating my surveillance of the outside of the market. Pulling the cart to the doors, I pushed them open and unsheathed my machete once more. The market was darker than the sporting goods store, though it had high windows lining the store front. Still, the back was lined in shadows and anything could be lurking at the ends of the isles.

I grabbed my flashlight and let its beam caress the rows of food and along with the mess of things flung across the tile floor. Some stores had been ransacked when the epidemic hit, but most were still generally intact. A few stragglers had made it and looted supplies before probably dropping dead when they attempted to escape the city or getting ravaged by the wild vampires that the virus had created. I stepped into the store slowly, watching my step to avoid tripping on the bottles, boxes and cans that blocked my path. The further in I went, the less of a mess there was, like the looters had not considered going too deep into the store for supplies. They'd had good reason for that.

It took a few minutes but it was well worth the peace of mind to do my rounds. Finished with my examination of the store and back storage area, I started to load up my cart with non-perishables that were on my list. It was a tedious job, dragging the cart along with one hand and holding the flashlight in the other hand, I was used to it and managed to dump a ton of supplies into the cart.

Finishing up in the store, I wanted to get outside to see if my mother and Jeremy were there yet. It didn't seem like much time had passed but it was near noon. Where were they? Pushing through the doors, I spotted the van parked to my left. Looking around for them, I saw nothing. *How could they be here, but not have come in and say hello?* I headed for the van and peeked inside. The keys were in the ignition and the back seat was filled with bags of supplies they had probably stuffed in there. Glancing around again and listening for any noise, I shrugged. They were probably in the store and I had just missed them.

I opened the trunk and started to fill the rest of it up with the stuff I had acquired. Once I was done, the metal cart folded up nicely and slipped in, too. Closing the hatch slowly so as to not make too much noise, I pushed at it and felt it click. I sat on the back bumper as I looked around again, feeling the tug of anxiety as I wondered once more where my family was.

Deciding to recheck the store, I hopped over the sidewalk and went through the front doors. Clicking the flashlight back on, I listened for movement but none came. I decided to call out to them, figuring it was safe since I had already secured the place.

"Mom? Jeremy? You guys in here?" My voice echoed in the emptiness, giving me a shudder as the large room seemed to grow dimmer as the midday sun no longer shined directly through the grungy windows. I licked my lips, feeling my throat close up as the air seemed to suddenly thicken and the staleness of it choked me.

I called out to them again and again but no answer came. I backed out and slammed the doors open, looking wildly around. The van was still parked in the same spot, nothing out of the ordinary that I could see. There was just no one else there.

Where were they?

My eyes fell on one thing that I had not noticed before. The driver's side door was slightly cracked open. My stomach lurched for a moment as I slowly stepped around the front of the van to look at the door. A smear of blood ran along the handle and up to the edge of the window. A bloody handprint of dark brick red in color, painted the center of the door. I gasped as my heart jumped, immediately drawing my machete out. I crouched against the van as my eyes darted around, looking for anything that would lead me to where they were. I searched the ground for blood trails but none could be found. If scavengers were out here too, they could have snatched them and I'd have been none the wiser. Not that I had seen any for almost a year.

I prayed for something but nothing came. I ran out toward the sidewalk that lined the street. It was quiet and desolate as ever. The sun reflected brightly on the dusty white buildings around me and fluttering trash floated by, riding on the breeze. My hair was flying in a halo as I wildly looked around.

"Oh, God, no, please! Where are they? Help me, please!"

I sucked back the sob that threatened to spill, not noticing the tears that already streamed down my cheeks. I ran to the corner of the sidewalk and glanced down both ways, desperate for any signs of them. Was Mom hurt? Was Jeremy? If I couldn't find the sign I needed, I could lose them forever. It wasn't something I was going to do, no, I couldn't lose them. As I was about to turn back into the parking lot, I spotted what I needed. A tire track was pressed into an old bag of stuff. Whatever had been in it was now smashed and imprinted with the wavy lines of a tire. I ran to it and studied its lines intently. It was fresh. The track was well defined and nothing interrupted it, no dust, no streaks of the sparse rain that had recently fallen. I looked in the direction the tires headed, but that was the only clue that anything had changed. I ran down the street but nothing came into view. I came to a stop, slightly out of breath but feeling the panic surge like an overwhelming asphyxiation. I bent over, feeling the world spin as I tried to tame it back down.

They're gone, they're gone.

No, no, no, no!

I fell to my knees and let my stomach release the knot of breakfast, spilling it across the pavement. Tears flooded my eyes as I finished and let the sobs rip through me and shake my body. How could this happen? Who would take them? I hadn't seen anyone or come across any scavengers in so long that it had become a world of just us three. We had often spoken of that, wondering together if we truly were the last humans left.

The thought of being left by myself jolted me up from my position. My machete was on the ground where I had dropped it. I scooped it up and began walking back, glancing around as I wiped the tears off my face and sheathed my weapon. I wanted to get to the van and follow the track. If I could find another clue, maybe, just maybe, I could find them in time. Trying not to think of the feral vampires or worse that may have captured them, I ran until I found myself back at the van. Flinging the door open, I cranked the engine. I slammed the door shut as I accelerated, screeching from the parking lot and out into the streets of Sin city.

14

Chapter Four

THE ENDLESS DRIVE and search had left me broken in despair. I had not found any signs anywhere of my mother and brother. I had returned endless times to the supermarket with no further clues of anything. The streets had not offered further hints to their whereabouts. I now sat waiting in the van, dried tears and dirt caked on my face as I pondered what to do as the sun descended just above Mt. Charleston to the west. Nothing made sense. Everything was so wrong and the pit of sadness growing in my chest arrested my breath. The dusk warned me in colors of orange and dusty red that the night threatened to make its appearance and the looming shadows grew.

I gritted my teeth and shook my head. Disbelief and denial flooded my head as I screamed, pounding my hands against the steering wheel, making the van shake.

This can't be happening! It's not real! Wake up April!

My hands screamed as the hits flared into a raging pain, turning them scarlet red. The ache was not enough to numb me, but it did send me into a spill of sobs. The last of my tears spilt down my face and soaked my shirt as they plopped onto the fabric.

I can't leave them here! I can't! That was not a possibility. How could I ever leave them for those beasts? How could I live knowing I drove away into the sunset without them?

I sighed, sniffling and wiping my nose. I knew the answer all too well; I would never be able to forgive myself when I finally did leave this place tonight. I would rather die looking for them and I'd never give up. They were all I had to live for.

Shifting the van into gear, the hum of the engine made my panic surge one more time but I swallowed it down into the pit of my stomach. I could almost hear my mother's voice telling me that it was fine. She would expect me to return home, to the safety of our sanctuary in the mountains. She had always stated as such. But I didn't want to. I could hardly breathe thinking of following her directions.

Her voice echoed in my head, making me nod slowly as if she could even see me. "Anything happens, you return here for the night. We get separated, or anything, don't let your emotions destroy your senses. You know what must be done. Don't look back."

Moving the shifter into gear, I gently pressed on the gas and drove across the empty parking lot to the street. Pausing at the edge of the concrete, as if any other cars would ever be crossing the way anymore, I took in a deep breath as the sun's last beams seared into my eyes. My foot pressed the gas once more and I slowly pulled away from the desolate city, leaving my heart behind.

Chapter Five

THE SUN SLUMBERED as I stared at the monitor of the security cameras. Its screen was split into four squares, each square displaying an image from one of the cameras that continually scanned the perimeter of the bunker. I sat on a steel chair that was ever so uncomfortable but it kept me awake, never letting my eyes waver from the screen. It was now burning itself into my retinas, making my eyes dry out. I hadn't changed and my grimy clothes clung to my skin. My disheveled hair flew in a crazy array of wisps and tangles about my head in a mangled halo, but I did not care. My feet ached, still in boots and sore from the endless search of the day. It was late but I was not going to be sleeping any tonight.

I prayed for them to suddenly appear, waving at me on the screen to let them in. I tapped on one of my katana swords that I had laid out on the desk before me. Its shiny steel surface gleamed under the fluorescent lights as I rocked the blade back and forth. The sun was not going to rise fast enough for me; the waiting agitated me down to my core. My nerves were jumpy and shaky as the overload of caffeine surged through my veins and made my head ache with a feverish pain. Rolling my shoulders, I stood up and stretched, walking over to the medicine cabinet to scavenge for some migraine medicine.

Finding what I needed, I sank back down on the steel chair. The hardness of it made my body protest even more. I grabbed a bottle of water I had left on the desk and swallowed down the two pills. I hated taking medicine if I didn't have to, but the caffeine and pain relievers were a necessity at the moment. I didn't want the migraine to get to the point where I would be debilitated and stuck in bed all night and day. I couldn't afford that when my mother and brother were out in the death-filled night. Rubbing my temples, I groaned. I had to stay focused. Glancing at the screen again, I jumped as a flash of movement stilled my breath. I scrambled closer to the desk and glowing monitors. The other cameras were still and had showed nothing so I waited, hoping my pounding heart would slow down as I anticipated whatever it was that had moved to round the corner to the next camera.

I didn't have to wait long; a blur of a figure came into view looking around as if disorientated. A girl or young woman slowly walked by, as oblivious to her surroundings as she was of me watching her. I gulped as I studied her slow, delicate movements and grabbed the camera's remote to follow her with the lens. I hoped the camera's movement was quiet enough to not be heard as I followed her in the darkness. It had a night vision lens and the brightness along the person's skin made me think of my mother. I hoped the vamps had not gotten to her and wondered if maybe it was her. I squinted to study the image closer, zooming in on the figure.

Suddenly, the girl turned her bright, reflecting eyes towards the camera. I held my breath as I watched her inch closer, like a cat in the night toward the camera and seem to sniff up at it, cranking her head to see it better. My lips were numb, pressed so tight together that they were surely white. I waited as she stood on tip toes to get closer. I stilled the camera and observed her. Her fair blonde hair was in tangles and her dress hung on her like shredded rags. Her face had the baby fat of youth with a bruise of shadows under her eyes. Her face was smudged with dirt, adding to the wild look in her bright eyes.

I wondered who she was. Was she a feral? Was she even real? I feared I might have been hallucinating in my sleep-deprived state. She seemed to lose interest in the camera but did attempt one last time to reach up and swipe at the camera. She was too short and missed. I began to suspect she was not human. But what if she was? Indecision bubbled inside me as I wondered if I should go out and see about her. I felt stuck, not sure whether to go or not. If she was a feral, I'd have to kill her. If she wasn't, I wasn't ready to let another human into our home, especially without my mother here to consult about it.

On a whim, I grabbed my katana sword and entered the code to open the heavy steel doors. I peeked out and shut it quickly behind me as I slipped into the cloak of night. I shined my flashlight around the trees and brush, heading to her last known whereabouts near the camera. The night was almost blinding; the new moon left the forest engulfed in a black hole of nothingness. The stars shined like pin holes in a canvas of night. I listened and kept alert, hoping the girl was either gone or not in the position to lunge at me.

I did not have to search long; she was standing at the van, which I had parked in the back of the house, and seemed to be trying to fiddle with the door handle. I had the keys so there was no way she was going to steal it. Anyone with carjacking skills would have had that van on the road by now. She seemed clumsy and unsure. I wondered why she was so fascinated with the van. I soon found out exactly what had caught her attention.

She had slipped down into a crouch as her face caressed the side of the door, near the smear of blood that had now dried onto the paint. She scratched at it and licked the dried flakes with her tongue, like a large cat lapping up milk. My disgust made the rage inside me burn. I wanted to smack her off the vehicle and my mother's blood, to make her suffer. The hatred rampaged through my head as I gripped my sword and pointed the flashlight into her face, briskly approaching her.

"Hey! Get away from there you animal!" I yelled as I got closer. My sword was already held out and set to cut her down. My voice startled her and she backed away and turned to face me. Surprise and fear flashed across her face as I came within sword's reach of her. Stepping back away from me, she winced as the sword flashed across her face.

"Who are you?" Her thin voice came out shaky and unsure as her eyes darted around at me. I paused, stunned that she had spoken. Feral vampires don't speak. I shook off my shock as I glared at her.

"It doesn't matter! Who are *you*?" I demanded. I nodded to the van as I continued, "you seek blood don't you?" I stepped one foot closer and she cringed, glancing behind her for an escape route. She had unfortunately gotten herself into a tight spot. The van stood in her way on one side and the wall of the house was at the other. She only had one way out for I was blocking the front. She glanced back to me and shivered as I stepped closer.

"I–I, wait, I don't know what you mean." She stuttered as her back pressed against the van. Her wild eyes reflected the beam of the flashlight, much like a cat's retinas would. This was always a definite sign of a vampire and it confirmed my suspicions. I held the sword ready and continued to approach her.

My hatred boiled in my veins, and the need to connect my blade with her neck felt overwhelming. I wanted her to suffer. My mother and brother were gone because of her. The vampires had killed everyone I had ever loved and they were nothing but blood hungry beasts that did not care about who they sacrificed. She may have looked young and weak, but I knew better. The monster lurking under her skin would rip me to shreds if given any chance. They had no mercy and neither would I.

"You're in the wrong place at the wrong time; I will make you pay for what you have done to my family," I growled at her. My voice was almost unrecognizable, even to myself.

"Your family? I–I don't know them! I've done nothing!" Her voice cracked with the terror that spread across her face. She turned and tried to climb up the side of the van to get away. I swung the sword back as I approached. Bringing it around, it easily connected with her neck as a piercing screech escaped her mouth but ended suddenly with the thump of her head on the shattered leaves below. Her headless body convulsed as its missing controller was now gone, slumping to the ground almost immediately. Her black-red blood pooled under the mass of her thin, childlike frame.

My heart was racing and I felt like throwing up. I hadn't had anything to eat all day or night except the caffeinated drinks I had used to stay awake. Dizziness and utter disgust from everything rushed over me at that moment. Her death had brought me no relief. She wasn't even a feral. What she had been was a mystery. *Ferals do not speak.* They had no speech at all. How could she be a vampire and be able to talk? It was an anomaly at best.

The nausea of what I had done overwhelmed me as I backed away from her corpse, now still and looking an odd, sickly-pale shade. I turned and ran to the door of the compound, punching several attempts into the keypad before it opened. I scampered inside and slammed the door shut, turning the locks into place as fast as I could. Her blood could attract others if any other vampires were nearby. I was so stupid! What if there were others with her? I could have easily died or have been ambushed.

I couldn't think anymore as I rushed to a nearby sink, letting my sword clank to the ground as I turned on the ice-cold water, dousing my face in splashes. The shock woke me up a bit more but the terror of what I had done remained. I wet my face one more time before turning the faucet off and looked up into the wild face that stared back at me. I looked like that girl, almost feral in my own human-like way. She hadn't had a chance against me at all. I was the predator now; she had been an ant under my foot.

I would have to burn her body in the morning but for right now, the exhaustion overwhelmed me. It was 3 am; I would have three hours to rest at best, if I could get any. I rechecked the door and motion detectors before slumping into my bed, kicking off my boots and slipping out of my dirty clothes. I pulled a clean shirt from a stack next to my bed and pulled it over; shorts were my jammies for now. Pulling my blanket up to my chin and stuffing the pillow under my head, I closed my burning eyes as my mind finally succumbed to a cocoon of restless sleep.

Chapter Six

THE ALARM RANG through my dreams, sending the fogginess of sleep out of my brain. I slammed the clock and rubbed my face, hoping yesterday had been a dream. One of my legs was dangling out of the blanket that twisted around my body. Sitting up, I sighed in disappointment as I stared at the two empty beds beside mine. I hung my head down and felt the sting of tears behind my eyelids as I tried to breathe in slowly. I had prayed so hard that it had all just been a torturous nightmare.

Readying myself, I prepped to venture out while the day awoke. Making sure I had all my weapons and some food and water to last me the day, I unlatched the heavy steel door and ventured out into the world, locking it behind me. Kerosene and a lighter in hand, I walked over to where the girl's corpse lay, still undisturbed.

Not like there was anyone around here to disturb a vampire's body.

I pulled her thin body over to the end of the cement driveway and placed her head on her chest before piling up dried brush and twigs around her. It was going to burn intensely; any flesh would burned hot and strong. The sun was still beneath the tree line, shadows shortening as it ascended. I wondered briefly if the sun would even burn this particular vampire. I wasn't going to chance her not burning. Once I was done, I lit a bunch of kindling and dropped it in the pile after dousing it with the lighter fluid.

The flames ignited quickly, licking her body with hungry fingers and burning her clothes up immediately. I watched, hoping that the smoke would not draw too much attention. Once she burned up, I would have to clean up the ashes and sweep the driveway. I sat impatiently as her thin frame was consumed, trying to keep my feelings about her at bay. At least it didn't take long. The fire burned intensely enough to pulverize her body. Fire did well disintegrating vampire bodies, they were so combustible. I sat and pondered why it had not gone up in flames at sunrise. This was indeed new to me.

I grew impatient and stood up, pacing the walk as I waited. When the fire had died down I grabbed buckets of water from a nearby water pump and doused the embers as they continued to crackle and snap. Nothing was left of the strange vampire now. Nothing but dust and ashes to even signify she existed. A sudden shame overwhelmed me. I had killed her before she could even tell me who she was. Feral vampires didn't speak. What, then, did that make her? Some sort of hybrid?

Shaking my head, I tried not to think about it so much, sweeping the mess of ashes and water off the driveway as quickly as I could. I had to get down into the city and search for my family again. I hated being alone, hated that my family could very well be dead now. No, I wouldn't accept it–I knew they were still alive, I felt it inside my heart and soul. Like a fire that still blazed within, it wasn't doused yet, like I knew it would be if our connection broke. That alone kept me focused this gloomy morning as I shoved the broom away into the garage and jumped into the van, turning the engine over and pulling out into the road towards Las Vegas.

The asphalt rolled under the car as I impatiently drove, agitated that I wasn't already there. I wanted to run through the streets, waking the dead. I had no plan, no investigative plot to find my family. But it was no holds barred. If I had to shake up all the hives of feral vampires to find Mom and Jeremy, I would. I would kill every last one of them if I had to.

My right hand drifted down to feel the hilt of my blades where they were leaning on the passenger side seat. I had brought my short katana sword and one machete. My crossbow, along with a quiver of arrows, would be strapped to my back if I needed it. It was compact and lightweight. I was prepped for war and I intended to win. Rolling my shoulders, I cracked my neck and felt my shoulders pop as I fidgeted in the seat, watching the landscape pass by as I pulled closer to the city. The debris in the road made me furious; I had to slow down to dodge the scattered mess. I wanted to be running. I was itching to kill the wretched creatures that had taken the only two souls that mattered to me.

Screeching into the parking lot of the supermarket, I jumped out of the van, strapping sheathes and daggers to my belt. Tightening the crossbow to my back, I made sure the quiver was stuffed full and the bow loaded. Last I pulled the katana and let it slide through my belt into place. It hummed in my hand and with a decisive power. The machete strapped to my right thigh and side nicely. I stuffed two flashlights into my belt too and slammed the door to the van, taking the keys with me. I wasn't sure if

I was expecting anything more than just ferals. They didn't leave the shadows of the buildings. But something had. Something had ventured into the parking lot to take Mom and Jeremy.

But any new hybrid vampires–if that's what they were–would have to pull the keys off my bloody, dead body to steal my ride.

I glanced around me; the midmorning sun was already warning me that time was running out. I nodded, acknowledging its reassuring warmth, even if it was just for my own assurance. Inside, the darkness of the buildings was always cooler than the outside. I'd take the open parking lot over the insanely claustrophobic cramped insides of the infested buildings. I started forward, walking briskly toward the road where the tire track I had found the previous day had pointed.

Scanning the street in both directions, I again saw no other clues. I groaned, knowing the immense search in front of me would not be easy. If my family was alive they were probably not near this place but far from it. Standing up, I decided to head in the direction the tracks were leading me and begin searching the buildings. The tall, dead casinos loomed in the distance, the same direction as the tire tracks. It was not beyond me to fathom that they had headed that way. Whoever took them must have taken up residence near the strip of the Las Vegas Boulevard. I wasn't sure, but what better place to start? It would take me forever to search every casino but I had a lifetime to spare.

I followed the road and made it to the Mandalay Bay's dusty, gold-hued windows. I stared up at the beautiful brilliance of its mirrored windows that reflected the sun like laser beams down onto the street. I smiled. I was willing to bet that most of the tower rooms in the hotels were not infested; the amount of sun pouring into them would be unbearable for the ferals. It was the dark pits of the main floor casinos that worried me. The rank hallways and hidden rooms were numerous in these buildings– having been remodeled so many times–would be the most dangerous. I remembered the bowels of some of these monstrosities, the halls that led nowhere and the underground basements that went on for miles, full of stored slots, tables, chairs and then some.

I sighed, quickly slipping into the parking lot and down the sidewalks overgrown with desert sage and tumbleweeds that clogged up the way. I remembered this place in all its glory. It was heartbreaking to venture into its lost beauty and wasted neglect since the epidemic wiped everyone out. The land had quickly snarled its grip around the streets and concrete jungles of the city. I worked my way through the weeds and overgrown grasses that had survived the lack of water and the summer's dry heat. It had been mild but not many plants had tolerated it. None of the colorful flowers in the neatly manicured displays had lived. The place had a haunted feel to it.

I gulped as I reached the main entry to the lobby of the casino. Studying my own reflection in the thick glass doors made my heart flit in anticipation. I pulled out a flashlight and my short katana sword. I hated the dark interiors; it was like walking into a swarm of snakes. I tried to slow my breathing as I pushed the first set of doors in, ready for anything with every step.

The inner doors looked undisturbed. I wondered if the ferals even used doors. Most places I had found them had the doors hanging by the hinges or torn off. These were solid thick glass doors with metal hinges. They were dusty but intact with nothing to signify vampires roaming inside. I wasn't about to take it for granted at all, though. One mistake or let down of my guard and I might as well serve myself up for dinner.

Pausing, my courage stuck in my throat as I pondered my reflection. I looked so thin and hard, so unlike the girl that had hung out with friends and danced at parties. I looked like a military black ops chick, geared up and all. My hair pulled tight in a ponytail, black shirt and black cargo pants. Dark cool eyes stared back at me, harsh and stern. I wanted to run from the woman that glared back at me, unrecognizable from just a year ago.

I pulled the door open and pushed the thoughts to the back of my mind. No time to think about that now. No time to ever think about that. The whoosh of stale air rushed at me like a sinister whisper. Clicking the flashlight on, I scanned the area before me. Endless chairs and slots stood dusty and dormant. Particles danced in the beam of light as I swept it around every nook and cranny. Katana in hand, I felt an odd coolness as I treaded inside. This place was undisturbed. Even the long-rotted corpses of people that I occasionally stepped over had been left where they had fallen. I glanced down to the ruin of carpet that ran all along the ground. Its dust untainted but for my own footprints. I doubted anyone had come in here or used it for anything. Even the ferals had not bothered with this desolate place.

I backed out after walking down one side of the casino floor. These buildings were death traps; too many hidden doorways and rows upon rows of slots and card tables to hide under or behind. I was sweating from the state of high alert that I had to keep up. The heavy canteen bumped against my leg as I moved. I was feeling the weight of all my gear. The night of bad sleep was going to catch up to me quickly if this continued. I sighed, marking this place as abandoned and headed back out into the brilliant sunlight.

The world looked the same. Unfortunately, nothing had changed. I headed down to next casino: The Luxor. Its dark windows were streaked in mud and old rain fall that carved little dirty rivers down its slanted sides. I wondered if any of the casinos were infested. I was sure they would be. But from the looks of the last one, the heavy doors were a hindrance to the vampires. The smaller casinos were probably a safer bet for them. I sighed. Just to be sure, I'd have to check out the main casinos on this intersection which was known as the Four Corners, made from the crossing of two main streets: Tropicana Avenue and Las Vegas Boulevard.

Luxor was more challenging than Mandalay Bay. The interior was more tumultuous, with various levels and the inner incline of the pyramid walls. My flashlight's range went only so far in the deep darkness. I hoped that whatever lurked on the upper levels wouldn't jump down and surprise me. It was precarious to search this one. I sighed, trying to calm my nerves as I stepped up the stairs and onto the second floor veranda level. It was full of overturned trash cans and snack stands with litter everywhere.

As I scanned the balconies that led to the top of the pyramid, I noticed what looked like clothes and other belongings dangling off the sides of the balcony walkways above. I also saw several bodies littering the floor below them, like the people had jumped at one point and fallen to their deaths. I shuddered, turning away to search the rest of the floor. One exhibit's display consisted of a dark hallway leading to a set of rooms. It looked vaguely familiar but the banners had long ago been torn away and nothing remained to signify what it had been.

A figure flashed into my vision. I swept the beam of light back to where I thought I had seen it and a shadow of a person stood on a riser before me. Licking my drying lips, I readied my sword as I crept closer to the figure. It did not move and I wondered if it was even alive. To die in a standing position and remain so was almost impossible. Once I was upon it and ready to strike, I baulked as I fumbled back away from it. The skin was missing and only muscles, tendons and sinew along its extremities bulged out. It was a Bodies display—preserved to show all of the inner anatomy and wired to stand in a playful position, throwing a football.

I let out a laugh. *Stupid exhibits!* I should have known—I had visited it once a few years ago. That I had forgotten all about it took me by surprise and I scolded myself as I tried to slow my heart rate down, dropping my blade to my side.

But my relief was short-lived. A feral vampire jumped toward me from the shadows, knocking me into the wall. Its snarls echoed in my ears and a foul odor assaulted my nostrils. My sword clanged to the floor and the flashlight spun in circles just out of my reach, lighting the place up like a disco.

Shit!

I struggled to capture my footing, not sure where the vampire had gone off to, though I could hear its growls echoing in the rooms. I pulled a dagger from my belt as I scrambled for the flashlight. As I lunged for it, my legs were seized, sending me flying forward again, smacking my knuckles on the cement floor. The pain seared up my arms but I had managed to clamp my left hand over the flashlight and turned to aim it into the creature's face as I kicked at it frantically trying to free my legs.

It grasped with its boney, thin hands, scratching and tugging as if its life depended on it. The deep blood-red eyes glared at me as it snarled, dirty fangs glistened in the light. It winced only just a bit under the flood of the light's beam but it was enough for me to sit up and plunge the dagger into an eye socket, sending it writhing and screeching. Blood and ichor poured from the wound as it convulsed violently. I scrambled back on my arms and up onto my feet, glancing across the floor to find my sword.

I caught sight of it not too far from me, picking it up as I turned back to the dying vampire. It hissed at me but seemed to weaken with the loss of blood. The pale grey of its skin seemed to gleam opalescent and turned whiter still as a pool of blood and other things grew under its face. I stood over its body and swung the blade down in a clean slice through the neck. The quivering creature stopped moving and all was still once more. I sighed, wiping the blade on the ragged clothes of the dead vampire. Their blood was sticky and black, reminding me of used up motor oil.

I felt oddly satisfied, almost giddy, as the adrenaline rushed through my veins, pumping like ecstasy into my head. It was always exhilarating and I was ready for more, wanting to let them come.

Making sure the rest of the exhibit rooms were empty, I returned to the second floor and stepped down a staircase to the main casino floor. It was in shambles too, with overturned tables, cards and chips everywhere. A panic had ensued here; I could almost feel its vibrations still lingering in the air. I scanned it quickly and made my way to the rear of the casino. If I had not visited these places before when they had been alive with flashing lights and the hum of people, I would have gotten lost for sure. Even so, the back hallways into the employee areas were nothing to be happy about. The long basement-like passageways were endless and had so many turns, I feared the way out would be a treacherous route indeed. Luckily I found an exit and came to find myself on the west side of the building, facing the huge parking garage of the massive casino, which it shared with two others.

Closing the door behind me, I breathed a sigh of relief and leaned back on the warming metal of the double exit doors. The sun blazed high noon on my face and the stale air from the inside of the building was replaced with fresher desert air. I inhaled it with pleasure, glad to be free of the stifling dark. Only then could I relax somewhat as I rubbed a knot on my shoulder that had seized up from landing on the ground.

I stared down the strip towards the next casino: the Excalibur. It was a huge looming giant that reminded me how big they were and how small I really was. It would take eons to search every building and the more time that passed, the less likely I was to find Jeremy and Mom. Stuffing the flashlight away and sliding the Katana into my belt, I hit the pavement running. The pillars and concrete of the parking garages flew past me as the wind whipped its fingers across my face, teasing my hair out of its ponytail. I loved running. It was the closest feeling I ever got to really getting away from it all. The land rushing by with the pavement smacking against the heels of my shoes and gulping lungfuls of dry cool air was exhilarating.

I skidded to a stop as I reached the sidewalk along Tropicana Ave. Glancing down both ways, the aloneness hit me again. I sighed, reaching for my canteen of water to take thirsty gulps of the sensational fluid. It was still autumn and the heat of summer was all but gone. The drifts of cool air were gaining strength as winter grew closer. It felt great on the sheen of sweat building on my skin from the run.

The Four Corners crossroad sat desolate and quiet. The litter that flew about seemed to sway in its own ballet like a star in a silent film. I still felt so small, staring up at the Excalibur and New York, New York casinos. They were enormous and promised me a thousand hiding places within. I felt almost at a loss. Should I search them all like the last two? Should I just randomly look in them? I could be way off the trail or close to it, I couldn't even be sure. I felt it was almost useless to search them all. They could be in a warehouse right off the strip, in the back alley ways that lined the outside edges of the boulevard or even farther, far away in the bordering cities of Henderson or North Las Vegas even. I hoped not. I prayed I was at least getting closer than anything else.

Chapter Seven

THE DAY HAD yielded nothing and my patience had grown extra thin. I hadn't even hit any feral vampire hives. I had managed to dispatch several lone ones, heading toward me in the bowels of the smaller casinos. Apparently, these were easier to break into for them than the larger casinos. Still, I was more frustrated than ever and my head ached with a throb that surged through my temples as I ended the day's search, driving away toward home, once again without my family.

The drive was even harder this time than it had been the prior evening. As I drove, feelings of failure and disappointment stabbed at me like daggers in my chest. The pavement seemed hypnotizing as the sun's light drained away over the horizon. I was leaving a little later than I had wanted but my desperation had grown to a fever pitch as I had frantically searched as much as I could in the last hours of daylight. Slashing down the ferals I had encountered left me more empty than satisfied. I just wanted to see my mother and brother's faces again–longing to see their smiles and listen to their contagious laughs and giggles in the loneliness of the night that awaited me.

Pulling up to the house in the mountains filled me with dread. Another night alone, another night left wondering what had happened to what was left of my family. Would I ever receive the answers to the questions that seems to run marathons through my head as I lay in bed at night, praying that the alarms would trip and it would be them banging on the door to come in? The deep searing pain I felt as I wearily peeled my equipment and weapons off my body, letting them clank onto the cold concrete floor inside the cell that I called home, ate away at my brain.

I showered the dirt and dried vampiric blood off my skin, temporarily easing the soreness of the day's activities. The water was amazing, hot and steaming. I remembered how absolutely thankful we had been to find that this underground refuge had a propane feed with a solar heater back up to heat water. Hot water, electricity–things I had taken for granted before–readily available only here. It had truly been a godsend.

I fell into my bed, barely pulling the sheets over my body before succumbing to the lure of sleep, so deep that for once, the nightmarish dreams eluded me.

CRACKING MY EYES open, I felt a sudden overwhelming anxiety that captured my breath in my throat. It was early morning and my body felt like it had been run over by truck. Sitting up, my joints popped and creaked as my muscles burned in protest. All the running and searching had been more than I had done in a while and had left me in a state of exhaustion.

I had to get up, though I did not want to. I could feel the desolation creeping into my mind as the urge to give up seemed to grow with each passing moment. To stay in bed and continue to sleep would be just fine with me, and this was unacceptable. Shaking my head, I tried to regain my focus. I had to keep moving, searching and searching until we were all safe again. I could not let this depression overwhelm me and threaten to freeze me into despair.

I quickly ate breakfast, gulping down an energy bar and some bottled green tea, and dressed for the day. I slipped on some dark jeans and strapped a machete to my right thigh. I stretched as I fit the weapons on. I hung a hatchet on an axe loop at my left side, leaving it at that. I was going to go light today. My body was not into hauling too many supplies and from the experience of the search yesterday, I wouldn't need as much as I thought I would. I checked my flashlights and slipped them into my many belt compartments. I filled the remaining pouches with water and snacks.

I finished off by pulling my hair into a tight bun that held at the nape of my neck. Done, I noticed again how gaunt I looked in the mirrors of the bathroom. I looked thin, but the sun had slowly burned its rays across my skin, giving it a slightly reddish, light brown hue. I'd forgotten to put sunscreen on the day before and groaned at the slight tingle of pain that emanated from the burn. I grabbed for a tube of the thick cream to slather on. The sun was intense here and a severe sunburn would be much more painful than sore muscles.

Exiting the compound, I loaded myself up into the van and headed off once more down the mountain. I wished I was closer to the city; the forty minute drive sometimes irritated me down to my core if I was desperate to get there, like I was today. I swerved around the debris, cursing under my breath that some of it had shifted with the violent winds that had swept through the valley during the night. It was still a bit breezy but not as wild as the night had been.

This time, after checking the supermarket area, I drove away toward the strip to be closer to my main search area. I had made it to the Flamingo and Las Vegas Boulevard intersection. That's where I had ended my search the day before. The short mile had left me exhausted. There were so many buildings to search that it had taken too long to get through that short part of the Strip. It had frustrated me to the gills.

I pulled in behind the Caesar's Palace casino, a place I used to hold a job at. The Forum Shops was a super-long mall filled with rich displays of expensive goodies. Now it was a darkened tunnel, probably full of vampires. I wasn't sure I wanted to start in the mall area. There were no windows in it, a completely enclosed mall. It was sure to be unsafe. The entire casino barely had any windows. I cracked a smile, thinking back to the reasoning for this. It had been done on purpose in constructing the casinos to keep people gambling their hard earned money away without a concept of time. No windows, no clocks. Genius on the part of the casinos but bad for me, in the complete darkness with creatures that wanted nothing but to slurp up all the blood out of my veins.

I decided to enter the back way, where the employee entrance was and I had gone in many times before. At least I knew this casino's layout well. Entering at the rear of the mall would be hazardous, but I'd have to go through there eventually anyway. Pushing the heavy double doors of the emergency exit, a black hole of nothing and dust swirled up before me, down a corridor into the insides of the building. I stood there for what seemed like an eternity. Nothing but the wind softly tossing about interrupted the air. I readied my hatchet and flashlight, wiping my sweaty palms on my jeans. I slowly entered, letting the doors behind me close softly, right into the bubble of black.

It was suffocating. The ventilation in these places was poor, even when it had been alive with electricity and air conditioning. It always had kept the smoke clouds from burning cigarettes lingering forever in the enclosed space. Now it was stifling and stale.

I walked slowly forward, reaching the vending machines full of old snacks that stood to one side of the wide hallway. An inlet to the public restrooms stood to my left and I contemplated searching them. I flashed my light over the doorway openings that stood opposite each other. Only the dust on the floor told me that no one had been here in a long time. A year of dirt streaked across the tile floors and all around me. I decided to forgo it, feeling pretty sure that no one had ventured down this way in ages.

The hallway opened up to a large dining and entertainment area where a huge aquarium stood, half full with murky water and the stench of death. I held my breath and pulled my shirt over my nose. It was strong here, maybe from the slush of dead fish that lined the top of the aquarium water. I wasn't too sure. Something told me to stay alert—the stench could very well be decomposing bodies in a hive of vampires. The place was wrecked. The beautiful faux marble displays and saltwater aquarium were filthy and disgusting now, a ghost of the memories I had of this place when I had strolled down these halls to work at Bath and Body store.

I didn't have to wait long to find out why the place was giving off a bad vibe. Three gaunt-looking ferals jumped into my view, snarling as their red-tinged drool hung from their fangs like gore. I wondered what they had recently fed on. It was not possible that another human was around. Or maybe I was wrong; I hadn't encountered any in so very long that to see one would be a miracle. I backed up into the hallway with the exit at my back, pondering if I should fight the three feral vampires or make a dash for the double doors where the sun's light would be more than enough to fry them.

I went for the latter after hearing another one plop onto the floor behind them. They crept forward, their hungry and desperate eyes scanning me greedily. I turned and ran for it. I could take out two, maybe three—but four? I was pushing it at that. I pumped my arms and legs as fast as I could, willing my muscles to move even more. The ferals were quick, super-human quick, and only my intense running and training had helped me keep out of their reach. The beam of my flashlight was zigzagging across the walls like an epileptic seizure. I wondered how much more I would have to run before reaching the doors.

I felt the grip of death as a cold, bony hands grabbed my left arm, sending the flashlight in my fist flying as I pummeled through the double doors. It sent a searing pain through my right shoulder, which had taken the brunt of the impact into the metal door. I felt the vampire latch its mouth onto my arm, gripping so tight with his fangs I thought my arm would snap. The sun's light wrapped around me like a brilliant fire, sending me and the feral rolling to the floor as I heard the vampires scream in pain. I rolled on the hard concrete, shaking off the tumbling body of the feral as I jumped to my feet, turning to aim my hatchet at them. I didn't have to fight anymore. The doors had gotten stuck wide open and the four creatures were writhing on the ground near me as their charcoaled skin hissed and cooked in the sun's rays. The stench that emanated from them made me want to hurl. I backed up away from them, my heart still beating insanely fast.

I pulled my eyes away from them to stare in horror at what had arrived behind them. In the shroud of the shadows, a dozen pairs of red gleaming eyes glared right back at me. The snarls rumbled inside the hall as I gasped. A huge hive of ferals were watching me hungrily even as they avoided stepping into the light. I backed away again, contemplating slamming the doors shut. Their faces were withered into a gaunt grey, looking more like zombies, except for the flashing fangs that gleamed in the dim light around their open mouths.

I glanced down to the now-still corpses of charred flesh and ashes of the four that had almost reached me. They were no longer a threat to me at all. I ran up to the double doors, slamming them both closed as fast as I could to seal the hive inside the darkness. I pounced back from the doors as I heard the thud of their bodies against the metal. Swallowing the hard lump in my throat and feeling the adrenaline pumping to the point of a headache in my head, I was relieved. Their needy moans interrupted my thoughts as I slipped off the sidewalk, still backing up. I stumbled to gather my balance and continued to walk away, heading toward my van.

Their pounding ceased and the doors stilled. They would not come out into the sun, they were smarter than that. They would let me go and search for me later, after dark. Luckily, they could not pick up a scent but I wanted to get out of there so fast that I literally was tripping over my feet as I made it back to the van parked in the street between two massive concrete parking garages. This place was the definition of a concrete jungle. The garages were not safe either, they were quite dark even during the day and shrouded from most light. They could be crawling with vampires, too. The entire city was infested with those vile creatures. I was vastly outnumbered.

I peeled out of there, jumping back onto the freeway of the I-15 northbound. I took the interchange to the US-95 and followed it back toward the mountains. My heart continued to race until I reached the outskirts of town and the city skyline shrank in the rearview mirror. The tires screamed their protests as I continued on, swerving dangerously around stalled cars and debris. Glancing down for a moment, I noticed the vampire bite on my arm just below my elbow. The blood seeped from the puncture holes which were drying into dark red, clotting drips that were also staining my jeans below it. The sight of the bite seemed to pull me back into myself and out of my jumbled thoughts, like a bucket of ice being tossed onto my head.

I slammed on the brakes, coming to a stop in the middle of the road. It almost made me laugh that I didn't pull to the side of the road like I had when other humans had been around.

"No one cares if I stop here! No one cares if I make it home!" I yelled at the windshield, pounding the steering wheel over and over until the searing pain caused me to stop. I was sobbing by then, gripping my arm and clutching it to my chest like an infant. I suddenly felt lost and small.

If the bite got infected, I would surely be of no use to anyone anymore. I swallowed back the last few sobs that tried to escaped my chest as I sat there, the desolate desert expanse before me on the dusty road. I hadn't left the city quite yet, but almost. The few straggling houses seem to sit there like silent watchers of my suffering. I sighed, wiping my face with a rag that hung on the back of the middle seat. I didn't know what it had been used for before but I tried to not think about it.

Instead, I grabbed a large bottle of water that was always left in the car for emergencies and poured its cool liquid over the wound, rinsing it out as best I could out here in the middle of the god-forsaken road. As the bottle emptied, I shook my arm to rid it of the excess water and pulled out the first aid kit from the back of the van. I sat in the rear hatch area as I smeared antibiotic ointment onto the punctures, making sure to cover the mouth shaped welts that accompanied them. After that, I wrapped it with gauze and an ace wrap, securing the band snuggly over my arm. I flexed my fingers and stretched my arm out, making sure it did not impede my use of it, but remained snug and secure.

As I stored the kit away and tossed the empty bottle to side of the road, I leaned back against the van and stared at the city. I had been so careless. A hive sat in that mall, definitely in my way and hungry now for my blood. I'd have to exterminate them. The shock of so many of them had left me skittish, like a coward. I cursed under my breath as I thought of my cowardice. How stupid to get so jumpy so easily. I had faced a hive before, why had they scared me so much this time? I rubbed my face and knew the answer immediately. I had always had my family to take care of. I had always thought that if I fought hard enough, I could save them from harm. Now they were nowhere in sight and I hadn't been able to save them anyway. I had run like a coward into the sun's sanctuary instead. I was nothing but a puny girl, trying to be a hero.

I gritted my teeth, grunting at my frustration. I sighed, knowing it was still too early to return home. I would search the exteriors of the casinos for the rest of the day. But first, I was going to make sure that this particular hive was exterminated. I would only rest if I knew that all knowledge of me was wiped away by their demise.

I hopped back into the driver's seat of the van and cranked the engine on again. Turning the wheel hard, I brought the van around and headed back toward the city. I would kill them all, even if I died trying. I knew I shouldn't have felt so strongly about it, but the rage burned inside me like a cancer, eating away at me and screaming to engulf me if I did not let it run its course. I wanted to take it out on them; the pain–the hurt. Here I was, without the ones I loved, scaring the piss out of myself by venturing into the shadows where I could breathe my last breath for sure. I hated it. I wanted to smother them in their darkness, so that they could meet the light, the ever-so-unforgiving sunlight and die for good this time.

I didn't care that they had been human once. They had been my neighbors, friends, acquaintances. I had found out immediately that once you turned, once you were infected, you were never the same again. You would disappear and leave a ravaged, hungry beast in your place. You could turn from a bite or, like most, from the contagious properties of the viral epidemic. Get either one, and you were toast. Some would die from it immediately, unable to host the devastating viral infection. Those were the lucky ones. I wasn't so lucky at all.

I pulled up near the double door exit where I had made my escape. I paused, scanning around me for any strange movement. The two large parking structures stood like mountainous gates to each side of this access road. The casino was in front of me, leading toward the right with its expansive Greco-Roman facade, as fake as it could be but nonetheless massive. I wondered if any of the rooms up there with the curtains still drawn were crawling with vampires. I found it funny that the casinos, for the most part, had remained intact. It was more of the downtown and older buildings that were crumbling to pieces. I guess they weren't meant to last forever. Still, if people were still around, maybe they would have survived daily use and abuse better.

I finally slipped out of the van, shaking off my reverie to concentrate on the mission at hand. Opening the rear hatch again, I pulled out a crate full of more-powerful ammunition: a grenade thrower, hand grenades and my crossbow. I smiled as I loaded myself up with all the goodies. I rarely used them because of the noise factor of the grenades. But this was no ordinary situation. I was willing to risk anything to take this hive out, even stir up the other hive pockets nearby. I almost truly wanted, no, prayed for them to show up and try to take me out again.

Go ahead, take your best shot. I'm ready this time.

I clipped on a wearable flashlight, one that hung around my chest like a beacon but was strapped down against me to avoid bouncing around and making it difficult to see. I stretched out and slipped both my machetes into my side sheaths, placed a couple grenades in a pack on my belt and held a grenade in one hand as I made my way forward, ready to swing the doors open and bring death to them.

The four vampires that had baked in the sun were nothing more than four charred piles of ash, softly floating away in the afternoon breeze. I frowned, kicking one of the piles and sending it into the atmosphere like a dance of confetti. Narrowing my eyes, I crouched forward to grab the handle of the door, feeling the warm metal under my fingers. It vibrated like it was on fire, almost burning my skin. Clenching my teeth, I sucked in a deep breath and pulled back with the most force I could muster. The ferals were not there. Nothing was there to even say they had been there. I propped the door open and readied myself, walking carefully inside, briskly but quietly. The light flashed around with the movement of my chest but created a nice area of vision for me.

I was already at the disgusting aquarium when I heard them. Glancing about the room, I saw them ducking out of store fronts and from behind pillars, dozens of them. I gulped, trying to keep my legs readied to bolt. I backed away a little bit and found that my movement made them hurry toward me even faster, groaning and hissing as I moved away. I retrieved four grenades, pulling the pins and waited as I held steady, my heart pounding like a drummer in my head. As I eased into the hall again, I pulled my arms back and flung the grenades, one by one, as high up as I could to the far walls. I turned to head out again toward the sweet sun that beckoned me from the opened double doors. I was not about to leave but gaining cover was a must with the grenades about to burst inside there.

The hall provided more than enough shelter. I felt the blast as the walls shook, kicking up dust clouds and bellowing like an avalanche. I backed out toward the sun to wait out the cloud of dirt, as it took out the visibility. The screeches were deafening as the sound of concrete and glass shattered the silence outside. Dust clouds billowed out, swirling around like mist. I readied my dual machetes, sucking in a breath before the cloud enveloped me. I ran forward into the middle of the large room as the dirt settled down on clumps of concrete and metal. All over were feral vampires in different states of wither, some shattered beyond recovery, some struggling under debris.

The blast had not leveled the large, round hall. Instead, it had broken enough pieces of the arched roof to open beams of sunlight that streamed down into the dusty room like spikes. Some vampires were pinned under concrete chunks and writhed as they burned beneath the intensity of sun. It lit up the room well enough for me to see as the ones left untouched lunged for me. I swung both machetes, chopping into the first feral as it bared its dirty brown teeth at me, its red eyes gleaming. Its head flew off with one swing and dark crimson blood spurted from its stump of a neck and down the filthy shirt that it wore.

I continued swinging my blades, catching several through the chests or arms, leaving them with severed limbs or on the ground, missing legs and screaming at me. One reached out, grabbing my leg and squeezing its fingers around my jeans with its long, dark nails digging in. I swung one blade down, severing the hand and hacked at its head with the other blade, the sound of bone cracking and tissue squishing under it with every hit. The hand held onto my leg and I shook it loose, trying not to think about how disgusting that was. I slashed through two more that had climbed over a fallen block of roof and attempted to grasp at me with their hands.

This was truly a fight of blade and teeth. I kicked one down and slashed its neck, then brought both blades to a cross in front of me and pulled back as the feral ran right into them, effectively decapitating itself with little effort on my part.

I had lost count of how many I had slaughtered. They were no match–I had become the monster killer in the room. My blades were sopping wet with thick clots of drying blood and ichor. The room took on a strong coppery smell as the dirt mixed with oily blood, swallowing the musty stench of the place with the overwhelming scent. I bit my lip to try not to think about the horrid smell. The aroma of death lingered with it, like a muck that tainted every surface of the place. The air seemed to grow thicker as I breathed hard, using up my energy quickly. The bite on my arm was screaming in protest as the muscle underneath the bite moved and stretched, contracting with every movement.

The adrenaline took care of some of the pain but I knew it would not last forever and really could not. Looking around as stillness overcame the room, I realized they were all down and dead. Every single feral that had leaped out at me was ripped to pieces, sliced into like cheese, bleeding guts and ichor all over the dusty marble floor. I waited, still semi-crouched with my knees bent and my swords out, still ready to slice into something else. Nothing came, though; they were all gone.

The silence seem to sober me up from my intoxicated state. I slowly stood up straight, examining the damage I had inflicted. A slight smile curled at my lips as I breathed in and out hard. It was an exhilarating high and I didn't want it to end. For that one moment, the pain of losing my mother and brother felt righted, even for just a minute. I knew this was what I was made for, to kill these insolent creatures and bring their hives down. They were as unnatural to this world as anything could be. My hatred boiled inside me and made my eyes blaze as I glared at the pieces of evil that were strewn about the room. Some were sizzling under the rays of sunlight, crackling and bubbling as they disintegrated. I wanted them all to burn; I wanted them all to suffer like I had.

Gasping, I realized that tears were streaming down my face and plopping down onto my shirt. I spun around, feeling as though the room was collapsing inward, even though it wasn't. The air seemed to thin out, small fires burned from the explosions and were growing in intensity as the bodies and trash fueled its fury even more. My eyes glanced about wildly as I felt the horror of what I had done creep into my chest and arrest in my throat. I grasped my blades and ran for the haven that only the outside air could give. Jumping over debris, bodies and rocks, I flew down the hall and spilled out onto the sidewalk.

Finally coming to a stop, my machetes clanked to the floor as I knelt over, breathing hard and closing my eyes, trying to calm the overwhelming anxiety that pulsated in my head. A bit dizzy and coming down from the adrenaline, I paused there for a moment, waiting for my heartbeat to slow and settle into a calmer pace. Standing slowly, I turned toward the double doors, seeing the beams of light cutting the darkness within like knives. Nothing came after me; they were all dead. Only I was left, standing alone. This feeling of fear and power twisted inside me like two piranhas circling each other, ready to rip into each other. I wanted to feel glad that I had killed the hive with little effort. I tried to shake the guilt off, telling myself it was okay, that I had done them a favor. They were no longer people–they were animals, unnatural and cursed. Putting them down was the only thing I could do for them now.

I reached down, grabbed my blades and slowly dragged myself to the van. Opening the side door and grabbing a rag that sat on the floor, I wiped the dark, sticky blood off my blades. I would have to wash them later but right now the fatigue was settling into my bones like a syrupy draught. I was feeling incredibly worn out and exhausted. It wrapped around me like a sedative. I slammed the door shut, leaving my blades on the floor of the van.

I looked around–the street's silence was almost too much for me. I wanted so badly to see another person, to have someone say my name again. The feelings that swirled inside me were overwhelming, almost making me want to hurl. I swung up into the seat of the driver's side of the van and cranked the engine. I gripped the steering wheel so tightly my fingers felt a tingle of numbness as I continued to sob. Drying blood streaked up and down my arms in intricate patterns. I wanted to scrub it off my skin and feel brand new again. Their blood was tainted and full of viral disease.

I wondered if I would turn this time, turn into one of them. I often wondered why I hadn't turned when the vampiric virus had vanquished everyone else. My mother, brother and I had fled the city when the nights were beginning to get a little too scary and deadly in our house. It had been centrally located near the sound wall built around the US-95 highway. It was an older neighborhood, meaning that the houses there had large yards and strong construction. Unlike the newer housing tracks, they were built to last forever. We'd had a nice huge spiked gate surrounding the property which had served as our protection from the outside, where the dead had increased and feral vampires had begun roaming freely.

We had boarded up the windows to the point that no light escaped when we lit our lamps at night. Keeping to the living room, we would take shifts sleeping and guarding, never making a noise during the long dark hours of night. The dead would make the noise for us. Outside I could hear the not-so-distant screeches of the feral vampires, hunting their prey. At first it was human screams that accompanied their hisses. Then as the population grew tinier and tinier, they had turned to capturing lost dogs and cats, pets of owners that no longer came home. I heard the dogs barking and the cats screeching back at the monsters. It wasn't long before those noises were silenced as well and the inhuman snarls faded as the neighborhood died and the lights went out.

I came back into the present as the street, now flying by in front of me as the van cruised down it, turned onto the freeway toward home. It was now about one hour from sunset and all I wanted was to forget the day and hide in my hole in the mountains once again. The sky bled translucent oranges and blues across the horizon as I rolled the window down, letting the air whip my hair around. I still felt suffocated, still felt an overwhelming angst within my chest that did not fade with anything but the air. The rush and noise of it made my mind a bit number, maybe even a bit clearer.

I raced through the abandoned cars and pieces of debris. The tears had dried into dirty streaks down my face and I once more felt the weariness growing in my bones and down my body. I wanted to keep driving, keep on until the road faded away into the endless desert plains and disappear with them. I knew that I couldn't and I knew that I had to stay here and keep fighting, even for nothing more than for the memory of my mother and my brother. For them, I would not let my spirit wither and fade. I would continue on, regardless.

Chapter Eight

AFTER A SHOWER I sat on the bed, examining the vampire bite on my arm. It was clean and looked like it was starting to heal well. I doubted I would turn into a vampire, I had been bitten many times before without infection, but I might as well lock myself in here if I did. At least I wouldn't kill anyone trapped in a cement tomb. I doubt I would be able to think enough to get out of here; the ferals didn't seem to have that kind of higher brain function. Even though they gathered into groups to survive better, they couldn't even open the heavy doors of most of the casinos. They were a bit zombie-like in that way.

I sighed, rubbing my face after bandaging up the wound to keep it from hitting anything or getting some other infection. My eyes felt dry and stung as I pressed my hand into them. I reached for a bottle of water on the table next to my bed and swallowed down the fresh fluid. It felt good on my scratchy throat. I hoped I wasn't getting sick. The desert seemed to suck the hydration from my body without any effort like a dehumidifier working to turn me into a stick of jerky.

I laughed at the thought and plopped back onto the pillow of my bed. I reached over to click the overhead light off which left me with only the soft glow of the security camera monitors to see by. I sighed, staring up at the pipes that ran overhead along the cement roof of this small sanctuary. Only the hum of the monitors and the fans that spun overhead filled the space. I hoped that I wouldn't have any kind of activity to deal with during the night. My body was already relaxing into a paralyzed bliss as the soreness of the day sat in my muscles and bones. I let my eyelids slowly meld together and the darkness float me into a temporary safe harbor.

MY EYES FLUTTERED as I woke with a start. Sitting up, I saw that I had been lying in what looked like a hospital bed. The smell of alcohol wipes and bleach assaulted my nostrils as I turned my head, immediately and instinctually scanning the room. I even checked underneath the bed I was lying in, hoping to not find a feral creature lurking there.

Where the hell am I? The lights were on and blared down on me like God's flashlight, examining me and making my eyelids flutter at the glare. How could there be electricity in this hospital? How the heck did I get here?

I swung my legs over the side, noticing I had hospital socks on and a flimsy white and blue gown that patients usually wore. I pulled at it, feeling quite naked underneath it. I shivered, looking around the room for my stuff but none of my clothes were there. My confusion made me curious as I stood up and shuffled to the door, listening with almost disbelief as I reached for the door handle. *Voices.* The murmur of them slipped through the door like a hum. My eyes widened as my heart seemed to jump with excitement. Could it be? Did someone find me? Other humans?

Overwhelmed with happiness, I swung the door open and stared at the nurse's station before me. I studied the nurses in their scrubs with their stethoscopes draped around their necks, busy at the desks. My mouth gaped open as the phones rang while they busied themselves, shuffling around papers and drawing up medications. They hadn't even noticed me yet but I wanted to run to them and squeeze them tight. I stopped before leaving my room, feeling like something was not quite right. I glanced down the halls on both sides of my door. They seemed to go on forever with so many doors, all closed and quiet. I wondered if there were many patients here.

I breathed in deeply, deciding to head toward the nurses and see why I was there and how I had gotten there. I padded softly on the cold tile floor, feeling the cool breeze of air conditioning swirling about me. The place was clean, as a hospital should be. The floor gleamed as the fluorescent light bounced off the freshly-polished and cleaned surface. It was almost too clean. I reached the desk and was about to speak to one of the nurses, whose back was toward me, when I let out a yelp as someone grasped my shoulder.

"Do you need something, miss?" A calm voice sounded off behind me. I swiftly turned, restraining myself from smacking her. The nurse eyed me suspiciously, her blue eyes gleaming as she studied me. Her dark brown hair was pulled tightly into a ponytail that sat softly on the neck of her purple flowered scrub top. Her pants were a solid purple and her lilac-colored stethoscope hung from her neck. My eyes drifted to her name tag and read the name "Grace." She wore light makeup and smelled like a combination of medicated soap and scented lotion.

"I–I don't know. Where am I? What am I doing here?" I asked softly. Grace gave me a concerned smile and waved me to a chair at the station as she grabbed a chart from a wall rack and flipped through it, reading the contents.

"Ah, Miss April Tate, right?"

I nodded.

"Well, it seems you are here for treatment of a viral infection." She smiled and looked up from the chart as I stared back confused. My fingers subconsciously reached over to touch the bite on my left arm. Feeling nothing but smooth skin I glanced down, sensing a shift in my surroundings.

"But how did I get infected?" I looked back up at Grace but found her gone. Looking around me, the same nurse's station remained but looked ravaged. The fluorescent lights were dangling from their cords and flickering in and out. Papers and charts littered the now-dirty and streaked floors. I shot up from my chair and gasped. Along the hall were the same nurses I had just seen working but now they were lying face down on the floor, lifeless, with the color drained from their skin. Their eyes stared out into nothingness, blank and dead. I shivered, stepping over them, and noticing I was no longer wearing the hospital gown I had awoken in, but jeans and a white shirt. I paused, catching sight of Grace standing in the hallway, facing away from me.

"Grace? What's going on?" I felt the hair on my neck stand on end as Grace turned around–she now owned the grey skin of a feral vampire and bared her fangs, flashing them at me as they dripped with fresh, red blood. A snarl crawled across her face as her red-black eyes gleamed in the nearly darkened hallway.

Oh shit!

I backed into the nurse's station, searching for a weapon in the trashed mess of the desks and chairs. Finally spotting a scalpel lying across what looked like a prepped table for a chest tube, I grabbed it and a cart of charts, swinging the cart behind me, just in time to hit Grace as she scrambled toward me. She was fast but not fast enough as I spun around a pillar. I hopped onto the desk, swiftly bending as I pirouetted back, bringing my arm with the scalpel in hand around in an arcing motion to slash her throat. The thick, syrupy blood poured out of the neat cut like a bucket being poured down her scrub top. I had not cut far enough through to decapitate her but it was near enough for sure.

I landed on the floor inside the quad of desks and scrambled back onto my feet as she reached toward me, gurgling as blood continued to spout out of her neck. Her eyes were angry but sallow as she began to turn paler, her life blood draining away. Grabbing a thick bedside chart, I swung it as hard as I could into her face, sending her head reeling across the tile. Her grey-skinned body convulsed as it dropped to the floor without its brain to command it.

I sighed, dropping the chart and looking around, hoping she was the only vampire around. When I didn't see any more I relaxed just a bit and started down the hallway. I avoiding the ripped wires from the lights above that swung into my path. I still couldn't figure out why I was even here. This was not right somehow; I was at home sleeping, wasn't I? I felt naked without a weapon and searched among the rubble for anything I could use to kill a vampire. Finding a broken bar off a transport cart, I gripped it in my hand. I was ready to pummel anything that came at me.

I made it around to the back employee hallway when I stopped, realizing the elevators might not be working. I pushed the button but the console was dead. I sighed, hoping I wasn't on the top floor; going down the stairwell was not going to be fun if it was infested with ferals. As I exited the employee hallway and made my way through the floor's main passageway, where I finally found the stairwell. I dodged a few gurneys on my way and stupidly swung the stairwell door open without scoping it out first. So why was I surprised when three feral vampires lunged at me immediately, taking me down and biting into my upper arms and my thigh?

I screamed as I kicked and hit as much as I could, hoping to get away from them, but they latched on and sucked my life's elixir away. The light faded in and out above me as I saw a shadow of a woman standing over me. Her eyes were not red but a desert sandy brown rimmed in a circle of gold. She snickered at me and bent down next to my ear. "You *are* one of us," she faintly whispered just before the darkness overcame me.

Chapter Nine

THE AIR AROUND me was thick and noxious, and seemed to set my breath on fire. My chest burned as I heaved the air in and out, sitting up in my bed. I was back in my compound sanctuary, this much I gathered from darting my eyes wildly around the room.

Oh thank God, it was just a nightmare.

Grabbing my bottle of water, I took a swig of cool liquid down my burning throat as I tried to control my breathing and my racing heart. The sheets were soaked and my body was drenched in a film of wetness from writhing in the bed. It had seemed so real and I had let it overwhelm me. I was usually pretty good at controlling my dreams, able to wake myself up before anything bad happened. Yet my control had languished in this dream and had left me flattened.

Shaking my head, I swung my legs over the edge of the bed and pushed my dripping strands of hair off my face. I hated nightmares; I had only wished to rest in a dreamless sleep that never seemed to come. I hoped my dream was not any kind of omen–that would not be good at all. The slickness of my shirt and shorts gave me a shudder as it reminded me of the coolness that the concrete emanated all around. Shivering, I stood up slowly and changed my clothes out for a fresh set.

I was about to pull on some new shorts when I noticed the alarm flashing on the console and the low beeping noise of the warning light. I froze, staring at the monitors, waiting to see what had set off a motion sensor outside. My heart wasn't cooperating anymore and continued to jump in my chest as I watched the screens.

Quickly, I grabbed a pair of jeans instead and pulled them on, yanking back my soaked black hair into a messy, low ponytail. Slipping on one of my hoodies for warmth, I sat at the monitoring desk and waited, hoping it was a false alarm and that an animal had found its way across the property. As the camera flashed to the driveway, I realized what had tripped the sensor. Two figures stood at the van, seemingly searching its windows and circling it round and round. I gulped. They were so close–I prayed that the soundproofing of my sanctuary was working its magic at that moment.

Staring at the figures, they reminded me of the lone vampire girl from the other day, the helpless one I had killed without hesitation. Pressing my lips together, I felt an urge to gear up and slaughter these two, just like the girl. That is, until I saw another two figures walk across the screen.

My heart jumped again. *Am I surrounded?* I sucked in a breath as I realized I had been holding it for a bit too long. *How many are out there? What if they find me?*

The questions poured through my head as I stared wide-eyed at the scene before me. I couldn't believe that they had come up so far into the mountains. Why would they do that? Was the lack of food bringing them to me? I frowned as I realized that my mother's blood was still smeared across the van's door and the light sprinkle of rain that fell on and off in the fall here had probably wet it enough earlier to bring out the blood-tainted stink all around the van. I suddenly regretted not washing the damn thing when I could've. It would have saved me this headache for sure.

I decided to get ready, just in case they barged through into my hideaway. I doubted they would, this place was fortified. Pulling on my socks and boots, I laced them tight and added some daggers to a bandoleer I strapped across my chest. My machetes sat cleaned and gleaming on the rack across from the desk. I pulled only one down, not feeling too hot on my left arm, and a hatchet to swing if need be. I was still tired but I was hoping I wouldn't be doing any fighting tonight.

The monitor's glow burned my eyes as I spent the next couple hours staring at the figures shuffling around. They had my curiosity up. Some glanced around the property and searched about for whatever they were looking for. Others were up in the cabin, checking it out, but none headed into the cellar for some reason or another. My hide out was safe. But the confused look on some of their faces made me suspicious. They were not the crazy ferals from the city who pounced without remorse and tore at a person with fangs. Like the girl from the other night, these ones walked more smoothly and did not snarl or look around crazed. I almost could mistake them for humans except for the glimpse of a fang every now and then flashing in the screen from their partially opened mouths. No, these were not feral, and this scared me most of all.

I thought I knew what was out there, but these mutants made me want to hide in my hole even more. I watched them for a good while until they disappeared from the cameras. I knew I couldn't leave without risking discovery during the night. I didn't think I could use the van anymore. I would have to find another car to use until they moved on but who knew how long that would be?

I groaned at my grave mistake, taking it for granted when I parked my van outside every day. It had been my only connection to our old life. Now I would have to let it sit for a while to make sure they suspected nothing was out of place. *More out of place than the blood on the door?* I huffed out a breath, shaking my head. I hoped they would just move on. This was so not a good thing; my little universe was crashing down, splintering into severed shards made to cut at every step. I wasn't sure there would be anything I could do if they discovered my hideout. Sighing, I was not sure what to do about anything anymore.

I sat at the monitors for what seemed like an eternity. My legs were kicked up on another chair while I leaned back, arms crossed on my chest while my exhaustion fought me to close my eyes. The hum of the equipment was lulling me to sleep, even though I had drank all the energy drinks I could without enduring any severe side-effects of overuse. I glanced at the clock on the wall; it was 4:15am, four hours since I had seen the strange hybrid vampires outside. I figured they had left by now, with sunrise nearing. I bet they didn't want to be around to enjoy that.

I sighed, slipping my weapon belts off to rest in the middle of the concrete floor. I went and slumped onto my bed, fully clothed. It seemed my will to be neat and tidy was waning as more time went by without my family. I shook the depression off me as the darkness embraced my weariness. I was going to need some rest, knowing that unfortunately, the game had now changed.

Chapter Ten

I WAITED UNTIL the sun had fully risen to emerge from my hideaway as carefully and as quietly as I could. I left prepared for a fight, no longer sure if the hybrid vampires were day walkers or not. Anything was possible. I was not about to walk out like a cow to slaughter. If it came down to it, I would die fighting.

As I crept out the metal doorway, I quietly clicked it closed behind me, hatchet in hand just in case I was jumped at close range. With my eyes constantly scanning the area, I waited minutes upon minutes, listening for any unusual noises. When nothing happened, I let out the breath I had been holding. My relief flooded me as I punched in the key code to lock the door and walked down the driveway, heading to the neighboring houses. I knew of several cars that had been left abandoned with the nice cabins that lined the roads in the Mt. Charleston community. I had spent many a youth church camp weekend up in these mountains. Some of the adult members had had cabins up here. It may not have been Aspen, but these houses were not cheap. Most had the log cabin feel to them and sat buried in snow in the winters. Right now, I wanted to get a new ride and hopefully someone had stowed a car in a nearby garage. But first, I would have to make sure no ferals were lurking about in the dark garages and houses.

The nearest cabin I came across looked like it might house something. I took the steps two at a time and tried the handle. It didn't turn in my grasp. Cursing under my breath, I ran around, checking doors and windows to find a vulnerable spot. Groaning when I found none, I took out the hatchet and positioned it to slam against the window next to the door. The impact sounded like an avalanche of massive chimes clinking onto the ground in a shower of glass, making me hold my breath. I scanned around the trees and the land, waiting for anyone to appear. Luckily no one came from outside or inside the cabin.

Reaching into the shattered remains of the window and avoiding the shards of sharpened glass, I turned the bolt that kept me from getting in. Rushing inside, I clicked the door behind me, surveying the cabin. It also seemed abandoned and untouched for what could've been eons. I quickly made my way to the garage door, pulling my flashlight out; it would be dark as night inside there. I swung the door open and flashed the beam of light across the space. It was empty except for some storage containers and shelves of old sledding equipment and bicycles. I had wished it would've been that easy but up here in the mountains most people hadn't made it back. I doubted they would leave a car in an unwatched house.

I moved onto three more houses before finding one that had been occupied more than most of the others, but no one had been there in at least half a year. There was the foul smell of old garbage sitting in the trash can. I wrinkled my nose, knowing I had to work fast. It smelled like whoever had lived here might be rotting upstairs. I held my breath after quickly scanning the rooms before me. Making my way to the garage, I flipped the lock open and turned the door handle. My beam of my flashlight showed me an older model Toyota. I wondered where the keys would be. Closing the door, I made my way around the kitchen and front door, hoping to find the keys somewhere common, on the counter or a hook somewhere. I found them on a hook on the kitchen cabinet catch all area, like a mini desk in the middle of all the action.

As I scooped up the keys, I heard a thump. I stopped in my tracks as I waited to see if it would sound off again, attempting to listen over the drum of my own heartbeat. The moments ticked by forever, but I never heard it again and chalked it up to a tree branch thumping the side of the house. I rolled my eyes, muttering to myself; I couldn't believe how paranoid I had become. I walked back over to the garage, opening the door to find myself immediately thrown onto my back, holding back a feral vampire who had slammed me onto the wooden floor.

I shoved back up at him, keeping his drooling fangs off my skin. He was incredibly strong, probably starving if he had been stuck in that garage for a while. I grunted as I tried to hold him up, jamming my forearm in his throat with my right arm, I reached down to my chest to the dagger bandoleer that I had crisscrossed there, quickly yanking out a thin sharp dagger. I jammed it as hard as I could into the side of his head, where the temple bone was thinnest, closing my eyes and mouth as the cold wetness of his fluids poured down onto my face.

Pressing up his weight, it was just enough for me to bring one of my legs up to thrust him off me and into the dark of the garage as he writhed and convulsed on the cement floor. I wiped at my face as best I could and ran ahead of him, unlatching the garage door lock and heaving it up. It rolled on squeaky rails and let in the late morning sun. The feral squealed in pain as it caught the sun's rays and sizzled into a blacken pile of ash. I dropped to my knees, breathing heavily as I recovered from the unexpected surprise attack.

I groaned, wiping at the stickiness that drenched my face. The black-red blood clung to my hair, face, neck and arms like a thick, rancid muck. Sighing, I frowned at the still-smoldering, smoky pile next to the car that I had wanted to take. I made my way back inside, finding the small hallway half bath where I grabbed the hand towel off the rack and wiped away what I could of the thick, disgusting ichor. Satisfied but knowing I now needed another shower, I turned to find the keys I had dropped by the door.

The car took a few turnovers before it started, showing a full tank of gas. Smiling, I shifted it into reverse, stopping in the driveway to slam the garage door back down to ward off any suspicion of disturbance. Jumping back into the driver's side of the car, I pulled out the rest of the way and headed back home to change.

Once inside, the sweet feel of the shower made me want to stand under the water forever. Remembering to conserve the heated water, I proceeded to scrub the nastiness of the feral vampire's blood off my body. The water swirled black and pink down the drain, like clouds of death, spinning as it fell into the holes of the pipe drain. Finished, I changed into fresh clothes and proceeded to cleaning my weapons, which were now caked in the clotted muck of blood. It would take me most of the afternoon to get them cleaned up. I figured my day was wasted. I hated not heading to town to search for my mother and brother but what good would I be in this anxious and spooked state? Unfortunately, it was time to lay low for a bit and this was the day to do it, especially with those hybrid vampires lurking about.

I dropped the belt of weapons and cleaned my hands again, knowing I had to stuff the little car into the garage before nightfall. I didn't want anyone seeing anything changed on the outside of my cabin. Walking out, I moved the car into the garage and closed the garage door down, locking it with the key lock. Luckily the owners of the place had left the keys to the garage hanging nicely by the door.

As I turned, my eyes landed on a sight that arrested my heart. Staring right back at me from across the road, in the shade of the trees, was a woman. Her chestnut brown hair floated about her in the breeze as she stared me down. I froze, mentally cursing myself for coming outside without a weapon.

So stupid!

I contemplated my options as we continued to look at each other, her eyes and face never wavering away from mine. Her skin was pale and her eyes did not shine red but a tiger eye color swirled in grey. I had never seen eyes like that. They shone like cat's eyes as she stood as still as a statue. I wondered if I should speak. Why hadn't she attacked me yet? I searched her silhouette for weapons and possible hiding spots that she could carry on her person. Finding none, I waited for her to make a move, wondering if she would.

"Hey! Who are you?" I called out to this stranger. She angled her head to the side, seemingly interested in my speaking. Her face sat still and frozen. "Um, do you talk? I asked you who you are!" My frustration leaked into my voice and she seemed to catch on to it. Her head snapped back up straight and glared at me–her eyes narrowing into thin little slits.

She seems a bit perturbed, I thought.

I chewed on my tongue as I held my ground, not wanting her to see any fear spilling into my face. I glared right back, daring her to make the first move. Her lips moved into a half smirk as she gave me a nod. She then moved faster than I could ever hope to, turning to run, and disappearing in a blur. I gasped; scanning the direction I had seen her run, squinting my eyes to try to catch sight of her.

"Ah!" I groaned, cursing at losing her in the forest. What if she came back with more vampires? This day was starting to look really bad for me. I felt my panic surge up into my chest as I spun around, glancing in every direction for the lone woman. No way was she human; and there was definitely no way she seemed friendly, either. This was starting to turn into a very dangerous place for me. My sanctuary in the mountains had turned into an island surrounded by beasts. I made my way back into the compound, locking the door behind me, ensuring that each bolt and lock was firmly in place. I felt small, like a rat in a maze. They must have been toying with me. How did they find me so far away from the city? I was going to have to leave, run farther away to find a safer place.

I slipped to the floor, burying my face in my arms and knees as I realized that there was nowhere to go. No place was safe. There was nowhere left to go in this world anymore. There were no humans left but me. Why would I think any place was safe? The warm tears squeezed out of from beneath my eyelids and made their way down my cheeks in a rush of warmth. I let my sobs shake my body as I cried and cried.

The horror of my predicament made me want to scream and fling things across the room. I held the destruction inside and bit down on my lip as the sobs eased. I hated this. The world had gone to shit and I could do nothing about it. What good was being a fierce warrior when a little despair broke me down into a sniveling mess? Losing my family had been inevitable. We were not meant for this world now, and to continue on was to be running forever.

I bent over, hitting the concrete floor with the sides of my fists, pounding it until the pain stopped me. Rolling over to my back, I stared up at the fluorescent light above me–glaring down its artificial glow and not giving one care for whom it lit up the room. I was sure that when I was gone, it would continue to glow until the power ran out or the bulb flickered out, all used up in its inevitable death. It would not remember me in any shape or form or be aware of anything at all. It too would stand forgotten and silent in desolate disrepair.

Not knowing how long I laid there on the icy-cold, hard floor, I finally picked myself up and dragged myself to the monitoring desk. I sat there for a few minutes longer, my puffy red eyes burning from crying and my arms aching. I watched the monitors, still lit up with daylight outside, but nothing crossed them. Maybe I had imagined the woman. But her porcelain face was emblazoned in my mind. I could still see her fiery eyes staring me down, attempting to slice into my head and sift through my mind as she pleased. In a way, I felt violated–my sanctuary was no longer pristine and solitary–no longer mine. She had trespassed, along with her comrades, into my only corner of the world. I wanted it to be mine again, quiet and safe. I wanted to reclaim its solitude once more.

Chapter Eleven

THE NEXT DAY I geared up at sunrise and readied to leave. Having not slept well that night, I felt strangely energized and awaited the day with an elated anticipation. I was relieved that the motion sensors had not gone off at all the entire night. Maybe the woman had been more scared of me than I thought. Or maybe she would be back later. Who knew? I wasn't going to let her ruin my plans to continue my search for my mother and brother.

The drive to the city was uneventful; it felt different in the smaller car than the minivan I was used to. It was almost cramped with the weapons I liked stashed in it. It would have to do for now. The meteor hammer I had brought along today was rocking in the chair, trying to roll out of the rope that cradled it. I didn't use it often but its deadly force was amazing when one got it right. I felt like swinging it around, smashing things. Today was a good day to do exactly that.

Once I arrived at the nearest gas station, I filled two gallon containers with gasoline for the mischief I had planned. Riding with the containers full was not comfortable when the fumes that seeped from them made me nauseous. Once I'd had enough siphoned from the station and several abandoned cars parked along the streets, I hopped back into my car and crossed over the freeway overpass to the Strip. I parked in front of the Imperial Palace, glancing down each way at the smaller casinos. If any ferals were lurking about, I was going to take care of them for sure. I wasn't about to deal with too much hand to hand combat today. Today was my retribution and I wanted to burn the place down.

I wrapped the rope around my chest diagonally and strapped one machete to my right side down my thigh. The actual meteor hammer ball I twisted into the rope loops so it wouldn't swing around and hit me as I moved. I grabbed one gasoline container and placed it outside the nearest casino, looking into the reflective one-way mirror tint that glared back at me on the windows. The woman that stared back seemed to change and flashed back to the image of the woman up in the mountains for a moment. I blinked her away, knowing how she gnawed on my mind but tried to clear my thoughts for the task at hand. I pushed in the door and scanned the front of the casino, illuminated somewhat through the deeply tinted glass.

This place was a mess–it had not been left undisturbed at all. The card tables were upturned and chips were scattered across the floor. The chairs had not remained untouched either; some were torn into two pieces, with their stuffing spilt out across the carpet. I stared back into the blackness at the rear of the casino, wondering what lurked in the shadows. The dark stared right back at me like a gaping mouth waiting to take a bite and rip me to shreds. I was certain I wasn't alone–only the boundaries of the sun's span kept a wall between me and whatever feral creatures awaited a taste of my sweet, crimson blood. I sneered, feeling the sudden rush of adrenaline rising to ready me for the thrill of the fight.

Pulling the meteor hammer off my body, I let the rope fall to the ground as I unwound it and looped it through my left hand. I let the remaining rope dangle and dragged it with my right hand as I walked forward. I was happy that the vaulted ceilings were so high; there was more than enough room to let me swing around my seldom-used toy. I felt ferocious as I pulled it along, feeling the familiar buzz along my skin that the ferals seemed to bring out when they were near. It vibrated up my arms and made my senses expand as they neared me. I hardly felt the smile across my face as the first of the wild ones crept over to me from a dark pillar on the edge of the room, hidden enough in the shadow so as not to make it cringe in pain from the sunlight outside but enough to let me see them with my human vision.

I started swinging the hammer, letting its momentum build as the rope hummed out its ominous whoosh. I loved the feeling it gave me, almost like a cowboy with a lasso, but this lasso could smash a feral's head to smithereens. Just as it stepped closer, growling and snapping its fanged mouth in my direction, I released the meteor hammer so it could do its work. The result was an explosion of thick chunks of brain matter and skull all across the wall and upturned tables.

His body hadn't even hit the floor before another lunged from behind a pile of tables that had been stacked together, apparently to shield them from the sun. His red, gleaming eyes narrowed as he hissed–his rotten teeth full of old blood and other things. Pale and dirty greenish-grey skin shone through the rips of his shirt near his shoulders. A once-healthy bicep muscle line peeked through.

He had to have been young when he turned, I was pretty sure of it. From the condition of this one, he had obviously been more dominant than the other ferals, not missing too many meals. His snarl grumbled in my ears, vibrating the air. I smirked back at him and, with a snap of my arm, flung the heavy metal hammer toward the spot between the eyes. His body flew back as the metal ball impacted with his head, amazingly not cracking his face in but sending his head flying off whole as it tore from the momentum. Blood erupted from the stump of his neck but I didn't have time to enjoy the spectacle. Two others popped out from behind him and lunged at me. I swung at them in succession, letting the momentum of the ball bash through them both, sending their bodies flying back into another group advancing behind them.

I backed away into the light from the windows, letting the boundary of the sun stop them in their tracks; the evil in their eyes filled with a desire so deep, they would stop at nothing to get what they wanted. I swung my weapon around in a continual spin, pummeling a couple more in their chests, sending them crashing back. I was willing to bet they would rip me to shreds without hesitation. I decided to leave the room to fetch the container of gasoline.

"So you want to play it rough, huh?" I laughed at the creatures, even though I was sure they could not understand. They were wilder than beasts, with no understanding except the desire to rip flesh and drink blood.

"I'm sure you will love to play this game for sure." I dumped the gas on them, heaving the container high enough to get the gas beyond them, into the casino. After dumping most of it on them and the surroundings, I smiled and waved as I backed out the door, their snarls never ceasing. Outside, I stepped back to find the outside ladder to the roof. Finding what I was looking for, I retrieved the pipe bombs from the car, which were all ready to go. Climbing the ladder, I lit one at a time and flung them across the roof to the area where the ferals were standing underneath the roof. I dove off the ladder, sending one lit pipe bomb inside the interior of the building before I ran around the corner for shelter just as the first of the pipe bombs went off, sending debris shooting up into the air and roof tiles flinging across the street as the top of the building collapsed. The ground shook and I had to cover my ears from the booms vibrating through my head. I was pretty sure I had woken up some of the other hives around me.

Once the last of the bombs went off, I returned to survey the damage. The front windows had exploded outward and dust and debris billowed out, making it hard to see into the building until it cleared a bit. I smiled, seeing the holes in the roof all the way to the rear of the casino. The gasoline, ignited by the explosions, was now consuming the writhing ferals with its burning embrace.

I hurried to set up the next casino the same way, not bothering to linger inside to smash them up as much. I wanted it to burn fast and fatal. The desire ran rampant inside me like a feverish plague engulfing my senses. Nothing would be better than to watch the city burn.

This casino was taller than the last. It had about four stories instead of the usual one or two of the smaller casinos. Inside, I contemplated the height of the roof, muttering to myself how completely not easy this one would be. I swapped the meteor hammer out for a hatchet and machete back at my car and grabbed the second gasoline container. Lighting the flashlights attached to a belt across my chest like a coal miner, I returned to the inside. I didn't see any ferals around but the smell alone told me otherwise and I knew that I was not alone.

I found the stairs and ascended as quickly as possible, keeping my eyes above me as I approached each floor. I was amazed at my luck in not finding any stragglers on the stairwell; it would not be easy to engage in hand-to-hand combat within the confines of this small space. Finding nothing, I reached the top floor easily and prepped to run into something as I entered the floor.

Finding mostly offices this high up, I scanned the darkness of the hallways slowly. I wondered where the damn ferals had hidden. Possibly the balcony of the second floor that looked down on the first floor? It seemed like the best hiding space that was easily accessible to them, from what I had seen. I made my way to the windowed side of the halls, knowing the sun's rays meant safety. I began laying down the pipe bombs, connecting the fuses and running them down the halls and into the offices. Once I had finished, I took the gasoline container and let out splashes of fluid all around the halls and near the pipe bombs. Once I lit it, I would have to dash away fast, down the steps and out the door before the roof collapsed. I wondered if I should just leave a trail of gas down the steps to at least the second floor and prop the stairwell door open to give me a better amount of time to escape.

Pondering my options, I nodded to myself. I think I could make it at least from the third floor. Sloshing the pungent liquid down the stairs, I made sure the fuse of the pipe bombs lay in the path of the gas to light up once the fire made it around toward the windows. I gritted my teeth as I completed the arrangement. I wasn't an arsonist and all I knew were from endless documentaries I had watched during the long quiet nights in the bunker with my family softly sleeping nearby. I wondered if it would work. It had better work. This was as good a place as any to try out my theory. As I made my way down the steps, I paused at the third floor, thinking about checking out what was on this floor before lighting the place up. My curiosity got the best of me, unfortunately.

Pushing the door open, I peeked into another area, an open room with many columns, and some tables pushed to the sides, like a banquet hall. I walked through the massive room, looking at the many different decorations that sat stored in the corners; I could make out some sunlight through the drapes of curtains along the same side as the windows above, on the next floor. Walking slowly down one side of the banquet room, the eeriness of the place seemed to drift about me and cling to the air in a cold embrace. I could almost hear the music that had once been played in this abandoned hall. Many a wedding reception or party had gone on here, it looked well used. Now, no one would ever dance here again.

Hearing a creak behind me and the familiar guttural noise a feral vampire makes, I turned and could hear footsteps approaching me from behind one of the piles of debris stacked high to one side. I pulled out my hatchet, expecting to take them down quickly. Instead I found what used to be a woman. She reached toward me with her long dirty nails and ragged clothes. I held steadfast but found my eyes drifting to something hanging from her chest that made me do a double take. It looked like a baby carrier strapped to her, the kind that let a baby face the wearer.

A sudden wave of nausea choked me, making me step away from her as the top of a baby's head flopped inside the carrier, the wispy hair still in place on the ashen grey skin of an infant. I heard its soft moan while the small hands curled and scratched at its mother.

I tripped and fell backward from the shock of what I had seen. The child was also a feral. It disgusted me beyond belief. Even if it was a vampire, it was still a small baby that I could not bring myself to swing at. The mother, yes—but a baby? Scrambling to get back up, I held the hatchet in my hand, thinking about running to the stairwell and heading out instead of facing this one. I didn't want to face her and the child. It was the stuff made of nightmares. It was so morbid and wrong on so many levels. Blowing up the building with them in it didn't seem as hard to do as hacking them to death. My heart was in my throat; that poor baby hadn't even had a chance at life.

Running towards the stairwell door, I had almost reached the frame when I found myself flying to the ground as another vampire shoved me. This one was bulky, his muscles protruding through the rips in his shirt. Thick arms wrapped around my waist as we rolled to the ground. I immediately hacked at his arms and face with the hatchet but couldn't get enough leverage to smash in his skull. His furrowed eyes glared at me in a hard, red, hateful stare. Snarling and snapping at me with his thick jaw, the hatchet hardly fazed him and his grip was solid as he bear-hugged my waist, making it impossible to kick him off.

Rocking my body, I pulverized his face with the hatchet before grabbing a dagger off my bandoleer and driving it into his eye socket. The squeezing ceased as he stilled, but the weight of his leaden body pinned me down. I stopped struggling to take in my surroundings. The woman with the baby was staggering my way but was still far enough away from me that I could probably throw something at her. I suddenly wished I had my crossbow to sink an arrow cleanly into her. I had some grenades attached to me but I didn't want to risk igniting the gasoline fumes that leaked from the stairwell.

I quickly realized that I had little choice; heavy, husky guy's weight had me stuck for the moment. I pulled the grenade off my belt and struggled a bit more with the husky man; his black-red blood poured onto my abdomen and chest. I tried not to think about how disgusting that was as I squirmed to free myself. I pulled the pin on the grenade as the woman edged closer, seemingly slow for a feral. I wondered how long she had been stuck up here. She had probably fed very little and was now feeling the effects of it, making her weak. Right as I was about to be freed from the dead corpse that held me down like a paperweight, another feral come about, throwing itself down on me and snarling as I scrambled to back away. Unfortunately, the impact of its body on me was enough to make me lose my grip on the grenade, sending it rolling down toward the stairwell.

I finally managed to kick this one back and jump to my feet, scrambling away from the rolling grenade and the third feral, toward the pile of overturned tables on the other side of the room. I dove the last few feet and slammed against the wall as the explosion shook the building and sent debris flying into the two ferals, along with a puff of dust and particles. Luckily, the tables took the brunt of the splintered mess that had flown my way. Dusting myself off, I coughed as the smoke in the room began to build from the fire that smoldered at the exit and ran up the stairs. I wondered what other escape I had, knowing the fire was crawling along the gas trail to the bombs above and below.

I glanced at the windows. I ran toward them and peeked down to the street below. I was still too far up for a safe landing but I had to think of something. I quickly grabbed the sheets that lay over the stored tables and chairs but were now dusted with debris. I knotted the sheets end to end as fast as I could and tied one end to the pillar closest to the windows. I threw a chair into the window. It splintered into a spidery crack but remained intact. Cursing, I grabbed the chair and smacked at the window again. After the third try the window blew out, letting the cool crisp air from the outside rush in, sweeping up more debris and fanning the flames. I tied the sheets around me and prepared to jump but the blast above me reverberated through the walls, releasing more chunks of concrete and wood.

The vibration knocked me to my feet. On my back, I struggled to stand, watching as the roof came tumbling down to smash into the floor. It made its way right down through to the next floor, the weight splintering the wood and concrete. Gasping, I avoided the falling pieces of concrete as

I tried to roll away, wrapping the sheet around me even more. I wasn't fast enough. I felt the ground lurch as it gave way underneath me. I fell until the sheet snapped tight around me. The sheet remained wrapped around my body several times, pinning my right arm to my side as I tried to frantically free myself.

I glanced down into the now empty hole below me. The debris had smashed a path down to the basement and the drop had to be more than thirty feet. I gulped, wondering if I would make it if I cut the sheet. I held onto the wrap with my left arm, feeling a raw ache on the side of my head where a warm wetness dripped down from it. The vampire bite in my arm seared from the pressure against it.

Damn! I was sure to have a seeping cut where my head had hit the side of the floor when I descended. Grunting, I wiggled like a caterpillar in a chrysalis, trying to break free of the restraints the sheets had become. Failing miserably, I stopped struggling and glanced around and above to see what I could do. Fortunately I was near the edge of the floor and wasn't too far from being able to grip it. Grabbing the blanket, I pulled up on it, hoping to loosen its grip on me just enough to pull my other arm free. It worked and I shook the sheet loose from my arm. Now free to pull my body up with both hands, I started the tedious task of dragging my weight up with my arms. I now thanked myself for busting my own butt to work out and even though I had been slacking lately, my efforts were still noticeable.

The cloud of dust swirled away from me, clearing up the air as I grunted and worked my way up. Once I was an arm's length away from the edge of what was left of the third floor, I reached up, grasping the ragged cement edge. It cut into my fingers with the sharp points of rebar and hard, rough concrete that crumbled a bit in my grasp. I gritted my teeth as I pulled myself further up the rope of sheets.

As I lifted my head up to look back onto the third floor, I realized the sheets were on fire. Flames licked at the other end of it, which dangled above as the fire slowly crawled toward me. I tried to grip both hands onto the ledge but the burning flames had eaten into the material so badly that my last tug made it unravel, sending me sliding back down. I dangled from the ledge by one hand, my arm burning as I held on for dear life. The part of the sheet that had been wrapped around me had loosened up enough for me to kick it off, sending it spiraling into the black abyss below like a rippling ribbon of fire.

Chapter Twelve

MY FINGERS GREW numb as the slight grip I had managed began to slip slowly from the edge of the jagged remains of the third floor. I couldn't reach the platform with my right arm, even though it was now untangled from the sheet's straight jacket embrace that had held me but a moment ago. I swung it up to hopefully catch on to the edge, only to immediately slip back off. I wondered if, or when, I did fall, just how many bones I would break. I was sure that it wouldn't really be an issue; I probably wouldn't survive the impact.

Shaking the morbid thoughts out of my head, I grunted as I tried one more time to reach the platform with my right hand. I was just inches away and the strain made me grit my teeth in pain and frustration. I couldn't reach it. No matter how hard and long I stretched, it seemed my left arm was somehow longer than my right. It seemed to have stretched an infinite length from holding my weight. I was sure I wouldn't be able to hold on much longer. Glancing down, I stared at the black depths below; the light from the windows was blocked by debris, leaving the place grey and dark. If I fell, I was pretty sure whatever ferals had survived the blast would be happy to finish me off for dinner. I whispered a small prayer to not live through the fall.

The fingers on my left hand reached the jagged edge and slipped off. The jolt of gravity and the feel of weightlessness made my body feel almost unreal at that point. For a moment, time stood still and the building hovered in my vision as I waited for my fate to come in that moment that seemed to last forever. When a hand gripped my wrist, the hovering feeling faded and the push of gravity embraced me again. My left arm was searing from the shock of being yanked upward as I was beginning to fall. I was sure I had dislocated my shoulder for the agony that followed made me fight to not lose consciousness. Turning to look up at my rescuer, I caught sight of flashing yellow and grey-brown eyes and long, chestnut brown hair. The woman grunted at the effort, pulling at my arm to bring me closer to the edge.

"Give me your other hand, you aren't that light!" She yelled out to me. I swung my right arm up, gripping her other arm. I held on for dear life and relished feeling the ground under my chest when I could finally pull my legs onto the hard, sturdy ground. Glancing up at my savior, who was now dusting off her black jeans and shirt, I wondered who she could be. My arms were numb and I rubbed them, attempting to regain the feeling back in them. I cradled my left arm as I stared up at the decimated ceiling above us. Standing up slowly, I came face to face with the first human I had seen in a long time, besides my family. Or so I thought she might be human. The pain in my left shoulder didn't help me focus.

"Thank you, I don't know what I would've done if…" I started, but she interrupted me almost immediately.

"Stop, don't thank me. You made a massive mess and you really ought to think these things through." The woman shook her head and rolled her shining eyes at me. I felt my face flush scarlet, wanting to give her a piece of my mind. She studied my arm and took hold of it with one hand and placed her other on my shoulder. Her sympathetic eyes found mine as she continued. "This might hurt a bit."

"I was just saying thanks," my voice was raspy and quiet but I was cut off when she jerked my arm, somehow getting it back into position with a strength I didn't know she had. I let out a choked scream, wanting to black out so I didn't have to feel the pain. I hated how small I suddenly felt; being at the mercy of anyone was not something I was used to.

"Forget it, I have to go," she spat out, more annoyed than anything. I gasped at the flash of fangs in her mouth, suddenly full of confusion.

"You're one of them, aren't you?" I asked, staring hard back at her, readying to grab one of the weapons remaining on my belt loop before she could retaliate.

The woman stopped in her tracks, having already turned to go. She pivoted slowly back, looking at me with her eyes, sizing me up. She didn't reach for a weapon but remained perfectly still, not saying anything, just watching me in a peculiar way. I stared right back, challenging her with my own eyes as I wondered why she would even save me. It suddenly dawned on me who she was and my skin peppered with gooseflesh as fear crept across me.

She was a vampire, didn't she need blood? Why would she leave me alive if I was her prey?

"We don't drink human blood," she cocked her head to the side, her beady gold-rimmed, grey-brown eyes reflecting the small fires flickering behind me; it clung to the wallpaper on the other side of the room. Pressing my lips into a tight line, I was suddenly at a loss of what to do.

This vampire had saved my life. She wasn't feral—she was another kind of breed, like the girl back home in the mountains by my van. Her face was now completely in my view and the streams of light that came down from the opened roof lit it up enough for me to see her more clearly. She was the watcher in the woods, the very same woman. The surprise must have been apparent for she did not seem angry, but began laughing at me.

"You really need to get to know how things really are, April," she said, watching my reaction to her knowing my name.

"How do you know my name, who are you?" I hissed, my voice acidic. I felt toyed with, like I was missing a piece of a great big puzzle that I thought I knew how to put together. But I didn't know how to put anything together anymore. The reality of it all was cascading down on me like a bucket of ice water, making me suck in my breath while I drowned in all my fear.

"I know everything about you," the vampire explained. "I know you hunt for your mother and brother, I know you are quite a warrior and deadly too. I'm not the enemy—you have no idea who is and that is going to get you killed." She huffed and turned as she started to walk away with a confidence about her that made me want to shake more information out of her.

"Who are you then?" I yelled at her back, enraged that she was ignoring me and feeling suddenly more vulnerable than ever before in my life. She beckoned for me to follow. I didn't want to go with her but as I stood in the ruin of the ballroom, I knew I had to. She might have the answers I needed to find my family. She was my one chance to learn what I didn't know. Everything was so fuzzy and confusing and only she could make it clear again. Reluctantly, I followed this vampire.

Reluctantly was an understatement.

Chapter Thirteen

I FOLLOWED HER to the stairway, where the now-dying flames had smothered the steps in soot and licked the last of the gasoline that I had laid down. I felt relief flood through me as we stepped through and descended down the stairs. My left arm was still aching something fierce and I rubbed it as best I could to ease the pain. As we reached the first floor landing, I grabbed my hatchet and readied to pummel whatever would fly through the door. Never did I even realize that my companion would take them out before I even had a chance to get to them.

Rain had begun to drizzle down in uneven sheets while I had been inside tearing the place up. It had begun to drip down from the holes in the roof; huge droplets plopped down on the mess that was now the first floor. Some of it had collapsed down into the basement. A few ferals turned as we entered but instead of attacking they seemed to cower and hiss as we made our way past them. They stood glaring at us in the shadows as if we were not welcome.

That was when it hit me. My companion was walking through the beams of sunlight that flashed in and out between the clouds above and had remained unscathed. She was a vampire and they cowered away from her but she was immune to the sun's light. I gripped the handle of my hatchet, more for security than anything else. It comforted me in some strange way. I would have preferred to have my machetes to hack into the drooling, sinister faces that surrounded me but the fight was not in me anymore. It seemed to have melted out of me from almost falling to my death and meeting this stranger. My rage had slipped to the floor like the fat plops of water dripping from above.

Before we left, one feral dared to lurch towards us only to end up in the woman's grip. Her fangs flashed as she hissed right back at the squirming feral in her grasp. Without warning, she clamped down on its neck and sucked on its blood. I paled, feeling suddenly small in a room full of predators. Disgusted, I ran past her and out into the drenched streets. I hunched over as my stomach lurched. Of course they didn't drink human blood, they drank other vampires' blood!

"Not very sturdy are you?" Her voice bounced out from behind me. I turned, still bent over, trying to swallow the heavy knot that had formed in my stomach that was trying to lurch up and out. I shook my head, taking in deep breaths as my hair dripped with water from the downpour above me. The street was already soaked and rivers of rainwater were rushing down the sides of the road, running into the holes of the storm drains at the ends of the sidewalks. My clothes were slick and clung to my skin.

I watched my new companion as she studied me; her honey brown hair clung to her face, framing it in long, slithering strands. She seemed to somehow understand that we were kindred spirits in a sick sort of way. I still didn't know what to think about her. My hesitation swirled in my head like a hurricane, scrambling up my senses.

We eyed one another for a moment, sizing each other up in the rain. Pushing my hair away from my face, I waited for her to speak. I was still too shocked to absorb what had just happened; nothing had taken away from the fact that this here was a vampire. No matter which way I looked at it, she could very well be responsible for my family's disappearance.

"Who are you?" my voice finally sounded as my fingers fidgeted over the handle of my hatchet. Nervous was not what I would say I was. Paranoid, with a dose of disbelief, would be more like it. I wondered how hard I had hit my head. Reaching back, I felt the raw patch of skin under my tangle of hair. My fingers came back with blood, swirling in the droplets and running like watercolors in the rain. The sudden ache to my head made me groan, accompanied by a slight lurch in my stomach. I hated being so fragile but my main concern was the vampire in front of me, staring hungrily at the blood dripping down my arm.

I held the hatchet ready, waiting for her answer.

"You don't have to be afraid of me, I told you, I don't drink human blood." She huffed back at me. I shook my head, not believing a word that slithered from her mouth.

"Look, I know you have a ton of questions so ask away, though I do suggest you return with me to our hideout. The sun will be gone in an hour and I'm sure not even you, miss vampire hunter, can take out the whole town after dark." The woman, if you could call her that, since she looked to be barely older than I was, wiped away the crimson drops that ran down her chin from her feed.

"Why should I trust you? You're one of them, an animal." The thick cold in my voice surprised me. Long gone was the gentile, laughing girl that had once been in my heart. I felt as cold as I sounded too, hardened and numb.

"Look, I'm not the animal here. I am a person, like you. My name is Miranda, I'm nineteen years old and I used to live here with my family too, you know." Miranda paused, almost choking on her words as she took a deep breath before continuing. "I am not a monster. I have just been watching you, seeing what it is you seek. You are the only full human left here that I know of and I was sent to investigate you. I want to help you find your family. I am also hoping that you can help save my family, too." She stared back at me, her eyes never wavering.

Now with her standing so close to me, I realized how her eyes had two distinct circles of color, one outer ring of gold and an inner ring of grey-brown. The sheets of rain made us both blink faster to keep the water out our eyes. I wondered if hidden in the streams pouring down her cheeks were also tears, just like mine.

I was wishing I had someone else there, like my mother, to help me make a decision. Her infinite wisdom would be useful right now. But there was only me, and only my own thoughts and choices would get me through the day. I felt paralyzed as the minutes ticked by, my head spinning, the dull ache now a piercing pain that made me want to bang my head against a wall. Not even the coolness of the water pattering on my hair and snaking down my strands could calm it. Nothing but the beckoning in the woman's eyes, a hint of hope spilling out of them, sent a renewed sense of peace washing over me.

"Alright." My voice came out like a child's, small and frightened. I straightened, bringing my eyes up to her gleaming vampiric gaze. "I'll go with you. But I take my weapons and you promise me that my life will not be in danger." I didn't know why I asked that of her, but something told me that if I did, I would know if she was lying to me when she answered.

"No one is allowed to harm you; we have strict orders not to." She paused. "Besides, we need you more than you will ever know." Miranda tilted her head down as she gave her answer. Her face was sincere, filled with curiosity and a sort of wonderment. I began to suspect that maybe she was right. Maybe I was the only 'full' human left here in Las Vegas. The way she stared at me, I felt like a specimen about to be dissected. Gulping, I pushed the thought way into the back of my mind as I nodded toward her. I prayed I wouldn't regret my decision.

Chapter Fourteen

"HOLD ON, WHERE exactly are we going anyway?" I asked as Miranda began taking a few steps in the direction she wanted to go. She stopped dead in her tracks, looking like she had forgotten about something and was wondering how to go about doing it.

"We're heading to the airport," she stated, still glancing around, looking a bit lost for a moment.

"The airport? Why on earth would you want to go there? There's nothing there. You really live at the airport?" My torrent of questions poured out of my mouth before I could press my lips together and stop the verbal attack. Miranda refocused on me and laughed, shaking her head at the seriousness permeating my face.

"The airport tunnel. We live down in the underground below the airport, where the tunnel is."

I continued to stare at her as she resumed walking, realizing she expected me to follow her.

"You're walking there? We'd never make it before sunset!" I sighed, swiping away my wet hair from my face. "We can take my car, it's right over there." I waved toward the car, wishing I could just drive home. Why do these things happen to me? It was bad enough I had to go with a stranger, but to her lair where surely more of her kind were lingering about? I snorted, pulling the car door open and sliding into the seat as I thought about the gravity of my situation.

Slamming my door shut, I gripped the steering wheel as I watched Miranda make her way to the passenger side. She plopped in next to me, happy to be out of the rain. She smiled, looking around my little car and eyeing the array of weapons strewn across the back seat. Her face fell ever so slightly but she tried to cover it just as fast with a flashing smile of fangs. I shuddered, turning the key as I pushed the lever into drive. The car hummed smoothly as I waited for her to give me a sign of which direction to go. The windshield wipers squeaked across the glass as the sheets of rain pummeled down. When she didn't speak, I turned to find her still staring at the weapons, the ones strapped to my own body.

"Shall I just drive in that general direction or do you want to be dinner tonight for some hungry, hungry hippos?" I huffed; surprised I could even crack a joke with my body aching the way that it was. I eyed her, watching her dual-colored eyes searching the blades and other contraband that were my own security blankets.

"So you do kill vampires a lot, don't you?" Her voice seemed smaller for the moment as she watched me. Watching her, I nodded my head.

"Look, they are not human anymore and they try to kill me any chance they get. Why does it matter?" My patience was growing thin with her, or maybe I was just worn out.

"They are vampires like me." She almost sounded angered as her tone grew tighter.

"They are not like you—you speak, you are in control of yourself and they are not. You are not a wild animal, like them. They are but remnants of what they once were, not what is. I find them to be very much like ferocious, rabid animals. I'm sure they don't think as much about me as I think about them," I spat out at her, disgusted that I even had to say those things.

I glanced back over to Miranda, waiting for her response to my words. Her face had gone blank as she now stared out the windshield, into the street. She seemed pensive, lost in her thoughts, for what felt like forever. I hated to interrupt her reverie but I was not going to wait until her memories released their grip on her mind. The sun was starting to set and the orange purple colors of the evening sky blazed like a warning of the dark soon to come. I needed to get to shelter fast, with or without her.

I pushed on the gas, turning my car toward the freeway that would connect to the airport. I could make it in ten minutes flat, leaving plenty of time to enter the airport tunnel to whatever lay underneath it. I hoped I hadn't miscalculated at all. I could already see some feral vampires gathering on the east sides of the buildings around us, hungrily watching and waiting for sunset. I gulped, thankful that the freeway was wide open and not really in the shadows of any buildings.

"So, how many are back where you live?" I asked, trying to ease the tension with my curiosity about my new 'friend.'

Miranda sucked in her breath and turned toward me. I kept my eyes on the road as the debris and broken down cars kept me alert, summoning my attention and making the trip interesting.

"Hundreds," she said quietly. I nodded, feeling my heart jump into a faster pace as I imagined the hordes of vampires that I was about to insanely waltz into. I suddenly felt the urge to whip the car around and head home. Gripping the steering wheel until my knuckles flashed white, I waited for her to continue. "It is an underground fallout shelter, fortified and well-built. After the initial chaos of the viral outbreak, those of us that had changed into vampires discovered we were not like the 'zombified' ones. We call them wildlings. We gathered together, at first hiding from both humans and wildlings alike. We then met another group like us that knew about this compound and it has been our home ever since." Miranda's voice was steady and calm as she described a chance meeting with an ex-military officer named Blaze, who had become their leader.

"So, does this 'Blaze' know that I'm coming with you?" I asked, afraid that I was going to run into some very surprised vampires.

"Yes, he has had me follow you for a while, ever since we discovered your hideaway. Sorry we disturbed you but we lost one of our own out there and had to return to find her. You wouldn't happen to know what became of her, would you?" Her tone was slightly accusative, making me sit up straighter in my seat.

"Yes, I do." I glanced at her quickly, wondering what she would do if she only knew what had gone down. "I killed her. She trespassed and I killed her." I turned back toward the road but kept her in my peripheral vision, hoping she wouldn't pounce on me and kill us both in a crash.

All I got was a sigh in return.

"I wish you hadn't done that. I understand your reasons for killing her, she being a vampire on your property and all. But I have to warn you, she was part of our group and some will not be happy to hear that you dispatched her so easily, without remorse." She watched me press my lips together in a tight line, absorbing her words with distain.

"Will they want to avenge her? Because if so, I might as well drop you off now." I waited as I slowed the car down, exiting onto the connecting 215 freeway toward the airport. I waited quietly for her to answer, knowing we were getting very close to our destination as the sun's light began to recede.

"They will not harm you; we are not allowed. Blaze will protect you. He is an honorable man and a great fighter, and no one messes with him." She chuckled a bit to herself, making me wonder what she was thinking about. "He's pretty much a badass if you ask me."

"A badass, huh? Well I hope you know what's going to happen, I'm going in with my gear whether you like it or not. I'm not above dispatching your pals. I only wish to find my family." My voice came out hard but straight and to the point. I glanced at her, wondering if she was now thinking she had made a grave mistake.

"You know," Miranda shot back. "I think that this is the start of a very awesome friendship. I don't like many in our group; they are not so street-wise and tough like you. I think we could benefit from your insight of the world. It may not be a nice place to live in anymore but here we are, alive and as well as we can be. I'm certain many will see you as a threat. But I can tell you right now that Blaze and I see you as the future of mankind."

Giving her a sideways look that pretty much said I thought she was out of her mind, I shook my head, half grinning at her words. She was out of her mind, that's all it was. I was out of my own mind for that matter. Feeling like I was walking into a lion's den with raw meat strapped about my body, dripping sanguineous blood down my clothes for the vampires to drool and snap at. I still couldn't believe I was doing this. I still couldn't believe that this was my life right now. The only thing I wanted was to find my family and everything I had come to believe in was now skewed.

Questioning myself was not helping. I could only hope that the road was spread out before me in the direction I needed to go. I had no leads otherwise, and I knew that there was bound to be someone there that could help me, even if I had to risk everything to find them.

Chapter Fifteen

PULLING UP TO the remnants of the underground freeway tunnel situated below the runways of the McCarran International Airport, I wondered where exactly it was that Miranda's hive lived. The tunnel had collapsed at the entrance, blocking anything from entering it. I studied the rubble of concrete and rebar dangling across the mess and shook my head, glancing at Miranda and hoping it was meant to look this way for one reason or another. The sun was fading fast, and unless we planned on dying when the hordes of feral vampires poured into the streets, we had to get to shelter fast.

I followed Miranda out onto the asphalt, leaving my car behind on the side of the road. I had my dual machetes strapped to my legs and belt and my bandoleer well-stuffed with daggers. I was willing to bet that whenever I did walk into her hive of vampires, I was going to get some challenging looks. I was dressed for war, still dirty, dusty and bloody from the explosions in the casino. My hair was in a chaotic disarray. I probably looked like hell. I really didn't care, feeling the day's events nagging at my sore muscles and bones. I was exhausted but I needed to get this over with, even if I had a slight hesitancy hovering in my stomach.

Miranda made her way not to the tunnel entrance but to a door on the side of the tunnel, still under the runway. Before the outbreak, planes would come rolling onto the expanse of concrete above, slamming onto the ground, making it shiver with their massive weight and rumbling turbine engines. Now only silence and an airplane graveyard filled the tarmac above. The city was desolate graveyard everywhere I went: a graveyard of people, planes and automobiles. The entire Earth was a graveyard.

I sighed, feeling eyes on me from all around, making my hair stand on end and causing me to pause often. I had to scurry to catch up to my newfound companion. She kept glancing back, as if she didn't trust that I would still be there and hadn't changed my mind. I almost laughed at the thought. I had never backed out of anything in my life before and I wasn't about to start now.

We came to a stop as Miranda tapped out a code on the door. My nerves were out of control by this time. We weren't alone and the feeling was gnawing at me as I closed the distance between me and the door. I rolled my head around, scanning the high points of the wall before us. Sure enough, that's where I saw them. In the crevices above, a gleam of cat eyes flashed as a couple faces bobbed into view, watching me like vultures from above. I studied them, narrowing my eyes to squint at their pale, porcelain skins, looking almost like they had powdered their faces. Miranda was pale but her time in the outdoors had tinted her skin with a hint of color. Those above me looked like they liked their cave-like home quite a bit.

I snickered at them, hearing them slightly hissing at me. Miranda opened the door and pulled my eyes back down so I could prep for an assault from any side, if it was coming.

It never did.

Miranda motioned for me to follow and I did, reluctantly. Making our way in, we entered a brightly lit hall that morphed into the inside of a huge tunnel. The bulky-looking doorman eyed me with disdain, baring part of his teeth and a fang that shone in the gleaming light. I gave him a toothy smile as I passed. He huffed and shut the door behind me, locking it with the biggest bolt I had ever seen. I turned away and continued on after Miranda.

She turned along the wall of the tunnel. It was brightly lit and had been turned into a massive chamber, with the opposite entrance to the tunnel also closed off. I figured it was likely that the entrances had been purposely blasted to collapse them, seal them off, creating an underground fortified bunker. I was definitely impressed.

"April, stick close to me. I have to take you straight to Blaze; not everyone will agree with you being among us." She motioned me closer and I lessened the space between us. I was feeling my confidence slipping as I eyed the hundreds of vampires now glancing my way, some curious, some ferociously angry. Some were now closing in and following as we made our way down the sidewalk surrounding the asphalt of the former street of the tunnel. I clutched one of my machetes, hoping it would not come to slaughter if they decided to attack me. I would take quite a few down with me if it came to that.

"You might want to let go of your weapon, some would take that as a threat," a husky voice said, sounding in the tunnel and echoing off the walls. I turned beyond my guide to find a man standing with his arms crossed near another door in the wall. Miranda stopped and swiveled back toward me; her lips pursed as she shook her head slightly and eyed my hand on my weapon. Watching the swarm of vampires grow thicker around us, I felt my heart racing a thousand miles a minute and worried that it was starting to look very bad for me.

I glared at Miranda, like she had lost her marbles. "Are you insane? I'm toast here! This is not what I had in mind." I turned and faced the now-growing circle of vampires, their reflecting eyes watching the scene before them. Some dared to edge closer; one tugged at my clothes, which I promptly slapped away. Snarls and a low rumble of growling filled the air around me, my hand once again on my machete. I huffed back at them, wishing I could pull out my blade and take them down.

A cool hand gripped my arm as Miranda shushed me and pulled me back toward the door that Blaze had swung open and now awaited us. We entered after him, a husky man with dark black hair. His broad shoulders made him impressive, tall but with well-built, smooth muscles that moved in waves under his dark brown shirt. His jeans fit him loosely but hugged his hips with a smooth black leather belt. I hadn't seen a guy in almost a year and my cheeks reddened as I tried to divert my eyes from his backside.

I heard Miranda lock the door behind us and we proceeded forward down a long hallway that led deeper into the underground. Evenly-spaced doors lined one side of the tunnel like a hall. Leaky pipes ran the length of it above us and the sconces lit the darkness just enough to see the tunnel in front of us. The unfinished walls were rough, without the smoothness of the concrete in the tunnel.

We silently proceeded behind Blaze and I began to wonder where exactly we were headed. My nerves were definitely shot now. My injuries burned as I flexed my hands, the raw skin inflamed and still riddled with bits of concrete and blood. I was sure that I would need a good scrubbing. A nice hot bath would do the trick nicely, though I hadn't had one of those since forever. It was showers or nothing now, quick ones at that.

We finally reached an area that widened and opened into a small room. A set of double doors led to the left and another lay to my right. Blaze turned and took the sight of me in. I blushed under the intensity of his gaze. His eyes also sported the dual ring of color, but the inside was a deep sapphire. I sucked in my breath, feeling almost mesmerized as I stared back into them. I wondered if they had the same hypnotizing effect as the feral vampires. To look into them was death, my mother used to say. But I was immune. Now, I wasn't so sure if I was still immune or not. These hybrid vampires were a whole different breed of something.

I couldn't read his eyes, they were still and intense. I tried to read anything off his face, but nothing came to me. He was as blank as a desolate pond of unmoving water. His chiseled face was handsome and hard. A lifetime of seeing way too much seemed to be etched in the faint lines on his face and his eyes, like fathoms of sea water that engulfed me as I stared.

Pulling my eyes away from his disarming face, I felt pathetic for staring too long. I glanced about the room to take in the simple surroundings in hopes of a clue as to why I was brought here. Nothing came to me as my gaze settled on Miranda, who was staring at the man as if awaiting orders.

"I'm Blaze, leader of this group. Miranda will get you whatever it is you need." He paused, turning to her as he continued. "Meer, get her set up with a shower and bandaged, she reeks of blood." Blaze took his leave and disappeared down the dim hallway. I was left puzzled, feeling like the stinky kid at school.

"Come on," Miranda tugged on my arm and pushed through the double doors on our right, bringing us into a small locker room with rows of metal lockers lining the walls and isles. I followed her in and past the rows to another room with benches and shower stalls. She reached into one locker near the showers and pulled out a bundle, handing it to me.

"Here's a towel. Get cleaned up and I'll come and get you when you are done. Shampoo and soaps are in each stall." I stared at her in disbelief, not wanting to let my guard down in any manner in this strange place. Miranda sighed. "Don't worry, no one will disturb you. These are the halls for visitors and higher guards of the compound. No one but a few of us live on this side of the hive. I'll let them know you're here. I'm going to scrounge you up a set of clothes and bring them to you." She smiled and turned to leave.

I stood there, alone in the cool air of the underground locker room, glancing about me and still feeling very unsure. I wanted to trust them, I had wanted the company of others for so long yet I had not realized it. I wondered how long it had been since my family had been taken. It felt like months though it had only been less than a week. The small amount of isolation had affected me more adversely than I had thought. I felt skittish and afraid, but not without good reason. This place was crawling with vampires, more civilized ones than the feral ones, but still. I wasn't sure that I felt comfortable enough to take a shower here quite yet.

I sighed, figuring what the hell, and proceeded back toward the showers. It was a semi-open room with four showers installed to the left of the room and a bench in the middle to put your things on. The right consisted of mirrors and sinks with counter space for more items. The simple white tile on the walls reminded me of subway tiles I had once spied in the subway in San Francisco. Las Vegas had no subways, only a monorail system that sat above the Strip's sidewalks and ran behind some of the casinos. The floor was made of cement, smoothed to a grey, non-slick texture that felt slightly rough under my boots. I sat on the bench, unlaced them and pulled my socks off. Standing, I reached over to turn the shower on, letting it run to test the temperature. Impressed that they had hot water here, I slipped my clothes off and tossed them onto the bench.

The steaming water felt amazing on my aching muscles, rinsing away the layer of dirt, dust and blood that had caked my raw skin. My hands burned with the heat but I gritted my teeth through it, using the soap to scrub the muck off of me. It made my injuries sting even more but it was worth it. When I finished, I let the water spray my face, loving the warmth and feel of it caressing my skin. Sometimes a shower is all one needs to feel renewed.

I grabbed the towel off the bench and rubbed my body dry; I ran it through my hair and wrapped it around my body. I looked around, wondering if Miranda really was going to bring me clothes or not. She had not returned yet.

I walked around the corner, back into the locker room to see if she was waiting. Finding not her but someone else standing and waiting made me gasp as I jumped back, my eyes wide.

"Who are you?" I took a step back, feeling foolish for leaving my weapons on the shower bench instead of taking at least one with me. A man waited there, still as a statue but now watching me will shiny steel-grey eyes rimmed by the tell-tale ring of yellow, marking him as a hybrid vampire. His skin was slightly tan and his hair was as black as a moonless night; it almost seemed to shine with blue highlights. He was handsome, in a mysterious way. His slender frame was muscular and his shirt and jeans where slightly loose but snug enough to show off his well-conditioned physique.

His face was still while his eyes, hard and gleaming like hematite, studied me for a moment. He then averted them to the floor and held out a neatly-folded pile of clothes to me. He almost seemed to bow slightly, maybe to lower his face even more, but did not move from the spot he stood in.

"I'm Rystrom, you can call me Rye," his eyes flashed up for a moment, looking at me through thick black eyelashes. He didn't seem too bothered that I stood there with nothing but a towel to cover myself with. My face flushed scarlet, not used to being looked at that way, with an air of being awestruck. I wondered if the hybrids could blush. If they did, he sure as heck was controlling it well. If they didn't, well, it was going to be interesting to find out how their emotions played out on their faces, if they did at all.

"Where's Miranda?" I clutched the towel tighter, hoping it wouldn't slip away from me at the most inopportune moment. At this demand, Rye stood straight up and brought his eyes back up to my face. His still features didn't move but his eyes twinkled with a slight amusement that made me seethe underneath my skin.

"She had a few things to take care of. She asked me to bring you some clothes." He held the pile out again, waiting for me to grab them. I hesitated for a moment, still unsure if I could trust him. His hair fell into his eyes as he averted them downward again, as if he wanted to avoid eye contact for a prolonged period of time. I wanted him to look at me. The urge was almost overwhelming and I wondered why. He was intriguing, more so than Blaze, in a way that I didn't understand. Again I wondered if the hybrids had the kind of mind control that the ferals had on ordinary humans. I had long ago known that I was not a regular human, not anymore. My immunity to their gaze had told me what I needed to know about that.

I stepped forward and reached out slowly to grab the pile from his hands. He let his arms drop to his sides, but did not turn to leave. His face was still frozen, blank as he could get it but his eyes–oh his eyes were full of something untold. I felt almost naked under the intensity of his gaze. I was torn on whether it made me squirm or made me tingle all over with a slight pleasure. The hybrids were beautiful, as though they were perfect specimens of all of humanity. I quickly remembered the pair of fangs that dwelled behind his perfect lips, which sobered me up just as fast.

"You can go now," I snapped, hoping he would get the message. I stepped away, still feeling foolish for letting my senses overload with his presence. I gripped the clothes to my chest, still wanting my weapons for comfort and protection.

"I haven't seen a human in so long." He lamented. He still didn't move but remained fixed in his spot, as though glued to the floor. "I am honored to meet you." He gave me a slight bow of his head and then turned to leave. "I do hope to see more of you." He had paused to say his last words before heading out the double doors of the locker room. A cool breeze from his movement whooshed passed me as he left, leaving me chilled with goose bumps up my arms.

I stood there, my mouth slightly open and still in a bit of shock, reeling from Rye's presence. He was even more disarming than Blaze and I tried to shake off the effect. It made me shiver as I groaned–pissed that I let the first two males I had seen in a long time do funny things to me. I was useless, like a love-sick puppy around them. I felt vulnerable and weak again and cursed at myself for such foolishness.

I quickly returned to the bench in the shower room and pulled on the new clothes Miranda had found for me. I folded my old dirty clothes neatly in a pile and strapped my weapons to my new outfit as best I could. They were a bit snug but fit like a glove, making my assets stand out a bit more than I'd have liked. I sighed, frowning at my modesty. I wasn't used to thinking about how I looked anymore. There had been no hybrids that could walk in daylight, were still civilized and intelligent, around to worry about. It felt like it had been easier to accept the feral vampires in their animalistic, crazed states than a vampire who didn't want to gnaw on me and drink of my blood. Maybe I was wrong about that but I really was at a loss on what to do or what to expect. There had been no one left to impress. Even now, I wasn't sure what to think about these vampires.

The game had completely changed.

Chapter Sixteen

"READY?" MIRANDA'S VOICE sounded from the cracked-open doors to the locker room. I stood up from one of the benches that lined the nearest isle, motioning to my dirty clothes pile, wondering what I was going to do with it. "Leave them there, they'll get washed and back to you." She waved me over impatiently. I scurried to the door and followed her out and down into the quiet hallway once more. I wondered if it would be Rye getting my dirty clothes and suddenly felt a bit self-conscious. I wanted to ask Miranda about him, about her and about Blaze. Heck, about everyone here for that matter.

"Where are we headed?" I inquired, keeping pace with her as we turned down the hall, not toward the tunnel meeting area but the other way, deeper into the underground. Her long hair was clean and lay in soft brown waves down her back. She had also changed into a clean set of clothes, similar to the ones she had worn before. Her slender figure showed smooth muscles under her form-fitting brown T-shirt. She was similar in build to me and I wondered if I was wearing her clothes.

I sighed, feeling my sore muscles still complaining with each stride. The hot shower had helped, but I was ready to crash. The day had worn me down with every little scrape and cut. I was hoping this so-called meeting wasn't going to last forever.

"To introduce you to the group, and see what plans Blaze has for us." Miranda said tightly, as though she was not looking forward to this either. I gulped, feeling her tension slide into me as we walked down the long underground tunnel, our footsteps echoing across the cold stone masonry of the walls. I subconsciously ran my fingers across the hilts of my machetes and bandoleer sheaths. I felt overdressed, like for a fight, but I didn't know what could happen when we arrived at our destination. I was willing to bet the distain in Miranda's voice was but a clue of what was in store.

We came to the end of the hall where she entered a code and a series of locks clicked in succession, releasing the door. She pulled it open to reveal a large room, brightly lit overhead with spotlights that strung along the tall ceiling, much like in a warehouse. Steel beams ran along the roof, braced with more beams, riveting the structured array. The room was filled with people. They casually hung in small groups or individually throughout the large room. The ripples of murmurs echoed in the airy space, but seemed to hush the moment we entered. I wanted to retreat into the sanctity of the tunnel but gritted my teeth as I followed Miranda closely.

The crowd once again parted for her as we made our way to an elevated stage, where Blaze awaited us. His face was hard, his arms crossed on his wide chest. He was still in the same attire as before, though this time I noticed a large knife sheathed to his belt on his right side. It was a Rambo kind of blade based on the size of it. I hoped he didn't have to use it too often.

Miranda turned as she ascended the few steps up to the stage, motioning for me to go faster, but I had stopped to stare at the hissing vampires that were closing the space between me and them. I wanted to swat at them but decided it was better to not piss them off. I glared back at them, disgusted at the display of fangs that accompanied their wild noises.

"Enough!" Blaze's voice boomed over us and the crowd seemed to step back away from me. Relieved, I continued up the steps behind Miranda where Blaze, now with his hands at his sides, awaited. She whispered to him and then left the stage by the opposite side. I felt naked, looking down at the myriad of faces staring up at me, some with anger splayed across their faces, some with curiosity flickering in their eyes. Nonetheless, I could feel the sweat beads gathering around my forehead and chest. My heart raced like lightning inside, making me wonder if I would die of a heart attack before anything else. The surprises I was getting of late were not helping.

"April, Miranda told me what has happened to your family," he said as he studied me. His eyes narrowed, pondering what he was going to say next. I glanced from him to the crowd around us, now engrossed with the scene before them. I felt naked and exposed. The hordes of fangs that lingered in the room were overwhelming, and my anxiety grew tenfold.

"Do you know why you're here?" Blaze's voice made me turn back to the burly vampire. His jeweled eyes gleamed under the bright lights above, making them look like blue fire. I shook my head, not trusting my voice for my breath had gotten stuck in my throat. "You're here because you are one of the only known humans left in Las Vegas. Most died or mutated into wilding vampires, changed from the deadly virus that killed everyone else. Not us though, we are not like the savage vampires you see on the streets. We are different, a hybrid of some sort. Changed, as you are, but somehow you have a resistance to it. No one has been left unaffected."

He paused, studying my features for whatever it was he was looking for. My face paled as I felt my blood drain to my feet. I tried to slow my breathing and bent my knees a bit, hoping not to pass out in front of the horde of hungry-looking vampires. They weren't skinny, but they looked a bit ravenous to me. I wondered again just how they all fed here. I was pretty certain that my blood must have smelt like a delicious entrée perfuming the room.

"April," Blaze's voice came to me as a whisper. I pulled my eyes away from the crowd to stare at him again. I wanted this over with, in so many ways.

"Yes?" I asked.

"We won't harm you April, we need you. The virus didn't affect you the same way it did us or the wildlings. We would like to sample your blood to see what sort of immunities you have developed. It would help us immensely." His voice was cold and serious. Hey couldn't even feign affection or plead in any way.

Sample my blood?

"N–no!" I answered. I took a step away from him and felt the panic surge as it overtook me. I had to get it together or I would die right there and then from either passing out, getting eaten by hungry mouths or die fighting. I was pretty sure they all weren't good choices.

"Please don't," Blaze requested. His tone made me freeze in my steps. My hand held my machete, ready to swing away. I was certain I was dead for sure now. I glanced around at the gasping and murmurs that echoed around the room. I was a rat in a maze. I had to weigh my options, which were pretty much none, so I put my machete back into place at my side.

"That's better. A bit skittish, aren't you?" he snickered as I pressed my lips together, finding him rather annoying and sounding like Miranda. I felt the beat of my heart slow slightly as I breathed in, willing myself to calm down. I still didn't want to give him my blood, even if it was for "research." Yet, he did have a point; somehow I was immune to this devastating disease that had killed everyone I had ever laid eyes on.

"I don't understand why you would need my blood or why I'm even here." I said. "All I want is to find my family and if you guys don't know where they are or you don't want to help me, then I have to go." This time I waited. I had a certain morbid curiosity of these beings. I knew they all had once been human but my fear kept my walls up around me–a deep sanctuary within myself. Could I ever accept these vampires as friends?

As for Miranda–I had gained some respect for her. Blaze, he seemed to be a strong leader here but still, I had no knowledge of their true intentions. I was afraid, pure and simple. Afraid to let them be my only recourse, afraid to no longer be on my own where things were predictable. Most of all, did it mean that I would never see my family again? It seemed that if I gave in to this craziness surrounding me, that I would lose my life again. A second death I wasn't willing to go through.

"I understand how skeptical you must be after dealing with the wildling vampires. I assure you, no one here will harm you. We need you, April. Our lives depend on you." Blaze's voice echoed in my head, making me suddenly want to fall down. The overwhelming emotions inside me wanted to spill over and threatened to do so. One tear slid silently down my cheek as I stared at his broad shoulders, avoiding his gaze. His hair was dark and shined under the bright overheads above. I risked a glance up, finding his eyes hard and still, waiting for my answer.

Miranda moved a little by the other side of the stage, noticing my distress. I wondered what she was thinking. Maybe she thought about just how weak and pathetic I was. The gravity of my situation made me want to crumble to the floor. I wanted to run out of there as fast as I could. Even though it was a huge underground warehouse, it felt like the air was stale and the walls were shrinking around me.

"Come on." Blaze came past me, fetching my hand as he brushed by. He pulled me along, down the stairs and into the locked hallway that held the locker room. Miranda was briskly behind us and locked the heavy metal door. Tears now stained my face as I stared back at both of them. My body shook and my voice failed me as I gulped down a sob. I wanted to hide–feeling so small and overwhelmed, especially since crying in front of vampires made me feel like a little child.

"Miranda, tell her what we know."

"Excuse me?" Miranda's eyes widened at Blaze, as though she couldn't believe what he was saying. "I thought we were going to wait until…." Her voice was cut off by Blaze's impatient tone.

"Now, Miranda. She can't help us if she doesn't know." His jaw was tense and his eyes glared at her as he waited for her to follow his order.

"Alright then," Miranda hissed. She turned toward me and handed me a tissue. I wondered how, in all this craziness, she had gotten a tissue. I accepted it and wiped at my face. My sudden arrest loosened at their words.

"We know where you mother and brother are." Her voice came out calm and serious, making my heart quicken as the worst possible scenarios jumped into my head.

"You do? Where are they?" I waited, wanting to shake it out of her. My breath seemed to quicken as my shallow breaths surged with her words. If she didn't tell me now, I was going to lose my mind. "Well?" I demanded.

"They are not here, first of all," Miranda said, feeling the tension radiating off of me. "A rival vampire group has them." She gulped, pausing as she watched for my reaction.

"You mean a group like yours?" I sucked my breath in. The time it took her to answer felt like forever.

"Yes. Although, they are not exactly like us." Her eyes studied my face as my stomach dropped inside. I was not sure if I wanted to know what made them different.

"What do you mean?" I inquired.

A silent conversation seemed to pass between her and Blaze, their eyes flashing to each other as they pondered what to say. My patience wore thin as I bit my lip to stop the harsh words that could sting from pouring out. I didn't know if I liked these vampires or loathed them. With every passing second, my feelings were beginning to waver toward the latter.

Finally Miranda sighed, giving a slight nod of her head as she slid her eyes back to me. I could tell she didn't want to tell me what she was about to say. I hoped that it wasn't bad news, but the dread crept into me anyway.

"They are mutated like us, vampires who can think and act human with super powers and can roam in the daytime. But," Miranda sucked in her breath, looking somewhat tired after the long day, "they use the wildling vampires as slaves. They have somehow transformed them to obey orders and keep hordes of them as their army of death. We leave each other alone for the most part but we have a double agent in their hive who keeps us informed. She told us that they have your mother and brother."

"Are they alive? Are they infected?" My voice quivered and I could feel the sweat beading once again on my forehead.

"Yes, they're alive and no, they're not infected. But they are well guarded in that lab of theirs. They are being treated well so far. They're just drawing some of their blood at frequent intervals to study and experiment on." Miranda paused as she let me soak it in with a mixture of relief and concern.

"So how do I get them out of there?" I asked, desperately wanting to have them with me now that I knew someone who knew where they were. The longer they remained in the clutches of rival vampires, the longer I risked not seeing them ever again.

"We're not sure; we'll have to consult with our contact again before we try anything, get a layout of their hive and possible numbers of their horde of wildlings," Blaze answered.

I turned toward the vampire leader, his eyes still blank as I scanned them for details. I realized my demands were great; to take on a whole other hive would be detrimental to this one if not done right. I felt suddenly concerned that I would definitely sacrifice them in a minute if it meant it would save my family. I averted my eyes to examine the spongy texture of the bricks lining the hall, afraid he would be able to read this off of me if I wasn't careful. I had to win them over somehow, get them to do this for me, or I was doomed.

"Okay, I'll do it," I whispered.

"Excuse me?" Blaze suddenly looked confused at my answer.

"I mean the blood tests. I'll do them, if you'll help me figure out how to save my family," I said. The gravity of my words filled me with serenity, something that I used to have so much of. This new determination had me suddenly focused and my anxiety had faded away. It was a like a fog had lifted with these few words and I knew this was what was going to be my chance at feeling alive again.

"Thank you April!" Miranda hugged me suddenly, causing me to almost fall over. She laughed as though she had expected the worst. I gave her a small laugh, her contagious mood making me smile. Blaze was also smiling but did not offer a hug. I gave him a tight grin as he waved for me to follow him down the hall toward the labs. I hoped that it wouldn't take too long for I felt like I could've fallen into bed and slept for days.

Chapter Seventeen

THE MOMENT I awoke, a panic surged through me. Where was I? My surroundings were completely unfamiliar, making me sit up with a gasp. The room was lit up by a dull overhead light that was a ways away from my bed. There were partition walls on each side of me, almost like the shower stalls had, but big enough for a twin size bed, a night stand, a small desk and a small chest of drawers lining one side of the wall. My boots sat tightly together on the floor where I had left them the night before. There weren't any windows, so I couldn't tell what time it was. I was still in the hybrid vampire hive, in my own makeshift room.

I quickly pulled my watch out from my cargo side pockets and glanced at the time. It was a wind up battery-dependent water-proof kind of watch and fortunately there were plenty of batteries to go around. I had raided and stored enough to last me a lifetime. It ticked quietly away and showed that it was six am. I slipped it around my wrist, something I didn't get to do too often since the risk of blood and guts spattering all over it was high.

I swung my legs over the side of the bed; having slept in my clothes had made it convenient to just get up and go. My dirty clothes were now clean and folded in a neat pile on top of the dresser. I wondered who had brought them while I had slept and felt just a little more vulnerable that I had not even woken up to their presence. I sighed, lacing up my boots on tight and running my hand over my mess of a ponytail that no longer resembled one. I stood up and opened the drawers of the chest and spied a new brush sitting in one drawer alongside a new toothbrush, a bottle of lotion, some Band-Aids and antiseptic solution. I wondered what kind of place this was that had new toiletries provided for each occupant.

I heard murmurs of voices echoing quietly along the cement walls. I finished pulling my rat's nest of hair into a pony tail and turned to walk out of my bedroom stall when Rye's presence startled me. He had been watching me tighten the band on my hair and a slight spark of amusement danced in his eyes. He was as still as stone and never said a word until I managed to snap at him.

"You scared me! What are you doing standing there?" I shook my head, grabbing the toothbrush and tooth paste and storming past him, not realizing that I didn't know where I was going. This thought made me stop just as fast. Groaning, I turned back to the steel-eyed vampire.

"I'm here to escort you through the facility. I assume you need to use the restroom, so I'd be happy to take you there first, miss…?" He lifted his eyebrow slowly as he waited for me to answer.

"Tate, my name is April Tate. Your name is Rye, right?" He nodded at me as I licked my lips, the harsh silence making me bounce on my legs back and forth nervously. "Well, you gonna take me there or not?" I felt like his slow-motion antics were meant to delay me in some way but his eyes never wavered from my face to give anything away. I felt a slight flush blossom on my cheeks and moved my eyes to the cool cement floor. It was porous and slick in some spots, laid in ginormous slabs all the way down the hall of sleep stalls. I didn't have the only bed in this section and I wondered how many vampires slept here. I did not like that fact that I had slept an entire night oblivious to the presence of others.

Rye began walking down the hall and I followed silently behind him. I studied each stall and wondered why they were all quite unused. Mine had been near the end and I didn't see any other people around to account for the murmur of voices I had heard earlier. No one but Rye and I were here.

"Rye?" I asked.

"Yes, Miss April?" he answered as he continued down the hall toward a set of double doors.

"Who else sleeps here? I thought I heard someone else when I woke up. I don't see anyone now." I studied the stalls and noticed just about two or maybe three that had a few other items in them but nothing with a truly personal touch.

"This area of our bunker is sealed off to the rest of the hive. Only Blaze, Miranda, you and I live here now." He pushed through the door and turned to his right and opened the door into a large locker room, similar to the one I had been in before. There was no one there either.

"Why is it sealed off from the rest of the hive?" My curiosity rose tenfold as we came to stop in the middle of the room, or rather Rye did. I turned toward him and waited for my answer. He was already watching me, sizing me up with a small squint to his eyes. He was extremely good looking; his pink lips were soft and beckoned a touch. I looked away again, wondering why I felt so stupid around him. It was not simple infatuation, but something else. I was hoping it was something else at least, some sort of vampire antics that I could not control.

"We are the leaders of this Hive. We do not sleep where the others sleep for safety purposes. We have had traitors among us before and this ensures that we remain safe when we rest and can monitor the hive without interruption."

I paused, darting my eyes back to his face, which was still as serious and unchanged.

"Leaders? I thought Blaze was the leader. You mean Miranda and you are also leaders?" I was very interested in discovering the hierarchy of this vampire hive. My ears were practically at attention to hear what he had to say.

"Yes, but Blaze is first in command, Miranda is second in command. I am third. Blaze is my cousin. We were in the military together, stationed at the Air Force branch here at Nellis Air Force Base, actually. This was our top secret facility where we both worked prior to the outbreak. We were the only ones who made it safely back here." He paused, watching for my reaction. I gave him none to work with so he continued. "We discovered that we had changed too but not like the wildlings. We were different. As we found others like us, we had to create order, to secure ourselves from the outside threats, so hence, the start of our underground home." He smiled and waved me toward the sinks and stalls. "I'll wait for you outside."

I nodded and watched him turn and leave. I wondered if he had to use the facilities like humans did. Maybe they didn't; they didn't seem exactly dead, even if the history of the vampire deemed him to be so. I wondered what made them different from the feral vamps. There was a major difference, of course. There was also an extreme difference between him and me for that matter. I swallowed down a dry lump in my throat, feeling suddenly alone once again. I was one of the last humans. What was to happen in this world when humans were finally extinct? The world would belong to these mutated beings. And they were as close to human as anyone would ever be again.

After brushing my teeth, washing my face and using the facilities, I walked out to find Rye patiently waiting. He was leaning against the wall and bouncing a small rubber ball off the opposite wall over and over. He pocketed it and turned toward me, smiling. That was a refreshing change.

"I'll lead you back to the sleeping quarters so you can change and put your stuff away. Breakfast is almost ready, are you hungry?" He seemed amused, watching my face morph into shock.

"What? You guys don't eat food…I thought…."

"You thought we just drink blood?" He gave out a laugh and shook his head as we continued to walk toward my "room." "No, we can survive on human food too, but if we forgo drinking blood for too long, we become very ill and weak." He stopped when we reached my area. He motioned that he would wait at the doors and left me to change, full of questions.

I felt stunned; Miranda had feasted on the feral vamp's blood quite eagerly. She could eat human food too and had not mentioned it. I got a feeling that human nutrition was not the favorite food group around here anymore. There was more iron at the top of the pyramid now. I shuddered at the thought and peeled my clothes off, putting them on a neat pile on the bed and slipping on my now clean outfit from the prior day. They felt good and soft against my skin, like a glove. I tossed my weapons on and belted the straps, feeling more like myself once I had finished. I quickly made the bed and headed out to meet Rye.

His face lit up a bit when he saw me coming. It made my stomach flutter, making me slip on my confidence. He seemed more human when he smiled, not the still, statuesque façade he had been parading on his face since I met him. Something told me to not underestimate him; he was a deep well full of life and knowledge of many things that he hid well. It obviously made him a good leader, to be still as stone and dependable as a leader could be. Blaze had more presence than Rye but this man was not a fool. I could feel his strength swirl around him like an aura. He could probably kick a lot of butt out there if he had to. I wouldn't doubt it one bit. And I wouldn't doubt that he had done so already, many times.

We followed the long, closed-off hall and entered into the large warehouse room once more. Along the farthest corner, long tables were set up and many a vampire was seated, eating up greedily and chatting amongst themselves. The echoing voices quieted some as we approached. Rye grabbed two trays off a pile at the end of the buffet-style line and a couple of plates. He handed one set to me and motioned for me to pick what I wanted. I kept one eyeball on the many vampires that now had their faces firmly glued on me. Their eyes felt like tiny little needles pricking me in the back as I tried to focus on plopping food onto my plate. I was starving but being the center of attention in a room full of fangs made my appetite diminish as my stomach twisted into a nervous knot.

I took a deep breath, watching my hand shake as I reached to pour some juice into a cup at the end of the food line. I spilled part of it and moaned slightly at my clumsiness. A hand reached over and took the pitcher from me. Rye poured the rest in, grinning slightly as he placed it on his tray.

"I'll carry it to the table. You're just a bundle of jitteriness this morning aren't you?" He winked and pulled me to follow him to an empty area at the end of one of the long tables. I sat across from him, darting my eyes toward the group nearest us. They whispered to each other as they glanced back to me every now and then. It was quite irritating and I focused my attention on my tray to avoid seething even more from their unwanted attention.

"Ignore them. They haven't seen a human in so long they're just not sure what to think." Rye shoved a potato into his mouth and chomped down, smiling playfully back at me. I was quite intrigued with this new personality that now flowed across his face. His grey eyes were twinkling, as though he had plans for shenanigans that day. I hoped he wasn't bipolar. I couldn't stand an unstable person right now; I was as unstable as one got in a difficult situation.

"I don't feel comfortable here. You don't think that any one of them would attack me, do you?" I asked. I shoved a bit of egg into my mouth and chewed, barely believing they had fresh eggs here. I would have to ask Rye about the food supply and how it was acquired.

"No, not as long as one of us is with you," he said coyly, winking at me, making me think he might be joking. I didn't want to find out if he wasn't.

I ate as much as I could with my stomach tensed up, which wasn't as much as I had wanted to. I knew I'd be starving before noon for sure. Rye grabbed my tray and shushed me when I protested. He dumped them out and returned, motioning for me to follow him again. The stares had diminished since we had first arrived so I was beginning to feel a little more at ease. He walked over to the opposite corner of the warehouse and down another hallway to another set of double doors. I recognized it as the lab where they had drawn my blood the night before. I wondered why he had brought me here again, hoping that they didn't need even more vials of my blood. I would be anemic pretty fast if they did.

"Why are we coming back here?" I asked.

"You want to see what they've come up with, right? Besides, Blaze has been here all morning, awaiting results." Rye smiled again, making me slightly at ease with his explanation. "He wants a cure more than anything. But, we have to help our hive stay alive first."

I crinkled my nose, wondering why it was that every question I had seemed to bring more questions. I sighed, following him through the doors as I glanced about the lab. The tables were full of vials, centrifuge machines and other machines that I was sure did the tests. There were fridges full of blood units on one wall, rack after rack of them. I wondered why they didn't just drink that blood. I doubted it would last very long with the amount of mouths they had to feed. Why this lab was not in the protected locked down area of the bunker was beyond me. I quickly discovered that there was a whole other freezer at the back of the lab, a deep freeze room stuffed full of blood.

"It's our emergency stash. If we're unable to leave here for days, we could survive for a while without venturing outside," Rye offered when he caught me staring at the clear glass doors of the freezers. I nodded, ripping my eyes away from the deep red blood inside row after row of bags. I wondered how they had acquired so many bags in one place. I shivered thinking about how many humans it had taken to fill freezers like that.

"Blaze, anything new?" Rye asked his huskier cousin. The leader slowly brought his eyes away from the computer he had been staring intently at to land on us. He smiled and gave me a nod before turning back to a person wearing a lab coat in front of him.

"This is Brian Sands, head hematologist of our hive." Blaze waved toward the lab coated man. "Brian, this is April, the only human we have found so far." Brian stood up, a scrawny and scraggly man with deep chocolate eyes and messed up, fading blonde hair. The ring of gold in his eyes seemed to almost clash with the deep brown of them. He reached out to shake my hand and sat back down.

"Good day, April," Brian said as he turned back to the computer screen in front of him. I waited as I craned my neck to see what he was looking at. The screen was full of gibberish and numbers that made no sense to me. I gave up staring at it and scanned the room, interested in all the equipment when Blaze yanked me out of my thoughts.

"April, we have isolated a compound in your serum that very well could hold the key to the immunity you've developed against the virus." I turned to look at him, his eyes studying me as if I was a very interesting item on display. The twinkle in his eye made me feel a bit guarded. He didn't make me as nervous as Rye did but he had a certain air about him that made me think twice before I said anything.

"That's good then, you don't need more blood do you?" I asked nervously, feeling a bit dumb for asking. Being around others was not comfortable to me. I realized how familiar my isolated lifestyle with my mother and brother had become. The cocoon we had created had apparently kept my social skills at bay. Now I felt like the new kid at a school full of people that weren't one bit like me. I wasn't quite yet sure how to feel about it.

Blaze gave a short laugh as he grinned, nodding as he stood up and pointed at the screen.

"No, we don't. Not yet. These are you antibodies here, the red are your blood cells. They are usually spherical and concave in a human, something we don't see anymore. Vampires like us, our cells are more like round spherical balls, bouncing around in our vessels, full of nothing but fluid, we have to ingest massive amounts of blood to keep our hemoglobin attached to our cells or we die." He paused, looking gravely serious for a moment. He waved me over to another monitor where another kind of blood was on display.

"This is a sample of a wildling's blood. See how withered it looks? This one had not fed in a long time. But they have the ability to fill their cells up once they feed and they look similar to yours but the surfaces of the cells are a bit rougher, like they're encased in a muck that sticks to them. These are the differences between the three of types of 'beings' left." He straightened up and sighed, looking a bit worn out for a moment as he rubbed his brows.

"So why do you need my blood? What can it do for you?" I asked, curious to hear an answer, if they even had one, to this outbreak that had ended the world.

Blaze's eyes rolled up to meet my stare. His eyes were now cold and a dark blue, like an ocean before a storm, no longer twinkling as they studied me. This made the hair on my neck stand on end as a chill passed through me. I rubbed my arms as he averted his eyes from my face.

"We are reproducing this antibody you carry in hopes that it could help us stay alive longer." His voice came out dry and rough as the room stared at him in silence with only the hum of the machines to interrupt the awkwardness. I pressed my lips together, realizing that whatever he was going to say next would change many things.

"What do you mean stay alive longer? Does that mean…are you guys dying?" My voice came out slightly accusatory. I sucked my breath in as I waited for an answer, fighting my impatience with every ounce of my strength. I had to wait for him to answer. I knew I didn't want to hear it, but what choice did I have?

"Yes, some of us. Not all." He turned toward Brian and gave him a nod. The hematologist nodded and hit a few keys on the keyboard to bring up another screen of blood cells. This was a time lapsed film that repeated over and over again. The red blood cells appeared spherical like their blood had, little balls bouncing around the screen. Eventually those balls changed colors, morphing into a sickly green that rippled the balls on their surface as they collapsed into themselves and then lay suspended like crumpled green bits of paper scattered in green fluid. It was sickening and I suddenly knew what was coming next.

"Some of us disintegrate, wither in a sense. We have no way of knowing when it will happen and the end comes quickly, usually within a week. We start to feel feverish, turn pale and sickly green. Then we bleed, our blood turning into a green sludge, pouring out of every orifice right before death. So far it seems only one in five of us suffer from this disease but we don't know how to track who is vulnerable. We have already lost about one hundred and fifty people. We bury them in the nearby water containment ditch, which has been dry for a long time. We usually set them on fire to disintegrate what is left." He shifted his weight, for he was still standing, his words wearing on him as he spoke. I soaked it all in, still waiting for him to bring up my own blood in all this.

"Your serum may be a vaccine for us to defeat this ailment. So you see, that is why we need you, April." Blaze was staring back at me, awaiting my reaction. My indifference surprised me. I didn't care if it helped them or not. They were still vampires–killers and dependent on blood. Whether they came up with a cure or not, I didn't care.

"Well, good luck with that. You got what you wanted. Now, are you still going to help me with what I want?" I narrowed my eyes at him, my voice spilling out icy and hard. I wanted to feel something for them, just to remind myself that I was still human, but I couldn't–or wouldn't. I wasn't quite sure which it was.

"We might need future specimens to make this work; you have to be on board to help us every time we need more samples." Blaze's eyes were open in surprise; he had obviously expected a different reaction from me. "It won't be much, I promise you that." His voice cracked in a slip of desperation. I shook my head and turned, surprising everyone and even myself as I headed out the door of the lab. The air inside had started to feel thick and dry, suffocating me. I ran down the hall a ways until I realized I had run the wrong way.

I stood staring down another hall and turned to run back but had followed too many turns to be sure it was the right way. I groaned in frustration as I slid to the floor and leaned against the wall, smacking my fist on the hard, cold concrete floor. I was rubbing the soreness on my hand when I heard someone approaching. I scrambled to my feet and came face to face with Rye.

His statuesque face was still and his eyes had darkened over like a coming storm. He was obviously angry but I stood my ground, waiting for him to speak first.

"What's wrong with you?" he snapped, taking a step forward, closing the space between us.

"What do you mean?" I growled back, my lips twitching at his disgust.

Rye tilted his head as he narrowed his steely eyes, sizing me up. "You think you're so righteous, don't you? This so-called mission of yours–killing the wildlings like animals–and for what? Just to find your family. Does that make you better than us?" He started shaking his head as he further closed the gap between us, a sinister grin dwelling on his lips. "But you're not better than us, April. You, my dear, are just another kind of vampire."

The heat of his breath seared my cheek as I pressed myself against the wall, pulling my head away from him, though my heart was racing. His warm nose brushed my cheek as he put his hands against the concrete wall and leaned in, surrounding me. I tried ducking away from him but he moved so fast I found myself pressed against the wall once more. My fear was mixed with want, fogging up my thoughts as I turned my head away, refusing to look into his gun-metal eyes. My hands pushed at his chest, but not with the force I would have used against an attack. My feelings were conflicted; I wanted to run, run so far that I would never see this place or his face again. And yet, I couldn't run. I didn't want to run, really. My feet would not budge and my heart longed for him to brush his lips across my cheek and press them against my own lips, with as much want as I felt.

He stepped away, breaking off a piece of my soul with every step he took. I let my eyes find his, my breathing fast and short, my heart in my throat, expecting to see malice and taunt dancing in his eyes.

But there wasn't any of that at all.

He looked more serious than anything else. Rye's eyes glinted bright like fire on steel, desire burning in them. He seemed as surprised at the feelings we had evoked as I was, if not more so. Sighing, his eyes lowered to the floor as he gathered himself once more. I could almost see his energy retract within himself until it no longer rippled about him.

When he was done, Rye glanced back up, once again sporting the stoic blank mask he'd had the first time I met him. I felt a twinge of loss without him near. I tried to shake it off but I knew the damage was done. I would help them, and not just because I wanted them to help me save my family, but because I could not bear to ever witness him wither and die.

"Come on, let's go back," he whispered, holding out his hand for me to take. I nodded, feeling slightly exasperated that the moment was over. Clasping his hand, I could see it shake before he curled his fingers over mine. He pulled me along, down the narrow halls and turns as if he could walk it in his sleep. I was pretty sure he could. I couldn't take my eyes off of him, a feeling of calm flushing over me as the warmth of his skin bled onto mine. I was glad to have met him. In a twisted sort of way, it felt right. I only hoped that no matter what, he would help me find my family.

Chapter Eighteen

RYE DIDN'T LEAD me back to the lab but he did lead me back to the room I had woken up in, the sleeping quarters. I had protested but he had shushed me with a finger to my lips, the longing returning to his eyes. He managed a slight smile and left quickly after telling me to rest up. I laid back after kicking off my boots, feeling more tired than I had thought I was. My lids sank closed as I let the dark embrace take me, replacing my thoughts for the time being. I was all too willing for this silent sanctuary.

I WOKE LATER, not knowing what time it was. The hum of the overhead lights was the only sound that hovered in the atmosphere of this underground bunker. I wondered where everyone was and how late it was. I checked my watch and realized that it was about one in the morning. I had slept for so long I had missed dinner. Sighing, I swung my legs out and stretched, wishing I hadn't slept so much. I would be up for a while now because of it. It hadn't occurred to me that maybe the vampires were nocturnal, even if they could walk in the sunlight.

I got my boots back on and ran the brush through my straggly hair, pulling it back into the ponytail it had fallen out of. Pretty sure I looked like I had just rolled out of bed, I stood up and flattened the wrinkles in my outfit. My stomach rolled, filling with hunger pangs as I licked my lips, feeling definitely parched. The dry desert air lingered down here too, sucking the moisture from my body. I had to eat and drink something but finding my way around this underground labyrinth would not be fun alone. I wondered what Rye was up to, if he was still awake or not. No one else was in the sleeping quarters; the place was as silent as a tomb. I walked to the door and hoped I would find him, Miranda or Blaze nearby.

The hive was vast. I was sure that it ran the length of the airport, at least. The long runways above used to vibrate above the freeway tunnel that led to this bunker, now forever silent. It had been so long since I'd seen a plane in the sky. This had been a place full of planes, twinkling in the evening skies like stars lined up and evenly-spaced as they came in to land. Now not even the bright lights of The Strip kept the night sky from showing the real stars, no lights to take over the natural brilliance of nature.

I wondered how long it would take for nature to overtake the city. It was already evident after one year of neglect. Weeds and litter were strewn across every street. Dead landscaping and crumbling trees were everywhere. A thick layer of dirt and mud stuck to the windows of the once magnificent Strip of Las Vegas and Fremont Street. Shimmering glass shards lay everywhere. No place was untainted by the viral epidemic. Apparently not even me.

I rounded the corner and came to dead stop. Before me stood a woman, dirtied and with wild hair. Her face was streaked with grime and rips ran through her clothing. Blood had dried in dark red and brown splats on her shirt and pants and the large Rambo-like knife that she fingered in front of me. She was ready to pounce, slowly shifting on her legs as she narrowed her eyes at me. Sucking in my breath, I instinctively reached for one of the machetes strapped to my side.

I was too slow.

The woman moved inhumanely fast, faster than even Miranda. She snatched my arm and twisted it behind me, forcing my fingers to lose their grip on my weapon as she pushed me to my knees and held the knife to my throat. The machete clanked onto the ground, far from my sight. Her breath felt hot on my neck as I struggled against her. She was incredibly strong, like there was a powerful beast inside her. My eyes bulged wildly, unable to pull my arm away from her as it burned in pain. I tried to claw at her with my free arm but she shoved me down to the floor, smashing my cheek against the rough concrete slab.

"Get off me!" I grunted, bucking as much as I could as she dug her knees into my back, making me groan instead. She was a bit smaller than me but she had me pinned pretty well. I stopped squirming as she brought the knife back to my neck, snickering as she whispered into my ear.

"Stupid fool, I could slice your throat like nothing." She pressed the blade against my skin, slightly dragging it along the surface. The sting of the blade on my skin made me gasp as my crimson blood slowly dripped down to the ground. She stopped suddenly, sniffing at the air and shifting her weight but still pressing down on my back painfully.

"You don't smell right." She stated. Her voice was now cracking and uncertain. She pushed off me and stood up, letting me catch my breath as I scrambled off the floor, turning to face her as my hand flew to my throat. It was just a scratch but my fear welled up in me like an overwhelming flood, my eyes wild as I stared at the filthy creature before me.

"What's going on here?" Blaze came storming down the hall, followed by Miranda and Rye as he pushed the woman out of the way. "What do you think you're doing?" He yelled at her as he pulled my hand from my bleeding throat. He let go and nodded, relieved to see that it was just a superficial wound.

"She's trespassing. I was about to dispatch her but…." The grimy woman snarled back at Blaze as she turned back toward me. "There's something off about her, she's not one of us."

"We know that! Take her to the infirmary, patch her up." He snapped to the two behind him. "Seraphin, go clean yourself up, you're disgusting! Then meet me in the debriefing room," Blaze yelled back at her, motioning for her to leave.

The woman's lips pressed tightly together as she glared back at him, her fangs flashing out from under her lips. She turned her hateful look toward me before spinning and running down the hall to who knew where.

I watched her disappear from sight, jumping slightly when Rye took my arm to lead me away. My hand held the cut, keeping it from oozing any more crimson blood down my neck. Walking slowly, I finally slowed my breathing as my thumping heart calmed its ferocity.

"What or who was that!" I said irritatingly, pulling gently away from Rye's grip. I didn't want to feel inferior or like I needed someone to care for me. I was used to being alone and doing it all myself. His touch made me seethe as I remembered how easily she had overpowered me.

"That was Seraphin, our double agent in the opposing hive. She's going to help us infiltrate the hive to find your family. She just got back and we haven't had a chance to tell her about the plan yet." He chuckled slightly but stopped as he caught the nasty look I was boring into him. He gave me a half smile but decided to keep his eyes ahead instead of suffering my stabbing look.

"She's on your side?" I was exasperated. I couldn't believe that violent and lethal wild-looking crazy woman was part of Rye's hive. I turned to look at Miranda for confirmation. She nodded and sighed.

"Yep, she's one of us. She's a little unconventional but she's the only one that would fit in with the other hive; they're not as civilized as we are, April. In fact, you think the wildlings are crazy? They have nothing on them." She gave a huff as she spoke of Seraphin. I wasn't sure if she approved of her methods but I was pretty sure that they had little choice.

"Let me see," Rye said as he tugged at my hand. I let my arm drop away from my wound. He draped a towel on me as he rinsed it out with saline, dabbed it with antibiotic ointment and taped a bandage onto it. I felt silly with the bulk of gauze hanging off the side of my neck but relieved that I didn't need stitches. Rye smiled and stepped away to wash his hands quickly in the sink. I began to suspect that the smell of blood was overwhelming for him. I glanced at Miranda who was trying to look busy rearranging a cabinet at the far end of the infirmary. Wrinkling my nose, I sighed. I would have to wash off the remainder of the blood and change if I was going to go near the rest of the hive.

"Is it hard to resist?" I said softly, swinging my legs as I leaned forward on the table I sat on.

"Hmm? Is what hard to resist?" Rye asked from the sink as he dried his hands, turning back to me. His face was slightly redder then before, as if he was straining to hold his breath a bit. I waited for his answer but I was already pretty sure about what he was going to say.

He exhaled. "Yes, it is hard to resist. Your blood, it smells amazing. I haven't smelled human blood in almost a year." He gulped as he stared at me from across the room. "It's like food to a starving man. The aroma, promising to satiate the hunger pangs that never end otherwise, even the wildlings blood isn't enough." He dropped the towel onto the counter and walked swiftly past me, heading for the door of the infirmary.

"Where are you going?" I jumped to my feet, not wanting him to leave but sure that I couldn't stop him if he wanted to go. Miranda had already reached the door and shook her head at me as he rushed out and left us.

"Don't," she said as I started for the door. "He can resist, but it is like torture to us." She sighed, rubbing her head. "Go to the left out in the hall and the first inlet on the left will be the showers. There will be a set of clothes there for you and towels. Wash off the blood and then keep going down the hall to the second left and that is our sleeping quarters. Get some rest. We will talk later. Right now we have to debrief Seraphin." I nodded to her as she let the door close behind her.

Sitting in the silent infirmary made me feel even more alone than ever before. I pondered Seraphin's aggression and chuckled at her name. I found it strange that everyone here seemed to have a strange name. I would have to ask Miranda or Rye about it later; maybe there was some reason for it. In the meantime, I went to shower the coppery stench of my blood off my body. I felt no closer to finding my family and the days were rushing by without a thought. After I rested again I would ask Blaze about how soon we could start the operation to rescue my mother and brother. I had waited long enough.

Padding out of the locker room, I entered the corridor, relieved to find no one in sight,. But the weight of isolation was making me feel just how much of a minority I was even now, after so long by myself. Now I felt even more alone despite being in a place full of people.

Chapter Nineteen

WHO KNOWS HOW long I had lain in bed, pondering everything that had happened in just the past few days. I hated being in this uncertain place in my life, it felt out of control and I didn't like it. My mind raced, wondering how I could regain my hold on the situation. It kept me up for hours, restless.

I didn't hear anyone else come into the sleeping quarters at all the rest of the night and it made me wonder if the vampires even required sleep. Maybe they had realized how different I was and what a hazard it could be to have a human amongst them. If my blood paralyzed Rye so, how would the others react?

Seraphin hadn't tried to drink my blood. I was definitely relieved for that. She could have easily ripped my throat out if she had so desired. I cringed at the thought as I subconsciously reached up to touch the gauze on my neck. I wondered what they were discussing in their debriefing of Seraphin. I desperately wanted to know and the wait made me feel like I could jump out of my skin from my fraying nerves. I hated waiting, it was worse than getting a tooth pulled.

I sighed, sitting back up as my anxiety made my sleeping impossible. I wondered if I should get up and search for the others. The place was pretty big and I didn't want to run into any more unknowns. These hybrids were fast, I was going to have to step up my game if I was to fight any of them and live. I sighed again, got up and stretched. I hadn't worked out lately and I could feel the slack in my muscles growing. I missed the limberness that exercise gave me. It was like meditation in motion.

I had on the loose clothes that they had provided me with; mine were once again blood-stained and dirty, hopefully getting washed by whoever did the laundry around here. I tried not to think about it as my fingers gripped my ankles, enjoying the slow burn in my muscles as they stretched and relaxed. I continued this for a few minutes before I stood up. Luckily, I healed quickly and my arms and hands were now feeling much better. Even the slice on my neck had stopped throbbing.

I grabbed my machete and gave it several swings and jabs, moving my legs along like a dance that I once knew. It felt fluid, like an old friend's embrace, partnering with me. Spinning, I let my bare feet grip the floor and swipe at an imaginary foe.

I paused to grab the second machete and began my routine exercises to condition my arms with the work of both blades, letting the air rush past with each movement. It refreshed me as I felt the intensity of it bring the sweat out on my skin. My training routine was calming in a most relaxing way. It let me get lost in my own thoughts as the metal flashed and my body became one with the dance. I'd had some formal training before the outbreak. My entire life I had been more physical than other girls, taking dance classes, karate and other martial arts training, almost anything I could get into. It was exhilarating and had hooked me right off the bat. That, along with a year spent watching my fill of videos on weapons training on the TV and DVD player during the endless hours in the bunker, had done wonders for my strength, agility and abilities. I was an excellent fighter; killing was what I was built for, a vampire hunter in every sense.

Like music in my mind, I let it take the movements of my body with it. I usually had music playing at these times but the silence provided its own. My kicks and jumps reminded my muscles what they should be doing. Practicing flips while holding two swords was difficult at first but once you got the hang of it, it was just a matter of keeping your center of gravity. It could either feel like the world has jolted you about or like you are flying. I preferred the latter and let my body take control of the movements without a problem. The adrenaline filled me up like an empty flask and I drank it in eagerly.

A movement in the room jolted me back into the present as I brought my blades up to the trespasser who had interrupted my solace. I held one of my weapons to their throat, ready to slice through it if I so wanted to.

Rye stood still as a statue as his deep steely eyes took my face in. I was breathing hard as I held my stance, afraid to move and not wanting to look away. His look was not of fear, hatred or anything of the sort; it was like diving into an endless pool of water that gleamed my own face back at me. He had said so much without a word and I wanted to dive all too willingly into his soul, never to turn back. I stood up straight, letting my swords hang to my sides, slowing my breathing as I waited for him to say something. How long had he been watching me? How long had he stood there, taking in my dance of blades, my private meditation, before discovery? It was a sort of violation but I wasn't angry. I wanted to reach out and touch his face, make him feel the exhilaration I felt at that moment. Make him feel something.

"How long have you been there, watching me?" I asked quietly. I watched as his eyes searched mine, making me feel the tingle of power that emanated from them. I was sure that if I hadn't been immune, I would have been toast at that moment, completely at his disposal for whatever he wanted. I was glad that I was immune to his vampiric manipulation but, in a way, I almost wouldn't mind letting someone else make a choice for me. I was alone now but this was someone whom I would let in. He only had to ask. I wondered if he even knew that.

"Long enough," he whispered back as his hand came up to my face, letting his fingers run slowly down my cheek, feeling more like a slight breeze than fingers.

I shivered under them. His touch was not cold, but it wasn't hot either. He felt human, if that was possible. Whatever hybrid strain of the virus had infected him, it had transformed him into a most intriguing man. I was certain he had been so beforehand but now he was downright disarming. I sucked in a breath, pulling my eyes away from him. I didn't want to, but I did. I denied myself what I wanted most as I turned back toward my sleeping area, placing my weapons back in their sheaths. I stared at myself in the small oval mirror that hovered above the dresser, my reflection looking flushed. My hair lay flat, sticking to my neck and temples; I wished I didn't look so wild then. I wished I had myself put together, made myself beautiful for him. But I wasn't. This was me. If he didn't like that, he could always leave.

I caught sight of him at my periphery. His dark figure approached slowly as he came up behind me, closer and closer. He laid his hands on my shoulders and clasped onto them as though he was drawing in my aura. I glanced up to the mirror, watching him move his face next to mine as my hair tickled his cheek. His warm breath sent ripples down my neck and tingled across my skin. I watched his eyes reflecting back at mine, making me almost smile as I thought about the myth that vampires couldn't see their reflections in a mirror. He was as clear in the reflection as I was. I reached up to touch and run my fingers up his black as night hair, letting the soft waves of it slide out of my fingers, watching his eyes as I did so.

My heart fluttered in my chest, making my breath feel harsh as I sucked in smaller draughts of air. He didn't move but closed his eyes as my hand made its way back down his crown and to his jaw, crossing his crimson lips. I wanted to feel his lips on my own, let them press tightly against mine and part to let my tongue into his warm mouth. I wondered if he felt the same. I had never fallen for someone so fast and a twinge of panic emerged as I realized that what I wanted more than anything was to fall for him even harder.

Rye pulled me away from the dresser and turned me to face him as his pupils dilated, making them seem like a small band of hot white fire as both rings of color thinned into circles of light. I wanted to know him, to know who he was before the outbreak, what he did, what he liked and what had made him happy. I didn't want to feel this way about anyone but I knew that it was now too late to stop it. Since it bothered me slightly, I briefly took my reluctance into consideration but threw it into the back crevices of my mind.

"April, I...." His voice came out in a nervous whisper, as though it was hard to form words when the air was electrified. His hands cupped my face as his eyes looked more and more entranced, as if I was a drug to be savored. It was nothing that I had ever felt before. His closeness made my body want to pull him even closer, until our souls fused and we would never part ever again.

"What is it?" I asked dreamily, wanting him to say something more, anything at all. I waited but he continued to let his eyes hover around my face, taking in every detail. I felt my cheeks flush under his gaze.

"I never thought I would meet someone like you. You're different; you're stronger than anyone I've ever met, even amongst the hybrids. I'll help you in whatever you need; I'll be there for you." His lips came closer as his words left them, brushing against mine. My lips burned at his touch.

Desperately our kiss deepened. Our lips sought out one another like a desert plant seeking out the slightest drop of water. His body felt amazing next to mine. Our arms held on tight, not wanting to let go of each other. Now that we had found one another, would we ever let go? Would the differences between our worlds and our blood keep us apart or pull us closer together? I wanted to know the answer to that, hoping that the desire engulfing us now would be enough to make it happen.

"Ow!" I pulled away slightly, bringing my hand to my lip which was oozing a sliver of blood where Rye's fang had grazed me. I looked at him in surprise before I burst out laughing. The look of sudden fear filled his eyes, concerned about the injury he had given me. My laugh made him stare back in confusion. I pulled him closer, letting my head fall to his chest, listening to his heart beating almost as fast as mine. It made me smile to know that he was just as flustered as I was.

"I'm so sorry, I didn't mean to–I should be more careful," he offered as he tightened his embrace, rubbing his chin against my soft hair. He sighed happily as we stood there, holding on to one another for dear life.

"It's ok," I whispered. "It's just a scratch." I licked the metallic taste away from my sore lip. He pulled away and held me at arm's length, studying my face as I returned his stare. "What's wrong?" I asked, feeling the nervousness slip back into my chest.

"I don't really understand why I feel this way. But this is something that burns inside me like a raging fire. I've wanted to tell you that from the moment we met. I want you to know something first, though." Rye paused as he took a deep breath, looking slightly distressed.

"Know what?" I asked with curiosity laced with uncertainty. I was afraid to hear what he was going to say but I knew that he had to say it now, no matter what.

"The year that we've been here, after we'd mutated, we discovered that if we fell in love with someone we would leave the ones we came with, even if we were married, to be with that person. It's like our new DNA compels us to want that other person, like two souls binding." He paused, sighing with some strain.

We sat on the bed as I continued to listen to his story.

"It was unexplainable at first but we discovered that it was something that was necessary, as if once we had mutated and found 'the one' we became mated forever. I don't know if you understand that, but I wouldn't have believed it either if I hadn't witnessed it myself."

I shifted on the bed as I listened, leaning my chin on one of my knees.

"So," I pondered, "if a married couple came to your hive and one of them bonded to another vampire they would leave their spouse to be with this other person? Like, forever?" My eyebrows lifted as I glanced back at him, surprised and slightly impressed. "What if the other person didn't want that? Do both of them bind to someone else or just one of them? What if you don't find this other half even if your spouse did? What then?" I studied his face, my heart now a calm drummer in my chest. I wondered if this phenomenon explained our feelings.

"Then we'd remain alone." Rye glanced at me, looking deadly serious with his now rounded discs of silver and gold. I wanted to kiss him again, to feel that fire he had ignited burn again in my chest. I glanced away, restraining myself as I smiled at the naughty thoughts that flashed through my mind.

"How many are paired in your hive? Does the other hive experience the same thing?" I asked quietly.

"Yes. Seraphin has confirmed that this is not an isolated trait. The other hive suffers from the same compulsion. Many of us are paired, many are not. It is random, it seems, and it looks quite bleak for some of us." Rye leaned back on the bed, slumping down with his hands on his belly, looking quite relaxed. I smiled and shifted to let my head snuggle his shoulder as he brought his arm around me. His closeness was like a calm in a stormy ocean. I had not felt so peaceful in a long time. I could almost call it happiness if it hadn't been for my constant concern for my family. If only I could have them with me, here or back at our bunker, safe and sound.

Still, I felt he had not told me everything, but I dismissed the feeling for now.

I smiled as another thought occurred to me. "Not so bleak for us, right?"

His hand rubbed my arm and pulled me in and brought his face close to mine, his eyes shining like beacons flashing across a dark ocean.

"Definitely not."

Chapter Twenty

THE COLDNESS OF the room made me shiver slightly. I rubbed the sleep from my eyes and glanced around, realizing Rye was gone. I was still dressed in my clothes from the night before, making me think that maybe I had dreamt up the events of the night before. Sitting up and looking at the spot where Rye had been lying when I had fallen asleep, I ran my hand over the bed, feeling a terrible loss without him near. It made me groan in frustration; I almost felt weak because of it. Falling for someone was not on my agenda, it had never been. It could be a liability in my search for my family but it didn't matter. I knew he had meant what he'd said about never leaving me alone and promising to help me.

Standing up, I found another pile of clean clothes on the dresser. Someone had brought it while I had been sleeping, maybe Rye or Miranda. I wasn't sure at all and it gave me the creeps to realize that they could sneak past me so easily. It was an unsettling feeling and I intended to get better at detecting them; it could mean the difference between life and death for me in the future.

I treaded to the showers and cleaned myself up. Donning the new pair of jeans and black shirt, I strapped my weapons over my body and sighed, wondering where everyone was. I was still restless, more so now than ever. Making my way back out into the hall, I paused and listened, hoping to hear Rye or anyone else for that matter. I checked my watch; it was early, seven in the morning. I was famished and was starting to feel neglected. I hated being dependent on anyone, so I decided to make my way to the dining area.

My neck had completely healed, as we had discovered last night. Rye had been impressed with how fast I'd healed. I shrugged it off, saying that I had always been a fast healer. Rye had looked at me with seriousness as he pondered what I had told him. Though he had shrugged it off as we fell asleep, I hadn't thought much of it.

I made my way to the locked door that led out to the large tunnel room where the food would be set up. I hoped being out there alone wouldn't put me in danger. I shrugged. What else was I supposed to do, starve? Not an option. I'd rather die with a full belly.

Turning the lock, I opened the door and stepped out into the tunnel. I closed the door behind me and heard the lock click into place. I gulped, wondering how I would get back in if I so needed to. I turned back and began walking to the far corner where the dining tables were set up. I grabbed a tray and began loading it up, ignoring the stares and whispers around me. The vampire in front of me turned to stare at me with widened eyes as his nostrils flared. I'm sure I still smelled like blood, or at least a little bit abnormal. I gave him a smile as the line moved on, and us with it. No one said a word but eyes aplenty dug into my back as I made my way through the food line and plopped down at an unoccupied table at the edge of the area. I prayed that I would get to eat something before anything started.

I had gotten halfway through my meal when it did happen. A burly, broad-shouldered man came to sit down in front of me, his eyes dark as coals, with a sliver of a gold halo around them. They must have already been dark in his prior human existence. His slicked back brown hair made me wonder how much gel he went through. It would be a sad day for him when the world ran out of gel.

I continued to shove food into my mouth and chew as quietly as I could, focusing my eyes on my plate, not wanting to start anything with this brick of a man. He had already finished his food and continued to stare as he tapped his fingers impatiently on the table. I could hear a soft rumble in his throat as if he was trying to intimidate me. I took a swig of my drink and looked up at him as I wiped my mouth.

"You don't belong here," the large man snarled. His hand slammed down on the table, making my heart lurch as I tried to keep as calm as I could. I wasn't going to start this, but I was intent on ending it. I would need every bit of my energy if he was going to make me fight. His lips curled back in a snarl as his eyes narrowed into little beads. I wanted to slip away now with my full belly, but I doubted I was going to get out without a quarrel.

"Did you hear me, human?" He said "human" like one would say "stupid." I stood up and took my tray to the trash, emptying what I hadn't eaten. I was about to place the tray in the dirty dish pile when I lost my grip on it as my body was shoved forward. I slammed into the wall and scrambled to turn and get on my feet but Mr. Burly Man picked me up by my shirt and held me up in the air as if I was a small child. My legs dangled but I tried to kick at him anyway and slam my fists into his chest. It had little effect on him and he would not let go. His smile was widening into a malicious taunt.

"Where are you going? No one is here to help you; they left this morning to check one of our satellite hives. Trouble is brewing and I bet you have a lot to do with it." His eyes were so black they seemed to swallow the gold ring that hugged his iris, like a full solar eclipse in the black holes of his sockets. I grabbed at his hands, uselessly scratching and slamming my own fists into his.

"Let me go!" My legs weren't even long enough to reach him and his arms were long with bulging muscles that held me easily. He began laughing at my efforts. The crowd around him was eerily quiet, obviously not sure what to do with the situation. I was sure there might have been some that would've helped me but they were too afraid of this man to try and go against him. I sucked in a breath and stopped flailing, feeling much like a fish on a hook. His grin widened at my supposed surrender, his glowing white fangs flashing in his mouth, looking as though they were growing longer.

He shook his head at me as though what I had yelled at him was a stupid question. "No, I can't let you go. You see, you're not mated and I'm looking for one. I think I might just stake my claim on you. You could give me loads of fun and when I'm done, you might make a tasty meal." He licked his lips and tongued the sharp points of his fangs as he dropped me to the floor. My hip slammed into the concrete with such a force it sent a numbing pain shooting down my leg, rendering me too stunned to stand up. I pushed up on my arms but my legs wouldn't cooperate. I pulled up on the wall and grunted as I reached for my machete.

He promptly slapped my hand away from it. My other hand flew to the one on my other hip as I tried to stand. He shoved it away and pulled me against him as I slapped him hard on the face, making his grin morph into a grimace of anger, contorting his face demonically. He growled at my horror as I again struggled against him. His body shook with his haughty laugh when he suddenly bent forward, his hot breath rushing past my neck and ear.

I realized with terror just exactly what he could have done if he'd wanted to. He could have drained me dry right there. There was no one to back me up and no one to even care.

Rye, where are you?

"You smell good, human, like the sweetest nectar, and I really miss drinking…."

He inhaled my skin like a rare perfume, making me cringe away from him. I reached up and snatched a small knife from my bandoleer, sly

113

enough so that he wouldn't notice. I swung it up in an arc, aiming for his head, but a flash of his arm flew by as I slammed my arm down, catching the knife in his forearm before I had gotten any closer. A gasp flew through the crowd gathering around us. I wanted to yell out at them to not just stand there but to help me out a bit. Darn bastards were no help at all.

Mr. Burly Man stared at the knife protruding from his forearm as he shoved me to the wall. My head bounced off the wall and the room spun as my sight wavered and threatened to throw me into darkness. I concentrated on breathing as I blinked and tried to focus on him. He was fuming. His lips snarled and a low growl was definitely forming in his throat.

He reached over and pulled my knife from his forearm, staring at the blood that was dripping down his arm and blade and splattering onto the floor. He came into focus as a surge of pain ran through my head, making me grip my temples to subdue it. I watched as a horror built inside me, my stomach dangerously queasy as he moved the blade to his lips and gave it a long, savory lick.

Gross!

I scrambled to my feet again. The world lurched, sending me off-balance. I was hoping I wouldn't lose my breakfast; it would not be worth this fight if I did. I began to walk to my right, the crowd parting just slightly, when I heard his booming voice hit me from behind like a freight train.

"You aren't going anywhere, lady," Mr. Burly Man said as I turned, watching him as he dropped my knife to the floor. It clanked and skittered across the cement to disappear into the crowd.

My head was throbbing but my anger was rising at his incessant battering. I wanted to get back to the tunnel and lock him out, make him remember that he was not a leader of this hive at all. I was sure what he was doing was quite against the rules and would not be tolerated by Blaze at all.

"Why don't you get lost? I'm pretty sure Blaze is not going to let you stay here once he hears of this," I stated to him, my voice calm and cold. I was sick of him already–I didn't want to dance anymore.

He gave a haughty laugh and shook his head. "Blaze is a nothing, a washed-out leader who is weak and oblivious to what really goes on here. You think he will save you? When I take you to my dwelling, he'll never find you and no one here will tell him for fear of my wrath. Right? Right?" He yelled at the vampires nearest him, making them shake and unanimously answer back in agreement.

"Yes, Charles!" Their voices squeaked out as they backed away from him, as if his touch would burn them like acid. He turned back toward me and sighed with delight. He was immensely frightening–his dark eyes gleamed back at me, malicious and psychotic. He had no problem doing what he was doing; I wanted to end him so he wouldn't hurt anyone else ever again.

I pulled out my machete, pushing the gasps that echoed around me to the back of my mind. I wouldn't let him win; I would die before he would ever have his way with me. Gripping the hilt, I bent my knees, ready to pounce on him. This time I was ready and I didn't intend to lose. I watched his sinister grin, one that made me sick. I wanted to slice it off, like the feral vampires I had hacked up before. He was no different a creature. He may have been able to talk and act more human than the ferals but he was just the same inside, wild and vicious.

I wondered if the virus had changed him or if he was just a dick by nature. I was betting on the latter.

I waited, gripping my blade patiently, letting him advance toward me. I was in no hurry. There wasn't any way he would win; I was ready now and nothing survived my wrath when I was determined. Even my head had stopped throbbing enough for me to focus. I wasn't bleeding but I was sure I would be full of bruises to agonize through later. I was going to end this now and if it was the end of me, so be it.

His smile wavered just enough for me to notice. His eyes narrowed even more as he watched me in my determination. I was sure no one had ever stood against him before, especially a small-framed woman like me, not even another vampire. I was willing to bet that he wasn't sure of himself for once, even if it was for just a single hesitant moment. He tried to cover up the edge of fear that flashed across his eyes but I had seen it, and that was all that I needed.

He lunged, yelling out as he rushed in and flung his full body weight at me, expecting to crash into me like a bull. I side-stepped as quickly as I could and turned to bring the machete around toward his neck as he dove forward. It connected and black-red blood sprayed from the wound as his head went thumping across the floor, leaving the heap of his body behind to crumble into a convulsing pile.

I held my stance, watching the blood drip down my machete to pool onto the floor, reflecting the bright overhead lights in its smooth surface. My breath came out hard as my eyes flashed to the crowd before me. Their whispers and gasps rippled across the room as they backed away slowly, none of them wanting to be the next to meet my blade. I stood up and walked over to Mr. Burly Man's body. I heard people repeating the name "Charles" in hushed murmurs. I gave him a swift kick, feeling my tension relieve with it. His head was a few feet away and I walked to it, bending down to swipe it up, holding it by the slick black hair that stuck out in every direction. I lifted it up above me to show the others. I wasn't above making it morbid. I wanted them to know that I was not weak; I would take down whoever crossed my path–Charles now being my prime example.

"Anyone else have a problem?" I snapped at the crowd. They shrank back, turning their eyes away from me, cowering like fools.

Tossing the head to the side, I wiped my blade off on his clothes. I scanned the room, finding Blaze standing silently near the door to our hallway. Shocked, I wondered how long he had been there, watching what had been going on. A slight anger flinched inside me as I read in his eyes that he had been there long enough and had not intervened one bit. I wasn't sure what to think or say about that but I was sure that this room was now suffocating me. As I approached him, we shared a look that told me we both had each other's mutual respect. He gave me tilt of his head and we both turned toward our living quarters, leaving the body of Charles for someone else to clean up.

I was sure that the mutual respect was going to garner me a lecture of some sort. I resigned myself to it as I made my way down into the branch of our private quarters as he slammed and locked the main door behind us. I sighed, turning slightly as he came toward me. His face was a mix of seriousness and…amusement? Confusion filled me as I wondered what was now going through his head.

What did it mean? My eyes ran over the rough concrete on the walls, feeling the stress of killing Charles hit me all at once. Leaning on the coolness of the wall, I slide down, tears flowing as I shook, the throb in my head returning with a vengeance. I didn't want him to see me like this; to show weakness was not an option for me. Yet here I was, my sobs filling the air and my tears spilling over my cheeks.

I rubbed my face on my sleeves and hoisted myself up on my legs. It wasn't supposed to be like this. I wanted my family with me now. I hated these new hybrids. The ferals were easier to control, they were not intelligent and had no sort of consciousness that I was aware of. To kill them, like wild animals, was nothing. Even when I'd had difficulties or had run into complications with them it was never emotional, never a decision that I questioned when I went in for the kill. Charles, on the other hand… well, he had certainly deserved his fate. I had been forced to the point of ending his bitter life but it wasn't what I had ever wanted to do. It didn't make me powerful and it hadn't made me any better than anyone else. In fact, I wondered if, deep down inside me, killing any kind of person was slowly having an erosive effect on my humanity.

Blaze said nothing. He didn't have to. He didn't even sigh or lecture me about killing off a member of his hive. Somehow, I felt that Charles would not be missed. A man like that had deserved what I did to him and more. The thought calmed me. At least no one else would ever have to suffer his wrath ever again. I was sure that he had taken advantage of many a woman. I had done this hive a favor and I sobered up with this absolution, looking up at Blaze as he held his hand out for me.

As we walked, he told me about the meeting with Seraphin. She had already returned to the opposing hive to prepare for our attack in a couple days. I felt impatient hearing his timeline–hadn't I waited enough? I willed myself to listen to the entire plan before I ranted; I didn't want to snap at him and tried my best to hold it in. Blaze's voice still held a hypnotic affect and it helped quell my anxiety, making me wonder if he was doing it on purpose. I didn't want to assume anything, though. I really didn't know him at all, or Rye and Miranda for that matter. I had to trust them with my life and the lives of my mother and brother. This was all I had and it was more than I'd had in a long while. Someone finally had my back, and my extended isolation had ended. I found myself hoping that it had ended for good.

Chapter Twenty-One

THE PLAN WAS simple: sneak our way into the opposing hive, set off explosives to shake them out into the daylight to rid us of the mutated feral vampires first, then we could pick off the remaining hybrid ones more easily. I was sure that I had a severe disadvantage with the last part. I was to find an injured hybrid with Rye and interrogate him on the location of my family. I was hoping it would be easy to get one to talk, for where we were going was not going to be an easy feat to get through. Their headquarters was located in the infamous Stratosphere tower. The entire casino and citadel was theirs. I hadn't even thought it possible that there was anyone else in the city but me and my family, assuming it was just another abandoned building. But apparently the bowels of it were filled with feral and hybrid vampires alike.

Blaze described how the mutated feral vampires were used as guards to every entrance but they were still sensitive to the sun and could only be used for this at night. The only thing they hadn't been able to genetically alter in the feral's DNA was their deadly kryptonite, the sun. Hence, the reasoning behind our daylight attack. Miranda had already shown me that the hybrids could walk in the daylight hours but something occurred to me as Blaze ranted on and on about which entrance Rye and I would take while he took on the front entrance, assuming the brunt of the attack.

My eyes went up to his face as my hand waved for his attention. He stopped his speech and waved at me to spit it out. "So, are you also as immune to the sun as I am? I've only seen Miranda out on semi-cloudy or rainy days." I was certain that something was off. He was a vampire and I had too-easily dismissed this question when Miranda had joined me. But it had made me wonder—why didn't they fill the streets like regular humans had in the bright Vegas sun and just live like we all did before the outbreak? With the exceptions of the feral vampires of course, they could have lived normal lives if the sun wasn't an issue.

The answer dawned on me before Blaze even answered back. "We are somewhat immune to the sun; we do not burn to ashes like the wildlings do if we step outside." He sighed, rubbing his temple as though the tension of talking about the plan had worn him out to the point of causing a headache. "But it is quite uncomfortable to walk under clear skies with the hot burning sun beaming down on us. We burn more easily than you do. It feels like being boiled alive. Quite uncomfortable, as you might guess." He shrugged and ended the subject at that.

"And what do I do once we are inside and discover where they're hiding my family?" My palms were sweaty as he continued, directing me to regroup with Rye and Miranda before attempting to rescue my family. I nodded, knowing how anxious I was going to be when the time came. I hoped that we made it that far, I hoped that we weren't going to be ambushed the moment we stepped into the dark underground of the enemy hive. I was also wondering if they had messed with the DNA of the feral vampires. What else had they been tweaking in their labs? I shivered as I thought of the hordes of things they could have been concocting the entire year I had lived in oblivion in the quiet mountains.

I longed to return home now. I ached for the sway of the trees in the wind, the scent of pine and mulch scattered throughout. The air down here was stale and recycled, making me feel all the more claustrophobic with nothing but concrete all around and above me. This tomb made me feel deader inside than I had felt in a long time. I hoped that once my family was released we could return to our bunker in the mountains, alone and safe once more.

The image of home brought me back quickly, realizing that it would never be the same. If this hive, one that had no ill intentions toward me, found us so easily, who's to say that any other hive that was less honorable wouldn't come my way? Especially after this battle, I was sure that my presence would be quite well known afterwards.

I shuddered. That supposed I survived this encounter at all.

RYE AND MIRANDA had come in as I was just about finished interrogating Blaze. Rye had smiled at me but it didn't reach his eyes. His seriousness concerned me until I realized I was still pretty bloodied up, with Charles's blood clinging to my shoes and shirt. I was positive he had passed by the mess of Charles's body in the dining area. His eyes studied me disapprovingly. I looked away but felt his gaze digging into me. I wasn't sure if this made me irritated with him or not. He hadn't been there; I'd had no choice but to eliminate Charles for my own survival. We went back to our sleeping quarters after the meeting in awkward silence.

"You okay?" he asked softly. Surprised, I glanced at him as he sat beside me on the bed, his arm embracing me from the side. I lean into him, relieved that he wasn't angry but concerned for me. I nodded, giving a slight smile back to him. His eyes told me he knew better, that he knew what had gone down. I wondered if he felt responsible for it. He would be the kind to resent the fact that he was gone when I was attacked. I valued his affection, his willingness to be my safety net now.

"I'm glad he's gone. He was nothing but a huge problem to all of us." Rye's hand rubbed my arm softly. His skin felt like cool, silken cloth and it reminded me of something, a memory long gone.

"Rye?" I asked.

"Yes?"

"Blaze said the sun hurts you. How does it feel? The burn, I mean. If you don't incinerate, how do you survive in Vegas sun?" I felt almost like I was intruding on his privacy but even Miranda did not seemed bothered with my questions.

"Like when you get a bad sunburn, that pain and raw feeling to your skin the day after? That's how it feels. We even catch some redness to our skin but if we stay too long in the sun we start to cook, smelling like barbeque."

I wrinkled my nose at the description, not liking the imagery at all. He gave me a grin, enjoying the fact that he could gross me out. I rolled my eyes, knowing how silly it was to think a vicious vampire killer like me could get grossed out. Well, a lot of different things had been happening in my life that had never happened before. I was sure my stomach was just not equipped for so many shocks so close together. Pressing my lips together as my stomach began to churn, I willed it to calm as the moments ticked by.

"Come on, I have something to show you." Rye tugged at my hand as he stood up, the moment obviously over. I wondered what he was up to, amazed at how comfortable I was with him already. He had basically told me we were meant for each other, though I was skeptical. I didn't want to jump into anything too fast, not when everything was so uncertain and the dangers ahead would be treacherous. I followed as he led me out, quietly keeping pace with him as he squeezed my hand.

We made our way down the concrete tunnel, away from the main area. I wondered where we were heading. How deep this place went, I could only imagine. The airport buildings were just above us. The farther we went into the tunnel the more I wondered if we would end up on the strip if we kept on. He took me through several locked doors that just opened to more and more of the underground maze.

I began to feel a bit paranoid as we kept on, being here, just him and me, alone in the deep tunnels of Las Vegas. My patience slipped from me and I came to a sudden stop, digging my heels into the ground. Rye spun around as my arm pulled back on his, his eyes surprised.

"What's wrong?" His eyes scanned my face; I'm sure it was full of suspicion and fear.

Shaking my head, I met his gleaming orbs and sighed. "Where are we going, Rye? It's endless. How far are we going? Why aren't we attacking for two more days? I'm tired of waiting." My desolate voice echoed in the lonely hallway, making me feel more like I was in a cell. I stepped back to lean on the cool wall, hoping it might help steady me. My uncertainty was drowning me, my impatience making me short tempered. I didn't want anything now more than my family safely back in my arms.

"I know you want your family back but these things take planning and timing. We can't just burst in right now, we have to wait for Seraphin's signal and she said to give her two days. We have to trust her—she is our only hope to get this right."

I rubbed my face, feeling the stress wearing me down to the bone. "I know, but I don't even know that woman. She's crazy! How she ended up as our only option is beyond me! She almost killed me!" I snapped. I did not like this plan and I wanted out of that tunnel, missing the sweet scent of pine and the sway of leaves rustling in the wind back home.

"You have no choice but to trust her. Besides, I know she's rough around the edges but I vouch for her. She's good and only she can do this right." Rye's seriousness turned his eyes into hard pebbles of grey, his face a blank sheet. I got a strange feeling he wasn't telling me everything again. I hoped it was just my endless paranoia nagging at me but this... this felt stronger than that.

"Who is she to you, Rye?" It was my turn to don a blank face as I watched his face morph into an expression of surprise. He turned away, letting his eyes stare off into the long tunnel, a memory flashing across his features. It wasn't a pleasant one either; it was truly filled with nothing but pain of loss.

"Seraphin was…she was my wife." He started walking again, motioning for me to follow. I knew he didn't want me to see his expression; his stride was just fast enough to stay in front of me. He continued in silence, making me realize that I had hit a very sensitive nerve.

"I–I'm sorry, I didn't know, Rye." I gripped his arm, pulling on him to stop. He turned to face me, looking vulnerable and sad. I could feel my heart stinging for causing it. "What happened?" I inquired, hoping I wasn't intruding too much.

He sighed, pursing his lips as he pondered whether or not to tell me. If Seraphin had been his wife, why were they not together now? Had she left him for another?

Suddenly it came to me as I sucked my breath in, my eyes wildly scanning his face. "She found another mate, didn't she?" He nodded as his lids closed to cover the memories that were probably flooding through his mind right now. I wanted to know everything: how Seraphin could have been his wife, who her mate now was and more. I wasn't sure if he would tell me but I had to find out. Maybe it was the slight tickle of jealousy that fluttered in my chest. I didn't know what else to make of it but being kept in the dark was too awkward. I needed to know.

"Her name wasn't Seraphin back then." The glowing halo of his eyes shined in the artificial light of the tunnel. It made them glow like an unnatural metal. He was handsome, more so than any guy I had ever met, and it was disarming to stand so close to him and not want to be even closer. "It was Angela before the outbreak." He let out a breath as his voice steadied.

"We all decided to choose new names after we discovered how changed we were. We were no longer human, we were something else. Our human selves had died with the outbreak and it was a way to start over." He sighed, slipping his fingers through mine. He tugged gently to start us walking again. I let him pull me into stride beside him as he continued.

"My name was Brian Reynolds before the virus took it all away." I listened to his story, of how he got married in a chapel on the Strip of Las Vegas Boulevard, how he had met Angela at a Starbucks while she served coffee behind the counter, how he had fallen in love with her flashy smile that seemed to charm even the grumpiest caffeine-deprived customer. He had been a goner when her pretty brown eyes had flashed up to meet his, mesmerizing him immediately. He wooed her from that point on, bringing her little gifts like flowers and small figurines that he would come across that reminded him of her beauty. Eventually, they got engaged and married. They had planned to start a family but after two years of trying the outbreak came and the end was not far behind it.

"Who is her mate now?" I asked, hoping it wouldn't sting too bad to answer my question.

Rye let out his breath. The tension sat on his brows, making him look as if his concentration was stuck on his face, creasing his otherwise smooth skin. He glanced at me, relaxing the strain on his face, bringing a smile to his face.

"She met Alan after we changed–he was a vampire in the opposing hive. He used to live here, amongst us, but felt that it would be too awkward to stay here after Seraphin left me." He was now watching the tunnel ahead of us, steering me toward a bend in the path. "I knew when she saw him that it was over. It was that fast, like severing an arm, fast, sharp and permanent."

"Somebody that you used to know…" I mumbled.

"What?" Rye gave me a confused look.

"Gotye. He was a singer whose song I heard when I was in school, not that much over a year ago. It's about someone treating you like you're a stranger after being intimate lovers." Biting my lip, I watched him, hoping I hadn't said too much. He gave me a slight nod as we reached the end of the hall where we encountered another locked door, bolted heavily into the wall.

"I heard that song. Definitely fits the bill." He turned the locks, grunting as they screeched to life. "Well, now it's all done and gone. She has Alan now. Me…," Rye winked at me as he pulled at the dusty door. "I have you now." His statement made me flush as I followed him into a darkened room. He pulled the door shut behind us and switched on another set of lights.

They flickered on, making me squint at the now-illuminated room. A staircase stood at one end of the room, leading upward. It looked like a small basement room and I wondered where the steps went. We should've been right beneath the airport. I wondered if that was where we were heading. Wouldn't it be full of feral vampires up there? I gulped as I watched Rye motion me forward, taking the steps quickly as though they were nothing. I scrambled to keep up with him, fingering my belt for a machete, hoping he wasn't going to hop into a dark space filled with crazed and hungry vampires. I wasn't in the mood to fight any ferals at the moment. Not that I ever really was but it was not smart to jump into it if you didn't have to.

I was about to ask him what exactly he was doing when we reached the top of the stairs. I stared down at the flights below us; we had gone up at least three floors before stopping. I placed my hand on the hilt of my blade, hoping and praying that I wouldn't have to use it.

Rye gave me a little squint and grinned, shaking his head as he grabbed the door handle. "Relax, there are no wildings up here. The entire airport is secure. We took care of that a while ago and the perimeter is heavily fenced." He shoved the door open, leading us into one of the large carpeted rooms of one of the terminals. This one was circular and had ports leading to jet ways that had been used to board passengers onto planes. Some of the gates were empty and some held silent planes, awaiting people that would never come.

The place was miraculously free of bodies or anything decaying. I wondered if they had cleared it out or if it had just been abandoned once the outbreak hit. I made a note to ask Rye about it once I had a clue about what we were going to do up here. The large windows faced out into the city, letting the sun's warm rays filter in from the west-facing windows.

I went to the clear glass, peeking out onto the tarmac. It was quiet and solitary here, making me feel safe in the light that I relished. Soaking up the light, I had not realized how much I had missed it. My hand came up to touch the warm glass. Spots of old rain and dirt encrusted the outside of the window but it was still clear enough to see the once-glorious Las Vegas Strip in the distance. I had been in this airport before but had never known about the labyrinth of tunnels beneath the terminals. Still, the surface was much more fascinating, even though it lay in suspended state of petrified neglect. My fingers slid down the smooth glass, making me want to touch the air around me. Sadness for the world I once lived in washed over me.

In my mind, I could almost hear the ground vibrate from the engines of the planes taking off. The way the massive planes sped up and left the earth behind had always fascinated me. I had ridden on planes a few times in my life and the guttural rush it gave you as the wheels left the sturdy runway always took my breath away. Watching the ground shrinking as it sped by outside the tiny plane windows had always made me wonder if I would live through the flight. I always did. Not even an airplane could bring me down.

Now the stretch of asphalt and concrete runways sat silent and the airplanes were like ghost ships, sitting and waiting. They would probably never reach the sky again.

Turning away before the knot in my throat threatened to open up into a gush of tears, I found Rye watching me. He was serene as he pulled me into his soft embrace. I nuzzled my face in his shirt, taking note that although he was a vampire he didn't smell any different than a man would. His scent was pleasant, that of a musky mountain wind. I inhaled, finally not feeling so alone anymore. His hand softly rubbed my back, sending a shiver down my spine as he kissed my head. I knew then that no matter what, things would be alright. Whatever lay in the days ahead, I would get through it as long as Rye was by my side. His strong arms held me in place and his sweet light lit my dark world.

Chapter Twenty-Two

"WHY'D WE COME here?" I whispered as we stood in the middle of the airport terminal. Rye's arms encircled me as we both stared out the tall glass windows. The night was approaching fast, our last night before the ambush on the enemy hive. The last night without my family. If it went the way I hoped, I would be embracing my mother and Jeremy in just a matter of hours. If only it would go that way. If only...

"I had to show you the beauty of it all again. We secured this airport soon after the outbreak. People fled the airport almost immediately when flights were suspended, so it wasn't too hard to do that. Only private planes and pilots had access, and those who could, left in the small planes. Otherwise, air travel came to a halt." Rye rolled his neck, stretching it as he spoke. "No one took to the skies; it was too big a risk to have a vampire outbreak in the air. Can you imagine what that would've been like? I'm sure most of the cabin would have been bitten before subduing a vampire. It would have been a graveyard up there." Rye sighed as he rubbed his chin on the top of my head. He was taller than me, but just by a head. His body felt warm and sturdy as I let him hold onto me. It felt like a slice of pure heaven, at least for a moment.

"Do you think we'll succeed?" I turned to face him, searching his eyes for truth. They gave me a flicker of hope.

"I think we're going to go for it, I wouldn't underestimate this hive, April. We are very strong and determined. We've been meaning to take them down, this city is a bit too small to support two large vampire hives and they have been destroying our food supplies."

"Wait, food supplies? What do you mean?" My eyebrows raised in confusion. Something told me that I didn't know the workings of this hive at all, that what I had seen was just the tip off the iceberg. I was starting to feel very small in a vast plan.

"Well, to the south we have a herd of cattle, sheep and pigs we raise to help feed our population. We keep them in guarded warehouses lining Lake Mead Parkway, near one of the hospitals off Eastern Avenue. Sometimes they raid one of the outlying facilities and get away with some animals. We've managed to stop them before they get too much but it puts a dent in our supplies and the attacks are increasing." His jaw tensed as he thought about the conniving opposition they had been facing lately. "It's just fate that rescuing your family has finally given us the incentive to counterattack." He smiled as he pushed a strand of my hair back, wrapping it around his fingers as he slid his hand down. I felt the tingle in the pit of my stomach, blushing as I turned back to face the window.

We sat on one of the rows of chairs that had once seated passengers waiting to board the planes. He had retrieved a couple of water bottles and snacks still packaged from a locked up safe that had been placed in the room. It seemed that we weren't the only ones that visited this area. It was like an observatory, quiet and surrounded by windows, where one could view the beautiful Las Vegas Strip without obstruction. It had been amazing to peek out those windows at night, when the lights shone bright, flashing their endless advertisements and previews of shows. It wasn't the same anymore though; the dead darkness of night brought no more twinkling billboards or crowds. Now nothing but silence and blood reigned once the sun went down.

I reflected on his words for a moment. "Yeah, you could be right. It is fate that brings us together now, of all the times it could've before." I wondered if I really believed my words the moment they left my lips, the doubt bubbling up within me again, making me close my eyes. I wanted to believe that we would win this battle. I had to believe it. There was no other choice.

I thought back to the first days after my family had been taken; the determination that had driven me back then had been like fuel on a fire. I was afraid the fire was dying inside me and that was something I didn't want to happen. As I opened my eyes, I felt the fire stirring again–I was ready to take anything on. I had not let it die completely; I had just let the thought of it slip out of my mind for a short while. My lips upturned as I felt the heat of my drive returning. My fingers itched to swing a weapon around and cut down some vampires, even if some of them would be the insanely fast and powerful hybrids. I was always game for a fight–holding a weapon felt more natural than holding a conversation. I would see my family again. Even if I died doing so, it would be more than worth it.

Rye tugged on my hand, breaking me away from my thoughts. "We should get back. Dinner is coming up and we want to be rested for tomorrow." I nodded, glancing back at the dimming light of the outside world as we headed to the door of the stairwell. My only regret was that the casino lights I so wanted to see light up once more never would again.

SERAPHIN GLARED AT us as we entered the dining room. She sat silently at the end of one of the tables, her plate scraped clean of food. Something laced the scowl splayed across her face as we got in line to get a tray of food. Was she jealous? I looked away, scooping up potatoes and chicken onto my plate. I wondered what she was thinking. Why was she here anyway? She was supposed to be in place at the enemy hive, waiting for our attack. I tried to shake my suspicions but felt her eyes burning into my back.

"Why is Seraphin here?" I whispered to Rye, hoping she couldn't hear my lowered voice.

"I don't know." He turned toward me without searching her out, making me wonder if he did that on purpose so she wouldn't know we had been speaking about her. "I'm sure it's not without good reason. Why don't we pay her a visit?" He winked and tilted his head for me to follow him. I groaned, irritated that he was going to put me face to face with his killer ex again.

As we approached her table, her glare never receded, sending daggers our way. Her face never lit up or cracked a smile at all at us; in fact, she seemed to be seething that we had come to her side of the room. Rye sat his tray down and plopped onto the bench in front of her. I scooted next to him but felt my appetite disappear as I lowered my gaze to my tray of food. It no longer looked appealing and the growl in my stomach had silenced the moment I had spotted her.

"So Sera, what brings you to this side of our little world?" Rye took a bite of his dinner roll, which was still soft, warm and steaming. I took a swig of my water and attempted to look busy picking at my chicken.

Her eyes narrowed into thin slits. A look of disgust filled her face, making what was a beautiful woman look increasingly ugly as her scowl grew. I wondered why she would act like she hated Rye so much. Hadn't she left him?

"You have some nerve to speak to me at all and sit here with that abomination." She hissed at me, making me drop my fork in surprise but I didn't move away. That would have shown weakness, something I didn't want to give her the satisfaction of seeing. Wondering for a moment if I should ready a weapon, I focused on her dark eyes. She was hiding something. What it could be, I hadn't a clue. Something was irking her too. Maybe it was Rye, maybe not.

"Back off, Sera, she is not an abomination. She's human, like we once were. You can cut the enemy tactics now, I want to know what you're doing here and if you don't tell me, Blaze will be happy to ask you." Rye's voice was icy, digging into the air like picks. This made Seraphin pull her stare away from me to look at him. I think she hadn't really looked at him much since she had left him because the surprise in her expression made me think that she had just remembered how handsome he was.

I wanted to bellow out a laugh but stuffed a bite of mashed potatoes and gravy into my mouth instead. I tried to stifle the sting of the jealousy crawling inside me, knowing I had no reason to feel that way. Still, she used to be madly in love with him, and he with her. I could only hope that he felt the same¬, or maybe even more, for me now.

"Well?" Rye pushed as he waited for her answer. Seraphin sighed, shoving her tray to the side and sitting back a bit, contemplating her next words carefully.

"I wanted to see you, Rye. I have something to ask of you." She darted her eyes at me but bounced them back to him right away. I felt that I shouldn't be there; she didn't want me there. Pressing my lips together, I wondered if I should take the hint and leave. Feeling the rest of the room staring at me from all around made me change my mind about walking away so they could chat. It was a bit risky but I didn't want a repeat of the Charles incident.

"Whatever you have to ask, go ahead, April should hear it too." He still looked serious but not angry. In fact, the confusion that swam on Seraphin's face now was bordered with hurt, as if she realized something she didn't want to.

"Fine, but she is an abomination, just like the other two. They aren't human, even if they look it." She turned to me and smirked. "Except they don't know that blood would make them much more powerful, if she could even stomach it." Tilting her head, she waited for my reaction as I absorbed what she said.

What?

"Stop!" Rye snapped. "Tell me what you want now or I'm done." He dropped his fork, apparently losing his appetite along with me. I bit my lip, holding back the torrent of obscenities I wanted to lay into her right then. I would never, ever drink blood. Never.

But what did she mean by all that? How could I not be human?

Seraphin's look hardened and her lips creased tight as her silence engulfed the thick air between us. I wondered if she would tell Rye what she wanted or if she just had. The questions tormented my head as I waited, not wanting to wait much longer.

In response, Seraphin stood up with a jolt, sending her tray crashing to the floor. Rye held his place on the bench but his usually calm and stoic exterior was quietly steaming. He was so angry, I hoped the two wouldn't battle it out right then and there. I darted my glances between them, feeling unsure of what to do next.

The dark-haired vampire let her fangs flash as her scowl morphed into a smile. She began laughing, letting her entire body shake with it. Confusion swam in Rye's expression, mirroring my own puzzled face. I wasn't sure where this was going, nor did I want to know. I wanted her to stop laughing, to turn and run as fast as she could out the door and disappear forever. Knowing I disliked her that much made me come back to myself, studying her that much more intently, wanting to know what was going on inside her head instead.

Her laugh drizzled down to a snuffled laugh as her eyes hovered over me. I straightened up, seeing tears now streak down her face. She was beautiful, in a fragile way. The dirt and grime had covered it well, presenting her as a savage animal when she had attacked me in the hall. Now, she was more like a porcelain doll with diamonds streaming down her face, her sobs now filling the air as she failed to stifle them.

"So you finally replaced me," she muttered to herself more than anyone, sniffling as she regained her composure. Sitting down again and hunching over, she stared at the table. "You know, my mate is dead now. He died in an explosion on one of the harvested casinos on the strip." Her eyes fluttered up to mine, her eyes shining with the tears still pooling in them. "You wouldn't know anything about that would you, Rye?" She turned back at her ex-husband and waited, the hatred gone and only desolate sadness remaining.

Rye's jaw twitched as his face stilled. He said nothing but stared coldly back at her. I was done with the tension and I prayed that it would end soon. I was tired of watching this ex-lover's quarrel, knowing it was about me regardless of what was said.

"Heh." Seraphin shook her head, wiping her face and standing up once more. She circled the table and came to stand between Rye and myself. Bending down, she let her lips almost touch his ear as she whispered, loud enough for me to hear, but no one else. "Give her blood. Make her realize she is one of us. No one will stop our victory and she will be all yours." She pulled away, her eyes slipping over toward me, her face stone cold serious as she sped out of the massive room.

It sent shivers through my entire body to hear her words. I was still confused but something dawned on me that made my stomach turn into rock inside of me.

"Rye?" My voice was a whisper, unsure and shaking like an earthquake.

He didn't seem to notice my plea, breathing in deeply, clearly affected by Seraphin's words. They had crawled into him and woven around his brain.

"Hmm?" He stood up as the spark returned to his steel-colored eyes. He pulled me up, too, and held my hand as I followed behind him, leaving the dining area behind. I didn't ask my question. I couldn't, at least not here. Not yet.

Chapter Twenty-Three

THE BED FELT amazing, but my head was making it impossible to sleep. Rye had left me to rest after he'd brought me back to the sleeping quarters. I begged him to stay but he had refused, stating that he had some loose ends to tie up before resting. I let him go only after he told me exactly what Seraphin had meant by giving me blood. He was so reluctant that I almost had to rip it out of him, telling him that he would have to deal with me no matter where he went. He had rubbed his tired face, sighing as he sank onto the bed beside me.

"She's right, April. They discovered this in the enemy hive. If blood is introduced to you or anyone from your family, you become stronger. A super human. You would have a vampire's strengths but none of our weaknesses; you'd also be much more powerful than we could ever be…."

"Wait, what?" I stuttered, interrupting his words. No, no way.

"It's true. There are no true humans left, only us hybrids, the wildling vampires and you, a type of super human and vampire hybrid. You don't need blood to survive but if you do have it, you'll become immensely strong and powerful, capable of killing a hybrid without breaking a sweat." He stood up then, looking extremely concerned as he turned to walk away but he hesitated, making me feel breathless.

I had nothing to say to that. Was that what they had been doing with my mother's and brother's blood, finding out all about them and their uniqueness? Blood made us a rare breed indeed. But what if the hybrids fed off of our blood? Would it help make them more powerful? I asked Rye this before he stepped out into the walkway toward the door.

He shook his head, shrugging. He seemed frustrated that he couldn't, or wouldn't, answer me. He didn't seem to know. I had wanted to ask him what would happen to a feral that drank my blood but he had also seemed uneasy to answer that. If a vampire had my blood, it could mean a dozen things. It could make them just as powerful as me or be as useless as a placebo to them. Who knew? I was hoping the rival hive didn't know or wasn't planning on finding out.

I felt suddenly anxious to get going to save my family. Time was running out. It had taken so long to get this far. I prayed they were still okay, that they had been left plenty alone and not tampered with. If they had been, what would I find? What could I do about it? I was definitely not sure and decided to try not to think about it. Tomorrow I would confront it; tomorrow everything would be known.

But tonight I had to rest, even though my mind was having none of that with the millions of questions running through it. I wanted it to be over; I wanted the normal life I had always thought I would have, a life of college, parties and homework. It didn't seem like so much to ask for yet here I was, without any of them and without any hope for the future but a bleak darkness that enveloped everything it touched.

Rye had left without saying goodbye, uncertain as to what else to say. Might as well be that way, for I had nothing else to say either. I awaited the daylight like never before as I pulled the soft blanket up to my chin and curled onto my side, the pillow under my neck and over my arm. The texture of the wall was looking far more interesting than anything else. Closing my eyes, I willed the sleep to come. I had lost count of the days without my family. I had lost the time so easily, never noticing how it had flown by without a glance. I would make sure my family was safe and rescued tomorrow. If it took drinking a vat of blood, so be it. There was nothing left for me to fear now and I was done being nice. It was time to get to know myself better. How else could I really know? What would it possibly do?

If I was human, it would do nothing to me, maybe cause my stomach to churn and make me sick. Otherwise, if what Seraphin had said was true, maybe it would be the edge I needed to win this, maybe it would be the difference we needed to overtake the hive and find my family that much faster. In the morning I would ask Rye for blood; I would drink it and see if it did anything. If it went well, I would be that much closer to my family. If not, I wasn't opposed to puking it right back up.

My eyelids fluttered, growing heavy like weights had been sewn onto them as I fought to stay awake. It was late and I would have only a few hours of sleep at this rate if I didn't stop my mind from racing. I let my eyelids close, savoring the darkness as it slipped into my mind and beckoned me to rest. Yes, I could rest. There was a chance the next sunrise would be my last. So for the time being, I rested.

Chapter Twenty-Four

THE EARLY HOURS rolled in much too quickly. I snapped awake at Miranda shaking my shoulder, whispering that it was time to get ready to go. I was never awake faster than at that moment, on my feet and moving. I had never gotten ready so quickly before either, almost forgetting to put my hair back into a tight pony tail. Of all days, I didn't need my long black hair in my face. Tucking in my shirt and strapping my weapons to my belt and bandoleer, I smiled at the bow and arrows laid out for me, along with several grenades. I was sure either Miranda or Rye had thought to bring me more stuff. I was certain to use it. After putting on a light jacket, I pulled on the quiver and hung the grenades along another bandoleer, crisscrossing the other one full of sharp silver daggers.

Glancing up before I left, I caught sight of my reflection in the dresser mirror. I looked like me, but thinner and just that much older. My blue eyes seemed to glow slightly, making them stand out from my skin. I could see my mother's face in mine as well as some of my father's strong features. He had mercifully died three years ago, quietly in his sleep. A silent heart defect, they had said. My mother had been devastated. I had been numb but strong for her. Jeremy was a bit too young to understand what had happened. The pain and loss fades with time, but it never truly goes away. Just another unseen scar on the soul.

I swallowed the slight anxiety swirling up into my throat as I pushed back a strand of my charcoal black hair, straight as an arrow, without a curl in sight. I felt a wave of comfort flow over me. I knew things would be okay, no matter what happened that day.

A smile crept onto my lips, letting the white of my teeth shine through, reminding me of that school girl I once was. Jeremy shared my smile and I couldn't wait to see his again. This was the most important day of my life. Nothing would keep me from them; I would make sure to do anything to bring them back. Even though I didn't look forward to drinking any blood today, I was going to. If it gave me an edge to win, it was a small thing to me now.

"About ready?" Rye's calm voice echoed in the empty room. Turning toward him I nodded, strapping my last machete in, tying it to my thigh. I kicked my legs up and rotated my arms around, making sure my weapons would not restrict my movements. Taking a deep breath in, I cracked a smile, returning his. His eyes were glowing this morning, like shiny steel balls that I had seen rocking back and forth against each other on office desks before the outbreak. The ticking and continual momentum had been fascinating to look at. Now these orbs shined back at me in the most beautiful eyes I had ever seen. An ocean of calm filled me with him nearby.

"Let's go," I said, and followed him out to have a quick light breakfast in silence with the others in the crowded main tunnel. I was quite impressed by how many were joining us today. The tunnel was full of hybrids, built like skyscrapers and geared up for a war. I took in the exhilaration of the atmosphere as murmurs rippled through the crowd, a mixture of light laughter and more serious chatting echoing off the walls. I let the energy fill me up, hoping it would be enough to get me through what I was going to do next.

"Rye, bring me some blood." I averted my gaze to his lips, avoiding his eyes, for I knew they would be filled with confusion. He shook his head slightly, his lips pursed.

"April, no, you don't have to do that…."

"I know." I shushed him, hoping he could see that I would not take no for an answer. I didn't want to fight him for it; I wanted all my energy left for the battle ahead.

"It might not work." He reached up and ran his fingers down the curve of my cheek, making me bring my eyes up to meet his. I could feel my skin tingle under his touch as it arrested my breathing for a moment. I could feel his concern but I kept it to myself. I didn't want to feel his anxiety, too. I wanted to be focused, determined to make it out of this game alive no matter what.

I think he saw this in my expression, making him slump his shoulders slightly, relenting to me. He gave his head a slight tilt, looking at his cousin Blaze who stood near us, loading guns and ammo into his armory. Blaze gave him a nod, having heard the entire conversation.

Rye tensed, taking a deep breath. His lips firmed as he pulled a knife sheath off his forearm, holding his wrist out toward me. I watched him, confused with the gesture. He continued to hold his wrist out to me and beckoned me to take it. I took his hand and looked down at his smooth skin, pale but with the shadows of blood-filled veins running underneath. I could almost see his pulse beating within the layer of skin, like a beacon telling me where to go. I gripped it tighter, trying to sync our heartbeats together as my breath sped up, nervous now that it was happening.

"What do I do? Just bite you? Won't it hurt you?"

"Shhh," Rye shushed. He grinned, his fangs flashing me, as though he had extended them a bit. He was excellent a concealing them when he spoke so the gleam of his sharp canines took me by surprise.

He pulled his own wrist to his mouth and bit into it, never flinching or making a sound. I fought the urge to cringe away, not knowing if it was going to be unpleasant or not. My tongue ran over my own teeth, even and straight. Lacking fangs made me feel more human but if drinking blood was to become a necessity, it might be a hindrance. My mouth was dry, parched like a desert as I watched his smooth, crimson blood leak from the puncture holes.

"Here," he said, offering me his wrist. I took it into both my hands, taking strength from his assurance.

He gave me a nod and held fast. I licked my lips and let my mouth engulf the wounds. The coppery swell of warmth overtook my senses immediately. I let it flow down my throat, its sweet syrupy texture making me feel a sudden rush through my head that surged through my skull and down my spine, all the way to my fingertips. I couldn't stop drinking, it was as if I had been left dry and this was the only way to quench a thirst I didn't know was there. It was exquisite, like silken honey. If this was what it felt like for the vampires to drink blood, I now completely understood the craving they lived with every day.

"Alright, April." Rye's voice echoed in my head like a distant dream. I didn't want to let go; I could hear his heart beat in my mind, the sound engulfing my senses like a gong sounding off. Something stirred in me that had never awoken before, something primal and fierce. I would not let go, I would drain him dry until his heart ceased to beat, until the light in his eyes dimmed. It begged me to, this primal thing that I did not fight–it wanted me to keep going and it took my consciousness with it.

I heard yelling and voices but they were so far away and so faint that I barely registered that one of them was Rye's.

I felt a rolling momentum as the room lurched under me and I found myself staring up at the brilliant bulbs lighting the tunnel. My tunnel vision was gone and Blaze was behind me, clasping my arms tightly and breathing hard. Why was he holding me, locked in his arms? I almost could not breathe. I wiggled in his grip, searching the gathered crowd for Rye. Lifting my head, I spotted him, on his knees and clutching his wrist as if he was in dire pain.

What have I done?

"Let me up, it's over now." I muttered. Blaze hesitated but must have felt it was now okay to let me loose. I scrambled to my feet and glanced between Blaze and Miranda, who I now saw had been standing behind Blaze. "What happened? What did I do?" I watched as Miranda helped Rye to his feet, his stance slightly unsteady. My confusion flooded my mind as I stared at them; no one offered an explanation as I waited.

I licked my lips. The remnants of his blood flashed me back to the drink. His paling face, his voice drowned out by the incessant need that had pulsated through my body, a fire engulfing me from within, needing a quenching that only his death would bring. My breath slowed and the horror that I had almost killed Rye for every last drop of his life made me run to him, desperate to remedy my actions.

"Oh my God, Rye, are you alright? Rye?" My arms hovered as I reached out to him. He pulled away swiftly, still clutching his arm. Anger and fear flooded his flashing steel eyes, making my heart sink. He knew. He knew I would have forfeited his life for his blood, it didn't matter what we felt for each other. It was that powerful a drive, so primal and unrequited.

"But I didn't know, Rye. How could I have known it would be like that?" I stepped forward again but stopped when he gave me a shake of his head. He turned to leave, almost stumbling to get away, giving Miranda a slight shove to let him walk unaided, leaving me there, arms as empty as my heart.

I had never wanted this. Never this.

Blaze came to my side and put his hand on my shoulder, bringing me away from where Rye had stood. Facing him, I wanted him to tell me what had changed. What would happen now? With Rye's blood coursing through me, what difference had it made? I hoped it had been worth it. I hoped that the results would be well worth the cost I paid, but I wasn't sure.

"Blaze?" My voice quivered under the shock of everything.

"Give him a moment, he'll come around." Blaze handed me a washcloth to wipe my face. I wondered what I looked like, my chin dripping with blood, standing in a mass of vampires. It was then that I noticed them, the others standing a few arm's lengths away from me, fear flowing through their blinking eyes. They had watched with interest but now they cowered away in nothing short of terror. I dropped the cloth, finding Blaze waiting for me, serious and contemplative. It was as if he knew what I was thinking. He gave me a tight grin as he started speaking again.

"You'll be a killing machine. I doubt any one of the others will be able to take you down. You almost got away from me before you came to your senses. I almost couldn't pull you off of Rye." He paused as the pain streaked across my face. I cringed at the thought of draining Rye. To think of what I could've done made me sick.

"So what now?" I asked warily, knowing the time crept closer to our confrontation with the enemy hive. "Is Rye too weak to help me? Why couldn't he give me some of the stored blood? Why did he give me his?" My feelings were a miserable mixture of anger, regret and remorse.

"You'll have more power with vampire blood; Seraphin noted this in the other hive's research. The leftover stores of human blood we have are for emergencies and as a last resort for food. Miranda is giving him some blood; he'll be right as rain in no time." Blaze handed me a small wallet that contained different types of lock picks neatly lined in the plastic. I took it and looked up at him, confused.

"They'll be chained up—you'll have to pick the locks. I assume you know how to do that by now, being on your own for so long." He winked as he turned to walk away, leaving me fingering the cool iron metal of the picks. Sighing, I stuffed them into my jeans where they would not slip out. To see my family chained up was going to be hard enough. I prayed I found them intact. I just wanted to see them again, hear their voices once more.

"We can do this, right?" I asked softly, hoping he heard me over the resumed murmur of voices bouncing around the room.

Blaze nodded, almost imperceptibly. "We can do this."

Chapter Twenty-Five

THE HIVE SPREAD out into a large circle surrounding the Stratosphere Tower Casino and Hotel. It was a wide perimeter and I was worried we were spread too thin to penetrate the building. Blaze reassured me as we peeked around from behind a pile of cars and garbage strewn across the alleyway behind the parking garage. Behind the casino were apartment buildings that had not weathered the ravages of time very well. Windows were smashed and doors hung on their hinges as they creaked in the slight breeze of the dawn. It was still semi-dark, but everyone could feel the sun pushing on the horizon. It was like a hum in the air, vibrating along our skin.

I could see well already, making me know that the vampire blood inside me was working. It was as if I had night vision goggles on and everything was clear and crisp. It made me wonder what I was now. I wasn't vampire, I wasn't human. I had no fangs yet I could see as well as my comrades as we crouched, awaiting our signal from within. Seraphin would be setting off explosives at sunrise to pretty much obliterate the feral vampire population guarding the citadel. I cringed as I thought of the ferals; these would be different than the others, the ones that were now tucked away in the dark crevices of the casinos on the south end of the Strip. These were more aware, stronger. But so was I.

I heard movement behind us and swirled around to come face to face with Rye. He didn't seem as pale as before but it was hard to tell in the dim light of the dawn. He didn't seem as exhausted either and his lips shone a darker color than when I had nearly drained him. I was certain they were red and filled anew with blood. He had fed well before he came, regaining his strength. I glanced down to the naked wrist where I had sucked. Two faint lines of teeth remained, nearly healed from the vicious draining I had administered earlier. I was glad he was healing but I wasn't sure if he was still angry.

I gave him a weak smile and he replied with a nod of his head as he scanned the area before us. He didn't return my smile and my heart seized with a searing ache. I longed to see his smile again.

Rye sniffed the air, taking in the early morning desert air filled with the unmistakable odor of feral vampires. "It should be soon. Seraphin has the bombs rigged to a remote control." I could smell the ferals easily, even if they weren't very close, in the outdoor air. Usually it was just in their dwellings where their withered bodies stank up the closed rooms. Here, I could smell it like skunk floating on the wind. Wrinkling my nose, I turned away from Rye and waited for the explosions to begin.

I didn't have to wait long at all.

The sun peeked like a sliver of gold over the eastern mountains, aptly named Sunrise Mountain, and the first pop and rattle of explosions began. The earth shook as it vibrated through the dirt and concrete, sending puffs of debris and particles into the air. I covered my head, afraid one of the thick fragments of cement would find its way to me. Smaller rocks and sprays of concrete littered the ground and rained onto us. I was relieved to have worn my thin jacket, for the shards and pebbles would have cut up my arms on their way down.

When the cascade of debris was done, it was time to run. We ran into the building, pushing the shattered doors to the side, drawing weapons. I pulled my bow out first, and began sending arrows sailing into the darkness wherever I saw movement. I would run out of arrows quickly, but it cleared my path effectively as I made my way into the crumbling mess of the casino floor. Everything in the place was upturned and literally almost impassable. Old dusty slots, stools and card tables were knocked to the ground, blocking the path. I kicked a few stools of my way as I sent arrow after arrow into the oncoming wave of feral vampires.

There were so many of them, pouring out like ants from an underground nest. Holes from the explosions riddled the roof and let the bright rays of sun pour in, setting some of the unfortunate ferals on fire, crumbling them to ash almost immediately. My quiver, now empty, ended up on the floor as I swung my bow to uppercut one feral that had managed to avoid the sunbeams shining down into the place. I hit him so hard with it, the bow snapped. I dropped it to the ground and pulled out both of my machetes. Gripping the hilts, I felt the adrenaline and blood surge within me. I felt invincible.

The blades flashed in the rays of sun as I sent them swinging along with my arms, slashing off heads like nothing. Hacking at their necks when I could, they fell into piles, forcing me to move farther into the chaotic mess. I spotted Rye to my right, his katana flashing. He jabbed and spun like a dancer, taking ferals down with every move. He was graceful and fluid, like he had fought all his life. I wondered if he had. My momentary glance ended faster than I would have liked when two ferals approached me, snarling and snapping their jaws as if they were wild dogs.

The differences were obvious up close. These ferals were much more muscular in build and their eyes were a more brilliant blood red, almost glowing as they took pains to remain in the darkness. They waited, wanting me to enter their realm just a bit more before pouncing on me. Their eyes were not as vicious and empty as those of ferals I had fought before. These were focused on me, with malice swimming across their faces. Their snarls seemed to morph into evil smiles. This made my heart jump, realizing that there was intelligence behind their expressions. I wondered just how much they could think. The other ferals had been so dead and lifeless that to see life behind the eyes of these made me more aware of them, more cautious.

I bent my knees, ready for their advances. They all-too-willingly lunged forward as I stepped out of the light. I swung my machetes in dual arcs, hitting one in the legs and the other across the chest. Their screeches joined the chorus of pain as their comrades died all around us. I hoped none of the screams were from our hive. I prayed that we were on the winning side; it was too hard to tell in the confusing wave of chaos.

One of the ferals was down but one remained in the fight despite his shredded legs. He pulled himself along on his arms, inching closer to me. I finished him with a hack to the neck and rushed forward. The rest of the ferals were beginning to scatter. Glancing around, I found Rye as he motioned me deeper into the building.

"Where are they keeping them?" I whispered. He shook his head and mouthed "Seraphin" before he was sent hurtling into one of the great pillars that held the room up. A hybrid vampire had jumped onto him and pummeling him with his fists. I ran over to hack into him but another got in my way before I could reach him. This one shoved me too, which seemed to be a popular fighting technique here. I caught my footing before crashing to the ground, turning and running to avoid another hit. The hybrid laughed, taking chase after me, but I was just a hair faster. His hand reached out and grabbed my jacket as I flipped the hilt of one machete in my hand to jab backwards into his stomach.

A screech of agony filled my ears, letting me know the machete had hit its mark. Yanking it out was another problem entirely. Underestimating my newfound strength, I had plunged it so deep into his chest cavity it was stuck on his spinal column. I yanked on it to no avail, leaving me no choice but to let him drop to the ground, writhing in pain, a blade sticking out of his chest. He recovered quickly, pulling himself up onto his arms, then up onto his legs as he lunged back at me, blade and all.

I pulled one of my knives from the bandoleer band across my chest. I was ready to swing my body weight with his, letting his momentum take me on a spin as I plunged the knife deep into his temple. The knife sank into his head like butter, up to the hilt. His body flew onto the debris before coming to a stop, a trail of dark blood in his wake. I landed lightly on my legs, bending them as I landed to absorb any shock. Smiling, I found that I liked this newfound graceful strength that the blood had given me. It was working in my favor in every way and the surge was a high I had never before experienced.

Scanning the chaos around me, my eyes could not find Rye. A flutter of panic hit my chest and I began to run toward the spot I had last seen him. Not finding him, I looked for the next person on my short list to see: Seraphin.

Her black-as-night hair was whipping around as she swung a hatchet, slamming it into some ferals that had remained behind as their comrades fled. A hybrid, clearly either her mate or close friend by the way they kept exchanging glances, was next to her fighting off another hybrid from their hive. I pondered why they had betrayed their hive for Blaze's favor. Had she lied about her mate being dead? I wondered if they would be executed if caught or if this went the wrong way today. I still had some reservations about her but now, seeing her diligently fighting and bringing the enemy hive down, I felt unsure, a bit confused, but relieved that she fought on our side. Even if trust was not yet won, I had a whole new respect for her and what she had endured by spending all that time in the enemy hive. She had risked so much and here was the culmination of all her work. I wanted to make it worth it for her, even if she wasn't my favorite person in the world.

I approached her cautiously, knowing her killing spree rage was turned up too high. I was right to hold back a moment, for the feral just in front of me fell before I could even get close to her. She was in front of me in a flash, hatchet poised to strike, when she paused, our blades lightly grazing one another. I gulped, glad she had seen me in time, telling her with my eyes that I was not there to harm her, but pleading instead.

"Where are they?" I inquired, hoping she could hear me over the snarls and screams that echoed across the casino floor. She straightened and nodded, motioning me to follow her. She took off in a blur of speed. I took chase after her, keeping my eyes wide open for any side attacks. We had not gone by unnoticed; Seraphin had to hack into at least two hybrids before we made it to the elevator shaft. It was rigged with electricity and I groaned as she punched in the key code, making the metal doors slide smoothly open. Of all the places in this building, I did not want to go up into the citadel of the Stratosphere tower.

Of course they would hold prisoners up there, it was almost unreachable.

I jumped into the elevator with her as the doors slid shut behind us. I was relieved to see Rye pass in front of the doors and smile as he nodded toward me. He was okay; we would be okay.

The lights inside were faint but seemed brighter after the engulfing darkness of the battle below. I shifted my eyes to Seraphin, who was standing perfectly still beside me, hatchet still in hand. Scattered drops of blood and ichor were splattered her clothes. She looked like a killer–deadly, dark and cold. I could almost feel her iciness pierce into me as the elevator moved, quickly gaining momentum until the lights of the floors flashed rapidly by. I'd forgotten how fast it moved, how it made my stomach shift to my feet.

I was determined to not lose my breakfast yet. Not when the end was so near.

"Why did you choose our hive? Your husband err…whatever that guy I saw down there is to you, he is not one of us. Did you lie about your husband's death? Why did you switch sides?" I asked her, my voice rough and guarded. Seraphin turned to me, her black irises flashing under the sickly artificial illumination above us. Her face was still like stone but her eyes told me many things. She wasn't trusting of me yet either, she eyed me curiously with a mixture of contempt and respect. I wasn't sure if this was good or not but she made me shift in my boots from the intensity of her glare.

"Who says I switched sides?" She sneered at me before turning back to stare at the doors before us. I watched her for a moment, hoping she meant what I thought she did. I wasn't sure of anything. Her words were cold comfort.

Our reflections stared back at us, looking gruesome and hard at the same time. I wouldn't want to face the two women that watched me right now. They looked like something out of a horror movie. I would've wanted to run for the hills before I'd ever face one of them. Blood and grime streaked my face, concrete dust from the explosions clung to my hair and the blood, making me look somewhat like I had been caught in a blood-streaked snowfall. I didn't look the same; my haunted but hard eyes made me want to do a double-take at the mirrored doors, almost sure that I was not really looking at myself but a stranger, one I would not want to ever confront. My hair was falling out of its tight restraint and wisps of night hung down in straight lines like wires. If I made it out alive, a shower was definitely in order.

The elevator's speed seemed to slow down and my stomach eventually crawled back into my abdomen. I watched Seraphin ready herself, pulling out a short sword to use instead of the hatchet. She was ready to run out into action. I wondered if I should too or hide in the elevator, waiting for the ambush. I wasn't sure but I readied my machete, the only one I had left, bending my knees to make a run for it but leaning against the side of the elevator to have a bit of cover in case these vampires used guns. I didn't use guns much. Rye had some with him but he had yet to use them by the time I'd lost sight of him.

A bell dinged right before the doors whooshed open. My hair flew back as the semi-vacuum of the elevator filled with cold air from the tower. Seraphin growled and pounced right out into the lit interior, immediately clanging weapons with a hybrid guard. I stepped out, waiting for the ambush and found none. Seraphin yelled at the guard, shoving him to the ground before plunging her blade deep into his chest. She yanked out the blade and swung it in a wide arc before bringing it down to hack off his head. The thump of the blade on the carpeted floor absorbed the sound of the cut as his head rolled off with the momentum of the blow. A spray of thick, crimson blood went with it, staining the floor. I was relieved there were no others here but I suspiciously glanced around, feeling that it had been too easy. Leaving only one guard at the elevator was not something a hive of intelligent hybrid vampires would do.

Seraphin waved me on. I followed her closely but took the rear position in case any others popped out. There were windows everywhere and I remembered these old gift shops that lined the hall. Now they were filled with couches and chairs. This seemed to be the meeting place of this hive's leaders, or maybe even their living quarters. I was surprised that they would choose such a bright area for themselves. The morning sun relentlessly poured in through the windows. I wished I had brought sunglasses, it was that blinding. Seraphin winced slightly as the rays hit her full on. We came to the end of the hallway and emerged onto the circular walkway that had been the tower's observation area.

I didn't know how she could stand the sunlight. Her skin was turning a slight shade of pink and her face was tense with the pain. I could barely see beyond the bright rays of light piercing the walkway.

I was tense, expecting something to happen and as if on cue a whirring hum filled the air, making us both back into the glass wall. My heart was fluttering as the walls vibrated from some machine gears spinning. I was slightly relieved to see that the noise was caused by slow-moving shutters that lowered over the windows, dimming the walkway.

Relieved that it wasn't some sort of trap, we continued onto the circular pathway. Through the slats of the blinds I could see the desolate city below. How serene it seemed from up here, bright and undisturbed. I almost thought I could see the little ants of people milling about as they had when I had visited this landmark so long ago. I blinked and they faded before my eyes. Only dusty streets littered in debris remained.

Gripping my blade tighter, I listened for any movement, the vampire blood still heightening my vision and hearing, making every creak and howl of wind louder than normal. The silence was disturbing. Seraphin crept quietly on, poised to strike but equally cautious. I admired the fluidity of her movements. She made no noise as she padded along and I felt quite like an obtuse ogre compared to her agility. I scanned the walkway ahead and the glass rooms of the interior, wondering if we were even in the right place. I knew there was another area above us and I was about to suggest going up there when Seraphin stopped and motioned me forward.

Standing next to her, I spotted what had her on alert. Two hybrids stood guard on our left at the bottom of a set of stairs. We would have to ascend them if we're going to find out where my family was. I was sure Seraphin knew that but I wasn't so positive she expected anything. She was not very forthcoming with information and I didn't quite trust her yet. I hoped I could trust her; this would not go well otherwise.

She turned to me and nodded, holding a finger up to signal our attack. I acknowledged her and readied myself to take down one of the guards. Together, I was sure we would be just fine but I was hoping this in itself wasn't a trap, either. I gripped my machete, its blade messy with drying, clotted blood. I loved my blade; it was sharp, reliable and easy to maneuver. It felt like an extension of my arm, especially now. The feel of the hilt felt like an old friend that hugged me right back. We had an understanding. I wished I hadn't lost my second blade. I made note to retrieve it if I possibly could when this was all over.

Seraphin jerked her hand down to start the attack. We ran into the small inlet where the stairway stood, looking like a majestic entrance to the heavens. Our blades swung at the guards who had been completely oblivious of our approach. Good, I thought, better for us that they were slacking off in their duties. They recovered quickly enough to counter our attack. Seraphin's was well-matched with foe; they paused briefly between each exchange as they sized each other up. This guard had surfer blond hair that was long enough to fly into his face. His blue eyes narrowed at her as he shoved at her when their blades crossed, almost sending her into a plate glass window.

My opponent was also quite skilled. His chocolate skin rippled as his muscles contracted. His hair short, closely trimmed and a shade darker than his skin. His eyes were an unnatural golden brown, making the gleam of the vampire's ring almost imperceptible. His face was hard and determined to finish me off. He was a good head and a half taller than me and I was pretty sure he ate little women like me for breakfast. I was surprised that I could hold him at bay.

He grew frustrated quickly and gave me a shove but I would not go down. His eyes pierced into me, a wild and disgusted look crawling across his face.

"What are you?" His voice came out in accented English, like his first language had been a dialect of French. I had taken three years of it in high school, just so I could visit France and the French colonies around the world. Now that seemed like a long lost dream, one I would never get to experience. His voice was a bitter, melancholy reminder of how different the world was.

"You're not a vampire," he snapped when I didn't answer. I gave him a slight sneer as I waited for his next move. I didn't want to chat, who chats with their prey? It was too dangerous to get too close. In this war, I didn't want any mistakes made; my life depended on that in every way.

He seemed to recover from his initial shock that I wasn't a vampire, though I could see he didn't believe that I was just a human, either. He was smart, I could tell from his intense glare as he readied his sword again. His teeth slipped from behind his lips as he smirked and jolted forward, arcing his blade. I narrowly dodged it as I crouched and spun out of its path.

The whoosh of air above me made me realize how close he had come to slicing my head right off. I jumped up and turned to meet his sword with my blade just in time, a sharp metallic twang ringing out over our yells. We held each other off, pushing against one another with everything we had. I could see sweat building on his temples as he clenched his teeth together. His dramatically white fangs seem to bite into his lower lip as he grunted to hold me at bay.

"You are no human and you are no vampire, either. What does that make you, woman?" As he studied my face through the grime and streaks of blood, a look of recognition passed over his features. He knew something and the longer I stared back into those golden brown eyes, the more I wanted to know what it was.

"Ah, the warrior daughter has come," he huffed as he stepped back, making me drop my stance and step away from him, too. Confusion filled me, wondering what he had meant.

I glanced about quickly for Seraphin and found that she and her opponent had retreated up the stairs and out of sight. I could hear their weapons clanging over the sounds of breaking glass and tumbling furniture. I sucked a breath in, waiting for Mr. Tall and Dark to pounce toward me again. I couldn't yet find his weak spot; he was a worthy opponent. His eyes seared into me, probably assessing my own weaknesses, wanting to tear me down sooner rather than later.

But I'd had enough of this dance.

"You know where they're at, don't you?" I accused him, watching his sneer grow wider. "Where are they, then?" My impatience came through in the acidity of my tone. I was tired of waiting–I had waited too long already and this man was just another obstacle in my way.

"Do you think I'd tell you? Look, mademoiselle, I respect your sense of family. There are not many left in this fallen place that do. But," he snickered, his eyes dancing in the muted light, "I have orders to kill you; you will never see them again." He raised his sword, pointing it at my chest as he charged at me, confident he would hit his mark.

The moment felt suspended in time. My anger at him for denying me what I wanted most ignited a new fire, one stronger than I had felt before. That this man could think this would be the end of me, before I had finished my mission, before I could hold Jeremy and my mother in my arms again and cry tears of joy, it was unacceptable. I wanted him to suffer as I had, rip his heart from his chest so that he would know what my pain felt like. I watched his movements, every twitch of muscle, every ripple that his body made as his feet landed on the floor. The moment slowed down, like an dramatic action scene in a film, giving me plenty of time to ever so slightly slip a blade from the bandoleer strapped across my chest.

He didn't notice, and I didn't even feel it when I let the blade sink into his chest, my hand following it through the warm opening. I felt the pulsating mass of his heart, jerking and shuddering as it realized it was no longer king of this vampire. I let my fingers wrap around it, feeling the life force shoot out of it as I ripped it from his chest. His face was twisted in surprise as he froze, paralyzed in the grip of death. Horror splayed across his features as he watched his heart beat in my hand. Its crimson fuel fountained down my arm and puddled on the floor. It continued to beat, succumbing to irregularity and finally stopping as the vampire's body slammed to the floor.

Even though my own heart was leaping in my chest I felt an overwhelming, hypnotic calm. I stared at the wet and veiny thing in my hand, like a token of battle. It made me feel a strange sort of ecstasy, filling my mind with pleasure.

"April!" Seraphin's voice pulled me back into myself. The horror returned with her voice as I stared at the organ in my hand, making me fling it to the floor, appalled and disgusted. My hand tingled, with the salty blood clinging in ribbons of clots and bits of muck. I wiped it on my pants and stared up at Rye's ex-wife. Her face was still, almost ethereal. Unlike me the rush of battle had not made her crazed and mad at all. I hoped I wasn't losing my sanity. Maybe it was the vampire blood inside me that had turned the world into such a strange and unfamiliar place.

I didn't know myself anymore. Ripping out a man's heart out was nothing I had ever done or trained to do. The blood inside me called for it, craving the hybrid's death, desiring blood and metal. I wasn't sure of anything anymore. This disorienting feeling made me want to question where I even was and what I was doing here in the first place.

I had to get a grip on this now.

Chapter Twenty-Six

SERAPHIN GRABBED ME and pulled me up the stairs. My senses were still normalizing from the shock of what I had just done. She practically dragged me along with her like a rag doll, up the staircase, never complaining. She had obviously done away with the other guard but I didn't see where she had disposed of his body.

We found ourselves on another floor, almost identical to the one below, except this one had a banquet room and a restaurant with a long hall dissecting the place like two halves of an orange. I glanced around; these walls were solid except the doors separating each section were plate glass. Another circular hallway followed the line of windows that surrounded the disc like the floor below. Where was everyone? Where was my family?

Seraphin continued to pull me along as we entered the old dining area. She sat me on a chair and took my machete from my side. I let her, not thinking much of it. I don't know why I let her, or why she did so, but her face was cold and serious. I hadn't quite recovered. That is, until she clicked something cold onto my right wrist, making me look down to see that she had handcuffed me to the chair. I jerked my head back up to her as she backed away, out of my reach.

No! I trusted her. She killed members of her own hive for me, no, this isn't making sense!

"Well done, Seraphin. You will be well-rewarded." A deep baritone voice boomed across the room from around a wall. I turned to see who it belonged to but couldn't find the owner. My nostrils flared as my anger seethed through me, glaring back at Seraphin. She was looking at me but not smiling, not sneering or anything for that matter. Her eyes were trying to say something. Or maybe I just wanted them to.

I wanted her to change her mind, let me go and get me the hell out of here. But why would I expect that from her now? Why had I trusted her at all? I was her competition now. Something told me that even though she had been paired off with another vampire, Rye was not so easily forgotten. I was sure of it. I groaned at my stupidity. I should have known. And Rye? How did he not know? Or Blaze? She had them all fooled.

"I apologize for the ruse. I don't like to toy with people." The baritone-voiced man stepped out from behind an area that had probably been an employee station to empty plates and refill drinks. His hair was a deep coppery mahogany, long and straight, tied at the nape of his neck. His features didn't match the color of his hair. I almost expected freckles but found a slightly olive complexion. He had to have been a mix of several ethnicities but I couldn't pinpoint which ones.

He stood tall, taller than me but not as tall as the warrior I had taken down at the foot of the stairs. His eyes gleamed back at me with strange colors; one eye was green and one was brown. That was a bit freaky in and of itself but the circles around each iris were not gold but a sickly bright orange-red, like rust.

"I've waited to meet you for a long time, April." His velvet tone washed over me like a wave of sleep. No wonder he was the leader of this hive. He was another mutation of some sort of vampire. His telepathic powers pushed at my mind, fogging it up and making the room spin. I tried to shake it off, breathing in slowly and closing my eyes.

"Where's my family?" I snapped at him. I felt clearer with the anger surging through me. I opened my eyes, narrowing them as I stared back at him. He seemed amused by my defiance. He waved Seraphin away and she complied, setting my sword on the floor and giving me a flighty glance before running out of the room and out of sight.

I'm going to kill her if I ever get out of this alive, I thought to myself.

"You have a fire about you that I like. Not like your mother or brother at all." He tilted his head, eyeing me like a specimen about to be dissected. "I should have aimed to acquire you instead of them." He rubbed his chin as he crossed his arms and seemed wave a thought away.

"No matter, I have you now." He smiled, looking genuinely handsome except for the fangs that slipped out like two tusks. I looked away, seething at his smugness.

I peered down at the grenades I had on my bandoleers, hidden under the side of my jacket. My small knives had been used up and were long gone. Seraphin had known I had more weapons; why had she left them? She had just taken my machete away. But even then, she had left it behind, gleaming at me from a just few feet away. I wiggled in the chair, hoping it wasn't bolted down. It was. Of course.

I watched him as he ranted on about my blood and that I would be the answer to the plague that now ravaged his hybrids and oh, by the way, his name was Christian. How appropriate, I thought. Apparently, his hive had been hit harder than Blaze's. That would account for the swelled numbers of altered ferals they'd had to use to defend the fortress. Daylight left them vulnerable. We had attacked at the perfect moment, information that could have only come from Seraphin.

I was beginning to feel that I was just a pawn in this game, that I didn't really know who was on which side anymore. I wondered if this man even knew that he had double agents in his hive. He must have known something was up by now. How much he suspected, I had no way to know.

"Look at me when I talk to you, mortal," he spat at me, reaching out and roughly jerking my chin up. I grimaced as his fingers dug into my face and glaring into his peculiar eyes. It suddenly dawned on me that he was most likely sick. His eyes should have both been brown. The sickly green one was an effect of the plague. I knew he was desperate for a cure, I could feel it in his touch. The sickness inside him made my own stomach lurch as he radiated his suffering onto me.

What kept him from keeling over? My insides twisted from his touch. I didn't give a damn about him, I wanted to spit in his face to let him know what I thought of him.

"Let them go and I'll give you all the blood you need to find a cure. I can smell the rot in your breath; you won't last very long without me. Let my family go and you might yet live to see another day—or night, in your case." I snickered, feeling his rage growing like a metastasizing cancer across his features. His hardened snarls made his good looks vanish, turning him into a monstrous devil.

Christian stomped away, pacing in front of the covered windows, glaring out the slats to observe the city. He knew I was right. I could see his mind wrapping around the thought of possibly having a cure with me as his guinea pig. He was frustrated and what had kept him alive until now was apparently failing him. I bet he felt like crap under that powerful exterior. I couldn't help but feel smug at pissing him off so. I wanted to laugh out loud at his weakness, so obvious once one observed him for more than a moment.

"I don't have to let them go. I have you now. You are no match for me and I will take every drop of your blood and turn you into a dusty corpse, with or without your consent," he hissed, walking around behind my chair.

I had other plans. My free hand had loosened a grenade and its pin. I held it in my left hand, the weaker of the two, but I was sure the vampire blood inside me would help me meet my mark. He was oblivious, for my back was toward him and he couldn't see what I was up to. I had to do it before he approached me again. I was hoping the explosion would blow him through the windows.

I wondered briefly if the shrapnel would hit me. It was a risk I had to take. I figured that if I hunched behind the chair I was cuffed to, I might avoid serious injury. It was fortunate I had only been bound by one hand. I was also fortunate that it wasn't an open-backed chair. I hoped it would be enough to keep me from the mess and shards that were sure to fling my way.

I whirled around and, dropping down onto one knee, flung the live grenade at the leader of the hive, hearing it clink on the shutters and glass of the windows.

"What the...?" was all I heard as I hunched down into a ball, my face pressed into the seat I had just been sitting in.

The explosion made the floor vibrate and shake in waves. Shards of glass and bits of metal and concrete scattered across the room. A cloud of dust particles enveloped me and reduced my visibility. I wasn't sure if it had gotten him or not but the howl of wind and the sudden clearing of the air assured me that there was now a gaping hole in the side of the Stratosphere tower. My hair whipped around my face as I looked up from the protection of my arms, which I had wrapped around my head. As I moved, a fiery shot of pain jolted me back into stillness. My left leg and arm protested, making me gasp and bite my lip through the agony.

I peered down at my arm first and saw crimson blood trickle out of a rip in my shirt. My leg had suffered the same fate; a sharp fragment of glass was embedded in my thigh, drenching my pants around it with dark, warm fluid.

Shit!

I reached over and pulled the shard out of my arm, yelping at the searing jolt that came with it. I tossed the red glass to the ground, pushing on the cut with my hand. I needed to stop the bleeding now. I ripped the bottom of my shirt into strips and wrapped it around my arm, tightening it with my other arm and teeth. I pulled on the stupid handcuffs and chain that bound me to the chair. I would need to pull really hard or get bolt cutters to get it off.

I had just finished tying a wrap to my leg when I realized I had forgotten about Christian. I looked up and over the chair, slowly pulling myself onto my good leg and peering about. He was on the floor, just in front of the gaping hole in the wall. His hair floated about him in whipping ropes of copper mahogany. He was lying face down and knocked out. His back was filled with multiple punctures that seeped with his icky crimson-green blood.

I yanked on the chain again, trying to squeeze my hand through the restraint. My skin rubbed raw into a nasty reddened, weepy sore. It probably would have hurt more but my leg and arm took precedence in that area. After a few minutes of gritting through my squirming to get the cuff off I sighed and sat back down on the chair, hoping someone else from our hive would make it up here soon to help me.

I jolted back from my resignation as I remembered the lock picks in my pocket. I fumbled to yank out the small rolled bag. I pulled out a couple pins but found it impossible to maneuver them with one hand. I dropped them to the floor, angry that they were as useless to me as paperclips.

I still hadn't found my family and worst of all, I was trapped. Being possibly mortally wounded made my endurance start to wane. I needed more blood. I could feel my body weakening under the strain of the fighting and blood loss. Eyeing my machete on the floor in front of me, I longed to hold it in my hand. I doubted I'd be able to hack this chain off but I would feel a lot better if I was armed instead of being a sitting duck on a chair next to a crazed, sick hybrid vampire and a hole leading out to oblivion. This had not gone as planned.

I hung my head down, warm hot tears forming in my eyes, maybe from the cool winds that made me shiver for a moment and stung my eyes, maybe from the deep failure I felt at that moment. I didn't know. I hated that my despair was bubbling up inside me. It was weak of me. I was stronger than that. I could kill hybrid vampires for goodness sake! I had hunted tribes of ferals that mucked up the city. I could do this and I would get out of here no matter what.

I was about to tug on the restraint one more time when Seraphin appeared before me, crouching and slipping the key easily into the lock. A muffled click sounded and I was free. I stared at her, not knowing exactly what to think or if she was going to finish me off. She gave me an assuring nod before a splash of her hot blood streaked across my face.

Christian was standing behind me and had caught her by surprise, slashing her across her neck and nearly decapitating her. She crumbled to the floor, writhing in pain, with her hand over the deep gash as her dark red blood gushed out from between her fingers. I jumped up and over her, diving for my machete.

I gripped the handle as I rolled painfully to my knees, attempting to stand onto my good leg. The pain screamed inside my torn muscles as I stood holding my machete at the ready. He could have killed me easily but he hadn't. He needed me alive. He needed my blood to cure his vile disease that was slowly disintegrating his insides. His face was a pallid green now, no longer the healthy glow he had prior to the explosion. The blood loss had cost him; both his eyes flashed a deeper puke green at me, both filled with the putrid color now. He hissed and snarled as he crept forward, his wild expression hungry for blood. My blood.

"Stupid human. Now I will have to feed off your blood first. You dare try to kill me? I have lived through more attempts than you can imagine. A puny human like yourself is nothing to me. You are but a speck in my eye. I will outlive you and your precious family, I promise you that." He was closer now, though his gait was unsteady, like he was still hung over with drink. I was certain I could take him, even with one arm and a leg functioning way under capacity.

"Just try it." I gripped the hilt of my blade, making my knuckles gleam white as bone. I tried to focus on this beastly man heading in my direction, with murder swimming in his eyes, a thirst for blood and vengeance making him lick his fangs.

His face snarled as he started at me, his broad body flinging itself, more than anything else, in my direction. I steadied myself, ready to jump at just the right moment. Patience was my virtue; patience was never more important to me than now.

At the last moment, I knew it was time. I lunged to my left, bending somewhat as I held my blade to his abdomen and let his oversized knife cut the air in a whoosh right over my head. He missed but I did not. My blade sliced into his gut, letting a spill of blood and ichor tumble out as I slid across the ground. I ended up rolling as my wound caused my leg collapse beneath me, breaking my slide and sending a ferocious pain, like knives, up my leg, rendering it useless. I tumbled across the ground and landed near the edge of the gaping hole. The wind rushed over my head, screaming in my ears as my hair flew wild and loose from its ponytail, blinding me in its dance.

I winced as I rolled away from the precipice, dragging my unwilling limbs with me. I looked to where Christian lay in a lump, hunched over. His left arm cradled his gut as he used his knife to prop himself up a bit like a crutch. He was barely alive, yet the vampire in him kept him breathing. His wild look was gone and instead the serenity of a man accepting defeat washed over him, making him look slightly gaunt but handsome once more.

I kept crawling away; I had lost my machete out the gap of the blasted window. I was weaponless but I was sure I could steal his knife away from him if I wanted to.

"You know what, April?" His voice came out raspy and tense, as if his lungs could not bear the stress of speaking. I didn't answer but continued my crawl across the floor, as far away from him as I could get. He watched me pensively, unmoving from his spot.

"I thought humans were all dead. I thought they were the weakest of us all." He let out a gurgled cough, shooting out clots of greenish, crimson blood. When he was done spitting the mess out, he glanced back toward me. I was closer to the door than I was before his fit and kept dragging myself along. "But you aren't the weakest. You'll be the last of us to walk this earth. You'll be all alone, with no one else, the fittest of the fit." He hawked again, hunching over and falling to the ground, moaning in his agony. I wasn't one to condone torture and I shuddered to watch him suffer.

To my shock, I heard footsteps running out in the corridor. I pressed my back against the wall, weaponless and hurt so badly I would be no match against anyone now. I grabbed a broken post of wood that lay beside me, still not willing to go down without a fight. I waited patiently as the trample of shoes spilled into the room. I dropped the wood when I saw none other than Blaze, Rye and a group from our own hive filling the room.

"April! You're hurt!"

You think? My sarcasm was thankfully all in my head.

Rye collapsed next to me, pushing my loose hair away from my face. "You're drenched in blood! Where are you hurt?" I smiled at him, relived to see his steel grey eyes.

"My arm and my leg on the–I can't get up now." I nodded down to the wraps on my arm and leg. He touched them, assessing how badly they were dripping.

"But your face and chest are covered in blood, where did he get you–your neck?" Rye's panic made me give out a haughty laugh.

"No, it's not mine. Seraphin got hit...she's hurt bad." I pointed to her crumpled body next to the chair. Blaze bent down to assess her but quickly glanced back up at me, shaking his head. His face tight and tense.

Rye gave a nod and turned back to me, the same hard look on his face as he took in the fact that his ex was dead. I would have to tell him her actions in the end, still not sure where she had stood but after it all, she had let me go. I was hoping that would be enough for me to forgive her betrayal.

"Rye, I don't think I'm going to make it out of here. Promise me you'll find my family...." I gulped down the stone that now formed in my throat as the tears began flowing. The air was feeling colder as time went on and blood continued to course rapidly from my leg. I could feel a threatening darkness wanting to embrace me, take me deeper into its clutches.

"No! I won't let you die. Here, you have lost too much blood and you need to drink. Go ahead, drink April. Now!" His voice was urgent as he pressed his wrist to his teeth and bit down, bringing his crimson life force to the surface. He brought it to my lips and I let him, clamping my mouth over the wounds. The silken drink flowed into my mouth, its warmth seeping deep into me as it went. It heated my core and brought me comfort, shoving the pain away from my broken body.

"That's enough, Rye. Let me give her some, too." Blaze came up to us and bit his wrist, pulling Rye's arm away from my starving mouth, replacing it with his own. I felt immediately better and the darkness pulled away from my vision almost as quickly. My body felt tingly, renewed.

When Blaze pulled away, I'd had my fill. I licked the last remnants of his blood off my lips, feeling the euphoria filling me up again and I relished it.

"Oh, wow." Rye's excited voice bounced in my ears and I turned to see what he was looking at. He had unwrapped my leg and the skin was a soft pink color, knitting together before my eyes. I shifted my eyes to my arm as Rye undid the tie on it and gasped to see the skin there healing as well. I smiled, amazed at the power surging through me.

"I've never seen any vampires do that," Blaze offered, his voice solemn as he observed the wounds. In just moments, I felt good enough to stand up. Rye helped me into his arms but the pain was not completely gone. I gritted through it as I held onto him. He smiled calmly at me but I was far from ready to let my guard down. I still hadn't found my family.

"Have you found them?" I asked quietly, hoping to hear something I wanted to hear. I waited but impatiently. I waited and fought the overwhelming urge to run out and continue to look for them.

"Yes." Rye's voice came out stiff, making me pull away from him to stare into his eyes. There was something he wasn't saying underneath his answer. He looked reluctant to tell me, his eyes pained as he avoided my gaze.

"What is it Rye, tell me what happened!" I pulled and yanked at his shirt.

"They're alive, April. Just barely, but they're alive."

Chapter Twenty-Seven

THE BATTLE WAS over but we were left with scars so deep, nothing would ever be the same again. And there were other wars to be fought. I had finally reunited with my broken family but my mother was weakened nearly to the point of death. Her only chance for survival was endless transfusions of human blood boosted with an occasional dose of vampire blood. I wasn't sure if that was what she would have wanted but I was pretty sure we "humans" could not be turned from the vampires' blood; our immunity seemed to prevent it, at least up until now. But we were no ordinary mutations. Something had to be done.

Her initial refusal of vampiric blood frustrated me to no end, but how do you change the mind of someone so traumatized, someone who did not wish to go on in a world like ours? She had lost her will to live. Even if Jeremy and I were there for her, she would not return from the deep chasm inside her mind that she had let herself descend into. She lay almost catatonic, lost inside herself. She accepted human blood to be transfused into her veins from the frozen stores in the hive but anything vampiric, even disguised as a unit of human blood, she'd somehow sense and would begin bouts of endless screaming until the unit was removed. That was torture to me in itself. I often left the room when this happened, hoping it would end soon. Despite her protestations, I felt that the little bit of vampire blood we'd managed to put into her body would help her recover.

Jeremy was much less affected. He was a strong young man and had remained at my mother's side at all times, when they had let him. They had left him alone, unsure of what to do with a young boy. Even the desire for a cure had not brought them to the point of harming a child, not one as young as him. Maybe someone my age, but not him. It had been his salvation.

I'm hunting game again, having brought my mother and Jeremy back to our mountain sanctuary for some peace and normalcy. But it's not the same and I fear we'll have to return to the company of others soon. My mother seems more at ease in the mountain air but she's still a shell of her former self. She had lost something in those missing days of her life. I have no idea how to get it back. She was no longer withdrawn inside herself but she wasn't the same either. Her spark, her light, was missing, and the darkness within her made me wonder what exactly had happened inside the enemy hive. She did not tell and I did not ask.

I miss Rye, even though he comes to visit regularly and see if I need anything. I never do, but his love keeps me going. Even though he wants more from me he knows that for now, this is enough. It has to be enough.

For now, the days rush by and the nights are mostly silent. The soothing hum of the camera monitors, Jeremy's soft snores and my mother's weak whimpers from her nightmares keep me company at night. They keep me calm as I wait for another dawn.

DISARMING

Reign of Blood, #2

Prologue
Resonating

THE DAY WAS fading and I stood staring out the car window. My backpack was strapped to my back, even though it was extremely uncomfortable sitting with it on. The window was cracked just a touch, and I could hear screams echoing over from nearby streets. It made the hair on my neck stand on end and sent a snake of terror through me. Who was letting out those blood curdling screeches? What was happening? I had hitched a ride with my best friend Sarah after a study session for a huge math final the next day. I was as ready as I was going to be, even though I hated math with a passion.

Another screech resonated across the houses, bouncing off the stucco and windows, making it seem as though the entire world was screaming. My eyes widened as I scanned the streets before averting my eyes to my cell phone, flipping through some websites I had wanted to check out to distract myself from the craziness. People were running chaotically, not a lot but a few. It just occurred to me that there had been quite a few people clogging up the streets on the way home.

"What the heck is going on? Some stupid rave we didn't get invited to?" Sarah groaned as she maneuvered around another crowd of people who kept jumping in front of the car and jaywalking across the street. Some had bags of groceries, some with bottles stacked in wheeled wire carts, tugging their load along as they flitted across the street. I glanced up from my phone and shrugged, trying not to think much of it.

"Probably, or some flash flood warning again. It's been storming for a week. The power probably went down again," I muttered.

"Oh, I hope not! I don't want to miss my show tonight! If it goes out again, I can't DVR it for tomorrow! Ugh!" Sarah cursed as another straggler popped in front of the car, making her slam the brakes. "Out of the road, moron!" she hollered out the window. I cringed at the glare from the man who gave the car a tap with his palm as he continued on across the way. Road rage was not uncommon here in Vegas, and Sarah was a poster child for it.

"I'll stick it on my DVR in case your power goes out. One of us is bound to have electricity," I offered.

"Thanks, that'd be great. I'll die if I miss another episode. I already don't know what's going on."

"You and your vampire addiction."

"Oh shut up, you know you like the show, too." Sarah swatted at me as best she could without tearing her eyes away from the street, making it easy for me to block her hand.

"Hey! I do, but I'm not dependent on them like someone I know. Can you say *addicted*? The first step to recovery is to admit it!" I swatted her hand out of my way as I laughed at her. She gave me an icy glare before weaving out of the crowd, gaining speed down toward my neighborhood. A thump on my window made me jump, and I frowned at the person. A woman with crazed eyes stared eerily at me as we passed. Was that blood dripping from her mouth?

In a flash she was gone, lost in the chaotic crowd. I shook my head. Studying had fried my brain, because now I was seeing things.

"I'd want to be a vampire if I could. They're all hot, and immortality has benefits," Sarah sighed, thinking of the life she could have in her head.

"Careful what you wish for, you might not like the fanged dental job or the bloody messes you have to get into." Arriving at my house just then, I jumped out of the car before she could swat me again. I slammed the door behind me and waved at her as she stuck her tongue out, rolling her eyes at me as I continued to laugh.

As her semi-new Honda rolled away, the screams caught my attention once more. The sun had just set under the west Summerlin Mountains, casting long, stretching shadows across the valley and streets. The chill it gave along with the elevated humidity coupled with the now cool September breezes made me rub my arms. I wasn't sure if it was so much the wind as the bone-chilling screams in the distance.

"April! Get inside!" My mother's voice brought my focus onto her. Hurrying through the gate that cut off our property from the street, I helped her shut and lock it. She looked as spooked as I was, and I waited until we were inside to ask her what the matter was.

"Something's wrong." Her wild eyes darted about the street before she twirled around and made a beeline for the door.

"You think?" I bit my lip as her icy glare pierced into me. I needed to shut my smart mouth. "Sorry, Mom."

"What's going on?" Jeremy's voice made me turn toward the living room where he sat in front of his Xbox, his game on hold in the middle of an all-out gun battle.

"Nothing squirt, keep playing. You might beat my score one day." I winked at him as he smiled, turning back to his game, newly eager to beat it.

"The news said there have been incidents… attacks."

"What kind of attacks?" I grabbed an apple off the pile in the fruit basket and bit down on the sweet, bitter fruit. Crunching on my snack, I finally noticed the stacks of canned food and water bottles littering the kitchen. My curiosity was getting the better of me when I realized the windows had boards nailed onto them and the sliding glass door had huge planks of plywood fixed across it.

"Um… Mom?"

"I don't know, they're saying people are turning into some sort of zombie-like vampires, pouncing on others, biting and sucking blood out of them." Her voice cracked as she shoved some more food into a cabinet, making a pathway to the hall where our bedrooms were.

"Why didn't you call me? I could have come home to help."

"Randy helped us." She looked up at me, knowing this statement would make me fume. "Besides, the cell phones are cutting in and out."

"Randy? The plumber? Come on, Mom, you know he only wants you for one thing. That's all he wants, he's a no good convicted criminal, how could you…?"

"That's enough of that," she snapped, giving me a stern look. "He has done plenty for us. He's coming back with more wood to bar the rest of the windows and bring more water." She sighed. Her eyes looked tired as the worry made her wrinkles deepen.

"Water? Why? We have the filter, we have water."

"No!" She shoved the cup I had grabbed from the drying rack before I could fill it with the water. I looked at her, shocked and unmoving. The water was running, clear and cool. The smell of chlorine permeated the air, reminding me to turn it off and wait for answers.

"Mom?"

"Don't drink it."

"Why?" her silence made my temper seep into my chest. "Mom, what's going on?"

She stopped shoving paper plates and cups into another area of the open pantry and sighed. The look she gave me showed me oceans of fear. This was bad, really, really bad.

"It could be a virus, or the water could be contaminated. No one knows, April. People are dying from it, too. The hospitals are full of bodies. People are keeling over out of nowhere. Or turning rabid…." She ran her hand through her messy hair, exasperated and looking extremely worn out. Her hands shook as she reached for more supplies. "We have to stay here, inside, for a while. Be safe."

I nodded slowly, letting her words sink in as I glanced back toward Jeremy. I knew she was right. She always was. Mom was as streetwise as a person got. She knew how to survive. She had made the few dollars we'd had during hard times stretch to feed us. She had turned her side internet business into a profitable one, bringing loads of extra income to supplement her puny teacher's salary. We had been able to buy a house with it. She had been self-sufficient ever since Dad had died three years ago.

Still, he had left an empty abyss in his place, nothing could fill it. Nothing ever would. Not even this Randy, who had endearing aspirations of filling the spot. Nothing could ever hope to replace him.

"I'm going to pull the SUV into the garage, get it stocked with supplies in case we have to leave suddenly." She disappeared down the hall, leaving me suspended in disbelief.

I solemnly grabbed a bottle of water to drink, cracking the seal open and gulping down the fresh fluid. The screams I had heard earlier crept back into my mind, making the gooseflesh spring on my skin anew as the comprehension spilled over me. What did this mean? A sudden surge of panic filled me as I remembered that Sarah was heading back to her place. I had to warn her, had to let her know what was going on and to load up her car and come back to my place. It was much safer here, with high walls and wrought iron. My mom had bought it because of the fortress-like feel to it, always so paranoid of intruders. Funny, I thought she had been nuts, but maybe she'd had some sort of sixth sense about it. Her uncanny intuition was scary at times.

Pulling my cell phone out of my jeans pocket, I noticed the "no signal" symbol and moved about the house until I found one or two bars staring back at me. Dialing her number in desperation, I waited as the phone rang and rang.

Come on Sarah, answer me, please….

The familiar beeping sound of her voicemail announcement commenced, and I cursed under my breath, hitting the redial as fast as it let me. I kept calling until the signal died once more, leaving me to wonder about and worry for my friend. I prayed she had made it home safely. I prayed the chaos of the world had not swallowed her up.

Chapter One
Outlined View

April

THE WORLD HAD vacancies. It was a run-down motel flashing its broken neon sign—dusty and forever waiting. It would remain empty and hollow, arid and vast. No one was coming to save us. No one ever would. I had resigned myself to this already, but it was bittersweet when my eyes would wander to the horizon, always waiting, always wanting to see the dust clouds move like a welcoming mat to new arrivals. But the desert was silent. And with its silence came the tumbleweeds, dancing by in their apathetic roll across the valley, knowing almost nothing would or want to stop them.

The wind was my lone companion here, offering its caressing touch and rumpling my long black hair, raking its fingers through it and pulling strands to fly along with it. It was comforting, this careful breeze. It reminded me that summer was approaching and spring was readily here. It reminded me that there is rebirth, and the earth continued on its axis, with or without us humans. It reminded me of so many things I prayed I would never forget.

"I miss Disneyland."

The sound of my brother Jeremy's saddened voice pulled me out of the confines of my head. I turned to glance at his small frame and dark hair, growing and wild as the wind played with it, too. His face had a few freckles from all the sun we had been getting lately. Sitting Indian-style next to him, I threw him a small smile, knowing exactly how he felt. He yawned and sighed, looking a bit bored from lounging on the warm boulders of Red Rock Canyon.

I loved it out there. It was a small vacation from the never ending rubble of the city and the confines of the cement walls of our mountain bunker. He was fine with outdoor explorations, but preferred to read books, watch old sitcoms on the television—recorded of course—or play the Xbox endlessly.

"What's wrong, squirt?" I reached out to give his hair my habitual rub, but he pulled away before I could get to him, shooting me a glare. This made me laugh, knowing that he was getting older with each day. He didn't want to be treated like the little brat that he was. He was a big man now. Having survived a hive of evil vampires that wanted nothing but to experiment on his blood had made him feel like he could take on anything. I was sad to even try to reason with him that he was still just a seven-year-old, fresh past his birthday.

"I'm bored!" He fingered a smooth pebble on the stone before snapping it up and flinging it out over the edge of the cliff. He watched as it bounced against the rock, ricocheting as it made its way noisily down the incline.

"Nice throw, Jer. I bet you would have been a star player on a baseball team." I leaned back onto my hands and enjoyed the midday sun. It was getting hotter every day, and the sun would be burning my light skin if I had not smothered it with sunscreen. I loved the warmth; it felt like life in a world full of withering death.

"Yeah, but I'll never be on a baseball team now. It sucks!" He stood up and huffed away, hopping across boulders until he found a small overhang. He crawled under it and bunched his legs to his chest, looking perturbed. I sighed. I knew how he felt, but I couldn't do a thing about it. Nothing whatsoever. The world was gone, his school pals were dead. Nothing was left. Nothing but the embers of the life we'd once had. Now we were alone. Alone with vampires and dust.

I stood up and lazily scanned the valley before me. The center was crowded with buildings and casinos. It had been so vibrant once, teaming with people and lights. Now it was as dead as the death it held onto. Houses rimmed The Strip in patched developments in varying states of neglect and decay. The valley was vast, so spread out, it was an eyeful. The view was breathtaking, and for a moment, it quiet and peaceful. But I knew otherwise.

"April, are we leaving soon?" My mother Helen's voice carried softly on the wind from behind me. Turning to face her, I could see the stark circles under her eyes and her pale skin. She was standing in the shade of a wall of orange-red boulders. They blocked the westbound afternoon sun enough to keep her in the shade. Her long black hair lay in tangles around her shoulders, frizzy and unkempt. She refused to let me brush it. She refused to do a lot of things and didn't seem to enjoy the warmth as much as I did anymore. This worried me greatly.

She was not the same person she had once been. My mom had been a strong woman, filled with determination and logical to a tee. After I'd saved her from an enemy hive of hybrid vampires, she had been returned to me, but she was not without wounds—wounds that would never heal. Helen had changed somehow, and I had yet to discover what had been done to make this way. She was a shell of the woman I had known my entire life. An empty house where the lights were all on, but no one was home. Nothing was the same. She was shattered and fragile.

"Yes, we're leaving. Right now, actually." I replied. I sighed, jumping down from my perch and motioning her to follow. She was no longer the one giving commands or instructions. She had checked out of her duties when an enemy hive of vampires had broken her down. I wanted my mother back, but from this, there was no recovery.

"Come on, let's go before we fry out here." I stuck my tongue out, trying to joke with her as I held out my hand to her. She was steady on her feet but almost fearful of the surrounding area. Agoraphobia was making her come out less and less. Her mental deterioration was continuing, but it had slowed down at least. She slipped her warm fingers into mine and let me lead her down over the smooth sandy rocks until we reached the bottom of the trail where our Jeep sat.

Slipping into the driver's seat, I waited until my brother and mother strapped themselves in before putting the car into gear. I was the only one who drove now. I liked to drive, but the silence in the car could become unbearable at times. We rarely talked anymore, unless Jeremy went off on a rant about whatever it was that he wanted to yap about. Usually it was about an episode of the Andy Griffith Show or the school work I had thrown at him. Helen had stopped teaching him his school lessons. She had been so vigilante to keep us at our studies even though it was the end of the world. So now I was the teacher. Though I had been a good student, long division, fractions and grammar were not my strong suits and I hated it.

It made me resent her a bit. She had abandoned us already, even if she was still here physically. How could she let herself go like this? How could she leave us behind as she withered inside her self-imposed prison? I wanted to slap her at times and shake the old Helen out of her. I held out hope that she was still in there somewhere, just lost in the crevices of the endless fields in her mind.

But how could I find her? What would make her return to this place, so empty, hollow and filled with loneliness. Maybe she had found peace some other way, deep inside the vast nothing inside her. Maybe she didn't want to return at all. Even though I understood her reasons for escape, how could I make her see what this was doing to us?

The thing was, I didn't think I could save her. Maybe no one could.

Chapter Two

Promise Me This

April

"WE FOUND MORE of them." Rye slipped down onto a park bench that sat just at the edge of the property where our bunker-slash-cabin was situated. He looked tired and rubbed his face as his gold-rimmed, grey eyes hovered near my face. He was devastatingly handsome and constantly made me avoid his gaze for fear that I'd get lost in his disarming looks. I didn't want to be in love with anyone. Love was a foolish, pre-epidemic notion. Love was not a necessity; it was a luxury I refused to indulge in.

Rye made it so hard, though. The way his presence sent shivers through me was irresistible and impossible to ignore. Sometimes I wondered if pushing him away would be foolish, especially when he looked at me with those steel-colored eyes of his. How could someone make me feel like an idiot with no words whatsoever? It made my chest arrest for a moment before I'd violently shake it off. No time for that. No time ever.

"More ferals?" I stopped cleaning my weapons as I waited for him to continue. "Were they burned up?"

"Yep. Not so many now, but a lot. They were lining the streets in heaps, like they had been pushed out the windows of some of the hotels." His lips thinned into a firm line, making him appear overly serious. I sighed, turning back to sorting my blades out across the table I had set up outside. There were ten blades, all sizes. Sharpening and cleaning each one took time, but it was an activity I saved for days like this, when too much was tumbling in my head and peace avoided me like a plague. It was soothing and calmed my frayed nerves.

I felt his fingers slip over my shoulders, giving them a tentative squeeze. My skin tingled with his touch, sending tiny sparks down my arms. I closed my eyes, and tried to control my breathing as he slowly kneaded my muscles, melting my tension away.

"What do you think is causing this?" I flung my eyes open, feeling slightly dazed yet relaxed. I continued to wipe down one particular machete, the one that I had chosen to replace my two favorite and now long lost weapons. I had grieved the loss of those blades, lost over the precipice of the Stratosphere Tower. It helped me turn my focus back to the conversation before I became a stuttering idiot from his touch.

"I'm not too sure. It's the weirdest thing." Rye's hands slid away as he propped himself on a chair across from where I sat, his eyes twinkling as though he knew how distracting he was. "Who would go out at night to shove the wildlings out the windows? It's suicidal." He ran his hand through those thick, black locks that never seemed to stay put. "And it's not like the windows are shattered. They look they were either never opened or shut after they did the deed."

"Hmmm," was I could muster as I thought things over. I wouldn't dare hang out in a hotel after dark. The risk of becoming dinner to hundreds of ferals was way too high. Who would be that crazy? The possibility of there being something else at work was unnerving, Despite the massage I tensed back up as I thought of there being another supernatural mutation out there. I really hoped there wasn't; there was enough stuff already lingering in the shadows, craving flesh and blood. "Nothing else has been discovered out there? Footprints? Blood?"

"No. Whoever is doing this knows what they're doing, and they're damn good at it."

"Have they come after any hybrids?"

He sighed as he shook his head, his frustration painted on his face, making the knots in my shoulders tense up even more. "No, not yet at least."

"Well, that's pretty strange. Not sure how to even go about seeing who is doing it unless…." The idea came to me suddenly as I stopped what I was doing and smiled, excited about the thought. "We could put night vision cameras out there, where there the feral pileups are occurring, and see who shows up!"

"No electricity, remember?"

"Duh! Battery operated of course." I rolled my eyes at the obvious and returned to polishing my weapons. Sometimes he was so stuck in the now that he didn't want to think outside his little box. Rye sat still, and I was pretty sure he wasn't smiling. Guilt suddenly ripped through me for being so insensitive. I wasn't used to apologizing, and I found myself frozen, my mouth uncooperative as I tried to voice an "I'm sorry." Instead, only a squeak leaked out as I watched him stand up.

"You're probably right. I'll run it past Blaze and go from there." Rye readied himself to leave, tucking away the few weapons he had also been cleaning, and brushed off the particles from his clothes. I paused and watched him, knowing my sarcastic remark had rubbed him the wrong way. I longed to tell him not to go, that I wanted him to stay and chat some more. I loved his voice, the little gestures he made while he spoke. But I couldn't. The words just never formed, and I didn't know why.

"Leaving already?" I mustered enough in me to ask him, jumping up and laying my hand on his shoulder. His warmth radiated through the material, enveloping my fingers and making me long to have his arms around me. Rye jerked slightly from my touch, and I pulled my hand back to my side. His face was no longer calm. A burrowed frustration lingered in his eyes.

"Yes, I got loads to do back at the hive." His solemn voice made my insides twist as I nodded, saddened but not wanting to upset him further. He gave me a wave as he said his farewells to my mother and brother. As he turned away and made his way down the drive, I let my eyes linger after him for a few moments. He was my best friend nowadays, but I didn't know how to let him in. Even though he and I had felt an instant connection, I had put my walls back up straight away after the battle at the Stratosphere Tower, not wanting to focus on anything but keeping my family safe again. I didn't know if he understood that. I didn't know if I was doing the right thing either. It felt forced and unnatural to keep him away. Even though my heart was being ripped into pieces, I didn't have enough willpower in me to let myself love him completely. Maybe one day. But right now didn't seem to be the time.

I sat back down, exasperated, but tried to shake it off. I missed him when he was gone, but his presence sent me into a tense state that I didn't want to tolerate for too long. I wasn't sure what to do about it. I wasn't sure I even had the energy to try and figure it out. If he was going to mean more to me, he'd understand. He'd wait for me, surely.

As I twisted my fingers, I wished I could say I was certain of that.

"APRIL." HELEN'S VOICE shook me from my sleep. I groaned and sat up glaring at her with puffy eyes.

"What's wrong?" I mumbled.

"I need you to come and help me."

I turned to glance at the red numbers on my bedside clock. 2:50 a.m. "It's late, Mom. Can't it wait 'til morning?" I muttered, rubbing the sleep away as I swung my legs over the side of the bed. The cool concrete penetrated the warmth of my skin, sobering me up some more as I waited for her to answer. I was exhausted. I had a hard time sleeping as it was, without her interrupting it.

"No. Now." She waved for me to follow her, her face stern and impatient. Her dark brown eyes glistened in the soft glow of the security camera monitors. It sent an eerie color across her pale skin and dulled out the dark coloring of her hair. She was wide awake and had probably not slept a wink all night.

I sighed. When she was determined, there was no telling her "no."

"Alright, one sec." My hoodie was balled up on the chair next to my bed. I grabbed it and pulled it on, zipping it up with a forceful tug as I grumbled under my breath. The nights were still cool, sending a ripple of shivers down my arms. Hugging myself, I stood up and followed her to the back storage room.

It was here that we kept extra food that we foraged: cans, bottles of water, bags of cereal, sugar, dried milk, dried eggs, dried everything. One end had a locked cage. It hadn't had much in it when we'd first come here, just some empty boxes, a sink and a latrine. I wondered often if it was a makeshift prison cell. Who would build that into a shelter? I hadn't thought about it too much at the beginning, but I did now because it now held more than that: a cot, a bottle of water and some stores of food stacked next to the cot. My mom's blankets and pillow were thrown on it, and a box full of her clothes sat under it, making me turn toward her in confusion.

"What's this?" I hissed at her. I was cranky and her strange actions were driving me mad lately. This was going way too far. "Why's your bed in there? What are you doing?" I waited for her to answer as she turned her cool, calm face toward me.

"I need you to lock the door for me during the night." At that she stepped into the cell and shut the door behind her with a click. I stared, mouth agape. I was flabbergasted and stood in my place, confused and shocked. Her eyes gleamed at me, unnaturally shiny in the fluorescent light of the storeroom. I could tell from her expression that she was not kidding. Whatever she thought she was doing, she had to be off her rocker. I really hoped she wasn't doing what I thought she was doing.

"What? No! Why are you doing this? You're not sleeping in the cage, Mom."

She was starting to lose her patience with me now as her face shifted to a darker shade of pink, flushing her cheeks as she stared me down. I didn't move, frowning as she refused to come out of the cage. Her fingers curled around the bars, her face hovered closer to me.

"I have to, April. While you and Jeremy sleep, I can't. I pace all night and the smell…." She bit her lip as she let the bars go and backed away, turning to start her pacing once more.

"What smell?" I asked. Curiosity had cooled my fury, but I was still seething.

Moments passed as she refused to answer. I waited, knowing she would talk sooner or later. Letting out a long drawn out breath, she stopped her pacing and turned back with fear pouring from her eyes.

"Your blood. I can smell it. Yours and Jeremy's. And it smells divine." She curled her fingers around the bars once more, narrowing her eyes at me as she stared. The darkness seemed to swirl in her orbs as my own widened in horror. "I might not be able to resist it anymore. You have to lock me up while you sleep, while your guard is down. I don't trust myself any longer."

Her dark blue eyes blinked. A storm of malice tumbled into them, making my breath stick in my throat and my mouth dry. The small sliver of golden halos peaked from outside the blue irises that reminded me of the expanses of ocean I so dearly missed. No, oh no.

I reached forward and pushed the lock together, heard it click and took the key out of its slot, my hands shaking with every movement. I couldn't breathe, could hardly look up at my mother as I took in the weight of what she had said, what she so plainly had showed me, mostly without even a word. The question now was this: if she's turning, what will she end up as? Feral or hybrid?

"Thank you, April. Don't open it until you're awake and don't ever leave me alone with Jeremy. You hear me? Promise me that." I nodded at her, though I could not bear to look at her. "One more thing," she added. "Promise to end it if it goes bad." She paused, awaiting my answer, desperation written across her worried face. But no answer came. I shook my head, not wanting to hear her words. "Swear it."

I reluctantly nodded, closing my eyes which now burned with salty tears. I didn't want to do what she asked of me. I wanted to turn around and scream at her that she could forget it. Why was this happening? The room spun and felt oddly suffocating. Yet I knew she was right and that I would want the same if the time every came. If the worst ever happened to me, I'd want the same. "I swear."

Helen settled down on the cot, taking a deep breath as she visibly relaxed. I did not, could not. "That's my girl. Now off to bed; you look like you haven't slept in weeks." With that she laid down as though nothing had happened between us and pulled the covers over her slender body before turning away toward the concrete wall that lined the other side of the cell.

I stood there for what may have been only minutes but felt like an eternity to me. I waited until her breath grew slow and even, until the silence became unbearable. My stomach was knotted up into a tight ball, and I doubted sleep would return after all that had happened. Time seemed different now. How it had come to change so much was lost on me. I had been tightly gripping the key to my mother's prison, and it had started to hurt as it dug into the skin of my palm, probably nearly breaking the skin.

How could this happen? Why? I couldn't even think anymore. My brains were mush, and my head ached as I finally slipped away to my bed.

Relaxing was impossible for the continued spill of tears on my face reminded me of the reasons that I tried not to look forward to anything now. She was right to protect us from her changes. The hunger would only grow from this point on. She had fought it long enough already, an internal struggle she had hidden well. I would have to get her some blood to feed on sooner or later, even if she were to turn into a hybrid.

After everything that had happened, in the end I wasn't sure if she would take the blood. Maybe she would choose starvation instead; she was capable of it. She would've never wanted to be this way. Even now, the withered part of her fought to stay. I didn't think she'd try suicide, but things had become so uncertain, I wasn't so sure anymore. I'd lost control over my surroundings so insanely fast, and it was all so unfair. Nothing I did fixed anything. It was a wonder I ever thought it could.

Chapter Three
Full of Wish

April

"YOU'RE NOT USING it right!" Miranda's irritation slipped into her voice as it hammered in my head. Another headache had ensued and I wanted to stop our training session straight away before I puked. I shook my head and waved her away.

"I'm not doing this today." I dropped the katana to my side and glared at the beautiful hybrid who was now the closest thing to a BFF I had as of late. Her dark brown hair was pulled tightly away from her face, making her glaring brown eyes stand out brighter against her pale skin. She ventured outside of the hive quite often, but avoided a suntan as much as possible. I didn't blame her, the sun made their skin flush an uncomfortable beet red as it began to cook under the UV rays.

Unlike the other hybrids, the daylight did not scare her away too often. Her slight tan was evidence of that.

"What is wrong with you today?" She snarled. My brooding was grinding on her nerves, leaving me to think she was close to stomping off.

I shrugged, heading to put the katana away. We stood in the driveway of my bunker where the sun didn't shine too much during the day. I didn't want to be too far from home with my mother the way she was. Jeremy watched us closely from the sidelines, sharpening and polishing the set of knives I had acquired for him. "First things first," I'd told him, "learn to take care of your weapons."

"It's my mom," I said to Miranda. "I don't know what's running through her head. She's distant, different. Wanting me to lock her up in a cell at night. She thinks she's turning into a monster."

"She'll be alright." Miranda's voice was soft and comforting. "Turning takes a few weeks, but it will be fine. I brought her some blood," Miranda offered, her stern tone fading as she remembered the reason why I'd be so out of sorts today. I'd hoped she'd understand but my mind was elsewhere. "She's all set when the blood lust hits."

"I know. And thanks. I was going to ask you about that. It's just, I don't know what to think about all this." I slipped down on the bench next to Jeremy, ruffling his hair. He didn't protest this time but gave me a tentative look. "She never wanted this. You saw how she took to the blood transfusions. She damn near lost her mind when she found out it was laced with vampire blood. She'll never drink it, if it comes down to it." I let a breath out, hoping to loosen some of the knotted tension building inside of me.

I was exhausted. Knowing what was happening to my mother locked inside her self-imposed prison was little comfort. I was only hoping that turning into a hybrid would help her mind mend from the torture she had endured at the hands of Christian's hive. It was cold comfort to know he was dead at my hands. My only regret was that it hadn't been long and torturous like he'd deserved for what he had done to her.

Miranda came to sit on the other side of Jeremy. "Look, it's going to be a bit rough in the beginning, but I'm sure she will be just fine in the end. It's not hard to be a hybrid. Just takes getting used to." She winked at Jeremy, who flushed as he averted his lingering stare to study the knives more intently. He had laid his small set out on the table in front of him and had been feverishly polishing the metal.

I nodded, pulling the hairband out of my dark hair, shaking it loose. It was growing longer and kept getting in my face when I trained. The last of the cool spring breezes were curling over my skin. Winter had been brief and mild, signaling that the summer was going to be intense with fiery, burning heat. I dreaded it with every cell of my body. The scorch would bring dry, sweltering air with the feel of sticking one's head into an oven on full blast. The stench of the rotting ferals and their infinite disgustingness would increase with it too. It was unimaginable. Definitely my least favorite season of all.

"I just can't shake the feeling that something really bad is going to happen, something I can't control in any way." I shuddered, but it was more than the breeze chilling me. I liked having a certain amount of control. One thing about the end of the world is that control is never going to happen.

"Nothing's for certain, April. Not even tomorrow. We just have to hope for the best. It's not much, but I guess it's just the lot that's been given to us now. I know it's not comforting, and I wish I had more to add. I just try to see the light in every new day. If I make it through, hey, it's great. If not, I don't think I'll be too upset. I'll be dead." Miranda attempted a half worn smile, half joking and ignoring how I stared at her like she was nuts. I shot her a twisted glare and shook my head.

"Um, Miranda?"

"Yeah?"

"Don't try to make me feel better, please." I gave her a stern frown, making her laugh out loud.

"Sure thing, April."

"What's it like?"

Miranda gave me a strange look and wrinkled her nose. "What's what like?"

"You know, turning." I picked the grime from my fingernails.

"Well," she stretched like a cat and then slumped back on the chair. "It takes a while. You just feel strange at first, like your skin is tingling. Oh, and the smell."

"What smell?"

"The smell of blood. It's hangs in the air like strong perfume, but it smells delicious." Miranda glanced at Jeremy, who was pretending to clean his daggers. I knew better; he was clinging to every word we said.

"Is it irresistible?" My stomach turned at the thought, though I quite enjoyed the taste of blood myself. That was the scary thing about it.

"Yes. It's like starving for weeks and feeling so incredibly thirsty, because nothing satiates it. Nothing. Nothing but blood."

"How long before you bit someone for blood?"

A silence built as I waited, causing me to look up at my friend.

"Not long." Miranda shifted uncomfortably in her seat, probably searching for words to make it sound better. I knew there were none. "A group of humans wandered into our hive before we had it completely secured. They saw us, thought we were human, too. Luckily it was just me and Blaze near the entrance, but I couldn't control it." Her gaze shot up toward the sky, searching for something to help the stab of regret fade. "They smelled amazing, and I knew what I was right then. Blaze tried to stop me, but his own hunger won out. We snatched them both and drained them until they fell unconscious. After that, the scent of blood drifted to the others, and there was no surviving that." She cleared her throat, aware that Jeremy and I were staring at her.

"So she's right to lock herself up." I glanced up to the blue atmosphere above us along with her. So much to fear, and now even more right here in our own sanctuary, where we should have been the safest.

"I'm afraid that, yes, she's right to do so." Miranda's cool hand brushed the wild hair away from my face, but I barely registered it. I felt the twinge of despair bleeding back into my chest. It was getting harder and harder to shake off. I was afraid that one day I wouldn't be able to.

"Come on, I'm starving. Food always makes me feel better." Miranda stood up, still holding her katana in its sheath. I gave her a slow tilt of my head and began to gather up our weapons. I was thankful I had someone to talk to now that my mother was pretty much incapacitated. I missed our chats, but Miranda's company was comforting in her absence. Even if she was a hybrid vampire, it was better than nothing. If I had ever had a sister, I would have wanted her to be like Miranda. Her optimism was contagious, which was exactly what I needed right now.

I watched the horizon as the sun slipped over the trees, sending the sky seeping into colors of purple and blue. I longed for it to stay, but it was a visitor who left every night. Still it was certain to return every morning. Even so, I wanted it to stay overnight, I wanted the sun to shine forever. But like the few certain things in this world, it was like clockwork, going on and on until the night swallowed it up. I hated the nights, hated them with every fiber of my being.

The nights brought death to life. Nothing was ever going to change from that now. I'd never get to leave this bunker, not ever. I'd never sleep in a normal room again, especially with the ferals and other vampiric hybrids out there. Who knows what was lurking out there. I had lived in a bubble of sorts since the outbreak. It had worked to keep us safe. It was the only reason we'd made it this far. All I knew was that it was me and my family against the world. Whatever was now left of it.

Chapter Four

Plague of Ash

April

"ARE YOU SURE this will work?" I shifted my weight on my feet, squatting down on the roof of the Aria hotel. The heat of the day was still radiating off the hot concrete, keeping me sweating as I worked and rigged up miles of cords and dozens of cameras. It was a great vantage point; I could see almost all of The Strip. It was a gorgeous evening, but I was not looking forward to spending the night up there in the dark, even with the stunning view, full moon and sparkling stars in the sky. Nope, definitely didn't look forward to being on The Strip at night. Not one bit. "I still don't think this is such a good idea."

I adjusted the night vision camera that I had been working on and peered through the eye piece to be sure that I had every piece of The Strip covered that I was assigned to. Rye was helping to set more up along the other side of the casino's roof. They were all battery operated, and each one would have to be changed out halfway through the night with fresh batteries to keep them going. A few had extended batteries on them, but I had not had time to find enough of the longer lasting batteries and have them all charged before dusk. We had them charging now for when the others ran out of juice, but it was better that we were there to make sure all the cameras worked the entire night so we wouldn't miss anything.

"It will work." Rye grinned over at me, his grey eyes flashing and reflecting the tangerine light of the sunset. It made him look even more handsome, like a photo-shopped cover model on one of the romance novels I had glanced at in the grocery stores when everything was still normal. Now I had a small stack of them at the bunker but had never gotten around to reading them. I wondered if the heroes in them were anything like Rye. He had an amazing build. If they were, I needed to get going on my reading for sure.

"I never agreed to stay up here like a sitting duck all night. I'm not too sure about that!" I groaned, dropping one of the batteries as I tried to clamp the camera into place. Securing it, I swept the roof and searched the ground for the battery. The light was already starting to fade and quickly. Rye found it under one of the pipes running the length of the roof and held it up. I reached over to take it gently, grazing his fingertips as he held onto it for a moment too long, sending jolts of warmth through my stomach. His sly grin told me he knew what he did to me. I felt the heat rise to my face and averted my eyes before I could see him get the satisfaction of watching me flush.

He's such a tease.

I felt the blood flashing across my face as I finally pulled it from his grip and jetted back over to stuff it into place. I was sweating buckets up there; at least the night would cool it down enough to sleep a bit. I had the second shift watch, so I had to get to bed soon.

"It's just one night. I'm sure we'll see something and won't have to come up here again. They've been consistent in dumping feral remains all over this city block all week, mucking up the streets in soot and vampire ash." Rye finished his own set of cameras and shoved the duffle bags that we had used to carry them up to the side. I felt his eyes lingering on me as I continued to work. It made me smile, knowing he was enjoying the view. At least I hoped he was.

"Who's they?" I turned then to meet his gaze. Rye pressed his lips together as I tried his patience once more. I knew he wanted to shake me sometimes; I was not an easy person to hang out with. Things have to be a certain way with me and this deviation from the norm had me worried to no end.

"I don't know yet. That's why we're doing this, remember?" I knew he was getting unnerved by my snappy comments but I had no patience for waiting. It was bad enough having to lug all this crap up dozens of floors through dark stairwells. This casino had been one of the few that had been cleared of ferals and secured around the base to keep them out. It didn't mean that nothing ever got in. There was always that risk. There will never be complete safety in any place anymore. "Besides, I distinctly remember you not protesting when we came up with this plan."

"Yeah, but I distinctly remember never volunteering for this," I muttered, switching on the camera as the last sliver of sunlight slipped over the western mountains. I wanted to say it was probably another hive of vampires stringing up the ferals and tossing them to the sun to wither into dust. Who else could it be? I didn't think there was any way there could be humans out there without anyone noticing them before, but the whole situation seemed so out of the ordinary to me. Anything was possible nowadays.

The world was in a suspended state of in between. The sun bled a tangerine-orange and sent reddish streaks throughout the sky, leaving the windows of the many casinos glowing an unnatural shade in their reflections. The shadows turned dark and blue behind the lit sides of the buildings. It was such a contrast, so stark it made me shiver, especially as I could already see the ferals crawling out of the shadows, free of their prisons to roam and feed.

"Okay, I'm done on this end, need any help?" I shifted over to where Rye was finishing up his set of cameras. His fingers worked with a smooth dexterity over the buttons and cords. He smiled as I approached, making me blush as his eyes told me so many things left unsaid. I knew how he felt about me. He had made it no secret how he wanted to be so much more than just friends. I loved how it felt when he kissed and held me, though I reluctantly pushed the thought out of my head. Pulling away from him had been more from my own insecurities about life than anything else. I didn't know how to be with him the way he wanted. How do you open to someone when there is nothing for certain anymore? Nothing but death?

He suddenly reached out toward me, stroking my cheek and giving me another grin that made me melt inside again. He did it without words and so easily it made my heart skip in my chest and my stomach drop. How did he do that without anything but actions? His skin was the catalyst, and my body knew it. He followed it with a sweeping embrace, pressing me into his body with his sturdy arms. It felt amazing, so comforting and protective of him. It was a moment of safe harbor, calming my ever flustered heart. Breathing in his skin, I noticed for the hundredth time that he smelled of clean linen mixed with a coppery taint. It didn't matter that he smelled of blood; the scent drew me in, and I was suddenly very aware of his pulsating jugular near my face.

Its soft rhythm made me wonder if the hybrids were really dead. They seemed more alive than some humans I had met in my lifetime. Save for the cooler body temperature and the gold haloed eyes, they appeared very human. Even their fangs retracted when not in use, a feature to make it hard to tell them apart from us. They were wolves in sheep's clothing, hunters of crimson currency. How he could stay so close to me and not crave it was a mystery. This made me suck a breath in and pull away for a moment. I didn't fail to notice the pain flash across his eyes before he turned back to his task. It stung me as well but I couldn't let him in. I didn't know how.

"Going to get some shut-eye." I motioned to the sleeping bag tucked in a corner of stairwell entrance, trying to make an excuse to put some distance between us. Or maybe it was for my behavior. He nodded, but I still felt his eyes follow me as I made my way to the sleeping area near a small storage room along one side of the roof. It was just a shack of a building, made in the shape of an L. The walls were a grey, plain concrete, streaked with dirt from the constant desert haze and scarce rainfall. It provided plenty of shelter on two sides of me. There was a chair nearby which Rye would occupy as the night went on.

I continued to feel his gaze burn into my back, leaving me filled with longing. It sent a ripple along my spine, sending shocks down my skin. I tried to shake it off as I slipped into my sleeping bag, bother me though it may. I suppressed my feelings deep into the dark places inside my mind I dared not think about now. Maybe one day, but for now, it was an impossible desire.

The night sky morphed into its darker twin as the colors faded and the darkness of night woke the city. In the distance, the snarls and moans of the feral vampires filled the air as they descended from their daylight tombs. It sent a different kind of shiver down my spine as I concentrated on breathing deeply, attempting to slow my frantic heartbeat down. It was unnerving, sleeping in the middle of the city, surrounded by fangs and death. I hated this and doubted I would get much sleep tonight, if any. I'd just have to do without.

"Going to be a long night, try to sleep some." Rye's voice was soft, but it did nothing to soothe my nerves. The chair creaked with his weight as he came to sit near me.

"Okay."

Rye

RYE WATCHED THE soft sway of breathing under the sleeping bag. He knew April was not yet sleeping, or maybe she was in some half-awake and half-asleep state based on the stillness of her sleeping bag. He wondered what she was dreaming about, if anything. Turning toward the darkened Strip, he could see clearly with his vampire eyes. The shadows of ferals running about, rummaging through messes and heading out toward whatever it was they were searching for. They were on their nightly run through the streets, blood-starved and desperate. Their features stood out, stark in the pale moonlight. They snarled with their ruined faces, morphed from what once was beautiful and human.

The night felt crisp, rich in coolness and doused with the scent of ozone. Glancing up at the stars made Rye mildly aware that while some things never changed, others were constantly in a state of flux. He had hoped that with time, April would return his affections like when they had first met. But after saving her family from Christian's hive, she had withdrawn from him in the most devastating way possible. The emptiness that had settled in the place of her love had left him hollow, cold and longing. She needed space, he got that. The post-apocalyptic world was no place to fall in love, or think of any future for that matter. Still, hope was all that was left to hold onto. Hope was all he had.

Straightening, he moved his gaze along the streets, but thoughts of April never left his mind. He longed for her to become his mate and form the absolute bond with him like the other mated couples in his hive. But she was not a vampire hybrid. She was a human mutation of some sort, which left him wondering if there could ever really be anything more between them. He'd never give up on her. If he was patient, she'd know how much she meant to him.

What if there were others like her out there? Maybe even another human hybrid that would be better suited to love her, one who could give her the life she craved, the life that was stolen from her when the epidemic hit. Could that be possible?

And then what? Would she choose a mortal man if she met one like her? What would happen then? He shuddered to think of it but tried to keep his thoughts on the task at hand. If he didn't, he would drive himself mad with worry and unreasonable jealously. It was bad enough he couldn't reach her anymore, but to lose her to someone else, someone who probably didn't even exist, was making him feel foolish.

The streets seemed emptier as midnight came and went. He was still wide awake and contemplated letting April sleep longer. Her rapid heartbeat had slowed as the echoes of the ferals' screams faded into the night. Where they had all gone was beyond him. At least he and April were safe for now in this building, high above the deadly grip of the hunters. But he didn't want to take anything for granted, so he never let his guard waver.

As the morning moved on, a shadow shifted in his periphery. It brought him to a crouch near the ledge to study the Sahara Casino down on the northern end of the street. The old rollercoaster that hung from the front was falling apart, bits of metal and cables dangling from the steel beams. Old billboards that used to cling to the outer walls of the casino's entrance lay shredded across the wall. The coaster led into the building through a gaping hole, but it was high up on the street, and he doubted the ferals would be able to reach it. He squinted his silver grey eyes and continued to scan the street surrounding the casino. Suddenly a flash of metal reflected the moonlight on the top part of the roller coaster. The building that housed it was smaller than the towering hotel behind it but connected itself nicely to one of the hotel floors. The windows had opened, and what looked like people had emerged, pulling ropes tied to staggering figures behind them.

Feral vampires.

Rye trained some of the cameras on them before flying over to April to give her a slight shake.

"April, get up, I see something."

"Mmm?" She sat up so quickly she almost rammed him with her head. She was instantly awake, which made him smile. It was amazing how fast she was on her feet and ready to pounce on something in a second's notice. "Where?"

"Over there, on the roof of the Sahara." He pointed her in the direction of the strangers, a trail of ferals roped in their midst. They approached the edge of the roof and studied the group below. The snarls echoed down the street as they attempted to snap and bite their captors. April's eyes widened in shock; she'd never expected to see the activity right in front of her.

"What are they doing with the ferals? Are those hybrids?" She narrowed her eyes to see better, hoping to recognize one of the captors.

Rye focused his stare on the wardens. They moved with grace, and there were a total of twelve of them. He studied each one's movements and listened with his enhanced vampire hearing. A male voice could distinctly be heard barking orders at the others as they worked to follow his commands. Several female voices echoed back, though Rye could not confirm how many were men and how many were women. He quietly relayed this information to April as she moved some more cameras to point their lenses in that direction. Rye didn't want to run the risk of the others hearing him either. If they were hybrids, they were a bit too far to hear them conversing quietly, but if he yelled they would definitely hear him.

"Can they see us?" April whispered as she came to crouch next to him, zooming one of the long distance cameras onto the group, snapping pictures as well as she could with the night vision in place. She looked excited, eager to discover the mystery of what was happening in front of them. Nothing thrilled her more, it seemed.

"I don't think so, but I wouldn't risk us being seen."

"What do you think they're doing?"

"My guess is they are waiting for morning."

"Why?" April turned her confused face toward him, waiting for an answer.

"To fry the ferals they caught to ashes, what else?" He shrugged and glanced back toward the group. He could feel the morning crawling across his skin even though the sun was more than an hour away from showing its face. Rye shifted uncomfortably, knowing he'd have to descend down the steps before the full spectrum of rays spilled across the roof from the sun and began to cook him alive. He'd have to leave April to tend to the cameras after sunrise, hating the thought of leaving her alone. He knew she would be just fine; it was an isolated island here, without any other buildings tall enough to jump from. He just hoped none of the guards down there would spot them before they got away.

With under an hour left until sunrise, the ferals had become restless. The guards had brought several more strung up and lined them up into rows near the edges of the building. They tethered them to a rigged up pulley system, making it clear that they had put together some sort of machinery for this. Was it only to drop the bunch into the streets below? Rye furrowed his brows as he rationalized their actions. Why bother? Why not line them up on the street instead? He had a creeping suspicion that this was done to make sure none survived the sun. It was to incapacitate them until the UV rays could have their wrath without a chance to escape into the shadows once the sun rose.

It didn't bother him that they were about to kill the ferals, but the mystery of the strangers made him antsy, and he wanted to hop on down there to see who they were. But why were they targeting feral vampires? And what was to stop them from targeting the hybrids next? He gritted his teeth at the thought, nicking his tongue in the process. It was uncomfortable to sit there in the warming air of the dawn, but he had to know what was going on. Glancing at April, who had been mostly silent, he saw that her legs were bouncing just a bit. She was desperate for action, too. A woman like her didn't stay cooped up for too long, not with so much to learn about the world around them. It was one of the things that he loved about her: her wild, antsy streak.

The male leader of the group was scanning the horizon, too, briefly lifting his head toward them. Rye and April quickly ducked down a bit more, watching to see if he had spotted them. His face lingered in their direction for an uncomfortable moment before turning away. Had he seen them? Had he spotted the cameras? Rye twisted his tongue inside his mouth with the suspense of it all, hoping the feeling of dread was just anxiety that was snaking around his abdomen.

April looked like she felt the same way, her body pressed against the concrete wall that lined the edge of the roof. He could hear her heart racing like a hummingbird in her chest, and her eyes were wide in horror. This definitely was no run-of-the-mill scouting mission. This was a whole other enchilada. Rye even felt her anxiety leak into him as he studied the group and hoped he wouldn't regret discovering them.

The downside of discovery was that it could really alter your days in unexpected ways.

Chapter Five
The Fall

April

THE SUN WAS snaking over Sunrise Mountain and tumbling its light across the valley. I watched it as the shadows retreated, running toward the west and blinding me to my right. It was much more intense in the morning, bright and overwhelming. The guards had waited patiently, tugging at the wrangled ferals like cattle on the edge of the building and shoving them into place with long spears and poles. I almost felt sorry for the wild things. If I hadn't had the unfortunate experience of almost being a chop-suey dinner for them on more than one occasion, I might've let the sympathy overtake me and run down there to save the day. But I didn't. I was merely left curious to see what would be happening at dawn, when the light judged them all.

Rye had waited as long as he could, but ended up descending to the next floor down, hidden in the shadows when the sun's intensity got to be too much. It was upon us before the group below. Without the protection of other buildings, he had stood there, panting from the pain. He had waited as long as he could, and I knew he would be watching them from the windows below. He had needed shelter; the sun was to burn bright and hot today, a cloudless and windless day. He would have to wait until I could drive him back to the airport in the van with darkened windows that the hive kept for emergencies. Still, I longed for his company, especially as I waited to see the end game these people had planned.

As I waited, I let my thoughts linger on Rye. I wanted to love him without restraint. His embrace still lingered on my skin even though it had happened so many hours ago. I could still smell him on my clothes. So much crap tended to get in the way for us and muck it all up. I still worried for my family, even after they were safe at home. Even so, my mother's fragile condition brought a new set of obstacles. My responsibility to her and Jeremy kept me from acting on my feelings for Rye. Now, with these new 'people' lurking about, I was even more apprehensive to get involved with anyone, even a vampire hybrid who could very well defend himself against many things and take care of himself.

The rays of sun intensified, smothering the air in its suffocating warmth. I watched the tied up ferals, unable to look away as they began to sizzle under the sun's wrath. Smoky wisps leaked from their bodies, smoke tendrils hissing from their skin as they screeched. It was ear piercing. The guards casually stood by the group and together they pulled some levers to release the ferals, tossing them hard against the ground, littering the street with their remains. Ash and embers burst from their bodies like confetti, tumbling to the asphalt into smoldering piles as row after row of them were yanked and sent over the edge. I would have cheered them on if it wasn't so darn appalling. I watched with a growing horror at the ease that the guards disposed of the ferals. I watched them work uniformly to achieve this task until the last of the wild things was sent over the edge, and nothing was left but piles of dust and flittering ash.

The guards quickly disassembled their pulleys and grabbed all the spears, running in through the opened window and making sure to shut it behind them. Just like that, they had achieved their goal of incinerating a batch of feral vampires, all without getting bitten and without a trace of their existence left behind. I was shocked by how quickly it had all happened. Not twenty minutes had passed since sunrise and the silence of the dead was louder than anything else on the horizon.

And what of these captors? They had appeared so human, so real. What were they? hybrids? Human? Or maybe, just maybe, they could be like me. The questions flooded my brain, leaving me exasperated and standing there staring after them for minutes before I realized that Rye would be getting worried if I didn't hurry up and join him. I quickly disassembled the cameras in the growing light and heat of the morning. My clothes were already beginning to stick to me as I worked, tossing all the equipment into duffle bags and hauling them one by one to the stairwell door.

Finally, I rolled up my sleeping bag and folded up the chair Rye had used and set them near the stairwell where they would not be visible. As I reached for the doorknob, Rye pushed it open violently and glared at me as I stood there, my hand still reaching for the door.

"What is taking so long?" he snapped. He began grabbing bag after bag to take down to the second floor, where a make shift sub-headquarters had been set up for the hive before I could answer. No one really stayed here much, so it was deserted most of the time. The windows were reinforced one way mirrors to allow us to see outside, but no one could see in. Lately it had been used a lot to plan and organize initiatives to see who was killing the ferals. Last night had been our watch and we had finally gotten them on camera.

"Nothing! I had to gather all the stuff." I frowned right back at him, shaking my head at his outburst. "What's the matter with you?" I huffed as I pushed past him and down the stairs with leaden steps.

"I saw them leave and I just thought it was taking a bit too long for you to get down here." He scrambled to keep up with me as I hastily burst through the second floor door, marching the bags over to the computers and dropping them in heaps, not caring to be gentle with the equipment. There was electricity here. It had been rigged with emergency generators in the basement so that the computers would work again. I loved having artificial light to work under instead of flashlights or lanterns. Still, it felt somewhat bare in here, and I hated the unused office feel of it.

"Well, sorry I'm not fast enough for you." I sighed, sitting down at one of the computers and pulling out a camera to fish out the SD card. Stuffing it into the card reader, I worked the rest of the morning downloading the videos and pictures, uploading it all to a portable hard drive to take to the hive. It was tedious work, boring and time consuming, but I welcomed the distraction. It gave me a solid reason to avoid talking to Rye.

Rye gave up on questioning me once he saw my resolve to ignore him and started on his own pile of cameras. Later, he tossed me a wrapped up cold sub sandwich for brunch. I hadn't eaten all night, so I grumpily thanked him before tearing into it. I was relieved that we had food and drinks here while we worked. A makeshift kitchen was set up in one of the rooms which had been some sort of office break room in the past, complete with a fridge, microwave, plenty of nonperishable snacks and a sink with running water, all rigged up by the hive workers.

Being hungry and exhausted while hanging out with Rye was not a good idea. Trying to keep things platonic was wearing on us both. It threw both of us into a bad mood after a while. I wished I could respond to his advances, but I just couldn't deal with a relationship, even with someone as amazing as Rye.

I clicked on one of the files near the time the strangers had started pushing the ferals over the edge. Staring at the different warriors, I studied their eyes. Did they reflect the light like the hybrids' eyes do? I watched and scanned over their faces in the zoomed in view, searching for the telltale reflection. Nothing.

"Oh my God," I whispered, shock filling me and making my breakfast ball up in my stomach.

"What?" Rye stood up from his chair and raced toward me, glancing at the video playing on the computer screen.

"They're not hybrids."

"How can you tell?"

"The sun hits most of their faces in a few of the shots. None of their eyes reflect the light like yours or any other hybrids' eyes do. Plus, none of them shun the sun like you do." I turned toward Rye, attempting to hide the gleam of excitement in my eyes.

I shifted over in my chair to let him peek over and observe the shots I had paused on the screen. His eyes roamed over the figures, taking in every detail. "Rye, they're human. They have to be." Turning back, I admired their human eyes and noticed how their skin tones were not so pale, like the soft translucent white of the hybrids. "Maybe they're like me. Maybe I'm not alone after all."

Rye frowned and leaned back in his chair, his face scrunching up as his lips turned down. "But you're not alone, April." The chair creaked as if answering for me.

"You know what I mean." I ignored his reaction and beamed at the screen, printing out the pictures of what felt like a discovery of treasure. After our work was done, I would take to the streets alone to clear my mind. Rye would let me, knowing how too much time spent together created more of a wedge between us rather than sealed the gap. Each time I left on my own, the longing in his eyes was more than apparent. It radiated from his entire being. He wanted to come, wanted to follow me through the streets, I could feel it. But I never invited him.

Maybe it was an old habit I had acquired in my year of solitude or just a means to escape. Either way, it helped me think without any interruptions, without any kind of distraction.

Sometimes being alone was good.

Chapter Six
We're All Monsters

April

IT IS SAID that time is unrelated to everything else. It goes on and on, unnoticing of our actions, our falls, our triumphs. Who's to care then, if time does not remember us? It flies by, fleeting, inattentive and disinterested in any occupants of this earth. What are we, then, if time thinks so little of everyone it passes? Time is truly apathetic to the many to whom a little empathy would mean so much.

The time I had spent watching the humans on the computer screens and thinking about them had left room for little else. I wanted to know more about them; where did they live, where were they hiding in this city? Why had I not ever seen them before? I had so many questions flooding my mind that it left me restless and stirred up my thoughts. I had been struck dumb with shock. For the first time, I had been truly baffled, left not knowing what to think. But I was also strangely exhilarated.

I didn't tell Mom too much about what I had seen that day. She seemed disinterested, further retreating into the shell she was constructing around herself as the days went on. The nagging hunger within her pummeled her senses, leaving her lost inside herself, muttering about delusions. Would it be long before she succumbed to it? How long before her delirium overwhelmed the person she had once been? Her moans and constant shifting around in her bed kept me awake through the long nights, making me grateful that Jeremy could sleep through it. He'd miss a hurricane if one ever came through here. I never did sleep soundly. It was a curse of sorts, to always be aware, to always know that monsters did exist in the world.

The click of the doorbell shook me from the semi-consciousness that posed for sleep. I sat up, jerked into awareness in a heartbeat. It didn't stop my heart from arresting in my chest, making me heave in a breath to calm the ache. Half pulling on my shoes and grabbing the machete that always was on my bedside table, I glanced back, relieved that Jeremy was still asleep. The back room where my mother now dwelled was as silent as a tomb. I nearly stumbled to the security monitors to peek at the view of the bunker's entrance.

A familiar outline shifted in the dark green of the night vision camera. Light reflected back from vampire-haloed eyes as Rye stared at me through the screen. He waited as I turned on the mike to speak to him.

"Password?"

"Nevermore."

I could almost feel his eyes rolling on the other side of the metal door. I clicked the lock open, allowing him to slide through quickly. I shut it as quietly and as swiftly as I could, keeping my eyes focused on the darkened blanket of the forest around the house. With the locks back in place, I finally turned toward him, placing the machete down at the surveillance desk. I plopped into one of the chairs, pushing back the wild hair that now shifted around my face.

"Rye, what's going on?" Rubbing my face, I yawned, feeling the fatigue roll through me. "It's really late."

"I have information on the humans we saw the other night." He rolled his shoulders, appearing tired also. "And…I couldn't sleep." His eyes met mine. Longing and sadness swam in them as he continued. "Plus, I wanted to see you."

I perked up slightly, all ears and definitely more awake. I stifled the urge to keep yawning and to let my eyes roll deliriously back into their sockets. Man, I'm so tired! "Oh, okay." I laid my head on the desk, waiting for him to continue, knowing full well I was ignoring half of what he was saying. "So spit it out already."

Rye laughed, his eyes twinkling with amusement. He knew he could prolong this torment by dragging out the details; he'd do it just to get a rise out of me. Sometimes I thought he could very well have a deeply hidden sadistic side. "Well, it could be just a rumor but…."

"But?" He had my attention now. I sat up, my back straight as I stared wide eyed back at him.

Yep, definitely sadistic.

"But we haven't confirmed it yet."

"Confirmed what?" I wanted to shake him. "What rumor?"

"Blaze heard it some time ago, a rumor that there was an underground city of humans—uninfected humans—under one of the larger casinos. In pre-epidemic times there was a story that one of the casino owners was some nuclear fallout paranoid guy who supposedly had a city built under his casino capable of sustaining its population for years without contact with the outside world."

I chewed on my lip as I thought it over. It was possible. There were a few bunkers I had discovered since I'd found the one in the mountains. None were as well fortified as our home abode was; some were impossible to enter. Some had been hit already and destroyed. This could very well be a true rumor, for all we knew. But how could we confirm it?

"Do you know what casino it was rumored to be built under?"

"Yes. The Wynn. But there are many possibilities."

"Hmm." I tapped my temple as I squeezed my eyes shut, thinking back on the days I'd traipsed throughout The Strip. I barely remembered the Wynn Hotel & Casino. It was so vague in my mind, I doubted I had walked through it more than once. Maybe twice. Not a good start at all. "Are you very familiar with the Wynn?"

Rye shook his head and sighed; he knew what we were up against. If there were humans down there that could wrangle up dozens of ferals, it would definitely be difficult to infiltrate. Their techniques and coordination were too good to presume that they would be merely ordinary humans. I doubted it. They could be highly-trained black ops soldiers, for all I knew. I was excited and disturbed at the same time. Could it be what I had hoped to find all this time, ever since the epidemic stole my life away? I wished there was more concrete evidence, but I'd take anything, even now, after all this time.

"Me neither." I slumped in the chair, letting my head roll over to where the small, curled-up lump of my brother lay softly snoring under the blankets. Thank God he was a sound sleeper. I would literally have to shake him awake if I ever needed him to evacuate during the dead of night. I wasn't that lucky. I don't think I'd slept through a night in over a year. "So what's the plan, Rye? Tell me you didn't waltz over here in the middle of the night without one." Eyeing him, I could've sworn I saw that pale, smooth skin of his flush ever so slightly. It was alarmingly pleasurable to see him shift in his seat.

"Well, the thing is, Blaze doesn't really have a plan yet. It's not going well. No one can decide what to do about this group. If we exterminate them…."

"Whoa, wait…exterminate them? No." I straightened up and gave him a death glare. He shifted again, knowing I didn't like this suggestion one bit. "Under no circumstances will that be our first plan." I gritted my teeth, seething but trying to think at the same time. That was their plan? Ridiculous!

"Look, April, it wasn't my plan. It's not really even a plan, actually. It was just brought up in case it was something we might have to do. We don't know what we're up against—a small band of vigilantes, or scores of humans? Who knows? We have to prepare for the possibility that they might not want to be found. They might be aggressive, for all we know."

"If they didn't want to be found, they wouldn't have come to the surface to lynch mob hordes of feral vampires in the first place." I threw up my hands in frustration. I knew Blaze's hive meant well; I understood their objective was to stay alive themselves. But this shouldn't be just their decision. They weren't human. Jeremy and I still were. It should never be left up to them. A human factor should always be involved when dealing with them.

Rye's silence made me glance toward him again. I willed my anger to subside as I took in his calm silhouette. I couldn't stay angry at him. He was right, it wasn't his fault. He was third in command, not the leader of the hive. No matter what kind of allies I had found in them, we were still two very different creatures.

"You know I support whatever it is you want to do with this, April. I came here to warn you, though. Blaze thinks that if they are exterminating ferals, we might be next on their list. It could cause an all-out war. Best we leave them be for now." He paused, but then decided to keep talking. "I didn't want you to hear it at the hive meeting or from Blaze without warning you first. It would not have been pretty to surprise you in that way. That's why I came here tonight. I knew you'd want to know."

He reached over, scooping my small fingers into his strong ones. I felt his semi-warm hands envelope mine. My own looked fragile and delicate. But as I curled the thin fingers inward, I felt their strength—a strength that could wreak havoc on anyone that got in my way. How deceitful it was to look so innocent and yet be so dangerous.

Finding his shiny, steel eyes focused on me, I knew that the same went for him and his kind. Beautiful to a flaw. Super strength and immortality did nothing to hide the monsters within. We all were, one way or the other. Were we all not vampires of one kind or another? Even when their kind of monster was only a thing of fairytales, stories gone awry all over the internet, books galore, paranormal vices to read well into the night until the sun greeted you with another day? Now I could only wish it was not real. Now it was nothing but a continual, nightmarish story that never ended, unrelenting with never any hint of what horrors would come next. Everlasting.

"Thank you," I whispered back to him, enjoying the warmth of his fingers. I traced the lines on the tops of his hands, feeling every bump, every indention on his perfect porcelain skin. "But if we let them exterminate entire hives of ferals, just like that, without provocation, then we are no better than the monsters." I cringed at my words, knowing the kind of hypocrite I sounded like.

Rye nodded, but I could tell he didn't fully agree with me. It disturbed him to hear me talk like that, as though the ferals were real people and the humans, no matter how malicious they may be, were real people too. It was worth it to find them, at least, it was to me. I knew then that I was alone on this. I'd have to seek out the humans on my own. He'd never allow it and neither would Blaze. They might do everything in their power to stop me from ever contacting the others.

In the end, I was alone after all.

Chapter Seven

Secret

Elijah

THE VIEW WAS everything one could hope for. He sat perched at the edge of the rooftop of the Palms Hotel & Casino, letting the soft breeze dance with the overgrown brown locks of his hair. The sun scorched his slightly tanned skin, but his medium-toned coloring kept the sunburns at bay. This was his only getaway, his one reprieve from the claustrophobia of the underground. The horizon was clear of smog, very unlike the skies before, when it was a bustling city. Only shattered rooftops and clouds for company now. He snuck up here whenever he could, which was rare.

It was an outdoor deck, hung high above the city streets and part of an old dance club he used to frequent before the epidemic. It still had an amazing sound system, and he had rigged up a generator to keep the place running. He'd also hooked one to a still-functional elevator. Fortunately, he wouldn't have to walk up and down the stairs to his favorite oasis in the hell that was life now. Nothing compared to the solace he felt up there. Even the few ferals that managed to infiltrate the casino downstairs in his absence didn't bother him. He exterminated them quickly with an array of traps he had strewn across the casino floor and along the way to the elevator shaft.

He'd frequently find them hanging from one foot, dangling and snapping their dripping jaws at him as he entered. Some traps dragged the ferals to the inner courtyard, where the sun shone brightly through the overhead windows, filling it with light and incinerating the intruders when the sun rose. He kept house here; it was a sanctuary he considered the closest thing to a home that he had at this time. The underground city of Vida was suffocating, and he needed to breathe. No one knew of this place, not even Sarah, his second in command. And definitely not the other ten human hybrids on his specialized security team. He liked it that way.

Elijah had spent the day rigging up solar panels and dozens of large batteries on the roof of the casino. Fuel for the generators would not last forever, and he had to come up with a better solution to sustain his home away from home. It'd taken a while to find enough raw materials to create his energy-producing station, but he had gathered enough to get it going.

He occupied one of the rooms next to the club as his own apartment when he wasn't underground, and it had every luxury a person would ever need. The ferals didn't wander this far up, making it an ideal place to live for now, a safe refuge he could run to if he ever needed it.

Jumping up from his perch, he headed over to the bar that sat nestled inside the club. He grabbed a bottle of beer out of the cool refrigerator and popped the top, cursing when he nicked his thumb on the cap's sharp edges. Sucking on the wound, he reached over to turn on the stereo system. The room filled with the thumping hypnotic tempo of the techno, vibrating the chandelier that twinkled above. The mirror ball spun into life, shooting shining stars all across the room. It was a relief that the club could not be seen from below, but he never lit the dance floor at night.

He bobbed his head softly to the beat, losing his thoughts in the memories, and stared through the windows to gaze upon the desolate blue sky outside. Somewhere out there was something better. If he could figure out how to escape his ties to the city of Vida, he might get there, maybe even see the ocean again. For now, it was the only life he knew, the only place there were others like him. He wasn't afraid to leave, it was just never the right time, the right situation. He was waiting for something. What it could be was a mystery even to him.

No one left Vida; it was forbidden. The underground human settlement was anything but home to Elijah. He was allowed to leave and scout for hives of crazed vampires or sites to fortify and keep supplied if they had to move. The "Zompires" were what he had dubbed the dead. Their absence of humanity and lust for blood was akin to the creatures in the zombies of movies he had watched many times in his "previous life." Never in his wildest dreams had he imagined he would be in the middle of a vampire apocalypse. Never had he ever thought it would leave him alive—but changed—after surviving the initial infection. He had not turned into a mindless cannibal, nor had he perished. Though that had not left him certain it was better to have come out alive. It had been nothing but a perpetual curse since then.

He lit a cigarette, sucking in the bitter smoke and letting it seep from his lips and nose, enveloping his face and making his eyes water. He would have to shower once he got back to Vida; the leader Katrina did not allow smoking and would pitch a fit if she knew he spent his days smoking out here. He didn't care. She could get mad if she wanted. He disliked her with every fiber of his being. He didn't really know why, he just did. Her strict leadership was overbearing, and she treated him, along with his eleven soldiers, like freaks of nature. Something was off about her, too, and he'd find out sooner or later what it was.

Flicking the stub of the cigarette over the edge of the platform, he watched it plummet through the air until it was no longer visible. He smirked, laughing out loud and throwing his hands up into a stretch. It was amazing to breathe the fresh air and let the hours pass without a thought. He was free for this one moment, and that would hold him over until the next time.

Elijah chugged down the last gulp of cold beer and dangled the bottle from his fingertips, his languid hand hung over the railing, swaying with the breeze. He studied the Rio Casino across the way—brilliant in its dirty red and purple mirrored windows. It had been a fun place to hang out, too. He'd wanted to clear each casino out from the Zompire infestations, but knew he'd never be able to do it alone. Eventually it would all fall to inevitable ruin anyway, no matter what he did to help maintain the buildings. Eventually the earth would swallow up the remnants of humanity, taking back what was hers in the first place.

He let go of the bottle, watching it descend into the oblivion below. Running his hand through his messy locks, he retreated and readied himself to return to his underground version of hell on earth.

April

THE SHATTERING OF glass had sent me running into the shadows, propped with my machete and ready to pounce. My heart sat in my throat, pulsating hard and pounding in my ears as I strained to listen for any further sounds. Stillness surrounded me, and my breathing was my only company. It had come from above, of that I was certain. I studied the small mess of glass that now marked the street. The glittering green glass had sprayed out into a circular explosion, sending its shards in every direction. I moved my gaze up into the sky, but nothing but blue and an occasional cloud filled the expanse.

The windows were all pretty intact in the tall Palms Casino. Months of exposure to the elements had left them dingy and streaked. Nothing betrayed itself in the sea of glass, leaving me baffled on where it had come from. I suspected that whoever had dropped it had not seen me. It had not come near my position at all.

I glanced at my goal on The Strip. I had parked at the Gold Coast Casino, an old haunt of my father's, intent on walking the rest of the way to The Strip down Flamingo. I had jetted across the street since I was going to keep to the southern end of the street this time. It didn't take long before I was walking to the entrance of the Palms. Its sleek doors looked dusty enough to make me think there wasn't anything out of the ordinary, but my gut told me otherwise. Someone was in there. I wanted to know who and why.

I shoved at the doors, only to be met with another set of heavy glass doors. Ferals definitely would find it hard to get into this place with the weight it took to push them open. But it wasn't impossible. I continued on, holding my weapon in hand, ready for anything that might come tumbling toward me.

Inside, the air hung still and heavy, making the darkness thick, even with the full daylight pouring in from the doors behind me. The absence of windows made the light diminish after a few steps in, and the dark tint lining the glass didn't help. I grabbed the flashlight off my belt and clicked it on. Sweeping the beam across the premise, I found nothing out of place.

It wasn't until I bumped into a row of slot machines that a stack of plastic buckets, which had been used in the days of coins, came toppling over across my path. A snap of a rope caught my attention as one of the buckets rolled into its lasso and was sent flying as the rope's slack pulled itself taut and hung like a noose just above me.

My heart was in my throat once more as I stared wide-eyed at the booby trap dangling before me. It swayed from the momentum, but hung empty. I didn't dare step further in, suddenly aware of the slurry of traps coming into my view: hidden stakes strapped onto metal poles and endless loops of rope draped across the carpet. It was definitely rigged up, and one false step would send me flying into the air by one leg or get me staked through the heart for sure.

It was brilliant. Why I hadn't thought of that was beyond me. I carefully took stock of the surroundings and discovered a small worn path to the right of the gaming area. It was not the first choice of anyone walking through here, which made it easy to hide and disguise the trap-free route. I snickered, making my way carefully to the path without setting off any more traps.

A gurgling sound drew my attention before I got to it. Turning back the way I had come, I held my blade out as I rounded a corner to find what had created the disturbance. A feral vampire hung by one leg, swinging and thrashing as I got closer. I examined its restraint, making sure it would hold before creeping closer. I watched as it twisted to look at me, its fangs exposed as a low guttural growl formed in its throat. He swung his arms at me, making the rope sway and creak under the movement. I grinned, finding it rather amusing. The trap was quite effective, rendering him harmless as he hung like a slab of cow on a meat hook.

I held my machete up and was about to slice through his neck when another noise startled me. I spun to my right and found a man waiting nearby, arms crossed, an angered frown pasted on his face. I didn't turn back, certain the feral was helpless enough that I could leave him swinging as I sized up the stranger. Surprise was not the world that described what I felt. Shock was more like it.

"Who are you?" I demanded, gripping my machete tightly, wondering if he was a human or a hybrid. Without answering, he stepped closer, into a ray of light that leaked through a skylight high above the card game tables. He wore a rumpled light blue T-shirt with well-worn jeans covering dark black boots. His clothes were worn but clean. Stubble colored his strong jaw and his dark brown hair laid in locks that threatened to cover his ears and fall into his eyes.

The look on his face confirmed that he had not expected to encounter any humans. The very fact that whoever had taken such pain-staking steps to keep the ferals from entering the bottom floor of this place made me think that they had not figured other humans into the equation at all. How this person was so sure there were no others, was beyond me. But I had certainly not expected to meet a hybrid vampire when Miranda had waltzed into my life, for that matter. My guess was that the traps were never meant for humans, but had been laid there for feral vampires.

We studied each other, and I knew then he had stepped into the light on purpose, for me to know exactly what he was. The sun did not bother him, and there were no golden halos surrounding his irises, reflecting the light. He looked pretty human to me, which was intriguing yet shocking. I wondered what he had been up to for over a year in solitude and why I'd never run into him before.

"I'm Elijah." He tilted his head to the side and continued to glare at me. "You're trespassing." He stepped even closer, making me back up, still holding out my sword. I didn't trust him, but I could not bring myself to bolt out of there immediately.

Now standing by the dangling feral, he shifted his eyes to the animal swinging in his trap. With a snap of his arm, he decapitated the snarling creature with a sword I had not noticed on him before. Stepping back to a row of slots beside the fallen creature, he pulled the lever on the nearest slot machine which sent the rope and the body crashing down in a mangled heap. I watched his every move, waiting for an attack. But it did not come.

"You shouldn't be here." He muttered, kneeling down to undo the restraint on the feral's leg. Finding it too tight to undo, he pulled out a hatchet and hacked the foot right off. Blood sprayed the carpet, but the rope was now free—and bloodied—but he nevertheless unraveled it and reset the lasso.

"What are you doing here?" I stuttered as I waited, unsure if I should let my guard down or not. He didn't seem as threatening when his eyes were not bearing down on me. Still, I trusted no one.

"Does it matter? I live here, so go away." Emphasizing the last two words, he refocused on me with the same daggered glare. I shook my head; I wasn't going to go anywhere yet. Not without the answers I sought.

Our stare-down continued as he stood back up and pocketed the hatchet. He wiped the sword clean on the dead feral's dirty clothes before placing it into a sheath attached to his belt. Obviously, he was pretty strong and intelligent to outsmart hordes of feral vampires for so long. I felt a sort of kinship with him, knowing we must have had so much in common.

Especially the human part.

"Very well then." He groaned and turned, heading down the unrigged path to an elevator. He hit the button, which lit up at his touch. My mouth hung open as the doors slid open and the empty car revealed a well-kept ride. "You coming or are you going to stay there with your jaw on the floor?" He smirked, the death glare all but gone. I followed him to the elevator and entered, positioning myself beside him, never letting him out of my vision. He gave me a curt nod and hit the penthouse button.

The lurch made me grab the side rails of the car. The last time I had ridden an elevator was at the Stratosphere Tower. It had ended pretty badly, with me beaten and near death. It was not a pleasant memory whatsoever, and I was pretty sure my apprehension was showing as he focused his eyes on me. It was like he was trying to probe my mind as we shared this tiny space. The end came quickly, with a slight ding as the doors opened onto the highest floor of the building.

If shock could permanently be stamped on my face, right then would have been a good time for it to happen. He led me into the old Ghost Bar, a dance club I had heard about and seen advertisements for on TV. He had it all rigged up with electricity somehow, and the lights on the chandeliers above the bar twinkled. It was pristine, like any minute a gang of partiers could waltz right in. But it was just me and this Elijah. And I still had no clue who he was.

"Not too shabby, right?" He beamed at my shock and headed toward the bar. A door stood right by the end of the counter, he entered a code into the panel beside it and then pushed it open. He motioned for me to follow. I was still awestruck, but I reminded myself to remember where the hell I was.

The bottles of beer lining the shelves of the bar were green, just like the shattered glass on the road.

I entered what was a comfortably-sized apartment behind the bar. It had a simple set up to it and one black accent wall. His bedspread was a striped black and brown, making it clean and crisp. It looked like a hotel room, but the decorative knives and swords lining the walls and sitting in glass displays along with the pictures of smiling people made it more lived in. One picture was of a woman, bright blue eyes and dark brown hair. Her perfectly white smile gleamed at me through the glass. Another had an older couple, white hair peppering their once dark strands and wrinkles cinching on their happy faces. I wondered who they were, what they meant to this man. I was definitely fascinated.

He walked to the mini bar he had set up in the center of the room and pulled out two glasses and a bottle of rum. He even had cans of soda, and my heart leaped at the sound as he cracked open a can and poured it into the liquor. I had not drunk any alcohol since high school, and that had been very little. But this little luxury was too good to pass up.

Elijah held the glass out to me as he took a swig of his own. "Come on, I don't bite." I stepped forward and took the glass, looking down at the little cubes of ice floating in the liquid, hitting the sides with the usual tink. I smiled, eager to taste the fluid. I took a swig, almost coughing as the burn tumbled down my throat and into my belly, setting it on fire. "Whoa there, not so fast." He laughed, handing me a dinner napkin to mop up the dribbles sliding down my chin.

I cleaned it up and set the glass down on the counter, staring at Elijah, wondering what to say. I had imagined this moment for months, but now, finally meeting another human, I had nothing to say.

"You never told me your name." He watched me tentatively, the anger gone from his face as he tossed back his drink. He was built enough he could throw someone out of a club if he wanted, but he didn't feel dangerous to me. I hoped my gut feeling was right.

"April."

"Well, April. It seems you are the first human I have seen in Vegas in a long, long time." He set his glass down and sat on the edge of his bed. He offered me the spot next to him, to which I shook my head. I was starting to feel a tad uncomfortable standing in a bedroom with someone other than Rye.

"Everyone's dead." I managed to squeak out. Sweat was forming on my brow from the liquor, and I was sure I was drenching my maroon shirt with stains. I had hung my machete on my belt in the elevator, leaving me free to wipe my dampened hands on my jeans. He watched my every move, which made me self-conscious, but the need to talk with him overpowered my desire to run.

"Yep, that's pretty much what's happened." Elijah sighed, scratching his head and staring out the window.

"How come you're alive?" I wanted to kick myself for sounding so stupid.

"I could ask you the same thing," he mumbled. His dark brown eyes found me again but crinkled with the large smile widening across his jaw. "Glad to meet you, April. I'm sure we would've been really great friends." Elijah stood up and held his hand out to me, still flashing his pearly whites as he waited for me to take the next step. I accepted, slipping my hand into his to give it a shake.

Instead, he pulled me toward him, spinning me around so that I faced away from him, and pinned my arm behind me. He easily yanked my other hand, which was trying to reach for one of my weapons, back behind me as well. I bucked up and down, trying to hit his face with my skull or stomp his feet, but he was well trained. He dodged my efforts easily, pulling me snug against his chest, his head cradling mine as he waited for me to calm down.

His rough stubble scratched my neck, making me pull away as his hot breath trickled down the side of my face. He smelled of cologne and clean linen. Pleasant. So why was he doing this? Up until that point, I had not felt a threat from him at all.

"The city is not safe. I wouldn't dream of harming you, but I'm warning you now. Go back to where you're hiding and stay there. Don't ever come back, and don't tell a soul about me, or I will kill you." With that, he pushed me forward.

I stumbled to the floor, catching myself on a chair with my arms, which now burned from the restraint he had me locked in not a moment before. I glared at him, wide-eyed and furious. He had his sword out and pointed down toward me, but made no move to use it. "I mean it. Come back and I won't be so merciful." He spat out his words, trying to look threatening. Was that concern I saw flashing in his eyes? In a second, it was gone, leaving only the cold stare.

My gut told me it was a farce, but my mind had me scrambling to get up to run out of the apartment, into the bar and out the doors to the lone working elevator. I shoved at the call button, fumbling with my machete in the other, just in case he came stalking around the corner or changed his mind about leaving me unharmed. The familiar ding came fast and I rushed into the box, turning to see if he was there. He was. He stood nonchalantly watching me as he leaned against the wall of the entrance to the club. His face was blank as he let his eyes glide over me and down to my machete, giving me a slight nod before the doors slid shut.

Chapter Eight

Broken

Rye

RYE WALKED TO his car as the sunrise's unseen tendrils prickled his skin and eyes, making him don his sunglasses. He hopped into the heavily-tinted dark grey Dodge Charger. The shiny exterior of the car was an inky, black pool under the scant moonlight. The air was already heating up, rolling over his skin like a wave of steam. Summer was heading their way, promising long days in the inferno of the solar glare, heating to obscene temperatures that made traversing about the land nearly impossible for him. He hated the summers in Vegas, swearing under his breath that he had to deal with yet another one.

The call of the northern west coast coursed through his veins, making him long for the wet and freezing temperatures of the sea-sprayed air. This place was nothing but dirt and death. Even the land had a way of withering the neglected buildings around him, claiming the structures back for itself. He sped down the mountain road to the even hotter and dismal valley below. How he had come to be anchored in a place like this was beyond his comprehension. He had the urge to keep driving, past The Strip and the disarrayed tangles of garbage, cars and tumbleweeds that littered the streets and highways. Keep on driving until the ocean met him with open arms once more. Only then would he feel safe and sound again.

Oh, how he longed for that day to come already.

Rye wondered if April would join him. He wondered many things about the human girl who had stolen his heart but probably didn't feel the same toward him. He had watched her pull away, watched her cease her loving embraces and holding of hands until the wall she had built up stood so high around her, he couldn't reach her anymore. Left out in the bitter cold. And he didn't even know why.

The hum of the motor made his thoughts drift. He had come to see April and found her lost in her thoughts and quiet. Dinner had been no better. He had tried to coax out of her where she had been all day long. Leaving her brother at the hive while she traipsed around town alone had sent up red flags. She loved to be alone, roam the city and do her thing. But he wanted to join her, to explore with her, spend every living second with her. Yet he didn't want to suffocate her and push her away. It was such a struggle to let her go and be who she was, but he had to. Otherwise he'd risk losing her forever.

His superior night vision left no stone or bundle of debris unseen. Rye dodged them easily, swerving at speeds that would make most lose their lunches. April hated his driving, and he had watched her bite her tongue as she silently prayed she would live through his hellish driving to see another day. This caused him to chuckle; these small things that made him think of her were the reasons why he kept coming around. He loved her, like he had never loved anyone, even Seraphin.

However, nothing made sense about April, not one thing. She's human, a human hybrid of all things. Made to fight vampires and drink their blood to pump her up into a fighting machine, like she was on steroids. He was a vampire, hopelessly in love with her. He wondered if he even meant anything to her because of this. Something was going on within her head and he'd give anything to break down her confines to ease whatever it was that was bothering her. Nothing he did sufficed. Nothing whatsoever.

He pulled into the airport, not spying as many ferals on the way back to the hive as he usually did. They stayed away from the hive for the most part, somehow knowing that the hybrid vampires fed on blood from the ferals, too. He found it odd that they would know this, but he brushed the unfamiliarity of it to the side as he hopped out to open the huge gate that was rigged to an electrical lock. He punched in the code and jumped back into his car, waiting as the gate creaked open. After driving down into an underground parking lot beneath the airport, he watched as the gate closed behind him, making sure no intruders entered before it shut.

Jumping out of the car, he made his way toward the double locked metallic doors that led into the hive. A series of locks squeaked as he punched in the codes, letting him through and shutting behind him with an automatic click. It was a double door entrance, making him wait a mandatory minute before the next door opened. Cameras focused on him as he watched the second set of doors screech open. He wondered whose eyes were watching him from the other side of the lens. Giving a curt nod to them, he walked into the massive hive's main meeting room, a large warehouse-like space made from enclosing the McCarran Airport underground bypass tunnel. Asphalt ran under his feet as he made his way to the other side, where another door led to the sleeping quarters of the three lieutenants of the hive—Blaze, Rye and Miranda.

The others watched him as he marched through, barely acknowledging them. No one challenged him; everyone knew who he was.

Blaze and Miranda were nowhere to be seen, making him wonder if they were already resting. The main meeting area was nearly deserted. With the sun rising outside, he was sure most had already sought the comfort of their rooms to rest. He shut the automated locking door behind him, stepped down the silent corridor and swiftly to his room.

Sliding onto his bed, he leaned back onto his arm and stared at the ceiling. The cold concrete was puckered and imperfect with its small ridges and porous surface. He had studied every crack and crevice over many, many months. He liked it here. It was silent and dark, giving him much-needed relaxation time, which seemed to be consumed by so many things lately. Letting his body lax into sleep had been difficult with so much on his mind, mainly April.

He hoped that this fiasco with the humans would make things clearer for her, make her realize that she wasn't alone or fulfill some endless need she harbored inside. He hoped that at the end of this, she'd come to realize that he needed her and that maybe, just maybe, she needed him too. He was patient, but he hoped it wouldn't be too long of a wait.

"RYE?" MIRANDA'S VOICE echoed in his dreams, making the scene before him shift violently to the dark concrete walls of the hive headquarters. He sat up as the end of his bed shook when she sat down. She looked cautious, probably expecting him to pounce on her for interrupting his sleep. He found himself slick with sweat and his heart thudding in his chest from the plagued dreams. "Are you alright? I heard you yelling at someone, I thought something was going on."

Her golden-haloed brown eyes reflected the dim light of the hall just outside his room and swam with concern. She lived in one of the rooms next to his; a long hallway of dorm-like rooms had replaced the long room of stalls and beds that had been their resting places for a long time. Here, the walls smelled of new paint and wood. The smell was sometimes strong in the stale tunnel air. But overall, it wasn't too unpleasant, except when it started to make him feel suffocated and hunger for fresh air, as he did now.

Rye gave Miranda a shake of his head, reassuring her that he was okay. "No, nothing, just a bad dream. Didn't have any dinner today." He chuckled, wanting to lighten the mood and steer her off him, but she was not so easily fooled. Miranda squinted her shiny eyes toward him, full of suspicion, not likely to let him off easy.

"You sure you're okay? Need anything?"

"I'm fine. Please, go back to bed." He waved her off, watching her as she slipped silently toward the doorway. She treated him like a little brother, much like April treated Jeremy. She gave him a curt not and disappeared like a flash. Her intentions were good, but he did not want her around when he was feeling vulnerable. She was second in command of the hive, set to take over if anything happened to Blaze. It was fine with Rye, but he hated to be seen as weak.

Sitting in the bed, he rested his elbows on his knees as his hands weaved through his hair, brushing back the beads of perspiration. The residual effects of the dream slowly ebbed away as his heart found a calmer rhythm. Closing his eyes brought an image of April floating into his mind. Why did she make him feel this way? Exasperated, desperate and wanting. He felt like she was pushing him away, like a nuisance, a fly buzzing around her head and annoying her to death. He wondered if he should just let her be, let her go.

No. He shook his head at the ridiculous thought and laid back against the cool, sweat-soaked pillow. He would distance himself a bit from her, but to be too far away would be unbearable. The connection he felt to her, the need to protect her in this devastated world, was much too strong to just let go. Maybe he should just tell her outright what she meant to him and find out what made her hesitate to return his affections.

It couldn't be that bad; but even if it was, he had to know. He would tell her the next time they met and make sure that no matter what, she knew that he would be there for her.

Chapter Nine
I'll Provide the Spite

Elijah

TEARS OF SOOT and despair disappear in the dusty moonlight. Or so it seems. Elijah wiped away the grimy residue caked on his skin and weapons. It streaked across his face, leaving a trail from his rough fingers. The mirror, unlike the reflection it now harbored, was crisp and clean, like the rest of the bathroom. It stood sterile, pure and white all around him. He leaned against the rim of the sink, letting the black ash trail along the clean porcelain, staining its perfect surface. He liked that. He wanted to smear around what was left of the zombified vampires' remains, which stuck to his clothes and clung to his hair. The burnt barbeque smell permeated his nostrils, making him remember the deed long after it was done.

He hated leading them to their deaths. Though they were no longer human and no longer resembled anything with higher thinking, he still regretted the fact that he was responsible for killing them. It was getting more and more difficult to push the guilt and horror of the world back into the tiny chamber inside his head, which harbored everything that had gone wrong in his life and hid the deterioration of his morality. Turning the faucet on, he let the warm water run and splashed it his face. The fluid churned black as he washed the grime away, soaping up his arms. He had to get a shower as soon as he could, but Katrina would be waiting for him at debriefing. She wouldn't like waiting.

Slamming the water off, he dried himself with a towel, continuing to stare into the smooth mirror before him. His reflection remained constant—slightly tanned skin and gleaming brown eyes glinted back at him. His shaggy brown hair was getting long, hanging over his ears, and needed to be brushed back for him to see without it in his eyes. Short stubble grew along his jawline, making him look like a rugged woodsman. He smiled at the thought. Elijah, the huntsman. *Right.*

Pulling on a clean black shirt, he smoothed the wrinkles down and jerked the door open, entering the cool, brightly-lit hallway. *It's too white here*, he thought to himself. *Sterile and plain.* Whoever had built this fortress had to have been a germ-a-phobe, he just knew it. That, or some mad scientist. The gleam of the clean walls and tile made him cringe. His thoughts wandered to a hospital he had visited before the epidemic. The smells had been nauseating, and the plain color scheme of the halls and waiting rooms just reeked of institutionalization. He wondered why they couldn't have painted it more lively, vibrant and happy. Why make a hospital look like one? The same went for this place. Why so much white? Was there a deal on white paint when it had been built?

That was why he loved his city escape in the penthouse of the Palms Casino. Every time he returned to the underground, he longed to leave again and go back to his sanctuary above the city streets. Thinking of his apartment, his thoughts wandered to the girl, April, whom he had chased off. He had been surprised to see a human alive aboveground. It was something he had not expected to see for almost a year. Supposedly everyone had died or turned. If by chance any had lived, they'd have been eaten by now. No, 'surprised' was not even the right word for what he felt about his discovery. He was stunned.

He couldn't ever tell Katrina about the girl. She would have them hunt her down and drag her against her will into the underground. He prayed she never came looking for him again. If she knew about the underground, it would be a death sentence for her, or at least a definite life imprisonment.

The underground city of Vida was the most boring and ordinary place on earth. It was inhabited by humans and hybrid humans alike. It had been the last place in Las Vegas left unaffected by the viral epidemic, the last stand. This made him smirk and almost laugh out loud. He'd never believed that. He couldn't believe it was the last place on earth that was safe, especially now with April roaming around as proof of life above. He could feel deep inside him that there were others out there, somewhere. This knowledge crept in his mind and surged through his bones like a sixth sense. One day he was going to find them. With or without Katrina's help.

The thoughts of the city's dictator made him groan. The plain, thin woman had claimed leadership of this underground, prison-like facility. She had run the place before the outbreak and God forbid someone else run the place in the wake of the epidemic. She was ruthless, with dozens of loyal followers. She was pretty close to being some sort of cult leader. Waco, Texas had nothing on her. She didn't hesitate to punish those who disobeyed. He'd had a taste of her wrath before, though she could've been harder on him. He believed she was wary of him, and maybe even had a soft spot for him. However, she kept tabs on all twelve of the hybrid humans living among her human followers. She barely tolerated their presence, and they knew this well. She would not let them forget it.

Elijah knew she was scared of them, of him, of their differences and their strengths. She used them as her ultimate soldiers but never forgot to let them know that they were not quite human anymore. She never neglected to remind them of their place beneath her, beneath the others, not once extending much courtesy toward them.

In fact, if Katrina could, he'd bet she would have thrown them all into a prison cell until they rotted. But they had their uses. So, until they became unnecessary, she used them for every little task which needed to be done. Elijah was made the leader of the twelve, mainly because they listened to him. And he did what he was told. Her hold on them was wrapped with the threat of being thrown into the unknown world, a world that was dismal and barren. That or death.

They had chosen to serve as her top security detail. It's not that they couldn't have overthrown her if they had so wanted to. But it would have been bloody. With all her faithful supporters, it would have been an all-out civil war.

It was best to avoid any confrontation with Katrina. Elijah couldn't quite put his finger on it, but there was something off about her. It made his skin crawl to be near her, and he didn't even know why. She emanated power as though it leaked from her pores. Whatever it was that was different about her, he didn't ask. He didn't really want to know.

He never looked forward to seeing her, and despised her more than anything. For now, he kept it to himself. Just like the existence of April, it was all kept safely in his mind. Katrina would never find out about her, he would make sure of that. For now, the task of annihilating the Zompires, as the Vidians had begun to call the wild vampires above, was her obsession. The half-zombie, half-vampire crazies were all that remained of civilization. This was a job he dreaded but he was satisfied that it kept her attention for now. He gritted his teeth the entire way to the debriefing room, wishing to be anywhere but here. As long as there was a "task" for the twelve, Katrina would let them remain in Vida undisturbed.

That was all he wanted, for now.

Chapter Ten
Holding Breath

April

I WONDERED IF mom would've approved. The old mom, I mean. The Helen I craved to see once more, the mother of my past. I peeked into the storage room just long enough to get a good look at the cage she now dwelt in. She left it occasionally, but only if I was there and awake. Otherwise, it was back into the prison cell she has made ever so comfy for herself.

The old Helen would probably not have approved. I could see her in my mind's eye frowning and shaking her head, disapproving of such an arrangement. She probably would have asked me to shoot her in the head. She would've made me do it already.

I felt defeated, like I was giving up on her as I turned away and flopped back onto my own bed. Night had crept over the horizon, and we had bunkered down for the evening. Rain had been threatening to fall all afternoon, and it now came down in sheets, keeping its ominous promise. It pummeled the walls, hard and unrelenting. I enjoyed the tapping sound; it brought life with it, something we all could use a little more of. When it rained here, it came down in torrential buckets, causing the valley to become flood zones with rapids all over the place.

I avoided the city when that happened. Even with the newly built flood channels, which remained intact, it was still dangerous to find yourself carried away in the swirling, dirty water. Some streets would flood completely and become impassable. Even some of the casinos were not left unscathed, filling up the first floors with muck and mud. If there were still people around, it might not have gotten so bad. But nature has a way of taking back the land, shifting the dirt and water to its own desires.

At least up here in the mountains we had no threat of flash floods, only the threat of mudslides covering the roads. I crossed my fingers that with every rainfall, the road to the city would remain clear. If we were cut off, it would take forever to dig our way out to get off the mountain. Not something I had time for.

I thought about the rumors of the underground city and the man in the Palms Casino—Elijah. I wondered if he was somehow connected to it. I doubted it, but I just didn't know. I felt the rumors must have been based on reality, like most are. Rolling over in the bed, I leaned on my arm, contemplating what it would be like underground. How big of a city was it? How many people were walking around in there without knowing I existed up here? What was it like to live there?

So many questions and I had no answers whatsoever. Not even one hint of how it would be there. It made my heart jump, leaving it anxious and fluttering in my chest. It made me restless, eager to get a move on, eager to find it, even if it was the last thing I did.

It had been a long time since I'd had some sort of goal. This was what I needed. I needed this to focus my thoughts. I was going insane not having anything to concentrate on, not having anything to give me some hope for the future. It was agonizing and tortuous. I wasn't the patient type, and having something to focus my energy on was a relief. It was a purpose, and I was going to find out everything I could about it. I was that driven.

"April?"

"Yeah, Jer."

"Do you think Mom's going to die?"

I turned back over, squinting my eyes as I looked at my baby brother. His face was a mask of concern, filled with features too old for such a young kid. It made my heart break, and I rushed over to give him a tight hug. "No, squirt. She's not gonna die. She might not ever be the same, but she's too tough a gal to die. Get me?" I ruffled his hair as I felt the hot tears leak from his eyes onto my shirt. He buried his face into my stomach and cried silently, never whimpering or calling out to anyone.

Mom was already gone as far as I was concerned. But how was it for Jeremy? What was he thinking about? My soul went out to the broken little boy still hiding deep inside the hard shell he had painstakingly built in the wake of being kidnapped. I wished there was something I could say to comfort him more, but the words were lodged in my throat and only silence remained.

Sucking in a breath, I licked my lips and attempted it one more time.

"Hey, it's going to be alright. You hear me, Jer? I won't let anything happen to you. I'll never leave you, and I'll always be here. Don't forget that, okay?" His head nodded softly in agreement as he tried to rub away the trails his tears had left behind on his face. He sniffled as I handed him a tissue. I was sure he didn't want Mom to hear him. He would just bury his head into the pillow if she happened to walk in.

It hadn't always been this way. Before they were taken by Christian's hive, he was stuck to my mother like glue, her little sidekick. Now, a part of him had been ripped away prematurely, amputated, leaving him ragged and torn, orphaned. I understood it, knew what it felt like, but I wasn't a little kid anymore. I'd been older when everything changed, and it had made a world of difference.

After he had settled back to sleep, I laid there awake, staring at the ceiling, trying to calm my mind with its erratic thoughts and endless chatter. I prayed for silence, even though only the hum of the machines filled the air. I felt more alone than ever, and I was desperate to find others like us. Not just for me, but mainly for Jeremy. He would need more than just me very soon, he would need things I could never provide. A family. Stability. If I could give him that, the one thing I actually could do, then I would do anything to do so.

MORNING CAME AND I had not slept at all. I had been busy formulating my plan to infiltrate the building by myself. First, I would raid the government center near the downtown area for a map of the interior of the Wynn. That way I would be prepared and ready to go into the casino without being too lost. Maybe I could even find a way down to the underground city. There had to be some sort of connection to it from the building, most likely in the basement. If I could make it that far, past any hives of ferals, I might just find the entrance to this rumored human city.

I was excited, exhilarated even. This was my purpose now, my focus. I was up at the first light of dawn, desperate to get going. Breakfast was readied in minutes for the three of us. This purpose had me humming to myself as I tossed the meal of powered eggs and ham steaks together from the storage freezer, adding some concentrated orange juice to drink. I settled down happily at the table, a sense of renewed purpose filling up my soul like food in my stomach. I even got weird looks from Jeremy, who was too sleepy to inquire about my elevated mood. My mother didn't even notice. She barely picked at her food as she sat there, lost in her own head.

I pushed her to eat, and she forced down a bite or two into her fragile, thin mouth. She was skinnier now, thinner than I'd ever seen her. Her lips were a light pale pink and slimmer. I gulped my breakfast down, my focus wavering as I watched her move her food around the plate, making it seem like she had eaten more than she had. "Mom, eat some more."

"I'm full."

"No, you're not. Eat some more, you're too thin." I urged her on.

"So what?" She hissed, dropping her fork and letting it clatter to the floor. "What's it to you?" Helen snapped—her eyes wide and wild. Was that a snarl slipping from her throat? "I'm. Not. Hungry!"

I held my hands up as if to tell her that it was okay. "Alright, just saying." I stood up slowly, backing away until I reached the sink to wash my dishes, turning to hide the tears forming in my eyes. Jeremy's face was frozen in surprise, shocked to see his mother react the way she had. His food was half gone, but he stared hard at his plate, as though he wanted to split it into pieces. My pain shifted to anger as I gripped the sponge to wash my dishes.

This was Helen now. Mom. A woman who had always been calm and confident. Helen, who never yelled but spoken firmly, like you'd expect from a mother. This wasn't her. I didn't know who this was anymore. I wasn't sure I wanted to know her anymore, not like this.

I gulped back my sorrow and watched the water swirl down the drain, taking the small soap suds with it. The huge lump forming in my throat made it hard to swallow, knowing my mother wouldn't care anymore if I did cry. But I wouldn't cry. I didn't want to see her apathy toward me anymore. The water spiraled around the sink, and I wanted to join it, down the drain, away from this place, away from it all forever.

"I'm going into town today, Jer. Do you want to come with me and hang out with Rye's people? Or…." I carefully formed each word, afraid my voice would crack if I didn't. I didn't want to offer the alternative. At least if he came with me, Helen could roam around the bunker freely, without fear of harming someone.

"Yeah, that's fine. It'd be nice to see Rye and Miranda again," he muttered, obviously having already lost his appetite as he shoved the food around on his plate, too. "Maybe Rye will be up for a rematch on Halo." He pushed away from the table and brought his dishes to the sink. I nodded to him and let him finish cleaning up. We knew our chores and did them without any protesting.

"Okay, well, it should be fun. Do you need anything, Mom?" I spoke softly, afraid to bring her wrath out again. She shook her head without looking at me, still lost in a distant thought, staring across the room and humming softly to herself. "Alright, just make sure you take a shower and put some clean clothes on. And your sheets need washing, wash day remember?" Biting my lip, I realized just how much I sounded like her, which made me cringe. Like the old her.

I saw the slightest of nods from her and I accepted that it was all I was going to get. Heading over to grab my gear, I loaded up my weapons and a bag of snacks and water. Never knew when one might need some back up food. Shoving some small LED flashlights into the pack, I turned to wait for Jeremy to finish dressing. He hooked his knife sheath to his belt and stuffed a metal zippo into his pocket. He had his own little emergency supply bag that he belted onto his hips before joining me to leave. Walking out the door, I called out a goodbye to Mom, who was still sitting at the table silently.

"Love you," I called out to her. I didn't hear the words returned before I closed and locked the bunker door.

"When do you think she'll be fully turned?" Jeremy inquired softly. I jerked my eyes toward him, studying his face as we walked over to our car. The rain had all but disappeared. The sun shone brightly behind the trees this early in the morning. Still slightly cool from the moisture in the air, the higher the sun hung in the sky, the faster it would all dry up. That's how it was here: pouring, grey and gloomy one day, then bright sunny blue sky the next, like nothing had happened.

"She won't turn."

"Yes she will, and you know that better than I do." His beady little eyes glared at me as I hopped into the driver's seat. I sighed heavily, letting my breath ease out slowly, giving me time to contemplate what I would say. I was still shaking from Mom's outburst.

"I don't know that, but it seems that it could happen soon if it does. It might not though, so don't hold your breath, Jer." I turned the engine, letting its welcomed hum break up the air between us. I was done speculating. If it happened, it would happen. If it didn't, then there was a God.

"That's why you don't leave me alone with her anymore, isn't it?" A small quiver lined his words. "It's not 'if' it will happen, it's 'when.'" He turned his gaze to stare at the passing scenery, now done with his complaints. I wished so badly that I could comfort him. But I wasn't the comforting kind, not all the time at least. I hoped that when the time came, I could be comforting enough. Seeing him this way broke my heart into a billion little pieces.

"Well, don't be so negative. We do what we must. For today, you hang out with Rye. I have to get a map of the Wynn, just for future reference, and it could be in a couple different places. Let him win a few rounds, K?" I heard him chuckle at the last statement, making the tense knot in my shoulders relax just a bit. "Oh, and Jer? Don't tell Rye what I'm doing. You know how antsy he gets."

He nodded. His anticipation of playing against with a real person had won over any suspicions he might have had about what I was going to do. I knew with that, he was hooked and eager to go. Who could turn down a video game challenge? Definitely not Jeremy.

Chapter Eleven
Last One

April

"WHY DO YOU always have to do things alone?" Rye's eyes narrowed as he took in the words I had just spoken. Leaving him behind to babysit Jeremy was not his idea of fun. He didn't mind hanging out with him, it was just that knowing I wanted to go searching for some hunting gear at my usual haunts sounded suspicious to him, especially the part where I wanted to go alone, even though that wasn't unusual for me.

I couldn't tell him the truth, if he knew I was going to search through the dark buildings of the government offices for blueprints of the Wynn Casino, it would make him furious. He would want to come then, and wouldn't take no for an answer. Instead I had told him I needed some alone time to breath and think about stuff. He accepted this reason, though quite reluctantly. I could tell.

"Don't be a nag. I know the risks as much as you do. I do this alone, like I always have. I don't need you or anyone to babysit me. Unlike Jeremy, I'm already an adult." My own teeth were gritting, holding back words I might regret. I wasn't used to working with another person or even answering to someone other than my mother. Though Rye was easy going and a comfort at times, I hunted alone. Period. Even with my mother, she had learned quickly that it was better to leave me to my own devices. He had to learn this soon or be tormented by my quirks.

"I'm not a nag," he sighed, rubbing his face and looking somewhat tired. "It's not safe. You know that. Why do you always leave me out of things? Is it because I told you Blaze doesn't want us to search for the human city, if there even is one?"

"*I* leave you out?" I huffed, almost laughing at the irony of it all. "I'm not the one making plans to exterminate feral hives and inadvertently joining the human genocide that is already happening. I'm not the one making plans to infiltrate an underground human facility without consulting a *human!*" I turned, already marching down the hall before I lost my temper. I could tell my words stung like salt to a wound, but I couldn't help lashing out.

"I need to get away from everything for a bit. If you have a problem with that, so be it," I hollered back to him. My patience was gone, and it wasn't even late morning yet. I was running out of daylight though, with every minute that ticked by, and I didn't want to spend it arguing with Rye.

Surprisingly, he didn't follow me. Maybe he knew me better than to continue to probe at the issue. He must have been getting to know me pretty well if he gave up so soon. Satisfied, I jumped into my car, gripping the steering wheel as I made sure Rye had returned to the hive's underground residence and had not followed me out. I was going to head back down to the other side of The Strip, toward downtown Fremont Street to get the blueprints of the Wynn Hotel & Casino. I had yet to find the right place where they kept the blueprint hardcopies. It was grating on my nerves not to have found it yet.

It sucked up my time so much, I had lost track of the days since I had seen Elijah. The Palms stared at me from every angle of The Strip, even from here, at the airport. He must have known I was searching for something. He had probably seen me once or twice sneaking around the Las Vegas Strip. His vantage point was pretty good from his penthouse. But if he knew what I was looking for, maybe he would understand. Of all people, he just might join me.

However, I had avoided his apartment since he had threatened me. He had made it pretty clear that he did not want me to return. Maybe when I found the underground city, I could approach him again. Maybe with evidence of others, he would be more forthcoming and less likely to stab me in the heart. Not that I didn't want to snap his neck myself for telling me to leave the way he had. It's just that I didn't think killing another human would be worth the trouble.

"Wait up!" Miranda's voice bounced into the car as she pulled open the door to the car and jumped onto the seat.

"Oh no, not you too!" I groaned, giving her a scowl.

"Hey, I'm so in when it comes to exploring. I need out of the hive sometimes, too. Too much testosterone, if you know what I mean." She winked, her dark eyes twinkling in the blinding light of the day. She threw on the shades she had hoisted on top of her head and wore a long-sleeved hoodie despite the growing heat, to cover her sensitive vampire skin. She fastened her seatbelt and waited for me to get going. An immortal that cared about safety. It was sort of ironic in a way, and it made me chuckle as I gave in and started the car, too grumpy to try to talk her out of coming along.

"Okay, just do me a favor: don't tell Rye what I'm—I mean, *we're*—doing, alright?"

"Oky doky." Miranda smiled at me then turned to look out the window without questioning me further. Sometimes I liked her no-nonsense style.

I loved Downtown. It used to be bustling with life before the outbreak. Small souvenir shops, island retail kiosks, zip line riders above our heads while the lightshow danced with multicolored LED lights, creating a unique experience. I'd never been anywhere else besides Las Vegas, but it was enough to escape the everyday mundane routine, escape to The Strip, escape to Downtown. A perfect place to blend in and disappear in the crowds. Loads of candy shops, ice cream and arcades to keep any teen busy. I knew because it had been a favorite hangout of mine and my best friend, Sarah.

But that was then. The memory faded from my eyes, and I no longer saw the twinkling lights or heard the dinging of slot machines as I approached the neglected city blocks. It was devastated. Some of the old shack-like houses looked even worse for wear, having been vandalized and wrecked during the initial outbreak. Longstanding motels sat with their windows smashed and the dirt caking them until you could no long glance inside. Celebrated wedding chapels stood with doors ripped from their hinges, and old arches were strewn across the yards where white picket fences were no long standing.

Weeds grew everywhere, the one thriving life form after the death of so many. They grew out of cracks and snaked through the edges of brown, dead lawns, stretching their fingers across the concrete, cracking it with snarling roots and littering the city with its dead cousins. Abandoned, neglected. Without order, the wild things ran rampant.

Reaching the government center off Main Street and past the casinos, I parked in the asphalt lot, unusually empty of cars. It must have been one of the first places to shut down during the outbreak. Most had sent people to emergency centers or shooed them away to their homes. Or maybe they had all left on their own accord, worried for their families, desperate to make it out of the city.

But none made it out. No one had made it. Or maybe they had. Maybe they all had gone to the underground sanctuary I was so desperately seeking. I crossed my fingers, praying the maps were inside.

Entering the building was easy. The glass that lined the roof still let in plenty of light, letting rays of sunshine stream down into the dusty corridor where the two floors stood dark and gaping down at me. I could see desks and shelves of books and paperwork lining this semicircular room. It was a shame there were so many windows; this would have been ideal for a hive of feral vampires. It was cool inside with thick rock and concrete walls. I shivered from the cool air. Miranda and I found the stairs behind the elevators. The stairwell was a bit dark, so we flashed our beams of light and sprinted up the steps three at a time until we reached the dimly-lit second floor. Only two floors to this place and no ferals in sight, my lucky day!

Finding the blueprints was the harder part. After telling Miranda what to look for, I checked each row of files on one side of the room and Miranda took the other. The place was nothing but file cabinets, rows and rows of them. I finally found the right area, but it was still tedious work, balancing a flashlight in my hand as I ran my fingers through each stack. Over and over I flipped through papers until my fingers were growing dried and sore with tiny paper cuts from the thousands of dusty files. I was thankful to not have to worry about any ferals jumping out at me; the place was abandoned. The short rays of sunshine were a welcome break in the wavering darkness.

Dropping the flashlight when I finally found the right file, I almost squealed with joy. "I found it Mir.!" I grabbed the thick rolls of blueprint after blueprint, glad they had them available and not lost on some microfiche film or scanned to a computer, which were almost impossible to view now. I guess it paid to keep paperwork. Things had reverted to the old ways, especially now that technology had failed us in more ways than one.

Miranda approached, grabbing one thick roll of blueprints from my arms. "Way to go, April. I'm glad you did."

After loading the blueprints into a large duffle bag Miranda had retrieved from my car, I dropped them into the back seat and studied the red and orange building that stared solemnly back at us. It was pretty enough, but now it stood like a lonesome soul, neglected and left to the forces of nature. No one would ever work here again. No one would sift through the cabinets full of files and knowledge, all about Las Vegas. It would stand for a while, maybe longer than some other buildings. I had made sure to lock it up tight. I didn't know when it would be needed again. If anything, at least there was one person left who even cared.

Maybe I was the only person left to care. Any which way, I was about to find out.

Chapter Twelve
Urban Decay

Elijah

THE WORST WAS over now. The debriefing had been, thankfully, brief. Nothing new. Just business as usual aboveground. Katrina had listened quietly as Elijah told her about wrangling up the Zompires and torching them with daylight. Her bright blue orbs stabbing into each of the Twelve as whatever ran through her head passed behind her eyes. No big deal, right? She never said a word all through it until she nonchalantly dismissed them with a languid wave of her hand, as though shooing away an annoying child. Not even a pat on the back for a job well done or anything. Nothing but her emotionless, cold shoulder. Her face was as blank as a slate. That was all one could ask for from that crazy old bat, Katrina. Anything more would not be desirable.

Settling in for the evening, Elijah was relieved to discover that they wouldn't be sent out again for another round of exterminations. He relaxed, happy that she had not seen through him and discovered his secret about April. Katrina would never know about her. It would endanger them all. April was his secret to keep for now, and it gave him a feeling of power to know this.

Elijah sighed, frustrated to find out why Katrina wanted all the Zompires killed. They only came out at night and lived in shadows during the long, hot days. They never came down far enough to breach Vida's city boundaries in the underground. Hardly a threat, really. He avoided them easily above ground, so what was she getting at? What was her ulterior motive to this particular mission?

He scratched at the growing stubble along his jaw. Katrina's motives were never quite clear. Most times he didn't care, but this had malice written all over it. His fingers smoothed down his beard; he needed to shave but had not made it a priority. More importantly, he needed to sleep for a good solid night. He was exhausted and tired of the drama that she usually pulled on him and his group. The searing stares, studying them like organisms and drawing their blood in endless rounds of testing got old fast. He didn't know what she was looking for or why. For all he knew, they were guinea pigs in a sick experiment ran by her.

So what if the twelve of them had superhuman strength and speed? They weren't vampires. They did not crave blood like the Zompires. But they weren't human either, that much was obvious. What they were was something in the middle, the limbo of the aftereffects of the epidemic. Whatever it was, he regretted nothing. He rather liked being superhuman. It made him special in a way that he'd never been before it had all gone down the crap hole.

What did that make April? It was curious that the young teenager had fought with him easily. He wondered briefly about her abnormal strength. Could she be one of them, too? He shook his head; he doubted it. She was just hyped up on adrenaline when he had twisted her arms behind her back. Still, she had been pretty fierce and determined to break free. It would definitely be better if she wasn't like them. Yet there was something different, but he couldn't figure it out, so he pushed it from his thoughts.

Maybe that bat shit crazy woman Katrina will exterminate us next, when all the Zompires are gone.

It definitely had crossed his mind many a time. He wouldn't put it beyond her. She was capable of ordering a lynch mob to shoot the twelve to death at any moment. But Elijah was going to be ready, watching and waiting to make sure it didn't happen. The closer they got to exterminating all of the dead from the city, the closer he'd be to getting rid of her suffocating presence. He looked forward to sticking a knife in her throat.

"Hey, Elijah, checking out for the night? We're going to play some pool for a while in the rec side of the room. Want to join?" A redheaded Sarah sat down next to him, flipping her long luscious mane in a flirtatious fashion as she waited for his response. She pointed toward some of the other twelve warriors busy playing the game. They waved back to her from across the room, which she returned with a prize-winning smile. Her black cargo pants fitted snugly over her slender curves, and her black tank top did the same for her torso. Elijah noticed it, but shifted his eyes away to his plate. She was a couple of years younger than him, but he felt worlds apart from her lively demeanor. He tore off a piece of the dried-out pizza he'd chosen for dinner as he gave her a shake of his head.

"Nope, not tonight, Scarlet." He winked at her as he said the playful nickname he had for his second in command. The twelve had their own system of ranks that Katrina was not privy to. It gave him some satisfaction that she didn't know everything that happened under their roof. What she didn't know gave them strength.

"Oh come on, you never join us anymore," Sarah pouted, picking on one of her pink polished nails while intermittently glancing at him. She was pretty girly and attempted to keep her fashion sense in every little detail. From her polished, smooth hair to her multicolored toenails and milky soft skin, she kept up her beauty regimen even after the apocalypse. She was barely eighteen and had been a model in her past life, just a year and a half ago. He knew she felt robbed of the famed career that could have been hers. What her life had been like before was definitely not comparable to what it was now. Life was pretty screwed up that way. Now, she got to gunk up her pretty manicured hands with soot, blood, and zompire decay.

"Sorry, I got to catch some zzz's. Haven't had much lately." He winked at her and polished off his meal. It should have bothered him that he didn't know much about her, besides the fact that her father had dragged her to the Wynn, knowing there was a shelter under it. He had been one of the lead security officers there and had brought his only daughter with him for safety before the doors closed to Vida. He had died not long after, a victim of the fatal version of the virus, leaving her all alone, transformed into the superhuman that she was now. But it didn't bother Elijah, if fact, the less he knew about everyone around him, the easier it would be to let them go.

Even so, Sarah had become his right hand woman. She was strong headed, stubborn and driven. He still felt a twinge of sympathy for her. *We're all orphans here*, he thought. But she was tough and he knew she'd be fine, with or without his empathy. Instead of bedding her and taking her for his own, he'd let her run the group as she wanted and never engaged in anything other than a platonic relationship with her. It wasn't what she wanted, and he knew that.

It was all rather depressing, the past, the future. It was all so bleak. He didn't want to think too long about it, so he hopped up and gave her a wave before depositing his garbage in the receptacles. Did he feel guilty knowing her eyes would be on him until he was out of sight as he exited the room? Did he even care that their less than perfect relationship was completely one-sided? No, he didn't care. He didn't have any feelings whatsoever for Sarah. It was like staring at a relative, a sister. Nothing made him feel anything anymore. All he felt was numb, empty and dead inside. He didn't know if he'd ever be capable of any kind of feelings for anyone else again. That's what concerned him the most.

Shuffling down past the stark, white halls to his quarters, he pondered on that. Since losing his entire family to the epidemic and putting them down, he had felt nothing. No feelings except maybe resentment. To fall in love would be impossible—or so he thought. He suspected that it had something to do with his superhuman powers. Maybe it had robbed him of the ability to love. He had seen a few of his twelve pair up as couples, but it wasn't for him. He hadn't seen any of the others in a different light. Not even Sarah, who was one of the only ones also not paired off. Sarah wanted more though, which he had noticed. He could see it in her gaze, in the way her hips swayed as she walked away from him. He wasn't blind, and he did like her. He just wasn't interested right now.

Heading through the door to his quarters, he slumped onto his bed and sighed, feeling the aches and pains of the day's work gnawing at him. He wasn't sleeping well, not since he had seen the April in his apartment at the Palms Hotel. Who was she? Where was she now? Wasn't everyone dead aboveground? If so, why was there a perfectly non-dead girl constantly lurking around the Palms, hoping to get a glimpse of him again? It didn't make sense.

He wanted to find her again, ask her questions and see if she really might be like him, a superhuman. But he had blown it. In his panic, he had threatened her with her life if she ever disturbed him again. He wanted to smack himself for being so shortsighted. If it was remotely possible she was a hybrid human like him and the other eleven here, she would need them sooner or later. Surviving in the outside world alone was not a life for anyone. But neither was imprisonment in the underground city of Vida.

He rolled over in bed, still baffled by April. How had she survived the nightly rampages of crazed, zombified vampires? No, there had to be some reasonable explanation for her survival. Maybe there was another human habitat nearby. Maybe. Regardless of the reason, he was going to find out. He would rest first, then seek out the girl in the dead city above to ask her those very questions.

Elijah relaxed in the room's silence. Nothing but the hum of the air conditioner filled the emptiness that hovered over him so many nights. He couldn't think about the thousands of pounds of dirt above his head. He tried not to think about the hungry, crazed mouths that snapped their jaws at him every time he ascended into the city. Their deteriorating and rotting faces were emblazoned in his mind for all of eternity, never to be forgotten. How could he forget? The epidemic had taken everything with it. All his family, all his friends, all gone in no time at all. He'd put many of them down himself and had waited impatiently for the virus to come and consume him, too. When that didn't happen and the change did not come, he'd been left confused, riddled with despair and regret.

The only reason he was even here and alive in this underground prison sanctuary was because he had been working as an usher for a show at the

Wynn. He had passed by the casino in the middle of the chaos in the hopes of grabbing any familiar faces before fleeing the city forever. Instead, he had found his former boss waving him down and begging him to follow. The executives had a safe place for those who were uninfected.

Curious, he had filed in behind everyone else, walking down long corridors and halls with endless twists and turns. He had been in awe that the electricity still worked down there, where the air was so cold and the smell of paint and cement clung to the walls and pipes. All the way down through specially built tunnels, stairs and reinforced door after door, he had finally found himself in the underground city of Vida. It was breathtaking how big it was. Stores and stores of food and necessities in warehouse-like room after room, each filled to the ceiling. Large greenhouses with artificial lights surrounded the main eating area, making it seem as though they were just a stone's throw away from the natural greenery of the outside world.

Yet it was a desert and death outside, and the artificial emerald green of the vegetation being raised and cared for here looked false and out of place to him. He was used to the sand, dirt, rocks and desert shrubs surrounding Las Vegas.

It wasn't until the doors were locked behind them—once everyone was processed, pictures taken, names recorded and blood tests taken to ensure that no one was infected—that he had realize he was trapped. No one could leave. No one else was let in. The infected were taken elsewhere, where they were probably exterminated right before they turned. It was something he had never dug into too deeply.

This sanctuary was vast, but not vast enough to keep him from feeling the suffocating panic that had settled into his chest and made him make a mad dash back the way he had come, only to find the doors sealed and guarded with armed men dressed in black uniforms and machine guns aimed at his heart. He had backed away, knowing he was weaponless himself and in no position to take down the armed men. Memorizing every exit, hallway and tunnel in the place, he knew he'd escape one day, somehow. He had to. This was no way to live. It was a tomb, a fortified suspension of life.

When the time had come to do Katrina's bidding outside the underground, he had earned her trust and had made his worth obvious as a leader, a warrior, a fighter. It had been a blessing in its own right. The time spent down below, trapped in the unrelenting underground, had taken its toll on him. Agoraphobia seemed to have taken hold of everyone and no one dared wander too far from the boundaries of Vida. Not even Elijah. The furthest he had made it was the Palms Casino, where he had taken up residence when he could. He had the chance to run now, but had never taken the first step to do so. What had kept him there, so frozen, so afraid?

Chapter Thirteen
Down the Rabbit Hole

April

NOW, TO SNEAK away to the underground. But how to
accomplish such a feat? That's what I wanted to know. Rye wasn't making
it easy. He appeared suspicious every time I headed near the door or
attempted to leave the vampire hive without him or Miranda. Was he on to
me already? Probably so, since I had hastily dropped Jeremy off with him
and had left without inviting him out whenever I went map hunting with
Miranda and a few times before and after that. I suspected that he had
interrogated her about our activities that day, but she was true to her word
and had said nothing.

I hated leaving him in the dark about it all, but I couldn't let him ruin
my plans to check out the underground city before I even got there. No. I
would put up with him as long as I had to and get down there. I would get
to the bottom of this rumor. But I had to do it without him holding me
back. So he remained in the dark about it.

For now, I waited. I waited as the days went by painstakingly slow,
waiting for the right moment. I dropped by the hive almost every day, and
every day Rye was there, waiting for me and making sure he knew
everywhere I went. I had to find a way to sneak away. I hated leaving
Jeremy at home with my mother, who remained locked up in the storage

room. But it was looking like I was going to have to do that to get enough time to investigate the casino.

So that's what I did. I invited Miranda to come stay with Jeremy for me while Helen remained locked up. For once I felt hope, the promise of something more in the heart of the city of Las Vegas.

I WATCHED JEREMY wave to me from the entrance of the bunker before he ducked back inside with Miranda and locked the door. Gripping the steering wheel tightly, I sat for a moment, twisting my hands around the rippled plastic, feeling the sweat building up on my palms. I could do this, right? I rarely felt so much doubt. I had to do this. I needed to. It felt like a compulsion so deep within to follow the road to the underground city to find the other humans.

Yet here I was, frozen in the driver's seat of my Jeep, waiting for a push from some outside force to make me go. A push that would never come. I was still surprised that Miranda had not offered to go with me. She had given me a knowing look when I had left, telling her I needed to blow off steam and go for a nice scavenging through the city by myself. She never probed further, letting me go without even a word of warning. It was easy with her. She knew I didn't want to elaborate and left it at that.

I let out my breath slowly, giving myself a pep talk and willing my foot to press on the gas. The car moved out slowly, as if it knew what to do by itself. I accelerated down the road and onto the highway, relieved that I was moving. *The first step is the hardest*, I thought as the asphalt sped by faster and faster. I was determined, and I knew that it was not going to be easy.

There were miles, literally miles of tunnels under the Wynn, under Las Vegas, actually. I couldn't tell exactly where they all ended up, but I suspected that at the end of one of them was a door that led farther and deeper into the ground. I was hoping there were not going to be too many feral vampires lurking about, especially since I was calculating that the human clan had probably already cleared them out of that particular casino. Still, every night was an invitation to the ferals to come inside and have a look around. New real estate. Maybe even the scent of human blood lured them in, who knew?

I gulped, hoping the humans were not aggressive. What if they were? They could kill me on site if they really wanted to. Then my brother and mother would be none the wiser of my fate, would they? *Whatever happened to April?* Who knows? For once I was more afraid of the unknown than the feral vampires themselves.

I shook the morbid thoughts from my head. It was grinding on my nerves, which I definitely didn't need, especially at this moment, when my doubt was at its greatest. My drive to the Wynn had gone quickly. I was almost dreading reaching the doors. I pulled into the garage where there was an entrance near the underground labyrinth that would soon be my mission to explore. It was relatively deserted, except for some stray cars and litter scattered into the corners of the concrete walls, propelled there by the rough winds of springtime. If any city should be called windy city, it should have been Vegas. It was never-ending here. Always kicking up dust and debris all over the place, flaring up my allergies. It was relentless. It was one reason I had wanted to leave this God-forsaken town after I turned eighteen.

It sure didn't look like I was ever going to be able to leave now. Where would I even go? Would it be any different from this ghost-town of a wasteland? It was highly doubtful.

Parking the car, I glanced around, watching for movement from the garage and the building itself. The windows of the hotel were one-way mirrors, reflecting back the multitude of floors of the garage. I strapped on the loose weapons I had brought on the passenger side of my car. Flashlights strewn across my chest along with a bandoleer of knives, which sat snug across my shirt. I chose two short katanas, easy to carry for they joined together into a short staff. I was hoping it would be enough to deal with ferals and humans alike. It was small enough to carry, but long enough to cause some serious damage further than an arm's reach. I secured them and then slipped on a flashlight headband to light my way and keep my hands free, smoothing back my hair under it. My long, black tresses were in a tight, low ponytail today. I thought I looked like a Christmas tree. But it was all in the name of vision.

I hoped I wasn't as noticeable to the humans with the lights. At least I had a quick shut off button in case I heard anyone. Slipping a loop of thin rope onto a clasp on my belt, I closed the door and stared at the double doors down a cement bridge that connected the garage to the building. I hoped the building was not rigged with traps. That would majorly suck.

It's now or never, I thought.

I puffed out my breath, rounding my cheeks like a chipmunk as I tried to control it. Who knew what was in there? Whatever it was, I was about to find out. I headed to the doors and peeked at their exterior. They looked undisturbed, and I prayed they were unlocked. A slow shove on the thick, tinted glass responded with a slight whoosh as the doors swung open and my intrusion sucked the air in like a vacuum. It was air tight and smelled of mustiness and old things. I took one last breath of the fresh breeze outside and slipped into the dusty darkness.

It was slow going, even though I had memorized the map. It had been difficult to read, being that it included all sorts of information on pipes and walls that looked all so unfamiliar to me. I was not an architect, and it had cost me. I had resorted to hand drawing myself a map of the labyrinth below after familiarizing myself with the ground-floor layout of the casino. I reached the stairs rather quickly and descended down into the main floor, keeping my ears on alert for any noise.

Dust floated across my beams of light, clogging up the rays and making the visibility short. I cursed as I made my way along the walls, dodging upturned chairs and garbage littering the dirty carpet. It looked like some flood waters had made it into this area; the floor felt gritty and was caked with drying mud. For the most part, it had dried in scattered puddles, leaving the floor incredibly messy but undisturbed. That meant no ferals had treaded on this mud at all. I took it as a good sign but did not let up my guard.

It didn't take too long before I made it past two dealer pits and dozens of slot machines and began to notice the familiar raunchy odor that had permeated my nostrils many times. I readied my katanas, hoping to find the lurking ferals before they found me. I snorted, knowing full well I was lit up like the apple in Times Square, a perfect shining beacon to pinpoint my spot.

Before long, I could hear it coming. One scrawny straggler, inching its way toward me like a tiger focused on prey. I must have looked incredibly savory, for it ignored the beaming lights blinding its searing red eyes and headed right toward me. For a half-starved beast, it was incredibly fast, its body looking bony and malnourished. A growl snarled through its withered lips, exposing rotting teeth and fangs. I took a quick step back before arching my sword right across its neck, sending its head tumbling and spraying ink-black blood across the cracked, muddy floor. Its body was left to twitch its last moments away near my feet. I dodged the puddle it had created near me and crept farther down the walls of the silent casino.

One down, how many more to go?

Another rounded the corner and stumbled toward me. This one was also withered but not as badly as the first one. Its wild red eyes glared hungrily, wanting nothing more than to rip into me. Its lips curled back, fangs glinting in the light of my flashlights. I let it scurry toward me before swiping one of the katanas across its body, watching as it sliced through easily, sending a spray of blood straight up and out, smacking into the roof and leaving a dripping splatter above me. It tumbled to the floor but continued to creep along the floor with its legs and one good arm. It reached out to me, fingers desperately curling in and out to grasp my clothes. I chopped the arm off and swung my sword one more time to decapitate the creature. I dodged the drips and was already past the body as it finally stopped writhing on the filthy carpet.

That was easy enough.

The trek through the darkness wasn't as nerve-wracking as I would've thought. I'd done this too many times to feel the fear penetrate any longer. It was still there though, checked into a hidden crevice in my mind and ready to pounce out if needed. But it was no longer my master, and I was no longer a slave to it. It wasn't the vampires that scared me; there were much more frightening things lurking in the darkness. Like humans. I hoped I could get in and out as fast as possible, only observing what I would find. If they were friendly, so be it. If not, well, I would deal with that as it came.

My patience was running low as I crept further into the building. It was slow going with debris and overturned furniture in my way. The stale air felt thick and made my throat itchy. Breathing in the toxic fumes of mold was going to take a toll on my allergies. I was glad I kept my prior regimen of taking my daily preventative meds going. The bottles were available in the old warehouse stores by the hundreds. I doubted I'd run out before they all expired. I never thought about what I would do when the effects no longer worked and the medications dried up from time. Any which way, the future would come. No matter what happened—or didn't happen—it was there, looming over my head.

It's not that I didn't look forward to the future. Who knows? Maybe it won't be as bleak as it seems it will be. I didn't know any of this would happen. I didn't know the world would die so fast outside my windows, withering in screams and blood. I could only hold out to find a future somewhere that resembled anything normal. Maybe that was the main reason I was down here. I was left wanting the normal, craving it like an insatiable disease eating at my insides. A normal where Jeremy could be a child, not some jaded kid raised on killing and scavenging like an animal. Most of all, I wanted him to have a life where he would have others besides me, especially when I am gone. Others to keep him safe and sound.

So I kept on, keeping my steps light on the ground. It was a relief to arrive at the double doors that led to the underground corridors. The great metal doors creaked in the silence, filling it with a pitch that made my hair stand on end. I cringed, hoping it would not attract any unwanted attention. I leaned on the door, letting my weight hold it as it slowly came to a close. The affirmative click made me sigh in relief. It was another barrier to attack from the ferals. I didn't really expect many down in these hallways—only those who had lingered in the dark from the beginning would be found here—but I highly doubted anyone would have wanted to remain here during the outbreak. I would be surprised to find anyone here.

Stepping on the smooth concrete slabs under my feet, I kept a constant vigil back and forth, ahead and behind me. My shoes left pressed imprints in the untouched dust that stuck to everything. Cobwebs dangled above and moved delicately like moth-eaten curtains as I passed. Certainly no wind had touched them since the breakdown of civilization. I hoped my disturbance was not tragic to the tiny critters left to stare at me as I passed. I welcomed them in this darkness; their tiny, unseen eyes were surely fixed on me. I shuddered for a moment before I assured myself that only humans had been affected by the virus. Thank goodness. Who knows what it could have done to animals. So far, none were infected that I had seen.

A distant shuffling echoed down across the walls, making me stiffen. I listened to it as it faded. I prayed I had just heard myself brush against a wall, but there it was again. Something dragged, like a broken foot pulled along as the other limped on as best it could. I immediately knew it wasn't human and gripped the hilts of my swords. I was ready for it, almost eager.

I turned the corner to find just what I wanted to find: a feral, its withered body barely able to move in the darkness. It paused, a single shiny red eye finding the illumination of my flashlights too bright, making it wince. Where the other eye should have been hung an empty socket. Pus and fluid dripped down its cheek and its flesh was rotting to the point of falling off its bones. Too hungry or too weak to care, it continued to shuffle toward me, a low guttural moan barely registering in its throat. It was so weak, I almost kept walking past it, but a quick swing of my sword and it was down forever, dark, inky blood oozing from its severed neck, spilling into an impenetrable black stain on the grey floor.

I stepped over its bag of bones body. It had been weakened and slow for so long, cobwebs had taken up residence on its shredded clothes. I felt narrowly disappointed. Where was the fight? I could feel my blood burning inside my veins for more than this. It was pitiful. I was used to the vicious feral fights with snapping jaws and scratching nails trying as they must to rip my flesh away. Not this. Not this lack of strength and an odd feral vampire or two to get in my way. Where were they all?

I sighed, remembering that this place had probably been cleaned out long ago by the humans. Not only that, their nightly cattle calls with the ferals were taking their toll on the population of the wild vampires. It was definitely noticeable now, especially here on The Strip. I wondered if the humans really wanted to hide anymore. This kind of extermination would not go unnoticed by others. Didn't they know that? Their genocide was going to attract a lot more than just feral vampires.

At this I gave a short haughty laugh. *Yep, attract other unsavory beings—like me.* Was I not here now, lurking in shadows and eager to infiltrate their solace? I was definitely going to find them, no matter what. I wondered if anyone else ever had similar ideas. If so, they hadn't come this way from the look of the dust and mess around me. I wondered if Elijah would have done the same as I was doing if he had discovered them too. Maybe.

How many entrances were there to the underground? It hadn't occurred to me before that there could be many of them. I gulped, hoping that I was the only one sneaking in at this very moment.

Finding the door which led even further into this labyrinth, I shoved through it to find a set of stairs leading down and down. Peeking around, I saw that it only led the one way. There was no staircase up. It had to be a private entrance of some sort. I shut the door behind me and crept slowly in to glance over the rails. The stairs spiraled down on and on, disappearing into darkness—I couldn't see the bottom. There had been no electricity so far, making me think that the underground city was sealed and self-contained in every way somehow. I hoped to find some utility lines to lead me in.

I took to the steps as stealthily as I could, wincing at every creak or shift in the metal. Most of the steps were concrete, but the inlaid metal was the noise maker. I sweated all the way down, the air becoming more and more stifling. It was like smoking a cigarette of dust, and I suppressed the need to cough as well as I could. My eyes burned and watered, streaming tears down my face as I descended farther into the dark. This place was like a tomb, and I hoped it would not be my last resting place.

Chapter Fourteen
Catch Me If You Can

Elijah

SLEEP EVADED HIM, always, like chasing feathers in the breeze, it was endlessly unattainable. Elijah sat on the untouched mattress, not wanting to stare for long hours at the unchanging roof tiles. He hated nights when there were no tasks to complete and he was left to dwell in his thoughts throughout the silent hours. It made him restless to linger with the ghosts of the past, the things that were never going to be the way they were supposed to be, no matter what he would have wanted.

Running his fingers through his messed-up locks, he let out a breath. He had wanted to do so many things in his life, and it was all gone now. Sailing the Pacific, traveling to every major city of the world, becoming a successful director—those things were no longer possible. They would never happen now. No matter how much he tried to devise a way he could still accomplish some of his hopes and aspirations, it all had ended with the outbreak, filling the world with demise and death. Would there be anything left of the other side of the world to see if he was even able to get there? He doubted it. He was pretty sure devastation like the kind that had occurred in Las Vegas was worldwide. Nothing would have held it in one place. It'd been an extinction sort of event.

Elijah slipped his shoes on and pulled on a plain black shirt. He had left his jeans on when he'd laid down, so he was pretty much dressed.

Wandering the hallways at night was a solace. Even with the dimmed lights, the white of the walls greyed out enough to seem more comforting than stark. He padded down the corridors, touching the smooth, painted cement blocks that composed most of the walls down here. It was pretty tough, but cold and unwelcoming. Still, he guessed warm and comforting was not in the building's blueprint plans when they had built this place.

He ducked into the control room where her highness Katrina usually sat during the daytime. Right now, without her suppressive presence, it was a sanctuary of sorts. All the cameras were doing their timed-out dance, flashing different scenes of the city across their screens. Some workers were still busy shuffling about their chores and running machines that required 24/7 operation. The wall of monitors had a sedative effect on him. He could breathe and watch the world pass him by. It made the compound feel bigger than it was.

Elijah gave a curt nod to one of the security techs who sat tweaking some camera angles. They knew his routine and left him to his own devices. He hovered over the switches, clicking them, looking for anything interesting or out of the ordinary. Usually there was nothing. Usually the monotony of flipping through each quadrant would wear him out enough to the point where he'd be able get some rest back in his room. He didn't expect anything out of the ordinary tonight.

He shouldn't have been so easily settled into his routine. He almost didn't notice when one screen flashed something unusual: a woman crept by, not quite noticing the camera until a second too late, just before she returned to the shadows. If Elijah had not been so intent on scanning the different scenes, he would have missed the flash of her presence, a presence that sent his heart jumping. It was her, the girl April, who had followed him into his sanctuary at the Palms and stalked around his apartment. It was the one who had haunted his thoughts since that fateful day.

Her dark straight hair was tied back against the nape of her neck. She had flashlights, small and square strapped across her chest and one on her head with a band holding it in place. She had already shut them off and was making her way by the bit of light filtering into the outer hallways of the compound. She had reached a side entrance that was rarely used. He wondered if she would figure out how easily she could slip in, just hot wire the door and she'd be home free.

He grinned, watching her furrow her brows at the simple contraption. They had figured Zompires would not be able to get it together enough to figure out a simple door lock. He almost laughed, thinking about how Katrina had never put into the equation that there would be other humans out there who would want to sneak in. She had written off all of humanity just like that. Her error had been a big one, one he'd hope would secure her downfall soon enough.

The woman, or girl—he wasn't quite sure for he hadn't asked her what her age was, though it seemed pretty certain that she was in her late teens, maybe early twenties—made her way in easily. She slipped quietly into the rear of one of the main greenhouses. It was lit up in there like twilight all night long with the full spectrum of light slowly growing as daybreak came. It was sufficient to see a lot of the floor, though the foliage and abundance of greenery would be sufficient to hide her for a while. Elijah knew she had figured this out and was now weaving her way through jagged rows of saplings, fruit and eucalyptus trees. Her black clothing hid her enough that no one noticed the svelte woman dodging people, sticking to the shadows and snapping quick, concise pictures of everything she saw.

She's studying us.

Elijah shook his head, amused by this revelation. Of all things, this human was studying other humans! Ha! But what for? What did she want to do with those pictures? Why didn't she just waltz right up to the door and introduce herself? She was definitely human and might have been welcomed.

Or maybe not. He frowned. Katrina was volatile and could decide she was a threat to the city instead. And what if she was a hybrid human? Could she be?

He craned his neck. Trying to keep up with her on the cameras was becoming difficult. She moved stealthily, quick and silent. Few humans had these qualities. She was an expert in her movements for being so young, well versed and definitely fit. Yet her route was not concise or straight, as though she didn't know exactly where she was going. Maybe she didn't, maybe she was just exploring. Either way, if Katrina saw that he was watching her instead of arresting her, he might be in heap of trouble. He wished he could go out there, grab her and disappear, and talk with her for just a bit. If only he hadn't run her off so quickly—he'd been too worried that she would find out about Vida. She had anyway, so chasing her off had been useless on his part.

Maybe she could tell him more about the world outside, how she had survived and if she was alone out there or not. Something told him that she had been out there all this time, surviving and living off of the shattered land. It was wondrous. He longed to know her, to hear her voice tell him stories of what she'd seen, of what had happened in her life so late into the nights when the dead roamed the streets and searched for her life blood. The way she moved like a stealthy cat, quietly and smoothly, made him want to stop her in her tracks and ask her a thousand questions, if not kiss her.

"What are you doing?" Katrina's abrasive voice behind him made Elijah stiffen. He turned slowly, inconspicuously clicking the monitor to another camera, far from the woman.

"Why, hello, Katrina. Can't sleep either, huh? I was just doing some late night work to sharpen my mind."

"Oh, cut the crap. What are you doing in *here*?" Her face looked puffy, as though she had rolled out of bed, run a brush through her loose, wavy hair and come straight to the control room. Could it be she was seeking him out? He wanted to snicker and say such out loud, but he pressed his lips tight before he could say a torrent of things he'd regret. She was irritated as it was, maybe from not finding him in his room.

"I can't sleep. Like I said. What's your excuse?" He turned back to the monitors, and flicked his eyes across them all, crossing his fingers and hoping April didn't appear on another camera while Katrina was here. It would not be good, not good at all.

"*Hmm*. I didn't think you liked camera duty that much." She came to lean on the console facing him as she crossed her arms. She looked different with her dark hair lying softly over her shoulders. Without makeup smeared across her face, she looked younger, fresher, he thought. He wasn't sure, but his aversion to her remained. Maybe it was his heightened hybrid human senses, but this woman was not right in the head. She sent a chill down his spine with just a look. He wondered how much sanity remained intact inside that skull of hers and what exactly made his skin crawl about her.

"Not much, but it's boring enough at night to help lull me to sleep." Elijah gave her a genuine smile, hoping she would just leave. Instead she sighed, turning to face the monitors and narrowing her beady eyes toward them.

Great.

"I feel the same way. Nothing like boring chores to entice the sleep to come." She reached out and clicked through cameras, viewing the different sections of Vida as though she was looking for something.

Come on…get on with it. Leave, he silently urged her.

Not finding anything of interest, she frowned, the lines around her lips betraying her age. Katrina was not that old, but her unsavory habit of smoking had done a number to add some wrinkles to her otherwise flawless face, making her look like she was in her late thirties, not thirty-three. She was older than Elijah by twelve years, but he often wondered if she had a thing for him. She made it no secret that she favored him out of the twelve, though for what reason other than his looks, he had no idea. He gave her no cause for thinking otherwise. He'd rather die than go there.

"Very well, I'll leave you to it, then. I think I'll have some warm milk and head to bed. Don't be up too late, tomorrow is a busy day." She gave him a warm smile, but he just averted his gaze. Finding this unsatisfactory, she was about to turn and walk away when she froze in her steps, her eyes widening in shock as she stared at the camera monitors.

"Did you see that?"

He sat up and did his best to act dumbfounded. "See what, Katrina?"

She rushed to the console, clicking the buttons rapidly until the screen flashed to the end of the secondary greenhouses that led to the main market of the city. Darkened and dim, it was abandoned at this time of night, but a sole silhouette of shadow gracefully walked across the camera, sending his blood running cold.

There she was, April, sneaking through the makeshift streets of their market. Elijah paled at Katrina's discovery, knowing he would be meeting this girl again in a whole different way than he'd planned.

"Notify security, get down there and detain her. She's not one of us," she hissed, pointing him out the door before he could even protest. He grabbed a radio and bolted out of there before she suspected anything, calling out to the security that roamed the halls at all hours to meet him in the market.

Damn!

Elijah broke out into a run to get to April before anyone else could. He sprinted down the staircase leading down the side of the large warehouse area that housed the greenhouses, taking them three at a time. His heart burned in his chest, making him determined to find her first. He knew the others were nowhere near that area, so it bought him a few minutes before they would come running. He wanted to be the first to lay eyes on her. He had to reach her before anyone else did, it was vital.

Pummeling through the last set of double doors, he slowed down, knowing that she was armed and probably ready to slice his head off if need be. He readied himself. He'd forgotten to get any weapons since he was off duty, but he was sure he could overtake her. Yet, he wasn't completely positive. It had just occurred to him that she might be highly trained. Maybe she would find him first and finish him off before he had any time to think. He hoped not. But she had seemed pretty strong back at the apartment. He wanted to ask her so many things.

He stopped as he neared the rear of the market, the rhythm of his frantic heartbeat booming in his ears, making it difficult to hear. No alarm had been raised besides via the radios that the security guards carried, to make sure she didn't sprint off and get away. She was, in essence, trapped. With few exits from the market to the outside world, she would not get away that easily. In a way, Elijah wanted to catch her and interrogate her. But he knew Katrina would not allow him to do that. She would throw her into quarantine up in the prison cells before even speaking to her. He shook the thought away as he came up behind where she was last seen, knowing she should still be in this area, somewhere close.

She was silent, this one.

He craned his neck to capture any slip she might make, straining to hear movements in the dark. His eyesight was pretty good at night, but not nearly as perfect as it was in the daytime. He hated how they dimmed the place to simulate nighttime. It was more for the comfort of the people than for anything else. It seemed useless since the sleeping quarters could be dimmed by each individual anyway. What was the point in that? He had no idea, but who was he to second guess Katrina's motivations?

There it was: a brief sigh, like a breeze in the still air of the city. Elijah catapulted from his position to where she was, just around the corner from him. Reaching the end of the storefront of one of the many small shops lining the makeshift street market, he paused once more, knowing she would be waiting for him around the corner. He hoped he had made it there unheard. If not, he was about to find out.

Slipping around the corner, he felt a sharp prick on his collarbone, causing him to freeze and suck a breath in. He hadn't been stealthy enough, obviously. April had been a lot quicker than he had given her credit for.

"*You.*" She hissed, a knowing glare staring back at him. "Why are you following me?" Her voice was liquid, smooth and soft as it echoed in the alley between the stores. She stood brazen, tall but not reaching his height, with ink black hair tied in a ponytail. Her shiny blue eyes captured what little light emanated from the street lamps. He held his hands up, radio still grasped in his palm, hoping to get her to stand down. Her jawline was well defined but feminine, along with the rest of her. In all black, she looked a lot thinner, but he would not call her a skeleton. This close to her, she didn't look a day older than seventeen.

"I live here. They're coming for you, and I suggest you do what they say," Elijah whispered back. If he could be the one to subdue her, she might stand a chance of not getting killed. His eyes scanned the length of the short katana she was using to pin him down. Another was gripped tightly in her other hand. He felt pretty sure she could use them proficiently and could very well hack him up into tiny pieces if she so desired. Her fierceness was intriguing, but he had to get control of her now, before all hell broke loose. "Put the weapons down. I'm not going to hurt you."

She huffed, pushing the razor edge of the sword harder into his skin. A warm fluid seeped from where it made contact, soaking his shirt, but his gaze did not waver from hers. He was hoping his reluctance would make her nervous, and as the moments ticked by, he could see it working as her hand began to quiver. He guessed that she would run when the others arrived. He hoped not. Instead, catching the slight hesitation in her stance, he reached up, pulling her arm along with the sword forward and caught her other arm before she could stab him.

He didn't expect a fight, but she had other plans.

Stars splayed across his vision as she cracked her skull against his, sending him stumbling back and forcing him to let her go. She helped him along with a good shove from her foot. He caught himself on the edge of a windowsill and hurtled his weight forward as she turned to run. He grabbed at her legs, and they landed hard on the floor, her grip on the dual swords loosening, sending them flying across the smooth cement.

Her attempts to kick him off were useless but annoying. Her boots scraped at his chest as she tugged and pulled, jerking her knees up and down. Her skin was smooth under his grip; only streaks of dirt and dust marred it and her clothes. She must have been bathing in the dust up above to look this filthy. He pulled himself up, locked her legs under his and grabbed her forearms to pin them down. He was definitely grunting from the effort to hold this wild one down. She was no sedentary thing. She worked out and it showed. Sweat gleamed on both their faces as he glared down at her.

"Enough!" he hissed, hoping the tone of his voice would make her stop. Instead, she flashed him a narrow, evil glare before continuing to buck her hips, hoping to dislodge his grip. It was exhausting for both of them, but more so for her than him. Eventually, his weight wore her out and her chest heaved to catch her breath.

"That's better." Elijah attempted to ease up on her arms but she squirmed immediately, bringing him right back to pinning her down. He shook his head but grinned down at her, grateful for the challenge. Not much kept his attention down here, but this woman was feisty and definitely worth his attention.

"What are you doing down here?" he asked, studying her luminous eyes, watching her hate toward him deepen. This was not the feeling he had wanted to induce, but he hoped to atone for it later. "How did you find out about this place?"

"Get off me, *Elijah*," she hissed. A low growl flickered into her words, which made him smile even wider. At least she remembered his name. He was getting a kick out of it until he caught scent of her blood, now seeping from her cherry red lips. Tilting his head, he watched it drip down her chin, mesmerized as it dropped into a perfect circle on the concrete. It wasn't so much the color or the consistency of it, but the smell that made his eyes widen in surprise. Her entire scent was off. She smelled too familiar, like the others—like him. Not quite human.

"What are you?" he whispered urgently as he heard footsteps approaching, echoing off the walls. He had smelled this scent before, and there were only a dozen people who claimed the same affliction. "You— you're not all human, are you?" The stricken look on her face made her anger fade and the fight temporarily subside. They were both shocked, even as the other security guards grabbed her by her arms and pulled her up. He let her go, a knowing knot forming in him chest. There was only one explanation: she was also a hybrid human, just like him.

Watching as the other guards relieved her of her weapons, Elijah stood frozen in his steps, ignoring the continued drip of crimson blood staining his shirt from where she had nicked him. Another hybrid? Living above ground? How they could have missed this was beyond him. He knew of the hybrid vampires, who pretty much left them to their own devices. Katrina didn't seem worried about them at all. But another *human* hybrid? How did she survive up above where the Zompires craved nothing but flesh and blood? How had she avoided them all this time by herself?

"Great work, Elijah." Katrina's irritating voice came up from behind him. He turned toward her, morphing his face into a blank slate of calm. She walked up to him and handed him a handkerchief. "You're bleeding all over yourself."

"Where are you taking her?"

"To the prison, of course." She glanced at him curiously, as if she could see right through to his soul. Elijah, however, knew better. The only power she had over him was the reason they, the twelve, had a place to live. If she had the chance, she would be rid of him and the other hybrids without a seconds' notice if she could. He knew she would. "Anything wrong, Elijah?"

The way she said his name made him cringe.

"No, of course not. I'll take her there myself."

She laughed, giving him a mocking smile. "I don't think that will be necessary. Besides, you're pouring blood. Go clean yourself up. We don't want to excite our other guest, now do we?" Katrina smirked, seemingly eager to throw someone else in with the *other guest*.

Disappointed and seething, Elijah held his tongue and gave her a nod, watching them drag April out of the market and down the corridor to the city's prison cells. It was an isolated area, quarantined for the people's safety. He might be able to sneak in there later, but it would not be without difficulty. He gritted his teeth as Katrina waved to him nonchalantly and left with the guards. He had missed his chance to talk with the girl.

But he had made a decision: he was going to enjoy killing Katrina, if it was the last thing he ever did.

Chapter Fifteen

Cheshire Smile

April

PULLED UNCEREMONIOUSLY ALONG, I let
the guards hold my weight, not helping them one bit. They cursed at me,
tugging and digging their nails into my flesh as I dropped my body slack,
giving them the brunt of my dead weight to contend with. Struggling was
useless and would just wear me out further. I wondered where they were
taking me. Wherever it was, I was not going to go into any prison cell
lightly. Especially not with some other guest they had mentioned.

Waiting for the most opportune time to escape was my only option. It
wasn't going to be easy. The woman who accompanied the guards had her
hawk eyes on me. Her very essence reeked of something unnatural, which
made me shudder under my clothes. Whatever she was, she wasn't human
either, but I doubted she was a hybrid human or vampire. I wondered how
many were affected by the viral outbreak down here in their, supposedly,
safe abode. If the virus had made it down here, was everyone immune?
And what the heck was Elijah doing down here? He seemed pretty
comfortable with the surroundings and I wondered what exactly he was
hiding. I had more questions than I'd had before arriving. I had to get out
of there before we arrived at the prison where it would be impossible to
escape. I had to get out now or never.

I shifted my feet, picking up the pace to be even with the guards. Immediately using their surprise at me finally helping with my own weight, I stomped on one of the guard's foot, pulling the other one on the side of me into him, where they collided into each other. I didn't count on the guard behind me to slice my back with his Rambo knife as I stumbled over the two trying to run forward. The pain in my back was agonizing and I stifled a scream as I fell, sprawling across the floor. As I pushed myself off the ground, I felt a sharp prick on my thigh. I kicked at the woman who held the now empty syringe in her hand, making her drop it before getting my footing and running ahead of the collapsed guards.

I had run around the corner and farther down the hall when my vision began to blur and my legs turned to jelly. Drips of blood spotted the ground behind me, and I felt myself melting to the ground before I finally let my body fall. I struggled to turn around and stare up at the fading ceiling, unable to move but hearing everything around me, including the chaos of the guards stumbling to catch up. The perfectly crisp, white tiles lining the floor were smeared with crimson fluid. It stood out stark against the pale, pristine color. My voice gurgled in my mouth as my jaw slackened.

The woman came to hover over me, giving me a most sinister grin as she mouthed to the guards to take me to infirmary first, then to the cell. She wanted me alive when I met my new cell mate.

I don't like the sound of that, I thought. Then my vision darkened and the world was silent.

SOMEONE WAS DRAGGING me once more, grunting and cursing at having to lug my dead weight along. My eyes were heavy and felt like lead had been melted into them. No matter how much I tried, I couldn't open them. The same for my entire body; it hung languidly with my legs occasionally bumping into my captor's bulky thighs. I was slung over their shoulder, jerking with every step they took. A stinging ache ran along my back where I assumed they had stitched me up. The slight itch emanating from my healing skin assured me that I was healing well, but I had lost a significant amount of blood, making me feel weak and dizzy.

From the rough, bulging muscles under my stomach, I could tell my holder was a male, strong and burly. I wondered if it was Elijah. He seemed to know more about what I was than I did, which concerned me.

If he knew about hybrid humans, could there be more out there that he had already run into? No wonder he had not taken any chances when it came to subduing me. He was also pretty strong—too strong actually. For a human male, his strength was abnormal, a lot like mine. Maybe he wasn't quite human either. I'd have to see if that was true, but at the moment I didn't see how I was going to accomplish that.

Being taken prisoner hadn't exactly been in my plans.

I heard other footsteps behind us, lighter and shorter, making me think of a woman's movements. Maybe it was that witch of a woman who'd had me stitched up to throw me into some cage with the other thing she had mentioned. What the point of that was evaded me. I wasn't looking forward to meeting "it." I had to get my body working soon if that's where we were heading. I didn't want to be eaten alive.

I tried turning my head slightly, but my neck barely cooperated. My hair was loose and thankfully hung over my face like a curtain. I managed to finally open my eyelids and peek around through a parted sliver in the strands. I saw high heels, dark maroon, confirming my suspicion that I was being escorted by the woman. The man holding me wore a dark brown shirt and black cargo pants. He didn't seem to have the right build to be Elijah. That was too bad, I would have liked to do some damage to him.

Testing out my fingers, I slowly curled them into my palms, making sure it wasn't obvious enough for Miss Dictator to notice. If I could gain control of my body before getting thrown into the cell, maybe I'd have a chance against whatever was lurking in there. The sedative was strong, and its lingering effects made me question what sort of heaping dose they had given me. I hoped I would get a separate cell from the "thing" and discover they had been joking all along.

Come on body, wake up!

"No, not that one! Put her in the cell with *him*," the woman's voice hissed. She sounded upset, but I was pretty sure it wasn't because of me. "I brought you a little snack."

This definitely was not going to be pleasant.

I wiggled my toes in my boots, happily finding them functioning well. Maybe I'd be recovered enough to survive whatever abomination sat in there waiting to devour me.

"Come near the bars and I electrocute you." The hard edge to her voice made my hair stand on end. There was an authority to her that I couldn't pinpoint exactly, but it made her dominant over the guard. I quickly concluded that yes, she must be some sort of supernatural, too. What she was, I'd yet to find out.

I was unceremoniously dumped onto a thin, stained mattress lining one side of the cell, but my captor miscalculated and I slipped off the edge, landing hard on the abrasive, concrete floor with a thud. No one seemed concerned about it since next came the slam of bars as they shut the door and the locks clicked. My wardens shuffled away without another word as I pushed myself up with my shaky arms to sit and glance around at my new home, searching frantically for whatever shared its space with me now. Seeing nothing, I studied the bars and cell. A prison cell. *Oh, yaay.* Complete with a sink and a commode with no privacy. *Great.*

I scampered up and leaned against the frigid bars. The hallway ran to the left of the room. More cells stared back at me from across the way and one cell stood darkened next to me on the left. There were only four cells, mine being the biggest and the darkest. Not really a prison so to speak, but more of a sort of holding cell. I wondered why I was here, what good it would do to hold me prisoner. Why they would put away another human was beyond me. Especially as food for some demented creature.

"Elijah! Let me out of here!"

"Cozy isn't it?"

The bars twanged as I launched myself back, ready to pummel the person behind me, but instead I just exacerbated the pain in my back. It surged through my skin, making me suck in my breath to keep from passing out. I flicked my eyes about to spot my cellmate, but he wasn't there. I saw nothing but shadows in the dim light of the holding cell. Squinting into the darkness, I watched as a figure emerged from it, stepping forward with eyes twinkling. One was a bright opulent green and the other the calm dark brown of dampened earth. Long, red-mahogany strands framed his face, reminding me of how it had whipped about in the howling wind, high above the city at the edge of the Stratosphere Tower.

I gasped, sucking air into my seized up lungs. My eyes widened in horror as the man of my nightmares sat solemnly watching me. There was no way he could be alive. No way in hell. I must've been hallucinating and I wondered if the medication they had used to knock me out was giving me delusions now. Or maybe my injury was way more severe than I had initially thought.

The man who stood before me was a ghost, a fragment of all things that had haunted the nights in my dreams. I was horrified and frozen in place as he casually leaned against the bars, flashing me a smile full of fangs. Amusement twinkled in his dual colored eyes, gleaming like marbles back at me. The golden halos around his irises reflected the dim lights of the cell back toward me, a hunter trapped in bars with the prey handed to him.

"Hello *love*, miss me?" he snickered, letting his hands dangle out of the bars as his head rested against them.

Christian.

He didn't look like the extremely sick and dying man I had last seen. He looked pretty sturdy, maybe bit pale and thin, but not too bad if you asked me. As a matter a fact, my shock slowly bled away as my anger toward him resurfaced, claiming back control of my body and making my heart jumpstart into a tumbling rage.

"*You!*" Poison for words spilled from my lips and I clumsily shifted my weight on my legs. They were working again, but I was still not as surefooted as I would've liked to be. Narrowing my eyes as they adjusted to the muted lights, I wanted to run over and clock him one across the face, and make him feel all the pain he had caused my mother. Make him feel the pain he had caused me, make him hurt for all of the life he had drained from her very soul.

He backed away a few steps as I approached, readying to pull his arms out of his sockets. He didn't look afraid but was merely curiously looking back at me. This enraged me even more as I curled my fingers into my palms, digging in my nails as I dared him with my eyes to come closer. I would show him a thing or two about vengeance if I could just manage to grab him without falling over.

Christian seemed to know what I was up to and did not stand within range. He produced a slight grin and kept it pasted across his face as a low, haughty laugh rumbled from his throat. I waited, squeezing my fists so tight I could feel the skin almost breaking from the bite of my nails.

"Now, now, April. Don't go and hurt yourself. I'd prefer not to smell the tantalizing scent of your tasty blood, if you don't mind." He sighed as his smile faded. He stepped back towards the rear stone wall of his cell and slid down, letting one of his legs extend in front of him and the other bend to let his arm rest upon it. He ran one hand through the dark red and brown strands that lay in long, thick locks covering his shoulders and back. He sighed, looking somewhat tired and pensive, as if he'd forgotten I was there. "Do yourself a favor and relax. You won't be going anywhere tonight."

Christian's eyes closed as though exhaustion had suddenly hit him. I was left unsatisfied and standing ready for a fight. My jaw ached from the tension I had let take me over, and I let my hands fall to my sides, unsatisfied. Watching him for any clue as to what was going on, I suddenly remembered that he was also a prisoner here. How had he ended up here when I had been so sure he had not survived our attack on his hive? How was it that he was very much alive?

"Aren't you supposed to be dead?" I stated more than asked, not wanting to settle down and sit quite yet. I wanted answers first, and I couldn't rest, or let him rest for that matter, until I had some. "How did you get here?"

"Doesn't matter how I got here. It only matters how the hell I'm getting out of this place." His multicolored eyes glowed in the darkness like cat eyes, making me look away. His grim face was unsettling.

"I thought you died. How did you make it out alive?" I tilted my gaze back toward him as I continued, "I thought I killed you."

He chuckled, rubbing his neck as he groaned. His eyes wandered back to me, serious and cold. "You damn near did."

He didn't move from his spot or let up his stare, making me feel somewhat exposed. Scanning the room, I realized he was right. He could've killed me if he'd wanted to. I wasn't going anywhere. I sat on the hard makeshift cot that was to be my bed for the night. I was trapped.

"But how…?"

"How what? How did I survive your disembowelment of me?" Christian sneered, knowing he had me. I needed to ask him so much now that destiny had landed us together again. I needed to ask him about what had been done to my mother. But I desired revenge. I wanted it for her, at least. The only thing he could do before I ended him for good was own up to what he had done. "One of my friends found me. Gave me some blood and an injection that remedied the sickness. He'd been sent to deliver it to me and arrived just after your group had left me for dead. If he had not come when he did, I wouldn't be talking to you now."

"Well, aren't you the lucky one." I muttered.

His lips pressed into a frown, staring at the metal bars around us. He slowly got up and stepped toward his own cot. The light above it had been busted, leaving his side of the cell in darkness. Lying down, he left his back exposed to me as his voice came out firm but sincere. "I know I don't deserve your sympathy or even your empathy in any way. But you don't know anything about me, April. I wouldn't judge anyone so quickly. Especially…." Christian swiftly shifted in the cot, turning to face me once more. "Especially since you left me pretty messed up, I was already delusional with sickness." He lifted up his shirt to show me the pale scar that ran along his stomach. It was pearly white, well healed but still a scar.

The translucent flesh entranced me, its unnatural appearance had me shivering. He was so pale, like he could use a few pints. "April, I know you have a million questions to ask me."

He'd caught me off guard with such simple words. I was disarmed in a jolt and I hated him for it. I bit at my lip, turning away to sit on my own disgustingly dingy cot. Closing my eyes, I wondered if I even wanted to know what he could tell me. What if he didn't know the answers, and there was no redemption for my mother? She was lost and broken. Nothing he had to say would make a difference, would it? The damage was still irrevocable, and there was no comfort in that.

And yet, a small part of me still wanted to know if he could fix her and still wanted to make him pay, make him feel the pain and wreckage he had left for me to clean up. To make him squirm under my grip for what he had done to her would be nothing less than satisfying.

"What did you do to my mother to make her lose her grip on reality? *Why* did you do that to her?" A quiver ran through my voice as I choked back a sob. Tears stung my eyes and I quickly closed them, trying my best to shunt the pain away. I had to have answers. Funny how things had turned out. He'd been dropped right in front of me once more, the source of my questions himself, of all people. Only he could tell me how to cure my mother.

"I didn't do anything to her."

"*Liar!*" I glared at him, sending knives at his back with my eyes. "I don't believe you."

Christian shifted again, coming to face me. Leaning on one arm, he let his eyes linger on mine until I wanted to squirm from the intensity. They were peaceful and sorrowful. Something told me he wasn't lying at all, so I relented to his stare and waited for his answer, feeling my anger dissipate into a prickling disappointment.

"I'm sorry it's not what you want to hear, April. But I didn't. She was in the care of my laboratory overseer, Rick Fortunato. Unfortunately, I was unaware of any methods he used on his 'experiments,' as he referred to his subjects, until right before Blaze's hive attacked mine."

Christian's face fell into a melancholy that made him look just a bit older than his years. His answer left me at a loss for words and all I could think about how much I wanted to know how old he was. He couldn't have been more than twenty when the virus had hit. Now he was stuck at that age forever, or so was the common belief that one became immortal when the change turned a person into a hybrid vampire. No one really knew yet if it was true or not. Not enough time had passed to see if hybrid vampires were truly immortal, frozen in time, or just aging really gracefully.

"I didn't know, I swear," he continued on. "I never knew he would try to change her into one of us. He told me the effects of a vampire transformation didn't take, but that was after he'd saved me. He said he'd had to mutate the virus to force any change on her, since she was human, but highly immune. That might've turned her mad, I don't really know. He never got a chance to verify the results before you guys burst in and took her." His frown made it apparent that he had not approved of the things this Rick Fortunato had done in his lab. "Is she alright? What happened after you were reunited?"

"*What happened?* She lost her damn mind, that's what happened! Before I got caught in this god forsaken underground tomb, she was locking herself in our supply room cage because she was afraid she was turning into a *feral* vampire." I sat up and put my head in my hands, seething at my thoughts. "She's afraid of hurting me and Jeremy. Now I can't even help her or protect him because I'm here, stuck with you, of all people." My head dropped back, bumping on the hard, unforgiving metal. Tears burned at my eyes, making me groan, frustrated at everything.

"I'm sorry." His face saddened, remorse swimming across it.

I groaned loudly, hitting my fists against the warped mattress, wishing so much that I could change things. "This is nuts!" I ran my fingers through the tangles in my hair, pulling and taking some strands with them. "But you, you look *fine!* She's not anywhere near fine. I can't fucking believe you're still alive." Shaking my head, I managed to open my eyes and wipe the spilling tears as fast as they came. "No offense, but you're an ass."

Christian huffed and smiled, making him look even less threatening. His sallow color was disturbing. It made me feel like I was looking at a corpse. He was not emaciated yet, but he looked like he had missed quite a few meals.

As the moments ticked by, the anger fizzled away, leaving me confused, lost and uncertain of my fate. Of any of our fates.

"Hey, how long have you been down here anyway?"

"Long enough."

"They're starving you." I stated. It was obvious. "Aren't they?" I cocked my head and scrunched my eyes as I studied the lines of his pale face. I hadn't bothered to do this before, back at that fateful battle up in the tower, when he had readily wanted to harvest me for blood before I nearly killed him by slicing him open. He had looked worse back then, sallow and green, filled with some mutating, vampiric withering sickness. But now his fair skin was translucent and smooth. His long maroon hair framed his face like a blood-fire halo.

Christian was not as repulsive as I'd thought he'd be; his eyes were definitely intriguing with their clash of colors. I was sure he had not been born that way, but the sickness and subsequent cure must've left him scarred in the most unusual ways. I wondered briefly who he had been before the outbreak, what had happened to make him who he was today, the leader of a vampire clan.

"Yeah, it's the new and improved slim-fast diet." He chuckled, but I could see the pain etched across his face. He was definitely suffering. It wouldn't be too long before he was weakened enough to incapacitate him or probably kill him. Could vampires even die? Did it mean they were not in any way immortal? I had always thought that they were. Maybe not. Who knows? Things certainly had surprised me as of late. Anything could happen in this crazy world. *Anything goes*, I thought.

Being stuck in an underground prison cell with Christian was no exception.

Chapter Sixteen

Never You

April

"SO, HOW LONG?"

"How long what?" Christian's irritation flooded his voice as my curiosity peaked. His face was pinched with pain periodically, making me wonder if starvation was that painful, or if my questions were driving him mad. Since we were stuck here together, with no way out, I figured I'd get to know him. Know thy enemy, right?

"How long before, you know, you kick the bucket?" I chewed on my lip, wondering if he was going to act all broody and uncooperative. It was going to be a hell of a long night if he didn't want to chat. I was wide awake, and I had no intention on letting him rest while so many questions dwelled in my mind.

Christian snorted and turned his gaze in my direction. Something told me he was doing the same thing I was: trying to peel away the layers that I had so carefully wrapped around me. It was my own armored wall that I had stacked so high not even I could get out. I was certain there was no way in, which was perfect for this moment.

"What? Gonna miss me?" he snickered. "I don't know. I've never starved to death before. I'll let you know when I find out." He shifted on the cot, sliding to the ground and crawling toward me. "Why do you care? You offering?"

"What? Oh *hell* no!" I shuddered and stood up, meandering to the bars and glancing down the hall. The place was as silent as a morgue. Concrete and the choke-inducing, stale air made me feel suffocated. I hated it. It was worse than Blaze's hive, mostly due to the bars that held me entombed in this place.

Christian leaned on the bars on one side of his cot and let one arm hang outside the bars, watching me pace as he relaxed. The halos of his eyes reflected what little light seeped over his side, making him wince from the brightness. I had the urge to slap him, like an annoying fly that kept hovering about my head. But he wasn't a fly. He was a full-fledged hybrid blood-sucker, now immune to the deadly vampire sickness that had caused havoc throughout his and Blaze's hives. I could see his hunger in every twitch of his lips and every flash of fang as he gazed hungrily at me.

"Oh come on, why not?" Christian closed his eyelids, sweat gleaming across his forehead as time ticked by. I definitely wanted to swat him across the face for his request. I couldn't believe he would ask me for blood. What the hell? I seethed in silence as I dug my heels into the ground. "Tell you what," he continued, "how 'bout we do this the right way, April." Nothing but calm radiated from him as he waited for me to let the fire inside me die down. I didn't want to listen to him. I already knew what he was going to say. "My name is Christian Hall. What's your name, beautiful lady?" The slight twang in his voice reminded me of a Texan cowboy. It was subtle, as though he had not spent the entirety of his life in the southern states but had moved there when he was quite young. I had to admit that I was curious about him too.

"We start over, a clean slate for both of us." He held out his pale hand.

An offer to start over? I really didn't know what to make of it. What was he playing at? Collapsing onto the cot, I leaned on my legs as I glared back at him. I sighed, feeling defeated.

"April. April Tate. And the pleasure is not mine," I hissed.

The smile Christian cracked made my anger fade a bit more as his hand returned to his side. He was amused by my little fit. His tongue ran along the sharp tips of his fangs, licking his lips but looking quite nonchalant about it all, like it was just a subconscious habit. His indifference made me feel pathetic, like I was over-reacting.

I stood up and approached him, staring him down, hoping to get a rise out of him. But would I? He was weak and hungry, craving nothing but to sink his fangs into my jugular. Still, I inched closer until I met the edge of his cot. Sinking down to my knees until our faces were nearly even with one another, I narrowed my eyes at him.

His hand reached over and carefully stroked my cheek. I wanted to flinch away, but I couldn't move my limbs at all. His eyes were hypnotizing and swirled into deep wells until I couldn't see anything but the endless emerald and brown abyss of their colors. My breath arrested and my eyes refused to close or pull away from his unrelenting stare. Everything inside me twisted as I suddenly felt a wave of nausea fill me. Breathing faster and faster, I wanted to pull away and find the air that my lungs screamed for. It was then that Christian reached out and grabbed my shoulders to give me a sharp shake, breaking the trance.

"Wake up!" A flash in my vision knocked me to the floor, leaving me gasping. All the while, my throat burned and my eyes felt like they were on fire. I choked down gulps of air into my searing chest, catching my breath. Finally, the silence engulfed me and calmer, slower breaths finally filled the void. My heart was pounding in my ears, but it eventually slowed its frantic pace.

What in the world?

What had happened was beyond me. I had never felt anything like it. It had been a rush, and the flash had been my sudden disconnection from him, from his touch.

As I regained my senses, still lying on the floor, I rolled my head toward Christian, anger burning in my eyes. "What did you do to me?" I demanded. The look on his face immediately told me that he seemed to know what he had done but was definitely as shocked as I was. His surprise made me feel a prick of fear as his voice slowly invaded my weakened consciousness.

"I–I don't know. That's never happened before…."

"Don't bullshit me!"

"I'm not." He kneeled beside me, slipping his arm behind my head and pulling me up to a sitting position. I frowned at him but let him help me back up. "I swear. I don't know what that was."

I groaned. Still dizzy from the shock which had incapacitated me. I scooted back to lean against the bars. I watched him suspiciously, wondering again why he hadn't already just bitten me. I was so close to him and now, kind of helpless. He could have drained me if he'd wanted to. Why hadn't he done so?

As though he could hear my thoughts, he answered back. "Not without your permission. I'm not that person anymore." His soft voice felt like a feather being dragged across my skin, making me shudder. He was so close he could have kissed my cheek. It was an invasion I didn't want, but I could not bring myself to shove him away. I sucked in a breath as I slid my eyes to meet his again. Would he try to control me again? How was he reading my thoughts?

"What do you mean, not without my permission?" I inquired, watching his face turn sullen as he avoided my gaze. It darkened, and I was left even more confused. I didn't yet want to crawl back to my cot. I did want to get the hell out of there and run from whatever it was that he had done to me, but in a way, I didn't want to run at all. Conflicted, I felt eerily scared. These were things I've found seductive in ways that were inexplicable.

"I will never taste your blood without your permission first. Not without your permission, *ever.*" His promise rippled along my skin, making me shudder again. "I apologize for the way I was before. I was deranged, crazed from the sickness, not myself. It's not like that anymore."

I didn't know what this was or why it was happening now that I was sitting so close to him, stuck in a prison cell. Was he sincere? My thoughts drifted to Rye, and I missed him more than anything right then. It was Rye who made my skin shiver and his voice that sent ripples of want through me. What was this, then? It had to be some sort of trick. Maybe if I moved away from Christian, it would go away. Maybe his hold on me would wane if I inched back just a bit. If this was some sort of persuasive influence, I wanted nothing to do with it. I called on every bit of my will power and crept back, slowly sliding away.

"Don't go, *please*, April…." He begged as he reached out for me. "I do need blood, but I don't need much. I won't hurt you, I swear." He sounded desperate, but I managed to make it back to the cot and pull myself into it. Why did I want to give him what he wanted? Why did I want to run back and let him sever my veins and suck my crimson life into him, just like that? My body ached to let him. I groaned as I turned away from him, hoping the ridiculous urge would eventually pass.

"What's happening? Why do I feel so strange?" I moaned, curling up into a ball. "What did you do to me?"

"I—I don't know, but…." A quiver shook in his voice as he continued. "I swear I didn't do anything to you. This only happens if…but…I'm not sure. Look, I know you won't like what I have to tell you, if it is what I think it is." He paused, waiting to hear from me and searching for words.

"Spit it out already!"

"We connected now, matched. Simple as that. I—I never thought that I would match with anyone, let alone you." I could feel his gaze on my back, probably secretly enjoying my shock.

"What?" I shook my head, not believing what I was hearing. Shifting on the mattress to face him, I scanned his face for trickery. It had to be there, right? "How do you know?"

"Well," he said, rubbing his head as he sat up and slowly breathing out as he thought of what to say. "This connection… you'll feel my pain, my suffering as if it's your own. It will be the same for me too, it goes both ways. That's how this vampire connection thing goes. We're now one. We can share each other's powers too. But," he let a long breath out, looking more and more tired, "this shouldn't be happening. You're a human, not a vampire."

"No!" I sat up and gritted my teeth. "You're lying!" He watched me calmly, complete despair spilling from him. "Why didn't we connect the last time we met? I don't believe you."

"Maybe the sickness blocked it somehow. I don't know, April, I swear I don't know. We're all new to this; it's not like I planned it," he sighed letting his head drop back against the concrete wall.

I felt my stomach drop as a creepy feeling of dread seeped into my stomach. "We can't be mates, that's impossible." I shook my head, unbelieving. "I love Rye, not *you!*" I dropped back onto the pillow, tears streaming down my cheeks, soaking into my hair and onto the cot.

What if it was true? Could it be his way of manipulating me to get what he wanted? Nothing made sense; nothing turned this chaos in my head into a calmer ocean.

"Not you." My sobs filled the air now, and a strong overwhelming exhaustion filled me. "Never you…."

Chapter Seventeen

Never Is A Promise

April

THE FLOURESCENT LIGHT seeped through my eyelids, making me groan and turn away from its assault. I didn't know what time it was, but I knew I had slept for quite a while and still felt like utter crap.

"Sleep well?" A voice jarred my memory, and it brought a loathing along with it as the events from the previous night echoed in the silence of the cell. I scanned around me and frowned, half hoping to awaken anywhere else but here in this hellish cell or some horrid, forsaken nightmare.

Christian's face came into focus and I pressed my already tense lips tighter together. He looked the same, if not a bit paler. The color did not suit him. His skin tone looked like it had once had a slight tan to it. But now it was transparent under the grey tones from the starvation. I sighed and sat up. He was on the floor and looked as though he had not slept at all in weeks, shaking uncontrollably.

"You talk in your sleep."

"What? No I don't," I muttered, throwing my legs down off the cot. My muscles ached, and my back was killing me from the stitches, not to mention the insanely uncomfortable cot. Running my fingers through my messed up hair, I was sure I looked frightful. But why would I care? I wasn't there to impress anyone.

"You look fine." Christian waved his hand at me as he leaned against the bars.

"Oh, so now you're psychic."

He shrugged and played with the shredded end of his shirt. He must have been wearing it for some time now; dirt and filth streaked the edges, leaving it threadbare and ripped. A slight wave of nausea rushed over me, making me clutch my stomach as it surged through me. I didn't fail to notice Christian flinch along with it. Had he felt it, too?

"Uuagrh…." I moaned as it receded, like a drowning ocean tide pulling away. "What's happening to me?" I gasped, my voice croaking in a strangled whisper. Hanging my head down in my lap, I took deeper breaths as the pain finally faded, leaving me clammy and slightly lightheaded.

Christian shifted, standing up to pace back and forth on his side of the cell. He was definitely agitated by something. Maybe he had felt the pain and nausea, but he'd recovered faster than I had. I wondered how long he had been feeling that way, since he seemed so used to it now.

"Make it stop," I begged as another wave tumbled through me, sending me crashing to the floor, writhing in its tumult. My hands turned clammy as I gripped my legs tighter to me.

"Hey, April." I felt his cool hand on my shoulder as he reached out and pulled me toward him. I sat up as the agony pulled away a bit. My breathing was rapid and shallow and I prayed I would just pass out. My vision threatened to fade to black as it shrunk into a tunnel while the room spun, reminding me of the seasickness of riding in a boat. I had ridden in a few in my childhood, and it had never gotten easier for me to endure. Just like then, all my senses were off, leaving me out of balance in every way.

"Don't fight it; it's better to just breathe through it." He had me sitting up, partly against the bars and partly embracing my torso to keep me from slipping to the floor. I sucked in ragged breaths as the sweat beaded off of me.

"I can't."

"You must."

"Please, make it stop!"

"I can make it stop," he whispered as I writhed in agony. "But you wouldn't want me to do it." His warm breath tickled my face, and I turned toward him. His words came softly and momentarily soothed the pain. I wanted to sleep and forget about this and him. His arms tightened as I swayed, slipping slightly against the cold smooth bars.

"What do you need to do?"

Christian leaned his head to mine, his dark brown eye gleaming in the dark right into my own blue one. The glowing gold halo surrounding his iris was the only difference between human and supernatural. "Give me some of your blood, just a tiny bit. Then you have to drink from me. It will heal us both."

"No."

"It's the only way, April."

"It can't be the only way," I whispered. My tears tumbled down my cheeks from the tension inside me. I didn't want to hurt anymore, it was excruciating.

"It seals a bond between us, but it will take the pain with it. Once I'm not starving anymore, this torture will go away. You're feeling my torturous starvation. It will make us both whole again, and we'll be strong enough to leave this place, this tomb." Christian's voice was a melody in my head as the room continued to sway. Why he had not bitten and drained me yet was beyond me. I was slipping with every moment.

"But if I let you, we'll be bound to each other, won't we?"

He nodded, his eyes betraying his concern.

"But that's no good. What about Rye? What will this do to us?"

Christian shook his head slowly and I understood the severity of this "cure." His sincerity made me want to scream. "I can't do that to him, he'll never understand."

"No, he probably won't. But you, as well as I, will die here otherwise." He tilted his head, watching me closer. "Do you want to die here?" I shook my head. "He never told you just how a vampiric bond between mates is truly formed, did he?"

I shook my head once more, wishing I had probed Rye more about it. "How fast will it work?"

"Not as fast as you'd like, but it won't be a long wait."

"I have to think about it."

"Of course." He continued to hold onto my weakened body, making sure I didn't slip farther down. I was definitely confused and uncertain of what to do. What could I do? I hadn't expected this, almost dying from pain that wasn't even mine because I'd somehow become matched with an enemy vampire. Just my luck. I wanted to laugh out loud at the irony of it all.

"I've never let anyone drink from me before."

"Always a first time for everything." His voice was sad and did nothing to reassure me.

Keep your enemies closer they say. I was pretty sure they hadn't meant it like this. How much longer could I endure these bouts of unbearable suffering? I was pretty tough, and I had a high pain tolerance, but even the strongest can be flattened by the smallest of things. The viral epidemic had taught me that.

Why had that wretched woman left me here with him? To watch me die? Since they had yet to return, I wondered if they even thought I was still alive. Probably not. She hadn't been very interested in me as she had been with Christian's reaction to me.

The room spun, forcing me to close my eyes and grind my teeth together. I fought unconsciousness as I curled into a ball. Regardless, the light darkened as I slipped into a sweet, soothing sleep. It was funny how sleep paralyzed the pain, until it breaks through with its ensnarling fingers to stir one from the oblivion of dreams. I wanted the pain to leave me forever and let me wander away in my memories and thoughts. Alone, pain-free and lost to the world.

THE HOUSE'S STUCCO was chipping off, leaving bits of grey under the red, earth-colored paint. I remember picking at it, watching the flakes fall into a pile of debris, like dead leaves off a tree. I'd pick the paint right off, until the gaping hole left the house's paint job looking like Swiss cheese. My mother would yell at me for being so destructive. Not my father; he would sigh and give me a tired smile as he retrieved one of the gallons of paint he had stocked for such occasions. I'd help him smooth it out and reapply the color to the wounds, like bandages to scars, drying to heal but remaining marred forever.

Most times, I would refrain from telling my mother about this, knowing her impatience with my small rebellions would probably drive her to madness one day. My father would just wink and tell me to go clean up before dinner, assuming the task of repairing the damage in secret. I'd return his smile and run inside, relieved I wouldn't have to face my mother's wrath. I loved her, but had always gotten along better with my father, more so than I did with her. We were always at odds. I wondered why that was. Maybe she had been right; I would always be more of my father's daughter than hers. Either way, we had been happy, but nothing ever lasts forever.

The night my mom had received the call that he had suddenly died was a blur of slow motion and flashes. I remember going with her to the hospital, sitting in the wretched waiting room full of plastic chairs that were hard and uncomfortable but easily cleaned. I'm sure they had to be that way in an emergency room, so much blood and vomit and tears had to grace these chairs pretty often. The smell of bleach and latex permeated the air, making me want to run outside just to be able to breath.

I hadn't cried yet. I was frozen inside. Shock had a way of making it seem like it was happening to someone else, surreal. The waiting room had blurred out in my vision and remained suspended in a slurry of noise and flashing lights. I barely noticed the endless influx of ambulance stretchers with patients rushing through the bay entrance and the dual door to the back. People crying, some complaining about the wait. Others arguing with the nurses in the triage area. It was chaos and static noise to me.

He couldn't be dead. He couldn't be. He hadn't been old enough to have a heart attack. He was young, in good shape and robust. Any minute he'd walk through the double doors of the nurses' station where the rows of curtains separated the beds of each sick person. Any minute I'd hear his voice as he called my name to come give him a hug because it had all been a mistake and he felt a whole lot better. Any minute now....

But the minute never came. I had sat there for what had felt like an eternity until my mother had emerged, puffy-eyed and exhausted, her hair disheveled and her nose flaming red from crying. One look at me as I stood up to hear any news of Dad had her stuttering as she mumbled about him being gone and how he'd had some hidden heart defect. Nobody could've known. There had been nothing anyone could've done, it was over so fast, but he didn't suffer at all.

I didn't remember much after that. Just a succession of images and voices. Me running out the ambulance bay doors and down the street, hearing her call my name into the wind and the rain coming down in sheets until it swallowed up her yells. The sting of raindrops, the burn of salt of my tears in my eyes. My hair whipping my face as it tangled up from the sopping mess it had turned into. My father was gone, and I was running like I could catch him before his soul left this earth forever. I wanted to catch him. I wanted to pull him back to earth and anchor him to the land permanently. We needed him. *Come back Dad, don't go....*

I SHIFTED IN my sleep, not realizing I was on the floor using Christian's chest as a pillow. He had managed to grab a blanket and pull it around me as best he could. He probably didn't feel the cold and his arm probably didn't cramp up under the weight of my head, but he didn't much sleep either. He was lost in thoughts that slipped into his own mind as the pain subsided for the night.

Or was it day? I couldn't really be certain. The only certainty I felt was the intense peace I felt lying next to him. I wouldn't know for a while, but he had felt happy and scared at the same time, wondering what it was that had happened to us that day. Between the worlds that divided us, we were still there alive and breathing, though barely. He whispered a soft promise that I didn't quite hear as he ran his fingers through my long black hair and let me slip in and out of delirium. As hard as I tried to listen and decipher his words, I faded into my dreams again before the jumbled whispers made any sense. It would take a long time before he eventually told me what those words had been.

Chapter Eighteen
Break

April

HOW MANY DAYS had passed while I was in my semi-conscious state? I would occasionally surface into lucidity but it would not last long, for the pain would return quickly and clutch me to its chest with an iron grasp. I wanted to die. I barely registered Christian there, urging me to eat as the guards shoved plates of sparse food and a cup of drink through the bars for me. From the looks on their shocked faces, they were surprised I was still there, still untouched and not drained of my precious blood. I'd get a few spoonful's down and tiny sips of water before the pain would sear through me again, tossing me into the black oblivion once more.

I wondered if I'd ever see Jeremy again and how he was faring. I prayed that Miranda would not leave him alone in the bunker with my mother. Helen was capable of anything now, even harming her own son. I should've been there, but my selfishness had brought me to this, trapped and near death.

I moaned in my sleep, my clothes were sticky and filthy from fever and days of missing a nice cleaning. At moments I'd find myself awakened, embarrassed to find Christian next to me. I was pretty ripe, and the constant soaking with dripping sweat did not help matters. I wanted it to be done already, but found no solutions for my predicament.

Rye.

Where was Rye? Was he looking for me? Did he know where to look? Had Blaze forbidden him to come searching down here for me in fear that a civil war might break out between his hive and these humans? I didn't blame Blaze one bit. I had underestimated these people, belittling their ability to keep me away, never taking into the account that I might not make it back out.

And the question of what they wanted with me was the biggest one of all.

"Eat some more, April. You're going to starve before I do." Christian's voice hummed in my head as I tried to keep my heavy eyelids open.

"I can't eat any more." I pulled my face away from the spoon he held out for me. To have him feed me like a baby was mortifying. I had to get out of here, at any cost. "I can't stay here anymore; I need to get out of here."

Christian dropped the spoon in the can that had been opened for my meal. Pork and beans for days now. It was like tasting metal now, and I couldn't stomach it for much longer.

"April, I can't break the bars. I'm too weak. I need blood, but...." He sighed, leaning against the wall. He sat at the end of my cot, his blanket permanently on me now as I curled up on the other end. I watched him curiously, baffled that he hadn't just taken my blood already. How does he control it? It must be torturous.

"But I don't want to be your 'bonded mate,'" I muttered. "No offense, but this isn't possible."

"I know that."

"So can I fight it? Is it possible to break a bond once it's formed?" My question hung over us like bricks. I doubted he even knew the answer.

"I don't know, April. I wish I did, really."

I gave him a tiny nod, knowing what he asked of me. If I didn't give him my blood, we would die here. I would never see Jeremy again. On the other hand, if I did give him a drink of my blood, I might have a new unwanted boyfriend, even though I didn't want it to come to that at all. I sighed; we were at an impasse.

I can fight it, fight the connection, I told myself. *I'm strong-willed and stubborn; if anyone can do it, it's me. I'll just have to stay far, very far, away from Christian.*

"So if I let you take my blood and you break us out of here, what guarantee do I have that you won't leave me behind? I can't even stand up." I was afraid to look up, afraid to see the wrong thing behind his eyes. But I couldn't stop myself and glanced up.

As his two-toned orbs flickered over to me, a twinkle of hope flashed in them. "Once I have blood, I'll feed you some back. I swear it. You'll be like new then, and stronger. Then we both make a break for it, leave this place. I won't leave you behind, I promise." He looked serious, and I wanted to believe him more than anything.

"Will you promise me something else?" I whispered as the tendrils of pain began to snake back in.

"Yes, of course." The words felt like waves of softness rustling over my skin, almost soothing. I shook it off, my body already twitching from the impending agony. "If I can't control our connection, if I start to think you really have become my mate, would you please leave me alone and stay far, far away from me? Please?" I wondered if he understood what I asked. I hoped he would. I needed him to.

Christian's face fell, and a look of doom painted itself across it, leaving his features solemn and dark. The sadness he emitted made me want to cry, and it made me doubt he could even do what I asked. Would he say no?

An eternal moment later, he whispered back. "I'll do what you ask. But I have to help your mother first. I have to atone for the things I've done before I leave. Okay?"

Another bout of pain seized my chest, and a sick wheeze seeped from my throat as I tried to breathe through it. Every cell in my body was on fire. Every inch and hair follicle protested and seized. I barely noticed that Christian was also having a hard time with this episode of torturous agony as he sat writhing at my feet. I couldn't think, couldn't breathe. I didn't want to endure it much longer. I knew whatever it was he needed to do, I was going to let him, for it was the only way out of this mess.

The pain receded, like a calming tide washing away. It left us both heaving from the intensity of it. As my breath slowed, I waited for him to continue, though he looked incredibly pale from this last assault. If we waited any longer, it was going to be too late.

"I have to take your mother to Rick, figure out what went wrong." He gasped for air and let himself fall into bed next to me. His breathing came ragged and harsh. "I think the end is near, April." His whisper reached my ears, sending me into a panic. Closing his eyes, he became very still. With what little energy I had, I slid down next to him.

"Christian?" He didn't respond, his eyes fluttering in and out of consciousness.

Crap! I hoped I wasn't too late. If he died, I knew that I would too. I had to do something.

I brought my wrist to his mouth. His lips seared like fire from the feverish heat that consumed him now. It gave him a slight blush on his pale, porcelain skin. He looked peaceful with his eyes closed, lost in some other place. I had to wake him, let him drink from me before it was all over.

"Christian! Wake up! Here, drink." I shook him, willing him to awaken. *This can't be happening.* "Please..."

Just then, his eyes fluttered open and rolled around until they focused on me. I offered my arm once more, waiting to see if he had enough strength to feed. "Come on, you need blood now."

He looked like he nodded ever so slightly as he reached up, his hands shaking ferociously as he fought to curl his fingers around my thin wrist. Bringing my skin back to the warmth of his lips, I braced for the agonizing bite. His fangs flashed as his lips parted. Then, faster than I could imagine, he sunk them into my wrist. I gasped, the brief pain replaced immediately by a calm, soothing euphoria. What dirty a trick to make the hunters soothe their prey with the bite that ended their lives. I felt the warmth of my blood gush into his mouth, his tongue swirling over the fluid hungrily as he sucked harder and harder.

Would he kill me? Would he bleed me dry?

As if to answer me, he let go at that very moment. I groaned at the receding block of pain, feeling the sore ache of the wound hit me as his fingers dropped from my skin. I watched in suspended surprise as his sallow, pale skin morphed into perfect, smoothed out flesh, a blush of color growing on his cheeks. Even his hair shined as though revived with life. I didn't feel better yet and let my head drop to the mattress in a tangled mess of black, stringy hair.

"April?" Christian's voice echoed in my head, too far away to respond to. I wanted to let him know that I was going to nap, to let my dreams take me away into some warm, quiet place where there was no pain, where my father waited for me.

"April! No, you're not, stay with me, Hun," I heard him grunt as he bit into his arm, letting the red, silky fluid drip from the bite and splatter onto my dried, cracked lips. "Drink, April, it's your turn to get better." He pressed his wrist to my parched mouth. The spill of wetness swirled over my tongue as the echo of euphoria returned. It was sweet and slightly sticky but tasted amazing, like the perfect food.

April….

I didn't know who it was that whispered to me as Christian's life blood flooded and swirled inside, fusing my own with this elixir. All I knew was that it was exquisite; its warmth penetrated my cold limbs and sent an electrifying surge through me. My strength was returning, and my fingers curled around his skin to pull him closer. I drank his blood desperately, wanting more and more.

"April… April, that's about enough." Christian jerked away, leaving me wanting. I fought the urge to pounce on him once more and finish my drink. It took all my willpower to clear my head of the strange fogginess that surrounded my thoughts. I was feeling more like myself once he pulled away, especially with the fatigue, pain and fever receding into oblivion.

"Wow!" I wiped the drips from my chin and studied Christian. He was smiling widely, his long hair hanging down over his face as he looked down on me. "I feel so much better! I never thought…." I stopped, wondering why his lips looked so enticing right now. The pull to get closer was overwhelming, yanking me like a leash strapped to my neck.

Leaning into him, I slipped my hands around his neck and pulled him toward me. I wanted to kiss his lips, hard and desperately, let the warmth of my skin penetrate his. The taste of metallic blood mixed in our mouths, left over from our drinks. Desire flooded through my body, demanding payment and wanting to feel his hands on me. His lips were equally hungry and insatiable. We kissed and ran our hands over each other, tugging and pulling our bodies even tighter together, as though we could fuse into one being, as though this was everything we needed.

No, stop!

A thought screamed in the back of my head and made me pull away from the trance with a jolt, back into the present. I snapped my eyes open, finding Christian still so close, kissing my neck and nipping my earlobe. I shoved at him, giving him a swift push which sent him tumbling onto the cement floor. He recovered quickly, his vampire reflexes already returning in full force. Looking at me, a surprised confusion replaced the wild eyes and desire spilled off of him in waves.

We sat there in silence for what seemed like hours. I was horrified by these feelings running so unchecked and turbulent inside me. I wanted him… badly. I wanted him like I had never wanted anything before. I shook the thoughts away and tried to focus back on the task at hand. We had to get out of there before we consumed each other to death.

"We have to go. *Now,*" I demanded, hoping he could focus enough to remember his promises. He gave me a nod, slowed his rapid breaths and stood up. He walked to the bars, took hold of two of them and pushed and pulled at them until the metal screeched in response and bent away. He was certainly powerful, probably more so than Rye. I wondered if the withering sickness had left him different, even more changed than he had been before. It left me apprehensive of what I had gotten myself into. What would his changed blood do to me?

He motioned me to follow and I jumped to my feet. The blood coursed through me, making my movements fluid once more, warming my insides as I felt it continue to strengthen me. I slid through the warped opening easily and hurried behind him, down the hall and out the unlocked prison ward doors.

Chapter Nineteen
Intentional Things

Rye

THE LAST OF the shattering glass settled around his boots. Miranda sat unmoving, her face tight but not one bit surprised. He had shoved their glasses off of the table, enraged and frustrated. "I can't believe you let her go alone." Rye's rage was cracking his voice, and his face changed shades of purple so fast he looked as though he was going to implode.

"I didn't let her go alone, she went on her own accord alone. I'm not her keeper." Miranda tilted her head, narrowing her eyes down to her now ruined breakfast. "And neither are you, for that matter."

"That's not the point!" Rye's rage surged, and it took everything he had to keep it wrangled. He slid down onto the bench across from her, not registering the stares and whispers from the other vampires eating in the cafeteria. He didn't care. They could stare all they wanted. All he wanted was to know what had happened to April. No word, no appearance for days from her, had him on the edge. Her mother and brother were also hysterical. April could take care of herself, but it was not like her to disappear without a trace for so long. "Do you know what the maps were for?"

Miranda gave him a shake of her head and sighed, looking tired but upset. "No, they were blueprints, not really maps. I know I should've asked, but you know how she is. She didn't want anyone to know. I figured she had told you, so I didn't ask. How was I supposed to know she was up to no good?" At that she stood and marched over to the broom and dustpan in the corner of the room. Returning to sweep up the mess, she avoided his burning glare.

Rye slumped. He knew she was right. April was an adult, and she had the right to privacy and her own doings. Still, something was not right. He knew it. *Where are you?* His thoughts held her in his mind's eye, making him feel as though the roof was falling onto him. Maybe he had suffocated her with his constant badgering and she had pushed him away for that very reason. Maybe she would have told him if he had not been so relentless to have her become his mate or be by her side all the time. He groaned at these thoughts and watched Miranda dump some of the mess into the nearest garbage can, feeling suddenly guilty that she was cleaning up the mess he had made.

"Give me that, it's my fault." He motioned for her to give him the broom. She studied his face briefly before handing it over. "I'm sorry. I didn't mean to take it out on you."

She nodded and smiled, her old self returning to her face. "It's alright. I'm worried, too. I should have been more inquisitive. It might have helped her now if she's in trouble." Her grin faded at that statement, her eyes shining with unshed tears. He gave her a nod and finished cleaning. After breakfast he would search again for any signs of April. He had avoided looking at the Wynn, since Blaze had told them to leave it be. But now, five days after she had gone missing, he was at his wits end. He'd go against Blaze's command and check out the Wynn for himself. There was no other place she could be. At least he hoped that would be the place. Even if the underground city was not under the Wynn, she had to be near there, he could feel it in his bones.

Finishing up, he headed to his quarters to grab his gear, hoping to not run into Blaze along the way. He would surely stop Rye from leaving if he discovered his plans. If he didn't find April soon, it could mean only one thing.

He couldn't think that. Not ever.

Rye grabbed his duffle bag and began arming himself, strapping on the gear that he rarely used. The feral threat was still there, but not so much now with the humans exterminating them on The Strip. However, if April had been caught by the humans and couldn't escape, he might as well be prepared to take them on. He opened his case of guns, knowing the humans would most likely be armed, too. There was no telling what he'd be up against. He grabbed his handgun and stuffed a few magazines onto his belt compartments cargo pockets, and into a zippered vest he wore to hold more ammunition.

Pausing briefly, he wondered if the humans had any idea about his kind, the hybrid vampires. If they didn't, they'd think of him as another human. If they did, they'd be sure to be on their guard. It grated his nerves a bit, not knowing what he was up against, but he didn't allow it to hamper his determination to find April. She needed him, he could feel that in the pit of his stomach. Maybe, just maybe, with this, he could prove to her that she needed him too, in more ways than one.

Leaving the hive was easy enough; no one questioned him and his suited-up-for-war threads. Being third in command had its perks, namely that no one asked him what he was up to for the most part. Only Miranda and Blaze had any authority to do so, of course. Speaking of Miranda, he spied her waiting near the hive entrance, also fully armed.

Rye stopped, frowning at her. She knew he was going to hunt for April and had probably assumed it would be in the underground. How did she do that? Where the hell was Blaze to busy her with some mundane task? He shook his head without a word. She raised her eyebrows and gave him a knowing look.

"Oh, fine," he grunted, stepping past her and into the exit hallway. It would be pointless to tell her not to follow him. Like April, she did what she wanted. She could always pull rank on him, too. Irritated, he continued on out the entrance and tossed his duffle bag into the back of the van. She did the same, slamming the door shut and jumping into the passenger side. She looked giddy, happy to be out of the confines of the hive. He couldn't blame her. He had also felt suffocated in the there—waiting and worrying.

The day was cloudy, the air thick with moisture from the recent rainfall. It was flashflood season, leaving most of the sun blocked by obnoxious clouds that threatened to dump their water all day long but failed to do so most days. That is, until they were so loaded they dumped it all at once, on one spot and flooded the area. So far they hadn't dumped their cargo onto the dried earth, but the humidity didn't make the growing heat bearable.

"I want you to know that I am totally against you coming with me."

"I know."

Rye sighed. It was no use to keep Miranda out of it, and at least he would have someone to back him up when Blaze told him off for disobeying. Always better when trouble had company.

"Headed to the Wynn?" Miranda's sing-song voice broke the silence. Rye nodded, still lost in thought and concentrating on the ravaged road. Why the hive hadn't just cleared the most frequently used roads was beyond him. He'd have to bring it up to Blaze next time he saw him, if he wasn't raging mad.

"We'll find her, Rye. She's resourceful. I'm sure if she's in a mess she'll find a way out of it."

"I know, it's just that, I don't understand why she doesn't trust me enough to help her."

Miranda shrugged and glanced out the window, the looming buildings of The Strip growing bigger as they neared the center of the city. "Maybe she just isn't used to having help. She's been alone a lot longer than we ever were. Just give her a break. Let the bird fly. She'll come back."

Rye shot her a worried look. He wanted to believe that, with every fiber of his body. What if she didn't come back? What if she was meant to be free forever? He shuddered in his seat, trying not to think bad thoughts. April would come back; he had to believe that. She was just curious about the humans.

He reluctantly realized that he was, too. What was down there? Were there a few of them or many? What would they think of him, a hybrid vampire? Were there others like April down there? His heart ran cold thinking that there might just be. Others like her meant that she would no longer be alone. She might find comrades among them. Would he, then, be the outsider if she no longer needed him for anything?

Driving up to the Wynn, he scanned the parking lot for her car. Not spotting it, his eyes ran over the parking structure, a tall multi-leveled thing that screamed of horrors inside. Maybe not, but the clouds in the sky would let the feral vampires roam a bit more freely and earlier out into the streets, just like he was doing. He'd have to proceed with caution and make sure they wouldn't get overwhelmed before they even got that far. He hoped that April had that much sense when she had entered here. The darkness holds many things. Some things were dangerous, with sharp teeth and insatiable hungers.

Entering the garage was easy enough; no ferals in sight. As they approached the third floor, he spotted the walkway to the casino and April's car at the same time that Miranda shouted "There's her car!"

He pulled up next to it, taking care to strap on his weapons first. He glanced around the car before jumping out. To his surprise, a lone feral wandered down the way between two abandoned cars, heading in their direction. It was moving slowly but would be sure to speed up once they left the car and their scent drifted toward it. Rye pulled out his sword, gleaming and shined to perfection. He felt disappointed that he had to muck it up already, but that was the way things went.

Heading toward it, he swung the sword with a snap, sending the feral's head flying into a red truck. Its body dropped immediately, spraying out dark black-red blood. He headed back to April's car where Miranda was inspecting the inside of it.

"She was here alright. She left willingly from her car." Miranda paused, staring at the double doors that led to the casino. "Well, at least we know where she went. I…." she stopped and turned back toward the rear of the garage, her eyes flashing in horror. "Rye, there's more!" She pulled her own sword out, not wanting to use her guns until absolutely necessary.

Rye spun around, ready to pummel another straggler but was shocked to find a herd of them, coming around the corner from the upper levels. There must have been twenty of them or more. He hoped April had not run into such an ambush, making him realize that there had been no bodies left around her car. She had not run into any, so why was there a bunch here now?

It dawned on him that this was no coincidence. Confirming it as the first of the ferals jumped toward him, snapping its jaws and stretching to reach him with languid fingers. They hung broken, like he'd been clawing at something for a long time. He went down easily but another replaced him just as quickly. Miranda was already piling a bunch up as she took on one after the other, slicing them up and letting their bodies thump on top of each other as they came.

Rye kicked the next one, sending it to its knees before decapitating it, its fingers still curling up toward him in one last attempt of scraping up a meal. They were also broken, the skin rubbed away to the bone. He'd only seen this on ferals that had been trapped, stuck in rooms or buildings where there was no way out.

As more poured out from around the bend, he quickly realized that most of them had the same affliction: broken fingers and torn skin all down their arms. Someone had trapped them, pinning them up somewhere to await a time to use them. Somehow they had been grouped together and let loose when Rye and Miranda had arrived. It was a trap, just for them.

Great.

"There's so many of them!" Miranda's voice was laced with doubt. Doubt that they could make it out of here. Rye glanced behind them. The doors to the Wynn Casino sat looming like a cathedral entrance. There was no way to go but inside. He'd have to bar the door the moment they got inside. He was sure there would be latches on the inside to lock the doors. The only problem would be if they were already locked.

"Mir, we have to go inside, there's no way we can take all of these." He grunted as one bit into his forearm. He pummeled a fist into the side of the feral's head and sent him flying into a few others. Rye swung his sword again, slicing through three ferals before pulling out his second sword. The dual sword fighting helped keep them at bay as he backed up toward the entrance. Miranda took the lead and ran to the doors, slamming into them. They swung inward, enveloping her with a billow of dust. Rye followed right behind, pulling the doors shut as Miranda pushed on them as hard as possible, waiting for the horde to slam into them.

Rye's hands flew up to the locks, one on the top and one at the bottom of the doors, sliding the last one into place right before the thunder of bodies slammed into them. One after the other they pounded the metal, over and over. He prayed the locks would hold. He helped Miranda off the floor as they turned their eyes into the swallowing darkness.

"Someone put them there. They were expecting us," Miranda's voice quivered. She produced a flashlight and sent the beam over the hall in front of them. It was quiet, deserted and still. Footprints stood out in the dust, stark against the dingy carpet. Only one set, which meant that whoever had penned up the ferals had not gone through the casino. Perhaps there was another entrance, another way in. For now, they had only to follow April's footsteps, the only clue as to where she had gone.

They proceeded on, taking the path of the smudged footprints and scanning the blackness of this cement tomb over and over again. Coming upon a fallen feral, Rye's heart surged. A clean cut to the neck signified that April had her swords with her and had made it this far at least. She must not have triggered any traps when she'd come this way before them. That trap had been laid out for further intruders, as if expecting someone to follow her down. He gritted his teeth, thinking about what that meant. If they expected more to come, or even just thought it remotely possible, then April had been captured, or they knew of her presence. He hoped it was the latter, because down this rabbit hole, there was no telling what would surface.

Chapter Twenty
Blood and Tears

April

I DON'T KNOW how he does it, but Christian knew his way through the city as though he had once lived there. We constantly dodged people, swept through doors and locks like nothing. I knew my face was a constant mask of flabbergast as I watched him work his magic. After a while, I suspected he was hiding more than he let on, and my curiosity was getting the best of me. Only the need to be silent kept my mouth shut until we had more privacy. If the size of this place was any indication, I wouldn't have answers for a while.

Finally ascending along hidden staircases and back hallways, we made it to what looked like a massive boiler room. Large generators hummed loudly and the place was in constant vibration as they worked. I prayed it was well ventilated; I didn't want to die from carbon monoxide poisoning and gas fumes down there. Christian motioned for me to follow him, occasionally putting his finger to his lips, hushing me to be even quieter. This irritated me, but I complied, knowing it was our only way out. At least any fumes would mask the hideous odor from my clothes. I felt sticky and nasty. Hygiene had not been a concern while in unbearable pain.

As we scurried through the rows of machinery and metal, it was a wonder he could hear anyone at all. He pulled me to one side, pressed his chest against me and lodged us into a crevice between machines. As one of the workers passed by, we held our breaths. I was surprised Christian didn't repulse me as I thought he would as his body melded into mine. Now that I was fully awake and feeling much better with his blood coursing through me, I felt amazing, almost invincible. If it had been up to me, I would have done away with anyone that got in our way. But Christian was more resolved and in control, keeping me in check and both of us in the shadows.

My body was betraying me. Feeling him so close was sending tingles all across my skin. My breath came in short gasps at his proximity. I shook my head, clearing it as he stepped away, pulling me along. I frowned. Discovering that our bond was so amplified when we touched, I yanked my hand from his, afraid to touch him, afraid of these feeling whirling inside. I didn't love him, but my blood screamed to be near him. It was intoxicating, and I hadn't been prepared for it. I resented him with every morsel of my being. It was never supposed to be like this.

If only Rye or even Elijah had been able to get me out, this would not have happened. That damn witch woman had ruined my life in more ways than one, sticking me with Christian, of all beings on this earth.

But did I hate him? Did I loathe Christian for doing this to me? It had been all in the name of survival. That much I understood perfectly. Now would be the final test. Would this be worth it? Would living through this be even worse than death would've been? Chewing on my lip, I tried to distract my mind with other things, like getting the hell out of there. The engine room was so long I thought it would never end.

Finally, Christian came upon a door on the left side of the massive room, tucked in a darkened area with some junk piled before it. Obviously it was not used at all, but this was where he was headed, so the pile was definitely problematic. He started shoving the stacks of plywood, metal sheets and a metal cart to the side. It wasn't exactly quiet work, and I cringed at every scrape of metal and every tap of sound we made. When the pile had been moved enough to crack open the door, we slipped through, miraculously unnoticed.

We found ourselves in a tunnel, similar to the huge wash channels outside in the city, but lined above and along the sides with large pipes running the length of it. Intermittent lights joined the pipework, but some were busted or burnt out. No one had come here in a long time, and I wondered where under the hotel we had ended up. If this was an abandoned entrance to the city, it was pretty much neglected. I hoped that meant that there wasn't much to fear. I doubted they would leave it so unguarded if there was cause for any concern.

Still, my insides twisted as we moved on. The air was musty and damp. One pipe leaked down the side of the tunnel, leaving an orange-colored rust stain mingled with green slimy muck snaking down the bricks. It pooled at the bottom and ran as a small stream under our feet, where the packed dirt squished, turned into patches of mud from the leak. I wondered where this led or if we were even headed the right direction. Again my suspicions about Christian's knowledge of this place made me wonder if he did know where we were going. I couldn't wait any longer; the need for answers pushed at me, unrelenting.

"Christian?"

"Yeah?" he whispered, glancing around as though we might have been heard. Relaxing when he heard nothing, he kept walking.

"How do you know where to get out? How do you know so much about this place?" I watched him stiffen as he came to a stop, confirming my thoughts. He did know more about this place than he had ever mentioned.

He sighed, finally turning his head partially toward me. "I used to work here. I helped build it." Resuming our walk, he said nothing further. I, however, had a thousand more questions.

"What do you mean? You helped in its construction? Did that lady know that? Does she remember you?" I bit my lip, attempting to be patient as the questions leaked from my lips.

"No, I never saw her while I worked on it. My job was to build the lab, get stuff ordered and in place. I worked the design of it and did some counter installs, supply stocking and machinery calibrations. I never actually got to work there, though. They used to lead us through this tunnel to access it, never through the main entrance so we didn't know exactly what it was buried under. We had our assumptions, but no one was allowed in with cell phones or any way to know the exact coordinates. This leads to a garage bay where they kept tinted passenger vans to transport us in and out. They were windowless. We couldn't see out at all. Top secret."

He was obviously uncomfortable talking about it, as though he had kept a little secret that he would now be killed for telling. I wanted to laugh, to tell him that it didn't matter anymore. Those kinds of promises didn't count in a vampire apocalypse. I doubted it would be of any difference to him, though. It was cold comfort to me. Either way, it didn't matter what his reason was to have kept this from me. Just that he hadn't volunteered this information had me seething. Someone had taken great pains to keep this city a secret.

"How far is the garage with the vans?"

"Not far." He mumbled something else, but I couldn't understand him. I shrugged and briefly glanced behind us to make sure we were not being followed. I was sure they would realize we had escaped fairly soon, if they hadn't already. I turned back and ran right into Christian's back. He reached his arm back to steady me, but his face was focused ahead of us. I peeked tentatively around his shoulder to see what he was now staring at.

Elijah.

Not just Elijah, either. Eleven other people stood their ground, blocking our way, weapons drawn and ready. I sucked in my breath before I stepped beside Christian, hoping Elijah was still on my side.

"Elijah?"

He narrowed his eyes at me, but his face grew hard as he glared at Christian. I took it the vampire was a bigger threat than I was. I took the moment to flick my eyes to the others standing beside him, fanned out into a V shape.

I wondered who they all were. I studied every face, but one kept me glued onto hers a lot more than the others. The lines of her face were sharp, her thin nose petite and perfect. Long red hair draped her shoulders on both sides in thick, tight braids. It wasn't the fact that she had a gun pointed in our general direction, but her eyes, blue like sapphires that gleamed in the obnoxious fluorescent glow above our heads that drew me to her.

I knew those eyes. I had laughed, cried and hugged the girl behind those eyes many times, over many years. I knew every freckle on her face, every line that crinkled between her brows. I had heard her laugh many times and braided that very shade of red hair too many times to ever forget it. I knew her face as well as I knew my own features.

Sarah.

"Sarah?" My voice sounded dry and scraped from my throat like sandpaper. Could it be her, or was my mind playing dirty little tricks on me after my near death experience? "It's you, isn't it?" I watched her flinch when her name spilled from my tongue, her eyes glowing brighter as they filled with unshed tears. I took a step forward, unaware of the uncertainty flaring up in not only Elijah's eyes, but the rest of the group, too.

"Stop where you are!" Her voice echoed in the tunnel, bouncing off the walls and vibrating in my chest. "Don't come any closer or I'll shoot."

I froze. I felt Christian touch my hand and pull me back a step. A knot formed in my throat, and I wasn't sure what was going on. Flashes of her smile and laughter rang through my head, making me dizzy and making me search her face for any sign of recognition.

"Elijah?" I asked, my voice squeaking. "Are you going to kill us?"

He did not move or answer for what felt like an eternity. Slowly, he shook his head, his messy hair falling slightly over one eye. I prayed to see the spark of his smile once more, the genuine friendship I thought he had offered me but had so unexpectantly rescinded. I wanted his friendship more than anything right now.

"No." Elijah motioned the others to stand down, and they obeyed without any questions, without any hesitation. I watched as they lowered their weapons and tucked them away. Relieved, I glanced at Christian. Confusion swam across his face as it did on mine, too. I waited for Elijah to make the next move. I wasn't going to push it, not with twelve warriors staring me down.

Feral vampires had nothing on these twelve humans. I would have rather faced a hive of snarling, snapping jaws than ever get into a showdown with these twelve. I waited, apprehensive to make any moves, afraid it would break the fragile, still atmosphere. I even held my breath, afraid it would be enough to disturb the moment.

Luckily, I didn't have to wait long.

Elijah huffed out a breath, and the eleven bodies behind him relaxed even more. Even Sarah, who had been ready to pounce, walked on over to peer at me, staring at my face as though she wanted to memorize it. I wanted to reach out and pull her close, squeeze the air right out of her. The joy I felt at finding her again was unbearable, and my arms ached to hug her. But I waited. Was it fear or apprehension? I didn't know. But I was relieved beyond words when she reached out and pulled me close, giving me the tightest hug I could ever imagine.

I prayed this wasn't a dream.

"April!" She stepped back, holding me out with her arms. "I never thought I'd ever see you again!" She stepped back in for another firm embrace. I let her tears fall and soak into my shoulder as she quietly wept.

"Me neither!" I laughed, and we both let our chuckles evaporate the last of the tension. "Wait," I said, studying her curiously. She smelled different, and the power radiating off her skin felt akin to my own. "You're a hybrid, aren't you? You're different, like me—I can't believe it!" I was so ecstatic, letting the surge of excitement fill me with such happiness.

"Yeah, and look at you! Wow! You sure are pretty bad ass yourself." She finally let go and stepped away, still smiling widely. "I heard you gave Elijah a nice run for his money." She winked. I glanced toward Elijah, who waited beside her. Surprised he wasn't upset, I gave him a tentative smile. This felt like home. Like the family I was missing all along.

"Are you going to let us go?" I asked him.

He shook his head. My face fell at the gesture.

What?

"No, I'm not going to *just* let you go." He sighed deeply, like he was letting a weight off his own shoulders, too. "We're going to join you and leave this inferno."

I smiled, stepping forward to give him a hug. I couldn't believe it. It was more than I ever could have imagined that I would find down here. "Really?" My tears were streaming down my face now, but I hardly felt them. "Are you sure?"

He laughed, and the others joined in behind him. "Am I sure? More sure than anything! We're tired of this tomb, it's time to go."

I nodded, wiping my face with my hand, not caring if I smeared it with dirt. I wanted to go home, the faster the better.

"Let's get out of here," he said, beaming. But his smile faded as another voice disturbed the air around us.

"I wouldn't be so sure about that."

Fourteen heads whipped around in the direction we had come, gaping in horror at who was approaching. Sure enough, the leader of the city of Vida stood smirking at us, as though we were nothing but fools.

"It's over, Katrina. We're leaving. We're done with your rules." Elijah weaved his way forward to stand in front of us as the group drew weapons once more. His glare narrowed at her, but she didn't even flinch at his daggered look. I stood weaponless, feeling naked without anything but my fists. But I was emboldened. We could take out this skinny bitch, no problem.

"Oh, Elijah. I had such high hopes for you. You can still change your mind, you know. Come back, lead the city with me. Be the ultimate leader." Her eyes flashed an angry red, like metal and car lights. I blinked to make sure I hadn't seen this illusion, but it remained. Her eyes were glowing crimson, like a feral's, but brighter.

What's this?

"No. I'd never join you, Katrina. You know that. You've always known that." He shifted, his gun still at his side as he watched her for any sudden movements. Apparently her appearance had been disturbing to him too.

She snarled, laughing as she stepped a little closer. A ripping, rubbery sound emanated from behind her as large, black leathery wings unraveled, ripping her shirt until it lay dangling on her thin shoulders. Her skin morphed into an inky black sheen and her fingernails grew into sharp, thick talons. "You don't know what you're doing, Elijah," she snickered. Her words dripped with sarcasm as her mouth twisted open, showing a set of perfectly sharpened black teeth.

Oh crap.

I stepped back, knowing that what I was seeing was more than I'd ever thought possible. She was a frightful sight, her long hair so utterly human but her red eyes, fangs and wings made her unreal, like a thing of nightmares, a demon in the flesh. What was she? Some sort of shape shifting horror?

"What the hell is that?" I yelled, taking another step back, right into Sarah. She gave me a knowing glance, slipping a gun into my hands as she turned back to the abomination before us. The shock in her eyes told me a thousand things. The twelve warriors had never laid eyes on Katrina like this. She had lain in their midst hundreds of nights and they had been none the wiser.

"I am the queen of all vampires, my dear." Her glowing eyes flashed again, giving the room a slight strobe light appearance. I held up my gun, steadying my aim between her eyes. "You can't kill me child. I am not as fragile as you are, *human*." Katrina hissed, snarling as her rows of razor sharp teeth grinned back at me.

It made me cringe and my blood run a thousand degrees of cold. I glanced at Christian, who was now armed with a sword, given to him by one of the warriors. At this moment, I was glad to have him, Elijah, Sarah and the others at my back. If I was going to die it would be with dignity alongside such amazing people. I gripped my gun, my knuckles turning white as I stared down the wicked witch of the western underground.

"Some things change." I let off a shot but watched in horror as she jumped so fast that she disappeared for a moment and then swooped down, disarming me and smacking Elijah, sending him flying into the brick wall of the tunnel. Sarah lunged, shooting off her own gun as she attempted to evade Katrina's talons. She almost did, but the sound of her shriek as the mutated woman slashed her shoulder with her long, pointy fingers made my blood run even colder.

"Sarah!" What the hell was that thing? How could we stop her?

I emptied my gun in her direction, though she kept dodging and flitting across the room, flying and dipping, turning and changing her course until my chamber clicked empty. Her cackling laugh echoed on the cement all around us as she picked us off one by one, knocking others to the floor and slashing at some. She was strong, but I watched her movements, memorizing them for any weakness.

There had to be one. There always was, right?

I ran over to Sarah and, she shoved her sword at me, attempting to slow the bleeding from her shoulder. A bright red gash interrupted her perfect skin, soaking her clothes with the bloody mess. "Take it! I can't wield it now." She gritted her teeth as she flung it toward me.

I mouthed her a "thanks," hoping to keep the demon witch from returning to her and finishing the job. The others were scattered all around, some fighting, some on the ground and a couple unmoving. I squeezed the hilt of Sarah's sword, attuning myself to its balance and shifting my legs to counter it. I needed to get close enough to do some damage but not too close. She was razor sharp on all edges, and avoiding them would be best.

Come a little closer, just a bit. Come on, you freak!

My mind was focused, though the fatigue and the wear of the past few days were already crawling back into my bones. I didn't need much, just one strike to incapacitate this bat. *Just one, come on, take the bait darling....*

Chapter Twenty-One

Breathe Again

Rye

MIRANDA TUGGED AT his sleeve, the echoing screams making her eyes grow wider. He had heard it too, his walk turning into a fast run toward the commotion ahead. They had finally found where April had headed. Sneaking into the hive had not been too difficult, even though subduing the human guards had been easy, too easy. Something was not right. Why put a trap like a horde of feral vampires to keep them out if they were not going to protect their entrance very well? Maybe their guards were distracted. Maybe something had happened. It could mean only one thing.

April.

She must have gotten out somehow, if she had been trapped down there all this time. Only she could cause such a ruckus to make all the guards disappear. It made Rye smile at the thought. She was amazing in so many ways. If anyone could escape this underground fortress, it would be her.

Once again, slipping through the underground city had been fairly easy. It was nightfall outside, and the ferals were probably swarming all over the place now. But here, it was a silent tomb. Everyone was most likely sleeping, if they kept in time with the hours above, it looked to Rye like they did. He and Miranda barely saw any humans during the whole trek through the underground warehouses. It was astonishing how much was down here. It literally was an underground city, with every need that could ever surface, met. The greenhouses were vast and beautiful with bunches of trees and plants. The large indoor pool made it seem as though the entire hotel above had been transplanted below. Room after room of stockpiles from canned food to endless rows and boxes of clothes filled the storage areas to the brim. It was breathtaking.

How this could have been built without the knowledge of the entire world was beyond him.

Luckily he had spotted April, but she had been so far down the catwalk, following a man, she had not heard him call out to her. By the looks of it, they were trying to seem inconspicuous, walking softly and sticking to the darkened corners. Try as they might, Rye had almost lost sight of them in the enormous boiler/engine room. The noise there was deafening, and the lack of security made it easy to weave through the forest of machinery. Staying in the shadows, he tried to predict which way April and her companion had gone. He'd closed his eyes and thought of her. If he were April, where would he hide?

Luckily, the misshapen pile of debris which partially covered a door caught his attention. It looked somewhat out of place, like someone had shoved the pile to one side to get to the door. Rye glanced at Miranda, who gave him nod. They agreed it was the most logical place to go.

Through the metal door they went, still mystified at the lack of resistance they had met. Upon entering and making their way down the tunnel, echoes of screams had vibrated against the brick walls and metal ceiling. The haunting shrieks coming from the far end of the tunnel made the skin on his arms prickle with gooseflesh. He couldn't even make out where they were coming from yet. The dimness of the neglected lighting here made it impossible. Even the darkness seemed to swallow them up as the tunnel progressed. The only thing leading them in the right direction was the yelling and screaming echoes which slowly got louder.

In full sprint, Rye didn't wait to see if Miranda was still following behind him. His gut told him April was there, maybe the one screaming, for all he knew. Whatever was attacking her and her companion was hurting them badly. He had to get there now, if not minutes ago. Pulling out his swords while running was not easy, but he did it, ready to pummel whatever came into view.

Slowing down as he approached, he wasn't prepared for what hovered above a group of warriors, all swinging swords and shooting their guns upward, toward a darkened blur that shot across the roof of the tunnel. It had black wings and snarled with a mouthful of sharp, pointed teeth. Otherwise humanoid and female, it was vicious-looking. Its red eyes flashed brightly and its talons dripped with crimson blood. Roaring, its screech bounced on the walls, making his ears ring and surge with pain. What the *hell* was *that*?

Rye ripped his eyes away from the creature to locate April. She was perched over another woman with long red hair who was bleeding buckets. He watched as she accepted the sword from her fallen comrade and crouched away, ready to jump and strike at the flying abomination. If she failed, it would slice her into a thousand strips of blood and gore. He couldn't let that happen, he couldn't let her sacrifice herself like that.

He sprinted forward, his swords swinging with the momentum. He wouldn't make it on time, and that realization hit him like a thousand darts in his chest. He could see the flying woman diving down, snarling and smirking at April, ready to take her talons to April's soft skin. His legs were on fire, burning with the effort of his full on dash to get to her.

In what felt like slow motion, he watched as April jerked her sword down, faking her path of destruction as she rolled to her right, tucking her body into a ball as the creature fell for the false move. Jumping up and now behind the winged horror, April brought her sword down, effectively slicing through one of the creature's wings.

An unnatural scream filled the air, making most of the soldiers collapse to their knees, holding their ears from the agony. The woman took to her feet, swinging her arm to backhand April so hard it sent her flying backward into the mud, the sword slipping out of her grip. Disarmed, she would not stand a chance against that thing one second longer. Without wasting another moment, Rye dropped one sword, gripped the other with both hands and pushed off the ground behind the monster. He pulled his arm back and arched his sword upward and toward her neck.

It met its mark, sending her head plummeting to the floor and the headless body, writhing behind it, sprayed a fountain of dark, reddish green blood. It jerked and spasmed across the mud as its lone wing thrashed and twitched. Finally, it fell in a heap, right on top of April. Rye hurried to toss the creature off of her.

The demon's body was surprisingly light, but he could feel its ferocious muscles under the humanoid skin withering away as its blood drained into the mud, making it black and sticky. It stuck to his boots and soaked his pants as he reached over to April and cradled her to his chest. She had been knocked out by the hit she had received, leaving her unconscious with a bloody claw mark where the woman's talons had sliced into her cheek. It stood out across her perfect skin, bleeding and bubbling with a green ooze that seemed to be festering before his eyes.

He shook her, called her name and willed her to open her eyes, but she didn't. He slid his fingers below her jaw to feel for a faint beat under her warm skin. He found it, but it was weak and thready, almost fading. He had to save her, but the only way he knew was with blood.

He bit into his wrist and dripped the warm, viscous liquid down into her mouth. It stained her teeth and slid down past her tongue. Hope surged through him as he saw a faint swallow, hoping it would work. But she didn't wake up, and her heartbeat became slower and slower.

"April!" He yelled at her, hoping to startle her awake. "Come on baby, open your eyes. A hand slid over his shoulder, making him jerk his head around to find Miranda. She was squatting next to him, having just checked the redhead who was also unconscious from the festering wound on her shoulder.

"It's poison. Her talons had some sort of venom excreting from them. I think it's lethal." She pointed over to one of the downed warriors, the first to be scratched. His skin was pale with a shade of green tint to it, his chest still and unmoving. "It's like the vampire withering sickness that turns us green, but works even faster." Her eyes searched his face, a doomed look slipping into her gaze.

"No, she's not going to die."

"The human woman is near death, too. It won't be long until…."

"No!" He glared at his commanding officer, unwilling to hear her out any longer.

Christian came stumbling over to them. His chest had been slashed by the creature, but it was already healing, weaving itself together. "Move."

"Don't touch her," Rye hissed at the hybrid vampire who obviously was the last person he had expected to see.

"If I don't give her blood, she dies." Christian met his stare with equal intensity, trying not to shove Rye away, though he wanted to with every cell of his body. The way he held April was too intimate, too close. He swallowed down the jealous feelings and waited impatiently for Rye to relent.

"I already gave her blood. It's not working."

"That's because you are not immune to the withering." He ripped away the rest of his shirt, showing blood smeared across his perfect chest. Where the creature's claws had slashed him, only healed skin lay under the telltale streak. "I am. So, *move.*"

Rye's mouth gaped in disbelief as Christian moved to cradle April in his lap. He wanted to shove him back, get him away from April. So this was the man accompanying her out of the underground. How would she have ever agreed to let him help her? She hated Christian with every fiber of her being. She blamed his hive for hurting Helen and breaking her. There must have been a good reason; April wouldn't trust anyone lightly.

Nicking his wrist, Christian let his blood drip into April's mouth. Her skin was paler and was taking on a green tint as the wound on her face swelled and bubbled madly. But the moment his blood touched her tongue, it seemed to halt the festering, bringing it into a full reverse as the wound began to heal and weave itself together until only smears of red and green fluid dirtied her skin. Christian handed her back to Rye and ran over to the fallen redhead to give her his blood, too. Within minutes, April and the others wounded by the creature were awake, glancing around and confused about what had happened. Only the one already dead had not responded, his body already cooling in the dampness of the underground mud.

Rye sat confounded. He let his surprise morph into happiness as April reached up to push a strand of his hair away. Her weak smile made him want to jump up and dance. His heart surged as her eyes flickered toward him.

"Rye," she croaked, her mouth sticky with red splatters of blood.

"Hey. Missed you." He slid his fingers down the side of her face where the wounds were mere pink lines slowly fading on her cheek. He wiped the leftover blood from it and smiled, pulling her closer and never wanting to let go.

"Missed you, too." She closed her eyes, looking tired and worn out. He was sure that her time down there had not been pleasant. He realized that he had forgotten about the human guards who were now circling around them. He stiffened, wondering what they were going to do. One of them, a man with brown wavy hair, stepped forward and knelt down to check on April. His grin looked friendly, and he appeared relieved to see her breathing.

"She's okay?" he asked. Rye nodded, still unsure of the man's intentions. "Good. She's a tough cookie." He stood and walked over to the redhead, who was now sitting up with a couple of the other human soldiers checking her out. He did the same with her before returning to Rye. His dark eyes scanned the tunnel behind them.

"We should go. I don't think she brought anyone with her, but I don't want to find out." He looked down, wary of the hybrid vampire. "I'm Elijah by the way. April's my friend, and we have chosen to leave the city of Vida and join forces with her." He cocked his head, an amused twinkle swimming in his brown orbs. "I guess that means we're allies, too." He held out his hand for Rye, waiting to help him up.

Rye nodded. He took the hand and stood up above April. If she trusted this man, it must be alright. The secrets she had been keeping lately were piling up, leaving a searing pain in his head. Helping her up, he was relieved to find that she could stand, but the sudden isolation he felt choked him and sat heavily on his shoulders. She had a ton of explaining to do. But for now, they just had to get out of there.

"Who's going to take care of the city?" Sarah's voice interrupted them, her uncertainty written on her face. "We can't just leave them down there. They have no leader now."

Elijah nodded. He turned toward the others and looked over them. "Anyone want to volunteer to take over?" Four of them stepped forward at his request, leaving him relieved that he wouldn't have to force anyone to do the deed. "Take her body back there, show them what she really was. It will convince her followers to reject the idea of revolting against us. Get things together, radio me and let me know what's going on and we will keep contact with you from above." They gave him a nod and started to retrieve Katrina's remains.

Miranda gave Rye a reassuring pat on the back. He knew the concern in her eyes was the same reason he was feeling awkward. He watched as Christian talked to Elijah, making motions with his hands in the direction they had all been headed before they were attacked. He didn't know what these two meant to April, and his eyes followed her as she eased herself over to listen in on the discussion.

The way her eyes hovered over Christian was disheartening. It was almost as if she had some sort of connection to him. He continued to watch them, keeping the flame of jealousy contained within. Something was off. He could feel it in his bones and in the air around him. He'd seen that look on others, other hybrids who had chosen mates.

Seraphin's face briefly flashed in his mind. He thought about how they had chosen their new names of Rhystrom and Seraphin once they had changed. The way she had loved him so intensely and then the way she had tried to avoid Alan's stare when he had joined their hive. She had flushed bright red whenever he had been near. Rye remembered the fear in her eyes when she had told him what had happened and explained away her affections for Alan, unable to fight the connection that called her to him. She couldn't have helped it. He was her mate and she had to join him, leaving Rye alone. There was no resisting the match. The hybrids were cursed with this phenomenon.

But what of the ones who never found their mates? What of the ones without any connection to another hybrid? Rye turned back to April, his heart sinking. Even if a person chose another, there was always the fear that a new vampire would become matched with a chosen partner, taking them away forever.

That couldn't be the case here, though. April was human. She was not a hybrid vampire, but a hybrid in another way. How this could happen was beyond him, and he silently prayed that it wasn't what it looked like.

They followed Christian and Elijah to the end of the tunnel, where a door to a darkened hangar full of windowless vans stood, dusty and undisturbed. Cranking the engines with the vampires stowed in the back, where the rising sun would not disturb them, they drove out of the hangar and into an underground tunnel, disguised as a floodwater drainage channel.

Surprised by how they had hidden the underground city's back entrance so cleverly and in plain sight, Rye let his head drop back against the metal of the van's interior, trying to relax in spite of it all. Miranda had suggested that they all head back to the hive where he was sure Blaze would not be happy to see them with new people. Closing his eyes, he sighed, happy that April had quietly slid in next to him in the van while Christian rode in another. She laid her head against his shoulder and closed her eyelids, weary from her ordeal as the van lurched and rolled over debris strewn across the waterway, heading home.

Chapter Twenty-Two
Raining Fire

April

THE ROAD HOME seemed longer now, with the knowledge of all I had seen in the past few days hanging over my head. After cleaning up in the hive airport headquarters and getting a good lecture from Blaze, I was finally heading home. Jeremy had been ecstatic to see me once more, squeezing me so tight I had to peel him off. He was staying at the hive now, my mother free to roam at our bunker in the mountains.

I smiled at the memory of his face. My kid brother had told me that he'd known all along that I would be back. Nothing would ever hold me back from him. "That's for sure, Jer," I had agreed as I took in his face, happy to see it outside of a memory while squeezing the bejesus out of him in a tight hug.

Now the road home to my bunker in the mountains called to me. I was desperate to see my mother, Helen. The news that Christian would help her was the best thing I'd heard all year. He would take her to the notorious Rick and have him fix what had gone wrong with her. She would be saved. That was all I could ever ask for.

I glanced into the side mirror, smiling slightly to myself at the black SUV following close behind ours. Sitting back in the chair, I caught Rye watching me in my periphery and flushed under his stare. I didn't dare meet his gaze dead on. I felt bad enough that my feelings for Christian were distorting everything I had thought was for certain. At least this unwanted connection had made me accept the fact that I did love Rye. Fighting the bond between me and Christian was tedious but necessary. We had avoided each other as much as possible, hoping the distance would keep us stable. But would it be enough in the end?

Putting the vehicle into park, I studied the outside of the cabin that stood above our bunker. It looked so peaceful, untouched by the ordeal we had gone through. I jumped out of the cab and slammed the door behind me. I was relieved to finally be home. It may not be the most comfortable place in the world, but for now, it was enough.

"April?"

I turned back to find Rye's warm smile, a smile that made me want to run back into the comfort of his embrace and breathe the calm of his scent. I could see that he felt the same, and it was okay with me. It didn't make me want to run. In fact, it felt like home to me. I wondered briefly why I had fought it so much before. The despair of it yanked at my heart, making my regret sting just that much more. I should have let him in sooner. But every day was a new day, and the past was the past. This tiny hope that blossomed in me as I grinned back at him made my heart happy. I knew he would take care of it, even when I didn't.

"Yes?"

"Are you alright?"

"Yeah, I think I'm going to be just fine." A strange calm wrapped itself around me like a cocoon. This moment was the best it could be, and for that I was thankful. I stepped forward, turning on my foot as I continued toward the bunker.

No sooner had I taken a step, an assault of air slammed into me like a brick wall, sending me flying back from the blast. Bits of the cabin flew over my head, landing in crumbled pieces, some on fire across the landscape. I collided with the jeep, the crunch of metal and glass hitting me as I kept on, rolling over the hood and onto the rocky dirt. It had knocked out the breath from my chest, leaving me dazed with the world spinning.

What the...?

A moment or two passed before the searing burn of air finally seeped back into my lungs. Secondary explosions sounded off from the bunker, shaking the ground all around me. Stunned, I could hear nothing but ringing in my ears, throwing my balance off as I struggled to push myself off the ground and back onto my feet.

Rye....

My eyes darted around, relieved to find him moving on the ground near me. I brought the view of the bunker into my line of vision, a knot of doom formed tightly in my belly.

Oh my God...Mom!

The sudden surge of panic enveloped me as I pulled myself up, awkward and unsteady, gripping the door handle to heave myself up. My skin burned like needles prickling the surface. I checked my arms and my shoulders, finding shards of glass and wood embedded in the flesh. The right side of my face was swelling rapidly from slamming into the jeep. Everything wavered as I stood up and peeked over the jeep to the inferno of what had been my home for over a year.

No....

"Mom!" My voice was a harsh whisper with my breath still struggling to filter through the shock of the impact, my throat stinging. "Rye?"

"I'm here." His pained voice made it clear he had not been spared the wrath of the explosion. He stood near me, his side scraped by rock and debris. Blood spots littered his shirt where shrapnel had hit him. If I had stopped to think about it, I was pretty sure I looked the same. Instead, reassured that Rye was okay, I stumbled toward the inferno that crackled before us, consuming the cabin and bunker in its unforgiving wake.

"Mom!" My voice was louder now, the ringing fading as I limped toward the heat of the flames. It seared my skin, an inferno that sizzled and hummed, stopping me from getting any closer. The fire roared from the inside of the bunker, a column of flame and smoke pouring out of the door, incinerating everything in sight. Nothing would be left after it was done enjoying the propane fuel and gasoline that fed it. Shattered wood and concrete littered the yard, some still smoldering from the explosion. The house was destroyed, leaving nothing recognizable. No one could have survived it. Not even my mother, who was, more than likely, still inside.

The scorching heat did not let me step any closer, leaving me feeling helpless, desperate to get to her. I couldn't even get near enough to peer inside at the remnants of the building without the heat of the fire threatening to sear my skin off. What had caused this? Who had done this? I didn't even notice the tears streaming down my now dirty face as my legs gave in and I slid to the ground, onto my knees.

Rye's hand slid over me as he knelt down and pulled me into a fierce hug, letting me bury my tear-streaked face in his shredded shirt. It wasn't until then that I realized I was sobbing, my face drenched with dirty tears, streaking my face. I couldn't save her, I never could. The likelihood that she had caused this herself was so high that I wanted to bury this information into the crevices of my brain where things were shoved for the purpose of forgetting. I didn't want to know anything anymore. I didn't know if I could handle it much longer.

"Rye? Helen...."

"I know, shhh," he whispered into my hair as I let the pain escape, shaking my body as I cried for everything I had lost. I was glad Jeremy wasn't there. He had stayed behind at the hive, enjoying the new people to challenge him on his video games. He would have run inside immediately the moment we had arrived. But he was safe, and that was the one thing that helped me as the pain ripped through me. She had done it while we were both still gone. But had I rushed in like I had wanted to when we'd arrived, I might not have been so lucky. Why had she waited until I returned to do this? Maybe seeing us pull up solidified her resolve to end it. I wish I knew. But now, I will never know.

Oh mom, why this? How did it come to this?

So I cried. I let the despair take me in its embrace, swallowing all of my senses and drowning my resolve. I felt it tear through my insides, pulverizing anything good I had ever felt, filling my world with pain, so much of it I wondered if I would ever know what it was like to feel no pain. Could I even remember such things? No, there was never no pain, there was always the hurt and disappointment waiting in the wings to take over when anything good ever came along, only to exit stage left just as fast. We must accept this, especially when that is all that is handed to us.

But I'd never see Helen again. I had been too late to save her. She had been doomed for so long, and in the end, nothing I could have done would have helped her. I knew that now. She had made this decision, probably ages ago. But it had been so sudden, so final. It had left me numb, unable to process it when it came.

Christian had pulled up right after the blast and jumped from the car after barely putting it in park. Running over, his eyes were wild and shocked as he looked at the blood seeping from my shirt, glancing over to the house and then back again. I could tell he immediately understood what had happened. He had come to help me, to help my mother. But now that purpose was lost forever in the all-consuming fire that had claimed her life.

There would be no atonement for him. There would be no absolution for any of us.

Kneeling down next to me, he waited patiently as Rye continued to hold onto me. I knew the ache that Christian must have felt, waiting there, unable to hold me, unable to take the pain away like he had done so before. It would be agonizing to him, like a different kind of starvation. I felt the ache in my own body as well with him so near. A strange subconscious longing betrayed my heart. It was easy to ignore these problems in the midst of devastation. It was easy to fall into Rye's arms when I wanted to feel nothing but numb.

I'd regret these thoughts later, when the smoke had died out and the embers were doused. I'd beat myself up for such things, for causing pain without ever meaning to hurt anyone. But I took what I needed, when I wanted it. I had left my mother to fend for herself in a fragile state. How selfish was that? I had done it without a second's thought, without concern for the consequences. I had to live with that now, no matter how much I didn't want to.

Epilogue

I RAN AND RAN...

I ran as fast and as far as I could, letting the asphalt race under my shoes with endless yellow and white lines passing me by. I wanted to run forever, to the ends of the earth until it ran out or the ocean came to greet me and swallow me up. It wouldn't be far enough or vast enough to kill the pain inside or numb the ache. Nothing would be able to do that. There was nowhere I could go to escape the breaking of my heart. Only time could heal me, and even that would never heal the scars that were left behind.

When my legs and chest burned from the effort, and I felt like my muscles would spasm from the exertion, I searched the cars littering the highway until I found one with keys still hanging inside. Cranking the ignition, I prayed the engine would turn over. A soft, hesitant hum greeted me and I slammed the lever into drive. I let the soothing sway of the vehicle numb me as I dodged the endless hunks of metal and debris in my way, taking to the outskirts of the city opposite of my home in the mountains.

I didn't care if the sun was close to the horizon or that the light would be gone soon, bringing the stuff of nightmares out to roam alongside me on the streets. I didn't even notice the miles as I let the car continue on through the hills at the edge of the valley. Over the mountain, to the edge of my world I went, down a road I once knew, one my father had taken me on over and over. I had every turn memorized, every building and sign emblazoned into my mind. I remembered because that was all I had left.

Memories. I hated them, loathed them, wanted to erase all of them and obliterate them from my head and yet, they were my only treasures.

Maybe it would be more merciful to be a feral vampire, to be oblivious of the way things used to be and were now, to be unable to register the devastation of the world. I envied them in a way. Envied the deterioration of their conscious minds. They didn't have to experience the pain of life and loss. Memory was a curse. It was a long and devastating torture that never leaves and never stops its endless rant inside our skulls. Try as I might, I couldn't make it go away.

I came to and found myself with my feet dangling over the edge of the Hoover Dam. I spied the murky water below, far beneath the pale waterline where it once stood. With no one to man the monstrous structure, it would inevitably fall into disrepair. Would it crumble to pieces? Would it shatter slowly, gently returning the flow to the Colorado River? Eventually it would, eventually the cement walls would buckle under the weight and the wear of time, giving in to the forces of nature and earth. I wondered if I would be alive to see it. I wondered if I wanted to be alive to see it.

I had never considered the fate my mother had chosen. I never would. It wasn't something I could ever want. Sitting here, contemplating her reasons, and trying to understand the complexity of everything. I let the tears slip out of my eyes and stream down my cheeks, dripping down into the still water below. I watched as the fish flipped over each other under the surface, breaking it with their sharp fins and slippery bodies. They squirmed as they grouped together, involved in some dance of their own. I wondered what it was like down there, with them. Dark and murky with filth and mud. Not that much different from up here.

I had not heard the slam of a car door or the tentative footsteps that closed in on me. I already knew who it was. I could feel it in the marrow of my bones. It was like static dancing over my skin and tingling in my fingertips. I pretended I hadn't felt it. The day had brought me nothing that I wanted. It had twisted my future and blurred the present so much, I wasn't sure my warped senses would ever recover. Especially not with Christian lingering around.

"Leave me alone," I muttered, hoping he'd get the message and leave me to dwell in my misery. Instead, he swung his black boots over the side and joined me on the ledge of the dam. I shifted to avoid touching his skin. He was too close. "How'd you find me?"

"I can always find you now."

I turned and glared at him. If I had known the dire consequences of binding myself to him, would I have preferred death over this? Studying his unusually colored eyes as they reflected my face, I felt utterly lost. I couldn't answer my own questions. It bothered me because I wasn't used to such confusion. I blamed myself for my mother's death, and I didn't loathe Christian's company like I thought I should.

The light darkened across the cloudy sky, and the sunset continued to fade. Knowing the wrath of night was upon us, we didn't get up, we didn't move. Eventually wiping the tears from my face, I retreated from the ledge. Without further words, I followed him to the car and let him take me back to my new home—the hive. Back to Jeremy. Back to Rye and Miranda.

Nothing was the way it ought to have been. Would it ever be? It would probably all eventually come crashing down anyway, but no one had given up on me yet. I had to let that be enough. I had to let it fill the emptiness inside that my mother had left behind and pull myself out of its grip before I let the despair win.

Another night had arrived, like many more to come and many behind us. The darkness poured its inky black veil over the city while I let Rye's arms hold me close, listening to the silence of the concrete walls and the soft thumping of our hearts. For now, sleeping in his warm embrace was solace enough, even if it was only a temporary peace.

AMPLIFIED

Reign of Blood, #3

Amplified

(The Curse)

A wary glance at ruined walls
Etched inside, much shunted blame
Every moment, a tick of passed time
Consumes, leaves my sky in flames

The curse above the desert floor
Wars of lesser things in disguise
And life stolen from their core
Reluctant chosen of blood and lies

Down the path, through masquerade
I'll avoid the fate of death
Unrelenting promises which I've made
Evolve to killer to give them breath.

Hunter or prey, neither kind I evade
Spill of blood drained by me
Worlds collide, empty days
Amplified and pressed into me.

Chapter One
Feel Human

TWANG!

The sword vibrated through my fingers as it hit the hard metal shielding of the door. I was almost ready to install it into the frame where a door had fallen off its hinges. It'd been temporarily fixed until a metal one could be found and welded into place, but the rusty hinges had finally given in under the pressure of one feral mob, crumbled under their weight. Elijah had woken up to find his little sanctuary in utter chaos. I'm sure he hadn't expected to get ready for the day only to find a mini-hive waiting for him on the first floor of The Palms Hotel & Casino. Imagine the rude awakening of finding him in full battle, already covered in dirty Zompire blood and mad as hell.

I'd offered to pick him up that day from The Palms. His penthouse was perched at the top of the massive high-rise, hence the reason I'd been able to witness the full-blown mess. At the appointed time, I'd made my way into the bottom floor of the place, already getting a sickening feeling in the pit of my stomach when I found the rusted metal doors knocked to the side and bent out of shape. It just so happened he was getting off the elevator to meet me and ran right into the lingering horde of bloodsuckers. It was lucky for both of us that the other had gotten there at the same time, or one of us alone might've been feral chow for the small but overwhelmingly hungry numbers in this little hive.

They were vicious, almost too violent for my taste. They moved faster than most did at this stage, so I knew they had recently fed on something alive. I'd usually find a small pocket of ferals in a starved, slow and harrowed state. Not this one. I slammed my sword against the metal, feeling its vibration in my grip after decapitating one of the Zompires. I couldn't help but feel bad for this sudden invasion into Elijah's abode.

It'd been my fault. I'd haphazardly tapped the pins back into the hinges the day prior, not even taking the rust and erosion of the metal brackets into consideration. That's what Elijah got for dragging me into his home improvement projects. I was a warrior, not a Home Depot junkie. That'll teach him.

Unfortunately, if we didn't make it through this assault, I wouldn't get the chance to chew him out for making me screw up like that.

I ducked as one of the ferals jumped at me, sending him flying through the air and right into one of the columns. His body hit with a dull thud, disorientating him but for a moment as I rolled and pushed myself off the floor, gained my footing and ran toward the atrium. I hoped the damn bastard would follow me. This one had at least two feet and almost two hundred pounds on me.

Where the hell was Elijah?

I didn't mind clearing out the crud and taking out the trapped ferals in the Casinos we'd set traps for. But this, this was ridiculous. It felt like an entire cluster of them had taken residence during the night, stuffing themselves in the tiny corners and hidden nooks of the place. Where the heck had they come from and what had they chowed down on to be so strong? It made me shudder to think that someone was now dead because of this group. Obviously they weren't stupid. Something about them was off in how smart they were. Why had they gathered here? Had they noticed how well taken care of it was and ventured in here to find a tasty human or two?

Whatever had led them here, they were a pain in my ass now. I turned to see if the feral with the huge biceps and dirty blonde hair that hadn't seen a shampooing in a decade, neither had his entire body seen a bar of soap in ages for that matter, come to a stop at the edge of the light. He snarled and looked up. The sun beamed down hard into the main casino atrium where an old fountain stood empty and some greenery Elijah had managed to convince to grow. It was the only thing keeping me alive as I took the moment to catch my breath, bent over my knees and huffing. The air vibrated with snarls.

Damn!

I'd have to figure out how to outsmart this particular creature. His red eyes widened, flashing fangs dripping with gore from his recent messy feeding. Eww. That was attractive.

I straightened and held my machetes up. "Come on! Not such a big bad wolf now, huh? Afraid of a little bit of sunshine?" I reached down to grab a chunk of cement debris which littered the casino floor. I flung it straight at him, hoping it would anger him enough to come sailing into the light after me. It hit him hard on the chest before bouncing off and ricocheting against a slot machine next to him, shattering the plastic face above the wheels and knocking it to the ground. The creature snarled even louder, exposing more of his disgusting teeth. He roared with a vengeance, thrashing at the chairs around him before picking one up and flinging it at me.

What the hell?

I jumped to the side, landing hard on a mess of gravel and rocks, feeling my skin painfully scrape right off. When I came to a stop, I made sure he was still far enough away from me before squeezing my eyes shut and pressing my lips tight. The pain was delayed, but it came rushing across my skin and down my synapses like an atom bomb exploding across them. I gasped, and tears squeezed from between my eyelids.

I huffed out a breath and opened my eyes, glaring at the beast with distain. "Okay, then. Don't want to play nice, huh?"

"Quit toying and kill it already!" Elijah hollered. I looked up to see him decapitate another feral right before a second one slammed into him, jamming him against the wall. "Oomf!" he huffed, the breath knocked out of him.

Crap!

I stepped toward him, but the feral crazy waiting for me scrambled to stand between us. Great. Just wonderful.

"Do you mind? You're in the way." I held up my machete, readying to bum rush the bastard and swing at his neck once I was closer.

The thing didn't flinch at my warning gestures.

"Don't say I didn't warn you," I yelled. I took off toward him, holding my blade to the side and ready to slice him up. He bent his knees, looking more excited the closer I came. He was overly confident that I'd be running into his arms and letting him rip my throat out. More reason to shudder. I let the sun caress my head, loving the warmth it gave me in the cold interior of the neglected building. Winter was over, but spring hadn't exactly jumped in to take over the show. Anything hidden from the sun was still radiating a frosty chill.

Thwack!

I swung the blade, hoping the momentum would get at least a good way through his thick, burly neck. It hit right where I'd wanted it to, but the damned creature grabbed the blade, which wouldn't come back out of his neck easily. I didn't let go as it loosened the blade, ignoring the blood and gashes in his own hands as he pushed on the metal. I pulled away, but my blade wouldn't budge. Not wanting to find his meaty fingers back on me with just one blade left, I hacked against his neck with the other machete, over and over, but his neck was tough, and I'd managed to just make hacking marks across it without much momentum. He rotated with me as I arched back, holding onto the blade near the hilt to swing me faster. If I let go, I'd go flying into a wall myself. If I stayed gripped onto the hilt, I'd be just within his reach in about five seconds.

Decisions, Decisions.

"A little help here!" I grunted, hoping Elijah wasn't as busy as I was. If he didn't get to me, I'd have to let go and fly into whatever object wanted to meet me. It didn't sound fun, but it was my only option left. I braced for impact, trying to get a glimpse behind me and hoping for a safe landing. As the burly Zompire dropped one hand off the blade and reached for me, I took the motion and let my body sway into it, letting go of the hilt of my stuck machete while my legs desperately tried to find footing.

I scurried backward, turning to see where I was headed. My second machete went flying from my fingers as I lost my balance. My feet flew out from under me, and I was pretty sure I was going to land hard.

A flash of white skin made me glance up as I fell forward, still stumbling to gain traction. My mother, Helen, was standing in her loose jeans and a flowing blouse that seemed to ruffle in a soft breeze. I was headed right for her, into her awaiting outstretched arms.

"Mom?" I gasped as my body turned, heading for the impact.

Instead, Elijah's arms encircled me. His strong, warm muscles and broad chest met my face instead of my mother's arms, instead of hard concrete and pain.

"Gotcha." He grinned and propped me back on my feet before turning to face burly Zompire.

"Elijah?" I stared at him, confused and swinging my eyes around to find my mother again. "But Mom was just there, she was just standing right there…." I found the spot I'd seen her standing and gulped. I was losing my mind.

"What?" Elijah only half paid attention as he smirked at the Zompire, just within reach of the light that shielded us now. "Come on, tough guy, it's more fun picking on someone your own size!" He let out a grunt as he started sprinting toward the beast, hunting knife in hand.

That was something, watching Elijah grab the man like he was a rag doll and saw the hunting knife through the tangle of arteries, jugular, tendons and bone. It almost made me sick from the bloody messy he was making, and looking like he was enjoying it with a mad gleam in his dark eyes and a wicked grin on his face.

Mom?

I looked away, still unconvinced that I had been seeing things. My breath returned to me as I found nothing and was able to turn back to

Elijah, standing at the edge of the light, drenched in blood, gore and chunks of flesh, huffing air in and out. The smile was still on his face as he continued to stare down at the burly Zompire's body. It lay in an unmoving heap, mangled beyond recognition.

"You all right?"

I could barely nod, but I did. "Yeah. How about you?"

"I think I need another shower."

My nervous chuckle came out choked, like the sound from a squashed duck.

"You don't look so hot." He wiped his blade on one of the downed ferals.

"Thanks." I leaned against one of the pillars, still scanning the surroundings for her. "I thought I saw my mother."

"Mind playing tricks on you?"

"Yeah, probably."

I found my blade and gripped it. Looking around for any more ferals, I saw that they were all dead. A bloody machete skittered across the floor, landing at my feet.

"Found your other blade." Elijah winked and walked back toward the elevator, where I knew he was headed to clean up and change, as if nothing had happened. I was left in the desolate silence of the casino atrium, letting the heat of the sun bring me back to life.

If that had been my mother, why had she flashed before my eyes and disappeared without saying anything? Why was she even there?

I pressed the tears out of my eyes and felt the warm liquid as it slid down my cheeks. I ignored them and grabbed another downed Zompire, dragging it into the sunny atrium and letting go before the flames burst across its skin and consumed the last of its rotting flesh. Even the burly one, who'd almost slammed me into wall art, was no match for the UV rays as I finally managed to drag his heavy mass into the light.

I worked like that for a half hour, cursing at Elijah for leaving me the mess. Maybe he needed his own space, too, but this was calming to me, piling up the bodies and watching the flames consume the last of them.

My mother had also been consumed by the flames. The fire had taken the last of her light, and with it, some of my own as well.

Chapter Two
Narrow Paths

SLOT CANYONS AND sand. Sand, all over this blasted place. In my boots, sticking to my fingers and clinging to the sweat on my face. I wasn't a girly girl or anything, I just wasn't a fan of being dirty. Thank goodness it wasn't muddy at the moment. The torrential rains which had been pouring down the last few weeks, unrelenting, like the sky had to take a major bathroom break, had subsided for now. Otherwise we'd have been swept away into the rivers these places became in a flash.

Stomp, stomp! Everyone turned around to see Elijah doing a funky dance, kicking up dirt, clouding up the air with flying sand. *Great.*

"What the hell?" I hissed, throwing him a nasty glare. "Not like my damn allergies aren't bad enough already without you kicking that shit up!" I covered my face with my shirt, sending daggers in his direction to let him know how much he was on my shit list for doing that.

"Fucking snake!" He pulled his shirt down, kicking the corpse of a snake he'd just pulverized to the side. He cursed even more under his breath.

I heard a stifled giggle from Sarah, who followed close behind me as she attempted to choke it back with a faked cough. It was amusing, to say the least, seeing a big guy like Elijah lose his cool over a snake. Let's not take into account that we were in the middle of a barren, sun-blasted desert. I swear, God meant this to be hell on earth. I would've joined Sarah in a chuckle if I hadn't been in such a foul mood from the constant barrage of dust in this pit of nothingness. My throat was raw and scratchy from the dust and pollen flying about. The rain had done nothing to settle it all down and relieve my itchy eyes. I used to work in a pet shop before my allergies made it intolerable, but snakes didn't bother me as much as spiders did. Those made me shriek like a banshee and sent me sprinting faster than an Olympic gold medalist.

"Focus, guys." Christian's agitation flashed across his face, and everyone quieted down. If someone would've told me I'd be in the middle of the desert with nothing even resembling civilization in sight and stuck in an overbearing but gorgeous slot canyon with him leading this group of human hybrids alongside two vampire hybrids, *near sundown*... let's not forget that... to find another secret facility which supposedly housed experiments on everything you could think of.... Well, I'd call that bullshit. Yeah, it was bad enough it had been my stupid idea to go there for some answers about my mother's suicide. But I wanted answers. I wanted to know the man who had driven my mother to the point of insanity.

Rye huffed behind me. Not a fan of Christian, *whatsoever.*

Who could blame him? Rye's jealous streak was something I tended to ignore, but it got downright annoying enough that I threw him a warning look. He reciprocated with an innocent smile, one that made me smile back and roll my eyes at the ridiculousness of it all. I'd dragged them to do this for me, and I had to show them some gratitude for doing so. None of us wanted to be there. Finding the notorious Rick was my mission, not theirs. Still, I was relieved I didn't have to do it alone. I was done with being solo. I'd spent far too long stuck in a bunker alone with just my mother and an un-relatable brother for company. Human connections kept me from losing my mind. At least that was something I'd come to understand about myself.

Then there were the things I didn't even comprehend. For one, Christian being my supposed "blood mate" didn't make things any easier. He'd tried to kill me once, when he was the deranged and sick leader of an enemy hive. But, unbeknownst to me, he'd been cured and imprisoned alongside me in the city of Vida. Katrina, the city's Hitleresque leader, had hoped leaving me with him long enough would make him want to munch on me for a little snack since he'd been starved before I'd arrived. I had to hand it to him, he had resisted it like a champ. I was thoroughly impressed. But when we'd touched, it had ignited a bond between us which had turned out to be more than unwanted. It meant I was his one and only, and all the intricacies that went along with that. This damned vampire virus had found more than one way to be a nuisance, and this had turned into a problem for all of us, especially when he was near me.

The bond had turned us each into some sort of pheromone drug to the other, and staying apart was the only thing that kept it in check.

Unfortunately, we both had to be on this mission, which sucked for all parties involved.

All right, I admit it, it didn't suck for me or Christian as much as it royally bummed out Rye, my vampire hybrid boyfriend. I still didn't actually call him my boyfriend, but it was close enough. When the world has swirled down the toilet, you pretty much avoid thinking about any luxuries, including love.

Jeremy, my brother, had stayed behind at the hive, our headquarters underneath the Las Vegas McCarren International Airport. It was home for now, even though we'd been spending tons of time in the underground city of Vida, where the last of the unmutated humans lived.

I wasn't sure yet, but Jeremy had been hinting that he wanted to move permanently to Vida. There were more human children his age there, so I couldn't very well disagree. Still, the crowds made me nervous and jumpy. He'd already adapted to it like he'd been there the whole darn time. Me, I stuck out like a thorn embedded into someone's thumb when I walked down the city's streets. I'd get terrified and curious stares all the time since I preferred to dress to the nines with my weapons displayed in my various sheaths, bandoleer and other holders. So I was the female Rambo walking about the place. Most residents left that up to the human hybrid protectors of Vida…the Twelve. Well, they were eleven now that one of them had died in the battle against Katrina, but that was beside the point. They rarely mingled with the humans and preferred to stay on the periphery. Walking around with my brother kept me in sight. Yep, it was mighty painful.

If Mom was still alive, she'd know what to do about Jeremy. Well, there'd be no decision to make, he'd be with her. No if, ands or buts. I wasn't maternal material, and I knew that, was totally cool with it. Each time I decapitated another vampire or dragged myself home with vampire guts and blood sticking to my skin, I really couldn't picture myself as the vision of domestic bliss.

"Keep your eyes sharp and weapons out. We're entering the monitored area of Asylum Fortress." Christian yelled back at everyone. "There's traps, by the way, and they're changed all the time to keep out intruders. I can't tell you where they'll be. I've been gone for a long time, so be careful."

I pulled out my dual machetes, ready for action. I didn't need to be told twice. This was what I lived for. I'd been stuck inside for a while, heading out only to clear out infested casinos or guard posts of invading feral vampires, duly named Zompires by the hybrid vampires due to their lack of humanity and lust for blood and flesh. This particular mission was dangerous, only because Christian hadn't returned to his hive's home base in the Valley of Fire in several weeks.

They had probably assumed he was dead and gone. New leadership was probably in command now. Christian's second in command had not been at the Stratosphere when Blaze's hive, our hive, had blown it to hell. He'd lost a major part of his troops, hybrid and mutated Zompires, but his second in command, Mercer, who from the sound of him was as cold as a vampire should be, wasn't there that day. Christian had described him as absolutely emotionless, stiff and perfectly calculating. I wondered how someone like Christian, who had a warm heart under his hardened exterior, had picked someone like Mercer as his second. There was a lot I didn't know about the other hive of the City of Las Vegas.

"Hey." Rye stepped up beside me, his long sword held in his hands and guns strapped to his waist. He wore all black with long sleeves and a cap. Blaze and Christian had also donned something similar. They looked paler than they usually did, even though I knew they had fed today. The sunblock fifty thousand or so they had smeared on made them look like painted aborigines. I couldn't even see his grey eyes underneath the heavily tinted sunglasses propped on his face.

"Hey." I wasn't a big talker lately. Losing family can do that to someone.

"Listen, I'm still not sure you and the others should be coming along. It's a hive full of vampires, and I don't think humans are part of this one, hybrid or not." His voice stung, though it was barely above a whisper. I didn't bother looking at him, fearing I would just snap at his unsolicited advice.

"Sarah and Elijah know the deal. They'd never let me go without them," I muttered. He was so overprotective of me, it got downright annoying. Sucking in a breath, I tamed my inner beast and threw him a soft smile. "Plus, you're here, too. You wouldn't let me go without you either, so you must understand."

Rye's face brightened, as if I'd told him I loved him. It was nice to see him smiling rather than frowning, which from my constant moping about lately surely had him doing that a lot. I had good reasons to be sad; I'd just lost my mother. She'd died in an explosion I believed she caused herself. I was still devastated, and it hadn't left me much room for happy thoughts. She'd been so together, tough and resilient. That is, until Christian's hive had stolen her and my brother and experimented on them. It had left her broken in body and in mind. The damage had been so irreparable that I'd been left to care for my brother most of the time before her death.

She'd feared she'd turn into a vampire, the one thing she could not tolerate. She'd had symptoms, yes, but I had assumed she'd become a hybrid vampire, not a feral. Well, the explosion she'd rigged while I'd been trapped in Vida had made sure she wouldn't become either one. I'd been too late, and it had left us, Jeremy and me, utterly alone.

I swallowed the bad taste the memories left in my mouth. Keeping my eyes focused on our surroundings, I felt the sun disappear below the mountains where the slot canyon began. The tall, smooth orange rock curved as it sent us around several corners, narrowing into walkways too small to fit more than one person at a time.

This was an unusual place for a fortress, but at the end of times, who would visit this popular tourist attraction now? It was a perfect funnel to pick off enemies one at a time. It made me nervous as we rounded the turns and nooks that littered the area. Flicking my eyes up toward the towering walls around us, I was sure that sooner or later, a perched feral hiding in darkness or a hybrid would drop in from above and do its best to slaughter us all.

Pessimism was my middle name lately.

Chapter Three

Mercer

"I DON'T WANT to sound like I'm freaking out or anything, but does anyone else feel like the walls are moving?" Sarah scrunched her nose up as she scanned the stone surrounding the slit we were quietly maneuvering. Her long red hair was pulled back into a tight ponytail spilling halfway down her back. It was braided into two thick braids, which I envied with all my heart. My own hair was medium length, black, thin and straight. Nothing spectacular.

"I feel it, too." The hairs on my back stood on end, not only from the feeling of being watched, but from the scant wafting scent of death slowly floating around us, its unseen tendrils wrapping around our heads like an ominous fragrance. "They know we're here," I whispered, gripping the hilts of my two blades tighter. The entire group was on alert, and we had stopped moving to listen to the echoes lightly treading across the walls of the canyon.

It was dead silent, not a good sign, but the Zompires weren't always silent. Their telltale groans and growls usually gave them away before they pounced. I was sure this was a trick of some sort, and I wasn't feeling reassured as minutes passed and nothing happened. The scent of death diminished, and we were left stunned and on edge.

"Come on, keep moving." Christian waved us forward and we cautiously followed, still listening for anything to give away the death awaiting us. I didn't like it, and I hoped we'd reach the fortress soon.

As we rounded yet another turn in the endless maze, I was beginning to think we were lost and wouldn't make it out before sundown, dying a miserable death at the jaws of a thousand ferals that probably lingered in the deeper recesses during the daylight hours. Though I didn't know where they hid while the sun burned down like a fiery inferno across the barren rock, I was pretty sure there were some ferals here who had managed to find shelter during the hot hours of the daytime.

Christian held up his hand, and we halted, studying the walls around us and behind, ready for anything. What were we looking for? Straining hard to hear something echoing across the canyon, I was getting tired of false alarms. I wanted blood and some fighting action. Enough of this hurry up and wait.

We continued on into a large opening in the canyon. The wavy walls hovered around us like giants bearing down on us, and the sand beneath our feet was cool and partially damp. I hoped a flash flood wasn't going to come through here any time soon. It would obviously fill with water when that happened. Though it would be a fast drowning death, it wasn't on my bucket list.

A crow cawed in the distance, and the rocks amplified its scream like a haunting melody. Something was wrong. I readied my blades as a horrendous gust of wind brought back the stench of death. Everyone was ready now, blades out and knees bent, hearts racing.

Clicking noises, followed by a variety of screeches and squealing metal, echoed across the rock. The walls opened, revealing small, coffin-shaped slots as some hidden mechanism turned, and Zompires poured out of them like pipes bursting. There were dozens of slots, and the things were piling out. I swung my machetes as the first approached me, slashing at its neck and sending its head flying. Another had its wild eyes trained on me before he met the same fate, his slick blood gushing like a fountain from the stump left behind. A chain rattled as it fell off his neck, no longer held in place by his head.

The chorus of clinking metal made me realize they were all chained by the neck, controlled by someone who could retract the chains when they wanted to pull them back into the holes. These were guard dogs, kept to attack the enemy at the entrance of the hidden fortress. They were nothing but puppets packed like sardines in the hidden encasements, starved and ready for anything living to chew on. *Great.* Who knew how many were holed up in the slots, as more and more poured out, hungry and ready for fresh blood?

"There's too many!" Sarah shrieked above the groans and screeches of the dead. Her sword slashed though two of them at one time, separating one from his arm and cutting the other cleanly in half. Swinging the sword around one more time, she decapitated the armless one, who was still headed for her, before finishing off the one crawling on the ground in a sticky pile of guts and gore.

This was going to be an epic mess.

Elijah had his foot on one Zompire, crushing his chest down as he took his spear and stabbed the fucker right in the head. Another was already rushing toward him, but he sliced through that one like butter with a huge hunting knife. He was covered with sticky, black-red blood, as was everyone else. It was a bloodbath. We were outnumbered, but definitely not out skilled. There was still daylight out, but the sun was beyond the ceiling of the canyon, throwing the entire path and clearing into shade, which was perfect for them to attack us.

I wondered who was holding the reins on these guys as I crossed my machetes on one charging corpse as he tried desperately to chomp his incisors down on my arms. A quick jerk and his head went rolling. His body twitched frantically until it fell silent.

Minutes later, the two dozen or so Zompires were all down, and the few left dangling from the chains were backing up, and not willingly. The chains were being reeled back into the slots carved in the canyon walls. I wondered where the coffin-like exits went, but the chains made one quick last jerk, rattling wildly enough that if anyone tried to enter while the doors were retracting, they'd get shredded by the chains. The doors slammed shut before I could get to one. I dropped my machetes and patted the wall to find any kind of opening. Scraping my fingers against the hard stone, I found nothing, not even an indention where the doors met the walls. Frustrated, I hit my fist against it before picking up my weapons and rejoining the group.

"Where's the entrance to this motherfucker? I've had enough of their games. You said there might be traps, but you didn't say it was a suicide mission!" I pointed a finger at Christian, anger surging through my veins as I ached for more blood. I hadn't had vampire blood in ages, not since I'd taken some from his veins, sealing our bond. It wasn't that I'd wanted to, but once you bond with a hybrid, the exchange of blood was necessary. Otherwise, we would have died.

Yeah, that was one of the worst days of my life.

Now digging a finger into his shoulder, I wanted to slap him. It didn't help that I also wanted to kiss him at the same damn time and see if he was okay. I think that infuriated me even more, especially since I could hear Rye chuckling at the sight of me going off on his number one enemy.

Damn them both to hell.

"I told you. They probably don't think I'm still alive. Mercer probably set this up after I disappeared. Looks like one of his sick contraptions." He stepped away, trying to control the stillness of his features, but I could see him steaming, too. So he didn't know this would happen, just wonderful. That deflated me a bit.

"Just get this circus moving already. Where do we get into this fortress of yours, Christian?" I hissed. Elijah was next to me as I stepped forward again, waving my bloody machete around like a mad woman. I liked action and getting things done. This unorganized mission was driving me bonkers, especially since I didn't plan on dying there. But someone, apparently, had other plans.

"Calm down, April. No need to expend all the energy on a vamp." Elijah spit out the last word like it was garbage. He wasn't a fan of the hybrid vampires, especially since he'd spent most of the end of the world exterminating the feral ones. If there'd been someone more skeptical about the hybrids, they'd really have nothing on him. He looked at the vamps like they were abominations of some sort. Hell, weren't we all some sort of mutated freak? It was really hypocritical if you asked me, but no one was asking, and he didn't care what anyone else thought of his antics.

I muttered under my breath and stomped forward, feeling foolish for losing my top, especially since Christian had remained so calm. Nothing grated my nerves more than not knowing what to expect. The city was predictable. This walking into an enemy hive was looking more and more like a trip into an asylum. I doubted we'd be welcomed by this Mercer. He sounded like cold-blooded psychopath.

I rounded the corner, still fuming, leaving my group to scamper behind me, and ran right into the meanest son of a bitch ever. Cold, calculating blue eyes drilled into me as I approached, making me halt in my steps. The seven burly body guards surrounding him not only were armed with guns, they also had hold of a bunch of feral vampires chained at the necks and torsos. If that wasn't a shocker of my lifetime. I wasn't ready for it. I had literally almost walked into the clutches of one of these ferals. His blood red eyes flashed at me as his jaws snapped wildly. He looked starved. So why wasn't he just turning around and pouncing on the hybrid vampire yanking his chain? Well, a moment later, he did try that, only to be zapped by a Taser baton as a reward. He hissed at the culprit but did not try to bite him again.

That's interesting.

I'd seen trained ferals before, back when Blaze's hive had attacked Christian's at the Stratosphere. Still, it made my skin crawl, and I eyed the eight vampires staring me down like killer animals. They treated these ferals like savage dogs, and it made me furious.

"Mercer." Christian gave him a curt nod but didn't approach him. The rest of us took his example and didn't venture any closer.

"I wrote you off as dead." Mercer's stoic looks made him appear frozen, like a marble statue. His dark black hair was cut short, almost buzzed to the scalp, and his skin was a golden tan, as if he'd spent some time in the sun. Golden halos flashed in his irises from the remaining light and made his bright blue eyes a buzzing neon color as he scanned them over us without a lick of approval. "Where have you been hiding these days?"

No one moved. Christian was the obvious ticket into this compound. I still couldn't see where the entrance was, just more turns and curves in the slot canyon walls. My stomach rolled, instantly complaining that this was not the best idea I'd ever had. Still, I had to speak to Rick if I was to find out what had really happened to my mother. "Well, as you can tell, I'm very much alive. I was caught in the city of Vida, under the Strip, for a while. Their leader was less than welcoming." Christian's face matched Mercer's, eye for eye, frown for frown, then smirk for smirk.

I saw why he'd pick this guy as his second. So different, yet perfectly matched in every way.

"What can I do for you?" Mercer tilted his head down, narrowing his eyes as he scanned each and every one of us. When he was done, the disgust on his face told me he wasn't impressed. Oh well, right?

"We need to speak to Rick." Christian stepped forward, close enough to almost invade Mercer's personal space.

"For what reason?"

"April's family was held in our station at the Stratosphere. Rick did something to her mother, caused her to change into something, possibly a hybrid. It drove her insane." He hesitated before he continued, "The change affected her mind to the point of driving her to suicide."

"Rick killed her." I stepped forward, drilling my glare into Mercer. He didn't even flinch at it, but I noticed a tiny drop of amusement dancing in his eyes.

He sniffed the air and the excitement grew tenfold on his face. "Human." His smirk slowly melted into a charming smile. "How so? Rick is human, just like you."

"I thought he was a hybrid human."

Mercer sighed and his grin faded. Apparently, we'd already pushed his welcome to the max. "He was. But he's developed a 'cure,' if you can call it that. It's far from perfect, but he no longer has a need to drink blood to survive. He's no longer one of us, just plain human." His fangs slipped out and a malicious grin spread slowly across his face. "I don't think he'd like visitors, though. He's quite the recluse."

"I don't care what he likes. I demand to see him."

Mercer's stare bore into me, and my skin tingled from the strain. He was an alpha vampire for a reason, but I was betting Christian could muster the same kind of threatening stare if he wanted to, if he needed to.

Right on cue, Christian stepped up to Mercer. He was obviously at least two inches taller than his former second and definitely bulkier. Mercer didn't back down, though. His glare shifted from me to his former leader, and a challenging eye match followed.

"I suggest you let us through. This is still my hive."

"It hasn't been your hive in months. I'm leader here now, and the hive does as I say."

"Mercer…." Christian was losing his patience, but he did well not allowing it to show.

"Your human army won't get far. I don't suggest you try to oppose me."

Christian snarled. Both had their fangs in full show now, their eyes flashing even brighter as their halos overtook the colored irises. Their growls made my skin crawl, but I readied myself to slice through Mercer's henchmen at any second now. His seven bodyguards shifted on their feet, similarly prepared for a fight.

"They are far from just human, even you know that, Mercer." Christian's words bled through his clenched jaw as he looked like he was actually puffing out to be even taller than he was a moment before. I swallowed the knot in my throat. Mercer had to let us in. I'd kill each and every one of them to get to Rick if I had to. "You know they could match us sword for sword, brawn for brawn, in combat. They have none of our weaknesses and everything we've longed for."

Mercer breathed heavily, his anger leaking from his glare as he flicked his eyes from Christian toward us and back again.

Mercer's second in command, a Hispanic male with equally short hair, spat on the ground and hissed. "Hybrid human scum." His fangs extended, and he looked mighty hungry for a fight. He was in front of me and eyed me like a filet mignon. Great. A psycho second is always fun to deal with. Bring it on.

"The pot calling the kettle black now, are we?" I huffed back. Flashing my machete, I threw him a wide smile and fluttered my eyelids. "Such atrocious manners."

"Philippe, enough!" Mercer's biting command made Philippe crane his neck to the side in surprise. Mercer glared at him until he stepped back, away from us, still fuming but focusing his anger on the grainy earth below. He looked peeved, but it was oddly satisfying to see his ego deflated with so few words.

"I apologize for my second. He craves the days of fighting and blood. We are a peaceful hive now and do not require such barbaric ways anymore." Another daring glare flicked over toward Philippe, and the second in command's presence was diminished as he flinched from his commander's gaze. He glared at the ground, his anger seething underneath his deflated exterior. I knew better than to ever trust this man. He was an explosion ready to happen.

"Come," Mercer said smoothly. "I will escort you through our facility. Welcome back, brother." He held his arms out and gave a tight, welcoming hug to Christian. The rest of us were left baffled, mouths agape at the sudden change in attitude.

What, no more fighting? I held back a groan and pondered tucking away my weapons.

Mercer turned, parting his warriors, who followed behind our group. I still held one of my machetes out, unwilling to put it away. The group oozed aggression, and I wasn't going to get caught unawares. I wasn't the only one on my toes, either. Elijah kept his oversized hunting knife gripped in his hand. Gotta love the guy, he understood the game even more than I did.

"Do you trust them?" I whispered over to him. The group had funneled back into two side-by-side columns. Christian was listening to Mercer as we made our way through the curves, turns and twists of the canyon with Mercer's group taking up the rear with their captive feral dogs in tow. As long as one of them didn't lunge at us, I was beginning to think me might actually make it back out alive. Still, I couldn't help keeping one eye on them and one eye forward.

"No," Elijah said. "Not one bit."

"That's reassuring."

"You asked."

Sometimes Elijah was too blunt for his own good. I'd grown to like his rough demeanor. He'd been leader for so long in Vida, he really had no social skills. Still, he had my back, and I had his. He'd become like a big brother, even more so than Blaze had ever been. I was relieved that he didn't seem to have any romantic intention with me, like Rye and Christian. I just couldn't take it if he did. Having a strong male influence around that wasn't out to tie me down was refreshing. Still, it made me sad that Sarah was highly interested in him, but he didn't show any interest in her, either. Or anyone, for that matter. I think he was completely missing the romance gene, actually. I decided I'd have to ask him about that one day.

"What if he tries to trap us?" I asked.

Elijah spun the knife in his hands and grinned. "We can take them, and their feral slaves. Been aching for some more action anyway."

I laughed but ended up clearing my throat as Christian and Rye both glared at me at the same time. *Geez. Can't have any fun at all.*

"I'm sure we'll get our chance soon enough," Elijah added.

"That's what I'm afraid of," I muttered as the group came to a stop in another opening in the canyon. This one was smaller than the one where the ferals had attacked us. Mercer waited momentarily as he stared at the wall right before a soft hum from all around us turned into a roaring rumble, and the wall began to shift. It slid smoothly inward, opening up to a dark hole within. As the dust that puffed up from its movement finally rested, I could see bright overhead fluorescent lights heading into a long ramp that led down onto the ground floor of what looked like one side of a large warehouse.

What is up with hybrids and warehouse hideaways? It reminded me of the warehouse fortress underneath the airport in the middle of the city which Blaze headed up. Lately, I hadn't been there as often as I used to go, especially with Jeremy taking to the citizens of the underground city of Vida quite well. He never wanted to leave. Who could blame him? It was the only place in Vegas that had other human kids there to play with. It was his paradise, but nothing but sheer claustrophobia for me.

We marched into the compound, and the large rock wall slid shut behind us with a slow, stomach-shifting rumble. I peered back at it, hoping the sinking feeling of doom sitting like a rock in my stomach would go away. The wall was painted black on the inside, reinforced with sheets of metal and steel. The entire place was like that: dark, black and very much confining. I could feel the air siphoning away from me in a rush to suffocate.

"Wow, who knew this was under all that rock!" Sarah spun around, in awe of the hidden fortress. It was definitely impressive, but it did little to stifle my dread.

"Yeah, pretty cool," I muttered. My mind was on the mass of hybrid vampires gathering to study us. More and more poured in from different halls and doorways, down the metal steps to the upper floor and out from behind the rows and rows of vehicles and storage containers that lined the belly of this place. If the city of Vida looked sterile, this one was the complete black opposite. It was all dark, dark and more dark. Most of these vamps probably never saw the light of day, especially isolated out there so far from any shelter except the slot canyons. Their pale skin was more proof of their reluctance to leave this sanctuary. Not my idea of the perfect place to live.

"Welcome to our underground fortress. It spans the size of ten football fields. We have living quarters in the third floor surrounding the warehouse and toward the rear. Greenhouse and animal pens are located on the ground floor toward the back, so are the stockrooms, deep in the mountain. Headquarters is just above us." He pointed up toward the stairs lining the warehouse and leading into a doorway off to the right. "Not much to look at, but it's home sweet home." Mercer gave us a wide grin, which only succeeded in making him look even scarier.

This Mercer was visibly relaxed now that he was within the walls of his home. I eyed the mass of vampires surrounding us and noticed that there were no humans. Great. I hoped none of them were hungry. We probably smelled appetizing to them.

"Where do you pen up the leashed Zompires?" Elijah's snarky tone was not lost on Mercer, who faced him with a sly smirk pasted on his lips. Maybe he wasn't so statuesque after all.

"We keep them near the armory. They are considered weapons." He turned and continued forward until he reached a set of metal steps leading up to a single doorway. "I believe Rick would like to meet you, too. Shall we surprise him?" He turned, punched a code into a keypad on the side of the door and flung it open. Shuffling in, I muttered my own little obscenities at the mention of Rick.

Oh, I bet he just can't wait to meet me.

Chapter Four
Circus of Lesser Things

"**WHERE IS HE** taking us?" Sarah whispered. I shrugged, but Christian had obviously heard us and immediately offered the answer.

"The Freaks Lab."

"Say what?" My mouth hung open at the pet name they had for the lab. It didn't sound very promising. In fact, the name did wonders to freak me out, and I fought to not turn and run away. Even so, another part of me was jumping up and down like an amused two-year-old, ready to play with the toys.

Christian frowned but didn't repeat what he'd said. I guess it was a sensitive subject. This only made my adrenaline surge, ready to trash the place for even existing. Any place with a name like that could only mean horrible things happened there, like what had happened to my mother. The darn two-year-old stopped clapping in my head and started whining protests. Yep, good times.

Mercer approached another coded door, and the locks clicked opened before he shoved at it to help it along. Inside, we all filed in and stared down at a room that really should have been a museum of Ripley's believe it or nots. I almost choked on the rancid bile tumbling up my throat as I took in the atrocities before me. Blinking hard and deepening my breaths kept me from losing my cool as the room narrowed in my vision and my disgust multiplied.

Row upon row of acrylic tanks filled to the brim with yellow-tinged fluid were occupied by bodies, mutilated beyond recognition. A collective gasp shifted through the group as we were silenced, our words stripped from our mouths at the horrid sight. Nothing I'd ever seen would have prepared me for this. My legs felt weak, but I stepped forward, hoping they wouldn't give up on me as I moved along.

The first tank held a large man, or what would've been a man in a past life. He now had large fangs jutting out of his upper jaw and wild, reddened irises that were enlarged so much, he looked bug-eyed and disproportioned. His skin was a tough, wrinkled and abused leather littered with scars and missing chunks, leaving his body gaping open, displaying sinew with tendons dangling from bones. The bulk of muscles underneath the remains of shredded cloth bulged abnormally and appeared to almost split the skin from their massive size. Thankfully, the thing was dead. I wasn't sure I could stomach seeing something like that alive.

Fortunately, everything else in the tanks was also dead. The corpses were all in differently morphed states and hung suspended in the fluid, like puppets left abandoned by their owners, awaiting their last dance. Mercer led us deeper into the lab, giving us little time to ponder the creepiness of the creatures whose eyes seemed to follow us as we made our way forward. It sent shivers down my spine, but at least I wasn't turning colors like Sarah was. Her pallor had intensified, matching her skin to the yellow fluid surrounding us and reflecting the dim lights overhead.

"Hey, you all right?" I slipped my hand onto her shoulder, and she gave me a weak nod but didn't dare to look me in the eye. I made sure to keep one step behind her in case she decided to spew what little lunch we'd had. She wasn't looking like she could tolerate much more of this. If she collapsed, she'd never stop beating herself over it. I hoped the next room would hold less gruesome displays.

At the end of the rows, the rest of the lab emerged, looking much like a regular chemistry lab I'd had in high school. Long black tables with shiny tops filled the room. Some had stacks of test tubes, clean and ready to be used. Others had sinks in the middle of their surfaces next to Bunsen burners sitting under glass vials with bubbling fluids of every color. Cabinets filled with all kinds of chemicals and refrigerators with packs of blood and bits of other non-mentionables lined one side of the room. It was well stocked and a lot bigger than the lab in Blaze's hive. I wondered just how many people had been destroyed in the confines of this place. Studied to bits, literally. It was the last place my mother had entered before losing her grip on reality, and I was pretty sure she hadn't been the first or the last to meet their fate here.

Her loss left an icy sliver of my heart empty and growing even harder as time went on. How do you let go of such pain? I hadn't, and doubted I'd ever be able to. Maybe by removing Rick's head from his body would I find some kind of peace. I was looking forward to it, more so than anything else I planned for the future.

Did I even have any plans beyond that? I brushed the thought away because I couldn't answer that question. I had no answers beyond the now. There was no future for me or anyone else like me. My desolation held its grip on me and wouldn't let go, but I'd think more on it later.

Speaking of Rick, the man sitting at one of the tables had whirled around in his chair to observe us with his studious eyes as we filed into room, filling it up well enough. He didn't look anything like I'd thought he would. He wore glasses, had sandy blonde hair and a lanky, thin body that looked ill-suited for fighting. His blue eyes twinkled with a hardened light of knowledge, eyeing each one of us up and down as he satisfied his own curiosity. Tiny lines were etched across his face from the corners of his eyes and into the chiseled line of his cheeks. There were no halos, no perfectly smooth and uninterrupted coloring to his skin which fitted the unnatural look of the hybrids so well. In fact, the signs of aging and slight discoloration to his skin marked him as only one thing.

He was human.

This revelation felt disjointed as I stared at him with sharpened daggers emerging from my glare. Okay, so what if he was human? It didn't brush away all the evil he'd done and was probably still getting at in the middle of this God-forsaken desert. Hell, it probably made him even more dangerous to still be in possession of his human traits, more in control of his insanity than the vampires whose cravings overwhelmed them without regard to life. Maybe he was a hybrid human like me, but that conclusion quickly faded as I heard Rye whisper the answer to me.

"He's not infected. Pure human, no hybrid to him. Not a hint of infection or mutation."

Great.

I'm not sure if Rick heard him, but his sudden smile told me he most certainly knew who I was and what we were talking about as well. "I wondered how long I'd have to wait to meet you, April." He stood up but didn't approach me. It made me wonder if he could possibly fathom the amount of hatred coursing through me at this very moment. No, he couldn't even imagine how much distain I harbored within my mind for this pathetic man. It was so strong it had sucked away at my life, bit by little tiny bit every day since my mother had killed herself. Each moment he breathed in life was a second my mother would never have ever again.

"The pleasure is not mine."

His smile didn't waver. Even in the presence of vampires, he seemed cocky, untouchable even. There was nothing more I wanted to do than to adjust that attitude, permanently.

"We've come for answers, Rick. Good to see you again." Christian offered his hand out to the man and they clasped and shook them, like old comrades. It only fueled my anger, but I pushed it down before I could burst and lose the fragile grip I had on my temper. I couldn't risk losing my mind in this place, it would only hurt the others with me. We were severely outnumbered, and my vendetta could wait until the answers I sought out were in my grasp.

"Christian. I knew you'd be too stubborn to just disappear. Good to see you're doing well." Rick squinted as he examined Christian's face. "The medicine I gave you, did you have any adverse effects from it?"

"No. I feel wonderful, actually." Christian looked happy, like he was recalling the times he'd been delusional and mad from the green withering, the vampire sickness. "If fact, I have great news about another use for it."

"Really?" Rick's eyes lit up, making him look even younger than he appeared. He may have been human, but he was aging very well. He had to be near forty, maybe mid-forties, but I couldn't be sure.

"Well, another mutation was living in that underground city I told you about. Her scratch was lethal, gave any victim an amplified version of the green sickness. But my blood counteracted the poison completely. It was truly amazing."

The scientist nodded, pushing his glasses up his nose as he listened. His eyes flicked toward me but never hovered long. He was smart not to do so. I practically ground my teeth down to nubs, my jaw aching from the tension. All I wanted to do was push everyone to the side as I ran across the rest of the room, grabbed him and slammed him to the ground to make him beg for his pathetic life.

"How did you know your blood would help? A mighty shame you couldn't bring me a sample of the creature's blood."

"I don't know, I just… when I saw them suffering what I'd suffered from, it just clicked. Yeah, it is a mighty shame."

I couldn't hold my tongue anymore. "A mighty shame? That thing almost killed all of us!" The fury inside was hell-bent on spilling out. "For all we know, you created it, too."

"Hold on now, April… we don't know that." Christian held his hands up, ready to hold me back if I stepped any closer. I hadn't even noticed that I'd been walking toward them the entire time. Rick sat back down, stiffening but not one bit nervous as I hovered near him. He was so smug, so certain of himself as he sat there calmly, never flinching. It made me steam even more. I'd give anything to snap each one of his fingers like tiny, insignificant twigs.

Still, I jolted forward, reaching out and managed to clasp my thin fingers around his neck, squeezing slightly. His eyes never wavered, taking me into their deep blue sea, narrowing in a dare to push this further.

Really? You really want to die so fast?

'Do it.'

What?

I gasped at his intrusion into my head, but my hands never let go of his throat.

"April. Let... him... go," Christian hissed as he stepped closer, only to be halted as Rick held up a finger.

"I'm all right."

"Not for long," I muttered.

He cleared his throat but made no move to shove me off. What was he doing? I watched him closely, waiting for a hidden weapon or something to shoot out and stab me. He was very capable of violence, I could feel it pouring off of him in waves. So why was he waiting now? Why didn't he just off me if he could?

'I need your blood, April.'

His voice in my head made me flinch. It felt awkward, like a fly buzzing in my ear, or a horsefly, constantly returning to irritate me with its hum yet impossible to evade. How was he doing that? I'd never met a telepathic person before. However fascinating it was to discover such a thing existed, it did nothing to quench the vengeance I so very much needed. His presence bothered me to no end.

'Do you want to be human again, April?'

The words drilled into my brain like ice picks, causing a throbbing headache to emerge. I was going to have his head for doing that.

Stop that.

The blue in his eyes grew darker, like a stormy ocean ready to pummel the coast on a wintery day. I wanted to pluck them out as the pain expanded down my neck and numbed my fingertips.

What are you doing to me?

'I'll stop when you let me go.'

I'm not doing anything to you.

'Yes, you are.'

I shook my head, trying to shake the fog that was blurring up my focus. I struggled to keep contact with his skin and dug my fingers deeper into his neck, giving it a squeeze. My lungs were halting, freezing mid-breath. "What are you doing to me?"

"Let me go, April." He spoke this time, the headache still throbbing from my contact with him.

"April, do what he says." Christian was reaching out to pull me off of Rick, but one glare from this chemistry freak was enough to make Christian freeze in his steps. Everyone behind me was shuffling nervously, not knowing what to do or what was going on.

"Stop!" I wheezed out a breath as my chest burned. The pain... I'd never felt anything like it before. *"Please."*

I let go, and my hands dropped to my side as I fell to my knees. The pain stopped immediately, leaving me to huff in and out while I stared at Rick through a veil of tears. If my hatred hadn't been consuming my humiliation at the moment, I'd have hopped onto my feet and run away from that unearthly beast or just slice off his head with my machete.

"That's better." Rick straightened, smoothing down his shirt and rubbing his neck where my fingernails had dug in, almost breaking his skin. He may have been powerful, but this man was mortal, fragile and human, just like me, if not more so.

"I'm not quite like you, April." His lips moved, but the words sounded far away.

"What? Stay out of my head!"

"You're special. A true human hybrid. Adapted to this vampiric virus in a most specific way. Made for supreme survival."

"What makes you not so special then?" I leaned forward, glaring at him, hoping to make him wince under the pressure my eyes emitted. "He's telepathic. He's reading our minds right now." I spoke more to the group behind me than to Rick as his grin grew wider from my proclamation.

The group collectively shifted in their places, and I could almost feel their worried looks flicking between one another. I didn't blame them. Having our minds read of anything we planned or thought about these strangers could be disastrous. Why hadn't Christian known Rick could read minds? Did he just not tell us? I was feeling less and less trusting of him as time went on.

"Because he didn't know," Rick answered.

Dammit! Okay, this mind reading crap was irritating me.

"Bullshit!" I swung my eyes toward Christian, almost as mad at him as I was with Rick. "He was your leader. How would he not know that?"

"Some things are better left unsaid until the time is right."

Christian didn't look pleased at all.

Some people just can't be trusted. My lips curled back to show him my hatred. I was already on my feet, backing up, feeling much better now that I wasn't in direct contact with his skin. Maybe the touch amplified his connection to my mind because now, his little inside mutters were farther away and much less painful, if not painless. Now they were just words, still echoing inside my head, an annoying intrusion, but there was no torment, no torture accompanying them.

Note to self… don't touch Rick.

At least, not until I could meet sharpened metal to his neck.

Chapter Five

Enemy Mine

"I DON'T LIKE this idea of staying here with the likes of them."
Sarah worked the elastic stuck in her long, substantial red hair out and
shook the vibrant strands, sighing as the weight of the locks fell over her
shoulders. She was still beautiful, as she'd been before all hell broke loose
and the world had gone to the gutters. I was still stunned to think how
much we were alike back then and now. Then, we had been besties and
done everything together. Now, we were both human hybrids and had
survived the end of the world against all odds. Somehow we'd been spared,
immune to the vampiric virus that turned people into mindless, blood-
seeking monsters. Or worse, left them dead.

"Me neither." Sprawled across the queen size bed with porn quality
satin purple sheets on them, I stared at the ceiling, contemplating what to
do next. This place was a full-blown hotel inside, including indoor pool
and windows! Can you imagine that? Windows to the outside world
strategically hidden by camouflage to appear to look like the red rock of
the slot canyon. If I wasn't so agitated, I might've actually liked this place.
Not to mention the three-shower-head bathroom with adjacent roman
sized tub to soak in attached to my room.

My family had lived a humble existence in a bunker hidden in the
mountains, and these bastards were basking in the lap of luxury. It was
unbelievable.

"Do you think this will work?" Sarah was staring out the window, watching the sun setting over the expanse of desert beyond the canyon walls. This section of the compound was built on a cliff, overlooking the vast and lonesome desert below. I joined her to see it fade away as the moments ticked by. I decided this place had been built before the plague. No vampire would add windows to the list of wants in a fallout shelter.

"Will what work?"

"Vampires and humans. Do you think we'll ever get along?"

"We're not quite human."

"I know that, April." She turned to me, a tight frown marring her pretty face. "You know what I mean."

"No. We won't ever get along. Is that what you want to hear? We'll never, ever, ever, ever get along. We're their food... period! Who wants to be the prey in a world full of hunters? We'll be extinct soon enough, and they will likely starve to death. No one wins."

"You really think that?" Sarah's green eyes glowed under the reds and golds of the sunset, shiny and full of naïve hope. We were so similar, yet the year apart in different situations had left us more different than I could've ever imagined.

"Yes, Sarah. I really think that. I wish I couldn't, but sooner or later, this is all over for us."

"When did you become so pessimistic?"

"I'm a realist."

"No. You've written us off already, like we were pitiful little chicks being sent to the coop to fatten up for slaughter. What happened to you? You used to be full of life, ready to take on the world. Where did that go?"

I huffed, crossing my arms and biting back the insults. "While you lived sheltered in the city of Vida, I was out there," I pointed out toward the horizon. "Where it was kill or be killed. Where starvation was just a supply run away. Where death lingered in the shadows, ready to chew on my flesh the moment I stopped being vigilant. I worried day in and day out for my family. I killed for them while you were tucked in safe. I was surviving."

Sarah's hard eyes turned liquid, tears pooling in them as the light faded, her jaw taut. She rushed past me and headed toward the door.

"Sarah... wait...."

Slam! The door vibrated on its hinges as I stared at it. I didn't know where she was going—most probably to her room at the end of the hall—but I was afraid I wouldn't see her for the rest of the night. The vampires would all be awake by now, and my anxiety was filling up my head as the moments continued and she didn't return. I contemplated going after her, but what good would it do? She might have gone to bother Elijah or at least hide there until she simmered down. How could anyone blame her? I was kicking myself for being so bitter.

A knock at the door had my hope zooming right back up. Flying to it, I paused as my fingers tapped the knob, feeling wary at all at once. I peeked out the peephole and couldn't see anything.

"Who's there?"

Silence followed by some shuffling reassured me that someone was there, waiting quietly. I backed away and grabbed one of my machetes lying on the bed and readied to cut up whoever burst through the door.

The knob shook and another knock resonated. "April? It's Rye."

I let out the breath I didn't know I'd been holding, relieved beyond the moon that it was Rye. It didn't last long, though. My anger at him for not replying right away had me wanting to sock him in the jaw.

"What the hell, why didn't you answer me when…?" I unlocked the door and was sent flying back onto the floor as it burst open, but my weapon remained locked in my hand.

"Mercer."

"April. I'm terribly sorry, I had to use a voice trick that comes in handy quite often to get you out of the door. Bad thing about having a compound fortress, it's really hard to open the doors if they're locked. Thanks for letting me in." Mercer's sly smirk filled my vision as he filled the doorway.

Christian walked in behind him, looking somber and defeated, followed by a vibrantly happy Rick. *Great.*

"What do you think you're doing?" I held the blade out, ready to slice even Christian with it. Three against one. Really? "Can't take me alone, had to bring back up, right? One woman, three men. Really appropriate."

Mercer wasn't too happy with my comments and motioned to Christian to grab me. He approached slowly, his haloed eyes shimmering against the halogen lamps across the room. He was my mate, supposedly. So why—and how—could he hurt me now? Even though I had committed to try to not fall in love with anyone, it sure wouldn't be Christian. But the pull of our bond made my stomach churn with every little traitorous step he took. *Dammit, Christian.*

"Don't touch me." I backed up. My thighs bumped into the edge of the bed, which I sidestepped to get around. I was cornered, but I wasn't going to give up that easily. "Why are you doing this, Christian?"

"I'm sorry. This is my hive. I have to take control of things right now."

"Really? Sounds like Mercer is in charge around here now, not you." I swung the machete, but he dodged it with inhuman speed and grabbed my wrist. Still, I punched him right in the knee until he buckled. Struggling to get back up, I took his momentary lapse to hop over him and head toward the window. I didn't see a way out, and the window had bars weaved throughout it. I spun around and held a slight bounce on my feet, hoping to find a way around him.

Rick stood behind them, but I could see him pulling something out of a small case he held in his hands. Uncapping the needle, he tapped it to get the bubbles out and then fixed his eyes on me. Whatever was in that syringe, I decided he'd better have planned to stick it where the sun don't shine. I stepped back toward the bathroom, hoping maybe I could at least lock myself in there to think of an alternative means of escape. Christian was nursing his knee, grumbling, but he wouldn't be down for long. Mercer looked as if he was going in for the kill. Rick only had to wait until I was subdued to plunge whatever he'd concocted into my arm. Like hell I was going to let him do that to me, ever.

"Don't make this difficult," Mercer muttered. His dark eyes reflected the lights shining from the vaulted ceiling. I felt a trickle of his vampire persuasiveness pass over me, sending a chill trickling down my spine. Narrowing my eyes, I smirked. Knowing his magic wasn't working on me made him furious, and I could see his lunge three seconds ago.

His slow mistake.

He flew past me right into the bathroom where I slammed the door shut behind him. Idiot. I turned back toward the others just in time to find Rick trying to stick me with the needle. I grabbed his wrist and winced. His telekinetic power zapped me as if I was touching a power outlet.

It was excruciating and left me breathless and fighting to suck in a breath, but I managed to twist his arm and pull it behind him, crushing his hand to make him let go of the syringe. Gritting my teeth, I fixed it into my fingers and positioned it to his throat. "I hope what you got in here doesn't do too much damage to humans," I hissed.

"Wait! Don't, please!" Rick paled as the needle dug into his neck, a pinprick of blood welling around it. His heartbeat was thumping under his chest, and I could feel it as I pressed my own against him to hold him in place. The electrocuting feeling he emitted stopped, and I shook my head to clear it.

"Now why shouldn't I?" I snickered. It was always better to be on the winning side. Christian stepped forward as Mercer made his way through the bathroom door, literally. It splintered into a thousand wood strips as he bounded into the room, red faced and furious.

"Please…." Rick swallowed as the sweat began to bead on his temples. His racing heart was a huge indication of what sort of poison I was holding. Good. Not so fun getting a taste of his own medicine.

"Let's play this game my way now." I shoved Rick toward the door to the hall and backed toward it, keeping a wary eye on both Christian and Mercer. "No one comes any closer or I off him. Oh, and Rick… tell me what this poison does."

"You don't want to know."

I tugged at his arm, causing him to yelp from the pain. "Oh, I think I don't, but I have the right to know what you were going to shoot me up with. Come on, we're all waiting."

Rick huffed and groaned as I stretched his arm even farther behind him. He'd have no use of it for an hour or so after we were done, but that would be his problem, not mine.

"It's an antidote."

"Oh? For what?"

"To make you completely human."

"I doubt that."

"It's true."

"Then why are the vamps staring at it like it's the black plague for them?" Did he think I was that stupid? Really? Mercer and Christian didn't dare get near us. They eyed the syringe with nothing but pure horror and an obvious smidge of intimate terror. Yeah, I had a weapon in my fingers, but I had to know what it was for.

"Because...." I loosened my grip on him as his voice croaked. He was straining too much and was sure to pass out if I didn't let him breathe. "It's an antidote to anyone's unnatural powers, from the Zompire plague. It turns everyone absolutely human again. No powers."

Well, well. Holy moly.

"An antidote to the plague?" I repeated in disbelief, my fingers shaking as I held it pressed oh so close to his pounding jugular. "What's it do to you? Kills your powers, too, right? You're pretty human already except for those telepathic tricks you're so good at agitating me with."

He didn't answer, just grunted as he pulled to attempt to free himself. Big mistake. I tightened my grip on his awkwardly bent arm. He gasped and paled. Yeah, that did him in.

"Well?" I wanted my answer.

"Yes. Even my telepathic power will be extinguished with it."

Ah. So he had attained his powers as a mutation from the plague. We weren't so different. Whatever he'd taken had left him with his mind powers intact but human.

Thank goodness the door was cracked open. I didn't want to let go of him to turn the knob. We slipped into the hall, and I backed us down the hall toward the way we'd come in. Now what? I kicked at the doors we passed to hopefully find one of my pals as I walked backward down the hall. I was still vulnerable, with no weapons and no idea where the hell I was going. This place was a maze, and I was severely outmatched. We'd been such fools to go there with so few warriors.

Finally I kicked one of the doors and Elijah swung it open, cursing at the noise. "What the fuck is... April?" His eyes widened, and he reached back inside for his weapons. He produced his hunting knife since our larger weapons had been confiscated when we'd entered.

"A little help here," I hissed. He immediately joined me and continued banging on doors as we passed. Eventually everyone in our group had joined in, and we held our ground at the end of the hall in a standstill.

"You won't get far out there. It's nightfall." Mercer's dark eyes dug into me like ice picks, and I was sure he would tear my throat out if he was allowed to. One slip and he'd pounce on us.

"I'll take my chances." I leaned in to whisper into Rick's ear. "Show us the way out, Einstein."

"Okay, just don't push the needle in anymore." His raspy voice made him sound like he was near fainting. What had happened to that crazy mad scientist who'd cracked my mother's sanity until it was broken beyond repair? Something wasn't making sense, but I pushed the thought back for later. I had more important issues to deal with at the moment.

"Well, don't make me."

"This way." I let him go and held the syringe pointed at him, nodding down to it. "You run, I stab."

He bobbed his head up and down and turned forward, pointing ahead. We headed in that direction. Once we'd turned down several halls and gone past the lab, I noticed Mercer and Christian were no longer following us. "Where did your fine leaders go?"

"Probably to round up everyone else in the armory."

Nice.

"Where's that?"

"Toward the rear of the facility."

"Any way to lock it down so they can't get out of there?" This wasn't sounding good for us at all. We had limited weapons.

"Uh… I… um…."

"Spit it out, human," Rye hissed. He had been next to me the whole time, but I hadn't noticed with my focus on Rick. I gave him a tight smile and nodded.

"Yeah. I can lock it down from my lab. It's like a quarantine mechanism we set up in case there was a severe mutation that got out."

I grabbed his arm and turned him toward the door to his lab. "Don't just stand there. Turn it on."

Chapter Six
Chemicals and Quarantines

"HOW SECURE ARE we in this lab? It's made of glass all over the place." Elijah pressed a hand against the cool surface of one of the see-through walls. He turned to view the hall in each direction, but no one was coming. Not yet. "I don't like the looks of this."

"It's a fortress, I assure you. The glass is extremely impact resistant and bullet proof. There is no getting in or out. It can also be sealed for quarantine protocols." Rick pushed his glasses up slowly with his left hand. His right arm was dangling at his side, probably dislocated. *My bad.*

"Get the armory and back section locked down now." Rye wasn't losing focus, and I was glad to have such stringent and focused warriors at my back.

"Okay, just one moment." Rick fumbled with his fingers as he hit a half dozen switches before turning three keys and flipping a bright red switch. A huge rumble shook the ground as the gates shut. Several monitors above this station displayed the rush of activity in the lower floors of the fortress. Only a few stragglers had been trapped outside the quarantine walls, and the bulk of the vampires ran at the noise of the large lockdown doors sliding down into place. I couldn't find Mercer or Christian on any of the monitors and wondered where they'd gone off to. I hoped they were trapped behind the barrier, but they would know about this feature and had probably made it out before we'd gotten the doors secured.

"How long before they get the doors back open?"

Rick settled into one of the rolling chairs, sighing as his eyebrows furrowed with pain. He held his arm, dangling uselessly at his side. "It's made to keep things inside or out. It could take them days to get it open again if they really, really tried to short circuit the system. They won't die in there; there's emergency supplies of food and water all over this compound." He grimaced as he rubbed his arm, the agony making him sweat and pale before my eyes.

I stepped forward, motioning for Elijah to help me. He threw me a knowing glance, and we both approached Rick. He flicked his eyes between us and paled even further. "I might need something for this pain... wait...."

"This'll just take a minute." I grabbed his arm and braced a leg on one of the solid metal counters bolted to the floor. Elijah wrapped his arms around Rick's chest and held on tight as I gave him a nice hard tug.

Rick's scream echoed through the lab, and I was sure the glass beakers and test tubes would shatter from it. I let his arm go and bent it, moving it around a bit to check mobility. This caused him further pain and had him passing out on the chair, slipping down before I braced his body against the chair with my weight. "Got a tough one here." I patted his shoulder after I propped him up enough so he wouldn't tumble to the ground. "Sorry about that. No, wait... not really sorry."

Plopping down in my own rolling chair, I felt the fatigue tugging at my bones. The sun had just barely gone down, but I was exhausted. What had happened to the days of staying up all night?

"You hungry?" Rye plopped an energy bar and a glass of water in front of me. Glancing up at his gorgeous, gunmetal grey eyes, also encircled with a reflective strip of a yellow halo, I found myself smiling at him. I hadn't really looked at him closely lately. He'd been around, holding me in bed, kissing my neck and making me feel wanted, but I hadn't really let him in completely. Especially with the crazy blood bind going on with Christian.

But at that moment, I made myself look, really, really look at Rye. I liked what I saw, and it warmed my insides with a spill of heat as his eyes hypnotized me. I took the food he offered, grateful that he could read my needs better than I could.

"Thank you. I'm more tired than I thought. Maybe I should eat." I unwrapped the foil covering and took a large bite of the thick bar. It was chalky and a bit tough to swallow, but hey, it was food, no matter how horrific it tasted.

"How are you feeling about all this?"

Ah, therapy time with Rye. Always the turn off for me. I frowned as I chewed.

"I'm fine. No, really." I chugged the water back and looked toward the rows of mutations nearby. A chill ran down my skin, but I tried not to shudder. "I still need answers, but this antidote... it really could be something." Rye's frown was prominent, and it made me wonder what he was thinking. "What do you think about it?"

"It depends on if it's for us hybrids or for the ferals only. If it's for us, we could all be turned human again, and with the state of the world right now, that could be really bad." He sighed, rubbing the fatigue from his eyes, making me realize just how exhausted and pale he was looking lately. "If it's just for the ferals, that'd be amazing, to save all those infected, but I have a feeling this isn't meant for the ferals at all. It's meant to make all those with extra powers, like us, like you and me, to make us normal and human again. Do you think everyone will want that? I don't. Who wants to give up power after having a taste of it? Who'd want to be utterly normal again?"

I nodded and pondered what he said. He had a point. Who could give up the powers we'd been given after so long and all the trials we'd faced? I wasn't sure even I could if it came down to it. What if it would be used as a weapon instead of the salvation everyone would initially think it was? That could be disastrous.

"I guess when Rick wakes up, we'll find out." I tapped my fingers on the counter, which reminded me of my chemistry classes back in high school. I looked up to see Sarah take another chair across from me. Her bright smile always lifted my spirit, and I was relieved that she was there with me. She no longer looked peeved at me, at least. No one better to have than my best friend.

"Would you take it?" I asked. She picked at her nails, frowning at her disintegrating manicure. Sarah always took care of herself, beauty queen style. Her flaming red hair was still pulled back into a ponytail, but she made that look stylish with smooth strands and a lock of her brilliant hair wrapped around the elastic. Me, I was the epitome of style neglect. My hair wasn't smooth, but fine and flat, pulled violently back into a ponytail with wisps escaping the tie's grip with each step I took. My face was free of makeup and clear, but I was no looker like she was.

"Maybe."

Somehow, our stark differences hadn't mattered so much before the apocalypse, but now? Now I caught Rye throwing her the tiniest of smiles before he looked away and fished out another energy bar from his supply pack to hand it to her. At least he was smart enough to have grabbed his pack from his room before escaping into this foodless lab.

I wasn't a jealous girl, but that one tiny look made me feel like a wallflower. Lately, now that Sarah was around me so much more, I'd felt inferior to her pretty face. Why that was bothering me now, I had no idea. I liked having my friend with me. I loved it, actually. Maybe it was all the company around me all the time. Before, I'd had no one except my family, and a year of it had turned me into a complete recluse. Breaking out of that habit was proving to be slightly difficult.

I just didn't know how to make it any better for myself. I was utterly clueless.

"I don't think I'd take it." Rye fished out his canteen and took a swig of water. "It's too dangerous. What if no one wants to take it? What good is it to take the cure and be defenseless? Unless it can be given in a mass dose to everyone, I don't see it ever going anywhere."

He was right, and the thought of everything being normal again made my stomach twist. So easy to just shoot up the world with an antidote to make it all all right again, but it wouldn't be easy. Nothing was ever easy.

Rick roused on his chair. Sweat gleamed on his forehead, but his pallor had subsided somewhat. Asleep, he'd looked harmless, like a school teacher, weak, pathetic. I knew better, though, and the urge to go and snap his neck again resurfaced. I sighed, closing my eyes to remember that I had so many questions to ask before I could kill him. Why is there always something in the way of a simple thing like killing someone?

I almost choked on the stifled laugh I let slip out. Everyone looked up at me for a moment, confusion flashing in their eyes. I must have looked like I was losing my mind, but I pretended to have almost choked on the energy bar sitting half eaten in my fingers.

"I'm okay," I managed to squeak out. They all turned back to what they were doing, and I refocused my eyes onto the now groggy but awake Rick.

"Where's your morphine?" Elijah let his gaze slide over the dozens of cabinets and drawers lining the wall. "You're going to need it."

"Third cabinet from the left on that wall." Rick pointed across from us and let his head fall back, his breath heaving from the pain. It probably wasn't as bad as it had been while it was dislocated, but he sure was a bit wimpy if you asked me.

I guess being utterly human did have its disadvantages. Even superpowers like telekinesis and telepathic abilities didn't make up for no tolerance to pain. What a pity.

Elijah grabbed a vial of morphine from the cabinet. After plucking some alcohol swabs, two by twos, a filter needle and a Tb syringe with a needle, he made his way over to Rick. I watched him expertly snap the ampule top off, suck up the liquid, switch needles, tap the air out and dilute it with saline. I wondered how much medical training he'd had.

"All right, give me your uninjured arm, show me a vein." He snickered as he snapped a tourniquet onto Rick's arm. Finding a vein didn't seem too hard for him, and he inserted an IV port easily. The smell of blood seemed to heighten Rye's senses, and I watched as he made his way to the farthest point in the large laboratory, away from Rick.

I sighed, rubbing my head. I was relieved that the blood didn't affect me like it did him. It was one advantage of being a hybrid human, not a vampire. Watching Elijah, I wasn't sure how a vampire would not want to munch on Rick's arm from the tiny amount of blood expelled from the IV site. Once he cleaned the site and slapped a tegaderm clear film on it, the smell seemed to dissipate, and Rye was able to come back to sit near me.

At least Rick didn't look like he was going to pass out again. His eyes were practically glassy from the nice dose of morphine he'd just received.

I jumped up and headed toward him, hoping he wasn't about to pass out again. "Don't knock him out, I still need to interrogate him."

Elijah cleaned up the mess of papers and needles, dropping them into a sharps container installed on the wall. "He's all yours, April. He's just feeling mighty good right about now, not knocked out." He stood up and walked away but not before revealing how tense his jaw was and how his fingers curled into fists with his hidden fury. He didn't have to hide it; I could feel it coming off of him in waves. The narrowed glare he threw me topped the cake before he made his way to take my place besides Sarah. His demeanor grew less intense as he turned to throw her a smile. She reciprocated and began her usual torrent of chatting about anything.

It was nice some people could forget so fast just what a predicament we were in. I was pretty sure Mercer and his gang were working diligently to get out of the quarantine area, and we were sitting here fucking around like it was afternoon tea. Yeah.

I took the seat Elijah had emptied and rolled closer to Rick, who watched me cautiously. I had to admit, now that he was stoned on the morphine, he didn't seem so scary anymore. I hoped he would answer my questions, or it would have all been a waste of my time and patience. Something told me that he held more secrets than I wanted to know. Regardless, I needed to know everything, no matter how deep or how far it went.

Chapter Seven
Soot and Ashes

"YOU LOOK LIKE your mother." Rick's beady eyes focused on me as I inched closer. I wondered what was running through that huge brain of his. If he knew what was good for him, he'd answer everything I asked, thoroughly and without any fancy riddles or avoidance. I hoped he knew this.

"I need to know what you did to her."

"She was an excellent patient. Very tolerant for the most part. Patient, too."

"Her name was Helen."

At those words he tilted his head, his eyes shifting to a faraway look. "I'm very sorry to hear she's gone. My condolences. Helen was an amazing woman."

"She was. Until you did something to her. I need to know what you did." I leaned forward. "And I suggest you don't leave any minor details out."

This didn't make him shiver or cower away from me as I would've expected, but instead, he lifted his chin to look at me straight on. He was cradling his injured arm but didn't flinch as I rolled my chair closer.

"When Christian brought her to me, I was very impressed by how strong-willed and tough she was. I wanted to break her down, make her mine in every way. By that, I mean I wanted to know exactly what made her immune to the virus. There are more strains of this disease than what you've seen. It's such an amazing entity in how it has developed, morphed and mutated as time has gone on. Zompires, hybrid vampires… they were just the beginning of the phenomenon which happened when it was released into the world."

"Get to the point." I could tell how much the subject fascinated him. My remark made his enthusiasm waver just that little bit. Still, he continued, ignoring my interruption.

"However, the human strains were what interested me the most. How is it that of all the living humans that I've encountered above ground, only you and your family remained immune to the virus? The people in Vida did well to quarantine themselves against any outside contamination during the time the virus was alive and actively changing people via airborne infection. Now the virus is no longer airborne but bloodborne. There's a good chance those humans who survived will never be exposed to it.

"So you see, your family is quite rare. Even the hybrid humans of the city of Vida acquired their particular mutations from exposure prior to going underground. I believe that you were immune even before the breakout occurred. Some strange genetic mutation that triggered your superhuman powers also kept you from turning into a vampire. I wanted to force a vampire mutation onto your mother, see if it could somehow still manifest and hopefully create a super hybrid vampire."

"So she was right, she was turning into one of them." I felt my heart breaking as he spoke.

"Yes. She fought it, though. She refused to drink blood, no matter how hard we pushed or starved her." He shoved his glasses up his nose, looking somewhat ashamed for a flicker of a moment. Damn right he should be.

"Well, I tested her blood over and over, and it looked like she was morphing as expected. I couldn't wait to see what abilities she would have. At that time, she'd stopped eating and become withdrawn. She stopped speaking, too. I think she knew what she'd become, before even we did."

"Of course she knew! She even thought she might be turning into a feral, a fucking Zompire! It made her lose her mind!" I seethed, ready to shake Rick into oblivion, but forced myself to calm down. I had to hear it all, no matter how much it was going to sting. I had to.

"Yes, well. I transferred her to the Stratosphere tower lab to start testing her tolerance to things that most vampires shunned. She passed all the tests with flying colors, but she was starting to wither away, either from her own doing or due to the changes. I couldn't be sure. I had returned here with a sample of her blood to figure out what was going on with her. If it was the virus causing her deterioration, then I had to discover how to counter it as quickly as possible. If it was her own doing, well, I thought maybe some antipsychotic meds might do the trick, because she was still utterly human."

"Did you give them to her?"

He gulped, looking outwardly distressed as his memories flooded across his vision. "No. Your hive retrieved her before I could return to try the meds. I also came up with the antidote when the tower was attacked. I had Christian's antidote for the withering sickness finished at the same time and came to give it to him when I found him barely alive. I had the medicines and antidote for vampirism for your mother, but…."

"We'd already taken her back."

He nodded, no longer looking at me. "Yes. You'd taken her from me before I could fix what I'd done."

"Would you have?"

He flicked his eyes back up to me, confusion swimming in them. "Would I have what?"

"Fixed her."

He licked his dry lips and let his head fall as he stared hard at the tiles at our feet. "I would've done anything to save her."

"Why? You didn't even know her. You did this to her. Why would you care if she died or not?"

He shook his head, closing his eyes and rubbing his face as he sighed. Why did he seem to care? Maybe he was so caught up with making super vampires he'd forgotten about the human aspect of it all.

"I knew her. I knew her before all of this." He waved his hand around the lab, letting out a slow, tired breath. His eyes met mine again, and the ocean of confusion had been replaced by a sea of loss and pain. "I knew her very well. I would never allow anyone to hurt her. She had agreed to help me until the vampirism took hold of her brain functions. Then I couldn't get her to respond to me properly. I never wanted to hurt her. I… I…."

"Knew her? What are you talking about?" Now I was totally thrown a curve ball.

"Before the outbreak, I knew her. She was a teacher at the same school I taught at. She turned me down for a date a few times after your father died, but we remained friends. That was before she left to do some internet business."

Shocker. Of course. Before her successful internet business, she'd been an English teacher. "So you knew her when they dragged her in? I bet you were happy to have her under your command."

"No, I knew about her, about you and your brother, for a while before they were taken. You guys were so thorough, this hive was unable to find you for a while. It wasn't until they tracked you to the city that day that they got her and your brother alone, without you. It was the only way to get her without a full on battle. If you weren't there."

"You had them take her?" My voice quivered, and I refrained from putting my shaking hands to his neck.

"Yes, April. I'm sorry. They had reports of your family, and when I found out it was her, I had to have her. One way or another. If I could show her what I was working on, then maybe she'd look at me as more than a microbiology teacher. I'd be more than just a smart guy to her. She'd have a reason to love me back."

"You stole my mother because she rejected you?" The rage was spilling over, and I could tell he felt every ounce of it as he sat up, his eyes widening at my rising fury.

"She was immune, unlike any of us. We had to have her help us. It was a coincidence that she was the one we needed. I would've never allowed them to take her if there were others to help us. Your family was the only one. Get it, April? No one else has survived this epidemic like your family did. No one."

"What about the twelve from Vida? You could've taken them."

"They didn't emerge from the underground until after the Stratosphere event. Otherwise I would've focused on one of them, April. I swear. I would've never hurt her, I couldn't have known she'd lose her mind and do what she did."

"But she did. She killed herself! You did that to her. It's all your fault!" I was on my feet, but Rye's arms were already around me, pinning me to his chest. "Let me go! I'm going to kill this motherfucker!"

"April...."

"Let me go!"

"Stop. That's enough. Nothing will change what happened. Nothing will bring her back."

"I know. I know that! I have to do this… let me do this." I continued to fight to no avail against him. He'd fed before he'd left our hive earlier, and I'd had no vampire blood in ages, nothing. Hell, I hadn't even eaten dinner, and I was paying for it now. That protein bar was sitting on the counter, only a bite nibbled from it. How dumb could I be? "Please," I begged, but slumped in his grip. He wasn't going to budge until my rage had dissipated. I knew that and let it morph into complete and utter despair. My sobs and tears spilled over, and he turned me around to hug me tighter.

"It's okay to be mad, it's okay," he whispered. I let my anger pour out into his chest, wetting his shirt, but I didn't care. It'd been so pent up for so long, I had no idea how strong it had grown. I did want to kill Rick. It'd been the only thing I had thought about since I'd watched the sputtering embers burn out at our bunker. Just like that, my world had collapsed. My mother Helen had been my anchor to sanity in this hell the world had turned into. With her gone, how was I supposed to care for my brother Jeremy and keep my wits intact? How was I supposed to do it? The world had turned into something I wasn't prepared for. No one could have prepared for this. How was I supposed to do this without her?

And it was all his fault. All Rick's fault.

THE HUMMING OF the machines whirring in the background kept me in a daze as I stared off into space and let the others shuffle about as they worked to take supplies from the lab, the cafeteria below and finish off the few hybrid vampires which had escaped from being quarantined when the walls had come down. Mercer had not figured out how to lift them yet, and by the way we could see him yelling at his troops on the cameras we'd managed to reroute so we could watch their movements, he was no closer to escaping than we were.

My fury had been expended, and I felt lighter, but as empty as a gas tank. It wasn't a good empty either. I felt hollow more than anything, as if a piece of my own machinery humming under my skin and keeping me alive and going had been ripped out and taken apart, piece by mechanical piece. I'd let the madness, the hate and the anger take over and had let it fuel each and every thought and movement I had made in the last few months. Now, without it, I was left vulnerable and weaker than I had ever been before. I had to fill it with something, some purpose or goal, and I didn't have any idea what that could be. How quickly vengeance ate away at one's soul without remorse, leaving nothing but a carcass of what we were before we let it overtake us.

Well, I had crashed and burned without even a thought on how to recover.

Hands slipped over my shoulders, warm and cold at the same time. I knew it was Rye. His scent wafted into my nostrils. I didn't want to talk to anyone, but he wasn't going to let me wallow in misery for long. He knew I would hate myself for it later. At least someone cared to know me nowadays. It did perk me up enough to make me snap out of it and look up to meet his eyes. A small smile attempted to form on my lips.

"Hungry?"

I shook my head.

"Here." He handed me a canteen filled with fresh, cool water. I accepted it and sipped on it slowly, still afraid to eat or drink. I just didn't have any desire to do so.

"Where's Rick?" I asked.

Rye studied me for a moment, and I knew he was searching for any deadly intentions in my question. "He's resting in one of the bunk rooms nearby. The morphine really knocked him out."

"At least one person is enjoying their beauty sleep," I muttered. I rubbed at my temples. The headache hovering behind my eyelids and forehead was throbbing, and I knew I had to lie down soon or drop from sheer exhaustion. The night had been extra-long, but dawn was just a few hours away.

"Come on." Rye slipped his fingers around my wrist and tugged.

"What?"

"We need to rest. Nothing is going on with the quarantine doors, so we have some time to regroup. You need to sleep."

I pulled away, shaking my head. "No way in bloody hell am I sleeping here. Their hospitality isn't really conducive to that."

Rye chuckled but grabbed my wrist again. "You're coming to lie down with me, or I'm throwing you over my shoulder after I hog tie you."

"You'd like that," I groaned and got to my feet. He was right, though.

"You bet I would." His devious grin had me shaking my head and chuckling. I wondered how he did that, how he could lighten my mood when I was so intent on soaking in my mellow blues.

I let him drag me to another bunker room which only had four bunks in it. I wondered if the one Rick was in was like this. I wondered if I could sneak in there after Rye went to sleep and slit Rick's throat.

I shook my head. Morbid thoughts wouldn't help me now. I still had questions for him, and I'd make his death long and painful, just like my mother's. Plus, I still had to ask about that antidote. His discussion about it had piqued my curiosity.

Rye threw himself onto one of the bunks, letting out a breath as he sighed in pleasure. I took the one across from him and untied my boots so I could lie down. How he could relax so easily in a place like this was beyond me. I hadn't felt safe to sleep without one eye open since I'd slept in my tiny cot bed in our mountain bunker. My mother had taken more than her life when she'd destroyed our home. My entire world had been there since everyone had died or turned into ferals. Now I had no choice but to plan a return to my old house in the city and scavenge for old stuff like photographs and what memories were left of our old life. It'd been so long since I'd been there, I was sure nothing was left to even go back to. We'd left it all boarded and locked up tight, but who knew if it had held against the end of the world?

"We'll have to exterminate them." Rye's voice interrupted the cool silence that had enveloped me. I pulled the thin blanket over me and rolled over to face him. "We can't leave them alive, not after all this."

"We could assimilate those who want to join Blaze's hive," I whispered across to him. Avoiding his eyes, I bunched the pillow under my head. I knew why he said those things. It was true. In this world, why leave alive those who wanted you dead? I wished there was a better way, but there just wasn't.

"Maybe. If there's too many, we'd never be able to control them if they don't like it in our hive."

"Who's to say they won't like it?"

"Blaze won't allow them to join. It's too risky."

I closed my eyes and hoped the darkness would allow me some rest. "I guess you'll find out."

"I guess."

"You don't oppose him much, do you?"

"No."

"Why?"

"You don't know him like I do. He's only shown the surface to you and the others. He even suggested killing your friends, the humans."

I sat up but couldn't fully since a bunk bed sat atop me. "What? Why didn't you tell me before?"

His liquid steel eyes flashed under the hum of the fluorescent light. "I wanted to, April, but he made me promise not to."

"And me? What about me? Did he ever suggest killing me?"

"No." Rye sat up, hunching down in the cramped space. "If he had ever suggested that, I'd have told him no way in hell."

"Maybe he's thought it."

"Maybe. But like I said, he didn't ever suggest it."

"Why not? I'm a much a threat as these people are."

"You were alone, April." A husky voice interrupted us, and we both turned toward the source. Blaze's face looked tired and dark, and I held my breath. How long had he stood there, listening in and knowing what we knew? He'd been quiet and reserved this entire time, taking it all in to ponder and digest. I'd forgotten he was even with us.

"One person can be more dangerous than an army," I whispered, and my thoughts went back to the destruction of Christian's hive at the Stratosphere. I'm not sure if I was angry, but tears formed, and I sucked in a breath to steady myself before I focused my eyes on the hive leader. "Just like you are more dangerous to others than they know."

Blaze contemplated my words quietly but didn't move. The color seemed to drain from his eyes. I've never really spoken with him much, not since he'd opposed my search for the city of Vida. Ever since, I'd stopped talking to him altogether and done what I wanted anyway. He was not my leader, and I was not his follower.

"No words have ever been truer." He narrowed his eyes on Rye as though mentally reprimanding him for what he'd told me.

"Don't worry," I said. "I'll be gone when this is all over."

Rye abruptly turned to me, his face masked in horror. "What?"

"If you wish. No one will stop you. You have your own free will." Blaze turned to walk away, as if he'd lost interest in our conversation.

"April, what are you saying? Why would you leave? Where are you going? What about Jeremy?"

"He's fine. He'll stay in the city of Vida. He already likes it there more than being with me. As long you guys leave them alone, he'll be fine." I emphasized my words about leaving them alone and narrowed my eyes at Blaze as he walked away, daring him to say otherwise. I knew he could still hear us.

"The city of Vida will never be under threat from us unless they attack us first. You have my word," Blaze answered over his shoulder before disappearing around the corner.

If I disliked Blaze any, I sure as hell hated him now. Even with his promise, I didn't like how he made it seem that he was doing me a favor by leaving the underground city alone.

"April...." Rye was on the floor, his hands on my arms. "You're not going anywhere. What kind of crazy talk is that?"

I turned and stared hard into Rye's gunmetal eyes, knowing I was going to miss them like the dickens when I did leave. "There's nothing here for me anymore, once I have what I want. There's a medical research facility in California that I want to take the antidote to. They can help replicate it, and we can all put this crazy virus-infested world behind us. I just hope there's still someone there who can help me."

Rye's mouth hung open like there was nothing more shocking I could say and withdrew his hands from my arms, though the reddened imprints of his fingers lingered on my skin.

"Not everyone wants to change back, April. You're going to plunge the world into a civil war."

"I don't care if I have to spray it like a pesticide. I will make everyone take this antidote, and life will return to what it was." My voice rose over his, and my chest heaved.

He shook his head and sunk to his knees. "Why would you want to take on that task?"

"For Jeremy."

"He's happy. Let him have his life down in the City of Vida. He's fine. Why do you have to become the martyr here?" His eyes turned from hopeless to focused and then bled into fury. He was losing his patience with me. Might as well. I was done.

"Because he may be happy, he may be a little boy now, but what about when he wants to leave? What will the world be when they emerge to try and repopulate the earth? It will be a wasteland, infested with vampires and ferals alike. It will be in tattered ruins. If I don't fix this mess, no one will. Rick may not want to help, but I'll make him and the rest of the world do what they should've done before this blew up into the wreck it is."

I yanked the blanket back over me and rolled to face the wall, hoping it was message enough for Rye to leave me alone. I was done talking. I'd made up my mind and not him, Jeremy, Blaze, hell, not even Sarah could convince me otherwise. I needed to do something. I couldn't just sit there and let the time go flitting by with nothing but ashes left to the future. Nothing but soot and ashes.

As things stood, there was no future. No future for me, for Jeremy. How could he expect to live secluded, underground forever? How could he be denied the blue of sky, fresh air and snowy mountains? Were they that naïve that the world would work out in the end? Were people so hopeless as to give up on the world and leave it in ruins? How could this have happened?

I closed my eyes, squeezing fat tears onto my pillow. My mother would've fought for it. I knew she would've. This was my future, our future, that I fought for. Why couldn't anyone else see it that way? As the dawn approached, I shoved at the turmoil in my head and begged for rest. It finally came but not without due payment of nightmares of a future filled with blood and death.

Chapter Eight

Truth and Lies

THE HUMMING OF the fluorescent lights illuminating the hall felt like a buzzing bee in my ears. I couldn't sleep, and what little I'd gotten had left me weary and itching to move from the lumpy bunk I was lying on. Blinking, I focused on the lump covered in the scratchy grey military-issue blanket across from me. Rye was dead asleep, his soft breaths barely noticeable in the dim room.

I swung my legs over the edge of the bed, careful to not make any noise, and pulled my boots on. I'd slept in my clothes, like I always did. Nothing beats being ready to go at a second's notice. Patting down the matted mess my ponytail had turned into, I frowned and decided to let it be. No sense in trying to impress anyone there. I slipped my travel pack on and was ready to go.

Sneaking into the hall, I glanced down the way toward the lab. It wasn't far but wasn't close enough to give me the heebie jeebies thinking about all the distorted things lingering in the tanks in there. It sent a shudder down my spine, but I let out a slow breath and decided to head down there anyway. I glanced around each door but only found empty bunks. It had me wondering where Rick was sleeping. Why did he make me feel that he was hiding so much more under that nerdy exterior of his? My gut feelings were usually dead on, and this one was screaming for me to talk more with him, alone. It wasn't that he'd given me any hints or anything like that, it was just a feeling that he didn't want to speak around the hybrid vampires, not about certain things. If I could find him, maybe I could squeeze out every little secret he held inside.

I followed the circumference of the lab, finding the place deserted. There were more bunks on this side of the lab, but no one filled the empty mattresses within, and I wondered where the hell everyone had gone. There were more bunks farther down the hall where Rye and I had slept, but I hadn't bothered backtracking to check them out. Maybe everyone was over there, and I'd missed them.

It wasn't a problem. I didn't really want to see any of them at the moment. I didn't want to explain my midnight stroll through this oppressive place.

I stopped, my heart drumming under my chest like frightened butterfly, warning me of something. Rick was nearby, and I didn't even know how I knew it. It was as if it was just a fact I'd been told somehow. I tiptoed farther down until I reached the last door of the hall of bunks. It was slightly ajar, and the darkness within told me he was probably asleep. I wiggled my fingers. They itched to reach in there and surprise the son of a gun.

Barge in or sneak in? I wasn't sure what I was going to do, but I crept in anyway, making sure the door didn't squeak as I focused my eyes into the darkness of the room.

"Are you going to kill me now?" Rick's disembodied voice hit me like an arctic wind. I swallowed but focused on the body lying in the bottom bunk.

My eyes adjusted, and I could make out his back turned toward me and his face hidden as he stared at the wall. Vulnerable. He was a pompous man if he felt he was safe within my reach. I realized I had the upper hand and slipped in, turning the small bedside lamp on as I sat down on the opposite bunk. He shifted and turned to face me, his eyes shiny under the reading light.

"No. I'm not going to kill you… yet." I didn't mean to sound so ominous, but I was tired of games. "I know there's a lot more about what's going on out there in the world, about this virus and why everyone is infected. I want to know everything, and you're going to tell me."

His nose flared as he studied me across the narrow void between us. His eyes squinted just a bit. His glasses were sitting on the bedside table. Still, he took me in as if he'd just met me and had to memorize each detail of this potential specimen before he could splay it open or let it sit in a tank of overpowering formaldehyde, posed like a precious work of art.

"I know a lot of things, April." My name on his tongue made me uncomfortable as I remembered how he'd used his telekinesis on me earlier. "Why should I tell you anything? And what specifically do you really want to know? Some of it matters, some of it doesn't. Your mother wasn't much for words, so I can't tell you if she was so unhappy here that it drove her to such a tragic end. I'm sorry I can't tell you much more about her in that way."

Now he was just pushing me. "Well, with what you did with her blood... the antidote... can you cure everyone? The sick ones, the ferals and the ones with the green withering sickness?"

It wasn't exactly the question I really wanted answered, but it would do for a starter.

He sighed, ruffling his hair and coming up to a sitting position. He leaned into his knees as he rubbed the sleep from his eyes. He reached over to clasp his glasses and perched them on his pointy nose before focusing on me once more.

"April, everything has a cure. There is a way to cure everyone, but I'm afraid the cure can be worse than the disease itself."

"What do you mean?" My palms were sweating, the anticipation harrowing.

"I mean there are those who would do anything to destroy it, hide it, use it for their own purposes, for power. There are those who would deem it necessary to make it mandatory for all to take the medicine. There are those who would refuse such an option. Maybe if we'd had this at the time of the outbreak it would've been more salvageable. But now, heading into a year and half after the event, nothing is the same, and it'll never be the same. There are hunters and prey, there are strong and weak, there are vampires and humans. Nothing will ever be the same as it was before. Do you understand that, April?" His voice was deathly serious, and his eyes were filled with a threat that made me flinch.

"You won't give me the antidote recipe, will you?" It wasn't a question. I stated it like a fact.

His lips curled up, showing off a perfect set of teeth. Tiny crow's feet framed his eyes as the smile met them. He could've been charming, in another life, for an older guy. I could see why my mother had liked him, if she had. I didn't believe every word coming from his mouth. But I only felt the burn of pure, unfiltered hatred toward a man who could withhold such things from humanity. It wasn't his decision to make.

"No, April. I can't give it to you."

I stood up, glaring down at him and feeling my heart surge like fire, begging release from my ribcage. He flinched, but only just. "You will give it to me. You have no right to keep it to yourself."

"And what will you do with it? Would you take the medicine? Would you turn into a plain human again when so many beasts and monsters still lurk across the world? Is that what you really want?"

"I don't know, but there are those who want it."

"And you are what? Their martyr?"

"It doesn't matter. It's not your decision. You're not God. You're not the Devil. It isn't yours."

"It isn't yours either, April."

I watched him through the pool of fury tears about to spill down my cheeks. My face flushed in heat as I tamed the hurt, the frustration and anger down into a tiny flame flickering in the pit of my stomach. I wanted to hurt him, but doing so would squash any chance for a future for myself, for Jeremy.

"Why won't you try to help others? You've done so much damage. Just give it to me, and I'll find someone who is more willing to explore the options. You don't want to, I get that. But you have no right to withhold it from the world. Why even make it in the first place? You're no king here."

Rick's face had fallen into tight, serious mask, and his eyes stared back in a pregnant silence. I hated not being able to hear his thoughts as he heard mine. I hated him with every tiny morsel of my being, but I held my ground, knowing I would take what I wanted soon enough, even by force. This was but a formality, his chance to make it easier on me and himself. I was ready to take him to the pit of hell, kicking and screaming, for the antidote. He would burn for not handing it over, but that would come all in good time.

What surprised me was that the moments kept ticking by, as though he was actually contemplating my plight and considering doing as I asked. Nothing would have been better than to do this the easy way, with his help. With him, the cure would be but a shot away, and not just for the ones that needed it the most, the ferals, but for everyone. Humanity could begin again. That was all I wanted, all I dreamed about anymore.

He sighed, straightening up, still sitting as he bore his eyes into mine. The darkness within and the slight hum of his telekinetic power brushing against my brain made me twitch. Dammit, what was the bastard up to now? It was always no good.

"I will not give it to you. You don't know what to do with it, and it will only bring chaos and more destruction than you've ever dreamed of. I won't let you do that. I may not have been the most righteous man here, doing what I do, but I will not be responsible for your careless deconstruction of what little remains of the world. That's what you'll be doing. There will be war between those who want the cure and those who wouldn't dream of taking it. You'll do nothing to bring peace or salvation to anyone. It will only bring more death, more pain. My answer is no."

Before he could blink, his glasses skidded to the floor, and my hand stung with a million tiny pricks of pain that burst across my skin as surely they did across his cheek where I'd slapped him with every bit of my inner hate.

"You'll do what I say, when I say." I grabbed his arm and shoved him against the door, pulling out my gun from my pack. "Or you die. Choose."

"Then you'll have to kill me."

"Dammit, Rick. You owe me this." My voice quivered. I was so angered by his stubbornness, I would have been okay jabbing the damned gun against the back of his head and blowing his brains out. I had to think, calm myself before it did end that way. "You owe Helen this."

At the mention of her name, his head dropped. I eased him back a bit. Obviously, the mention of my mother had an effect on this guy, for whatever it was worth. I had to use it for all the power it could give me.

"I'm truly sorry about your mother. Really, I am," he said, his voice cracking.

Seriously? The guy was about to cry. Great. He was nuttier than a squirrel's hoard in winter. Did he really think I was going to feel sorry for him? Unbelievable.

"Look, I don't know who you think you are, but what you did to her, you need to make up for it. You can't do anything for her now, but she'd want you to help me. I knew her better than you ever could have."

He looked up at me, sniffling like a little weasel. "What do you mean?"

"What do I mean?" I restrained myself because I was about to strangle him. "I mean, if she really meant something to you, you have to understand that this cure... it's our salvation. And she would've wanted it and given everyone a choice to be cured or not. She would've never wanted it to be just your choice, Rick."

His tears remained wet across his cheeks, but I could see I was affecting him in some way. Maybe he could listen after all. Maybe he wasn't as lost as I thought he was. I was far from trusting him, that would be a battle for another day, but if I had his cooperation, it was going to be a whole lot easier.

After what felt like an eternity, his head began to bob, softly nodding. He waited for me to continue, but I found myself at a loss for any meaningful words.

"Come on," I said. "We've got a lot of work to do." I stood up and headed out the doorway into the darkened hallway where nothing met us but the humming of distant machines and the slight buzz from the lights. I heard him shuffling behind me hesitantly, but with each step, his stride turned more confident. I just hoped that he wouldn't stab me in the back like Christian had. His betrayal was still fresh in my mind, and even though he wasn't my boyfriend, our blood bond still messed with my head so much, it was enough to make me want to stake the bastard the next time I saw him. It hurt me, the thought of his love turning against me. After all we'd gone through, I had become soft, trusting and naïve to believe he'd never put me in danger. He had, and he would do it again.

Blood bonds suck.

THE LAB WAS quiet, like a lonesome, eager pet waiting for its master. The master was Rick, who trudged along through the freak show of tanks, specimens, limbs, and whatnot, like it was another day on the job. I still couldn't understand how he felt so at home there with death surrounding him. I guess it wasn't much unlike the way it was above ground, outside in the city where all the buildings were infested with evil and teeth that just wanted to rip your flesh. Except he had it a lot better. These things weren't trying to kill him at every turn. They just sat there and stared at us as we moved through the lab with their unwavering frozen stares, like they knew something we didn't.

"Where do you keep it?" I asked.

"Where do I keep the antidote, you mean?" He fiddled with a drawer and yanked out a ring strung with more keys I've ever seen. They jingled as he moved, and I winced at how loud they echoed across the counters and walls of the empty lab. I hoped no one heard us, it would ruin everything. I wished I didn't have to do this alone, but if Rye, Elijah or Sarah knew what I was doing, everything would be over in a millisecond.

"So, April," Rick said, "what do you think you can do with this antidote?" He flipped through the key ring, letting them jingle like a tiny song tinkling in my ears. It occurred to me that he might be stalling, but I wasn't going to assume it. I didn't know this man standing before me. Heck, he'd known my mother, in our past life, when time was abundant and death but an afterthought. He could know things about me that I'd never told anyone but my mother. Would she have even known she'd be giving up such secrets without a second thought? Back then, when a conversation over a cup of coffee in the teacher's lounge was as innocent as waking up for the day, she could have told him anything.

The thought was unsettling, and I found myself twiddling my thumbs as I thought about it. What guarantee did I have that he would help me? I wondered how well he had known my mother before this all happened, before the world fell to pieces and he became a mad scientist. I almost laughed at the thought. It was sort of funny to think that Rick was a normal science teacher once upon a time.

"What's taking so long?" I asked. "Don't you know where you keep it?" I stepped forward toward him, but he sensed me and backed away until his back hit the cabinets.

"Don't touch me!" His harsh whisper stunned me, leaving me to stare at him.

"What the… are you insane? I'm not going to hurt you." That's when I heard it, one tiny step where the rubber of the sole of the shoe squeaked on the shiny tiles, and I knew he hadn't directed the comment toward me. I flicked my eyes behind me and saw a sword swing into the air just in time for me to duck under it, swipe my leg back toward the intruder and hit their ankle full force as I dropped to the floor.

The sword went flying across the tiles, but I didn't wait to see where it went. I was already up on my feet, catapulting onto the stranger before he or she was able to get up. I straddled them, yanking out a knife from my hip holster. I dug my knees into their shoulders and upper arms while my feet pressed into the sensitive area of their inner thighs. They yelped, obviously in pain.

The attacker was wearing all black, with dark jeans, a long-sleeve shirt and even a dark mask covering their face. From the feel of their body, it was a man, but he was small and I was able to hold him down even though he kept bucking his weight up at his hips to try to shake me off.

Grunting with the effort, I managed to pull off the mask. I gasped. "Mercer?" He stopped bucking and dared to throw me a smirk. "What the fuck?"

"Quite impressive, April. You're as fascinating as Rick said you would be."

I made the mistake to look back toward Rick, who was holding that same fucking syringe. Mercer took that distraction to buck me off and encircle his arms around me, squeezing hard enough to make me drop my knife.

Shit!

"Don't worry, April." Rick wasn't smiling, which was surprising, considering he was about to shoot me up with something. "It's not the antidote. We set you up for capture, and you walked right into it. Thank you, April. You played your part so well, you made it all too easy."

"What the hell do you mean? What is that if it isn't the antidote?" I struggled against Mercer, who now had me pinned to the floor, and his hot breath on my ear made me cringe. I swore to God if that was a hard on I could feel bulging down there, I was going to lose my mind. Or he was going to lose something.

It wasn't my imagination. The psycho was getting off on this. *Perfect.*

"Sorry, April. This might sting a little bit. It's just something to make you for sleep just for a while."

I managed to pull away some, and Mercer struggled to keep me in one spot, tightening his grip with his arms encircling me like a straitjacket.

"Rick… please… don't do this! You have to help me! Don't let him have me. Please…." I felt the pinprick stab in my arm, a tiny spark of pain.

I always hated needles. The medicine worked fast, and the room began to sway while my struggling body went lax. Mercer led me down to the floor.

"I've got the girl. Come quietly, everyone's still asleep. Over."

I could hear them speaking to someone in the crackle of a radio. My body no longer responded, but I could still hear him, and I could still hear Rick shuffle around with keys as he probably went to remove the real antidote. *Damn you, Rick.* Why would he do this to me? Where was everyone? Rye was probably still sleeping, and the others, too. I was such a fool to do this alone. Now what would become of me?

"Is she out?"

"She might still hear us, but she's pretty out of it. She won't give us any trouble for a while."

"Good. We can have a lot of fun with this one."

"You'll do no such thing." This voice was cold with a hint of anger in it. Was it Christian? Was he actually there? Why didn't anyone know they had gotten out of the quarantine? How could they all sleep through this? What was going on? "We have to leave the area and close it down like before so they'll think she broke in on her own accord. Just keep to the sections with no cameras." It *was* Christian. That traitorous bastard!

"I'm still your second in command," Mercer snapped back. "I'll be in charge of her. Your blood bond will cloud up your thoughts and risk our mission." Mercer's snarl did nothing to faze Christian as he muttered a rebuttal that Mercer didn't immediately oppose. I could feel his heart beating through his relentless grip on my arm. I wasn't sure who was carrying the bulk of me, but Christian was making sure he wasn't touching me. Now I knew just how much the bond was affecting him. I had always had more control over it than he.

"Mmmm…."

"Rick!" Mercer hissed. "She's waking up, dammit! Hit her up with another dose now." He shifted, still digging his fingers into my skin. Another sharp prick in my arm burned the muscle like liquid fire, but I couldn't scream. I could do nothing but let the darkness overtake me.

"I added some sedative this time. That should knock her out." Rick's dry tone told me he wasn't happy with the situation at all. Well, that made three of us then.

Their voices faded as the medicine flowed through my veins. I hoped that when I woke up, I would still be whole and untouched. Mercer scared me, but I had faith that my bond with Christian would keep that vulture away as I lay dead to the world.

Chapter Nine
Memory is Cruel

I HEARD BIRDS chirping, but it wasn't real. No, it was more like the flapping of their wings had brought me back to the beaches my parents would drag me to when I was small, before my brother had been born. Days spent digging into the fine grains of sand and dragging buckets of seawater to my piles of dirt to make it easier to sculpt it into a masterpiece were precious memories. I could feel the same powdery sand under my skin as I shifted and the scent of ocean permeated the air.

I had to be dreaming. This wasn't something from the present, and my mind shuddered as it fought to regain control of the dream, throwing darkness around me like an inky black smoke. But the fog was too rich, too thick to brush away, and I slipped back to the beach of my ten-year-old self.

The scenery turned crisp, bright, and I focused on the shoreline before me. The sun burned at my scalp, prompting me to glance around for a hat or towel to throw over it and keep the rays off my skin. I had a tendency to burn easily.

"April." My mother's voice echoed in my ears, far away, as though it was underwater or through a thick wall.

"Mom?" I spun around and finally laid eyes on the woman who I considered to be one of the most amazing and beautiful women I've ever known.

"Here." She handed me a scarf, and I promptly wrapped it about my head and donned the sunglasses dangling from her delicate fingertips. Her nails were smooth, manicured to perfection, but with only a thin layer of clear coat to make them shine. Her hands were beautiful and strong.

"Thanks, Mom." I gestured toward the tumbling waves and prepared to barrage her with questions. "What are we doing here?"

She plopped down beside me and let out a deep rushing breath. "Oh, my dear. Have you forgotten to enjoy things already? You have to look around sometimes, take in the beauty of the world. It can disappear without a moment's notice. Look at the water. It's strong, unshakeable. The sand, smoothed over from centuries of being tossed about. Notice how fine it is and it feels like heaven under your feet. Why is it so hard to see the simple things?"

I huffed and turned back toward the water, watching as wave after wave pummeled the shore like a raging beast.

"People die out there, Mom," I said as I contemplated her words. I had always been too old for my age, or so she had said. An old soul trapped in a young body. It had prevented me from enjoying my childhood like any other ten-year-old, and it had stolen my innocence along with it, replacing it with the blatant knowledge of just how cruel and dark the world could really be. "Millions have died already. There's no hope."

I bit my lip, and the taste of coppery blood hit my tongue.

"Darling, I know it seems as if there's nothing to care about anymore. It seems impossible with such a bleak horizon in sight. I know how you feel." She sat quietly beside me, and I waited for her to continue. "Nothing I say can make you feel better. I know that more than anyone. Just promise me you'll pause and look around now and then. Enjoy the burnt orange of the sunsets. Breathe in the crisp ocean air, savor the taste of wild strawberries and watermelons we find now and then treading through untouched greenhouses. You can't forget these things. You mustn't. Promise me."

I peeked at her sideways and scrunched up my eyes. She had hers closed and was letting the ocean breeze rush past her face and ruffle the long fuchsia scarf she'd wrapped around her unruly hair.

But wait… she was dead, wasn't she?

"Mom?"

"Hmmm?"

"Why did you leave me?"

She didn't turn toward me but just stared off across the waves. I breathed in the faint smell of coconut lotion and waited for her response. When she didn't move, I opened my mouth to speak again, but her image flickered.

What the…?

I scanned the beach and found it empty. My eyes swung back to my mother, but she too was gone.

No, no, no....

I jumped to my feet and felt the air turn frigid as I spun, searching for the birds, the few people who had occupied the beach just a few seconds ago.

"Mom?" I called out.

Only silence answered back to me.

"*Mom!*" I hollered and ran toward the shore, but there was no one.

No one but me.

I was still alone in the world, and everyone was dead. Everyone but me.

"WHAT EXACTLY ARE you saying?" Mercer's voice came out snappy, as if the person speaking to him had irritated him for the last time and was in danger of being extinct.

"I mean... the girl. Her blood isn't compatible with any of the antidotes."

"Rick shot her up with all of them?"

"No, sir. He used them all on the samples of her blood he took."

"None of them are working?"

"No, sir."

I heard a smack and then the thump of something heavy landing on the ground. "Get the hell out of my face and tell Rick he needs to hurry up. I'm sick of waiting for results from that pencil-necked twit."

"Yes, sir." The other person got up and limped away. The scent of his sweat permeated the air, and a nervous charge hung in his wake like static.

"Maybe she's the final product of the virus. Lethal and all powerful. Immune to any antidote because she's not really infected per se, but the result of a human body's perfected defenses against it via adaptation."

Christian.

I resisted the temptation to jump off the hard mattress I was lying on to slam my fists into his pretty face. His dark red hair haunted my memories, as did his two-colored eyes. Brown and Green. Two different hues that so perfectly represented his duality. I loved his eyes, though. They called to me in dreams and tormented me whenever I met them face to face. The sadness over his betrayal hurt down to the core, and I fought to keep my breathing rhythmic and slow as my heart felt like it would burst. How could he do this? I thought he had wanted to win my heart and be my mate. Even though I wouldn't have given in to him so easily, if he'd been patient, with time… maybe we could've been something more.

What was I saying? I flicked my eyes open and tried to move, only to find that my wrists and ankles were strapped to the metal frame of the bed. Great. Why hadn't I noticed that before opening my eyes? I was a sitting duck.

"Hello, princess." Christian's voice was warm and welcoming, making me hate him even more. A chair scraped along the cement floor, and I focused my blurry vision onto him as he leaned in toward me. "I was hoping you'd wake up soon."

I closed my eyes, tugging at the restraints to no avail. I'd been drained of blood, left weak. What had they done to me?

"Water," I managed to whisper, but I couldn't do much more. It hurt to speak, to breathe. Only dizziness greeted me, even though I was lying down. So cold.

"One moment." I heard him rustling about followed by the distinct sound of liquid pouring into a plastic cup and a crinkle of paper before he returned to my side. "Here, love. Sip from the straw."

I blinked as I felt the plastic touch my cracked lips. I let it past my teeth and sucked in the fluid, my stomach clenching with waves of nausea as I paused to breathe past it before I could sip some more.

"Where am I?" I croaked. How long had I been out? It must've been a while because my throat felt like it had been dragged through sandpaper, and my lips had a layer of dead skin that cracked as I spoke. I licked them and tasted the taint of blood.

The memory of the ocean came rushing back to me, and I tensed up, remembering my mother. Tears blurred my vision again as I gulped back a sob.

"Now, now. You'll be fine. I promise you."

"Where am I?" I hissed it this time and managed a nice frown as I focused back onto Christian through the tears that I fought to restrain. I had the urge to damage that pretty face of his like I'd stabbed up his stomach. One day, I promised myself, that would be on my to-do list, right at the very top.

"We're still in the same facility. We've quarantined off the area where Blaze's group is. Don't worry. They can't get in here like we could get in there. They'll never find the way in. They're trapped there. There's no way out from that quad. It was a way to trick them into closing themselves in. They fell for the false sense of security."

"Bastard." I closed my eyes, feeling a bit better, but my head was still aching fiercely.

"April, let's not be so harsh. It's for all our good that we did this."

"Fuck you, Christian."

A haughty laugh echoed from behind my head. I couldn't see him, but I knew it was Mercer.

"My, my. She is a feisty one. Just like you said. You lucky bastard."

"Go to hell, Mercer."

His hot breath flared across my cheek, and his face appeared right next to mine.

"Come on, Mercer, back up," Christian said, looking annoyed.

"Listen here, *precious*. I don't care if he's your mate or not. I'll still kill you with the first wrong step you take. And for your information... we're already in hell, if you haven't noticed, bitch!"

"Back off," Christian said again. He put his hand on Mercer's chest, throwing him a look of warning.

"Temper, temper," I said, laughing at how quickly they had begun to bicker. Maybe I could use that against them. I let my head rest against the flat pillow under my head. "I need to pee."

"Pee yourself."

I laughed again and shook my head. "What? Afraid this little drained human is going to beat you up? Aww...."

Mercer stomped away, cursing under his breath. Feeling a tickle at my feet, I looked down to find Christian undoing the restraints.

"Sorry, he's sort of insensitive."

"No kidding."

"Come on. I'll take you to the showers. There's a toilet, towels and fresh clothes there. You stink, by the way."

"You smell like a rose, too." I scrunched up my nose up and eyed him straight on. "How long was I out?"

"A full seventy-two hours."

"Geez...." I let my head drop back as he slid over to undo my wrist restraints. "Is that true? Can the others not get out?"

"Oh, they can get out. It'll take them forever to do it, but it's possible. This place took years to complete. It was built before Vida was."

He helped me sit up, and I rubbed my sore skin. The grime under my nails and my cracked skin made me frown. "How do you know of all these secret projects?"

"I used to work for the government. It was my job to oversee the labs and chemicals being shipped into these places. There's dozens of fortresses, all across the country."

"You're kidding, right? Do you think humans made it to them at all?"

He shifted on his feet, still bent at the bedside. He stared hard at the cement floor. His long, dark red hair framed his features, making his eyes shine in the dark.

"I don't know. Probably. Quite a few made it to the ones here in Vegas, surprisingly."

I stood up and waited. He stretched up before me. His height was always impressive.

"All right, then," I said, looking up at him, "lead the way."

Chapter Ten
Where All the Things Meet

RICK WAS TINKERING with an assortment of vials and liquids bubbling over Bunsen burners. In his protective glasses, lab coat and gloves, he was the epitome of a chemistry teacher, lost in concentration and every so often jotting down notes in a notebook splayed open on the counter nearby. Slipping onto a stool the next table over, I watched him with curiosity as he mixed the chemicals, siphoned drops out and dropped the fluid into trays filled with other fluids and gel.

This lab was much smaller than the other, but it had clearly been stocked in advance. Several vials were obviously blood specimens, some the rich red color you'd expect them to be while others were the dark black-red of feral blood. Blood was the new gold in this day and age. There was nothing more precious or more fragile than the red, viscous life sloshing about in our bodies.

The urge to grab one and tilt it into my hand to watch the blood flow back and forth in small, tiny waves was overwhelming. My fingers itched to touch the glass containers, so I stuffed them into my pockets and remained seated on my stool. Besides, it was easier to not reach over and snap Rick's neck if my hands weren't available.

I wondered which vials held my blood as I craned my neck to read some of the labels. When I'd mentioned to Mercer about being a drained, little human, I wasn't kidding. The effects of the anemia made me overwhelmingly exhausted, thirsty and lightheaded if I stood up too fast.

After taking a shower and wiping the steam off the mirror of the bathroom, I'd found an unfamiliar pallor of yellowish gray to my skin, replacing the previously healthy pink glow. It had made me wince as I took in my reflection, my lips a dusty pink, pale and delicate. It had flared up a bit of resentment toward Mercer and Rick, but I shook it off momentarily, promising myself they'd get their just desserts in due time. These freaks had to slip up sooner or later, and I had to recover from the draining before I could even think about fighting with anyone.

I hated feeling helpless. Already so used to being a hybrid human, which had given me so much strength and agility, I felt a sense of utter loss at being drained. At least I was sure to recover fast. Still, if only I had some vampire blood, it would speed up the process.

I cleared my throat. Rick didn't even look up. "Rick."

"I'm quite busy."

"I don't care."

He put down a vial and smiled as he finished dropping a couple tablets into it, causing it to fizz up. "I knew you were stubborn, but you really need to let me work."

"Worst of the worst."

He peeked over his glasses, shiny blue eyes framed with tiny crow's feet wrinkling around them as he continued to grin. "Helen would chat with me sometimes, when I was able to see her, and she spoke highly of you and your wild ways. She had so much respect for her wayward daughter. She was very proud to be your mother." Was that a hint of sadness in his voice?

It only caused the anger to resurface inside me, and my mood darkened at the mention of my mother. I flicked my eyes down to the black counter, willing the bubbling resentment away.

"Sorry, I didn't mean to upset you."

I shrugged. "Doesn't matter." But it did. "Did you find anything in my blood that makes a difference?"

Moving his eyes down in shame, he swirled the vial in his fingers until the fizzy liquid turned a pale violet and then morphed into a deep maroon red.

"Well, I've found several differences between your blood and your mother's." He lifted the vial and poured it into several test tubes he had propped up in a rack. "I've isolated several red blood cells that defy the definition of a blood cell. It's like they're super red blood cells, filled with energy and resistant to injury. Your T-cells are abnormally large, too. In fact, the entire makeup of your blood is mutated compared to a normal human's blood. It's not very obvious, but I see the differences." He peeked up at me again, a serious but excited twinkle lingering in his eyes. It only made me shift in my seat even more. "It's like you've adapted to this virus, assimilating it, and it has enhanced your entire body."

"The Hulk. That's me. I'm relieved I don't have to turn green, though."

He laughed, and so did I. As much as I despised Rick, I was glad the somber mood was gone.

"Well, not quite, but not too far off. You could very well be the answer to the antidote problem."

My ears perked up at this, and I waited, impatiently, for him to tell me more. My knees knocked under the table, and I buried my hands deeper in my pockets to hide my fidgetiness. "What do you mean?"

"I mean that the antidote was having some issues working without any side effects."

"What sort of side effects?"

"Well, some people... err... vampires... died from it. They're body couldn't separate from the virus without tearing up the person inside." He wrinkled his nose and dipped a dropper into the vial he'd just mixed, letting one fat droplet ease onto a slide.

I gulped. "So why in the hell were you were going to shoot me up with that crap?"

"Well, we hadn't tried it on a human hybrid yet. Your mother's blood hadn't converted to hybrid, and it was impossible to test how well it would work."

"I could've died, and you didn't want to test it on my blood first?"

"I wasn't given a choice. Mercer wanted it tested on you immediately."

"And if it had killed me?" He didn't answer. "Who would you test it on then?"

"I don't know, April. I'm working blind here. I really didn't want to do it."

"That doesn't make me feel better."

"I'm sorry. I'll have to show you what it can do later."

He was silent as he worked and didn't look up again. I was left stewing at his words. Moments later, I was still steaming, tapping my fingertips furiously on the black tabletop, but he'd decided I'd calmed down enough.

"Look, I know that would've been the better route to take, get a sample of your blood and test it on that first. But Mercer is very impatient and even convinced Christian to help wrangle you up. I didn't know what his real intentions were until I got to your door. It was only then that he ordered me to inject you with it. I'm really sorry."

"You can shove that apology where you know it will hurt most, Rick," I hissed and pushed off the stool, sending it toppling over. Bad idea. The room spun, and I grabbed at the table to steady myself.

"Whoa, there, cowgirl." Christian's hands were on my sides, holding me up. I wanted to hit him in the chest with my frustration and hurt, but I just let him hold me instead. I was tired, and it was making me think all screwy. It wasn't a good position to be in. Weak, vulnerable.

"I'm going to lie down." I shoved his arms away, but he didn't let go.

"Did you eat anything?"

"Yes, breakfast." I glared at him, but his twinkling eyes found it amusing and not dismissive as I had wished it to be.

"It's lunchtime already."

I hung my head and closed my eyes. I decided the fatigue might fade some with food. I relented. "Okay. What's on the menu?"

"Steak."

My eyebrow lifted, questioning the choice. "You have steak?" My question would've been unusual before the end of the world. Now it was so foreign to talk about meat. Fresh meat, at that.

He nodded. "Yep. Fat cows and sheep in the underground pastures. Just like the City of Vida."

I grinned. A steak might be good for me. Iron, protein. I was game.

"Got any hamburgers?"

"With the works."

"About time something goes my way." My mouth was already salivating, but I swallowed it back.

"Indeed."

Now that the room wasn't spinning like I'd just gotten off an amusement ride, I managed to keep up with Christian as he headed toward the dining room. He ordered a burger with the works for me. I glanced around the crowded eating area and cringed. It was full of hybrid vamps. Lots of them, with hungry eyes and deafening whispers as I passed them by. Déjà vu sucked eggs. I wasn't ready to fight, not here, not against these vampires. I had no weapons, no juju, nothing. I wouldn't stand a chance.

"Don't worry. They have strict orders to not touch you."

"I've heard that one before." I groaned and turned away before I let their haloed stares wear me down and make me want to bolt for the door. I wanted my hamburger.

Christian's eyes flashed at me, deep and determined. "I'm serious. It's an immediate kill order for anyone who comes near you, no warning."

"What about you? You've touched me."

"I'm exempt. But I, unlike them, have no intentions of killing you."

"What about Mercer?"

Christian flicked his eyes away and accepted the two burgers handed over by the cook. It was piled up tall with all the fixings, making my mouth water even more. In my mind, I was already savoring each and every delicious bite.

"He's not to be trusted." He kept his voice low as we left the grill and reentered the rows of venomous stares.

I pondered this while he led me back toward the room I'd been in earlier. It had a small table and two chairs in it. I figured it was probably best he took me there anyway. We were away from the prying eyes of dangerous folks who looked like they wanted me gutted and spitted.

I had to figure out how to escape, but I really didn't want to yet. I wanted that antidote, and I was all ready to stay as long as it took to get it. It wasn't for me, though. I was never going to take the damned serum. I liked the way I was, but there was a whole new world out there that could use it. Once I had it in my possession, then I would figure out what to do with myself and get the heck out of there. Not until then. I was just hoping it wasn't going to take long to get it. I was already missing Jeremy, Rye and all of my friends.

The thought of them sent a sharp pain through my chest, and I sucked down a sip from my soda to cover it up. How I longed to be enjoying this burger with them. Jeremy would love it. He'd eaten one every day we'd spent in Vida. That and heaps of pizza loaded with all kinds of stuff on it. It'd been a good time, seeing him scarf down his favorite pre-epidemic favorites. The virus had stolen so many such pleasures away.

Jeremy would understand my plight. If I told him that I wanted to save more people from Mom's fate, he'd be completely aligned with me. I knew it. The thought rewarmed my frigid insides as I shoved an enormous, mouthwatering bite into my mouth.

Chapter Eleven
Salvation Is Love

Rye

"HOW THE HELL did she get away?" Rye paced the floor, unable to calm the raging fire consuming him ever since he'd discovered April was missing. "How did they get her? We were supposed to be secure."

"Calm down." Blaze's set jaw let Rye know he wasn't immune to the disappointment either. Their enemy had effectively locked them out of their isolation area and snatched one of their own from right under their noses. "We'll find her and get her back."

"Why are we sitting here, then?" Rye paused, staring out the glass wall of the lab. "She could be dead by now. Or worse."

"We're trying to find the way they came in. Patience."

"They're not trapped, we are. Leaving without her isn't happening."

Blaze sighed, rubbing his temple and staring out the glass wall alongside Rye. "Christian betrayed us. He was our only link to this hive. If we stay, we risk being decimated by their ranks."

"We can't leave!" Rye's eyes widened at the suggestion. "She's their prisoner. I can't leave without April." Rye shook his head, aware of the danger they were in. "I won't leave."

"We have to go. Knowing April, she'll figure a way out anyway."

"You did not just say you're fine with abandoning her here."

"Rye." Blaze grabbed his shoulders and tilted his head forward to meet him eye to eye. "This is April we're talking about. If anyone can get themselves out of a mess, it's her."

Rye continued to shake his head, unable to fathom what his cousin was about to do. "No, I can't."

"You will come with us. It's an order." Blaze let go and headed toward the sleeping quarters where the others were waiting. No one would be happy with the news, but he knew Elijah and Sarah wouldn't object. They knew April as well as he did. They would return to patrol the area for April, but it was now up to her to escape. The fortress was impenetrable, and they had no knowledge of the place, no guide. There was simply no option but to leave and let April figure it out from the inside.

Rye smacked his wrist on the glass, and a dull pain instantly enveloped his hand. As much as it pained him to leave her behind, he knew Blaze was right. They were sitting ducks there, waiting for a slaughter. Still, the thought of leaving made him sick and desperate to save April. But how? How could he save her?

Rubbing his throbbing wrist, he sighed and felt his heart ache. He'd make sure to patrol this area every day until April was found. He'd be there when she figured it out. She would, too, knowing her stubborn, conniving resourcefulness. She was the only person he'd always bet on.

"Let's move out!" Blaze's voice echoed down the hall, and Rye grabbed his pack and headed over to join them. His heart was racing to the tune of his boots pounding the tiles as they evacuated the hive. He hoped April would forgive him and sent a silent message of love and support to her.

I'll never leave you.

His silent prayer to her made him feel a bit calmer, but it still was devastating, like when he'd lost her to the City of Vida for days upon days without news, without a way to locate her. This wasn't any easier; it was actually worse because he knew where she was, he just couldn't reach her. She could be just a few yards away, on the other side of a wall, but she was all alone.

"I'm not going anywhere."

Blaze's agitation was slipping past his usual mask of stoicism. Rye didn't care if he pushed him too far. He'd planted himself in place and refused to move.

"You'll die here."

"So be it."

Blaze's shiny halos flared to life, his anger flushing the color of his skin. "Fine. Rye, it was a pleasure knowing you." Blaze pivoted away, and the others followed closely behind. Rye sat down at the control panel, scanning the cameras and watching the others in their quarantine. There was no sign of April, no sign of anything out of the ordinary. They were even still drilling at the escape door, hoping to open it.

Their continued charade made him laugh and shake his head. The bastards were stellar actors. They still acted as though they were desperate to open the door. It was that or they really didn't know that someone had come and taken April through a hidden route. From the looks of it, the entire hive wasn't privy to this information. It made him wonder where the possible hidden entrance could be.

Now that he was alone, he had all the time in the world to find it.

A tap on the tile floor had him jumping from his chair and drawing out his gun. Crouched and poised for an attack, he groaned as Elijah and Sarah stood with hands up.

"Whoa, buddy, it's just us."

"What the hell do you want?" Rye stuffed the gun away and plopped back onto the chair, switching camera views to another part of the facility.

"She's our friend, too." Sarah sat down on a swivel chair next to him and started scanning the screens. Her long red hair was in a thick braid draping over her back. She was beautiful, and Rye knew she was April's friend from high school. That little fact made him relax, happy to have some small part of April there with him.

"Blaze has no authority over us," Elijah said. "We choose our own paths. He's heading back to his hive and said if we didn't return within a day, he'd write us off." He didn't join them but walked to the glass wall that led into the corridor. Peering out to scan both ends, he secured the control room before he settled in next to Sarah.

"Fair enough. I have to get her out of there. How could Christian betray her like that? I hate his guts, but isn't he prohibited from putting her in danger? He's supposedly bound to her in some sick way." Rye's face contorted at the thought of his competition. He'd noticed the way Christian stared at April. She also had some sort of emotional attachment to the enemy hive leader, which was an obstacle itself. She'd controlled the attachment by avoiding Christian in every way possible, a fact that made Rye very happy. Still, he was close to her now without any barriers between them. This sent Rye into a steaming rage, and he tapped his fingers impatiently on the console. It sickened him and made him even more desperate to find her now.

"I don't see any views of their cafeteria or any sort of prison-like cells to secure someone in. My guess is that the lack of cameras in those areas is intentional. I suggest the best course of action is to scope out any entrances and blueprints we can find and find another way in. Once we do, we'll have to target these areas; it's likely they're holding her in one of them."

Sarah hopped up and started ripping cabinets open for any blueprints of the place.

Rye watched her, impressed with her thoroughness. "Where'd you find this one?" He flicked his eyes toward Elijah, who shrugged and yawned.

"Came with the territory."

"She's hybrid, right?"

Elijah nodded. "There were twelve of us enslaved under the City of Vida's dictatorship. When April killed Katrina, we were freed. We owe her everything."

Rye nodded and turned away from the burly human warrior. He wasn't sure what Elijah's attachment to April was either, though he had no reason to feel threatened. He was pretty sure that Sarah had laid claim to the hybrid human leader already, but he wasn't sure.

"Found them!" Sarah bounced back into the room, spreading several rolled-up blueprints across one of the tables behind them. She smacked her gum, which she then twirled around her finger, stretching out the elastic substance before popping it back into her mouth. Rye gave her a tiny smile as he moved his gaze onto the papers under her hands.

"Where did you find them? I thought they'd be in a more secure location."

"I figured they'd be in the most obvious place that they'd think we wouldn't look."

"Where's that?"

"Storage closet at the end of the hall."

Rye wrinkled his nose but resumed orientating himself to the blueprints. It took a while to go through all of them, but as the three of them studied the papers, they came to a unified conclusion.

"No way that it's that easy."

"No wonder they got past us."

The bathroom at the end of the dorms was the hidden entrance. It was the only area left unmarked. It left a hole in the blueprints like someone didn't really want to include it on the paper but had to so that the structure looked intact. The cavernous fortress was massive. It held huge living quarters with everything needed for survival, including water collection and filtration machines, livestock quarters, a massive greenhouse for food and herbs. It was a well-oiled machine and had been constructed over a period of years. The other hive had it good here, and it made Rye just a tad bit jealous that they had endured such harsh weather in the city to construct their makeshift bunker under the airport.

"Let's head here first." Elijah pointed out the armory and was already heading out the door when Rye and Sarah moved to catch up.

"He doesn't waste any time, does he?" Rye asked.

Sarah giggled and almost skipped along next to him. Nothing ever seemed to get her down. "Yeah, he's pretty to the point. No bullshit." She winked, making the blood rush to Rye's face. She was pretty and so upbeat; he could see why April liked her. They were polar opposites in every way. Maybe April needed Sarah's chirpiness to keep her head out of the murk she was constantly submerged in.

He hadn't really thought about what April had been like before the virus killed off most of the population and turned everyone else into blood drinkers. Had she been as happy and carefree as her friend here? It saddened him to realize how the world had left April—disillusioned and desolate. Her moods had become more unstable since her mother had died. She'd even left Jeremy in the City of Vida with his friends' families instead of caring for him. How had she become so hopeless?

"Here it is." They arrived at the bathroom and headed to the last stall. It looked the same as all the other toilets, but the wall on one side of it had to be hollow. Elijah spent the next few minutes touching it and pushing on the tiles to find the trigger to open it. Finally, he gave up and let Sarah have a go at it. After a few minutes, she had it swinging open after pulling the flusher handle up instead of down.

"That's the stupidest lock I've ever seen."

"You couldn't figure it out, could you?" Sarah rolled her eyes at Elijah, who shook his head as he frowned at the toilet.

"Come on. Let's get April back."

Chapter Twelve
The Never Ending Hunger

"I NEED TO show you something." Rick motioned me down the hall, and I glanced at Christian to make sure it wasn't a trap. The damned bastard looked as confused as I was, so I was pretty sure there wouldn't be any funny business. Christian was hard to read, but our connection somehow hinted to me what he was feeling. It sucked most days because his emotions were often filled with desire. Today, it was muted and full of curiosity.

"What is it?" I followed along, cracking my knuckles to try and relieve some of the tension. Christian was right behind me, but it did nothing to reassure me.

"You'll see. It's very important and might convince you of things you otherwise wouldn't believe." Rick's smile gave me the heebie jeebies. He looked too happy, and I wondered what experiment he was going to throw my way.

I was getting tired of this endless labyrinth of cement and metal. I tried to not feel suffocated, but the lack of windows in the central area of the fortress I'd been held in was making me claustrophobic. Occasionally, the air would feel noxious, and I'd have to slow my breaths to calm my fluttering heart. Panic didn't look good on me, and I had to hold myself together.

We made our way to the smaller lab, and as we entered, I noticed the large window on the opposite side of the room. It had been darkened, covered in a blackout curtain. I wondered briefly why a human like Rick would blot out the sun, but I found out not a second later exactly why he kept the light at bay.

He pointed through another window, this one leading into a large, padded room. In it, chained to the other side by its wrists and ankles, was a feral vampire. It hung there, head down and limp as if it was resting or dead. I narrowed my eyes as I stared through the glass. Its ruined clothes were shredded but still clung onto the muscular body. I could tell it'd been a man at one point in life. Now he was nothing but a wild beast, a predator focused only on flesh and blood.

I wondered how Rick had come across one so intact. His flesh wasn't split open except for where the restraints were rubbing away layers of skin as he had pulled and tugged on the chains. His hair was missing in some patches, but for the most part had been kept free of knots. It grew wild over his eyes and touched his shoulders.

It would've taken several warriors to hold this one down long enough to chain him up. Maybe he'd been sedated, though I'd never seen a sedated Zompire. His muscles bulged from the immense strength the vampiric virus had given him in death. Even his legs looked like they'd bust through his ruined jeans. He still wore shoes, though quite worn with holes at the tips. It made me wonder how he'd come to be there.

"What are you doing with the feral?" I asked.

Rick smiled, as if a distant memory had clicked. "I've only met one other who called them ferals. Usually it's wildings or Zompires." He flicked his eyes to me, and it morphed into a pained sadness. "Your mother used that term, too."

The mention of my mother would've normally sent me into a seething rage, but the presence of the chained-up creature had my focus, and I wasn't going to leave until Rick told me what he was up to.

"So what do you need him for? He looks like one of the biggest ones I've ever seen. Is he sedated?"

"Not at the moment. We did have to tranquilize him when we captured him. Took several darts to put him down, and he still took out six of our warriors. Not a bad show of strength."

I peered in, leaning closer to the glass. "Will those chains hold him?"

"Oh, yes, they're the strongest metal chains available. They've held bigger things than him." Rick went to the freezer standing against the wall and punched in a code. It beeped, and the door swung open, revealing row upon row of cylindrical vials. They held but half a milliliter each, like vaccine bottles I'd seen at the shot clinic. He pulled a drawer open next to the fridge and produced a single use syringe and separate needle. Unwrapping both before twisting them together, he plunged the needle into the vial and pulled back a bit of clear liquid.

Was this where the antidote was held?

I pulled my hungry eyes away from the fridge and focused on the feral in the room. Something bothered me about him, as if I knew him. But how would I ever have met him? I didn't remember knowing anyone so bulky. It was a feeling, a tingle across the hairs on my neck, that told me I did. It'd been ages since I'd seen a feral this intact. Most had crumbled into various states of decay and decomposition, like wild zombies who fought to stay satiated when there was a lack of blood. This one had not had a lack of blood meals.

Rick turned the handle on the steel door leading into the room and entered, syringe poised and ready. I wondered how cautious he should be with the sleeping feral. He seemed awfully confident walking in there without extra protection. Maybe those chains were capable of holding King Kong.

Even so, my stomach flipped as I pressed my hands against the glass and watched him get closer to the sleeping beast.

It still hadn't moved. The soft movement of his breath lifted his shoulders in a rhythmic repetition. Was he still sedated? His hair was slick with dirt and oil from the lack of a wash, and it hung down over his face, hiding his features. It could be dark blond or light brown, the dirt made it difficult to tell. The same went for his skin color. Underneath the grime and dried blood, he could be Caucasian or possibly Hispanic. My impatience had me wanting to tap my fingers on the glass to know where I'd seen him before. Rick couldn't wake him up fast enough.

As if he'd heard my thoughts, Rick reached out and stabbed the feral in the thigh muscle. He yanked the needle out just as fast before he jumped back as the feral roared to life. It thrashed, sending the chains rattling, and Rick backed out of the room, hurrying to open the metal door before slamming it behind him. I glanced at Christian, who shrugged. What the fuck had just happened?

"What the hell?" I put my hands on my hips, but a thump made me turn back to the room as I also stepped back. Rick was busy setting the deadbolts on the metal door before another thump slammed the door, and he jumped back.

"I'm not exactly sure what's going to happen." Rick bounced on his feet, staring through the window, excitement spreading across his face.

"What?" I stared in horror and turned back to the feral since he'd stopped thumping against the wall. Instead, he stood at the window, his hands pressed against the glass, wrists still in chains where his blood was streaming down his forearms. He· was huffing and puffing, with a snarl stamped into his features and his eyebrows furrowed so deeply, I wondered if his skin would burst from the pressure.

But that wasn't what worried me the most. He was staring at me, his eyes still rimmed with red, but one of them was morphing into an orange blue like the color of the sky at sunset. He hissed as I stepped forward, his face calming the closer I approached. The one partly blue eye narrowed at me, flicking between my eyes in some sort of repressed recognition.

"What's wrong with his eyes?"

"He's morphing." Rick stepped closer to the window, obviously calmer but rubbing his fingertips together as he also observed the creature.

"Morphing into what?" I never looked away. I couldn't. It was like watching a car accident pile up, with each car tumbling into the next until it was nothing but a mass of blood, guts and twisted metal.

Rick turned toward me and smiled.

"Into a human."

My eyes widened, and I stepped closer and pressed my palms to the cool glass. The eyes blinked at me, no longer filled with rage, but with desolation and a memory of something I should have seen before. But now it was easier. His face smoothed out and the eyes cleared into a blue I remember seeing a lot of with my mother.

"Randy."

"What?" Rick muttered, bouncing on his feet as he watched the feral morph.

"His name is Randy."

Both Christian and Rick turned toward me in disbelief. The scientist's mouth was dangling open.

"You *know* him?" Christian was at my side now, glancing between the ruined monster before us and me.

"Yes," I leaned my forehead against the glass, my gut twisted into a tight ball. Thank goodness I'd yet to eat. "He was my mother's boyfriend. They were dating when this all happened." My breath caressed the glass, fogging it up some, making Randy touch the soft mist as if he could wipe it off.

I hadn't cared for Randy at all, even though he'd done nothing but nurture and support my mother. Helen had loved him, but she had never shown it much around us. She was tough as nails, but I knew she'd had soft spot for this man. I'd tried to convince her he was nothing but trouble, but my argument had slid off my mother like oil to water. My motive hadn't been all unselfish, though. Randy's attention toward my mother meant sharing her with another man who wasn't my father, already dead for three horrid years.

That reason felt childish to me now, stupid even. Any tie to my mother would've been welcomed at that point. Even if it was Randy. He'd never treated me like anything other than another adult. He'd been respectful and had even taken my side on several arguments when I'd fought with my mother. He'd been good for her—for us—and yet I had rejected him as a father figure no matter what he did.

Now there we were once more. He knew me and I him. I balled my fist against the slick glass, sweaty from my damp palms, and I wanted to hit the slab of window. What would he turn into now? Would it return him to a natural human state, or would it leave him as broken as my mother had been? I couldn't bear to see him suffer if this didn't work. Or what if it killed him? What if this was toying with fate and would just hurry up the inevitable? Another death of someone close to my family would not be good.

I swallowed down as the cool glass felt slick under my skin. He howled inside, scratching at the glass and fingering the chains digging into his wrists. Agony ravished his body as he collapsed to his knees, breathing hard and wincing from the changes occurring all over his body. His hair began to fill in where it'd been torn out. Missing pieces of flesh filled in with scar tissue, and his fangs retracted back into his skull, as if they had never existed.

Would this work? The miracles that could occur…. And if it didn't? The horror it could unleash….

No matter where I turned, this virus was still tearing at my flesh and mind bit by tiny bit. It was like a pool of piranhas, ripping into my life without remorse, just wanting to satisfy the never-ending hunger.

Chapter Thirteen
A Primal Need

THE DAY WORE on, and I felt increasingly restless. How long were they planning on keeping me prisoner? I was already feeling better after a few meals and knew I'd be healed up very soon. Christian had made frequent trips to see me, trying as he must, to pacify my impatience and growing anger. But I had tired of the situation, and no soothing words or attempted friendship from him now could change that.

Knowing Randy was recovering in a barred cell near the lab made me impatient to get out of there and release him, too. He may have not had time to marry my mother, back when they were together, but I knew he would've if she'd have said yes to him. He was family, and I couldn't leave him to rot.

As daylight approached, the hallways dimmed so the vampires could rest. They even dimmed the cell blocks. There was a cot just outside my room where Christian slept. I wondered why he'd been chosen to guard me. Maybe they didn't trust anyone else. Maybe he'd volunteered because he didn't trust anyone either. All I knew was that I wanted out of there, and sleep wasn't an option.

"Hey," I whispered through the bars. I hated being locked up. It reminded me of my time in Vida, waiting to die at the hands of this very same vampire. "Christian, wake up!"

He must've been exhausted, because he'd been asleep without moving for almost three hours.

"Yeah?" He finally rolled over and squinted his eyes at me, groggy and slightly disoriented. "What is it, April? Need anything?"

"Can't sleep."

He swung his legs over the edge of the cot and shoved back his long, straight auburn red hair. Seeing him look so tired and waking up made me feel confused inside, and the familiar longing that the damned bond made me feel swelled up within my chest. I pulled away from the bars and sat on my bed as he stood up and opened the door, pressing the electronic lock behind him. We were locked in, but I had seen the code.

It made me wonder if he'd purposely shown it to me or if he'd let it slip in his sleepy state. This thought alone made me watch him as he settled into the bunk next to mine and stretch out. He would be asleep in no time if I didn't speak. Why he made me choke on my words mystified me and didn't let me relax whenever he was around. You could say it was fluttering butterflies like having a high school crush on someone, but I didn't like it. Not one bit. It had been forced upon me when he'd bound himself to me down in the bowels of Vida where we'd been left for dead by Katrina.

It was all her fault I had these uncontrollable feelings overtaking me every waking moment. Even though she was long dead, the resentment I held for that raging vampire anomaly still caused my blood to boil. If she hadn't stuck me in that cell, I wouldn't have had this problem.

I chewed on my lip. I had to keep him awake. Maybe if I could keep him from sleeping now, he'd be knocked out later, and I could sneak out.

"You're sleeping in here?"

"This bed is more comfortable than that piece of crap cot out there. You don't mind, do you?"

"No."

"Good. Now try to get some sleep."

"I told you I can't sleep."

"Why not? What's bothering you?"

"Why are you being nice to me when I know Mercer wants me dead?"

"He doesn't want you dead."

"Now who's full of it?" I huffed. I was tired of these mind games and wanted to finally get the story out of him. "Look… I haven't asked you this before, but I need to know. Why did you betray me? I thought you were my mate. I thought you were supposed to be on my side." I rubbed my eyes and turned to face him, cradling my head in my arm. The dim light seeping in from the hall lit up his haloed eyes, and they glowed like cat eyes in the darkness.

Christian let out a long breath, knowing he wasn't going to be sleeping any time soon. "Okay. I'm sorry you think that way. We haven't exactly been 'mates.' You told me to leave you the hell alone. I did. What do you want, April? I can't hide these feelings I have for you, and you've forced me into this misery. I won't let Mercer hurt you. We need you. And I never betrayed you. It's not what you think. Your blood is the solution to this epidemic that has us enslaved… drinking blood, living in the shade. He'd never jeopardize that. He wants it even more than I do."

"How do you know that?" His argument hadn't convinced me just yet.

"Because those ferals out there, those beasts you put down like they are nothing but the rot beneath your feet, they were people once. Wouldn't you want to save them if there was a chance you could? Wouldn't you want to be a part of the cure, the savior of all mankind?"

"I… I don't know."

"April…." There was no reasoning with him about it. I had never wanted to be part of any revolution. Yes, it would be nice to save those who were lost, turned into wild savages—that's why I had tried to get the antidote from Rick—but the past few days had made me reconsider that idea. What if it didn't work? What if the cure turned out to be worse than the disease? They were going about it the wrong way, too. Kidnapping wasn't exactly diplomatic.

"I want my mother back. I want my family back. That's what I want. And because of your meddling—Rick's experimentations…." I said his name with disgust. "I have nothing. How's that for a cure? How do I cure death? Tell me how to do that!"

Christian waited for me to finish my rant, which was probably the wisest thing I'd ever seen him do. I could see why he'd been a leader once. His quiet observations and ability to listen was superior to Blaze's. This small detail filled me with the fear that this hive was more together, more united in their cause than ours. That could be costly if both sides went to war again.

"I'm sorry about your mother. Truly, I am. I didn't kill her. She chose her path, and no one can undo that for her. Rick may have tampered with her sanity, but I didn't kill her, April." He was on his knees before me now, scooping my hands into his while I sat up on the bunk, shocked to have him so near, so close. I held my breath. "I didn't kill her, but you blame me all the same."

He looked defeated, his frown making my heart race to correct his misery. Why did he make me feel that way? I forced back the spill of emotion and gritted my teeth. I had to stay together, or everything would collapse in upon itself.

"Please don't touch me," I whispered, and he dropped his hands onto his knees. The effect of the touch has not left him unscathed, either, and we now both fought to keep our positions. How could he have lapsed so easily? It only took a touch, one caress of his skin, one unguarded bump to ignite the fire within that claimed me as his and him as mine. I prayed that such a connection would fizzle out after so long apart, but time had done nothing to stifle this urge. I swallowed the dry knot forming in my throat as I searched for the words to say, to make this end tonight.

I loved Rye. If only we had this sort connection, if only the man standing before me was Rye, I would have been all right.

But he wasn't Rye. He was the enemy no matter which way I looked at it. Still, the desire burning in his dual colored eyes had me struggling for control with every gasping breath.

"Why is it so hard to push you away?" I closed my eyes, my heart pounding hard enough under my lids that I could see starbursts under them. His scent filled my nostrils and pushed at my own longing, snaking into my head and stirring it up into a mush. I hated it, but the more I fought it, the more it hurt to move, like a knife embedded in my side.

"Because we're meant to be together, April. I know you'd sever this in a moment if you could, but only death can undo it. We are bound for life." He reached out and slid his hands over mine again. "Why fight it?" He inched closer to the side of my bunk, and I began to shake, fighting the urge to skitter back and press my spine against the wall. Anything to run from his scent, his gorgeous eyes and long, silky hair. I'd never really looked at him as I did now, and I found each angle, every tuft of hair and patch of smooth skin alluring. Why, if he was right, did it feel so wrong?

"Christian…." I licked my lips, my eyes trained on his. Damn this unnatural attraction. It was exhausting to fight it, but I kept at it. Eventually it felt as if that side of me, the opposing part that disagreed with everything involved in this bond, was hidden behind a thick plate of smoky glass. That April was screaming and pounding on it to no avail as her voice faded away.

"Yes?"

I blinked at him, feeling the fight slip from my grasp and the protesting in my head silence. "Kiss me."

The confusion played across his face while his eyes searched for truth in mine. I wasn't sure what he'd see there. For once, I wasn't the girl I'd once been, full of confidence and ready to kill everything in sight. No, this girl had just had her entire foundation pulled from underneath her leaving nothing but a wide abyss she had to cross, one uncertain step at a time.

My heart was going to burst from the excitement. If I could just get a taste of him once more. One little taste, maybe I could satiate the hunger until I got out of that place. Maybe he'd give me the much needed blood I needed to gain my strength back. Maybe if I relented, it'd give me what I needed to push the thought of him from my mind until later, when I could think without him being so close.

Just this once….

"I… I can't fight it." My words softly escaped my lips, sounding so far away, it was as though another April had spoken them.

He closed the gap between us, his lips slamming into mine in a voracious attack. I felt his fangs extend and nick my tongue. The pain was pleasurable, and I relished the taste of blood swirling around our tongues.

The taste of him was a rush I'd been seeking for an eternity. It was the ultimate high.

"April… I've needed you for so long. You have no idea how torturous it's been without you."

His kiss deepened, and he pushed me back so that we were both on the bed. I let his desire ignite my own, and it was impossible to escape. It wasn't blood that I wanted anymore, which I found curious, especially since that had been the initial trigger for touching him. No, this time it was whatever bound us filling me up with pleasure and singing its happiness. It was where it wanted to be, in the arms of this man. As the clothes slipped off and the minutes wore on, his kisses sent fire across my body, and running my fingers across his skin and the scars I had made on his abdomen, I felt safe, happy even.

Even the screaming inside my head wasn't missed as we each took what we wanted from the other. Each touch felt like flames, licking across my skin in hot pleasure. I wanted his lips to kiss me and his fingers to pull me even closer, until there was no separating the line between us. And so we did, until the fire flickered down to embers and our hearts quieted down into a slow, steady rhythm. As we lay there in the quiet of the daytime while the sleeping vampires were tucked away and the world was silent, I fought to keep the happiness afloat. I felt loved as he twirled my hair and stroked my skin until his energy ebbed away and sleep overtook him.

I didn't leave right away. I couldn't, with everything that had happened. I touched his sleeping face, sliding my finger softly down his cheek and feeling the pleasure seep into my skin from this one simple gesture. This bond was some sort of magic, a trick of mutated DNA that I had finally given into. Though I planned to never let it happen again—I wasn't expecting to see Christian ever again after that day—I felt a tiny sliver of sadness at the thought of losing him.

Once I was sure he was completely asleep, softly snoring and unresponsive to my movements, I slipped out of bed, pulled my clothes and boots back on and entered the code on the finger pad. Holding the bars so that the click wasn't overly loud, I pushed at it slowly and it opened wide enough just for me to squeeze through. I closed it behind me gently, making sure Christian was still gone to the world. I watched his slow, deep breaths of slumber, and it warmed my frigid heart to see him so vulnerable.

I turned and headed toward the future. Back to Rye, to Sarah, Elijah and Jeremy. I needed to leave this place so far behind, I would never be able to turn back. I searched ahead to find the armory and carry out my plan. I needed bombs. Lots of them.

Chapter Fourteen

Belly of the Beast

SARAH SIGNALED TO stop and wait, waving her hand out behind her. It'd been three days since April had disappeared, and time was of the essence. They had waited as Elijah returned to Blaze's hive and loaded them up with weapons. It had taken a while for him get back carrying so many supplies. The narrow canyon was only passable on foot. The rest of them had waited patiently and studied every possible route on the blueprints. Sarah had it all memorized within a day. Rye had spent his time pacing, ready to lose his mind in anticipation. Patience wasn't his strong suit.

Sarah jerked her head up and listened to distant footsteps pass down the hall they were about to turn into. Moments passed before she gave the all clear. She was swift and quiet on her feet, and Elijah was enjoying the view from behind. As though she felt his eyes upon her, she swung her head around, sending her long braid swinging over her shoulder, and threw him a knowing smile. Elijah pressed his lips together as she turned back and kept on. Rye came up next to him and threw him a shrug, smiling as he passed by.

Why was everyone so smug? Elijah held back a grunt as he followed behind. He'd made it clear to Sarah that he wasn't interested back in the City of Vida. The constant stress Katrina had put him under and their frequent missions to secure the Las Vegas Strip around their sanctuary underneath the Wynn was exhausting, leaving him little time to give much attention to the seductive redhead. Finding out that she'd been April's best friend had surprised him. It had made him realize how little he knew Sarah. It'd been humbling to discover that she had her own fascinating secrets.

So maybe he was intrigued by her now. Things were vastly different outside the City of Vida. Where they had lacked freedom before, they now thrived in it. April had been a wonderful tour director, introducing them to the entire city above ground, something they'd not been allowed to do much on their own before. This had loosened them up. Of the twelve hybrid human warriors he'd been commander of, four had remained in the Vida to keep it safe and under control, and one had died in the battle against Katrina. Of the other seven, only two had joined April on this trip to the Red Rock slot canyon fortress: Elijah and Sarah. Most of the twelve had worked in pairs. Mated or not, they had partners. Elijah had never taken a mate. He'd been the elected leader from the beginning and couldn't show favoritism. It left an odd number, and Sarah had been left to do most tasks alone or with him, naturally making her his second. He'd never seen her as anything more than his second in command; it wouldn't have been appropriate.

Now things felt oddly different. Elijah wondered about the prickling of feelings stirring within him whenever he looked at Sarah. It was confusing, for he'd never liked her as anything more than just a friend. Maybe it was this newfound freedom to roam, to go wherever he pleased, which had released his repressed emotions. He couldn't quite put a finger on it, but he knew he'd have to make a move for her sooner or later. The competition was growing.

Glaring at Rye as he slid into a doorway, he felt the grip of envy. Rye knew exactly who he wanted—April—and would do anything for her. It must be nice to know what you wanted. On the other hand, April wasn't exactly reciprocating Rye's affections. Elijah had briefly wondered if April would be interested in him but decided against pursuing her because of Rye's dedication to the girl. It was obvious Rye would not be willing to let her go any time soon. Still, if she'd ever approached Elijah for a roll in the sack, he doubted he'd be able to resist the sassy, dark-haired beauty. She was every bit a woman warrior, and he liked that.

It was those same traits he adored about Sarah. So why did Sarah cause such confusion? She'd always made it obvious she wanted him. It was hard to admit defeat and give into her. She was so beautiful with her pouty pink lips and voluptuous breasts, not to mention her well-trained physique. She'd been the object of many other men's affections in the City of Vida, but she'd brushed them off without a second thought, as if they were just not good enough.

Maybe that was it. He didn't want to mean nothing to her. He wanted to be good enough.

"Come on!" Sarah's hushed voice brought him back to face her. Her bright green eyes narrowed as she smiled, catching him staring at her. "Eyes ahead."

He clenched his jaw, hoping the dim lighting in the walkway heading out over one of the warehouses would cover his flushed skin. He avoided her eyes and peered over a short concrete wall, fingering the large hunting knife at his side. The massive room below looked like it was a storage area and infrequently used. There were several Jeeps in various states of repair or in pieces for parts. Several wooden crates were stacked up almost as high as the walkway and were arranged in rows draped with long swaths of drop cloths.

No hybrid vampires in sight. Elijah waved at the others as they continued their careful trek into the heart of the underground fortress.

"This feels too easy," Rye muttered, gripping his sword. They were hoping to kill any resistance as quietly as possible. Something was wrong, and it ate at his nerves as they crept along. Why wasn't anyone near the secret entrance? Christian and Mercer must have felt very secure that it wouldn't be found if they left it unguarded.

"Where do you think they're keeping her?"

Sarah peered across the room and pointed to a far door on the bottom floor. "That one leads to the main living quarters, right next to the cells where prisoners are kept. At least, that's what the blueprints show."

"We can't just walk into the living quarters. There's an hour or two of daylight left. It's probably filled with them right now." Rye sheathed his sword and brought out his guns, knowing they'd be walking into a sleeping hive. It was best to be prepared to kill.

"I know that." Sarah rolled her eyes and smacked her gum. Where the hell did she get gum? Elijah smirked at her snarkiness. "What do you think I am, suicidal?" She pointed at a metal staircase. "This is the back way." She took the stairs with swift, soft steps and was on the ground sprinting through the rows of cargo like she was running through a field of wheat. Elijah admired her carefree nature, even though she really wasn't that naïve. It was her mask, a front to make others believe she was more vulnerable. If he hadn't known her for so long, he would have wondered who the hell she thought she was. But he did, and it made him smile.

He made his way down the same way she had gone, swift and light on his feet. His bulkiness made everyone believe he'd be rough and clunky on his feet, but that wasn't the case. Being a hybrid had its advantages, including being able to move fast but quietly.

Sarah was crouched at the doorway, already sticking pins and her lock picking tools into the slots. This was a regular doorknob without any kind of electronic key pad or lock. For a back door, it was simple and unprotected. Elijah just hoped it wasn't a trap.

"Got it!" Sarah jiggled the lock once more, and a tiny click resonated in the silence surrounding them. In the massive storage area, the sound felt like it echoed across the pallets and metal, amplified. She slowly opened the old door, and the hinges began to groan. She cringed and stopped, listening for anything or anyone who could be coming down the way. When nothing happened, she slid through the doorway, Elijah and Rye hot on her heels.

The darkness within shifted as their eyes adjusted, and they found themselves at the end of a very long hallway. Hopefully no one would be coming around the corner to trap them in this maze. It could be the end of a useless walkway that led to the warehouse. Either way, the far-off echoing voices were so faint, they seemed to come from quite a distance away. Rye took the lead, and they shuffled close to one another until they came to the bend in the hall.

Peeking around the corner, Rye's tension visibly relaxed. "It's an abandoned barracks. Which way, Sarah?"

Sarah stuck her head out to scan the room then pulled back to talk with them. "There's a door on the end to the right. Through that door is the cell block. She should be in one of the rooms there."

A small squeak on the tile made them all clamp their lips together and turn toward the barracks. Someone was in there, and the risk of discovery was high.

Rye pressed his back to the wall and dared to peek into the room again to find out what was going on. He was so surprised to see April heading back to the cells, trying in vain to make her boots stop squeaking on the tile. Her face alone made his heart burst with love. It was obvious she hadn't noticed them yet because she took each step swiftly and softly as she turned into another hallway right ahead of them and proceeded to leave the room. She was laden with a large army bag, half full but apparently heavy. She shifted the strap on her shoulder and cursed under her breath.

"April!" Rye called out softly, afraid she was being pursued.

She froze in her steps. He hoped she wasn't about to shoot a weapon in his direction. They would be in plain sight if she would just turn around.

She whipped around and held out a gun. He wondered where she had swiped it from. He stepped out into the room and held his hands up.

"It's me, April. It's Rye."

Her hands shook, and she didn't look as thrilled to see him as he thought she would. Still, who knew what she'd been through down there? He hoped she hadn't been subject to the torturous experimentation her mother had endured. He waited and could feel the others hesitate behind him. April's eyes were wild, like a frightened predator. Not exactly an invitation to run and hug her.

He waited, not sure if she was in a killing high or ready to pounce on him. Deciding the best course of action was to talk to her, he licked his lips and hoped it would shake whatever it was she was experiencing.

"April? Are you okay?" He swallowed, his mouth dry.

"April, it's us." Sarah peeked around Rye to study her friend. April looked like she hadn't slept in days, even though she was clean and looked like she'd bathed. Still, the haunted look in her eyes made Sarah glance at Rye and then back to Elijah.

"Rye? Sarah…?" April's voice shook, and she dropped her hands, letting the gun dangle in her fingers. Bright, glistening tears streamed down her cheeks as she sobbed silently. "You shouldn't have come." She shook her head like they'd interrupted her train of thought. "You can't be here."

Rye took the opportunity to run to her, and she collapsed into his arms. "April, we're getting you out of here."

She shook her head again, her gaze searching his face as she let him hug her. "I can't. I need to find the antidote before I leave. I lined the bunker with bombs. I have an hour left to find it and get out of here. Oh, Rye… I've made a mess of things."

Rye brushed away the loose strands sticking to the thin sheen of sweat and the wetness of tears on her face. She pulled away, and his heart seized.

"Let me go." She stepped back, eyeing him and the other two through her tears. "If you want to help me, thank you. But I'd rather you go now. If you can't, I understand. This isn't what you came for."

She turned and held her gun back up, wiping her face with the back of her hand.

"We're going wherever you go. April, what's going on?" Rye followed behind, keeping his eyes trained on her back, but as they entered the next hall, he ripped them from her to resume his scan of the surroundings. Stupidity got you killed. Losing control of emotions was a definite risk. So why was April losing it? He'd never seen her so distraught to see him. That couldn't be good.

She only shook her head, making him clamp his lips together. Whatever had her shooken up, it didn't look like she was going to divulge what it was any time soon. At least, not here. It didn't sit well with him and made his imagination run wild as they continued down the halls without a disturbance. April looked determined, and he wondered if she even knew where she was going.

"April," he whispered, trying to catch her attention. "Where are you going?"

Her lack of response sloughed off his patience, and he tightened his grip on his guns. The place appeared abandoned, but thinking about April made him sloppy as they turned the corner, and he almost ran into her.

"Crap, Rye," she hissed as she did her best to not fall over. Footsteps at the end of the hall had them scrambling to press themselves against the wall as they came closer. The clicks of the boots on the tile floor had the count at about five of them. They could take them, Rye just didn't want to bring anyone else to the fight while they were at it. He pulled out his swords after tucking his guns away. He handed one to April as she tucked her gun into her jeans. Her lack of weapons made him wonder how she thought she'd be escaping this place once she had managed to do whatever it was she was doing. Except for the lone gun she had acquired somewhere, she was weaponless.

That has never stopped her before, he thought. The bunch of vampires made it to the corner, and the band of infiltrators jumped the group. Behind them, Elijah and Sarah slipped in and took out the two back guards. The last one had jumped back and was already dashing back the way he'd come when they'd attacked.

April took off after the rogue and reached him in time to slice the sword diagonally across his back. He groaned as he toppled over, slamming his face into the ground and knocking himself out. She hopped onto the fallen figure and thrust the sword deep into his back.

She remained there, perched on the vampire's back as she huffed and puffed, looking even wilder than she had before. A strange feeling flooded Rye as he watched her reach down to pull the blade out of the guy's back and touch his blood with her fingers. Her fingers went immediately to her mouth, and she sucked the blood off of each one.

He flinched away and checked the hallway for more soldiers. She had looked somewhat pale when he'd pulled her to him earlier, and the thought of her being drained nauseated him. That was the reason she was probably starved and weaker now, though she had shown them she was on the road to recovery. But what had the draining done to her mind?

"You okay, April?" he asked while turning back to find her finally satiated and licking her lips.

"I'm perfect now." Her eyes remained hooded in ecstasy. "Let's find the lab. I need to see Rick again."

"There's a lab on this side of the quarantine?" Sarah wrinkled her nose as she swiped her sword across the fallen vampire's clothes to clean the blood off. "It must have been added later. It wasn't on the blueprint."

April stared at her friend as if she didn't know her at all. "You memorized the blueprint?"

Sarah nodded, looking like it was no big deal. "I've had an enhanced memory ever since the change."

April eyed her friend for a moment before bursting into a chuckle. "I still can't get over you being a killer hybrid human. Just thought I'd never see the day."

Sarah scowled as Elijah laughed. "Why not? I can be beautiful and fight like a man, too."

"You sure can." Elijah threw her a rare grin, and a blush flared across her face. Her pale skin flashed like a red light, and she was left speechless as they proceeded farther down the hall, April already so many steps ahead of them all.

"April, stop." Rye grasped onto her arm, hoping she wouldn't swing back with her sword.

She stopped in her tracks, turned and drilled her eyes into him. "What?"

"What's wrong? Why are you acting so strange, and why won't you answer me?"

Her anger melted into anguish as she stared hard into him. He felt his heart pounding as Elijah moved forward to scout for more vampires. Sarah kept to the rear.

"Come on, love. What's going on?"

"I—I...." She swallowed and turned away. Whatever had her upset wasn't easy to get out. "I can't do this right now, Rye. I'll tell you soon, I promise. I just can't right now."

Rye nodded and let go. It crumbled his resolve to pull it out of her, and all he could do was walk away. Joining Elijah, he hoped that when this was all over, there would still be something left between them. The feeling of foreboding twirling in his stomach told him otherwise, but he tried to shake it off.

"It's just around this hall and through the double doors at the end," April stated dryly. Her voice came out stiff and calm, as if she hadn't almost lost her nerve a few moments ago. Her face was now a still mask with cold eyes. She refused to look in Rye's direction, choosing instead to trudge ahead and swing the lab doors wide open without scoping it out first.

"What the fuck, April! Wait!" Elijah grimaced as he ducked into the room behind her only to find her facing just one other person. Rye had sped up to join them in the lab.

"Rick."

The man stood from his chair and backed away, eyes widening at the sight of the four of them. "April? What are you doing here?" He walked backward and bumped into the wall swinging his head both ways to find an exit. He was surrounded and looked like a cornered animal. She wasn't the person he'd been expecting to see today, if ever again.

"I want the antidote, Rick. And...." She walked to a doorway that led into a small hall. "And you're going to let Randy go, too."

He shook his head as he watched her approach, glancing at the tiny containment block down a small hallway on one end of the lab. "You shouldn't take him out of there. His results have only been negative once." Elijah had a large hunting knife pointed at Rick's throat, so he stopped talking.

"Where are the keys, chief?" Elijah smirked as Rick's eyes widened at the massive man pointing the knife at him. He reached into his lab coat and held them out.

"Thank you for your cooperation."

Rye stared at Rick and then flicked his eyes to April, who snatched the keys from Elijah. She motioned toward the scientist. "Tie him up."

Rye followed her down the hall to a row of bar-lined cells modified for prisoners who needed medical treatment. "April... who's Randy?"

Chapter Fifteen

Battle Scars

NOTHING WAS GOING to get in my way. I was ready for anything. I slammed my way toward the cell blocked infirmary where Rick had kept Randy since injecting him with the antidote a few days before. There was no one there, never was. I'd visited Randy for the past two days, watching his continuing transformation in fascination. Where skin had been ripped open now lay new skin, taut and healing. His face had been left mostly intact as a feral, which was fortunate since I'd seen a ton of ferals without faces or with a good chunk torn off.

It had taken him almost a full day to begin to speak. He'd started with short wails, grunts and unintelligible noises that had me shaking my head that I didn't understand. His vocal cords had to heal, and they took forever to do so. Once he could pronounce simple words, much like a toddler learning to speak, he could finally whisper simple sentences to me.

"Helen?" His voice was hoarse.

I'd shake my head, looking away. It hurt too much.

He'd met me with silence, settling back on the cot in the cell he'd been moved to once he'd been deemed safe enough to remove from the padded observation room. His wrists were still healing from the handcuffs digging into the skin, leaving the skin purple and yellow but regenerating where the top layer had been rubbed off.

We'd had no further discussion about my mother. She'd left an abyss of emptiness in us both. Instead, as his words came easier, we'd spoken about the world outside. He told me his memory wasn't good from the time he'd been lost in the fog. He described it like floating in a nightmare, where nothing made sense and noises bounced off the walls and echoed in his head. He knew it was a possibility that he'd killed people in his feral state. He took it pretty well, considering. I knew he'd been in prison for something before the outbreak, but I'd never asked him about it. Maybe it'd been for murder. It wasn't as if anyone was innocent anymore. These days, that was a luxury only little children possessed.

"So what now?" he asked. His hair had grown thicker, and his eyes were now their normal blue color. Still, he wasn't unscathed by the virus. He'd be left with scars from quarrels with other ferals and possibly victims. His body was peppered with slashes, bite marks and nail scratches. I guess we all wore our scars differently.

"I guess we'll see. I have to get out of here. I need that antidote and need to figure out how to give it to the population. Or find someone who can distribute it more effectively than in a shot."

"That's not your job, April."

"I know."

"So why do you want to do that?"

He'd frustrated me in our talks. I'd sat back in the creaky folding chair outside the bars of his cell. "I don't know. Maybe it's a purpose that I'm here for. I've felt lost since my mother died. Like her death stole this fire that I had inside. Snuffed it right out. It's been... difficult."

He'd nodded and not asked any further questions.

But it was my turn to ask questions. "What are you thinking of doing?"

He would shrug, leaning back and closing his eyes. He'd slept a lot; recovering must have taken a huge toll on his body. I couldn't imagine how it felt as his body morphed back to human. So far, Rick's test samples of Randy's blood were promising. He was not a hybrid, not feral but not quite human. What he would eventually end up as was a mystery to us all. Still, it had to be better than being a feral, right? Zompire no more.

Now here I was, grabbing the keys from Rick to release Randy. As I unlocked the cell door and rolled it back in a loud clang of metal, Randy stood up and joined us. I hoped he'd have enough strength to escape with us. Sarah and Elijah eyed him suspiciously. Those two really didn't trust anyone. Probably a good thing. I had trusted too much, and it'd been my undoing.

"Let's go," Rye said. He was at my side, looking at Randy with apprehension, narrowing his eyes as if conveying a threat to him with only a look. "No funny business now. We don't exactly know if this antidote worked, do we?"

The last part he'd directed at Rick, who stood a few feet away, shuffling his feet side to side as his fingers nervously rubbed the hem of his shirt.

"I'm positive he's fine right now. His body is just adjusting to the rapid change back to normal. The antidote speeds up healing, so he may look different every hour until it's done."

Rye nodded, but his eyes never left Randy. "It's time to go."

"All right." Randy nodded, exited the cell and following us down the hall.

Sarah waved at us, pointing toward the door. "I think we've been spotted."

Cameras against the lab wall showed us the chaos spreading throughout the hive. Dozens of vamps were gathering nearby, Mercer yelling and gesturing to get the group moving. They looked frantic. I scanned the screens for any sign of Christian. It wasn't that I didn't want him to escape, I just didn't know what to feel about him anymore, or even Rye, for that matter. The escape was a welcomed focus, and I pointed to a satellite armory untouched by the hordes that were gathering.

"We don't have much time left. The bombs are timed for twenty minutes from now." I peered up at Sarah, Miss Photographic Memory. "How do we get to this armory and then out? I can delay the timer if we get back to it."

She smiled, a wicked gleam growing in her eyes. "I saw that on the blueprint. It's this way. I know a way out from there, too. It'll take us back to the dusty warehouse we came in through."

Perfect.

THE TREK TO the armory ended up being more difficult than I'd hoped. The moment we left the lab and headed down to a deeper level—one Sarah thought would be free of guards—we were ambushed. I was still low on weapons, having only Rye's second sword for defense. The gun's ammunition was low, so I was reduced to slicing my way through the wave of vampires as they headed toward the same armory. At least they were light on the weaponry, too. Otherwise, we'd have been terribly outnumbered.

"Girl… move!" Elijah snapped behind me. His bulk shoved me aside, and I turned just in time to watch him slice open another vamp's chest, one who had obviously been attempting to get to me. The slick plop of blood and guts splattering across the clean tile floors mixed with the slap of bodies colliding. I peered down at the convulsing vamp who'd almost gotten me. Damn, I was getting too lax.

"Thanks!" I yelled back to him before spinning and cutting down another figure who had pointed his sword at us. I fell to my knees, jamming the side of the sword against his legs and sending him flying over the metal and crashing to the floor. I didn't have any time to recover since the hall had filled with more vamps. I'd even lost the others in the mass. The bodies piled up on both sides of me as I pushed forward, slicing, swinging and shoulder-butting the vamps out of my way. I just hoped we were winning.

At that rate, there was no way we'd make it to the armory in time for me to disarm the bombs. Final resting place? I really hoped not. I kept on, punching and slicing my way through the crowded hall.

Until, that is, the stars spilled across my vision when someone hit me from behind, sending me flying into the wall. Hitting full force with my side, I struggled to regain my breath as my ribs screamed in protest and the pain made the air feel like fire. Still, I saw him coming and managed to flip toward my left as his sword rammed into the wall where'd I'd been leaning.

"Try that again!" I yelled, though with my lungs still seized, it sounded more like a rough hiss. I glared at the vamp, a medium-sized man who was slender but fast. He cracked a wicked smile as his dark eyes gleamed.

"Thanks for the invitation." He brought the sword up again and sliced it downward, but I managed to stop it in time with my own blade. Pushing hard against him, I made it to my knees but couldn't shove him off enough to stand. I thought for sure he'd have the best of me, but he was holding back. Why?

"Kind of short, aren't you?" I muttered. He really wasn't, he was at least two inches taller than I was, but his comrades towered over him. I guessed his speed and strength made up for that. His slender physique made him faster and more dangerous than his fellow vamps.

"Height makes no difference." His lips curled back, showing off his sharp fangs. I wasn't impressed and didn't give him any satisfaction. Instead, I huffed to push him back again, but only found that we were at a standstill.

Crap! My arms were on fire, and I could feel the tiny muscle fibers beginning to shake from the strain. If only I was at full strength, this guy would've been toast.

"What? Mercer sent his peons to take us down? Not much of battle, is it?" I laughed, garnering the effect I had wanted. The vamp narrowed his eyes, his frown deepening as he pushed back against me. Only then did I notice he didn't have any halo rings around his irises. What the hell?

Another type of hybrid?

Well, ain't the world a candy store?

410

"Rick fuck with you, too? Your haloes are missing," I snickered, hoping to rub him the wrong way.

My words confused him, as if they might've hit some sensitive thing that he'd hidden deep down. He pushed me back with a final rough shove but backed away and stared at me with disgust.

"How do you know anything like that?" He didn't look scared but stunned. I was hoping it would be enough to catch him off guard.

"He fucks with everyone. Don't you know?" I spit out a mouthful of blood and glared at him. My body was tiring, and I could feel every bruise, ache and cut from the fight. Even the adrenaline wasn't helping, and I stumbled back, trying my best to hide the weariness. The others were still fighting, but a bubble had formed around us, keeping me and him encircled. Just as I backed away, I found the room where I had initially run into Rye and the group. I took that moment to turn, burst through the door and run past the cell blocks, which were now empty, and down the hall. I found myself in a dusty warehouse lined with piles of crates, canvas-covered vehicles and junk stacked to the roof.

I didn't have to wait long for Mr. No-Halo to rush into the room behind me. I slipped behind a stack of crates, still sealed from delivery, and took a moment to rest. I was breathing hard, and the burn of my broken ribs seared through me with each intake. The pain worsened with each movement, and I worried it was more serious than it appeared. I held the bloodied sword, gripping the hilt so tightly my fingers felt numb.

"April... that's your name, right? Christian told me all about you. He's got some sick fascination with you, like you're his mate or something insane like that." The man let his blade drag across the cement, sending up a loud, echoing screech probably meant to grate on my nerves. What kind of a sick bastard was he?

Glancing around, I took in my surroundings, looking for the way out. There was hidden walkway circling the entire room up above. A cement railing hid it from sight since it blended in so well with the walls. I could see it, though, and followed it around to find the doors that had to be up there somewhere.

"I wish I could've met you under different circumstances. We have so much more in common than you know. I'm Felix, by the way. It stuns me that you know Rick did something to me. Most just assume I didn't morph all the way. You see, I was a hybrid human, much like you, April. But Rick had to go and mess with things, claiming he'd fix me, cure me...."

I hoped he wasn't asking for sympathy. I was all out. His voice echoed, making it hard for me to pinpoint where he was. Apparently, the others hadn't yet noticed our absence, for no one had followed us into the warehouse. I took a chance and peeked around the edge of the row. Finding it empty, I crept along, silencing each movement as I struggled with the tiny breathes my damaged ribcage allowed for. If I didn't get some blood or get out of there soon, I was pretty sure Felix would overpower me without dripping any sweat.

"Do you know what it did to me?"

I sure hoped he didn't expect me to keep up the conversation. I kept limping on, my chest feeling like it was being squeezed. Pneumothorax? I was pretty sure one of my lungs was punctured because the tightness had turned into wheezing, and my vision swam as the pressure increased. *Crap!* Where was everyone?

"It made me an outcast to both humans and the vampires. But that's okay. I'm stronger, faster and more powerful than any of them now."

So much for his mental health. Not stronger there.

I made it to the end of another row and stopped, the wheezing now louder. Pretty soon I was going to lose consciousness, I was sure of it. I glanced around, trying not to breathe, for each inhalation only made it worse. I was out of options, and it wasn't looking pretty.

"April?" I spun and held the sword out, shaking violently as Felix approached. My sword was at his chest, but his was pointed down to the floor. Why didn't he just kill me?

My heart was bursting, I was sure of it, and I sank down to my knees, dropping my sword as I collapsed against a pile of burlap sacks and garbage. I hoped I hadn't landed in anything disgusting, but only dust billowed around me as the squeal of air replaced my voice and I gripped my chest.

Felix narrowed his eyes, studying me as I struggled to breathe. I could see the conflict swirling in his normal-looking brown eyes. His dark hair covered his ears, and he suddenly reminded me of someone. Someone I had known so long ago.

"I—I can't…." I gulped, pressing my eyes together and letting my head thump back. This was it, the end had finally come. One darn broken rib and anemia had done me in. Tragic, wasn't it?

Felix's indecision spread across his face like a wildfire before he dropped his sword, pulled out a small knife and dropped down beside me. He pulled my shirt up and checked my side. What the hell was he doing?

"Don't…."

Before I could protest, he shoved the knife into my side. Pain and panic gripped me for only a moment before my vision failed and the squeal of air no longer filled my ears.

The pain was gone. It faded along with everything else as I slipped into unconsciousness.

Chapter Sixteen
Return

THE VEHICLE BUMPED along the road, making me hit my head against the frame of the window. Air rushed by, drowning out the sound of voices inside with me. I briefly wondered where I was but found only confusion and a foggy memory. The last thing I could remember was the warehouse, the fighting and the intense pain in my chest. I flicked my eyes open, and the bright light of day made me squint once more to adjust to the blinding sun shining above the rushing landscape.

"Hey." Rye's hand circled over mine, his thumb making soft patterns across my skin. I glanced down and noticed my hands resting in my lap. Shifting, I yelped, sucking in a breath as the pain from my side reminded me of my last moments in Christian's hive and why I'd passed out.

Wait… where was Felix?

A boom echoed behind us, and I suddenly knew the fate Christian's hive had found by my hands.

"I—I was… where did… how did we get out?" I settled back down, slowly craning my neck around to see which of us had made it. A cloud of dirt hovered across the horizon in the direction we'd just come from. Somehow, we'd escaped before the bombs I'd set had gone off. How? I wish I'd been there to see how we'd accomplished that. The exit must not have been too far away.

"We stole one of the jeeps from the warehouse," Rye said. "Elijah hotwired it after we found you on the floor, bleeding."

"I couldn't breathe," I gulped, my throat sore and dry. "One of the vamps we were fighting… he… I think he saved me after I hit the wall and broke a damn rib." The effort it took to speak without pain was too much to handle. I bit my lip to steady my breathing, which eventually buffered the pain.

"Don't talk. You definitely got something going on there. Is that why you cut your side? Your rib jabbed your lung?" Rye pointed down to my right side, and I slowly reached around to touch the bandage wrapped around my torso. The rough bandage had been done up fairly quickly, from a first aid kit, I suspected. Still, I wondered where the mysterious stranger had gone off to and why he'd bothered to save me.

Kind of made me feel guilty if I'd just thanked him by blowing him to smithereens.

"Where's Sarah?" I managed to squeak out. I cleared my throat and immediately regretted it. I was being stabbed all over again as my side screamed with torment.

"Here, chica." She hung over the back of the front passenger seat and winked at me. I could see Elijah driving but no one else in the car. "Just you three?"

"Yeah. Who else? Definitely not your boyfriend, Christian."

Elijah smirked. "You made quite a mess of the joint." He had no regrets. I had to remember to live that way.

"I armed a lot of bombs."

"So that's what you were doing when we found you." Rye watched me, thoughtful as he processed the information.

"Well, that plan worked like a charm. Though we almost didn't get out on time." Elijah kept his eyes on the road, but I could feel his slight anger that we were almost blown to bits.

"What about that guy, did he make it out?" I wondered out loud. Elijah and the others looked at me questioningly. "You know, Felix. He wore all black and was one of the shorter guys. He followed me into the warehouse." The blank looks on their faces confirmed that they hadn't seen him at all. I sighed and rubbed my eyes. The exhaustion still hung on, gripping my bones and burning at my muscles like liquid fire. Maybe I had imagined the guy.

"Not sure who you're talking about." Rye narrowed his eyes into the distance. He was trying his darnedest to remember who I meant.

"Just as well." I let my head drop back, trying my best to reduce any movement. "What about the antidote?" I panicked, reaching to pat around for the small bag I'd strapped to my side. I'd taken what I could after smashing the fridge door before leaving the lab and stuffing the vials into my small black fanny pack.

"You looking for this?" Rye held it up. The bag swung in the sway of the jeep as Elijah dodged an abandoned car in the middle of the road.

"Give it here." I held my arm out, knowing I couldn't struggle with him for it.

"Why do you need it? It's not up to you to distribute it." His eyes stared at the pack, filled with a dark sadness. "It should've been incinerated with the rest of them."

"Give it to me, or I swear to God I'm going to deck you." My nostrils flared, and I shot him a daring look. If he thought questioning me now was a good idea, I didn't care how much it would hurt, I'd make him hurt along with me. "Rye…."

The pain flashed in his eyes momentarily before he lifted his chin and composed his features. Solemnly, he held the pack out for me to take, which I snatched and gripped onto like a treasure.

"You'll find nothing but trouble in those vials."

"It's my trouble to find."

"I just don't get it. Why try to save the world?"

"So optimistic, aren't you, Rye." I looked back out the window, the arid landscape flew by, and I let the conversation die. Even when Rye tried to ask me if I was in pain, his question went nowhere, for I refused to answer any more of them. I was lost in my thoughts, a plan forming within.

We arrived at Blaze's hive where the four of us had taken up residence. Even though I wondered why Blaze wasn't with them, I didn't have to think on it much when I saw him waiting at the entrance for us, looking relieved but reserved. He'd left, I could already figure out that he'd had little faith Rye and the others would find me. Exiting the Jeep took some effort, but Elijah lifted me into his arms without even asking and carefully carried me into the underground headquarters of Blaze's hive. I hid my anger as we passed Blaze, too tired and in too much pain to start something.

To my relief, Jeremy was safe in the City of Vida. I didn't want him to see me in such a ragged state. I'd rather he not see how weak I'd turned out to be or what I'd put myself through for our future. He didn't need to know such things.

Once in the infirmary, Elijah left with Sarah, laughing together, finally relaxed after the ordeal we'd faced. Rye, of course, stayed behind, sitting on the bed next to mine until the doctor checked me out, stitched me up, and notified me of a continued pneumothorax, a pocket of air between my chest wall and lung, but that he would just put me on an oxygen mask for a day to reverse it. I let him affix the mask—a plastic contraption with a plastic bag dangling from it—to my face. The hiss of oxygen drowned out any conversation I could have or listen to, so I closed my eyes, hoping that made it clear enough to Rye that I wanted to be alone. Once the doctor left with the vials to refrigerate them—after much protesting on my end, he'd agreed to give me the key to the mini-fridge he'd stick them in—all I wanted was silence.

But Rye didn't leave. Instead, he took up his silent vigil in the bed beside me and let me rest. At least this time he knew better than to push me. I couldn't be less uncooperative, so it suited me fine. I pulled the thin sheet up to my chin and turned, staring up at the IV inserted into my arm. It had blood dripping into the saline solution, and I had noticed a slight shift in the way my body felt. Still, I knew it wasn't a full transfusion. And it was human blood, not vampire, but any little bit would help.

With the sweet nectar dripping into my vein, morphine circling in my head and the constant whoosh of the oxygen mask, I let my eyes flutter shut until I couldn't fight the lethargy anymore. Sleep was a lover gone far too long, demanding its overdue embrace.

Chapter Seventeen
Running

THE TARMAC WAS a graveyard. Weeds strangled the asphalt and slipped through the cracks that had formed under the deteriorating runways. There was no movement in the blinding daylight, but these were the hours I liked best.

The horizon displayed an array of neglected buildings on The Strip which were bleached white from the unrelenting sun. It made everything look brighter than it used to, a long time ago. At the same time, if one looked closer, it made the vegetation pop out even more. It crawled up the sides of the buildings, choking the cement and beauty away from what used to be.

I was sitting in the highest tower of the air traffic control building. It gave me a 360-degree view of the entire valley, for the most part. The distant mountains looked like far-off massive peaks of rock. Peering across the runways, I stared at the distant Red Rock Mountains with a somber mood. What had happened to Christian and his hive? If I'd been awake during the escape, I would have known for sure, and this wouldn't have been my worry. I'd blown up the place. It was what I'd wanted... to finish the deed, severe these bonds and finally feel safer. It had been the once-in-a-lifetime opportunity to rid the valley of Mercer's evil and possible future retaliation.

I just hadn't thought about how lost I'd feel at losing Christian. It was so final, a strange feeling.

It made me seethe as I ground my teeth, my jaw tense and sore from the tension. There was nowhere for me to go that I felt right or happy anymore. Even visiting Jeremy in the City of Vida, run by the few of the original twelve who had decided to stay to keep it going after Katrina died, couldn't keep me in any better spirits. I was restless, agitated in my own skin. I jumped up from my seat to walk the length of the tower. I hated sitting still. I felt like I was suffocating, but I didn't know how to make it better.

Christian's death was just a catalyst. I freed myself of one jam only to find myself searching for another mess.

What was out there? What was left of the world now that the vampires had ravaged the human population down to nothing? Was there any kind of normal left? Besides the City of Vida, there were no signs of humans anywhere else in the valley.

The small seed of hope had been planted in me when Rick told me of the antidote. If I could find someone I could trust to reproduce it, maybe I could help people become human again. But who could I trust? Not Rick, he was probably dead with the rest of them anyway. He'd been Mercer's rat and untrustworthy. Not Blaze's chemist, who only knew rudimentary things about science and hematology. Who then?

I knew the answer before I even realized it. I'd have to leave the city. There was nothing left for me in Las Vegas. There was an entire world out there to explore, to discover, to help if I could. There had to be more people out there somewhere, scientifically inclined people who could reproduce the antidote, even perfect it, right? I had to take the chance and find a way out of there before I went mad and I could no longer tolerate my own insanity.

Jeremy would forgive me for leaving, even though I intended to return. That was for certain. I just had to let him know that I would never forget him and I was doing this for us, for our future. If, by chance, I didn't return, I'd have to make sure he knew how I felt about him. My little brother was now living a life that suited him well, but it had left me out in the cold. He'd understand if I said goodbye, just in case.

I left the tower and descended back into the underground fortress. I was going to pack up to go visit Jeremy and then hit up my car, stashed in Vida's expansive underground garage, and leave this place for a good long while.

I was just hoping I wouldn't run into Rye on the way out.

"WHERE ARE YOU running off to?" Sarah was sitting at the edge of my bed in the private room I'd been given within the commander's corridor of Blaze's hive. I'd walked into my room to find her there, as if she had already read my mind. Her stuff was packed and ready at her feet. Damn if the hybrid effect hadn't made her intuitive in more ways than one. It was scary, actually, but I had to grin slightly at her challenge.

I didn't say anything and went on to stuff my own things in my bag and strap on as many weapons as I could carry. I looked like I was ready for combat, but whatever I took would be all I had, so I had to take almost everything.

It was comforting to know I wasn't alone on this quest. Luckily, some things never changed between friends. She could always read me, and I her. She waited quietly as I finished packing some clothes and whatever food stores I had in the room before I lifted it onto my back and gave her a nod. She joined me without a word, and we headed out into the halls of the hive.

I had to leave quickly, while the daylight kept the activity at a low. Rye and Blaze were elsewhere, probably still in their chambers asleep or conducting important hive business in the main area. We all had our own sleep quarters. It was better that way. Even though Rye had wanted to share one with me, I couldn't give up the chance for privacy, something I dearly needed in such a large hive.

"April?" Sarah's voice broke through my thoughts.

"Yeah?" Our footsteps were light on the cement floor. We could wake anyone at any time, especially once we left the hall.

"Don't be mad, but Elijah's coming, too."

I stopped in my tracks and turned toward her. If looks could kill, that would have been it for Sarah. "What? Why did you tell him?"

"He understands us more than you know. Besides, he's good in combat, and we could use more than just the two of us."

I sighed, not willing to argue. She had a point, but still, I couldn't stand not being included.

"Where's he at?"

"He's our getaway driver." She giggled at this, but she immediately stifled it as I shushed her. Of course she would find this funny.

"Not funny."

"Lighten up, April, it's hilarious. We can pretend we're bank robbers or are getting away with murder."

"That never sounded fun to me."

"Oh, come on!" Sarah let out a breath. Maybe she was already regretting coming with me.

"I'm serious. This is a serious mission." I went into the infirmary, quiet and empty at this hour, and headed straight for the vaccine fridge. Luckily, the antidote could be left at room temperature, but Rick had told me that keeping it cool made it last longer. I had a little cooler to stuff it into, and I plucked cooling packs from the freezer to throw in as well. I grabbed the vials and placed then into the portable cooler, zipping it up and clutching it to my chest like precious cargo. It would warm up after a while, but it would at least keep them longer than using nothing at all.

"Okay, let's go." I started for the hall but stopped. "Wait."

Sarah turned a puzzled face to me, her eyes widening as comprehension passed across her face.

"I need to get Randy. He can't stay here alone. If we find someone to perfect the cure, he's the one we need to make sure it works."

She nodded and pointed toward the back of the infirmary, where a locked door stood alone against the stark white of the wall. I walked to it and peered inside. It was another room with two cells inside and a desk on the other side of it. The hive's doctor, John, sat at the desk, meticulously jotting down notes in a huge ledger. I knocked on the window, and he stood up and opened the door.

"How can I help you, April? Your ribs feeling okay?"

I nodded, stepping into the small room. It was an observation room connected to the cell where Randy lay sleeping on a thin mattress. "I'm good, John. Just need to take my friend with me."

He looked hesitant, narrowing his eyes as he thought my request over. I could see scenarios playing out in his mind as he thought about what to do. When I thought he was about to protest, he cleared his throat and held out a key on a ring.

"He's still very much in tune with the feral circadian rhythms and vulnerable during daylight. I have a bad feeling that the vaccine is not permanent, so I do advise extreme caution when the night approaches."

"Thank you, John." I took the key and paused, confused by his immediate cooperation. "Why would you let him go so easily?"

John scratched his dark hair and sighed, looking tired. "He had a rough night. Restless. None of the sedatives I gave him worked. I'm afraid there's nothing more I can do for him. I'm afraid he'll regress back to his feral ways unless you fix that vaccine of yours. As a doctor, letting him go so he can find better treatment is the best thing I can do." He reached out and placed a gentle grip on my arm. "Do be cautious. During the daytime, he's harmless. But I can't guarantee your safety at night."

I nodded. "Thank you. I'll keep that in mind."

I unlocked the cell, and Sarah helped me drag Randy out. He woke up a bit, but only enough to step along with our help. He was so groggy, we had to steer him as we hurried out.

We scurried the rest of the way down the hall and out toward the exit doors. I knew the moment we walked out, we might be reported to Blaze. But Elijah was already chatting it up with the gate guards and they were laughing like the best friends that they were. Most likely, he had smoothed the path for a clean escape, and we walked past him and out into the arid, warm late morning of Las Vegas. We jumped into the awaiting Jeep we'd stolen from Christian's compound, and I was impressed to find it full of gas and stuffed with food. Maybe Sarah's intuition went a lot further than I thought. I gave her a funny look, and she returned it with a happy, toothy grin.

She's scary. That is all.

We stuffed Randy into one of the back seats where he snored softly and shied away from the light of the sun. I remedied that by draping a dark shirt over the window, anchoring it with the window itself. I jumped into the driver's seat, slammed the door and got ready to crank the engine, but I didn't find any keys. Elijah opened the door and glared at me. "Move over, I'm driving."

"Says who?"

His face didn't move, but instead, he waited until I complied. Sighing, I slipped into the passenger side without any further argument.

"We have to visit Vida really quick. I have to say goodbye to Jeremy."

He nodded and shifted the Jeep into gear. Sarah sat in the back seat and stared at Randy, eyeing him up and down to make sure he wasn't about to pounce on her before she clicked her seatbelt on and leaned back in her seat. As we maneuvered out through the gate of the hive, I looked back, knowing I'd probably never see it again. A flood of sadness filled my stomach, enough to jerk my eyes back to the road in front. Rye was back there. He may have been a bit overbearing, but I did love him, and leaving without a goodbye was going to gnaw at me forever. Still, if I didn't do this, I'd continue to regret not at least trying to get the vaccine fixed. Which was worse? Could I give up on love, or could I give up on a promise for a better life? Neither felt like a good choice to give up on. I couldn't win.

So I did what any girl should do when faced with such a difficult decision. I shoved it so far down, it became an afterthought, a forgotten memory. Out of sight, out of mind. It wasn't right, and it wasn't what a good girl would do, but it was all I could manage to keep the fragile cracks in my heart from splitting open and pouring out the blood within. I needed to bottle it up, tuck it away and forget it even existed. If I ever saw Rye again, maybe it wouldn't be so bad. Maybe he could forgive me. But like so many other things in my life, I had a feeling it would come and bite me on the ass. Until then, I'd cope by avoiding the topic at all costs. Swallow that puppy down and hope I didn't choke on it.

We pulled up to the City of Vida and entered quietly, in a slow rush that made me sweat as I thought about saying goodbye to my only living relative. It was the right thing to do, leaving him here. He wouldn't be happy on the road with me, let alone safe. Here, he'd have everything he'd dreamt of when we were stuck underground in our bunker, with just me and my mother for company. He had his companions who were fun and exciting to be with. He had an adoptive mother of sorts who loved him as her own. He had food, shelter… safety. What more could I have asked for him? Not much, except to be with him, too.

As we reached the row of "houses" which were just apartments along one of the city's long hallways, I swallowed back the lump forming in my throat. They'd done loads to spruce it up, covering the whitewashed look Katrina had maintained and exchanging it for colorful paintings made by the city's residents. All down the halls were drawings of rainbows, graffiti, sadness, laughing, hearts and flowers… anything you could think of. There were walls of hands painted on by toddlers, children and the elderly. Here was the life he needed. Here was where our paths split. I only prayed those paths would intersect again.

Jeremy was in his new family's apartment, where he had his own room. He and his adoptive brother, Leo, were playing a video game. They were yelling at the screen but quieted down when Leo's mother, Allie, opened the door for me. Elijah and Sarah waited in the hall, knowing that this was a private family moment. Allie and Leo excused themselves to go make lunch in their small kitchen. The place was cozy, quaint and lived in. The way life should be. An array of sports equipment filled baskets on the side of the couch, and the place smelled of delicious homemade food I hadn't yet had the luxury to taste.

Jeremy played with the remote of his video game, pushing at the colored buttons and knobs as he avoided my gaze. He'd grown a foot in just a few months, and it made me want to pull him into a tight hug. Time was flying by too quickly.

"Hey, kiddo."

"Hey."

I slipped down onto the couch next to him and smiled, he'd grown so much in the days I hadn't seen him. No one had told him of my ordeal, which was for the best. I didn't want him worrying about me. Why should he worry when I was worlds away from the life he led now?

"Your hair needs a trim," I said as I pushed a thick lock of his brown hair away. It refused to comply and flopped back into its original position. I stopped trying to tame it when he pulled away.

"Are you coming back?"

Shocked, I waited a moment before speaking. "Of course I'm coming back."

"Where are you going?"

Jeremey wasn't intuitive like Sarah, but he was way more intelligent than I gave him credit for.

"Not sure. Maybe out west, maybe east. It depends on what we find. We might have to wander for a while."

"Thanks for letting me stay." He tugged at a string dangling from a loose seam on his shirt.

"You belong here, squirt."

He nodded before breaking down and slamming into me for a hug. "Promise to come back?"

"I promise. Hey…." I pulled back to look into his huge, tear-filled eyes. My brother, my only sweet love. I felt the tears prickling behind my eyes, too. Oh, how I'd miss him. "I'll always come back for you."

His sniffles were muffled in my shirt, and I rubbed his thin back. How had he gotten thinner and taller? Where was that short pudgy kid I'd known not so long ago? I'd missed so much. "Make sure you don't lie about that," he said.

"Never, Jeremy. Never."

Chapter Eighteen
Leaving Las Vegas

I WASN'T SURE how it ended up being decided that we should head to the Californian coast, but that was the direction we'd taken after leaving Vida. Elijah insisted on driving the entire way, leaving me to let my mind wander. Watching the city disappear into the rear view mirror left me feeling numb. There was something sad about saying goodbye to the only road I've ever been down. The last of the scattered houses at the edge of the desert valley disappeared, and the slow trek through a highway riddled with vegetation, stalled cars and debris made the ride feel like it lasted for eons.

Still, we'd make it to California before dark. We hoped we'd be able to camp outside one of the major cities in an abandoned house somewhere. We wouldn't have time to scope out possible hiding areas before nightfall to figure out if the cities were infested or not, so it would be safer than trying to shack up within the city limits of Barstow or San Bernardino. So far, there was little sign of life on the road, which suited us just fine.

The memories resurfaced along with each mile of road traveled. I remembered taking this trek many times with my parents, heading to the beach on impromptu fun trips or going to Disneyland, where all your dreams were supposed to come true. I huffed at the thought and ran my fingers through my dark strands. It was cool enough to keep the windows down since we weren't traveling at high speed, and the fresh desert air was delicious when I breathed it in. Sarah was sitting up front with Elijah now, and I watched as she chatted his ear off. I'd occasionally notice her hand land on his arm, or she'd reach over and poke him playfully on the shoulder when he tuned her out. I didn't blame him. She could go on and on, and I had already blocked her out myself.

Still, I think her feelings for Elijah ran a lot deeper than she let on. It made me smile, happy my friend had found some sort of distraction in the world after. They'd spent a lot of time together in Vida, and from what Sarah had told me, she'd been his right-hand man… err… woman. It was astonishing to see the transformation of my friend, who'd been such a girly girl as much as I'd been a tom boy. To watch her fight was like watching someone else take over her body, a possession of an intensity that could relate to.

I chuckled and went back to sharpening my large hunting knife. The thing was huge and made me feel like a female Rambo, but it was one of my favorite blades outside my dual machetes. Even the double katanas had nothing on this. I scraped the stone across the surface and relished the sharp noise it made. It was calming and didn't bother the others, as the wind rushing in through the window hushed the scraping sound down to a distant shuffle.

It was impossible for me to do nothing on this trip. When my weapons were cleaned and sharp enough to slice through the metal of the car, I sat back, one knee up to lean my arm on as I stared out across the horizon. We were going a little faster as the miles stretched on, swerving now and then to avoid debris. There were fewer cars out on the open highway, reminding me of how fast the virus had taken ahold of the cities. Most hadn't had a chance to escape its clutches the way my family had. Most had died within the city limits, gripped in the chaotic mess of death, blood and sickness. It made me somber to think that so few had tried to escape before the virus had taken its victims. If you hadn't died from the virus right away, you had to stay behind because you were either taking care of a sick loved one or you had become food for one of the thousands of hungry, soulless creatures that began roaming the streets from dusk until dawn. How we'd survived even a couple nights in our house in Vegas, boarded up within, was beyond me. Randy had been part of it.

As I thought of Randy, I turned to watch his steady breathing. He was all healed up now, with only faint pink flesh in areas betraying the missing pieces he'd had in his previous ruined state. The sun didn't kill him, and he didn't burn to ash, but the effects of spending so long as a nocturnal creature meant he felt extreme fatigue during the daylight hours and suffered from extreme sensitivity to the sun. It was bad enough that it burned him to a crisp in no time if he laid out in it. Strange as it was to have him back in my life, it brought the memories flooding back, memories of my mother.

I still didn't understand her motives in the last moments of her life. Maybe the grip of madness had just been too much for her. It made no sense, though. The woman I'd grown up with, the one who'd kept us alive at the end of all things, wouldn't have done that to herself. She never would have given in to suicide. The thought kept hounding me, adding to the pile of questions she'd left me asking. I knew Jeremy hadn't asked the same things I had after her death. His coping mechanism had let him accept her loss long before her death. He'd watched her wither away, like an old person slipping into dementia, a death of the mind before the body. Maybe that was how he'd survived it so much better than I had. He'd accepted her death long before it had come. He was amazing, I had to admit that. An old soul trapped in such a young body.

He'd be fine, even with me no longer at his side. I knew he'd understood the situation before I had even had a chance to explain it to him. Thank goodness he was wiser than I was. Otherwise, my guilt would've eaten me alive.

The Jeep slowed to a crawl, and I sat up, peering over toward Elijah to see what was going on. If we didn't make it to the outskirts of San Bernardino before the sunset, we would spend a night without sleep for certain. "Hey, why are we stopping?"

"I have to take a piss, if you don't mind," Elijah grunted. Sarah rolled her eyes and turned around in her chair, smacking the ever-present gum in her mouth. How she'd found so many packages of gum to carry around with her always baffled me. Of course, I didn't exactly keep an eye out for it.

"Any more gum?"

"Uh-huh." She nodded and dove into her bag. She rummaged around for a minute before tossing me a small rectangle of Hubba-Bubba. Of course she had the good stuff.

I stuffed the huge, rubbery chunk into my mouth and chewed, letting the flood of sugary bubblegum flavor fill my mouth. "Been a long time since I had some of that."

"Good, right?" She smiled, already hanging off the back of her chair. "Are you excited? I haven't left Vegas in forever." Her big toothy grin made me laugh. I had to agree wholeheartedly.

"Yes, I'm actually looking forward to seeing the West Coast again. Been landlocked far too long."

"I know! I wonder how Hawaii is. My dad took me there for one of his visits to the the Marine Corps base on Kaneohe, Oahu. It was gorgeous! I loved the beaches there. The water was cool, but nice enough to snorkel. He tried to teach me how to surf, but I sucked and kept getting pummeled by the waves over and over again. That wasn't my idea of fun. I loved the sun though. Sand and sun, best stuff ever."

I nodded, amused by her story. "I've never been to Hawaii. I wonder how the epidemic played out there. You don't think they were spared, do you?"

She shook her head. "I doubt that all the passengers on the planes were clean when the planes stopped running. I bet it spread there like wildfire, too."

"What about the islands that don't have an airport?"

"Could've been filled with people from the ferries, maybe. Who knows? Maybe there's a hidden paradise unaffected by this crap." She slipped back into her chair, snapping the seatbelt back on as Elijah jumped back in.

"All right! Let's get this show on the road." He smiled at both of us, wagging his eyebrows over his sunglasses. We both laughed, and I was thankful for the relaxed atmosphere. Randy slept through it all, but it didn't matter. I was happy for the first time in months.

Even the uncertainty of the future couldn't have brought me down at that moment. Every mile took me closer to something I knew I was meant for, even if I had to leave my heart behind in Vegas.

"So… L.A. or San Diego?" Elijah questioned as he swerved around yet another wreck. It was an old SUV, burnt and shattered, with twisted metal and glass splayed around it. One look inside found me staring at the charred skeleton of its unfortunate driver. It silenced our group as we made our way around it. I only wished this wasn't the norm nowadays. All the vehicles had some sort of damage or had been left abandoned, doors open where the passengers had fled into the desert and died from exposure or vampire.

We'd been fortunate that we'd even survived this epidemic at all. It made me even more determined to get the antidote to someone who could use it in the best way. I hoped we found them in California.

"L.A. first. Then, if we don't find anyone who can help us, San Diego," I answered. Nothing made me more anxious than thinking about what we'd encounter once we got there. I just hoped we'd find what we were looking for sooner rather than later.

Chapter Nineteen

Ordinary Days in Infinite Ways

"THIS IS GOING to have to do." Elijah pulled onto a dirt road leading to a far off house, hidden near the base of one of the smaller mountains before the road entered the pass into San Bernardino. We hoped the pass would be clear enough to get through, but it was getting late, and the slow pace had us running out of time before the night brought the creatures of darkness out.

I peered over Elijah's shoulder and studied the road before us. There was a small church tucked into the hills nearby. More houses appeared as we went over the hill, but the entire area was deserted. At least, I hoped it was. The shadows were growing with each passing minute, and we would have to gear up for the night's stay, taking turns on watch.

Glancing over toward Randy, who was miraculously still asleep, I hoped that his inner clock was a good indication of when we could expect the ferals to awaken. Their influence still lived in him, and I wondered just how human he was now. Or was there even enough left of him to overcome the time he'd spent in the virus's grip? Would the feral ever really be extinguished? He'd been hard to rouse during the day when we'd stopped for lunch. He'd awoken, drowsy and quiet, and even munched on a sandwich I'd handed to him. He'd eaten it silently, avoiding interaction as though he wasn't all there yet. He'd refused to leave the shade of the gas station overhang we'd taken shelter under to eat and relieve ourselves. He'd donned some sunglasses scavenged from inside the trashed convenience store, and they were still on his face now, blocking the evening dusk as it came rushing at us.

"This one looks sturdier than the other ones and isn't a trailer. Plus, it has bars on the windows." Elijah pulled the Jeep into the driveway of a small adobe-style house, reminiscent of the Mexican villa homes I'd seen on a vacation to the south in my youth. I remember walking into some of the houses, transformed into small museums about the culture of each area. It was always cool inside, despite the overbearing heat of the outside and always smelled like the rich, salty earth of the underground. They kept the heat out and they kept it mighty quiet inside, too. I'd enjoyed those places. They were like ghosts in my mind, still haunting me, reminding me of times past.

We shuffled out of the Jeep, even Randy, who stumbled out into the evening, not yet as awake as we would have liked. As soon as we entered the house and swept it for ferals or any non-desirable, he slipped down onto one of the beds to continue his snooze. The sun was a powerful influence on the ferals, and I'd only seen its sedative effects up close on Randy. Pretty soon, the shadows would be long enough for him to walk across the outside of the house without any fear of the sun touching him, and he'd be fully conscious, like his fellow feral creatures. That was precisely when we needed to go on alert.

"Any supplies, take them. We don't know if we'll find much in the city." Elijah pointed toward the pantry, and I nodded as he made his way to the garage.

"Hey, so what are you going to do?" I frowned at the thought of him ordering us around while he didn't do his part in scavenging.

"I'm putting our Jeep in the garage, backward, for a quick getaway. Any other questions you got while I'm here?" He tapped his foot, glaring at me. I waved him off, shaking my head. He could be such a jerk when he wanted to be, but he was pretty harmless. I sauntered off to join Sarah, who was busy filling trash bags with cans, unopened food boxes and bottles of water.

"Wow, pretty untouched, huh?" I said, opening one of the cabinets in the kitchen island. Inside, I found only cookware and pans, so I moved to another cabinet.

"Yeah. Major jackpot." She tossed something at me and hit me in the shoulder.

"Ow! What's that?" I bent over and grabbed the package. It was a box of fruit strips. "No way. Haven't had one of these in ages." I ripped it open and took a bite. "Dang, if sugar wasn't God's gift to earth, I don't know what would've been."

Sarah nodded, her own strip stuffed into her mouth as she chewed. That girl found sugary sweets no matter where she went. "I got first watch," she said, "so I want to be all hyped up to crash later."

"You're insane, you know that?" I tossed the rest of the box she had thrown at me into the trash bag and dropped some bags of rice into it as well.

"Yeah, well, we all need our quirks to stay sane nowadays, right?"

"I guess so."

"So what's up with you lately, April?"

I paused, shoving back a loose strand of hair as I stared out the window. The sun had touched the bottom of the western mountains and seemed to be bobbing there like an apple about to take a dip.

"What do you mean?"

"You know. You and Rye, that Christian guy. I don't think the others noticed, but I saw how you looked at both of them. I know you're mated to that redhead, but man, he gives me the creeps with his weird eyes. Plus, he's probably dead."

"They're just different colors, that's all." I didn't like where this conversation was going.

"I know that. Still, I'm sure it's pretty crazy to be bound to someone like that." She sighed, tied up one of the bags and pulled out another from the dusty roll. "And what about Rye? The guy is nuts for you, but you beat him off like he has leprosy or something."

"I do not."

Sarah stopped what she was doing to put a hand on her hip and glare at me. "Oh, come off it. You treat Rye like crap. You also avoided Christian even though he was nuts about you, but after he went and kidnapped you with Mercer, he's so not cool in my book, so... what's wrong with Rye?"

"I don't know." I squirmed and opened another cabinet to avoid looking at my friend, even though I felt her eyes on the back of my head. "I never wanted to fall in love. It's not something I've ever wanted."

"Why not? I'd kill to have two men fawning over me." She sighed and started dropping more cans into the bag. The pause gave me a moment to choke back the sudden rush of tears threatening to flow from my eyes.

"When there's so much death around you, love turns into a luxury, a petty indulgence." My eyes stung, and I sniffed quietly. "Why fall in love when life is not guaranteed? It could be stolen from you in a split second. All love brings is loss."

Sarah remained silent. My curiosity finally got the better of me, and I turned to find her staring at me, a pathetic, sad and shocked look pasted across her face.

"Really?" she said as I looked up. "That's sad, April. You're so depressing. I get that we can keel over or get attacked by the wildings at any time. And then there's the crazy hybrid vamps. I get how someone can think love is not worth having and life isn't worth it since we all die sooner or later anyway. I get that. But how did *you* become so hopeless? So cold? Where is the April I used to know?"

"She's dead."

"Bull."

"It's not bull. I'm not that girl anymore. Neither are you, Sarah. Where's the fashion conscious girly girl who wouldn't dream of breaking a nail swinging a sword around? Tell me you haven't changed either, Sarah."

Sarah's freckled face turned an obscene red as she practically steamed from the ears. I immediately regretted my outburst, but it was too late.

"I may have to kill things to survive and scavenge for food. I have to get dirty and do things I never would've done before, but deep down, I'm the same. I still love having fun, painting my nails, looking nice, and I care about my family and you. I'm still your friend. I'd never give up on you. I'm just concerned that you're doing this to hurt yourself, this not letting anyone in." She sucked in a breath. Her eyes focused on me, seemingly close to tears as a sheen of fluid shimmered across them. "I'm not dead inside. You need to really think about what's going on in your head and all around you and for goodness sake, quit dragging along people if you can't tolerate them."

"Who made you the keeper of whoever loves me?"

She groaned and was tugging at her hair when Elijah reentered. His eyes darted between the two of us, amused. "What's the ruckus about? Come on, we've got to make sure all the doors are barred and not waste time chitchatting."

Leave it to Elijah to knock some sense into us. We followed without looking at each other again. From the way Sarah kept tugging at a loose lock of hair, I could tell she was still irked by our conversation. Hell, I still was. Maybe she was right, though. Maybe I was the one who'd changed so much I didn't even recognize myself anymore.

Would the April from two years ago have acted that way? What would she have done if she had to choose between two men who both set her skin on fire and made her question all the rules about love? She'd have chosen one for sure. She wouldn't have strung them along with her insecurities and indecision eating her up alive.

How I'd let it get this far was beyond me. I was so disappointed in myself, and it dug into my chest as I helped Elijah lock all the doors and shove cabinets and sofas against them while Sarah draped the windows with dark linens and shut the blinds in every room. We closed all the interior doors and piled into the living room after we were finished, feeling the night creeping in.

Randy was wide awake now. He sat on the floor, chewing on a protein bar we'd found in a cabinet. I slid down on one of the mattresses we'd dragged over from the bedrooms. I stared at the ceiling, studying the stony imperfections, and breathed in the dusty atmosphere. Randy offered me one of the bars, but I refused. I wasn't very hungry after what Sarah had said to me. I couldn't get it out of my head, and I turned to watch Elijah settle on a thin rollout camping mattress. He chugged down a bottle of water and pulled off his boots. At last, he lay back onto a pile of pillows and let out a long breath.

Sarah loved him, I was sure of that. So why weren't they an item? Maybe I wasn't the only one who was confused. I shook my hair out of the severe pony tail I'd had it pulled into all day. My scalp hurt from the band, and I rubbed it furiously before flopping back onto the pillow. The place was comfortable, I had to admit. If Randy hadn't been pacing the floor, I would've passed out in minutes. My watch was the last rotation of the night, near morning, so I had to get some rest. It wasn't cold enough for a blanket, and it lay haphazardly crumbled at the bottom of my mattress. If it got cooler, I'd pull it over me.

I propped my head on my arm and looked up at Randy. "Why's the daylight still messing with you?"

"Yeah. It's weird. Like I'm still on that vampire routine. Everyone would sleep when the sun came out. It was like clockwork. Each morning they'd all flop onto the ground and just pass right out the moment the sun came up. You could feel it pushing on your bones when the dawn approached. Like the light would be so much brighter, and it felt like it sucked your life away, even if the sunrise was still an hour away. It's like an extra sense built into you. Can't shake it yet."

Interesting. I just hoped it was a residual effect and didn't mean he was still very much part feral. The latter thought gave me a shudder.

"Would you tell us if you felt… off again?"

Randy stopped pacing and flicked his eyes toward me. "Of course I'd tell you. I may still feel different, but I feel… human. If you get what I mean. Those days…." He waved off into the distance, staring as if remembering another life. "They were like nightmares I couldn't wake from. Murky, filled with rage and feeling like I wasn't in control. It was definitely a beast inside that took over, and I was just an unwilling participant."

I pondered his words and got a slight chill. I reached down and yanked the threadbare blanket over me. It was horrible to think that those creatures I had killed, the ferals, could still be human inside. Their humanity might have been buried deep within, but they were still there. Would I be able to kill another now that I knew that? With the antidote, could all of them become like Randy? More human?

I closed my eyes. I knew the answer to that. I'd do what I had to do to survive. If it meant killing a feral who was attacking me or the ones I loved, I wouldn't hesitate. Even if Randy turned back and was threatening us, ready to rip my throat out and drain my blood, there was no question about it.

Elijah was snoring softly, and Randy eventually left the room to join Sarah at a quiet game of cards. I stared at the light from the little battery-operated lamp until my eyelids grew heavy enough to close and allow me rest once more.

Chapter Twenty
Can't Hardly Wait

"APRIL," ELIJAH'S VOICE echoed in my head. First it was so far away, I thought it was a trick of my mind. Then it came louder, along with someone shaking my shoulders. "Wake up, sleepy head."

I blinked, and the light slowly came into focus, making Elijah's face glow in the flicker.

"I'm up." I swiped at his hands, but he only had to lean back since he was kneeling next to me, chuckling. I stretched and scanned the room to find Sarah asleep on Elijah's mattress and Randy nowhere to be seen. "Where's Randy?"

"He's been in the garage, pacing but trying to keep quiet, so he went in there, circling the Jeep."

"Restless much?"

Elijah shrugged, looking like he couldn't care less. "Probably. Your turn for watch. Move, lazy. I want my two hours of sleep."

e ripped the blanket off of me, and I muttered a threat or two toward him as I grabbed my boots and headed to the bathroom. I washed up with some bottled water and tinkled in the disgusting toilet before I shoved my boots on and headed back to grab my bag. I pulled out my weapons as Elijah watched me from the mattress. As soon as I stood up, he rolled over and conked out.

Damn, I wish I could sleep so soundly on demand. That would be handy trick in a world like this.

Shaking my head, I dragged myself toward the kitchen. I peeked outside the window and saw nothing but black. I closed the dingy, thin curtains quickly. I knew if there was anything out there, we'd be hearing it soon. Ferals weren't quiet. At least that gave their prey some advantage over them.

Grabbing one of the kitchen table chairs, I sat and leaned back, my head settling against the hard and cold clay wall. In another life, this might've been an energy-efficient paradise. Desert paradise. I hadn't seen any greenery yet, and I hoped California still had some. Memories of palm trees, tall grasses, orchards and miles of soft, glittery sand made me smile. I could have used some surf and sand right about then. Jeremy would've loved it, too.

A thump coming from the garage had me shooting to my feet in a second, machete in hand. I listened for a moment, not sure whether it was just Randy in there or if something had joined him. It was our first night with Randy, so I wasn't sure how it was going to end up or if the night would enhance his feral tendencies.

I heard nothing but silence, which still didn't convince me we were safe. I had to check on Randy, and I hoped I wouldn't be walking into a trap. Elijah hadn't mentioned anything unusual about Randy, so I had high hopes he was just fumbling about in the garage. Slipping my fingers over the cool brass knob of the garage door, I leaned forward to listen to any noises from inside. It was a thick metal fire door, so the noises were muffled by it and made it difficult for me to identify anything.

"Dammit, Randy," I muttered and gripped my machete tight. "I really don't want to use this on you." I stepped back as I turned the knob, preparing myself for the worst. Ready or not, here I come.

I yanked the door open and peered inside. A single lamp sat atop the hood of the Jeep and Randy, facing away from me, was standing still next to it, staring at the garage door.

"Randy?" I checked both sides of the garage before I stepped forward, closing the door behind me. The hairs on my neck stood up, responding to a static charge in the air. It could have been the sunrise approaching, but wouldn't Randy be feeling it, too? The way he was standing there, like a carved statue with tattered clothes and hunched shoulders, made me nervous, and I really hoped he hadn't turned feral once more. Still, my breaths come in short, sharp intakes, and the sweat began to form in itchy beads across my forehead.

"Randy?" I repeated his name as I stepped closer, gripping the hilt of the machete with my sweaty palm. Would it be rude if I poked him with the machete? I hoped it wouldn't agitate him from his meditative state, but I'd rather do that than give him a hand to pull me over with. Yeah, I could see that panning out real well in my head. With that picture haunting my mind, I reached out, letting the tip of the blade tap him gently as I called out to him again.

"Don't come any closer, April."

I froze, squeezing the blade handle while I kept it ready. "What's going on, Randy?"

"Apparently, the antidote only works temporarily."

I swallowed, feeling it scrape down my throat in an attempt to get past the sandpapery dryness while the sweat dripped down my temple. "What do you mean?"

He shook his head. His long, dark blond locks moved gently with the motion, but he had yet to turn around. "I wish it would've worked completely, but the virus is so strong, it won't let me go." He continued to shake his head, muttering under his breath.

"Randy, turn around and tell me what's wrong. Maybe we can find out how to fix it."

"You can't fix me." The despair in his voice took me to a place I didn't want to go. I realized that my decision to kill Randy if he turned back might have been a bit premature. Could I really do this?

"That's what my mother said," I replied. "She didn't let me help her either. What good comes of that?"

Mentioning my mother made my stomach knot up, but I did my best to ignore its choking grip. My eyes never left Randy. There was too much to lose from such a misstep.

"The fangs, they emerged a few hours ago. I thought I could fight them, but they came. The scent of everyone's blood was driving me mad, so I came out here to walk it off, hoping to get far enough away that I could stay calm. But you know what the worst part is?" His head snapped up, and I could see his chest filling with breath as he began to huff it in and out. "The worst of it is my eyes. I checked them in a mirror when they started to started to ache and burn like they were on fire. They're red again."

He jerked around to drill the blood red irises into me, and I stepped back. Until that moment I thought it might have been psychological, but he was right. The antidote was wearing off.

He was feral, but not quite. His fangs dripped with saliva as he stood his ground, breathing in madly, trying to tame the beast with each struggling breath. In his eyes, I could see the shiny irises reflecting as his natural blue flashed in and out, as though it were battling against the feral red. It was a sight to behold, and the shock kept me from turning around to run. It spiked my curiosity even through my stifled terror. A ring, a bright yellow halo, circled the red with a hint of reflective gold, branding him as a hybrid now. How could that be? Was he possibly still changing? He wasn't human but he wasn't feral, either. What was he evolving into now?

"Randy, I'm going to step back and go back into the house. I'll check on you when the sun is up, okay? Maybe you'll be fine then. We can figure out what to do when the others wake up." I stepped back and he growled, a deep guttural sound that seemed to vibrate along my arms and into my chest, rumbling like an earthquake. I backed away even more, trying not to go too fast or too slow. He was like an animal, ready to pounce, and I couldn't make any sudden movements. Instead, I crept backward, and the growls faded into a listless hum as his breathing deepened and he closed his eyes.

"I'm so sorry, April. You should have left me in the compound. I'll bring nothing but harm to you and your friends. I should go."

"No, just wait, okay? Wait for the dawn."

"You're right, though. I can feel the sunrise coming. It makes the beast withdraw some. I feel calmer every second." His eyes flipped open. They were now a funny reddish blue that looked almost brown, the way paint does when it mixes wrong. His fists clenched tight then loosened. He stretched his long, clawed fingers, only to curl them tight into fists again. "I really should go."

"Please don't. I need to know what's happening to you. We're so close to the city, we'll find a cure."

He kept his eyes closed but turned back around to face the garage door. "Okay. But only one more day. I don't know how long I can control it. It's writhing inside me, like it's trying to break out. I'm not strong enough to hold it in. It's been far too long since I was human. I don't think I know what it feels like anymore."

My back touched the garage door, and I reached behind me for the knob. "Maybe it's something you just have to get used to again. The control. You've let the subconscious rule for too long, the wild side. You have to chain it up and take control. You can be human again, Randy. I know you can." *Turn the knob… push the door open slowly… shove it closed. I can do this.*

I turned the knob, and his head jerked up at the sound. He began breathing harder as he straightened and sniffed the air. Things weren't looking good for me. I pressed my body against the door, and it creaked open. Each squeal made me cringe as I watched him turn his head, still sniffing the air like he'd detected a tasty, bloody steak. His fists curled up once more, and his shoulder twitched in anticipation.

One final push, and he jerked around, staring at me with full on reddened eyes and a snarl carved into his face. He was no longer the gentle Randy who'd told me stories in the cell of Christian's underground hive. No, he was now the fighting beast within, and I had to get the hell out of there. I made it into the kitchen a moment later and shoved with my entire body against the door, slamming it shut as he slammed into it from the other side, causing it to bounce open slightly and then close with a click. I fumbled to turn the lock before the door shook violently as he pummeled it again. I held my body against it, feeling my heart die even more as I heard his desperate growls on the other side.

"Let me in!" His nails screeched against the metal as he clawed at the door.

"What the hell is going on here?" Elijah was behind me, his wide palms pressed against the door to help me hold it. I peered up at him, relieved to see his groggy but familiar face. "Randy?"

I nodded and turned to grab one of the chairs around the kitchen table. I shoved it under the doorknob, and we backed away, still staring at the door. My heart was beating wildly, and I scolded myself for feeling so spooked. Had I not killed dozens of ferals? Had I not enjoyed the thrill of slashing them to bits?

I shook my head, still feeling my heart sink, and I wanted to just break down and bawl my eyes out. This was different. I had never killed anyone I'd known before the outbreak. Not like this. It was a whole new ballgame, an unknown arena where no one really won the games. I knew Randy, and knowing how much he was fighting for control made me feel even worse. I ran from the kitchen, barely making it to the bathroom to heave out the contents of my stomach, the measly snack I'd had earlier. As my stomach settled, leaving me with just the sickening dry heaves that let up after a few minutes, I spit out the disgusting mess in my mouth and closed my eyes as I shrank back to sit on the floor. Leaning against the cold, jagged stone of the natural adobe wall, I let my strangled breathing catch up. I needed to catch up.

Oh, Mom. What do I do now?

Sarah peered in on me, holding the battery-operated camping lamp while she handed me a washcloth. It had been doused with cool water, and I wiped my face and mouth with it, thanking her for being so thoughtful. Back in high school, she'd always be the one to pick me up when a guy broke my heart or some idiot from the popular crowd jabbed at me, just to pick on someone. No one had ever picked on Sarah. If they did, she'd let them have the biggest verbal smack down ever and had left them looking more embarrassed than they'd ever left me.

Nothing like the best of friends.

"Need anything?"

I shook my head. "No." I sipped from the bottle of water she'd offered then sighed. "Is he still trying to bang the door down?"

"Nope. He stopped, and I haven't heard anything else from him." She stepped back to peer around the corner where Elijah was still in the kitchen, keeping watch at the door, before turning back toward me. "I think the approaching sunrise is wearing him out."

"This is all my fault." I rubbed my face and wiped the sweat beading across my forehead.

"Don't blame yourself, girl." Sarah smacked some gum as she leaned on the doorframe of the bathroom. "How were we to know he'd turn during the night? The first few nights he was in quarantine at Blaze's, he was fine. No issues."

I nodded, rubbing my face, and huffed out a breath. "I know. It's just so unfair."

"I know."

I got up and headed out into the living room, deciding to pack up our supplies to be ready to leave once the sun broke past the eastern mountains. No point in sleeping now. I pulled a rope from one of the supply bags and hung it on the chair barricading the door. If Randy was to survive, we'd have to tie him down from now on. It seemed barbaric, but if we were all going to make it through this, keep him alive and find a cure, we had to do it.

After gathering up the rest of the food we'd found and stuffing our gear away, we peeked out the windows and studied the landscape as it slowly transformed into morning. We decided it was about time for the wild, savage things to retreat into the shadows.

Elijah returned, his huge hunting knife gripped firmly in his hand. "Okay, who wants to check on Randy with me? I say if he tries to kill us, we put him out of his misery."

I winced as I joined him. Not quite the plan I was thinking of. "Look, let's just try to keep it civil," I said. "I need him alive."

He blew out a disappointed breath and nodded, a wicked gleam shining in his eyes as the morning light poured in through the windows, reflecting off his very human eyes. "Yes, ma'am."

I rolled my eyes and headed to the garage door, hoping beyond hope that Randy had passed out from the sunrise and overexertion of the night. "I'll open the door and you grab him. Got it? I'll tie him up, just hold him as best you can or knock him the hell out."

Elijah smirked. "Let's get this party started." He flipped the knife in his hand as he bent his knees and faced the door, looking like a linebacker ready to slam into the opposing team. I had to admit, he was pretty no nonsense and to the point. Plus, it was always an advantage to have a burly guy like Elijah on your side. Just what we needed right now.

"Okay, ready... set... *Go!*"

He lunged forward and I yanked at the door. I was expecting to hear the screeching growl from Randy, but I instead heard nothing. Zilch. Nada. Only silence and the soft hum of the lamp still sitting on the Jeep. Randy was passed out on the ground, face down, as if he'd fallen and refused to move. Okay, so the sun still had quite the effect on him, and it was startling to see him vulnerable when just a few hours before he had been so incredibly frightening.

"Well, that was easy." Elijah poked at him with his boot, but he didn't respond, so he reached down and flipped him over with a good, hard shove. He waved me over and pointed toward Randy. "He's all yours!" He cracked a smile while I frowned and rushed over, whipping out the rope to tie his wrists and ankles together. He was going to hate this when he came to, but it was for the good of everyone involved.

"Okay, done," I said.

Elijah opened the back door of the Jeep and heaved Randy's slack body into it like a rag doll, not caring if Randy's head thumped against the other side. This just made me frown deeply, and I avoided his happy smirk as I made my way back inside to grab a couple of bags of supplies to toss into the back of the Jeep. By then, Sarah already had the garage opened along with propping the door into the house wide open. She was tossing bags of supplies out to put into the Jeep.

"How do you put up with him?" I asked her, shoving a trash bag of food into the cargo area. I decided to keep my own bag with me in the cabin so I wouldn't have to dig for my weapons when needed. We always had to be ready to jump, grab stuff and run.

"You get used to him."

I wrinkled my nose as Elijah, who was chewing on a bag of mixed nuts with his shades on, studied the road down and back into the hills on the horizon. "I don't see how."

Sarah laughed and slammed the hatch closed. "It's an acquired taste."

"Yeah, like shitty, cheap beer?"

"Be nice."

I stuck my tongue out and went around to the empty side of the back seat where I plopped my bag in between me and Randy before I slid into the cool comfort of the seat.

"Sorry about the rough ride, Randy, but it's just going to have to suffice for now," I muttered as I slammed my door shut. He moaned slightly as he turned to adjust his body, blissfully unaware of anything that was going on. How lucky he was to not notice much right now.

"All right," Elijah said, "did everyone hit the loo? 'Cause I'm not stopping, just so you know." We all mumbled, and he turned the engine over. After pulling the Jeep into the driveway, he jumping back out to close the garage door, leaving the house as we had found it. I looked at him questioningly as he hopped back into the vehicle. "Hey, can't leave a messy trail for people to find us."

He had a point.

We got back onto the highway and traveled down the pass, which was excruciatingly slow due to the increasing number of abandoned vehicles. We were getting close to the city, and I knew we'd eventually have to abandon the freeway and use the side roads to get to the coast, but I didn't mind.

It was the start of a new phase of my life, and I couldn't wait.

Chapter Twenty-One
Breath of Life

THE RIDE DOWN the pass was slow and tedious, with cars blocking the road everywhere. My stomach was already feeling twisted, and the constant turning and curves made me even queasier. I remembered my parents speeding down the hills in this area when we'd traveled through it on several occasions. Now it was a mess, strewn with debris from crashes, twisted metal and just... stuff. Lots of it. People's luggage, furniture and various other items they'd thrown out of their cars in a hurry to get the heck out of the horror engulfing the world. I wondered why some were heading toward the city. Would it not be the dumbest decision to head toward the chaos? The other side of the road was also an almost impossible trek. There'd been more people leaving than staying. We'd have to remember to take this side of the road on the way back to Vegas.

Were we ever going to go back? I rubbed my eyes as I glanced at Elijah and Sarah. What had they thought about all this? There'd been few words between us, and I knew they meant well, but I really didn't know what they expected to get out of this adventure. Maybe there were no expectations. Maybe they would do anything I asked, even if it meant never returning to Vegas again.

I didn't want to put that kind of pressure on them, not yet. If they were to decide to return before I was ready then I would let them go, of course. I wasn't their keeper. We were all free souls here.

I focused on Randy, who muttered in his sleep on and off and cringed away from the window when the light would shift and hit him right on. He was the least free of us all. He was trapped inside his own body which didn't want to expel the virus it so desperately held onto. Did he need another dose of the antidote? Would it kill him?

I wiped my hands on my pants. It made me nervous to think of such things. If I gave him another hit of the antidote, would we be ready to accept what could happen? I'd have to ask Randy, when he was more lucid and communicative, if he ever would be again, before the night hours sucked his humanity away.

He shifted in his seat again, the ropes still snug against his wrists. He never fought it, accepting his fate to be tied up instead of free. How it saddened me. It put me in a somber mood as I turned back and stared wearily out the window. We passed San Bernardino more quickly than I thought we would. The neglect was apparent there, just like in Vegas. I'd hoped to find a better place, anywhere, where the devastation had not been as widespread as it had been back home.

"There it is!" Sarah yelled and bounced on her chair, pointing toward the horizon. The ocean finally came into view in all its glittery, blue majesty. I had to admit, it was stunning, and I hadn't felt so excited in a long while. I cracked the window open and let the rush of ocean air tumble in, sniffing it like it was a drug. Sarah was doing the same, hanging out her window, letting the sea breeze tangle her hair and squealing with exhilaration.

"Ocean, baby!"

How do you stay in a bad mood with the ocean nearby? The smile on my face made my cheeks hurt as the breeze whipped my hair into a disheveled mess, but I didn't care. It was amazing, even when the Jeep jerked to avoid yet another abandoned vehicle. Once we were on the beach, I was going to shed my boots and dig my toes into the warm sand and hit the waves running. There was no doubt about it. One thing I'd missed from my younger years was the feel of the grainy sand underfoot, digging for shells as the cold ocean water rushed over me, sucking my feet down as it retreated but begging me to tread farther in. I never swam out too far. My fear of the unknown had somehow anchored me to the shore where my feet could always graze the sand so that the ocean could never truly claim me. It was tragic, I knew that. Still, I'd enjoyed the water until the sun had burnt me to a crisp and my skin was raw from the constant rubbing of sand against it.

There was no beach in Vegas. Here was my only reprieve, where I could jump into memory and forget what was really going on around us, even for just a moment.

And so, as we reached the shores of Huntington Beach and Newport Beach, I was eager enough to jump out of the Jeep as it slowed to a stop and run the rest of the way toward the froth of waves and roar of the water. Once at the shoreline, I barely remember ripping my boots and socks off my pale feet and jetting into the water, up to my thighs and farther in until I floated chest deep and the waves attempted to knock me over.

The water was freezing, and I gasped as each wave pelted my head and my temperature dropped enough to send my lips quivering. Still, I splashed the water about, watching the drops gleam as they turned into faceted rainbows. It made me laugh, and I didn't stop until I saw Sarah jumping in, clothes and all, joining me in the exhilaration of it all.

"Elijah! Get in here, you big ogre!" she called out, waving him over as he approached the waterline. He didn't jump in right away. In fact, the way he stood there with his arms crossed and a frown creasing his face, I was sure that underneath his sunglasses and hardened exterior, his eyes were disapproving our enjoyment. Whatever. He could be such a party pooper.

"Someone needs to keep watch while you have your little fun."

Sarah stuck out her lip and pouted then glanced over at me and winked before she dove under the surf and disappeared. What was that woman up to?

Minutes passed, and I was getting nervous as I spun around, eyeing the waves for Sarah's bright head of red hair. I saw nothing, but Elijah dropped his arms and looked about as spooked as I was, having chucked his sunglasses down. He yanked off his boots, barely hopping out of them before running into the water and diving in yelling for Sarah.

I had to get a better view of the water, so I swam closer to the shore to look around. Where the hell had she gone? I knew better than anyone else that she knew how to swim. Why was she doing this? Whatever her reason was, it wasn't funny, and I was going to ring her neck the moment we dragged her out of the water.

"Sarah! Sarah!" Elijah's head emerged, water droplets flying from his locks as he yelled out, scanning the waves before diving back under. The wait to see him resurface had me on edge as I stood on my toes, still not seeing Sarah return from the depths. A sudden flash of orange caught the corner of my eye, but it disappeared before I could confirm it.

"Elijah! Over there!" I hollered, pointing madly as he resurfaced, spit out a mouthful of water and turned in the direction I was pointing. That was all he needed to redirect himself and dive under the froth of waves once more. The moment he went under was the moment Sarah popped up, not far from where I'd last seen her. She treaded back in, laughing hysterically and turning a bright red as she pulled her sopping wet tail of hair back to squeeze the excess water out. She marched toward me, still laughing when Elijah popped back up, focused on her and dove in her direction, raging mad.

"What the hell, Sarah!" He started high-stepping through the water as it hit him hard on the back and shoved him forward, causing him to stumble before he caught his balance. "I swear I'm going to make that death wish you're aching to fulfil come true!" He spat out a mouthful of water as he pushed forward and stomped through the knee deep surf toward her. She tried to run but couldn't outpace him in time. She laughed as he picked her up and swung her over his shoulder before heading back into the water, cradling her only to swing her body out into the coming crash of waves.

I shook my head, glad I was finally enjoying a bit of the fun I'd intended to have. After rinsing the sand from my arms and pants, I squeezed the water out of my pony tail and waited for them on the shore. The waves lapped weakly at my ankles as I sank into the sand. Tiny holes bubbled up through the sand as the water retreated, and I watched the earth slowly suck me down until my ankles were covered in the stuff. Seaweed and debris littered the shoreline, looking much like it had before the vampiric virus had hit, except maybe it was a tad bit worse. There were no people on the beach to gather up and dispose of the trash floating ashore. No one barbequing at the fire pits lining the beach barrier to the parking lot. No beach towels lined up against the glittering sand. No oiled-up bodies or canopies to block the view. No screams of squealing kids or laughing bunches of teens drinking their illegally obtained beer and playing beach volleyball until they were as tanned as leather.

It was eerily quiet. Even the cars in the parking lot sat under a layer of sand that caked their windows and piled up around the tires, aching to overtake the beach once more. It'd been left alone too long. The asphalt had disappeared under the shifting sands. It was all over the place, even up the steps of the lifeguard towers, laying in drifts that hadn't been there the last time I'd visited.

The land was still very much alive and taking back the earth from the long dead humans.

Studying the skyline, I spotted the pier down a ways and wondered if it had suffered much from over a year left to the elements. It appeared intact, but there were piles of seaweed tangled on its legs and barnacles clinging to the wood where the water periodically receded before filling up the shoreline once more. The stores and shops atop it were still there, but many windows were obviously smashed while others were boarded up, as if someone could be living in there, watching us.

The feeling of eyes peering back at me crept up my spine and down my arms, making the chill of the water as it dried off my clothes in the warm Californian sun feel even colder. So we were not alone, but who knew what was up there looking at us across the seashore? It was at least a mile or two down the beach, but I wasn't sure if I wanted to go there. To find others was one thing, but I needed to find those who could help us replicate the antidote and perfect it, not those who would find sanctuary on a long forgotten, rotting pier. Still, it would be a good hiding place if the ferals were afraid of water, which they might very well be. It was hard to know if they were because there were no bodies of water in Vegas where I could have tested such a theory. Lake Mead was miles away and too far from anywhere to appeal to them.

If only there was an island out there free of infection. That would be something to look into. Maybe, if somehow we did get to Hawaii, they would be Zompire free. Wouldn't that be nice?

I shook the thought from my head and turned back to watch Elijah and Sarah toying with each other, splashing water and repeatedly shoving each other into the waves. Their laughs clashed with my darkened mood, and I tried to push the gloom away, but it always managed strangled me somehow. Why couldn't I just enjoy myself? I had to try to make an effort to feel alive again, especially since there was so much I still had to do. Feeling dead inside wasn't conducive to do the task I'd set out to accomplish. It wouldn't help me any. I had to bring myself back to life, not just for me but for Jeremy.

If I'd ever see Jeremy again.

I gulped down the bittersweet longing suddenly surrounding me. I missed him already, and though I knew he was safe, having fun where he belonged, I couldn't help but feel like I was missing something so dear to me, something so vital it was ripping my heart out, and I was left but a shell walking around, empty and worse than any Zompire. If I was going to be any good for my baby brother, I had to fix this broken soul first, before I could ever love anyone else, before I could again find some semblance of a normal life.

Chapter Twenty-Two

Soot and Sand

"HEY, SPACE CADET!" Elijah slapped a cold, wet hand on my back and brought me out of my reverie. I was still sitting on the sand, almost dried off from the warm sun hovering above. "Where'd you go?"

I smiled as he sat down next to me, dripping and messy. "Just thinking." I had to admit, at least it didn't bother him to be all wet and caked with sand. He made things look so easy. Sarah was out of the water, too, but had run back to the jeep and was now bringing back three towels and some water bottles. She dropped one of the soft towels on me and handed me some of the water, winking as she plopped down next to Elijah. I hadn't even noticed how thirsty I was until the first gulp passed my lips, and I downed half the bottle in just a few swallows.

"Thanks."

"Anytime. Isn't this awesome?" She hugged the towel around herself, her lips a pale tint of purple as the cold sucked her heat away.

"Yeah, it's really great."

"Almost makes you feel normal, doesn't it?"

I nodded, sadly peering across the shore and into the blue horizon. "Yeah."

"Did you feel them, too, April?"

"The pier?" I asked.

Sarah nodded, taking another sip of water. "Yes. There's someone in the shops up there. Want to check it out?"

I shook my head. Wisps of my dark hair slapped my face. "I don't think the ones we need would be holed up on a beach pier."

"You never know."

I turned toward her, giving her a stern stare. "I know. I need people who'd find a more secure location. They won't be easy to find."

Sarah didn't look convinced. "You don't know that. One thing about an apocalypse, people don't think clearly. But when it the world has fallen apart, where would you want to really be in the end? I'd choose paradise over a hole in the ground and surviving in the dark. Wouldn't the beach sound better than the bloody hills?"

"That's ridiculous." I sighed. Leaning forward, I pressed on my thighs and traced a swirl into the fine sand with a finger. Dusting off my hands when I was done, I looked up to find Elijah and Sarah watching me.

"What?"

"When did you get to be such a downer?" Sarah toweled her hair and looked away, disappointment written all over her features.

"I'm a downer? Being logical isn't a downer. It's called thinking with my head on straight and not in the fucking clouds like some people are all the time." I stood abruptly, threw the towel over the crook of my arm and stormed off toward the Jeep. Her words made me furious. Who did she think she was? She never had any concerns or worried about anything. She'd lived above ground only briefly. I'd lived over a year in the elements. The only thing she'd ever worried about down in the City of Vida, the lap of luxury, was whether she'd break a nail practicing with her swords. It irritated me to no end, and I ignored her calling me back as I made my way to the Jeep.

I yanked the backseat door open and jumped back as Randy's body half fell out. He didn't awaken, but his skin began to smoke and sizzle under the intense afternoon sun reflecting off the white sand. I tossed the towel onto his face, grabbed him and started to shove him back into the Jeep. Finally, huffing under his weight, I managed to shove him back to the other side of the seat where the sun didn't shine into the window. I peeled the towel off to find him flushed red from the exposure to the sun. His skin had tiny darkened lines on it that made me wonder what was going on. Something was definitely wrong, and I didn't know what to do about it.

Was the infection doing this, or was the antidote the cause? Either way, I was afraid it would kill him if I didn't do something soon.

I reached underneath the seat and yanked out the small cooler bag with the vials of the antidote. They were still cool but not cold. I hoped what Rick had said about the antidote staying viable at higher temperatures was true. Pulling out an individual use syringe and needle, I popped the top off one of the vials, screwed the needle and syringe together and plunged it through the rubber. After aspirating half a milliliter, like Rick had done with the initial dose, I dropped the vial back into the cooler bag and turned back to Randy, who was still sleeping.

His reddened skin looked angry and sensitive to the touch, worsening with each minute. The sun hadn't affected him this much the day before, confirming my fear that his feral nature was very much alive underneath it all. I hoped he'd forgive me if he was in any amount of pain, especially when he woke up. I ripped an alcohol pad open, rubbed it furiously on his bicep and aimed the needle toward the muscle while holding his arm down.

Here goes nothing, I thought. Clenching my jaw, I stabbed the needle into his arm and shoved at the plunger. As I pulled it back out, I watched a drop of darkened red blood seep from the puncture site and trickle down his arm. It wasn't blackened yet, a good sign. He hadn't responded at all to the shot, not one flinch, not one movement. I had to observe his chest moving to verify that he was still breathing. His shallow breaths reassured me, but I had expected something to change in him with the second dose. Anything would be nice.

Several minutes passed before I fell back against my seat and let out a frustrated breath. Nothing was happening, and I was running out of time. If he was frying under direct sunlight, he'd be full feral much too soon and would probably rip us to shreds if we didn't extinguish him first or tie him up good. The stupid antidote was supposed to work. It was supposed to! How could such a thing be presented to me and be taken away so quickly? It pissed me off to no end, and I smacked the chair if front of me until my skin stung with angry sparks of pain.

I focused my sight out toward the shoreline to find Elijah and Sarah still sitting where I'd left them, deep in conversation. Elijah was even making hand gestures up in the air as he told his story. Sarah's high-pitched laugh echoed across the drifts, joined by several seagulls who'd hovered and landed next to them in the hopes of a snack.

There used to be thousands of seagulls along the beach. Now there were still a few, but much fewer than before, when the beach was thriving with morsels of food for them to steal. It made me laugh, because I'd had my sandwich stolen by those flying rats before.

The thought of food made my stomach jerk in an angry growl. I reached into the back where the food cooler was and dug around in it for something palatable. I came up with a can of tuna and a couple sealed packets of Ritz crackers. Using the can opener we'd stashed with the cans, I squeezed the fluid out onto the sand and used the crackers to scoop the bits of tuna into my mouth.

I missed having sliced bread, mayonnaise and mustard to slather all over the sandwiches. Sometimes we got lucky and found some mustard or ketchup, but most of the time the mayonnaise was always going bad from sitting out in the heat for far too long. I swore if I found a good jar here in Cali, I'd enjoy it to the max and take it back to Vegas with me.

I sighed, washing down the food with more water as I watched the birds bantering with each other along the sand. Some of them would occasionally dip into the water, fishing for food. I wondered if they found any. We could try to catch some fresh fish if we were going to stay here for an extended amount of time.

Glancing over back toward the pier, I felt eyes on me again. It made me uneasy, but I didn't feel as uncomfortable as I had before, just curious. Who was in there? What did they think about us showing up on their beach and just making a day of it?

I sighed. The old me, before my mother died, would've thrown caution to the wind and jumped at the chance to check it out. What had changed so much? I sat there, just thinking about things and not acting irrationally as I once would have. Maybe my mother's death had killed a lot more of me than I'd originally thought. No sense of adventure anymore whatsoever. It was one of the few things that had kept me going when I'd lost her and Jeremy all those months ago. That determination and impulsive behavior had been both my bane and savior before. Now I felt like a shell of myself. Empty… hollow… dead. I had to find that part of me again somehow.

I swung back toward Randy and let out a yelp, gasping for air as I found him watching me with deep, blood red irises. It was hours from sunset, and he was wide awake and very feral in appearance.

"Randy?"

His eyes darted around the vehicle, focusing outside for a moment before finding me again. His pupils were tiny, showing so much red it made me wonder if I was speaking to Randy or the feral monster inside.

"Are you all right?" I moved slowly to grip the knife sheathed on my hip. He was tied up, but I didn't trust him to not lunge forward and take a decent chunk out of my flesh with those razor sharp fangs. Better to be safe than sorry.

"What's happening?" He closed his eyes, breathing rapidly while his eyelids fluttered madly. Suddenly, his body began to twitch and tiny grunts escaped his lips. "It burns." The ropes held his arms and legs together, but his back arched as he bucked and fought against the movement.

"Randy!"

I tried to keep him from smashing his head into the window as his body convulsed underneath mine. *Crap, Crap, Crap!* What if this was an adverse reaction to the second dose of antidote? What if it killed him this time around? I wished I'd been smart enough to have asked Rick what would happen if a second dose was given to a feral. Now I was getting a front row seat, and it was horrific. It could have even been some anaphylactic reaction, and I didn't have anything to counteract it. What if the first dose hadn't really worked well enough and this one was just going to send him over the edge and kill him? I regretted giving him the second dose as his seizure continued.

"Randy, come on… just breathe." He finally slumped, his chest still and his eyes firmly shut.

"What the hell happened?" Elijah's voice boomed behind me, and I turned to find him and Sarah staring with mouths wide open as I pushed on Randy's body. Sarah started running around to the other side to yank open the door.

"Pull him out, we need to give him CPR."

"No!" I yelled and pushed her hands off him. "Don't touch him! He'll burn in the sun, that's why he's all red!"

She drilled her eyes into me when I smacked her hands away. She shifted her gaze toward Randy, who was still, but his chest was finally moving with soft, shallow breaths. His twitches became more subtle, and his choked grunts had silenced.

Sarah stepped back, looking grim and tired. "If he burns, he's a feral. Let him burn."

I clamped my lips shut, avoiding her gaze, knowing if I met her eyes I'd want to smack some sense back into her. Maybe it was me who needed some sense smacked into me, but I couldn't give up on Randy yet. I had to see this through to the end. There was simply no other option.

"I'm going to forget you said that," I managed to hiss past my frowning lips as I got Randy's body to cooperate and maneuvered him into a neutral position so he could breathe more easily. He was motionless throughout the effort, confirming that he was out once more. I settled back in my seat and ran my hand through my hair. "I gave him another dose of the antidote."

"Why the heck would you do that?" Elijah was shaking sand out of his jeans and pulling a dry shirt out of his bag, as if nothing had happened. He had such an unconcerned attitude about it all, it made me want to slap him for being so insensitive.

After pulling off the half dried shirt, he yanked the new one over his rock hard body. He just had to go and do something like that in front of me. I closed my eyes to try and not think about how awesome he looked when I was so pissed at both him and Sarah. It made me miss Rye in more ways than one. Rye had always been a pretty sight to look at shirtless, and I knew he'd know when to keep his comments to himself.

The thought made me even more depressed as I opened my eyes once more when Sarah and Elijah hopped back into the Jeep. I turned toward Randy and found him fast asleep again, unharmed, as if nothing had happened. I wished he'd be able to tell me more about what was going on inside him, give some sort of clue to what kind of war was raging under his skin. Now I'd have to wait, and he probably wouldn't awaken before the feral beast did.

Elijah looked up and stared at me through the rear view. Even with sunglasses on, I could feel his gaze burning into me.

"If he so much as breathes wrong, I'm offing him, April. No ifs, ands or buts. Got it?"

I nodded, swallowing down the dry, sandpapery knot in my throat. "Got it."

Chapter Twenty-Three

By Chance

"WHAT ABOUT THERE?" Sarah's voice echoed in my head, and I peeled my cheek from my arm, which had been leaning against the door of the Jeep. I'd passed out hard after Randy's reaction to the antidote. We'd decided to locate a suitable place to spend the night, and we still had several hours before sundown but didn't want to get caught by surprise. We needed time to fortify our hideout before the ferals came out. I was pretty sure California had more vampires than Vegas did. Maybe more toward L.A. or San Diego, but we were pretty near them. These beach towns weren't exactly huge, but they ran into each other for miles upon miles without a break, blending into one another, making it seem like it was one long and endless city. That could be bad. Really, really bad.

The building Sarah had pointed out was more of a lighthouse. It was off in the distance, surrounded by sand dunes and swells of scrubland. I wrinkled my nose at it as Elijah pulled off the road and headed down one of the sandy roads toward it.

"Looks good as any," he said. He grinned and slammed down a gulp of beer. He'd found it in a convenience store we'd scavenged which had collapsed from some heavy rains. Underneath the crumpled awning it'd been fairly intact, and he'd managed to pull out a couple of six packs of beer that had remained half buried in dirt. He'd dusted the cans off and pulled the tab on one, taken a sniff and then a nice, large swallow of the fluid. The smile on his face told us he'd found something he absolutely loved, and he'd practically launched himself into the damp earth to dig out as many as he could find.

"Pay dirt!" he'd yelled as he shoved a couple six packs under his arms and lugged them to the Jeep.

At least someone was getting a treat. The other stuff we'd found was akin to the same crap we'd found in any forage: beef jerky sticks, dented cans of Spaghettios, ravioli, some salvageable individual packs of fever meds, bags of chips and loads of candy. Tons of it.

Well, maybe we were getting some treats, too, but real food would've been nice right about then.

"Should you be drinking and driving?" Now Sarah was acting the mother hen.

"Oh, don't start. I can handle my alcohol. Besides, I won't really drink that much until later. Need to get the place up to snuff before we can party." He winked at Sarah, turning her scarlet as she bit her lip and turned away. Man, the girl had it bad for him, and she was so transparent. I almost laughed but held it in as I studied the dunes around us, hoping ferals didn't like sand. If they didn't, this was a perfect home base until I found what I was looking for.

If I found what I was looking for.

We pulled into a spot near the lighthouse and studied the building, lonely against the horizon.

"Okay, April, you take to the back, I'll go in through the front. Don't forget to call out if you find something. This isn't a solo mission, you know."

I rolled my eyes. My reputation for working alone plagued me like a skunk attack. "Yes, *sir.*" I emphasized my words and threw him a dirty look before grabbing my machetes and a flashlight. I was ready to pummel anything that got in our way. One glance toward Randy reassured me he was out for the count. Still, I cracked the windows and locked the doors. If he woke up delirious again, he might inadvertently kill himself by opening his door and frying in the sun. Not something I needed right now. Elijah handed me the keys, and after he clipped his hunting knife sheath to his belt, he checked the rounds in his gun and strapped on his katana.

Sarah was doing the same. Her long sword looked overbearing on such a svelte girl. How she handled herself so well with the weapons always impressed me. No matter how long I'd seen her fighting, it was like watching a stranger. She could probably say the same thing about me.

She caught me watching her and gave me a tentative smile that didn't reach her eyes. Okay, so she was still pissed at me for pitching a fit earlier. I sighed and headed toward the lighthouse, ready to take some ferals down if I had to. Sometimes it felt good to start a fight and make something bleed. I missed it. That was my mission, and I couldn't wait any longer.

The bottom part of the lighthouse was like a small cottage. Tiny windows faced the ocean and the front where we'd parked. They were salted and caked with over a year of water spots, impossible to see through, especially with the sun still glaring behind us and reflecting off the glass. I groaned and kept on, hoping to find a second entrance in the rear, leading toward the beach. The deep sand was hard to trek through, and I could feel it filling my boots as I sank into it.

Cursing under my breath, I made it around to a wooden pathway leading off the deck from the back door and down through an opening between the grassy dunes and off toward the beach. I stopped and studied the surrounding area. It was easy to hide there. The hills hid everything from anyone coming around the corner. It could be good or really, really bad. Good that I could sneak up to the door without being seen. Bad if anyone else did the same to me.

Walking up to the door, I took a moment to hold my breath and listen. The seagull cries across the beach mingled with the hollow sound of the ocean. Even the slight breeze rustling the grasses intensified as I tried hard to filter the noises and listen for anything suspicious. When nothing stood out, I peered at the old wooden door before me. It was smooth and worn down from time and the constant assault of ocean air. I reached out and turned the rusty knob, cool and gritty from lack of use. It turned slowly, crackling as the rust flakes spilled out from it and flew away in the gusts of wind. I stopped and listened again, hoping there would be nothing here to find, either alive or undead.

No scratching, moaning or screeches. There was nothing human echoing out either. If I was going to get this done already, I better just do it. I shoved the door in with all my weight, and it swung open, filling the dark atmosphere inside with a huge cloud of billowing. I hurried in, my blades in position as I scooted to the side of the door and let my eyes adjust to the dimly lit interior.

Nothing lunged at me, nothing came bearing arms or tumbled in my direction growling with blood drenched fangs. I let out the breath I was holding and continued in, hoping it remained abandoned all the way through. The wind thumped on the door, and I worried it would make it slam sooner or later, so I reached out and pulled the door softly shut before continuing.

I found myself standing in a small mudroom of sorts, converted to a tool and storage shed. Several tools hung from the wall, though for what they were, I didn't know. I didn't see a garden around anywhere. I figured you could still rake the sand, so the long-handled tool with hundreds of teeth had some sort of purpose. The others—a trowel, shovel, fertilizing, pruners, a spade and what looked like a Japanese gardening knife—left me baffled. I hoped it would make more sense as I continued into the little house.

The next room was a hall that ran down to a back staircase leading up into the tower of the lighthouse. The air was stale and felt musty, thick and unused for a long time. I wondered if Elijah had explored the front of the cottage yet. I didn't want to run into him by accident and end up chopping a limb off. If he was in the building, he was remaining excruciatingly quiet, as was I. Making my way past the hall, where a small room lay to the left, I found nothing. Across from it was another short hall that looked like it ended in a kitchen where a small breakfast table sat under a dirty window.

I focused on the small room to my left and peered in, pushing the door slowly as I let the contents come in to view. An old rocking chair, a reading chair and several bookshelves lined with leather-bound books of all kinds circled the room. Piles of books lay on two side tables, and reading lamps sat amidst them. There wasn't a desk, but it appeared to be a reading room of sorts. The two worn ottomans told a story of many hours of use. It made me smile. If I could, I'd check out some of those books later, see if there was anything I'd want to read for the long, restless nights I was anticipating.

With that room cleared, I headed toward the kitchen area. The moment I turned into it, a creak of the floorboards made me freeze in my steps. I let out a breath when I found Elijah standing at the doorframe to the kitchen from the other side.

"Whoa… it's just me."

I pointed behind me. "Staircase back here, I'm going up."

"Okay," he said. "First floor's clear. I'll heading up the front stairwell."

We threw each other a curt nod and turned back toward our destinations. The stairs looked foreboding and disappeared into the ceiling like a black hole without much to look at from down below. I swallowed. Going up there would be a great disadvantage for me; my head would be a tempting target for anything waiting up top. As I ascended, I decided to pull a small knife from my belt and stopped as I reached the top of the stairs, before I'd become visible to anyone waiting for me. I swung my hand back and tossed the small blade up onto the top step, waiting for movement. When none came, I crept up slowly and found the second floor, much more open than the first.

This opened to a circular living area where there was recliner with a lamp and small table next to it. Like everything else, it was covered in a thick layer of dust. No one had been through there in ages. Even the wooden floor lacked any sign of footprints. It was reassuring, but I still had more levels to check. Who knew how big this place was? There was one bedroom with a creaky-looking brass frame bed and a single light on a lonely table next to it. The sheets were flat, made up one morning and never turned back down, forgotten. I crossed out of the room to where the wall hid a small hallway of windows to the outside.

The view of the ocean was impossibly beautiful, and I had to pause to admire its brilliance. I loved it and was so happy to be able to see it again. It made my heart jump with the excitement to have the beauty of the water so close. It was humid, but it didn't bother me. My skin begged to be drenched in its richness. Nothing felt better than that. It was what I'd needed to feel renewed, even in the face of the unknown dangers to come.

I turned back to find Elijah watching me. He'd entered the hall of windows from the other side. His nonjudgmental eyes twinkled as he followed my gaze toward the horizon.

"Gorgeous, isn't it?"

I nodded, smiling that he understood.

"Come on, we'll have a few hours to enjoy it. The spiral staircase starts here, and the living quarters end. Both floors are clear."

"Okay."

I joined him at the base of a scary-looking spiral staircase. The stairs stuck out from the wall of the tower without a railing on the open side.

"Ladies first." He smirked and wagged his eyebrows. I gave him a dark look, readjusting the machete in my grip.

"You're going to pay for that," I said before jumping onto the steps, not daring to look to the side. I wasn't afraid of heights, I just didn't want to know just how far I'd have to fall if or when I did fall. Okay, so I was a fiery pessimist. So what? I didn't really care what others thought about my attitude. I focused on the task and made my way up the creaky stairs.

They seemed to go on for miles, with no end in sight. I hated not knowing what I was heading into. Still, the call of the ocean outside was better than the arid desert I was used to. Nothing could dampen my excitement from being near the water, not even an imminent attack above.

The only thing missing was Rye. I gulped back the sadness that wanted to creep up my throat like rancid bile. I hated feeling guilty about something, but I really didn't know what else to do about it. I'd left him behind. That was the fact of the matter, and he and I would have to deal with the consequences when we saw each other again. *If* we saw each other again. I wasn't so sure we ever would.

Chapter Twenty-Four
Not This or That

WE WERE NEARING the top, where the stairs were swallowed by the ceiling and led up into the lantern room of the lighthouse. I prayed that since it had to be full of sunshine up there, no ferals would be crawling all over it. Maybe ferals were the last thing we needed to worry about. If there was someone or something up there, it would be conscious and probably more dangerous than a feral.

Right before I popped my head over the threshold, I paused, waiting to hear the telltale noise of a stranger. I heard it as I stepped up, just in time to drop weapons, duck and avoid getting my head chopped off by a swinging blade. It met with the metal around the stairs, twanging in a violent pitch. Whoever had tried to get at me was now backing up, waiting for me to try it again. I took their pause as a way in and sped up through the entrance, jumping to roll across the floor and slamming into the wall. Luckily, I avoided the assailant. They were caught by surprise as they scrambled to follow my path, only to have a leg pulled out from under them by Elijah.

Surprise, Surprise.

The thump of their body crashing into the floor and their blade skittering across the metal far from their grip happened so quickly, they couldn't catch their breath in time to retaliate. They laid there, frozen in surprise, with hands up in surrender.

It was a woman. "Stop!" she said. "I surrender."

Elijah pointed the tip of his blade to her throat. "Why'd you try to chop my friend's head off?" he snapped. His eyes narrowed on the stranger as I stumbled over to drag her off the ground and frisk for more weapons. She had a total of six blades on her. One stuffed in her boot, three were on a belt, one strapped to her thigh and another had been tucked under her jacket in a secret pocket. She continued holding her hands up in a show of faith. It made me want to slap her on the back of the head and scream at her for trying to kill me.

She refused to answer and flicked her eyes to the floor.

"Who are you?" I waited patiently as she shifted her gaze to eye me up and down, assessing what I was with her nimble, dark-haloed eyes. She was pure hybrid vampire. Not hard to see that with those telltale rings. Though what she was doing in a brightly lit room at the top of a lighthouse was beyond me. Most hybrids hated the sun, though they could venture out in it, it would always burn their skin.

"You're trespassing in my home." Her scalding hiss was low and accusatory. Her stare was relentless, and I hoped she wasn't thinking about getting her blades back. That would be the day. Elijah would get to her before she ever got the chance to lunge at me.

"You're home? You live here?" I was surprised. "Quite a place you got here. Looks very much unlived in. So try again."

She frowned, staring hard at the machete in my hand, which I'd retrieved from the stairwell. "I just moved in."

"Yeah, okay." I sighed, rubbing the tiny headache creeping into my temples. "So what would a hybrid want with a bright ass lighthouse? Not really your style."

"It's no concern of yours."

Elijah shoved her to her knees, and she grimaced as they dug hard into the floor. "Wrong answer."

She turned to glare at him, throwing him a disgusted look as she narrowed her eyes. "Sanctuary. I was looking for sanctuary."

"From who?" I asked.

She chewed her lips before pressing them tightly together. Whatever she'd run from, she wasn't willing to divulge much about it. I hoped we could change her mind. She could very well know someone who could help me with the antidote.

"Lark."

"What's Lark?"

She frowned, closing her eyes as if the name caused her excruciating pain.

"Not what, who."

"Get to the point." Elijah poked her in the shoulder, and she yelped, reaching over to rub it.

"Okay," she sighed. "Lark is the leader of my hive. She's been conducting experiments on my people, and I protested. She wouldn't listen and even subjected me to some of them. I escaped, but they're after me. She doesn't take too kindly to people escaping."

"Where's your hive? Is it far from here?"

"No, it's actually not too far. I figured I'd shack up here for the night. Just like you, I thought a lighthouse would be safer than the usual hideouts. I need to feed before I can travel more. She deprived us of blood, it was one of her reconditioning experiments." The woman sat onto her calves, tired of stressing out her knees. "You don't want to go looking for them. It's too dangerous."

"And why would that be? What's your name, anyway?" I knelt down, drilling my eyes into hers. She looked afraid, nervous and desperate in a way. She kept averting her gaze from me and pulled away as I crept closer. Maybe she was more afraid of the scent of my blood than anything else. A starving vampire was no joke.

I wasn't sure what she was running from, but it sounded like another Mercer and Christian sort of hive to me, people determined to study the different strains no matter who suffered.

She huffed at me, unwilling to continue the avoidance game we were playing. I wasn't sure, but she looked reluctant to tell me her name. It spiked my curiosity as I waited for her response. Right about the time I was wondering if she'd speak again or not and Elijah seemed this close to giving her an encouraging shove, she decided to enlighten us.

"It's Raina. And you don't want to go looking for them because you'll become their experiment, too. They won't hesitate to try out their new antidotes, serums or anything they can on you." She sniffed and finally met my stare. "Especially since you're a human."

Studying her composure, I watched for signs of a lie slipping past her lips. When I saw none, I peered up at Elijah, who apparently was doing the same thing. He shrugged, already looking bored and increasingly impatient. After much deliberation, I stood back up, offering her a hand to stand.

"Okay, Raina. I believe you. But you have to tell us where this hive of Lark's is. Otherwise, we get to tie you up, no matter what." I offered her a cheesy grin to relax the atmosphere as she tentatively took my hand. Curiosity, tempered by a healthy amount of caution, made me want to probe her for more. What had she been doing in the last year and a half since the virus hit? She didn't look much older than I was, and it made me recognize the detrimental effects it'd had on others my age. Maybe she'd been through more than I thought. Maybe she needed help, and we were put there for that very reason.

Who knew? I just felt a sort of kinship with her, more so than I'd had with Sarah after reconnecting with her. Sarah would always be my best friend, but this girl had lived through the same experiences I had. She was not much older than me and could show me so much of how the world had been effected here, in a whole other section of the world.

"Look, I'll tell you where it is. Heck, I'll show you, too. But don't expect me to waltz in there with open arms and kumbaya with Lark. Make no mistake, she's not your friend. She'll trick you, earn your trust and twist her words to manipulate you into her sick games."

"What did she do to you that you're so hard up on her?" interrupted Elijah, who was leaning on the windowsill peering out across the expanse of ocean. His hard eyes met hers, challenging her to break under the slight pressure he exerted.

Raina shifted her weight, shuffling her feet as she looked away from the weight of his stare. "It doesn't matter. Just know that she will. I know her better than anyone else there."

"Really?" I stepped toward her, feeling some impatience creeping into myself. "Prove it to us. How so?"

Raina's dark eyes flicked up to meet mine, challenging in her own way. She was intimidated by Elijah, but not so much by me. Why was that? "Because… she's my sister. I know her better than anyone ever could." This heightened my curiosity, and I wanted to know her more. Still, I trusted her as far as I could throw her.

"Why would your sister want to hurt you at all? Sounds like a family quarrel to me."

Sarah chose that moment to jump up through the hole in the floor, katana in hand and looking around, still in warrior mode. "The outside's clear. Randy is knocked out cold on the couch. I tied him to it, so he won't be going anywhere soon. Unless he chews his way through the ropes. But it would take some gnashing and a lot of time." She tilted her head at the girl still waiting before us. "Who's this?"

"This is Raina. Apparently she's taking refuge here, and we interrupted her humble abode."

Sarah snorted. "Here? Really? Who'd live in this dump?" She peered around, wrinkling her nose at the place. I actually liked it, so I rolled my eyes at her comment.

The silence that followed along with Raina's scowl filled the moment with thick tension. It made me shift on my feet. Sarah looked perplexed, and I didn't blame her.

"Did I miss something?"

"She said her sister is the leader of a vampire hive near here that's highly dangerous," Elijah said. "They supposedly don't know she's here. Not sure whether to kill her off now or keep her for use later." He was picking his fingernails with his hunting knife, looking bored as he leaned on the windowsill.

Raina crossed her arms at his remarks and averted her gaze toward the windows. The expanse of blue ocean was endless across the horizon, and it reflected in her haloed irises. A darkened look hooded them with a sense of sadness and longing. I wondered what exactly she was looking for, running away from her only family to this desolate place. I hated to find out if she'd been abused or something worse than that. Maybe we should heed her warnings. This whole thing gave me a sickening knot that clenched my stomach into a hard, apprehensive rock.

"Whoa… looks like I missed all the fun doing the dirty work downstairs. Why is it I get stuck carrying the heavy dead weight of a crazed vampire through the sand while trying not to burn him to a crisp while you guys get a history lesson about the hives in this area? Next time, I'm going in first." She circled back toward the stairwell but paused before she continued down them. "I say we listen to what she has to say. She might have some useful information. Never know." She shrugged and hopped down the steps two at a time, like the height didn't bother her at all.

I wished I could be so carefree and naïve. Sometimes the things we lost in the vampire plague were the things I still needed the most.

"I'll tell you whatever you want to know. My sister can be ruthless, but she's a scientist and bent on curing this disease. Even if it means making the problem bigger, or worse."

"What do you mean 'worse'?" Raina had my attention now, though I felt like it wasn't going to be a happily ever after tale.

"Lark… she's gained her position of power because of her smarts and ruthlessness. She would even sacrifice her own flesh and blood for the cause." Raina's voice shook as she took it upon herself to sit on the gritty floor, Indian style. I felt awkward left standing and hovering over her. Compelled to join her on the floor, I slid down and matched her position. Elijah lifted an eyebrow at me, but he could see that she was pretty harmless at that point. He let out a long breath and then stomped down the stairs, shaking his head and mumbling his opinions under his breath. As his head disappeared through the hole in the floor, I focused on Raina, giving her my full attention as she picked at her dirty fingernails.

It had escaped my attention until now that she was disheveled, hair wild with a film of oily dirt which clung to every exposed part of her body. Even her clothes looked wrinkled, slept in and ragged. I wondered how long she'd been hiding from this sister of hers.

"Lark wasn't always so horrid. Like I said, she's a scientist. Incredibly intelligent. First of her class at the university. Valedictorian, actually. She studied physics and genetics. Who majors in that crap? The intelligence gene completely skipped over me, though. I never graduated with honors or made it past my first year in college." She nervously chuckled, picking at the sand stuck in the ridges of her boot treads.

"Anyhow, when the plague hit and she found out that everyone we knew had either died, turned into some sort of blood-seeking creature of the night or warped into some weird human vampire mutation—like me—

she became obsessed with finding a cure. It was so consuming, she ended up trying a lot of what she came up with on herself."

My eyes widened. "What? What do you mean?"

Raina sighed. She closed her eyes, suddenly looking very tired. The fatigue caused her to look much older than her years. She was young, but from the terrified innocence still present on her face, I knew she had seen a lot.

"She's not like me anymore. She's… morphed into something else."

I groaned and ran a hand through the flyways escaping from my ponytail. "I've dealt with a pretty strange mutation of the virus before. Like a large bat woman with fangs and poisonous blood who could make herself look human. She sort of like that?"

Raina shook her head, her eyes looking more interested in my story now. "Really? No, not quite like that. She's… well… the wild vampire ones that hide in the dark until dusk comes, she's a lot like them. But she has none of their weaknesses. She can walk into the light, but her appearance has been damaged from the constant self-experimentation. She's quite frightening to look at, actually."

"Explain."

"Well, you know how the wild ones look?" I assumed she meant the feral vampires, so I nodded. "Well, her flesh isn't falling off, but it's really discolored. And her eyes are all red, and not just the irises. It's really off-putting. Plus, her fangs hang outside her mouth, like a saber-toothed tiger's would. It's disturbing, and I never could get used to it."

I swallowed. The visuals her descriptions gave me were horrifying, and I was sure that no matter what, Lark was hideous. "Go on."

"Her hands are long, the fingers so thin, they look like sticks. Her need for blood comes and goes, but when the urge hits, she could very well kill whoever is standing right next to her. She usually warns us when it's getting that bad and stocks up on blood, so she usually avoids it, but accidents do happen."

I cringed, wondering what sort of genetic manipulation Lark had gotten herself into. It was fascinating, in a sick, demented way. "Would she be willing to work on something else that could help?"

Raina stared at me in confusion, wrinkling her nose as her eyebrows tensed together. "What sort of thing are you talking about?"

I smiled, for once feeling somewhat excited and hopeful at the prospect of meeting this frightening creature who used to be Raina's sister. "I have an antidote. It worked on one of the feral vampires, the ones you call 'wild ones.' It turned him near human, but the effects are wearing off, especially at night. He returns to his demented state after a while, but I have some of the antidote with me."

Her eyes flashed open, shock slowly blanketing her youthful face. "You have it with you? That would be like gold to Lark. She'd kill you for it if she knew you had it."

I pressed my lips together, suddenly worried by her prediction. "You don't think she'd be willing to work with us on it?"

Raina pulled her battered legs to her chest, hugging them as she cradled her head in them, rocking as she thought about my question. "I don't know. Maybe. If you have something she needs, she'd keep you alive at least. Maybe you three would catch her interest."

"How so?"

She peeked up, the haloes around her irises reflecting the light and shining like gold discs spinning on a turntable. "You three are different. Human but not so. What are you, anyway? I've never seen a human mutation like you. There are the regulars, the untainted. Then there's the wild ones and others like me. But you… there's never been anyone in our area who was exactly like you and your friends." She sniffed the air and stared out the windows again, as though she were remembering something.

"That vampire downstairs. He's different, too. Not fully a wild one, not fully human." She inhaled again, and it made me suck in a breath slowly through my nose to see if I could smell the same thing she had. I couldn't. "He's tainted, but you did something to him, didn't you? The antidote?"

I nodded, but guilt began to tear through me for the first time since I'd shot Randy up. Maybe we should've left him alone. Maybe this entire mission was a failure. I didn't know, but whatever he was downstairs now wasn't what I'd ever wanted for him.

This Lark chick was my only ticket to finding out if I could save him. Every night that passed, my hopes of curing him grew dimmer and dimmer. Every minute that ticked by, he was slipping away from the humanity he so craved to embrace once more.

I'd make Lark work with us, even if it cost me everything.

Chapter Twenty-Five
No Less than Ordinary

I KNOCKED THE spoon around in the metal can as I smashed the contents into an unrecognizable mash. Spaghettios. I used to love them, but now the pasta and sauce tasted like the metal it'd been sitting in for far too long, and the texture felt like a gummy paste in my mouth. It hadn't gone that bad, I just didn't feel much like eating. I wanted to get out of the lighthouse, and was antsy to get my mission going and meet this Lark woman already.

Patience was not my virtue.

"Hey, eat. You're getting too skinny. Guys don't like toothpicks." Elijah nudged me as he spoke with a mouthful of green beans. I made a face and looked away. He had the manners of a gorilla, but I knew he meant well.

"I'm not a toothpick." I glanced at Sarah, who flicked her eyes away from me, avoiding my gaze.

"I'm just telling you like it is." Elijah laughed, sending a spray of food bits flying from his mouth, some of which landed on my arm. Frowning, I made a show of wiping it onto his sleeve and letting my breath out in a long, extended sigh. He was probably right, but still. I just didn't have much of an appetite lately. Not since my mother had died.

Munching on food around the soft flames of the fireplace made me wonder how Rye was doing. I was really taken aback by how much I missed him. Christian was lingering in my mind, too, but not like Rye. My feelings for Christian were definitely different than anything I felt for Rye. I hated that I'd made such a mess of things. I didn't deserve either one of them, and it killed my appetite as the guilt rushed through me. I set my can down and sipped some water from the bottle sitting in front of me.

Elijah offered me a can of beer, but I refused it to his utter, nonchalant disappointment. He shook his head and chugged the darn thing down himself.

The flames of the fire flickered across the faces of the others. Elijah was taking first watch, so I had to try to get some rest before my turn came around. Raina offered, but we didn't quite trust her yet. She instead shrugged and settled on one of the mattresses we'd dragged into the main living room. The more rooms we could lock up, the less space we had to patrol. She'd been silent, eating her two cans of random, label-free food and sipping from her bottle of water. We'd found a lot of food at the last place we'd stayed. It was as if the owners had never had a chance to even think about food when the world died. They had probably just been out somewhere when the virus hit and not been able to return home. We'd never know.

The fire crackled and sent small puffs of smoke up the chimney. Elijah had made sure that it wouldn't be too visible, even though we were far from the city limits and out on a fairly desolate shore. He'd decided it would be fine, and I hoped he was right. All we needed was to attract a horde of ferals. Or worse, Lark's tribe. I didn't want to become one of her science experiments, but I also had to talk to her and figure out what to do with the antidote. I hoped she'd be willing to work with me and get this going, for everyone's sake.

There was always the chance that this lady was bonkers and wouldn't take any offer into consideration, but I had to hold onto the tiny shred of hope that lingered inside me and told me this was the path I had to take. This was what I was supposed to do. If I didn't and I failed in helping others the way I thought I should, there was a huge chance that my life was over anyway. I couldn't live in this post-apocalyptic world. I'd remain the shell of the girl I'd once been, empty and unable to enjoy life.

I couldn't do that to myself. This mission was my drive to live. I had to live again, somehow.

Scooting away from the fireplace, I pulled my boots off, yanked a sheet over my legs and lay back, feeling the old mattress sink under my weight and creak. It was comfortable, but I really never noticed things like a comfortable bed or clean sheets anymore. I could sleep on the open ground if I had to. I slept, I ate and did my necessary tasks. Repeat. There was no real thought to it anymore. I'd turned into a robot. I'd let this endless day to day oblivion suck me in easily, readily with open arms. There wasn't much to it, really. Maybe I was emptier than I thought I was.

I felt old, frozen and lost. No one else could save me, and I had resigned myself to that. If I was ever going to change, it would be all up to me.

The light of the fire danced across the ceiling and made the shadows stretch and flicker as the night wore on. I tried to close my eyes and fall asleep, but my mind was running at full speed. I hated not being able to sleep. It left me exhausted and unfocused. In the morning, I'd need it more than anything, and I couldn't make my head shut off. I groaned as I twisted in the sheet and turned toward the darker side of the room.

"Can't sleep?" Raina's voice echoed behind me, and I turned around to find her lying back with her arms cradling her head and her eyes closed. "I usually can't sleep either. I figured if I just rest my body, it's enough. But…." She flipped her eyes open and looked at me like she was staring right into my soul. "You've got a lot more going on in there than I do. It's about that antidote, right?"

I nodded, suspicious of her intentions. Trusting no one was an old habit, but trusting this girl I'd just met was something I just couldn't afford to do, especially when something about her didn't jive with me.

"If I can cure some ferals, it would be all worth it. Even some of the vampire hybrids. It would be one step closer to normal again."

She propped herself on her elbow, her gaze never wandering from my face. It made me fidget, so I closed my eyes and waited for the inquisition to continue.

"And what about those like you? The human hybrids? Don't you want to find a cure for yourself, too?"

"I don't think a cure for the human hybrids is a priority. We don't have the blood lust, the deterioration of the ferals. If we can find one along the way, so be it. Awesome. But I need to find something for the vampire strain first. I think that takes precedence right now."

Raina chuckled, an annoying sound that made want to sit up and swipe at her. Instead, I frowned and turned back toward the wall. I was done talking to her if she was just going to laugh at the things I was working on.

"Sorry, I'm not laughing at you," she said, apparently sensing my frustration. "I just think it's kind of odd that you'll be leaving the human hybrids alone. You'll still be special, but you'll blend in with ease. We'll be nothing more than ordinary again. You'll still be stronger, faster. I feel like that just means you'll rule over the rest of us. How will that be any better than it is now, with people like Lark in charge?"

The bitterness in her voice didn't escape my notice, and I felt the iciness of her intent. Sarah returned to the room and plopped down on her mattress, striking up a conversation with Raina as I lay there seething. Something told me that meeting Lark would tell me a lot more about Raina than the girl was letting on. Maybe Lark wasn't the one I should've been concerned about. Maybe it was this Raina I had to keep an eye on.

Listening to their soft chatter, I closed my eyes and forced my brain to stop its incessant banter. I hated doing this, cutting my thoughts off to sleep. It was a forced relaxation, and it rarely got me the rest I needed, but I needed silence, inside my head more than anywhere else.

The morning would confirm any suspicions I had about Raina, and I'd find out if my life was going to mean anything at all. If Lark could do what I needed her to, then it was all icing on the cake from there. This had to work. It just had to.

Chapter Twenty-Six
Enough

THE DARKNESS OF the room slowly shifted from pure pitch black to the dim light of the moon shining through the tiny windows lining the tops of the walls. It streamed in with long arms, caressing the floor around me in rectangular patches of light. Blinking for tears to soak my dried-out eyes, I focused on the lumps around me. Raina's slow breathing surprised me, because she was a hybrid vampire, and they were usually awake during the night. Maybe she hadn't slept for days. It made me wonder even more about her.

Still, what had awakened me? Sarah was still on her mattress across from me, and the fire had burned down to softly glowing embers and didn't provide any more light. Afraid to move too much in case an intruder was lurking, I tried to listen to the space around me.

Nothing.

I sat up and scanned the room more thoroughly, snatching my boots to slip them on and tie them taut. I grabbed one of my machete blades out from underneath the mattress. Listening further, I heard voices echoing softly from the next room. Elijah was still on watch, and it was probably near the time to wake me for watch, so I figured I'd just get up and see who he was talking to. I hoped it wasn't someone who shouldn't be there. Just in case, I crept slowly toward the door to the hall that led straight to the kitchen where he'd set up to play cards on the tiny breakfast table.

Making it to the archway leading into the adjacent room, I strained to listen for the voices. They had paused, as if they were listening for someone, too. I hoped they hadn't heard anything and continued talking, that way I could determine whether Elijah was in danger or not.

"Well, I'm sure she'll be happy to see you, regardless of what you think."

"I don't know. She's going to mad as a hatter, I know it. It's just, I'm glad you told me before you left. I really would have lost my mind sitting back there without word, without knowing what had happened."

Rye? My mouth dropped open as I listened to the voice that whispered in my dreams and had soothed me during the nights I couldn't sleep and cried and cried until the tears wouldn't come anymore and the pain turned numb. The same voice would whisper sweet words that made my skin tingle when his lips touched my skin and his kisses sent jolts of energy flying through me.

The one and only voice that haunted me for leaving him behind.

A sigh and a chair scraping against the floor followed. "Hey, I know how much you love her. You're good for her. She just doesn't know that yet. Give her some time, she'll come around."

My surprise twisted from confusion to anger to from longing and back again. I wasn't sure how to feel about Elijah telling Rye where we'd gone. How did he know we'd be at the lighthouse? It seems that this destination was more premeditated than I'd initially thought. I wanted to hop in there and give Elijah a good screaming attack about how he needed to step away and stop manipulating my life. How dare he? How could he betray my trust so much? The anger surged, and I took deep breaths as I tried to wrangle it under control.

Still, Rye was here. Wasn't that a good thing?

I sighed, tired of battling my emotions. I wanted to see him, yes. In fact, seeing him was feeling more urgent as the moments ticked by. I needed to see him, hold him. Why? I had no idea why. Maybe… maybe I had succeeded in destroying the hive back at the slot canyon. Maybe Christian had died in the explosion, which would mean our bond was broken. I was no longer mated. I was… free.

The excitement of the possibility of this made me almost giddy. I wanted to jump up and down and squeal in happiness. Had it been so bad to be mated to Christian? No. But that wasn't the point. The point was that I didn't love Christian. I loved Rye. No matter how attracted to Christian I'd been due to that sick bond, it wasn't worth not having Rye's love.

This epiphany made me breathe out a sigh of relief. I knew what I wanted, and it suddenly became clear to me what I'd been missing all this time. I smiled, and a calm washed over me as I let myself feel the happiness of having Rye back with me. I walked into the kitchen and stopped to peer at both men. I didn't want them to see that I was happy yet. Let them suffer for putting me through this. It didn't matter in the end, but I could have my fun.

They both turned to face me. Rye paled, and Elijah began picking at his fingernails. Nervous much? I wanted to snicker but trained my face into a stoic mask. It was just going to be much funnier this way.

"What are you doing here, Rystrom?" I asked. My voice was low and monotone, frigid in every way.

Rye winced at the sound of his full given name but stood up and focused his eyes on me. "April, how are you?"

"I'm fine."

The silence grew heavy, and he shifted on his feet nervously as I weighed him down with my stare.

"I couldn't stay behind. I was going crazy. You know that. You may not have a bond with me, but I'm bonded to you, through and through. I love you, April. I made Elijah tell me he'd let me know if you ever left and bring you here. I'm sorry if I had to do this behind your back, but you have to know… it pains me to be away from you. I can't stay behind." He stopped shifting and was completely still. His face darkened, and the seriousness of his words sunk in like a bittersweet nectar.

"You told him?" I feigned disbelief at Elijah, giving him a dose of my death glare.

He nodded. "I told you, there are some people who really care about you. You shouldn't cut them off because you don't know what you want."

"Who made you the expert?"

Elijah's jaw tensed, and he stood up from the table, shaking it enough that the house of cards he'd built collapsed.

"I'm headed to bed. It's your turn for watch anyway." He stomped off, leaving a tumbling breeze as he exited the room.

I focused on Rye's boots, well worn, caked with dirt and scuffed from miles of walking and use. His pants were frayed along the bottom seam and were equally worn and stained. The dark green fatigues were faded beneath the dirt. They were a favorite of his. I think he owned several pairs of the same style.

My eyes slowly made their way up to his shiny belt buckle and over his snug but clean black shirt. He looked like soldier, but not quite in full uniform. His dog tags were tucked under his shirt, and I'd never really studied them before. His sleeves lay unfolded and straight, pulled taut against his rounded biceps and wide shoulders. The line of his collarbone fused with his neck, and the slight stubble that covered his skin made him look tired but incredibly handsome.

Finally I fixed my gaze on his shiny grey eyes, which were almost silver in the bit of moonlight slipping in from the kitchen window. The halos rimming his irises flashed, blending their metallic gleam with the silver of the coloring of his eyes. They were framed with thick, dark lashes, matching the smooth midnight locks. Silver highlights reflected the light, making his hair appear peppered with silver. I knew better. His hair was soft, thick and black as the darkest night of a new moon. His pale skin almost glowed, making him look even more ethereal. It was enough to make me hitch my breath and freeze us in our stare.

"It's good to see you again." His voice broke the silence. I couldn't even hear Elijah rustling behind me, probably already asleep on the mattress I'd just abandoned.

"It's good to see you, too." Why was I at such a loss for words? Here was the man I loved, and having him there, in my time of need, when I needed his comfort, his strength… he was always there.

"I missed you." Rye reached toward me, and I suddenly felt like either running away or slamming into him in a rush of passion.

"I missed you, too." I stepped forward, bringing my blade up to set it on the table. As my fingers left the hilt, I met his gaze once more. "I'm sorry."

He closed the space between us, his arms encircling me without hesitation, without fear or apprehension. Without any resentment. I let him pull me close. His body met mine, and I melted right into him. His chest smelled amazing against my face, a scent so familiar and comforting. I let my shaking arms lift up to embrace him back.

"Don't be sorry. Just don't do it again." His fingers stroked my hair, gentle even with the rough calluses from constant use. I rubbed my cheek against his hardened chest, and it felt good against my tired eyes. I didn't want to let go. I never should have.

"I just didn't know what you'd do when I came here without you. I didn't think you would have let me go if you'd known. But I wasn't positive."

"I'm here, aren't I?" He pulled away a bit, cupping my chin to bring my face up to his. "Hey, I love you. I'll follow you, wherever you might go. Anywhere, I'll be there for you. Whatever you want to do, wherever we end up, it's you and me."

My heart was on full-blown overdrive. I could feel the blood rushing to my face, and all I could manage to do was give him a smile, but apparently, for Rye, it was enough. He pulled me back against his chest, his arms never wanting to let go.

And that was enough for me, too.

Chapter Twenty-Seven
Sacrifice

WE DIDN'T GET to celebrate long. A loud crack resonated throughout the lighthouse as the front door exploded inward. The impact sent me sailing back into a wall as Rye dove through the doorway behind him. The dust rained down on me as I fumbled for my blade, which was still sitting precariously on the edge of the table.

"What the hell?" I yelled. "Rye!" Where had he fallen? I managed to reach the table and my blade. I gripped it with a bloody hand, bleeding from some cut I'd managed to obtain while falling backward. The air choked me as I stumbled to the left, back toward Sarah and Elijah, hoping they were ready for whatever was coming from the other side of the doorway. I could already hear them scurrying into the kitchen after me. I only had moments before they'd be on me, ripping my throat out, taking the precious red life from my body.

"Run!" I screamed, falling into the room and finally getting my legs to work as the ringing in my ears began to fade enough for me to hear the footfalls behind me. One glimpse forward and I found Elijah and Sarah running out of the room through the set of doors ahead. This place was almost circular, each room leading into the next behind it. They reached out and pulled me into the room with them. Elijah managed to slam the door and lock it before a barrage of bodies slammed into it from the other side. He shoved a chest of drawers against it as it vibrated. Dust poured down on him as the room shook. I didn't know how many people had poured into the room behind me, but it sounded like a lot.

I jumped back, turning to find Sarah at the other door, about to check it out to see if we could exit the room. I scanned the rest of the room. I couldn't find Raina.

Where the hell had that girl ended up?

"Where's Raina?"

Sarah shook her head, peering into the hall behind us. "I don't know. She was gone when the explosion happened. Come on, it's clear." She tugged at my shirt, and I followed, feeling Elijah's body shoving me forward.

"Rye went the other way around," I managed, the pain in my arm distracting me as we moved. I glanced down and found a large splinter of wood jutting from my arm. I winced at it and tried to pull it out, but it wouldn't budge, and I feared it was wedged between the bones in my forearm. "Shit, it's stuck."

"Here." Elijah grabbed my arm and took the splinter in his other hand. Before I could even brace myself, he gave it a hard yank. The searing pain from the deep gash in my flesh made me sweat, and I could feel the blood drain from my head, willing me to black out. I fought it, biting down my teeth until my jaw hurt. I felt like I was about to pass out, but the warmth dripping from the hole brought me back to the present.

"Here," Sarah said, pulling off the button down shirt she was wearing over her black tank top. She ripped off a piece of the fabric to wrap around my arm. Her fumbling was much steadier than mine would have been if I'd had to do it myself. I was thankful she and Elijah were with me. Even so, as she finished tying it snug against my injury, making me want to keel over from the dizzying pain, I worried for Rye and not myself.

"We have to find Rye. He's alone," I urgently whispered. Sarah nodded and took my elbow, tugging me along as the door behind us began to splinter apart. We ran down the short hall to the back stairs, pushed open the door leading to the stairs and headed up.

It wasn't smart to go up. We'd either be trapped or forced to jump. How would we survive whatever had popped in on us? Had Raina betrayed us and brought this wrath onto us? So many questions ran through my head in my attempt to stifle the need to collapse. It may have just been a flesh wound, but I was still bleeding profusely. I'd have to wrap it again soon if I was to stop the gush of blood.

We made it up the steps and to the circular room. Elijah dropped the hatch leading down the stairs and flipped the switch over to lock it. It was a measly metal slide lock and wouldn't hold a barreling beast at all. Still, there was nothing to throw over it and hold it down. I scanned the room for an escape route other than going up the spiral staircase. There was only a single window, and it looked barely big enough for us girls to fit through.

I glanced back toward the others, and Elijah was already nodding at my observation. "Go! I'll hold them off."

Sarah shook her head violently, her face reddening as she dug her feet into the floor. "I'm not leaving without you!"

The latched door bounced as they braced themselves for another impact.

Elijah's expression remained calm, if not very determined. "Get out of here! Now, before they get through!"

"No!" Sarah began sobbing, and Elijah flicked his eyes up to me, begging for help.

"Sarah…." He swept her into his arms, stroking her long red hair and kissing the top of her head. "It's okay, I'll be fine. You get out of here. I'll hold them off."

"I can't just leave you here," she sniffled peering up at him with wet eyes. I'd always known she had a thing for him, but seeing them together, I knew it went deeper than either had ever cared to admit. Elijah's caresses were calming in the madness surrounding us. I turned away from the two to give them a moment and went to work on the window, trying to hold back my own devastation at losing sight of Rye. He'd just returned to me, and not moments later, had been literally ripped from my arms.

"Go with April. We'll figure this out."

Sarah nodded, gathering herself up from the crumbled mess she'd become. It was fascinating to watch her do that. She was usually so together, so laid back and unfazed by anything. Watching her have to pull herself together was a rare sight. But she did, and she was back to her calm, warrior self in no time at all, even with puffy eyes and a red, tear-streaked face, she would always look beautiful.

Elijah smiled, let her go and walked over to the hatch where he pressed against it with his feet, hoping to keep the enemy at bay a bit longer. "Go," he mouthed and gave her the brightest smile I'd ever seen from him.

She turned away and grasped the window, which I had managed to get halfway open. She shoved at it with all her might, and the metal frame screeched open the rest of the way. She waved me through, and I didn't wait for her to finish gesturing. I took one last glance at Elijah, who watched us with calm, silent eyes, more accepting of his fate than we were. I gave him a curt nod and darted out the window, landing hard on the small rooftop below. I jumped to my feet and peered over the side.

A dark figure rustled in the bushes below, where the sand drifts were high and pressed against the lighthouse walls as if they were going to one day swallow the place whole. At least it would be a soft landing. Still, I narrowed my eyes to study the person lurking in the shadows as Sarah dropped behind me. She pressed her fingers onto my shoulder, giving me a sad smile as I pointed toward the nearest drift of sand. She stepped forward, readying to jump, when I grabbed her arm and pointed at the figure in the tall grasses, who was watching us closely.

"Who's that?" Sarah squeezed her eyelids together, straining to make out the features of the man. It looked like a man, broad shoulders and dark hair….

"It's Rye!" I almost shouted his name but turned back toward the window. There wasn't any movement from inside yet, so I was pretty sure Elijah was still holding them back. It made my heart sink to know that Sarah's beloved wouldn't be leaving with us. Maybe we could circle around and cut off the attack from the bottom. There was still hope to catch them by surprise, as they had us.

"Come on!" She tugged at my good arm and turned to hop off the edge of the roof. I watched her tumble down the embankment. I followed, closing my eyes as the sand whipped around me. It wasn't as soft of a landing as I'd wanted, but it was good enough. My arm screamed in protest as I rolled over it, causing stars to spill across my vision. I hoped I didn't pass out from the pain, and gritted my teeth together.

At the bottom of the sand dune, Rye lifted me up and pulled my good arm around his. His embrace filled my nostrils with his calming, manly scent that I remembered always enjoying while lying next to him. Why did it seem more intense now? Our bond was growing. I could feel it. If we shared blood, I was certain it would seal the deal. I smiled at the thought but found Sarah's wild eyes searching the lighthouse windows desperately, making me lose the sense of euphoria right away.

"Elijah's trapped," she said.

Rye nodded and motioned me toward the grass-covered dunes in the direction of our Jeep.

"I have an SUV hidden behind some dunes. I didn't want you to hear me pull up, so I parked a bit away."

"Where's Randy?" I whispered, wondering where the poor guy had disappeared off to. "He was tied up in one of the rooms, and we couldn't get to him in the chaos."

Rye shrugged, shaking his head. "I don't know. I didn't see him. I wasn't able to get back inside after they rushed in. It wasn't me they were after."

My eyes widened. The antidote was in the car, in the small cooler stuffed under my chair. I had to retrieve it. I hadn't told anyone exactly where I'd left it, and I knew that was what they were looking for.

"The Jeep."

"I have the keys," Sarah said. She pulled them from her pocket, and I thanked our lucky stars that she was as paranoid as I was and slept with them on her.

I grabbed the keys and looked off in the direction of the Jeep. "Come on."

We made our way around, sinking into the deep sand, which made it that much more difficult to run. I hoped that if the others saw us, they'd have just as difficult a time coming through it after us. My arm throbbed, and with my good arm around Rye, my machete dangling from that hand, I was close to useless unless I got some blood.

"Rye," I said through clenched teeth. He looked at me, and I gestured that I wanted to sit down. He slid me to the ground and I sat, wincing in pain and feeling exhausted. "I need blood."

He looked up toward Sarah and then back to me. Sarah kept watch and peered around one of the dunes toward the lighthouse. Her eyes were shiny and dark. If she was crying, it was impossible to tell. I was pretty sure she was looking for Elijah.

"Mine or Sarah's?"

I studied his eyes and smiled. His soft touch on my arm made me feel so much better, and I knew what I had to do.

"Yours."

He nodded and brought his wrist up to his lips without hesitation. Has he let his fangs extend, he looked dangerous. His halos flashed brighter, and the razor-sharp edges of his teeth looked lethal enough to rip a throat out. He bit into his wrist hard, barely wincing from the pain. He brought it to my mouth where I licked at the drops of blood seeping from the punctures. It tasted metallic and harsh, like a mouthful of copper pennies. It'd been a long time since I'd had any blood. We both knew what would happen to me. I'd become stronger, inhumanly strong, and heal with unbelievable speed. It was exactly what I needed, and I fought myself so I wouldn't completely drain him of the precious fluid. The taste had turned into something delectable, like pure, sweet honey.

I pulled away, breathing hard as I felt it spread through my body. My mood shifted from the cold feeling of fear to the hot, burning inferno of hate and vengeance. I closed my eyes, relishing the turbulence inside me. It was pure energy, euphoric and scary all at the same time. I wanted more, but this would have to do for now. I could already feel the pain of my wound subsiding.

I flicked my eyes open and threw Rye a wide grin. "Okay, I'm ready. Let's get Elijah out."

Chapter Twenty-Eight
End Game

WE PEERED OVER one of the dunes, scanning the perimeter of the lighthouse for movement. It was eerily quiet, but my senses were on overdrive. The sand was constantly moving under my feet, filling my boots and making me sink into it if I moved too much. I narrowed my eyes on the lighthouse, checking each window and entrance for signs of Elijah or Randy. I hoped they were still alive. If they were dead, I'd never forgive myself. Sarah was desperately searching, too. I knew the stakes were higher for her and made sure I was focused on the target. Any sign of an easy way in or of either man, and we'd ambush the group who'd taken us by surprise.

This time the tables would be turned. The confidence pumped along through my veins and made me feel invincible. I couldn't wait to get into combat. I wanted to kill something, drown my pain with a meeting of blade and flesh. This primal need filled me up and pasted a wicked smile across my face as I licked my lips, watching the hybrid vampires roaming about the lighthouse. They had no idea what was coming.

"Come on." I motioned to the others and headed toward our Jeep. I paused. Someone was inside. I could see them moving around violently as I got closer to the vehicle. I approached one of the windows and peered in. The darkness made it hard to see, but drinking Rye's blood had heightened all my senses, including my night vision.

Thwack!

I jumped back a tiny bit when Randy's face and hands appeared on the other side of the glass. He growled and flashed his fangs before realizing it was me. He quickly calmed down and sat back, huffing and puffing. He'd recognized me! If the feral inside was weakened from the second shot of antidote, he was probably aware of what was happening. Apparently, our visitors had locked him in the jeep after finding him in the lighthouse. But why hadn't he been able to get out? Further inspection showed me the child locks were on, and he was tied to the back seat so he couldn't escape out the front doors.

Was he feral? Was he human? I hadn't known if the second dose of the antidote had had any effect on him, but I now had an answer. Still, he wasn't fully human, and he'd have to stay tied down until we figured things out.

"We'll be back, Randy," I said. "Just wait."

We made our way back up to the lighthouse. When we reached it, we saw that the front room where they'd entered was empty, and we tried our best to not make any noise as we approached. Where had they gone? The moment we cleared the front door, the room was flooded with light and we were surrounded by hybrid vamps. Some flashed reddened, haloed eyes at us, while others had normal colors with haloes. I could see what Raina had talked about with the mutations Lark had been messing with. Even her soldiers were not left unchanged by her tampering.

We pressed into each other, facing out in a tight circle. We were surrounded, and it was not looking good for us in any way.

"Who are you?" I asked. The soldiers kept a tight circle around us, and I hoped they weren't intent on killing us just yet. Abruptly, they spread apart to let someone through. A woman. And she looked just like Raina. *What the hell?*

"Raina?" My surprise leaked out into my voice. I swallowed it back and replaced it with a ferocity that left me wanting to rip the girl's neck out.

"Sorry, April. I can't have you running the show." She leaned forward, studying me with beady little eyes. She turned to the others, looking at them as if they were insects ready to be pinned to a board. "I think we should keep this one and kill the others. No, wait…." She straightened, and the smirk spreading across her face made want to slap it off her. "Keep the one in the Jeep, too. He's all messed up already anyway." She turned and was about to exit the room when she suddenly stopped and began to turn back toward us.

"You traitorous bitch!" Sarah yelled and jumped forward, aiming for Raina. One of the soldiers slammed his fist into her stomach, sending her crumbling to the floor, wheezing for breath.

"Watch it, Ginger. I have your boyfriend. He's perfectly safe. I can see what you like about him." With a haughty laugh, she waved at someone behind her. They retreated and returned a moment later, pushing Elijah before them. He stumbled in, bloodied but fierce as ever. They had his hands tied, but he appeared to be okay. "Any more from you and your pretty boyfriend loses his pretty face."

Elijah snarled at her and flicked a concern look toward Sarah as she sat in a heap on floor. Raina laughed, but a commotion behind her made her turn to see what was happening.

The soldiers were parting for someone else, and that person had Raina paling faster than a bleach-soaked shirt. "Lark? I... I...."

"Just what do you think you're doing, sister?" Lark stepped into the light emitting from a flood lamp one of the soldiers had propped against the corner of the room. This woman was a lot like Raina. So much so I knew they must have been identical twins at one point in life. But this one had red irises surrounded by pale skin and a thinner frame than Raina. Where Raina appeared healthy, filled out, but disheveled, Lark looked like death itself.

"I was gathering specimens. You never let me finish what I'm doing." Raina's fear had morphed into anger as her voice shook, and she crossed her arms as her sister approached. The red irises focused on her as Lark reached forward and wrapped her bony fingers around Raina's throat.

"Never defy me again. I wanted them brought to me peacefully. You ruined our chances for their trust. Get out of my sight." She shoved at Raina, sending the girl stumbling backward where a wall of Lark's soldiers caught her, to her obvious disgust. She jumped back to her feet, straightening her clothes and shaking off the helpful soldiers.

"Fine. Do it your own way. You'll never succeed. I'm tired of your endless lab experiments anyway. Find another scout to do the crap work for you." She spit on the floor and stormed past her sister, making a show of brushing shoulders and knocking aside those who stood in her way.

The adversity between the two had me curious to know what Lark would have to say about all this.

She watched her sister flee with the stillness of a statue then faced us and motioned for her guards to untie Elijah. Once loose, he growled at them but kept his hands to himself as he rubbed the raw skin on his wrists. Sarah finally managed to get to her feet and rushed into Elijah's arms.

This woman looking at me appeared fine, if you could get past her skeletal appearance. Normal, even. Too normal. The intelligence in her eyes told me she was something extraordinary, even though she smelled of a hybrid, tainted, but a mix of vampire and human. Something was different about her, but it was really hard to decipher what exactly that was.

Her shiny, red eyes found mine, and she walked over, looking me up and down.

"You must be April." How did she know my name?

"What do you want?"

"My sister Raina is the best scout I've ever had, but she tries too hard and wanted to find the cure faster than I did. She usually brings me the unusual, the lost, the ones I can use for experiments." She sighed, looking upset as she glanced out through the door and into the dark ocean air. "Now she withholds information and experiments with people herself."

"She's a traitorous bitch!" Sarah's shrill outburst made wonder if she was going to jump Lark. Even the guards stepped up closer to make sure she didn't try anything.

"Yes, you're right. She's not trustworthy, even to her sister." She sighed, and a weak smile formed across her face as she watched Sarah steam. "So much life in this bunch. I like that." She paced back and forth, looking studious and concerned. I watched the line of her soldiers, hoping for a lapse, a break in their vigilance. "Look, I don't want to fight. I need your help."

"Not the right way to ask for it," I muttered. "Let us go." She wasn't going to become my best friend forever by treating my real friends like crap.

She halted in her steps and frowned, glaring at the soldiers behind her. "I'm sorry for the brute force, but my sister can be a force to reckon with. She was my second in command and called my soldiers out without my approval. I will remedy that immediately so you will know we really don't mean you any harm." She waved at them to put their weapons away, and they shuffled on their feet, looking apprehensive, but did as they were told. "Please… forgive me. I meant no disrespect. It's just, Raina is not quite herself."

My teeth and fists were clenched, but I relaxed as Rye's fingers wrapped around my hand.

"Get to the bloody point," I said. I was tired of games.

Lark smiled, looking hopeful. Oh, I would listen to her proposition, but that didn't mean I had to be nice to her about anything or even accept it.

"I want to make a deal. This antidote that my soldiers say you have… I want it. I know you have some, but my soldiers failed to find it for Raina. Can we make a peaceful negotiation and trade for some of it? I promise no harm will come to any of your party. If you have more than one dose, I'd love to have it all."

"No."

"Come now," Lark said, looking shocked by my abrupt answer. "Okay, I don't need all of it. Just as much as you can spare. How about half? How's that? I really would love to work on it with your group, but I don't know if you're willing to work this out after such a rough start."

I could feel my face burning from the deepened frown creasing my cheeks. "Why would you want to work with us? What if you betray us like Raina did and turn us into one of your experiments? I don't want to end up like that. None of us do."

"I know you don't trust me. How about a promise? I swear on my life that my people will not disturb you as long as you're here. We can work on the antidote together, and I promise I won't attempt any unwilling experiments on anyone. That is not our way, truly. Would you do this for me then?"

Sarah was back on her feet, leaning on Elijah but almost recovered from the blow she'd taken. "Your word means nothing to us," she said. "Raina said you did such things to people, but you say it was her. How do we know which of you to believe?"

Lark's hardened glare focused on Sarah, but she did nothing to argue. Instead, she turned to wave down one of her soldiers, possibly one of her lieutenants, and then back to us as he whipped around and told the entire army to fall back.

What the...?

Lark waited until there was no one left in the room but her before speaking again. "There. My troops have pulled back to the road. The wild ones do not bother us here, so it's quite safe to leave if you wish to do so. I do hope you consider my deal, because I want to help you find the antidote. I can help your friend in the car out there." She pointed out through the shattered door, toward the Jeep where Randy was trapped. My stomach clenched at the thought of saving him, and I struggled with the options before me.

If I struck a deal with this woman, would I live to regret it? If not, would Randy?

It was a hard road, and as much as I didn't trust this woman, I had no choice. I just wished she had approached us rationally in the first place, not like this, not with force, even if it hadn't been her fault. Her rein on her sister appeared weak, something she'd have to remedy indeed.

Reluctantly, and to the protests of Elijah and Sarah behind me, I stepped forward and held out my hand to seal the deal. I had found what I'd come for, and by the excited twinkle in this woman's eyes, she had also found what she was looking for. I was going to stay and make sure she kept her end of the bargain.

"On your word and on your life that you will keep us safe while we work on this antidote, I accept."

Epilogue
Things We Lost

STANDING AT THE edge of the world, watching the tumbling waves rush up onto the sandy beach, I gripped my arms to my chest, the weight of it all suffocating me. I wanted to save them all, not only to bring some sort of hope and purpose to their lives again but to ultimately save myself, too. But could ferals, hybrids and humans ever be equal again? Would the differences continue to keep us apart, even after the cure? Weren't the history books filled with people fighting over the slightest things? Still, if I could, I'd do everything in my power to help the world achieve some sort of peace.

It'd been two months since we'd found Lark and her hive. It was full of a wide variety of mutations she'd created in her well-meaning attempts to find a cure for the virus. They weren't completely messed up people, not like the freak show lab in Christian's hive. Some had subtle discolorations to their skin, hair or eyes. Others had longer fangs and reddened irises but were otherwise powerless compared to a hybrid vampire. Still others had increased strength, stamina and fighting abilities. These super soldiers were recruited into the ranks, but no one was ever tampered with beyond what they consented. Raina had lied when telling us about Lark's hive. Why? My only guess was sibling rivalry, or she'd just really wanted to mess with our heads.

Through much coaxing, Lark had taken samples from all of us and tested them against new variations of the antidote, with a few promising results. We even visited her hive, to Sarah's utter disgust. She still hated anything to do with Lark or Raina. Still, we found Lark's hive to be accepting of our presence. I had to give it to this lady, she worked tirelessly to find the right combination of antibodies from all our blood samples and mixed them with the antidote. For the first time since I'd discovered the existence of an antidote, I felt we could really figure it out and save people.

Randy had been quarantined with us in the lighthouse, our temporary headquarters since it was near Lark's domain, but still our own sanctuary. He'd spent the rest of that first night tied to a kitchen chair but hadn't flashed any fangs or growled at any of us as we worked to barricade the demolished front door with plywood until morning. It was strange how calm he'd become, and it gave me hope that subsequent injections of antidote would continue to keep him calm until the right antidote could be mixed and given to him.

In his more lucid moments, he'd listened to Lark's proposal to try the new antidote on him once she got it near perfect. I was astonished by this and made sure he was making a conscious decision when he'd agreed to it. I would've hated it if he'd ended up making an error without really thinking it over.

"I know what I'm doing, April," he'd said.

"How can I be sure you really do?"

He'd stared at me, his eyes a marbleized mix of red and blue, a sign of his fight against the virus.

"You can't be sure of anything in this life at all. If I die, I get to see Helen again. If I live, I live. Win-win, if you ask me. If it fails and I remain feral, I know you'll do what you have to do with me." He smiled. Never sad. Never forlorn. I wished I could be so brave.

"Of course."

Sarah and Elijah became official, an interlocked pair, finally admitting to their mutual feelings. The days passed, and they'd enjoyed each other's company, walking along the beach and watching sunsets from the top of the lighthouse. Who knew they could be so in love? It was inspiring to see that tragedy could result in people realizing it was time to take a chance on love. They were perfectly matched in every way, and I just wondered what had taken them so darn long to realize it. It's never too late, I guess. Even in a post-apocalyptic world.

And what about my own fragmented love life? What about Rye? I'd let it sink in that he was the one for me, knowing with certainty that I finally knew what I wanted. I felt it in my bones, down to the very marrow within them. When the days passed and we held onto one another like we would never spend another moment apart, I knew it was real. It was as real as the way he got my heart racing with a smile and sent tingling rushes of pleasure shooting across my skin when he touched me. As real as the taste of his blood and the way it filled me up until I could hear his heart beating with mine as we exchanged blood, mating us together for life. He exhilarated me, and I hoped I did the same to him.

From the looks I'd catch him giving me when he thought no one was looking, I did. It was all I needed, and the happiness he gave me kept each day in the right.

Lark proved to be true to her word. She sent frequent updates and allowed me to work side by side with her on occasion. She'd concoct different antidotes and choose a volunteer to use it on. We painstakingly labeled each new mix, testing them on ferals we caught on expeditions during the night, deep into the cities of the California coast. We took them from different parts of the state to ensure we evaluated all possible strains of the virus. We even procured some from Las Vegas. Though we always found more and more variations the further we dug, it only brought us closer to finding the cure.

What we did with it would be entirely a collective decision. First and foremost, the infected ferals would be given the adjusted antidote, that decision was unanimous amongst Lark's hive and Blaze's. Rye kept the lines of communication open between them, always trading the information from Lark to Blaze and back on trips back and forth between Las Vegas and the coast. He even returned one day with a sight to surprise even me. Felix.

He'd survived the bombing of Christian's hive, escaping before we had. He'd approached Blaze's hive under surrender, waving the white flag. His information that the enemy hive was completely obliterated, including Christian and Mercer, was confirmed by Blaze's many scouts. Felix's desire to help us with the antidote, even trying one of the latest batches on himself, had given Blaze more than enough good reason to send him with Rye on his trip back west.

Lark had taken an immediate liking to Felix, finding their mutations very similar, even though Felix was more filled out than she was. He'd also been an asset to her as she continued the tests, taking one for the team and subjecting himself to endless blood draws and tests by her. I was glad he took the focus off Randy, who'd been changing more and more each day, becoming more and more human and leaving the feral beast to slumber, hopefully forever. He had to continue getting a shot every three days to keep it subdued, but that was better than anything he or I could've hoped for.

In the end, I returned to Las Vegas. I needed to see my brother and ensure that he was still happy. We'd exchanged letters through Rye as he made his way back and forth, but I needed to see him for myself.

Sitting in the confines of the underground City of Vida, I watched his soccer championship game against some older kids. He really was a sight to see, sprinting across the expanse of the underground field, and the normalcy of it all brought me back to my own childhood. He kept growing, like an overfed weed, never stopping, always different each time I saw him. I knew he'd never forget me. We were family, and it never got old to see his face light up when I did get around to visiting him.

This was what happiness was to me, even though I knew I would continue to fight with myself. No matter what happened, I could find the places and moments of contentment I so longed for. I'd fight for them, one bloody battle at a time. I knew my mother would've smiled at me and agreed. Oh how I wished she'd been able to hold on, just a bit longer. But then, would we have been where we are now if she had?

For now, the fight in my soul had quieted and was slumbering like a gentle giant. I'd probably have to reawaken it one day, but hopefully that day was far off in the distant future.

RESONANT

A *Reign of Blood* Prequel Story

0.

Weeks after initial viral outbreak

I WANT TO smash every single window.

Why the hell am I even here?

I close my eyes. I can still see everything I want to forget stamped behind my lids, but it sticks to my brain like forgotten lollipops embedded into the couch. I can't wipe it off or make it go away, and that pisses me off to no end.

I flick my eyes open and continue to pass them over every nook and cranny, every brick and niche of my old house. How can one place cause me so much anger… pain? Well, maybe it's not so much the place itself, but what happened outside these walls while I hid inside that will forever scar my precious soul. How I haven't lost my mind by now, I'll never know.

The sun burns into my back, and a thin film of sweat forms on my neck, reminding me that summer is ending but still holding on with tooth and nail. I'm standing in the middle of the road of a perfectly normal neighborhood. It could be a quiet midday siesta time, or everyone could still be at work based on the serenity surrounding me in maddening stillness.

Yet it's not. It's deader than a cemetery after midnight. No one will come out to greet anyone. No one will run out and ask me if I'm suicidal for standing in the middle of the road where someone could come careening around the curb in their family SUV and slam into me. Not a soul is alive to do so.

You see, I'm alone. Alone here in the remains of my city, Las Vegas. It's abandoned…neglected…nothing but a memory swimming in my head now. Everyone is dead. All the people I knew are either gone or sleeping in the deepest darkness they can find in this ever-bright desert town. Not a soul roams the street during the daylight but me and what's left of my tiny family.

"April, what's gotten into you?"

My mother's voice echoes in my head as I watch our old house waver from the tears fighting to fill my eyes. She's not here but hunkered down hiding with my brother Jeremy to keep the sun off their backs and to keep the harm far away. I'm back in town, staring at our old house, about to walk in and get the rest of the memorabilia we were unable to grab when we left in a rush while all hell broke loose. This isn't our home anymore, and that's why I'm madder than a hatter.

I wish it still was. Oh, how I wish nothing had ever changed. Why did it have to happen?

I peer around to the windows of the other houses. Some are decimated, shattered, broken into and looted. Others sit untouched, silent and watching me... observing me as they stand guard in the desolation. Still more, like ours, are boarded up to keep the nightmares out... or to keep the monsters trapped inside.

But no one is here. I know because I've checked. I've broken into all the houses that looked boarded up and secured. But who can run from a virus that flies through the air and takes control of the very thing you need the most; your body, your mind, everything that you are?

"I'm here! Why not kill me too? I'm waiting!" The dizziness as I spin makes me stop, but the answer doesn't come. I think I hear a lonely crow caw at my interruption of its perfectly tuned day. It's the only response to my breakdown, and I worry it will never change.

1.

First Night

"WHAT IF YOU look them in the eyes? Will you die?" Jeremy shoves another mouthful of mac and cheese into his already puffed-out cheeks. I wish I knew. I haven't looked one of the feral vampires in the eyes... yet.

"I don't know. I wouldn't try it though. I heard you'll freeze or become their slave." I laugh and cross my eyes, sticking my tongue out to make him smile. His toothy grin as he chuckles makes the gap between his upper front teeth stand out. My brother still smiles, even when the world is slipping away from us just outside the window.

I slip my fork onto my plate before taking it to the trash can. We've decided to stay the night in our house. It's sturdy, elevated, and surrounded by high wrought iron and breezeblock walls. It's an island unto itself, a sanctuary on our residential street. Sure, it isn't pretty on the outside with its crumbling paint job and fortress-like appeal, but in the middle of the chaos turning our neighbors into bloodthirsty animals, it's as good as it gets. Inside, the house feels cozy, safe. I still make sure to check the barred doors as often as possible, hoping our vulnerabilities are taken care of.

Our furniture is barricading the doors we don't use often, and the windows have been sealed with not only plywood, but are also glued shut. They are double plated and impossible for a human to break through with even rocks and especially bare hands. A high-powered rifle might make it through, but luckily, the creatures have no use for such things. It's them we hide from now, as the evening turns to full dark and the moon shines high over the rooftops of the houses along our street. The second floor windows have bars on them, so we left them alone. I make sure to enjoy the night sky and peek out through the curtains to watch the stars twinkle and the lights of the city flicker as the power plants continue to run, probably unsupervised by now.

How long will we have power? How long will the comforts of our lives be available to us like they had before? These things we're losing, the luxuries, the modern world itself, will we get it back soon? Or has the sun set on that world forever?

These thoughts make me draw the curtains shut as tears make their way to overflow my lids. I can't let them fall. I can't give up yet. It could be just a fluke, a temporary disaster which the government is surely on top of, flying in hazmat workers and CDC people to figure it out and clean up this mess. How long will they take? When will it end?

This is just the beginning, and I'm afraid to ask anyone how long it will last.

Tonight, we'll sleep in the living room. Together. My mother is already draping sleeping bags, pillows and blankets across the couches and the floor. This way, we'll be together to escape to our van in the garage if something went awry during the night. We've covered all the windows so none of the light from our lamps can sneak out into the night and bring unwanted guests our way. I really hope this is enough to keep us safe.

"We need more pillows." My mother gestures to me to help her spread a sheet across the array of mats she's laid out on the floor. "I put our best blankets into the van already, so we're using our old ones." She seems to be chatting to keep herself busy as she moves about the room, but I don't believe she cares for any response. I tuck the sheets under the mats and peer over to watch Randy, my mother's boyfriend, take a swig of cold beer.

The man is drinking, and we might die tonight. I have nothing but loathing for Randy, so I flick my eyes over to the pile of blankets my mother is sorting on the couch. I grab several and place one on each mat. He brought lots of supplies earlier, but now he's relaxing on the couch, flipping through TV channels to find any news on this strange outbreak. He may have been a nice enough guy to get all that stuff to prepare the place to keep us safe, but watching him drink now makes me realize his true nature which I've suspected all along. He puts up a good front for my mother, but to me, he's a lazy, two-faced alcoholic. How do I trust someone like that?

So what if he was trying to replace my dead father? I didn't like him. I couldn't explain it. Maybe I was too stubborn to let Randy in. It didn't really matter much anymore. I chose to loathe him, and I just couldn't help pointing out everything wrong with my mother's choice for a companion.

I finish with the blankets and swiftly leave the room, heading upstairs to grab the pillows off all the beds. I want to sleep in my own bed, but my mother won't have it. It makes me seethe that I'll have to listen to Randy's soft snores during the night. It's hard for me to sleep as it is, let alone with others breathing around me. The thought makes me frown as I return to the living room and start dropping pillows onto the mats.

"Quit frowning. You'll get premature wrinkles." My mother lifts her eyebrows as I glare at her. She knows I dislike Randy, but if only she knew how much I hate his guts. I force a smile to get her off my back and choose a mat, one near the window, so I can listen to the movements outside and hopefully warn my family if I hear anything unusual. I don't believe I'll be sleeping much tonight.

"Can I watch some cartoons?" Jeremy takes the mat next to me, and I'm relieved I won't be next to my mother, or Randy for that matter. I give him a genuine smile and turn down my blanket, shoving my legs under it before I fluff up the pillow and stuff it under my head. I stare at Jeremy, who's now gotten the remote from Randy and found his favorite cartoon channel still working. The local stations were the first to go, but some national ones are still broadcasting, and a few are reporting on the same situation happening across the Southwestern United States.

"So how long are we holing up in here?" I close my eyes. I don't want to see the agitation in my mother's face.

"I don't know. We have supplies for a few days, but it all depends on how bad it gets."

A screech echoes through the walls, and we all jump. I'm sitting up now, my heart racing.

"That's really close," I whisper, trying to calculate how near the source of that scream could be.

The TV flickers as the lights waver and then go completely off.

Minutes pass, but no further noises fill the silence. The lights finally flick back on, and Jeremy turns the TV right back on as I lay back down and pull my blanket to my chin. The chills running through me can't be warmed, for my soul feels colder than an iceberg.

"What if they come?" I ask to no one in particular.

My mother sniffs. Jeremy hugs his legs to his chest and stares hard at the cartoons flashing across the screen. Randy keeps drinking.

"I suppose we run. That's the plan." Randy snickers at me and drains the last of the beer in the bottle before placing it gently onto the coffee table. Six are already lined up in a neat row.

"Run where?"

He shrugs, scratching his goatee. His scraggly dark blonde hair shakes as he stretches. He's not ugly, but I don't understand what Mom sees in him. He reeks of alcohol, and the smell wafts about the room in waves, making me turn away from him to stare at the wall, crinkling up my nose.

"Probably as far as we can get from the city. My brother's got a cabin up in Mt. Charleston. We can head there for a while. Less of a chance to run into people."

I have to admit, it isn't a bad plan. "What if we don't make it there?" I can hear my voice crack, but I don't turn away from the solid, tan wall I'm studying. Each chip in the paint looks more and more neglected than ever before. We were supposed to repaint the living room once... what was it? Two or three years ago? That was the plan before my father died.

Plans always change, no matter how hard we try to prevent it.

Randy doesn't care to paint anything. He fixes things up all right, but interior decorating is low on his list of things to do.

"Well, April…." He emphasizes my name enough to make me cringe. "If we don't make it, then we won't have very much to worry about anymore, will we?" He laughs and pops the cap off another beer. It only makes me want to grab it from his hand and fling it at the wall.

THE NIGHT CRAWLS on slowly, and I listen to every tiny noise, every creak of the house shifting around me. I can't rest. I don't think I ever will again. Not after this.

A thought hits me for the first time since I got home today. Sarah. Where is my best friend? I've failed reaching her in spite of leaving voicemail after voicemail. I haven't heard my phone go off all evening. The cell towers are probably all down by now.

I scan the darkened room. Only one lamp is still glowing, set on the step up to the hallway. In the sunken living room, I can hear everyone's breaths softly filling the air with sighs and snores. Hoping to not awaken anyone, I slip my phone out from my purse lying next to my head and flip the screen on. The screen lights up the room like a floodlight, and I squint at its brightness. Adjusting to it as I pull my blanket over my head to keep from waking the others, I check my texts and find none from Sarah. No calls. Not even a viable signal.

Great.

I turn it off and stick it back in my purse. It's useless now, a piece of junk plastic and glass. How am I going to get ahold of her now? Could she be dead? I shudder, hoping that isn't the case. There's no way of knowing if anyone is safe unless they're still in their homes and barricaded in. Sarah's house isn't close enough for me to walk to, and I sure as heck am not going to go there at night, not with those creatures still roaming the streets.

The screeches are more distant now, but occasionally, I hear screaming. That, combined with the nearly constant barking of dogs, makes me want to throw my hands in the air and give up on sleeping for the night. The others are passed out cold. Why can't I knock out as easily as they do?

The night wears on, and the lamp flickers a couple times before morning. I watch it, praying the electricity doesn't give out, hoping the night and its demons do not yet win. But the day might bring even more bad news. Will we be able to fight whatever is coming? If we fight, is there any chance we could win?

2.

Flickers
The Second Day

I AWAKE TO shuffling movement, blinking the sleep from my eyes as I watch my mother gathering things up and stacking the mats to the side of the couch.

"April, get up." Her voice is tense, and I sit up, peering about the room. Jeremy is awake, watching cartoons on TV again. A bowl with leftover milk sits on the coffee table. Hair mussed up, he looks half awake.

"What time is it?" I rub my face and untangle my legs from the blanket. I'm still wearing my jeans from last night, afraid we'll have to make a run for it in the middle of the night and be caught in jammies.

"It's about seven-thirty." She pulls my blanket from around my feet and begins to fold it. Her hair is pristine, as if she's already primped herself for the day. I'm wide awake, and I wonder if I'm the only one who couldn't sleep last night.

I groan. "Why are we up already?" Normally, we'd have school this morning, but with the state of things, it wasn't going to happen.

"Can't sleep all day. We have to make provisions. Plan... map out a plan." Her repetition spikes my curiosity, and I finally notice Randy is missing.

"Wait... where's Randy?"

At the mention of him, my mother stiffens. "He's gone to help some friends. He'll be back soon. He just wanted to make sure they were okay and ask if they want to join us on our trip to the cabin today."

I scratch my head, the tangles catching on my fingers. I reach for my purse and yank out my brush. "Did he tell you the address of the cabin?"

She freezes, drops the blanket and pales. Her eyes widen, and I wonder if she's going to pass out.

"Mom?" I realize why she's shocked. "You didn't ask, did you?" I shake my head and sigh. Of all things to not know, she doesn't know where the cabin is and Randy, our only link to it, is now gone.

"What if he doesn't return, Mom? What if something happens to him? And you didn't think to ask him exactly where we were going? What if he can't get back here? What if he leaves without...?"

"He wouldn't do that," she snaps and glares at me, but I'm already seething too much to even be upset at her stringent words.

"Maybe. But if something bad happens to him, we're fucked!" I stand up, squeezing my lips into a tight line.

"You will not speak to me like that."

I don't say anything else, but I feel the fight in me struggle to stand still. I move away from the living room and up the stairs where I shove the bathroom door and slam it shut. I decide to hit the shower to calm down. Might as well. It could be my last since our chance to escape just blew off into oblivion.

Afterward, I sit on the lone step into the living room. I'd sent Jeremy to take a shower, too, feeling the dread of the days ahead creep up on me.

"Well, if he can go help his friends, I want to see if I can get Sarah."

"No." My mother doesn't even look up from what she's doing, or not doing is more like it. Her fingers twist the end of a handkerchief over and over again. It belonged to my father, but I know he's not on her mind right now. It's Randy who has taken that spot.

"Why not?" My whining makes even me cringe. I hate this confinement. It makes me feel like a caged animal. What irony, to think the beasts are out there now, free, while we sit here inside the prison.

My mother, Helen, doesn't answer me. Her long, shiny, golden brown hair is woven into a braid sitting over her shoulder, the victim of her endless torment as she alternates between the hankie and the end of her braid.

I let out a breath and lean on my knees, my black, straight hair draping over my shoulders. I can't go anywhere. Randy took our second car. Only the van sits untouched and ready to go in the garage. I don't want to risk the van, our only lifeline to get out of town when we have to, and yes, it's when, not if. I can feel the future rushing at me like a great, barreling beast ready to trample me down into the dust, demanding payment of blood and flesh. Morbid I know, but that's what awaits us now.

"If he doesn't come back by tomorrow, we should go find the cabin ourselves. There can't be that many up there, right? One of them is bound to be the one." My logical brain clicks into action, and I feel a sliver of hope. We could go there without Randy. It's better than nothing; better than staying here, in the deathtrap of a city.

Mom twists her hankie again before bringing her fingers to her lips where she's chewed one nail down to the nub. I frown at her nasty habit and am glad I never picked up on it. Unfortunately, Jeremy has, and he's drooling all over one of his thumbs while his teeth click on the ragged edge of his nail as he gnaws it off. I hope he hasn't gone feral.

No, we're safe. We have to be. Why haven't we turned yet? What makes us so different than those out there running amuck in the streets and screeching as they hunt for blood in the night? Maybe we won't change because we aren't out there mingling with the infected. I hope that was it. Still, the danger that any one of us could turn during the night scares the bejeezus out of me.

"I can't sit here and do nothing, Mom. Let me go after Randy. I can see if his car died or something on the way to his friends' house. Where do they live?"

Silence. That's all I get from my mother. She is disintegrating before my eyes. I can see it. It isn't reassuring at all. Only now do I see just how dependent she has been on Randy's strength. Would she crumble by herself? She never needed anyone before, even after my father's death. Even so, this isn't the kind of problem anyone would expect. No one could've predicted the mess we're in.

"You don't know where they live, do you?" My accusation comes out low and heavy with the sinking feeling I have growing within my stomach, filling each pressing question.

She shakes her head.

Dammit.

"Mom…." I groan and rub my face. "Where are we supposed to go, then?"

"We'll figure it out."

"What? No, you don't even know where to go now."

She slams her fist on the table. I didn't notice her getting to her feet to pace the dining room. The noise makes me jump, but I don't ask any more questions. I know the answers to them already.

"Fine." I stand up and head over to slump next to Jeremy. "But when the morning comes, things will be changing."

She says nothing, and I take that as the end of our conversation. It suits me fine as we watch more TV, occasionally having to turn it back on whenever the lights flicker.

MORNING'S HERE. Another restless night. I'm up before the others, unable to attempt any more sleeping. My mother still tosses and turns, constantly reaching next to her, subconsciously touching the empty mat where Randy should be. It makes my heart squeeze for a moment as I feel her longing, but it also ignites my determination to go find him and get more food and supplies.

I grab a duffle bag sitting near the front door. Lacing up my boots, I can feel my mom watching me, but I don't meet her eyes. The question is coming.

"Where are you going?

I pull out my shoulder holster for my 9mm and strap a sheath to my thigh for a machete, which had belonged to my father. I was okay with the machete, but I know how to use a gun thanks to him.

"Out."

"Where?"

I flick my eyes up to my mother and do my darnedest to not roll them. My hand flicks out into the air. "Out there."

She says nothing but watches as I finish prepping. I'm turning to walk toward the garage when she grabs my arm, holding it with an iron grip.

"Don't look for Randy." She pauses, swallowing as her voice breaks. "Get as many supplies as you can. Food. Guns. Water."

I nod. Her face is stoic, but I see the tears fighting to slip from her eyes.

"Okay."

"I'll see you back here before sunset." With that, she lets go and turns away to go sit on the couch near a sleeping Jeremy. The silence lingers around us, but it says so much, it's overbearing. Something tells me things are never going to be the same after today. For her, for me, or for anyone else.

3.

Personal Missions
Three Days after Viral Outbreak

I TAP MY fingers on the glass, hoping nothing moves inside the store. After I wait for several seemingly eternal minutes, nothing comes. I hope that means the coast is clear, especially since the overhang on the front of this store blocks the sun effectively. It's a perfect retreat for those human-like creatures roaming about while I'm in town to scavenge supplies. I may be just seventeen, but out of the three of us, I'm the most physically able to get in and out of the city quickly. It's a tough assignment, but I chose it and will do anything to help my family survive.

Clutching the hunting knife I have in a sheath buttoned to my belt, I slide the fingers of my other hand over the gun in its holster at my side. I'd taken shooting lessons with my father when he was alive, and they sure are coming in handy now. If one of these crazy vampire-like people tries to bite me, I'll be ready.

"Hey!"

I turn to find an older man limping his way toward me. His face is pruned, tight with a permanent frown pasted on his lips. The white hair on his head is thinning and wild, lifting up with the soft breeze of the early morning hours. His clothes are disheveled, and a cane with dozens of scuffs and nicks on it helps him wobble along.

I suck my breath and turn my back toward the window, my fingers on the gun, but I don't answer him. Sometimes, the people that I've met after the first day haven't yet turned. It was hard to tell, but I'm starting to see the signs. They can still walk in the light, but have become sensitive to it. They're usually injured or sickly and the real sign is the bloodshot eyes… eyes like this man's.

"You hear me, girl?" he yells, like I'm deaf or something. I nod, hoping he stops approaching. I can feel my blood freeze inside my veins as he sniffs at me… sniffs!

I gulp and clear my throat. "Yes, sir."

"Damn kids nowadays. No respect, 'specially now, with the whole darn place going to hell in a hand basket." He shakes his head, grumbling under his breath, words I can't decipher.

I contemplate running, but this store hasn't been looted. In fact, as I flick my eyes to peer through the window, it looks downright pristine. We need more food. We need to load up with as much as we can to leave the city. We have to leave. Staying is not an option in this pandemonium. Movement in my periphery makes me swing my eyes from the store to the old man, then to a couple of people sprinting across the street. I have to go inside so I won't be seen. Running into anyone is risky.

"I'm just leaving." I step back. The old man is almost within arm's reach.

"You stop right there. I won't take this from a malnourished little bitch like you. I'm hungry. I need… I need…." He stops in his tracks, shaking a finger at me as if accusing me of a dire crime. He immediately crinkles his brow, confusion spreading across his pale face. His lips are a faded pink, cracked and in need of some hydration. The tired appearance of his bloodshot eyes morphs slowly before my own.

His irises spill with blood, and his faded blue eyes slowly shift to a darker brown and brick color.

"I… I… I'm so thirsty." His consciousness fades before my eyes, and I can see it as plain as if he was standing in broad daylight. He isn't. He's left the safety of the sun for the large overhang I'm standing under, the shade darkening the sidewalk enough for the disease to jump into action and take the reins from his very soul.

Shit!

I step back, grabbing my knife and pulling it into my grasp. I ready myself for close contact while he stands frozen for a moment, his mouth twitching. His finger, still suspended in the air, shakes as his body betrays him. The man who'd been there a moment before, fades completely.

Another step back. At least the sun isn't far, but I'm still kicking myself for having to miss out on the good loot in this store. Most of the meat has gone bad already, but some freezers still have frozen meat available, slowly thawing in the cool September air.

He lunges. His wobbly legs still uncooperative as the ferocity of the virus kick starts his energy, and he comes flying at me. He's still slow enough for me to slam the knife into his chest. His fangs extend out as his jaws snap toward my neck. I shove him back, slamming him into one of the columns holding up the overhang. It's large and thick, wide enough for me to push his body against it as I fumble to grab my knife.

He lurches toward me, and I lose some footing as his strength grows. I'd have been a goner if he was younger, healthier and sturdier. This frail shell of an old man is struggling to push me away, but still inhumanly strong. I grunt as I shove him back once more, slamming him back against the column, sending a flurry of dust over our heads.

"Come on!" I grip the hilt of the knife again, my forearm against the man's throat and collarbone. His teeth click as he snaps them, attempting to rip out a chunk or two of me. I finally manage to pull back on the knife, slick with dark red blood, and slam it right between his eyes.

He goes limp, dropping to the ground as his body twitches and the red irises flip into the back of his head. A low growl manages to escape his mouth before he goes silent and still.

Dark, sticky fluid makes my fingers feel colder, and I reach down to wipe them on the old man's clothes as I breathe hard. My heart is hurried, ready to burst from my chest as I grab my knife and leverage myself against the guy's head to pull it out. He doesn't move, his fangs still hanging in place with sticky saliva dangling from them in strands, and it makes me want to puke as I step away from his fallen body.

Collapsing against the windows of the store, I let my heart and lungs catch up as I stare in horror at the old man. I've never killed anyone before, but that isn't what's bothering me.

I enjoyed it. This… this euphoria. I can feel it coursing inside, like standing in flames, lighting me up from within. I smile, knowing more about myself in this one moment than I have in seventeen years.

I'm still holding the knife, and the blood has run down the side of my jeans. I stare at the coagulating blood, gritty under my nails, my vision tunneling on the glistening fluid. I shake my head, and my chest tightens as I peer out into the street. The daylight washes everything out, and I scan my surroundings for any more intruders, hoping there aren't any.

No one. Not even a trace. The world is quieter already, three days after the initial outbreak. Or is it the sudden panic flooding my chest that keeps me from hearing anything?

My eyes land back onto the old man, and I briefly wonder if the sun will burn him into a crisp. Vampires are allergic to that, aren't they? Maybe. That is, if the legends and stories about vampires are true. Every fiction has a sort of truth to it, right? I have to believe it, for the feral vampires I've seen spring out of this insanity prove it beyond the shadow of a doubt.

It reminds me of something, and I feel a sudden urge to jump into action. Bending down to wipe my knife and hands as best I can on the old man's clothes, I feel but a hint of guilt. Shouldn't I be panicked—or crazed—after killing someone? Instead, I feel little to nothing, and a brief concern flashes in the back of my mind, but I put it away, like an old book back onto its shelf, for later.

Shoving the knife back in its sheath, I ready myself to drag his heavy weight into direct sunlight. Time to test all those stories and lore.

I grunt with the effort. I'm not a puny skeleton or anything, and the variety of physical activity I religiously keep up has left my body toned and lean. Even so, weightlifting is not my thing, and it's biting me in the ass now as I try to get a good grip on the man's body. Hooking my arms under the guy's armpits, I lurch back, digging my feet into the ground and heaving his weight into me.

It seems damn near impossible. The guy might as well weigh a ton. The inches I gain make me sweat, and my muscles burn from the effort as I grunt away, literally wanting to scream with frustration. I could've sworn the guy appeared lighter than he is. Now his dead body is as resistant to my efforts as a loaded sack of bricks. It takes me several minutes to gain any inches, but the moment I get his torso into the light and the beam of sun hits him, he ignites in my arms, and it singes the hair on my limbs as I scurry back, away from the scorching flames.

A couple of my fingers ache with a prickling sensation, burned at the tips. I shake them wildly to air them out, but the damage is done. At least my face hadn't ignited. That would've been tragic and mighty painful. I sit on the gritty sidewalk, feeling cool through my jeans as I watch his body smoke from the fire consuming his body. It consumes his flesh and turns it into ash, like a mad, ferocious beast, as hungry and voracious as the man had once seemed prior to his death. It's a sort of irony to watch this beast eaten by an even greater, uncontrollable and more unfeeling force.

4.

The Truth about Untruths

I'M NOT SURE how long I walk, but the moment I see it, I know I have to prove something to myself, before the sun sets and it becomes too dangerous to experiment. The church's steeple looms high above, piercing the sky with its spire as I watch a flock of pigeons flutter about the belfry and coo as if nothing is wrong. But everything is wrong, and the sanctuary within calls to me, like in the days of my youth, when my father would take me to church, and I'd listen to the dry lectures and do my best to not lie down on the bench during sermon for a quick snooze.

The memory snaps me back into my mission, and I let out a slow, longing breath as the vision of my father fades. He will never see the mess the world has become. He'll never have to deal with the ramifications of every action the way I do in these horrid times. In death, he is the luckier one, but I can't give up. I have my mother and Jeremy to protect.

So I march up the steps of the massive building, pristine with its wooden doors, brass knobs and stained glass windows. The beauty of it all eludes me as I press my bloody handprint against the cool doorknob and rotate it. Shoving the heavy door open, I enter the cool foyer before clicking it shut behind me.

The sound of soft voices singing echoes throughout the place, bouncing off the walls from the great sanctuary beyond another set of doors ahead. I'm sure the people inside know what's going on outside, but they make no effort to lock the place down. They put so much faith in the safety of this hallowed ground. It makes me wonder if there could be something to that. Either way, I'm on a mission and need to find out if what was said about vampires could work on these mad creatures.

As I make my way to the double inner doors of the sanctuary, I pause and find a wooden cross hanging above a picture of the Christ. I peer at it for a moment before I snatch the cross and stuff it into the belt of my pants.

"Sorry," I whisper to the picture of Jesus looking on with kind eyes and a halo lighting him up. My guilt over stealing wanes quickly as I push on the sanctuary doors enough to get a good peek inside.

There are a few people sitting in the pews, and some singing in the choir area behind the podium where the priests or pastors lecture. I'm not sure what sort of a church I'm in for some look the same unless you read the name. Before I proceed further, I see what I came for. A stoup stands in the back of the sanctuary, still and alone. I get giddy and then remember I have nothing to put the holy water in. I let go of the door and back up into the foyer, flicking my eyes about to see what I can use to carry the water.

The foyer has few options. It's neat, bare and free of clutter. I start to think I might not find anything here and will have to return later when I spot the trash can. Sprinting over to it, I flip the top up and hold it as the hinge keeps it from coming off. Peering inside, I see an empty bottle of water and, just my luck, it has the top to it screwed on. I pluck it out, uncap it and shake the remains of water out of it.

Perfect.

Slipping back into the sanctuary, I walk softly to the stoup and pull the top off it. Luckily it isn't locked, and I dip in the bottle for a bit of water, rinse it out and chuck the waste water to the carpet before I let it sit in the basin and fill to the fullest.

The place has gone quiet, and I barely notice it until I look up while screwing the cap back onto the bottle. The water is tinged pink from the blood that has seeped off my skin and tainted the water with its grit. I hope it still works, but the stares I get have me giving them a weak smile before I turn and head right out the doors and then to the outside world.

I hope I get to test it before I get home.

Sure enough, the overhang where I had killed the old man has several new ferals lingering under its protective shell against the harsh afternoon sun. The three sitting under it watch me studiously as I approach. I meet their challenging glares for a moment before looking away. My fear blooms as I wonder if they can control people with their minds, like the stories say they can. They hiss at me, and I get my answer as I find that already one person has gotten too close. His body shows no signs of struggle; no scratches or other defensive wounds from what I can see. He lies face down on the shaded concrete, spread eagle, as if willingly sacrificed. Surrounding the body is a sticky puddle of what I know to be blood. He's probably better off now. I just hope he doesn't come back as one of these feral creatures.

Reassured that the three are no longer humans, I turn toward my awaiting van in the alley next to the store. I hope it's still there and cross my fingers that no one has looted it yet. I still want to hit that store up, but want to test some theories out first. Slipping the key into the lock, I shove the side door of the van open and get an extra magazine for my favorite 9mm semi-automatic pistol along with a machete, for good measure. The machete is a crude weapon, which I taught myself how to use with lots of online video tutorials. Sometimes they show more blade use techniques in my martial arts classes, but I hadn't gone deeper into that portion of training yet. I wish I had. No better time than now to need it, right?

I shove the door closed, contemplating whether to lock it or not. If I have to get away fast, the locked door and fumbling with the keys could be tragic. But if I leave it unlocked, theft is more probable. I sigh and leave the driver's side door unlocked and lock the rest, hoping it won't bite me in the backside in the end.

Heading back around the corner to the overhang, ready with weapons, I frown to find another feral has joined the group. The apartments down the way must be where they're coming from. I frown, but it gives me more of them to try my weapons on. The four turn as I walk into their line of vision, and they begin to snarl, hiss and snap jaws at me. Their eyes, once normal colors, are now deep crimson, red as blood.

There's no way I can't admit I'm scared. These creatures are like Hell itself and filled with the ferocity of wild animals. The ones who've tasted the fallen man in the puddle of his own blood have the crimson smeared around their mouths and dripping from their teeth. Even human teeth look dangerous when covered in red, sinewy gore.

I swallow the desert forming in my mouth as my tongue sticks to the roof. It makes me lick the dryness of my cracking lips. Note to self, get a drink and some lip balm when I blow the doors down on this joint. It's now or never.

I bring the gun up and aim for the last feral from the left, pulling the trigger to hit him square in the chest. He staggers back, falling to the concrete, but a moment later, pushes off and snarls at me, looking madder than ever before. I gulp and shoot again, this time at the head, and it makes a fine mess of what used to be the right side of his forehead. His eyes loll in his head as he stumbles to stay upright before crashing to the ground in a loud thump.

Okay, so hits to the head slow them down... significantly. File that away in the 'important' memory box.

Next, I yank out the water bottle I have stuffed in a loop of my pants. Unscrewing the cap, I step closer, hoping to get as many of them with the holy water as I can. Almost within arm's reach of one of them, I hold the bottle out and shake it furiously, soaking the ferals with the fluid.

The screeching is horrendous, and as soon as I empty the bottle's contents onto them, I drop the plastic to the ground and cover my ears. The sound pierces the air like arrows shooting into my eardrums, and I grimace. It's my turn to stagger back, but I glance at them long enough to see their skin sizzle wherever the water has touched them. The one I hit full blast in the face also crumbles to the floor and into the sunlight with half his body in the bright light. He immediately combusts, and his body shakes violently as the fire consumes him more quickly than anyone can pull him away from the fiery sun. I watch in fascination, but the others don't seem to notice the feral's peril, for they are hissing at me again, madder than ever.

Their melting faces make my stomach tumble as I fight to stay upright without hurling the small lunch I had earlier. I still have two more ferals to dispatch, but instead of my resolve growing stronger with each kill, my knees become weaker and weaker.

I can do this. I know it.

I breathe in deep, hoping it centers me enough to take the last two out.

"Okay," I breathe out, bouncing back and forth on my feet. "Two down, two to go."

I put the gun away and feel for the cross at my belt. I have to get close to use it, which makes it impractical. Still, I have to know if it works or not. I hold out the machete and step closer. My hand shakes, but I breathe even, slow breaths, knowing that if I don't stay in control, there will be no surviving anything today.

People run down the street, probably from the same apartments these four came from, and gasp as they see the monsters I'm facing down. They don't stop to help, but why would they? They just keep on sprinting past, bags in hand as they yell at each other to hurry. Hurry to where? I wonder.

"Don't look. She's good as dead," I hear one say across the road from me as he shoves luggage into his car and his wife sits trembling in the passenger side. She looks ill, pale even. I wonder if she's sick, if she's caught this virus devouring the remains of the human race. They look like they packed in a hurry. Probably tried to hunker down in their small apartment before it got too much to handle and they decided to run. Whatever drove them to leave in a panic, it was probably too late for them now. As her husband flings himself into the driver's side, she dons sunglasses and still hangs her thin, pale hand over her eyes to shield them from the sun.

I don't think it's me who's going to be dead today. The beige sedan screeches its tires as he slams on the gas and speeds away. I know I can probably follow its path and find it wrecked down the way. The woman is shaded in her spot and the windows are heavily tinted. It's only a matter of time before there will be enough shade for her to turn, and he will be her first victim.

My focus returns to the two before me as my slick hand grips the hilt of my machete. They continue to push at the boundaries of the shade as the sun shifts across the sky. In a matter of hours, the ferals can have anyone unfortunate to linger on the streets. But they will not be having me.

I bend my knees, suck in a breath, and let out a wailing battle cry as I run toward them, blade out and ready to cut away the death in their eyes. I swing at one first, then the other, sending both stumbling back from the deep slices across their bodies. In the shade now, they don't look bothered that they are bleeding profusely from their chests. They continue to come, so I shift on my feet and ready the blade to swing higher at the first one to reach me. I hit his neck, and though I get deep enough where blood pours from the wound, it's not enough. He continues to come at me, and I shove him back as we slam against the wall of the pillar.

I push off and spin as the other feral comes hurtling in our direction. She hits the other on the pillar, and they both turn toward me as they find their balance. I pull back the blade for another swing at the other side of the man and run toward him, hoping the woman feral goes flying to the ground when I slam into him. He's between me and her, and I can use him as a shield after I get his head removed from his body.

I swing as he comes at me, roaring like a beast as his dirtied hands reach out toward me, aching to taste my blood, just a little sip….

The machete hacks at his neck and slips though the remaining bone and tendons holding his head on. His head goes spinning to the ground as his body crumbles. I barely have time to swing about again as the woman makes it to me, and I slam into her side. The momentum throws her off balance, and she trips over the body of the fallen feral. I pull out my hunting knife, jump onto her writhing body, and plunge it into her heart.

Her body twitches, but she's still alive. Blood is pouring from each wound, which gives me enough time to yank the crucifix from my belt to press it to her chest. It sizzles, and I have to yank back as another finger burns from the flames erupting at the contact point. The cross clanks to the ground, but the flames leave behind a very specific charred outline of it. I smile at knowing this, but I'm not sure how it will help me much since I have to get right up close onto a feral to use it. My jeans are getting spotted with the sticky mess pooling under her, especially after I pull out my hunting blade and grip it tightly. Stuck, I can't move off her yet because she's still squirming, so I slam the blade straight into her right eye socket.

She jerks, sputters and gags on the blood streaming from her mouth before going still. Only a small exhale lets me hear the residual life leave her. Blood is all over the place, leaving me smeared in her black and red blood. It's darker than normal, and I use her thin sweater to wipe it off.

She begins to twitch again, causing me to jump to my feet, grab her arms and yank her toward the sun, a few feet away. If they don't die from stabs to the head, I'm going to have to remove a lot of heads if I can't incinerate them first. The thought makes me want to puke as the sunlight sparks on her flesh, setting fire to her soft, pink sweater. I stumble away from the flames, land on my hands, and finally lose my lunch.

I stay there, hunched over and feeling the world spin while I spit the nasty from my mouth and catch up on my breathing. I peer over at the fallen ferals in the shade and hope they don't try to get back up, too. I'll have to drag the ones that weren't decapitated into the sun to make sure they don't resurrect themselves as soon as I recover. My muscles ache as a fiery burn engulfs them. My fatigue seeps back in from the lack of sleep and poor nourishment during the past few days. I have to eat better, take better care of myself, for there will no longer be doctors or dentists or anyone to help put me back together.

The loneliness this evokes makes the tears well up in my bleary eyes, and all I want to do is sob as I sit back on my heels. I have no friends anymore. People are dying all around me. I hear a distant screech of tires and then the inevitable crunch of metal as a car crashes some distance away. People scream, but the lack of sirens verifies my utter desolation and confirms the end is near.

I have to get up, I tell myself. I have to go into that store and get supplies. We need them. Plus, this place has guns next door, in a small pawn shop I can hit first and then pull my van around to fill up with any food to be found. The sun will not wait for me to finish. It has already given me so much already, consuming the feral wastes and shining on my back, a soft, warm but lonely comfort.

So I get up. I get on. I grab everything in sight, including tons of lip balm to feed the bad habit of licking my lips to utter rawness. I grab some more 9mm handguns, along with a few shotguns. Ammunition gets dumped into duffle bags as I grab what I can. I have to hurry. The shade out front could bring more ferals before I get done inside the stores. Luckily, the doors have pull-down gates, so I drag those suckers down to stave off the crazies while inside. I line up my bags and place them at the base of these gates until I finish my scavenging, stuffing them to their zippered brims. Only then do I pull the gates up and shove the bags into the van.

I return to pull the gates back down, for good measure. Maybe they will serve to keep the place feral-free so when I come back for more, there might be something worth salvaging from here. Maybe not. There will be a lot of maybe nots in my foreseeable future. I can count on that.

Cranking the engine, I slam on the gas and watch for more crazies out on the road. Already, I find I have to swerve around stalled cars, with victims stuck inside with ferals, their family members turned and ravaging their bodies. Some have managed to hop out of their cars after someone inside turns, only to turn themselves and die in the fiery ash as the sun lights them up. It's a harrying ride back home, and I hope nothing has disturbed my family in my absence. I pray I don't find either of them turned. I don't know if I can do what I have to do if that happens. It would be asking me to do the unthinkable, the one thing I can never do, ever.

I shake the thought from my mind and head onto the residential road leading to the cluster of ranch houses where our home stands, in a western Las Vegas neighborhood. I lay my gun in my lap as the van speeds away on the bumpy road, back to my new life and the only ones left I love.

5.

Nothing But to Wait
Days after

MY BODY ACHES, reminding me of the prior day's ordeal. I still remember the people I've slain. The memory of taking them down rolls through my brain over and over, like a bittersweet torture. I don't know how anyone could've ever killed anyone and not lost their minds over it. But I must move on. There is no choice now but to do so.

I pick at the remnants of my dinner: Spam, green beans and canned corn, no butter. I miss butter. Thinking about the fatty, slick taste of it makes my mouth water, but I find that the memory is fading already. We ran out of butter the moment the electricity went out in the city. Though there are patches where the electrical grid still continues to function, we'd find ourselves in the dark. At night, I'd watch the flames flickering on the candles my mother kept lit all through the treacherous night. The nights were filled with screams, screams that kept me awake. I'd feign sleep as I listened to the ravenous screeches outside our walls.

The neighbors, the people I once knew, have transformed into something else, something vicious, insatiable and violent. I'd watch them for a bit in the darkness of my room upstairs, peering out through the crack of the window curtains as they scattered, running down the street, chasing whatever unfortunate soul had crossed their path. Those who weren't careful, those who made the mistake to attempt to leave after dark, they were the ones dead now, lying splayed across the pavements, torn and shredded, their clothes left in tatters and the blood pooled across the dark asphalt.

I had to look away, though it was almost entrancing to watch them. These once humans…. What are they now? What does that make me now?

"April?" Jeremy's voice jerks me back to reality, back to the present of the campground we'd fled to. I smile at him as I scoop up another spoonful of food and chew it without tasting.

"What's up?" I rub my hand over his soft hair, which is brown with some golden highlights. His chubby cheeks puff out as he smiles, giving me an eyeful of half baby teeth with emerging permanents which look awkward at this stage. His teeth have corn stuck in them, and I laugh.

Have to get him to floss more. There will be no dentists to fix any tooth damage from now on.

My somber mood returns at that thought, and I slump in my chair, chewing the ball of food sticking to my mouth. I swallow it down though, chasing it with a cool soda. Right now, food is still plentiful. The abandoned markets are all over the place, some raided, some untouched. I wonder what will happen when we've eaten it, or other scavengers, the survivors, have taken it all. What then? Will we be reduced to hunting and digging out worms from deep dank holes in the ground?

I shudder at the thought.

"Mom?" I turn to find her scraping the remains of her lunch into a garbage bag. The campgrounds are cooling down, and we need to find permanent residence before the real cold hits. Though it doesn't get below zero here, in the mountains of Southern Nevada, it does get down into the 30s and 40s and even the 20s higher up. I shiver and go to sit on a rock near the fire. I hate camping, but we've take refuge in our van where we all sleep during the night. That way, if we're attacked by anything, we can move out of here fast. Sleeping in tents is out of the question now.

My mother doesn't answer. She looks pale in the bright sunlight as she dumps the bag of remains into the trash can near the restrooms. I watch her pensively as she turns around, looking so incredibly sad and worried, still strangling a worn handkerchief in her bony fingers.

It hits me then, and I don't push her to answer me anymore. Randy, her boyfriend, never returned from saving his friends. She has to be going out of her mind because of it. If only he hadn't run out to help them. If he'd only stayed with us, with her, he'd be safe. Just another thing I hate him for.

How he could put my mother second to saving others when all the world is falling down into the open pit of hell irritates me, and I feel like jumping up and down, rejoicing that he's gone. Good riddance. I never did warm up to the guy; he could never replace my father. Oh, but he tried. He tried over and over to be a father to Jeremy and me, to be a good companion for my mother, who obviously adores him. I just never warmed up to him, and I almost feel bad that he's probably dead, and I never let him in. I never see the good in people, so all I can remember about him is the bad, really. It just angers me to know how easily my father had been replaced. How could she forget him so soon?

She hasn't forgotten, I tell myself. The struggle to move on is etched in every line of her face, in every tear she's shed. We all need to move on from loss, from death….

I sigh, dumping my leftovers into the trash and rinsing the plate off in the bucket of water my mother fills to wash dishes. It vaguely reminds me of camping with my father, but I shut down the memory train before it gets me all worked up and derails me again. No need to continually torture oneself.

"April, can you load up the van, please? We need to search for a more permanent place today."

"It's already noon, Mom," I protest, drying off my plate and sticking it into the box in the back of our van. "If you wanted to look for a place, we should've left earlier."

She shoves the small cooking pot and a bag of cans into the van's rear hatch. Jaw tight, I realize I'm pushing her and decide to follow along. Pressing her will only end in an argument, and I'd love to avoid it. I pick up the bucket of dirty dish water and dump it onto the fire.

Jeremy is already sitting inside. He waves and presses his face against the window, making crude faces. I stick my tongue out at him as I shut the trunk door of the van and head around to sit in the passenger seat.

Mom slides into the driver's seat and squeezes the steering wheel with an iron grip. Scanning the campsite, she lets out a long, shaky breath before she grabs the door handle and closes it with a finite slam. Turning the key, the engine roars to life, stifling out the noise in our heads—the memories. I slip the seatbelt on, wary that her mood has never been so foul. Randy's been gone a few days now, but waiting for him to return is like waiting for the sun to go supernova. It might never happen. If he does, he won't come back the same, will he?

I wrap my arms around me and stare out the window as the landscape rolls by. The same scrawny and bare deciduous trees, starved and thin, sparse from living in this arid desert, stand tall, reaching for us with their withered, spidery branches. I want to see something more alive, greener. The occasional coniferous trees, which still possess some greenery, are a small comfort. It makes me feel the desolation of the world heavy on our shoulders now. A pulling, sinking feeling leaves me drowning as the wind whips my hair up into my face.

6.

Resonant Hope

"HEY!" I SHOVE at the debris in my way. "I think I found something." Kicking at a sheet of plywood, I manage to jam the edge of a metal cart into my side. I groan, press the spot with my hands and breathe out slowly. The tender spot throbs.

"Are you all right?" My mother comes up behind me and touches my shoulder. I nod and straighten, hoping I didn't hit it too hard. I rub at it furiously and point toward the door I'd been uncovering.

"See that? A metal door. Looks like it could lead to the same place as that one we saw outside. What do you think?"

She helps me move the last of the debris—metal poles, boxes and a dresser—out of the way, seemingly random junk clearly arranged to hide the location of the door. It spikes my curiosity as I reach out to touch the cool, streaked metal. I hope it opens. The other door on the outside of the cabin had been locked, with no visible way to get it open. Trying the door latch, I find it locked, but a small green light turns on to my right where a keypad is hidden under a small metal cover. It's slightly opened, as though whoever used it last didn't bother to close it all the way.

From the looks of this place, it hasn't been used in a long while. Maybe it's a safe room, a panic room of some sort. Whatever is in there, no one has come to check on it in a very long time.

The cabin stands in a hidden alcove, just atop a small hill in the mountains of the Mt. Charleston area surrounding the west side of the Las Vegas valley. We used to come here during the winter to slide down the snow-covered hills and build snowmen as the flurries floated softly down onto us. We'd play until the cold became too much to bear and our fingers were downright frozen.

It was the one area there are no people, at least none that we've yet run into. It seems we're the lucky ones to make it out of the city alive. Those who make it to the highways, die off soon enough, infected or incinerated in the daylight, even chewed up by their family members. It's horrifying to pass by their wrecked cars, metal twisted and blood everywhere.

Fortunately, not a lot of people live in their Mt. Charleston cabins. These are for summer vacations or winter snowboarding trips. In the middle of fall, no one is around.

Lucky for us, I guess.

"Let's check upstairs. Maybe there's a code written down somewhere." My mother turns around and heads swiftly back upstairs to look. Jeremy is sitting at the top of the stairs, too scared to be in the cabin alone. He jumps up and joins her as I follow behind. I hope she's right. To find a reinforced room to live in during the night would be a godsend. Our chances for survival would jump a thousand fold from what we have now.

I find my mother pulling out drawers, shoving the contents around before closing them quietly. I'm pretty sure she would be slamming them if she wasn't afraid it could attract people, or worse. She's still upset about losing Randy. We'd had no choice but to leave when we started finding scratch marks on the outside of our house. I wish we had left sooner, but that's how it ended up. Mom waited for him. Then, at the break of dawn one morning, she'd herded us into the van, pulled out of our house and left it behind, probably forever.

"Here." She pulls out a notebook and a dangling key attached to its spiral wire. "The code is in here plus a checklist of supplies inside the bunker." She looks up at me, tears glistening in her eyes. "It's a bunker, April. A real life bunker we can use and be safe."

I nod, and we scramble back down the stairs to punch in the numbers. I guess whoever owned this place never thought they wouldn't make it back. They would be in there if they had.

This thought jerks me back into action, and I pull the gun from my holster as Mom reaches over toward the keypad to punch in the numbers.

"Mom, they could be in there, the owners."

She glances at me and nods, then steps to the side to give me a full view of the room when she opens it.

"Ready?" she asks.

"As we'll ever be."

She punches the numbers in, and the green light flashes. A low but audible click hits our ears. My heart is pounding furiously, knowing that whatever greets us from within will determine our future.

Mom pulls at the handle and yanks it open, hiding behind it in case we get bombarded. Dust bellows out in small puffs, but not enough to obscure my vision. I grip the gun, my finger ready on the trigger as I creep forward into the darkened room before us.

"Flashlight, Mom," I whisper, and she pulls the flashlight out from her belt loop and flicks it on, peering around the corner and sweeping the room with its cutting beam of illumination.

My chest tightens as I enter the room with her behind me. She continues to sweep the room, but it looks like a good-sized place, so we explore it further. A desk with monitors sits dusty, but the console is lit up. As we step farther into the room, motion sensors detect us, and the overhead lights flicker on, flooding the area with bright, artificial light.

My mother flicks the flashlight off, and we stand in the center of a large room with a door that leads to what looks like a bathroom. There's a small storage area toward the rear of the room. Another metal door to our left must be the one we'd seen before, leading to the outside. There are two metal beds with mattresses, a TV, a small coffee table near it with a sofa lining the wall. A kitchen runs along the rest of the wall, and a small breakfast table with four chairs sits in the middle of the room.

I move on toward the back and flick on the light of the bathroom. A mirror faces me, and a shower to the right with a curtain drawn stands next to one toilet. The wall next to the door is piled with toilet tissue rolls, all wrapped in plastic. Cleaning supplies sit under the sink area but are left in the open.

Turning the light off, I move to check out the storage room to the left of the bathroom. It's piled high with canned goods, nonperishable items, and bottles of water along with drums full of it, too. There are even toiletries and large boxes filled with new and used clothing. After doing a round through the room, I walk back to where my mother and Jeremy are standing, watching me.

"It's good. It's got all we need."

"It has electricity, too, and even a filtration system. Where's the electricity coming from?" My mother peers up at the ceiling and studies the lights and electrical cords plugged into the wall.

There's a generator hum nearby, but it's faint enough to not be noticed much. I wonder where it is and hope it's not noisy enough to attract people, or worse, ferals. "I'll find the generator, but I think I saw solar panels on the roof of this place, too."

I check the metal door at the side of the room and try it. A beep sounds off as I open the door, but it doesn't alarm. The cool, mountain air trickles in, and I take a wide breath of it before I set out to find the generator. I find it, buried under several concrete breezeblocks with a small fan ventilating it out through a tube that goes all the way to the roof of the house. It's virtually silent and must run off pure solar electricity from the looks of it. I hope so. I'm not sure where I'd be able to find enough gas to keep it going.

I head back to the opened door to the bunker and step in, shutting it behind me.

"It's outside, buried but ventilated. I think it's all solar, but I'll have to check out where the batteries are kept. I don't really know much about a system like this."

My mother nods, and we both turn toward Jeremy who is turning the TV on and is all giddy at finding a video game system hooked up to it.

Meeting my mother's eyes as we face each other, I see something new in her expression, something that makes me smile again. Hope.

"Let's unload the van."

I agree and follow her back out to grab our supplies, then hide the van in the cabin's garage.

Evening arrives, and we settle into our new beds. We've dragged another frame out from the basement and used one of the mattresses from a twin bed in the cabin for a third bed. We make sure to lock the doors and set the alarms as the notebook specified.

I lie in my bed and study our small sanctuary. Cameras kept eyes on the perimeter of the cabin, but nothing moves in the stillness of the quiet night. Outside are the monsters, down in the city where the virus has pretty much decimated the human population by now. Inside here, we're safe, cocooned in our own tiny world.

This only brings the questions I've suppressed back to the surface as I lie here, listening to Mom's and Jeremy's soft breaths while they sleep. How long will this last? Will we become infected and turn into those crazy, vampire-like ferals out there? Will they come and get us eventually? Will we die of something sooner or later?

When the answers don't come to me, and sleep finally takes over my senses, I hope only to dream of nothing. Not the nightmares surrounding us. Not the end of the world. If this is it, then it is the end and there's nothing left to figure out. If it isn't, well, tomorrow will be there, no matter what comes our way.

ELIJAH:

THE MIEL CHRONICLES

A *Reign of Blood* Companion Story

by J.T. Lewis & Alexia Purdy

Mythos

The workings of heaven are shrouded in mystery and myth, leaving us to only theorize as to what awaits us when we pass.

Generally speaking, we like to think that we all fall into two distinct groups: those that live a good life and go to heaven, and those that don't and are destined for *another* realm.

There are those among us however, that are special cases.

These are good people that have committed a horrendous crime, such as murder.

What makes their cases special however, is the fact that by committing these egregious acts, one could argue that they have made the world a better place.

The premise of *The Miel Chronicles* is that there is a heavenly court that is forced to consider these special cases, holding in their collective hands the fate of the souls that come before them.

Three archangels make up the Court of Souls, but only one among them recognizes that these souls cannot be judged on just the outward facts.

He alone will take it upon himself to dig into the sordid details surrounding the crimes in question. But he is a busy entity, and unable to traverse the world in search of evidence.

Miel, a lowly angel that can walk among us, travels the world in his stead. Tasked as an investigator by the archangel, her job is to gather facts. But more than that, she must capture the emotions that led to the act in question, as well as any evidence of repentance.

It is this recording of emotions in the *Journal of Souls* that will ultimately clear, or convict the soul.

These are the journeys of Miel, the Keeper of the journal.

ELIJAH:
THE MIEL CHRONICLES

A *Reign of Blood* Companion Story

The salvation of this human world lies nowhere else than in the human heart, in the human power to reflect, in human meekness and human responsibility.

Václav Havel

Rashnu stood behind his desk, looking out on heaven with his hands clasped behind his back. His nerves were shot; at least they would have been if he possessed that uniquely human condition. Perhaps his current outlook would be better described as frayed...a harried and frayed soul.

The court was busier than it had ever been, thanks to the viral outbreak in the southwest United States.

Rashnu let out a sigh of frustration. Whatever name one might assign to what he was feeling now, he had about reached his limit of patience for it.

Idiots! He mumbled under his breath.

He spoke of God's chosen people, the humans that inhabited earth, for it was their own doing that had created this dire situation.

If left unchecked, it could spell their complete demise!

The love the archangel normally felt for the human race was strained to its limits.

How could they have let this happen?

While he knew who was ultimately responsible, he couldn't shake the feeling that someone somewhere should have been able to stop this...this...apocalypse!

It was not foretold that this would happen!

The souls of the men responsible had been branded; there would be no redemption for them. They were firmly in the camp of Rashnu's dark brother whose name was never spoken here.

"Good morning Your Grumpiness."

Rashnu sighed again as he turned to greet Miel, his impertinent investigator. He often ignored her willful attitude in deference to their longstanding working relationship, but today was not one of those days.

"Sit down and shut up Miel. I have little patience for your antics this day."

Removing her messenger bag, Miel took the seat at the front of the desk. Knowing some of the pressures that Rashnu had been under lately, she took no offense to his outburst. She knew that she pushed the boundaries of angel propriety on a regular basis with Rashnu. Although she felt no compunction to stop in general, she would rein it in for the remainder of this visit.

At least she would try.

"Our job has gotten infinitely more complex with this outbreak Miel," Rashnu started, diving immediately into the case. "The others on the Court of Souls have shown little flexibility in dealing with the carnage surrounding this. Mithra and Sraosha both contend that killing someone to save oneself is still murder.

Miel leaned forward anxiously. "These things, these vampires…haven't their souls fled their body?"

Rashnu glanced up with a pained look. "That's the rub. Eventually the soul leaves the infected body. Those souls are judged not by what they have become, because they have had no choice in that matter. They are judged strictly by their life previous to the virus."

Standing, Rashnu turned once more toward the window behind him, letting the beauty of heaven around him pacify his frayed soul.

"No, the problem is that those infected can be dangerous before the soul has fled the body. In fact, I think that is when they are the *most* dangerous!"

Turning around, he latched onto Miel's faded blue eyes.

"The humanity still within them can appeal for help from those around them, even though at that point they cannot stop the wildness infecting their body from attacking any that reaches out to help."

Slumping into his chair defeatedly, Rashnu leaned his head into the palms of his hands.

"It is at this point that many of those that have turned are killed as the uninfected try to save themselves."

Rashnu again caught Miel's eyes, "As long as the Court continues their asinine refusal to acknowledge this particular situation, our job becomes almost impossible."

"Do you think a single but very compelling case could help sway them?" Miel questioned the archangel. "One that not only shows their repentance, but describes the unavoidable situation they are in at the moment?"

Rashnu's eyes seemed to soften as he considered this. "You know, that might just work. If the other judges could be convinced that these actions are nearly unavoidable if one is to survive this cataclysm…"

"And *not* fighting to survive," Miel jumped in excitedly, "is tantamount to committing suicide."

Rashnu felt a twitch at the corner of his mouth. Not knowing how to smile, the archangel would never have associated the movement with anything so utterly human. Nevertheless, he felt a small pulse of positive energy creeping into his being.

Nodding, "It's worth a try Miel, but it must be some of your best work ever. Even if they can contain the outbreak to the southwest, there are just too many souls crossing over too quickly. We must strive to present one of the most compelling yet all-inclusive stories to the court."

Leaning forward seriously, "Considering what is going on down there, this may be the only journal entry you have time to obtain Miel. This one story may have to suffice for thousands of souls!"

"Better get started then," Miel said as she rose from her seat. Slinging her messenger bag over her shoulder, she took a step away from the chair before stopping suddenly. A confused look enveloped her as she glanced down at her feet.

"Your feet?" Rashnu questioned. "Are they feeling somewhat leaden at the moment?

Miel nodded as she rotated her shoulders, looking uncomfortable as she slid the shoulder strap of her bag to a different spot.

"Does your bag feel like it weighs more now too?"

Miel's eyes sought Rashnu's, the blue of her eyes now tinted with the hint of confusion.

"Yes! What does it mean?"

Rashnu nodded in understanding.

"It's quite simple Miel…you are carrying the weight of the world on your shoulders now."

The sliver of sunrise breaking free of the eastern skyline found a home on Miel's closed eyelids as she faced east, letting the light warm her soul. The millennia of sunrises she had experienced never ceased to comfort her during her time spent on earth.

She loved it here.

The beauty of the world around her rivaled that of heaven in her eyes. The cycles of birth, life, and death fascinated her. Even the fickle elements were a joy to experience for her, countering the beautiful yet overly predictable weather in heaven.

But she loved the people the most. God's chosen, whose free will allowed them to screw up things royally from time to time. Even allowing for that however, the human race continued to amaze her as she traveled amongst them. No matter where in the world she was, she would find those that energized her soul.

Sunrises were the best though. No matter the mission, she would always stop to take in the glorious breaking of a new day. It was one of God's greatest gifts, the promise of a new beginning.

An unseen breeze suddenly whipped at her sun bleached golden hair, sending wisps of it dancing behind her. Sighing contentedly, Miel opened her pale blue eyes and glanced around at what remained of the once lively Las Vegas.

Pulling up the wide-brimmed hat by the strap, she lowered her chin and pushed it onto her head by the crown. Raising her head once again, she scanned her surroundings with a practiced eye.

It was time to get to work.

Moving down the deserted street purposefully, she would have cut a striking figure had anyone seen her. Though having the weathered look of long travel in her faded jeans and hiking boots, all eyes would be drawn to her because of her uncompromising beauty.

Except for a few special souls however, no one would remember seeing her after she passed, although most would continue their day with a lightened heart.

It didn't take her long to meet one of the new inhabitants of the city. Crossing through the shadow of a building, her ears were assailed with a screech from her right. Turning toward the noise, she casually observed the quickly approaching apparition.

Covered in blood, the feral vampire reached toward her with its claw like hands to attack. In the flash of an eye, her palm was on its forehead. A bright glow emanated from her touch as her attacker stopped dead in its tracks.

Studying the animal through her touch, Miel was saddened by what she found.

Nothing.

The soul of the once human had abandoned the body, leaving only pain and an unending hunger. She could feel the damage to the internal organs, and the overpowering fever that probably racked the body constantly.

Deciding quickly, Miel sent a pulse though her hand that stopped the wildly beating heart in the mutilated body.

The body slipped to the ground, finally relieved of its pain.

Saying a quick prayer of forgiveness…for her as well as the now dead beside her, she continued down the street.

Her progress was slowed as she continued to encounter the beasts anytime she moved out of the now scorching sunlight. Time after time she had to dispatch one of the pain ridden vampires as they tried to attack her.

Her soul cried over the devastation surrounding her, even as she purposefully strode through the city in search of a redeeming soul.

Another screech approached her, and again she held up her hand to stop the approaching animal. Ready to send another pulse that would stop this one's heart as well, she suddenly felt the glimmer of a soul.

Putting her other hand behind its head, she lowered it to the sidewalk as she tried to coax the soul out of hiding.

The facial features of the vampire gradually softened before the now clear green eyes suddenly focused on Miel's face.

"You!" It came out as a hoarse whisper.

"I remember you!"

The man lying on the sidewalk grinned, his sharp fangs now evident.

"You came through my town in Michigan when I was little."

The man suddenly looked confused, "But how? That was over thirty years ago…you still look exactly the same!"

Miel smiled at the man. "That's right Henry; you gave me your snow cone."

"That's right!" Henry replied in amazement. "You looked so weary from your travels, and it was such a hot day. You were wearing an old Army coat, even though it was at least ninety degrees outside.

Miel glanced down at the cuff of her coat, the same one she had been wearing that day.

"You should leave this place," Henry said suddenly. "You are in danger here. Something has happened…"

His words trailed off as he seemed to be trying for an explanation.

"I'll be ok Henry," Miel replied while she reached into her bag. "But I needed to give you this."

Removing her hand, she now held a grape snow cone in it. Bringing it too his mouth, she gently held his head up so that he could take a bite.

"That's really good," Henry said after swallowing some of the icy treat. "My throat has been really dry for some reason."

Nodding, Miel leaned closer to the ravaged face. "Can I tell you a secret?"

Henry nodded as Miel dropped her lips close to his ear. "That snow cone?" she whispered, "The one you gave me all those years ago? It was the best snow cone ever!"

Henry grinned contentedly as Miel placed her hand on his forehead, the soft glow sending him to his reward as a single tear made its way down the angel's face.

Miel was getting worried as even hours later; she had yet to sense anyone that could save the souls of the survivors.

Maybe they are all gone, she thought to herself as she walked past yet another casino. *Maybe I will need to travel far from the city to find the one that I need…the one everyone needs.*

Sighing inwardly, she decided to enter the casino on her left. Maybe there was someone holed up there.

Entering into the darkness, she felt dozens of eyes on her. Too many to deal with at the moment, she made herself invisible as she continued on into the building.

Making her way past the devastation within, she continued into the heart of the building before she felt it.

It was only a faint feeling however, so she continued on, her faith renewed as she climbed over a pile of gaming tables. The vampires were everywhere here, attacking the weaker of their kind as they awaited the darkness of night.

Miel pushed her way though a splintered door and into what was left of a theater. The sense was stronger now, and it seemed to be leading her toward the stage.

Pulling herself up on it, she passed through the curtains at the back of the stage and into a closet that had once been used for props. Confronted by a large steel door, she placed her hand upon the metal.

The sense was strong here, but she needed to get even closer.

Waving her hand in front of the door, she soon found herself in a long hallway. Moving down the corridor, she soon encountered another, and then another door. Making her way through these, she continued down into the recesses of the earth until she finally reached the final door.

Touching it, she smiled as she felt the soul on the other side. Quickly reaching into her bag, she pulled out the old leather-bound book and opened it to a blank page before settling herself on the floor.

Concentrating on the connection she needed, she almost didn't notice when it happened.

Imperceptively at first, the letters started appearing on the page. Then an image materialized behind the writing. It was as if Miel was looking up from the page of the writer himself as he penned his thoughts that may just save his soul…and quite possibly the souls of a multitude of others. Miel watched as the dark-haired man confessed his sins, the book on her lap recording it as evidence of his remorse.

She just hoped it would be enough…enough to save Elijah.

Nothing prepares one for the end of the world. No one could ever fathom the way the world dies. I saw it myself. I lived it.

It was the worst day of my life.

I remember staring out my apartment window, watching the stream of people running across the pavement.

I wish I could say that I'd been a good man, the kind that jumped out and helped every person, woman and child.

But I wasn't.

I'd hid in my apartment until the hour I could no longer wait anymore, knowing I would have to get the hell out of town after seeing who would join me from my job at the Casino. Remembering that day, I'd cared nothing for the throngs of strangers with wailing children who would inevitably cross my path along the way.

The monsters I had encountered were vicious, brainless things. The night would bring more of them with it, and nightmares would've been nothing compared to the slaughter to come that dusk.

How would a regular Joe like me have made it out there? I'm average height, a bit on the husky side, but muscular. I'd done some construction work to make ends meet when my job as an usher at the Wynn Hotel & Casino hadn't been enough. I'd always been huge on watching Bruce Lee films until I had all his moves memorized. Even then,

I'd still crave to learn more from the endless classes in martial arts I'd managed to scrape enough together to take.

Still, I'd felt ill prepared for what appeared to be a sort of apocalypse. I had wondered if I'd even last long enough to make it to my place of work before fleeing for the hills. Sweat had pooled under my pits and my shirt stuck to me like it was a second skin. I'd been scared. Holy beloved, I was going to do exactly what I said I would. I'd been on a mission: Get those I'd known at work and let this world go to the birds...or vamps, that is.

Good Riddance!

I had to do it! Staying there would've put more than just a target on me. It'd be a sure death sentence if those hungry, dead people had swarmed the apartment complex. That place was packed tight with families and the like trying to pay the low rents and survive. One little infection would've spread like a wildfire on a dry, drought plagued meadow. Hell no. I was going to get out of there.

I'd zipped up my backpack and strapped it on. One last look around my apartment made me realize I'd never return to it, but it was somewhat calming to push that life deep into my head. Stepping outside, I had narrowed my vision onto the street below, waiting for the terror to begin.

The slam of my car door luckily had done nothing to attract anyone to me, which was good since the streets were emptying out in the setting sun. It had been about an hour and half before the last rays of sunlight would disappear and the horror of night would be upon me. Throwing the car into drive, I had peeled out of the parking lot and steered around the complex, doing my best to avoid all the stragglers who had tried to wave me down as they pleaded to take them with me.

Where had they thought I was going? The streets were going to be hard to get through no matter what or where I went that day. I doubted I'd be able to keep anyone else alive for too long, besides myself. I remember shaking my head as I peeled out, trying to not look in the rear view, trying not to feel the dread growing within me. I still hear their sobs, their screeching starting to blend into the far off hissing of those vampire-like hunters haunting the air.

I wasn't going to let it affect me...people died stopping to help others. It'd been highly dangerous to venture out alone and there'd been no one in the world I trusted enough to stop for. The only reason I'd been headed to my work place was because there were a few acquaintances working that night whom I did somewhat care about. Whether I cared even a little bit or not at all, they were the only ones I ever really had contact with.

You see, I hadn't let anyone in since my family had died. It wasn't worth the pain which was sure to follow when I let someone into my life. My precious family had consisted of a brother, a sister, mother, and father...all gone in one twist of fate. They'd been left shattered, just by coming to visit me at the wrong time...one moment of fate. When they turned, I never really had a choice, did I? What made me immune to this ugly death had not been given to them. I wished it had. More than anything.

I felt the stab of pain shift inside me when those memories fought their way back in, it'd made me clench my jaw tight, like a rock. That flicker of pain would always inch its way in carefully, if I let it. But I'd always send it retreating back into the corners of my mind where I could deal with the agony some other day, if at all.

It was then that I'd had to slam on the brakes, filling the air with the acrid scent of burnt rubber. I'd found myself glaring at a woman limping her way across the road. The crowds had turned thicker up ahead, near the Las Vegas Strip and this woman had completely blocked my path when she moved awkwardly slow along the asphalt.

"The Fuck! Get out of my way!" I'd shouted at her through the windshield. Then, I'd hung out my window and hollered at the woman again. Her eyes had finally found mine and to tell the truth, I hadn't even noticed her torn up dress and disheveled hair until her dead, reddened eyes were glued on me. I hadn't been sure she'd understood me, but it hadn't mattered when I'd noticed the blood streaking down the front of her blouse, I studied how the blood matted in her hair, making her look somewhat oddly hypnotized. I'd even done a double take. I'd wondered briefly what'd been wrong with that broad.

Of course, I'd found myself opening my car door and had been halfway out when I'd caught her approaching, shuffling along slowly on a bad leg. Her foot hung out under her dress hem, twisted and broken to the side. Her ankle was swollen, discolored with bruising while blood seeped from an inch long cut along where her tibia was sticking out, splintered and sharp.

How had she walked on that shattered leg?

"Are you alright...?" I asked her. She'd been a fright to look at.

My eyes moved her up toward her face and I tried to really look at her, taking in each miniscule feature and blemish that had blossomed across her ashen white skin.

If I hadn't known any better, I would've said she looked dead.

She was inhumanly pale from the obvious amount of dropped buckets of blood she'd left behind across the pavement from her broken leg and her torn out throat. How could anyone have been moving with all those injuries?

"What the fuck?" I had shrunk back into my car, grabbing my gun and holding it in my hand as I attempted to take in the meaning of it all. Locking the door, I had rolled the window up hastily, just as her ragged nails, caked with blood, dirt and skin, tapped the painted metal of the hood. Her fingers had begun to grasp onto the car to hold herself upright. I thought these things couldn't live in the daylight. I thought only at night they came out...

"No way!"

A harsh whisper was what my voice had turned into, but I knew better than to believe I wasn't in danger. My shock had worn off and a deep, embedded instinct had slammed me back into reality as she made it to the driver's side window and slapped her weak wrists against it. She then bared her teeth as she snapped them at me.

Her eyes...the irises were red...and her teeth...Oh my God...there were fangs in there...

"Vampires don't exist," I'd told myself. "Not like that."

This couldn't have possibly been real. Didn't the sun kill them? But, this woman had fangs! Not the fake ones they sell at Halloween stores. Oh hell no…these were the real fucking thing.

Next, I'd swept my eyes across the parking lot of the warehouses I'd settled between and realized my fatal error. I had been sitting in the middle of a vast shadow emanating from an array of apartment buildings. Each casting their own short pieces of darkness, they eventually joined those from some oversized warehouses that hogged the industrial side of the road.

Shit!

There were others walking about as confused and disheveled as this lady, but then I noticed it.

They were avoiding the light at all costs.

Their boundaries were the edges of the looming, evening shadows which hid the scorch of the setting sun from these creatures.

A stronger thump then slapped at my window and brought me back to the woman scratching at the car to get in. No words came from her mouth. Nothing but a hiss of desperation ever made it past her lips as her nails broke off while she hit the door over and over again.

I shook my head at her, not really registering that she could no longer understand my gestures. Her mind was gone, her body twitched in some unreal energy as she then reached down and picked at the door handle, trying in vain to remember what the gadget was for, as if that memory was edging the boundaries of her insanity.

Of course I'd slammed the locks down and made sure they stayed down before I cranked the engine again. This brought the attentions of some of the others lingering about as I shifted the gears and peeled out of the death shadows. Some of those people jumped into my path, others came darn near close enough to warrant a jolting bump against the metal sides of my car, sending them flying in all directions.

Blood streaked the metal and small dents had appeared whenever I swerved to turn away from another body, another and then another. The world had morphed into madness before my very eyes…a madness filled with blood and fangs.

As my car made it to the warmth of the sun's light once more I had pressed the gas pedal even more furiously as the time ticked away. Each shadow would bring more of these creatures as they followed me while I maneuvered my way toward the casino. This area had been hit hard, but the farther I'd gone the less of the strange monsters I seemed to see. Instead, a more normal crowd had hurried along there, trying to pack into their cars and busses to leave the city. Others were walking by foot toward the strip and government centers in hopes of some kind of salvation.

Would there be any to be found?

I had made my way around these clumps of people, hoping that they knew what danger was quickly approaching as they abandoned their houses and took to the streets in an utterly chaotic mass.

I had to make it to the Wynn before the sunset completed its dip under the western mountains. I had to find the few I had gotten to know over the last year, even though I hadn't taken the time to know them very well at all. After that, somehow, I would have to get the hell out of there.

The lobby had been a chaotic mess and being trampled was a high risk. Employees as well as guests pummeled each other to escape the building as fast as they could. I hadn't seen anymore weird demented people there, but I was sure they were coming like a wave of death. Order ceased to exist and all the rules had been thrown out the window.

"Elijah!" The old man Eddie had rushed past the hurried crowd to reach me, taking a few bumps as he dodged the barreling crowd.

"Eddie," I waved back as I rushed forward to meet him halfway. "What's going on? Where's the crew from the theatre?"

"You have to follow me. There's no time to find anyone else, I've already rounded up everyone backstage. You have to follow me. Now!" He had tugged at my sleeve like a madman and I had given him a short, affirmative nod, glad I had decided to grab my bag just in case I didn't make it back to the car.

"Okay, let's go."

He had turned and headed toward the walls to make it past the barrage of people heading toward the exits. It'd been suffocating to say the least but we managed. After a bit, I did offer to go first, since I was taller and stockier than the fragile old man, and people tended to get out of my way faster. He never did protest, but pushed on behind me as we slowly made our way through the rows of slot machines and dealer tables down toward the main theater.

Reaching the theater doors, he had hastily unlocked them and we slipped inside. Eddie swiftly turned and locked them behind us, letting out a breath of relief after doing so. I'd been curious about this, but never asked about why he'd locked them. There really hadn't been any time to think with all that racquet and screaming coming from outside the doors.

"No one else comes in," he had whispered and pointed toward the stage. I'd nodded and headed down the aisle of the abandoned theater. Suddenly, the lights had begun to flicker, powering down until there was nothing but a blinding darkness. Moments had passed only to find them lighting up to full brightness again. Pausing, I had scanned the theater and waited for Eddie to catch up to me. The black of the theater had led me to believe that the generators would not be kicking in after the lights went out tonight. That was going to be really, really bad.

"What do you think is going on out there? Do you think we should leave town?"

Eddie had rushed past me, shaking his head as sweat beaded on his shiny bald scalp that now reflected brightly the lights overhead. The peppered white hair that ringed *the side of his head clung to the side of his sweaty neck as he took the steps two at a time up onto the stage. He always wore his hair a bit long for an old guy.*

"Nowhere safer than here."

I really hoped he knew what he was doing.

"Where is everyone?"

He then waved me forward, pointing toward the backstage doors.

"In the back, they're waiting for me. I figured I'd return within the half hour with anyone I found, but you were the only one I recognized and the only one willing to come with me. We've got to head down and lock the doors before it's too late."

Before we ever reached the backstage doors, someone leapt out from behind the tall theatre curtains, and slammed into Eddie with a high pitched screech.

"Eddie!" I yelled, but I had been too late. The creature, or person, whatever it was, had a firm grip on Eddie and it had latched onto his arm with its sharpened teeth. It greedily sucked the blood as the fluid slipped down from the corners of its mouth, bubbling from its breathing and desperation to drink.

Eddie's screaming for it to let go haunts me still.

He'd beat it with his other arm until I grabbed a piece of a table leg from some broken props thrown carelessly to one side of the stage. Returning quickly, I smashed the wooden prop into what looked like a woman with long blond hair, now caked with old dry blood. The stench of death and gore clung to every inch of her body.

"Meg?"

I'd recognized her, hesitating for only a moment before Eddie's cries brought me back to my senses. I realized she was no longer our beautiful stage manager, but a wild, insatiable beast who wanted nothing more than to rip us into tiny, bloody bits.

Yanking at her clothes, I had managed to pull her tiny body off Eddie easily, throwing her to the side like a trash bag. Her body thumped against some boxed risers that were used to elevate singers and other actors on stage. Taking the broken table leg, I had pointed the sharper edge of it toward her and ran forward before shoving it straight through her heart. Then, I pulled it out and slammed it back into her as fast as I could. The last time, I drove it into her forehead.

The sickening crush of bone and mush made my stomach flip, but I'd kept on slamming the point in and out of the pulp that was left of her head.

"Elijah…"

Eddie's voice stopped me. Huffing, I'd stared at the bloody chair leg in horror. Meg was no longer Meg, or even that beast of a thing she'd become. She'd turned into nothing but a pile of bloody horror which I had now effectively put down.

"Elijah…help me."

Disgusted, I tossed the damn leg to the side and hopped back up, making my way towards the fallen body of Eddie. He was huffing, his pale skin sweating profusely as he clung onto his fractured arm. The vampire, or thing, had chomped down hard with its teeth to suck on the blood.

"Here," I said as I ripped the bottom of my T-shirt and wrapped it around the bite. Tying it down, I'd hoped to keep it from bleeding any further.

"*Come on; tell me where we're going Eddie? Eddie? I think we need to keep moving.*"

Eddie was losing it at that point, fading in and out of reality from the pain of my wrapping his arm. He shook his head, letting it hang down between his knees as he composed himself.

"*Help me up, we've got to move.*"

The door at the entrance of the theater behind us boomed, as if someone was smacking right into it. I had stared at it and waited to see if it'd just been someone bumping into it or a figment of my imagination.

Another boom sounded off, followed by another and another.....scratching.

"*They're coming.*" Eddie's haggard voice willed me into action and I'd yanked his good arm over my shoulder to hoist him up.

"*More of them...right? Like Meg?*"

He nodded weakly, his shallow breathing worrying me.

"*Okay. Backstage doors, right?*"

He managed a muffled yes as his head dangled down.

"*Alright, stay with me, old man.*" I drug him toward the door ahead and used my free arm to yank it open.

My eyes widened in astonishment at the barrel of a shotgun.

On the other end of the gun was Anita. A seamstress, she usually worked on the costumes and jeweled head pieces of the actors of the show. Now she held a gun on me, her tiny trembling fingers worrying me as they shook at the trigger.

"*Whoa now, it's just me...and Eddie.*"

"*Elijah, oh thank God! Eddie!*"

She proceeded to drop the gun and ran hastily toward us. Immediately checking Eddie, she pressed her bony fingertips into his neck to check for a pulse. Scanning the rest of him with her studious brown eyes, she recoiled as they landed on the bloody wrap on his wound.

"*He's bit!*" She turned her terror filled face toward me and shook her head.

"*He can't come with us.*"

Tears sprung out of her large brown eyes and slid down her porcelain cheeks, dark streaks of makeup already stained with a previous cry. Her long hair was in tangles, sticking out of a long forgotten braid lying tattered down her back.

"*It's too late for him...he's bitten.*"

As if I didn't know that.

"*What do you mean? We can't leave him.*"

"*We have to...*" The shudder in her voice hadn't been very reassuring.

A loud crack then echoed across the theater and screeches filled our ears as more creatures entered the theater behind us. The doors had splintered, leaving them a decimated mess.

"*We gotta go...*"

She tugged at my arm desperately, but I didn't let go of Eddie.

"*I can't leave him!*"

She nodded but still pulled me toward the group behind us, now exiting the backstage room into another door at the back of one of the costume closets.

"Where are we going?" I asked. I lifted Eddie into my arms and followed behind. The adrenaline had made his weight seem like nothing.

"Where it'll be safe." Anita stated. Her accent returned in full force when she was scared, and this counted. Her tears were long forgotten as shock settled back into her features.

Another woman stood beside the new door, letting the others go first. Her hard dark eyes found me and stared, like tiny onyx daggers speculating my every move toward her.

"You can't bring him in here," she hissed as she bolted the door behind us. I had never realized the costume closet had a lock on the inside of it. Who locks themselves into a costume closet? It was barely a room, barely even a closet, but I'd found it peculiar.

I shook the thought out of my mind and pressed on.

"He's not going anywhere, but with me," I had growled at her. My patience was gone and I had no room for arguments, especially with this dark eyed stranger who I suddenly found quite stunning.

Her cold, hard fingers laced around my arm and gripped it tightly.

"He'll turn, like the rest of them and kill us all. I can't let that happen." Her eyes were a serious sting at my chest.

"Who the hell are you?" I asked as I stared her down, trying to send her a challenge to go ahead and try to stop me. I kept walking when she didn't offer a response.

She finally spoke as she rushed to cut me off at the end of the costume closet. "I'm Katrina; I oversee the City of Vida."

"The what?"

Eddie groaned at that moment and I paused to slide him down so his back was propped against the wall. Next to him was a brushed metal door that looked to be heavily reinforced. A large wheel was attached to the locking mechanism, making it look like something from a submarine.

She frowned at me as her eyes flicked warily toward the door we had just come through.

"The City of Vida," she repeated. "It's below us, underground. It was built for disaster protection. We'll be completely safe there."

Another thump sounded behind me, the closet door this time. I quickly clutched at Eddie as I readied to hoist him back up on into my arms.

"Leave me, Elijah."

Eddie's harsh whisper had startled me. Turning toward him, my eyes widened in shock. His one iris was turning blood red while his other one lingered a chocolate brown. He looked downright stoned.

"You have to," Eddie moaned. "I don't feel right, and it's taking over my senses. Can't think right…I don't want to bite any of you. Please, leave me."

I'd set him back down next to the massive metal door and shook my head. "No Eddie, we've got to get you to some medical care, ASAP."

He mumbled his disagreement. "No...no medicine can cure this now." He waved at his broken arm and pointed toward his mouth. I lifted up his lips to check his mouth and swiftly pulled away.

What the hell?

Sharpened and pointed, I couldn't believe my eyes! His fangs were coming in. But, it was so fast, so soon...

"You'll be one of them..." I swallowed as I told him this. My mouth had become a cracked, desolate desert. My heart broke.

Eddie pointed at the gun Anita had been offering to us nearby and I scooted over to grab it.

"Kill me."

"No, I..."

"Do it!" He glared at me, his other eye now morphing brick red and brown. He looked as if his strength was swiftly returning as his words muffled into a groan. He closed his eyes with the noise but a moment later, flung them back open in a fury.

"Do it or I'll be the one killing you!"

His eyes pleaded as a single tear of blood tinged red slid down his cheek. "Please...don't make me..."

I nodded and stood back, listening to the incessant thumping and smack of fists against the door behind me. It was reinforced, but not the hard metal of the entrance to the dark hallways beyond. Time had finally ticked down to nothing and the sound of cracking wood and drywall filled the air, along with small puffs of dust as the hinges loosened from the wall behind us.

Looking down at the old man, he gave me a faint nod as he held my eyes. I positioned the gun, sucked in a breath and squeezed the trigger, knowing just how final the sound of it was.

I couldn't even glance at Eddie then. He was gone, forgotten and lost to the world. My heart was in my throat, feeling like it would choke me.

The whole group had jumped at the sound of the gun, turning to watch from behind the entrance to the long hall. Worried whispers followed as they once again turned and continued moving forward.

Anita ran toward me, hugging me tight before tugging me back to the entrance as the door behind us splintered. An inhuman screech suddenly filled the air behind us, causing panic to shoot through the hallway as people shoved at the ones ahead of them.

"Hurry!" Katrina screamed as we passed the door's threshold. Four others quickly joined her in pushing the heavy metal door shut. Just in time she spun the wheel to set the lock as a barrage of thumps emanated from the other side of the metal door. Katrina then fell to her knees as the other men leaned against the wall, exhausted.

"There are several more doors," Katrina managed with an exasperated breath, motioning everyone to keep on moving. "This will hold well, but we must continue down and lock the rest of them behind us."

The group edged forward, frightened looks darting back toward the metal barrier that now kept us alive and separated from the carnage of the world behind us.

What were they? These things...?

543

I stared at my filthy hands and wiped Eddie's and Meg's blood off them. It was a long and silent walk past the next several gates before we reached a stairwell. We started descending down and down, past the known depths of the casino, past any place I ever knew existed. Far down into the belly of the Wynn casino, we'd found a new home while the one above us crumbled to wasted bits. Dust in the wind.

The City of Vida we found was massive and well-constructed. Layers and layers of living space existed for the few lucky ones who'd made it down here.

Was it luck to have been ushered this way before becoming infected?

What destiny was it to have been saved from such a fate by my friend Eddie, only to have him succumb to the very thing that sought to infect me?

A sadness filled me to know he hadn't made it this far.

Before entering the final gate, we'd been stripped of our belongings and my pack had been searched for anything which could be considered dangerous. I gulped as I watched them rummage through my stuff and confiscate my weapons.

I suddenly felt naked without them. Would I ever see them again?

I'd had to soap up in the decontamination showers too, my clothes replaced with scrubs to remove the dried blood. I was examined for any bites or infection and my clothing burned before I was allowed to join the others.

What of those found infected? What had become of them? What was to become of us?

Days would go by, then weeks. I remember standing at the last heavy metal gate to the world above, waiting and watching to see if others would come through them.

Would they ever come and announce the world was once more safe again to tread?

Would the ominous thumping of the infected reach us all the way down here? Or had those creatures moved on to easier prey as they turned into feral things…wildlings?

The thumping never came, but I had continued to sit and stare at the gate for weeks on end. There would be no rescuing here, but that was not the top concern I'd had.

I'd killed Eddie. I'd killed him without a moment's hesitation.

And what of the theater director, Meg…what about her?

I'd been sure she was a goner, like the rest of the crazed, dead people turned vampires out there. But, had there been a slim chance she'd just been feverish, delusional and crazed from sickness?

What if we'd just given it a few days and the world would get over this crazy illness and all would be righted?

And if it did, what would that make me now?

A killer…

The word murderer had swum in my head in the endless nights of waiting, watching and listening for any news from above.

Maybe if someone around me had really understood what I was feeling it'd been easier. As it was I shoved it down into the pit of my stomach where those events could be hidden until the day my fears could be put to rest. As it was, everyone had been so involved with their own concerns and fears that no one even noticed my anguish.

Eddie had been forgotten by everyone here, dismissed from existence as fleetingly as the days of the past. How could I ever live with myself like this?

Maybe I was damned, a worse fate than that of the infected above ground.

Though nothing ever did come from the other side of that God forsaken metal door, I'd quickly discovered I was trapped. Nothing came in, and no one left this underground sanctuary either.

We weren't even allowed to touch the barred metal gate in front of the doors. I'd discovered that when I'd been wrestled to the ground with machine guns pointed at my head after I attempted such a thing. It was useless to fight the guards, appointed by whom I sure would've liked to have known.

I am trapped, a prisoner of a different kind. Not only am I physically imprisoned, but also spiritually by my lack of redemption. I've suffered through my guilt with no salvation in sight for my damned soul.

For now, I can only wait and hope the day for absolution will one day come for me in this pit of hell.

Miel closed the Journal of Souls and ran her hand lovingly along the edge of the binding before replacing it into her messenger bag.

Would it be enough?

It was a heartfelt confession, and Miel felt it was enough evidence to free his soul when he left this world.

But what of the others?

Would it be enough to convince the Court of Souls that this was a unique situation? Would it pierce the hearts of the other archangels enough to understand that when people are fighting for their lives, that sometimes they have to do things that threaten their soul…if only to survive?

Miel stood and made her way back up the hallway.

Even she had almost missed the soul hidden within the ravaged body of Henry. If it had been that elusive to her, how could they expect a human to know what they were really facing?

She knew that her work on this was not yet complete; she would have to strive to gather more evidence…if there was any left to be had.

That was her job…and she was *very* good at it.

Making her way out of the ransacked casino, Miel found a patch of light, even as the sun made its way toward the western horizon. Sliding the hat off of her head, she let it glide down her back until stopped by the chin strap.

She needed the sunlight right now; she needed the rejuvenation it offered to her soul.

Turning her head, she watched as a pair of uninfected men loaded a car with their belongings. Wary against being attacked, one of the men noticed Miel, nudging the other man and nodding her way.

Turning to go, Miel started walking toward the impending sunset, following the glowing orb as it too left the ravaged city behind.

The two men watched with interest as she passed, quietly observing her until she disappeared into the waves of heat.

As one, the men then returned to their labors, the recollection of the mysterious woman now lost from their memory.

In its place however, was just the smallest seed of hope.

ABOUT THE AUTHORS

ALEXIA PURDY

Alexia currently lives in Las Vegas, Nevada—Sin City! She loves to spend every free moment writing or playing with her four rambunctious kids. Writing has always been her dream, and she has been writing ever since she can remember. She loves writing paranormal fantasy and poetry and devours books daily. Alexia also enjoys watching movies, dancing, singing loudly in the car and eating Italian food.

J.T. LEWIS

Mystery abounds in the books of Amazon Best Selling Author J.T. Lewis. Living in Southeast Indiana with his wife and daughter, J.T. has always loved a mystery. Striving to bring readers a story packed full of action, adventure, and suspense has led to his current selection of titles.

His first full length novel, Murder! Too Close To Home, has been voted #1 on Goodreads Best Debut Mystery Series list. The second in the series, Gabriel's Revenge, was released with much anticipation in

July 2012. Both of these titles belong to the Adventures of Gabriel Celtic series.

His newest series is called The Adventures of Young Gabriel Celtic, a Middle Grade series that focuses on the misadventures of Gabriel Celtic as a youngster. Always inquisitive, he follows his intuition in search of mystery and adventure. Unfortunately, things don't always turn out quite like he planned.

Also look for JT Lewis' Pepper and Longstreet YA mystery series. Having been compared to the old Hardy Boys and Nancy Drew mysteries, Pepper and Longstreet at first seem an unlikely duo.

Having discovered Jacob Longstreet standing in her kitchen one day, the ghost of a Civil War soldier soon becomes Pepper's friend, as well as her partner in solving mysteries. Together, they find themselves in the most unlikely of situations as mysteries unfold around them.

An electrician by trade, at night JT Lewis morphs into a fictional detective with a keyboard, a transition that suits his need for creating exciting stories for his ever-growing audience.

Printed in Great Britain
by Amazon